Escaping the Aventine

by

Mads Hennen

DORRANCE
PUBLISHING CO
EST. 1920
PITTSBURGH, PENNSYLVANIA 15238

Dorrance Publishing Co
585 Alpha Drive
Suite 103
Pittsburgh, PA 15238
Visit our website at *www.dorrancebookstore.com*

ISBN: 978-1-6470-2394-2
eISBN: 978-1-6453-0323-7

For all those who live in their own Aventine,
Remember, patience pays off.

And for Anna, who was there from the very beginning.

Chapter One

The library was silent except for the whistling of wind as it howled across the open windowpane beside me. My bare feet dug into the carpeted floor as the muscles in my legs tensed, ready to spring to the side toward the window as adrenaline scorched my veins and my heart throbbed in my throat. I was so close to the fresh air, I could smell the snow on the treetops down below and feel the icy nighttime breeze on my arms. I felt totally electrified. There it was, no longer beyond the invisible cage of two-inch-thick plate glass:

Freedom. I didn't have time to be afraid of falling to my death if I failed to catch a support beam when every fiber of my body was urging me toward that rarely open window. *Go now,* I thought. *Now or never!*

I flinched when I noticed Quinn's jaw clench. He was almost right beside me, poised like a hound ready for his master's permission to strike. If I made so much as a move, he'd reach out with his long arms and catch me. I knew my pupils were dilated—the dim lights in the library suddenly seemed too bright—as I glanced frantically from Quinn to James, who was watching me with an almost amused air of curiosity.

"Excuse me," James remarked softly, gentlemanly as ever. He slowly reached up to remove his reading spectacles. "What are you doing?" The serene sweetness of his low voice would have me believe he was utterly calm, but I knew better. He was completely still, like Quinn, and rigid with alarm. He was far from calm and I could see the thunderstorm of his hideous temper brewing in his grey eyes.

"I...," I stammered, my mouth suddenly dry. I swallowed, gulping, as a cold sweat broke out over my upper lip. I glanced once again to the open window.

"Daisy," said James, a little sterner. "What are you doing?" I made the mistake of looking back at James only to see that glare he was famous for, the singular warning sign that his temper was about to rear its monstrous head. Panic seized my beating heart as the winter wind howled outside. I forced myself to look outside, hearing Kit's gentle chiding in my mind, *eyes on the prize*, but James was too arresting and Quinn was too close….

It was already over: I'd failed to escape. The corners of my mouth quivered as I began to cry. My courage was spent and it made me feel so small and pathetic. All these months of preparing, waiting to spring on an opportunity to get away from this place, and the first chance I got, I choked. My shoulders slumped in defeat. I bowed my head, grateful when my hair fell to cover my face as I sobbed quietly. My cheeks felt hot, and I wanted to throw myself on the floor at James' feet—I hated myself with a burning passion for it.

"There, there," James sighed. "My dear Daisy." He visibly relaxed and slipped his spectacles into his pocket. I couldn't stand the wetness of tears on my face so I swiped at them with trembling fingertips. I knew Quinn was still wary as ever, but when I looked at James, he was pinching the bridge of his nose and shaking his head.

"You're so tired," said James. "You don't know how tired you are, Daisy." The threat of his temper was gone when he looked at me now with trained kindness. "Why don't you let Quinn take you to your room?"

I was too ashamed to speak. I dried my hands on the front of my fawn-linen frock and nodded, looking away from James' pity. Quinn grasped my upper arm with such strength, I would have winced if I hadn't been so humiliated. He began to lead me out of the library and I forced myself to spare one last look at the open window, hoping to sear the image in my mind down to the last detail so that I could punish myself by thinking of nothing but my failure once I was locked in my room, probably for a week.

I gasped when, instead of the vast night sky, I saw Liza step out from behind the bookshelf nearest the window. James turned on a snap when I recoiled, which made Quinn tighten his grip on my arm. Liza's keen violet eyes were blazing with a fiery defiance I couldn't possibly have mustered as she stared right at James. Her stance was brazen for a young woman of her stature;

James could strangle her with one hand if he had a mind to, she was that much smaller than him—and she was barefoot, no less.

"Liza!" James exclaimed, surrounded by a nimbus of chagrin. I couldn't tell if he was more surprised than furious. I had never seen him bemused like this. Quinn wrenched me behind him and took a step toward Liza. "Quinn, do not get any closer!" Quinn froze, not daring to disobey James' sharp command. "Liza, come away from there at once, please." I'd never heard his voice so uneasily thin, so close to being frightened. Liza took half a step backward, edging closer to the window, and Quinn started for her again.

"Not another step, Quinn!" James snarled. Again, Quinn stopped. I was too petrified to move, too startled by the harsh ringing of James' voice. James forced a kinder tone when he said to Liza, "Please, Liza. Be a good girl and come away from the window."

Liza held her chin high, though I could see a shiver of trepidation flicker past her irises. "No," she said. For the first time in my life, I had finally witnessed someone disobey James the Master. My knees threatened to buckle as my stomach dropped into a vacuum of horror to see James adopt an unimaginably threatening posture.

"I fear that Daisy has set a very poor example," James explained carefully through sharp teeth clenched in a grimace. "It's time to stop this nonsense. Come away from the window, Liza. Now." Kindness was absent in that command.

I could see Liza's mind whirring behind her eyes—she'd always excelled at thinking on her feet, I knew she was weighing her options at breakneck speed: If she jumped, she had the brutal cold and dangerous forest to contend with. If she stayed, she would have to face James and his violent temper.

James took a short step toward Liza but immediately held back when Liza edged even closer to the precipice.

"Easy, Liza," James warned. "Don't be a fool." Liza wet her lips. I'd never seen anyone look at another person the way she was looking at James. There was a brilliant, wild vehemence in her eyes that made her look almost scary.

"I will no longer be your prisoner," Liza uttered gravely. She whirled around and jumped from the open window, disappearing from sight instantly as she fell with outstretched arms. I screamed loudly and burst into tears. Quinn and James ran to the window and I cried out for Liza over and over.

"What are you doing?" James bellowed at Quinn. "Get after her! Go downstairs and get every damn guard after her!" Quinn did not need telling twice. He sprinted from the library at a speed I didn't think possible for a man of his build, hollering for his fellow guardsmen to follow him. A moment later, the alarm blared over the speakers. I shrieked again when James grappled onto the adjacent pane of glass and leaned all the way out of the open window, holding on by four fingertips while balancing on the tiptoes of his shoes as he hung outside and looked down.

"LIZA! IT IS THE DEAD OF WINTER!" he roared furiously. "GET BACK HERE NOW! STOP! WE BOTH KNOW I WILL FIND YOU!"

Liza was alive, then! She must have caught hold of the support beams underneath the compound and was climbing down—*alive!*

"Liza!" I cried. I was both terrified and overjoyed. I prayed, "Oh, Liza! Run!"

With a contemptuous groan, James pulled himself back into the library. He slid the window closed and clicked the bolt into place. His eyes were ablaze with fury when he turned back to me, his features twisted with malice. I realized how much trouble I was in when James balled his fists at his sides, the frigid night air rolling off him in a wave.

"It would be best, I think, for you to come with me." James took my arm and pulled me hastily out of the library.

"James," I whined, suddenly shaking in fear of him. "I'm sorry, James, I didn't—"

"Be quiet," James snapped. I shut my mouth at once. We were bustling down the halls so fast, I would have stumbled if James hadn't been holding my arm. The servants were peeking out of the kitchen, dismayed by the alarm. I could hear their hushed voices, whispering and wondering what could have happened to make James this angry.

"Sir," said Douglas, James' second-in-command, as he fell into hasty stride with us. "We've obtained a visual on the girl. She's made it to the east end of the undercarriage—"

"Damn!" James hissed.

"But," Douglas went on urgently, "she's still got a hundred feet of air below, and we just received word of a pack of volpines right under the compound."

James paled, as did I. I had never seen a volpine—let alone the forest floor itself—but I had read about them in my schoolbooks. The thought of Liza being chased down by one of those nightmarish monsters made me sway where I stood.

Tugging on my arm to keep me upright, James stopped short of the west wing where the Masters' rooms were, and it seemed that Douglas and I were waiting for James to speak before we could take a breath.

"Call Donovan," James said curtly. "Tell him to send in the swordsmen, and under no circumstance are there to be any firearms used."

"Sir," Douglas replied incredulously. "The volpines are great in number, surely the more proficient gunmen could—"

"I will not risk a stray bullet finding Liza before we do," James declared. "I need her back *alive*." That was the end of it, apparently, because Douglas gave a quick nod and dashed off. I started to sway again, mostly at the idea of Liza being shot.

"Daisy," James said. He turned me around to face him. "It is imperative that you understand the seriousness of this predicament. Because of your stupidity," he seethed the word, disgusted, "Liza may die. If I didn't think there was no choice for me but to now go below with the guardsmen and try to find her before that happens, I would drag you back to your wing by your hair. Now, you will go back to your rooms and stay there until you are sent for."

"Sent for?" I asked.

"If any harm comes to Liza," said James, fixing a hard glare at me, "I will have every guardsman in the compound flogged for his incompetence. They will then, in turn, hold you accountable for their slights, as this very necessary rescue operation is entirely and indisputably your fault." Without waiting for my response, James reached back and struck me across the face with the palm of his hand. I yelped and spilled bodily into the floor, my cheek stinging and my ears ringing. The servants in the hall heard the loud slap of James striking me, and my subsequent involuntary cry, and came forward to help me get to my feet.

"None of you will lift a finger to help her to her room!" James thundered. "She's done enough this evening. Get back to your work!" He stormed off to the his wing, slamming the door behind him.

I wasn't in any shape to feel sorry for myself in front of these people. With the little dignity I had left, I got to my feet, my knees knocking together, and slowly made my way in the opposite direction James had gone. I was completely despondent. I could hear nothing over the wailing alarm echoing through the halls, not even my own whimpering. I craved the solitude of my windowless room, the comfort of my plush bedding, and the lonely skylight over my bed through which I could stare at the synthesized stars projected by the lamp I knew was there to mimic the true sky outside and pretend I was worlds away.

I found the Tribute wing soon enough. The doors slid open upon my approach and quietly closed behind me, muffling the wail of the alarm as they sealed tightly. I looked up and saw that Kit and Armand were waiting for me. They stopped pacing the moment I came through the doors, their expressions aghast when they noticed the tears in my eyes.

"Daze," Kit rushed forward and lifted me off my feet, holding me tightly in his arms. "Are you all right?" As soon as I heard the concerned waver in his voice, I began to cry again. Kit crushed me to him, stroking my hair soothingly with his hand. "Daisy," he hummed, swaying back and forth. He hushed me and tilted my head so that it rested on his shoulder.

"What happened?" Armand demanded urgently. "One minute, we were walking back from the gallery and the next, the alarms go off and the guardsmen throw us in here and tell us to stay put! What the hell happened, Daisy?" I assumed the look Kit gave him was caustic, because Armand did not press me again when I didn't answer.

"Daisy," Kit said softly. "Are you all right?"

"Yes," I croaked. I locked my arms around his neck and clung to him, my always safe Kit, whose sleek, sunny blond hair was so like mine, and whose brown eyes were always warm and caring.

"Your cheek is red," Kit remarked, gently prying me away from him. He carefully took my chin between his thumb and digits and turned my head so that he could see my face in the lamplight. He winced when he got a good look at it, as did Armand.

"Who did this to you?" Kit asked, his dark brows furrowing. Another bout of shame overtook me. I shook my head and shut my eyes, unable to answer.

"Daisy, you must tell me. Who did this to you?" I was taking gulps of air, trying to steady my nerves, but I couldn't keep from crying. Eventually I was able to croak out that it was James who hit me, which spurred Kit and Armand to exchange horrified glances.

"All right, I'll bite!" Armand exclaimed. He would have sounded braver and more fed up if he hadn't hushed his voice. "What did you do?"

"I managed to get into the library," I began, holding tightly to Kit's arms to save myself in case my knees gave out. "The window—it was open, and I—"

"Oh, tell me you didn't do what I think you did," Armand groaned. "James caught you trying to escape, didn't he?"

"Yes," I admitted. I gritted my teeth and kicked myself, hard, in the shin.

"Daisy, cut it out," Kit rebuked me, trying his best to be kind. "So what if he caught you? We knew this could happen. I wish he hadn't hit you, but it could have been worse—"

"It is worse!" I pulled away from Kit. I took a wheezy, shuddering breath and fell into the chair behind me.

"Daisy, sweetheart, I'm really trying to be patient here, but you are not giving me any reason to not panic!" Armand berated. "How could it possibly be worse than getting caught?"

"Liza jumped out the window!" I sank back in the chair and covered my face with my hands, too upset to watch the likely gut-wrenchingly scandalized expressions Kit and Armand made. The whole thing came pouring out of me, in hysterical bursts: how Liza must have sneaked into the library behind me, how James had nearly flung himself out after her but instead sent away for Donovan and his swordsmen to go retrieve her before the pack of volpines could get to her. Gradually, Kit and Armand both sank into chairs across from me, each silent and ashen, and clearly as sickened as I was. Finally, I told them what James had said to me before cracking me across the face—how he and everyone in the compound who worked for him would hold me accountable if Liza was not found alive.

"It's a miracle she survived the jump," Kit murmured after a few minutes of shocked silence. Kit was one to take a diplomatic stance in the face of crises, as he was constantly pointing out whatever blanket positivity there was to cover a situation.

"I beg to differ," Armand replied bitterly, sounding a lot like our tutor, Graham.

"Oh?" Kit rounded on him. "You don't think Liza surviving what would have been a three-hundred-and-fifty-foot fall by catching a support beam defies the staunch probability to the contrary?"

Armand guffawed, looking in disbelief around the parlor of our apartment for spectators who were not there. "You've got to be joking! So she survived jumping out of the window! Great! And what do you suppose James is going to do to her when he finds her?" Kit said nothing. He looked away from Armand, but he must have been just as cynical about the idea as Armand was, because he didn't look at me.

"If Liza dies," I said slowly, in a voice that didn't sound like it belonged to me, "he'll kill me."

"We'll never let that happen." Kit's response was automatic.

"Kit's right, Daze," Armand agreed, his tone earnest and dry at once. "It's unlikely James himself would do it, but those guardsmen he'll kick the daylights out of for not rescuing her might!"

"Damn you, Armie!" Kit yelled angrily, getting to his feet. "What's wrong with you?"

"I'll tell you!" Armand shouted. "I said from the very beginning, this escape-the-compound business is a stupid idea! Liza is an idiot for thinking she stands a chance! And I'm sorry, but Daisy just signed our death warrants!"

"Don't you go blaming Daisy," Kit growled. He squared up to Armand, who was without question both taller and meaner than himself.

"No one escapes," Armand said, a menacing shadow darkening his features as he glared at Kit. "That's the only thing we know for sure about this life. No one escapes." Armand stepped away from Kit and looked to me. "I wish we could be free just as much as you do, but this is insanity. And if Liza dies, our lives will be nothing but miserable until we beg James to kill us."

"Shut your mouth, Armie," Kit warned.

Armand continued, blatantly ignoring Kit. "What do you imagine James the Master will do to us if Liza survives and he doesn't catch her? What will he do when the singular truth of this world is threatened by the escape of one little girl?"

The notion was unthinkably horrible. It dawned on me that all of Armand's objections to finding a way to escape hadn't been cowardly at all, that his insistence that we find another way to gain our freedom without risking so much had actually been reserved, even clever.

"I hope they find her alive," Armand said dejectedly. "James will beat her silly and we'll clean her up, and that'll be the end of it." Wordlessly, Armand turned his back on Kit and me and retreated to his bedroom. His words fell heavily on me and I worried that I wouldn't be able to stop crying ever again.

"He can be a real bastard," Kit decided. "He's the cruelest when he's afraid. Remember that." He crossed the room and pulled me up to my feet. "Come on. I'll help you to bed. You need to sleep."

"Oh, I couldn't possibly," I moaned.

"You must," Kit disagreed. He smiled sadly as he looked down into my eyes and lightly brushed the unmarked side of my face with the side of his thumb. "You wear your shame as plainly as you wear that frock." He gestured to his own linen garment, which was cut differently to fit his masculine form but otherwise identical to mine.

"These are not the clothes of prisoners, Daze," Kit said. "They are suits of armor. We're only strong when we're together, remember? Don't punish yourself for not going through with it. I'm glad you didn't. You could have died jumping out that window."

"I'm not glad," I said. I meant it. "Maybe if I'd jumped, I'd have—"

"Left me here all alone, with Armie?" Kit's attempt to cheer me up was wry and ineffective, but he still chuckled dryly. "I don't think I'd survive in here without you to keep me sane."

Maybe he was right. As much as I hated myself for having choked up in the library, the thought of plummeting to my death and never seeing Liza and the boys again was not a warm one. The more I replayed the memory in my mind, the more I foolish I felt. And then all I could think about was the look in Liza's eyes when she stared at James.

"What was she thinking?" I asked Kit. We called Kit the mind-reader of the group, for he had a knack for accurately guessing what any of us was feeling or pondering at any given moment.

"Liza has always been the bold one," Kit pointed out.

"Bold? I think you mean competitive," I said. I was only sort of kidding.

"Either way," Kit replied, "maybe bearing witness to your hesitation gave her the strength to go through with it. She might be the bravest of us, but she looks to you more than you think she does."

"Maybe," I replied, pondering that idea carefully. Liza was older than me; I found it hard to believe that she would ever look to me for guidance.

"Or maybe she was less afraid of James than you were," Kit guessed. His honesty didn't sting me like it would have Armand; I had the imprint of James' hand on my face to prove that I had every reason to fear him. James had only struck Liza once, as I recall, but even that had been an underreaction to what she'd done to deserve it.

It had been just shy of four years ago, when we had dabbled in martial arts as part of our schooling. We'd always been encouraged to exercise familiarity with each other, but when Kit and Armand's roughhousing started to lose its innocence, James decided we needed a fitness regimen into which the boys could channel their aggression. Ultimately, his hope was to shape our adolescent bodies to be graceful and sure instead of wobbly and gangly. James insisted that we always have the best tutors for our studies so naturally he hired an instructor through Donovan's connections, a master of hand-to-hand combat known only as "Yuki." Once we were proficient in the basics, the four of us would pair off and practice together. James had taken a particular interest in overseeing these training sessions as in his youth, he had been something of a fighter himself—on more than one occasion, he even joined us on the training mats.

Kit had not been wrong when he said tonight that Liza was the bold one, but I was also in the right. The girl was competitive and at eighteen, she had been more eager to prove herself than ever. Our sensei favored the boys and often spent nearly the entire class focused on their form and movements. James was happy to assist with mine and Liza's training. He once told me he found my sheer will to look intimidating to be endearing, which I chose to take as a compliment. He also confided in me that he'd been small for his age when he had learned to fight as a boy, and encouraged me to keep working at it.

Liza he found to be fiery, "promising" was the word he used to describe her after he'd watched her spar with one of his guardsmen trainees. On the day James had hit Liza, our training had gone fairly typically at first: Yuki had taken Kit and Armand aside to carefully correct their stances and I was on the mat, having been knocked down by Liza yet again. James had been watching and came over to suggest Liza try her tactics on him, implying that a larger and stronger opponent would not be so easy for her to defeat. Liza agreed, excited for the challenge, so James proceeded to take a defensive, if not amused and even lighthearted position.

Of course, Liza's daring wit had gotten her into trouble with our tutors dozens of times before, but when she purposefully punched James squarely in the face hard enough to make his lip bleed, the entire floor of the compound went deadly silent. James was taken aback by the hit; obviously, he hadn't expected her to be able to put so much force behind her fist. Laying any kind of hand on him was a flagrant violation of the laws of the compound, let alone a closed fist. James had hit Liza right back—he split her upper lip in return and knocked her to the floor. Immediately afterwards, Kit had been so upset by it that he refused to partake in any more martial arts training. Armand and I had been shocked by the whole ordeal, but both of us had to agree that Liza had been wrong to strike James like that, and when Liza told me privately that James had hit her so hard that she'd felt her teeth rattle in her skull, I had joined Kit's recusal of the martial arts.

To this day, I could see the pearly white scar James had left on Liza's lip. The strike had been brutal to see, but even Liza admitted it was an underreaction—James had killed men for doing less and we all knew it. Perhaps it was true that Liza didn't fear James as much as I did. Or maybe she counted on the knack she had for extricating herself from hairy situations, like inexplicably catching a support beam after jumping out a window.

"You'll drop like a stone if you don't lie down," Kit said, pulling me out of the past and into this daunting reality. "Come on, I'll help you." I let Kit lead me to my room and helped me pull back the down blanket on my bed. He diligently ensured I was tucked in comfortably before crawling on top of the covers beside me. We had more freedom in our Tribute quarters than anywhere else in the compound, but there were strict rules regarding how we spent our sleeping hours. As young children, the four of us would pile in one bed and fall asleep giggling and singing to each other. Once we reached adolescence, however, sleeping together was deemed inappropriate and the tutors carefully spelled out the rigid code of conduct by which we must abide: we must not share our beds with anyone, being the key take away.

It didn't stop us from embracing the close company of each other for comfort, though. Tonight, after the upsetting tribulations I'd gone through, Kit held me in his arms as I dozed in bed. I knew he would leave as soon as I fell asleep, but I would have exhausted myself from weeping if I'd been left alone for the rest of the night.

"Worlds away," Kit murmured to me as I stared up at the twinkling stars through the skylight. I slowly drifted off, the droning alarm still blaring distantly in the compound. In my dreams, I was surrounded by sunlight. I could hear birds and smell sweet fruits, even freshly chopped wood. I heard a woman's voice calling my name in a delighted but far away memory. I turned into the shadow to search for the woman calling me and suddenly felt so cold....

The dream twisted into a nightmare as James came for me. No matter how fast I ran, I could never get away from him. I could feel his fingertips graze my back as he reached out to catch me, the claws of a demon's hand digging into my flesh as I screamed for Liza—but Liza was gone, she jumped out of the window, and James was roaring after her, *"We both know I will find you!"*

I woke up as a strangled cry escaped my throat. I saw up in bed, daylight pouring in through the skylight overhead, and breathlessly put my hands over my racing heart. My head was aching, and I was sure my cheek was still swollen. I slipped out of bed and went into the washroom, thankful that I had a private one so that I wouldn't risk running into the boys before I had a chance to see how unkempt I looked. I clicked on the dim light and reached down to turn the knob on the bathtub, filling the basin with steaming hot water. I stripped off my linen garments from yesterday and finally braved the mirror after turning on the brighter vanity bulbs that lined the glass frame.

My brown eyes were swollen and red from crying. I frowned to see the puffy appearance of my skin, as though I'd had an allergic reaction. I placed my hands on the sink basin and leaned in close to the mirror with my face turned. There was no redness now, but the shadow of a yellow bruise traced along my cheekbone. Liza's bruise had been much uglier after James had struck her on the training mat. Did that make me feel better?

I ran a brush through my hair and grimaced to find so many knots and tangles. I glimpsed myself in the mirror when I turned to shut the bathwater off before the tub could overflow and hardly spared my reflection a second glance. I never paid much attention to myself naked, mostly because nudity was far removed from my life in the compound. I'd studied art with the boys and Liza under Graham's tutelage, of course, and I was familiar with anatomy, but I was not keen to admire the body like others my age—especially the boys.

Armand commented once that Liza's breasts were fuller than mine and she'd pinched him hard on the arm for saying so; in addition to Liza pinching Armand, a disgruntled Kit had warned him he was "on the fast track to being a scoundrel!"

I never really grasped why the comparison was such an inflammatory thing to point out, for it was true as far as I could tell. I'd learned from studying literature and art that something as simple as a pair of breasts had started wars among men, which was ridiculous to me. And then our anatomy tutor and resident doctor, Jada, assured me in earnest that the tricks of copulation and intimacy of our kind were irrelevant to me here at the compound and I had no reason or interest, really, in proving her wrong.

I shook my head and pushed the irreverent thoughts from my mind. I switched off the vanity lights and climbed into the tub, breathing through the sting of hot water on my tired limbs. I listened for the wail of the alarm but I heard nothing—of course they wouldn't let the alarm sound now that the sun was up, but did that mean they'd found Liza? I was anxious to know but I forced myself to stay in the bath until the water went cold. What could be waiting for me outside of our wing, if Liza was dead?

I drained the tub, dried my hair, and dressed in fresh linens. I even plaited my long hair back before I felt compelled enough to leave my room which by my astonishment wasn't locked from the outside. As I made my way to the kitchen, I realized I hadn't put on my shoes. We rarely wore shoes around the compound; James only insisted the servants and guardsmen keep to the stringent dress code. Life as I knew it had gone out the library window after Liza, and it made me wonder whether or not I should have put on my shoes even to venture into the kitchen.

"Good morning, Daisy," said Graham. The tutors were the only people in the compound allowed to enter our wing, aside from James and Donovan. It wasn't unusual to find Graham around the apartment, usually drinking coffee or reading one of the rare books James would procure to suit Kit's taste in literature. This morning, Graham had a large ceramic cup of coffee in hand and was leaning against the marble countertop, probably supervising Armand while he cooked over the stovetop instead of working with Kit at the table.

"Good morning, sir," I said. Kit looked up from his workbook at the table and pursed his lips sadly. Armand switched the stove off and expertly transferred the omelet he'd cooked onto a plate. He noticed me and nodded.

"Hi, Daze," he said. I could tell he felt guilty for his harsh words the night before because he never called me by my nickname. "How'd you sleep?"

"Poorly," I sighed, taking a seat at the table across from Kit.

"She had nightmares," Kit added stiffly, jabbing at Armand for his rough manners last night. He quickly went rigid when Graham cleared his throat and made knowing eyes at him, clearly displeased by the implication of how Kit might know how I slept the night before. I nervously looked at Graham, whose stern features were outlined by age, and waited for him to rebuke me for bending the rules. He was about to make a stern opening statement, which would likely be along the lines of, "Now, Daisy," when he noticed the bruise on my cheek. His face fell. He set his coffee down and pushed back his sleeves, turning around to pull a second ceramic mug from the shelf. He poured tea from the pot on the stove and brought it to me, then quickly retrieved his coffee and sat beside me.

"Now, Daisy," he said (I couldn't help but smirk at having guessed his words), "it is my understanding that you got into a great deal of trouble last night. Despite your part in what went on, Master James behaved in an abhorrent fashion towards you. I will gladly risk his discontent and apologize to you on his behalf." Graham's voice was deep and measured, which lent his words and sentiment a rich gravitas. I might have found solace in the secondhand apology if I knew it was genuine. Then again, I knew he could be reprimanded for speaking on James' behalf so he must have been greatly concerned.

"Not much has been disclosed to the non-essential staff," Graham went on, "about what went on last night. I spoke with Quinn this morning when I

arrived, but he merely explained that we are to go about our work as usual."
He paused to take a sip of coffee. "Kit and Armand told me that you had been
through an ordeal and should be excluded from studying today. I greatly admire their discretion, no doubt out of respect for your feelings, but I confess
I am very interested to know what went on. Are you able to tell me any details,
so that I know better how to move forward with you today?"

I sipped my tea and slowly looked at Kit, who gave a single and nearly un-
detectable negating nod of his head. I knew he was right—I shouldn't give
Graham any insight about what happened. I found it too hard to believe that
none of the tutors had heard about it, or that they would be denied information. And anyway, why wouldn't they tell Liza's tutor why she wouldn't be at
the compound for class today?

"Sir," I said to Graham, mindful to keep a neutral tone. "It is too horrible
for me to rehash so soon. And I am too worried about Liza." I saw Armand
nod in approval out of the corner of my eye. He was always reminding me to
keep answers clipped and concise when speaking to the staff.

"I understand," Graham said. I could tell he was disappointed.

"I am sorry, sir," I said. "Please don't think I distrust you. I really am so
tired…," my voice caught in my throat. I felt nauseous suddenly as James' voice
echoed in my memory. *You don't know how tired you are, Daisy.*

"Master James did not forbid me from instructing you today," Graham
said. Maybe James did feel sorry for hitting me last night—that would explain
the unlocked bedroom door, the non-explicit consent for me to participate in
my studies.

"It would be better than sitting around all day waiting," Kit urged quietly.
I knew he was right. If I holed myself in my room with nothing to distract me
from the gnawing, raw failure that set in last night, I would surely waste away.

"I'd like to work today, if you'll allow it," I said. "Sir," I added quickly.

"Very good, Daisy," Graham said, a proud smile spreading on his face. "A
very wise choice, indeed." He got up to finish his coffee and wash his cup in
the kitchen sink. Armand had just finished wolfing down his omelet and slid
around the other side of the table so that he was right next to me.

"Smart, sweetheart," he said.

"Lay off, Armie," I said, scowling.

"No, really," Armand whispered. "You did the right thing. We have to keep acting normal and not tell them anything about last night. We're going to be good little students, and you're going to keep your nose down and pretend that nothing happened."

"He's right, Daze," Kit whispered. "They're either testing us, or they've hushed it up for a reason." He widened his eyes knowingly, unable to voice his suspicion aloud, that Liza must be alive. She must have successfully escaped and survived the volpines, otherwise everyone would know what happened, especially me.

"Very well, pupils!" Graham said rousingly. "Clear up breakfast, Armand, so that we may get started. Today will be geography and sketching; I thought we might bridge into cartography this afternoon."

Over the next twelve hours, I realized that maintaining a clear head by keeping myself thoroughly distracted wasn't as difficult as I would have thought. I followed Graham's sultry baritone voice through the major continents, oceans, and mountain ranges of our continent.

The Quake, as it was known, was the singular event that resulted in the birth of the Master System. Seventy-odd years prior to my own birth, the continent of North America had been split by a violent earthquake that broke the vast plates into five main pieces. The smaller remnants of North America dotted the east coast, at least the parts that hadn't been washed away in the terrible storms that followed the earthquake. Formerly known as the Midwest, the Central Plates were four continents that were roughly the same size. My childhood history lessons told of gruesome battles for independence and land seizure in the second largest continent, the Northwest piece that was now called simply Dakota, and even worse power disputes in the southern continents.

Concerning Dakota, there is current speculation among environmental experts that the creatures we knew as volpines originated from the volatile continent due to an accelerated mutation of the common grey wolf. I had witnessed Graham debate this theory with many a young tutor's apprentice, who seemed to always insist that the presence of nuclear weapons in Dakota before the Quake resulted in the existence of volpines, beasts that were best described as fox-wolves the size of horses, but my dependable old teacher never failed to find a solid reason to refute such a claim. It was easy to imagine such terrible creatures had come from Dakota, an assumption that seemed appropriate based on the awful events that transpired there, but the proof of the volpines' genesis simply did not exist. Indeed, these monsters were merely one of the hundreds of new variations of life that the massive tectonic shift had shaken loose.

The Quake irreversibly changed not just North America but the entire globe. History lessons described the shift in international unity after the Quake as "a fitting book end to society as we knew it" as land was gobbled up and all semblance of organized politics went by the wayside. The rest of the world left North America to its own devices just as its residents washed their hands of the foreign bodies that could not—or would not—extend a helping hand.

The Aventine was our compound, hidden away in the West Masterlands. As they did everything else in their domain, the Masters controlled cities, townships, farmlands, and each in-between development that the survivors of the Quake settled in. Those who did not ascribe to the Master System—I understood them to be the sworn enemies of the Masters—were the Free Factions. These were the only group of people I knew of who were disgusted by the idea of offering Tributes to the Masters in exchange for protection from the threat of the infidels who called Dakota their home and any other hardship that might find them in their lives outside of a compound.

Drawing maps of each continent in my sketchpad was difficult. There was so much land in the Masterlands that was protected by the Masters' military, I couldn't label many of the cities that were nestled too close to the forest near the coast. Still, on a day like this, I put all my focus into my work. When tired of maps, I sketched still-life scenes from the study and hummed errantly under my breath as I went.

When Kit, Armand, and I left the Tribute wing to go fetch supplies from the art studio upstairs, we were relieved when no passing servant or staff member so much as looked at us. They feared James more than they wanted to see for themselves that Liza was not with us, and I felt a surge of affection for the boys, who protectively kept me between them at all times. Still, it was too quiet for our comfort. The halls usually bustled with activity during the day, with merchants and craftsmen buzzing in and out of the Masters' chambers like diligent worker bees. While there was a lot of movement in the common areas, I couldn't help but notice the absence of the very tan outdoor workers or the cheery-looking delivery agents who brought in food and lumber. Part of me suspected that James had turned away all the passersby to keep the servants from spreading gossip…but could James be so afraid of a scandal?

At night, after Graham left us, Armand and I worked in the kitchen while Kit played the piano in the study. Armand had a penchant for baking bread, so he put me to task peeling and slicing zucchini for the savory loaf he would cook for our dinner.

"Remember when Liza tried to bake bread?" Armand asked as he kneaded the dough.

"How could I forget? It prompted our first lesson in fire safety," I recalled, cracking a smile for the first time that day.

"Strange, wasn't it? That so many faces weren't around the studio today?" Armand wondered.

"I noticed the same thing," I replied.

"James may not have been in today, at all," Armand guessed.

"But would there be guardsmen inside if he was still out there?" I asked.

"I'm not sure, but the alarms went off just before sunrise," said Armand with a stifled yawn. It didn't occur to me to have asked him how he'd slept this morning—evidently he hadn't at all. "The tradesmen wouldn't have heard it by the time they got in." We shared an eager expression.

"She must have gotten away," I said quietly.

"It's a speculation," Armand reminded me. He was so quick to guard himself that I often wondered if he ever let himself feel excitement or hope.

"I know," I replied, to ease his cynicism. I thought about what he'd said last night when he'd asked me what I thought James would do to us if Liza really escaped, and by doing so made a mockery of the laws of the compound?

"Get the lemons, Daisy," Armand instructed. "I'll teach you how to zest the rind."

"Zest?" I teased quizzically. "You mean, peel?"

"No," Armand replied wryly, "I mean zest. That's the term. Good grief, Liza never gave me this much fuss when she helped in the kitchen…."

"Apart from the time she set it on fire?" I chided. Armand laughed and I heard the piano music stop from the other room for just a moment. That must have been Kit appreciating Armand and I laughing together.

I loved the sound of Kit's playing. After the martial arts fiasco and the four of us pursuing separate avenues of specialty study, Kit discovered a love of music that even James openly admired. James found him a separate tutor for violin and piano, an impressive fact with which I tried to bargain for my own separate tutors in gymnastics and ballet, to no avail. James wouldn't hear of it because Liza was more driven in gymnastics, he'd explained, so if he was going to hire an additional expert who would demand an even higher pay than my ballet teacher, it would end up being for Liza, and she'd just get bored of it and give it up anyway.

After dinner, Kit and I cleaned the kitchen and joined Armand in the study where he'd built a fire so that we could sit around the hearth and read together. I sat on the floor with some pillows and leaned against Kit's legs. He read James Joyce while Armand scribbled some notes in his sketchbook. I tried to read my own book, but when I realized it was a novel Liza had lent me, I couldn't focus. I went to bed after assuring Kit that I didn't need company.

"You coddle her," I heard Armand murmur as I padded along the corridor to my bedroom.

"So what?" Kit sighed, set on not engaging with Armand.

Sleep claimed me almost as soon as I laid my head on my pillow. I really didn't get rest last night, so I was relieved at how easy it was to bat away the tormenting thoughts that tried to steal me away from slumber. My dreams took me back to the sunny place where I could hear a woman call my name. I tossed once in my sleep when I dreamed of Liza, but I didn't relive the library escape. It was a peaceful dream, in which Liza was singing and braiding my hair.

The next morning was almost normal. I woke up, bathed, and joined the boys in the kitchen for breakfast. Graham brought Jada with him this morning, and she insisted on looking at my cheek.

"It's far from silly," Jada said grimly when I tried to insist she leave such a trivial bruise alone. "On a face like yours, it's better to be safe than sorry." She leaned in and carefully applied a salve to the side of my face. "Graham has a daughter just a few years older than you, you know," Jada whispered. "He can't help but worry over you when you're hurt. It's the father in him." She flashed a dazzling smile when she finished dabbing salve on my cheek. "There, good as new!"

"Thank you, Doctor Jada," I said automatically.

"You're welcome, Daisy," Jada replied warmly. "You let me know if you need anything. I'll be around." She glanced down and gestured to my frock. "That needs longer sleeves, honey. You've grown since the last time I saw you!" She laughed when my face reddened—I liked and trusted Jada enough to feel comfortable when she made observations about my body, but it felt embarrassing to bring it up in front of Graham and the boys.

"As you say," I said, fidgeting with my sleeve.

"I'm happy to put in an order with the tailors," Jada said, putting the bottle of salve into her leather satchel.

"I would appreciate that," I said, trying to mask my confusion by keeping up with my manners. It was strange for her to offer to visit the tailor on my behalf; I had to imagine she had dozens of more important tasks to do instead.

"No problem, honey. A bit of shopping sounds like just the thing, maybe I'll stop by the tanner on my way there. I could use a new bag!" Jada was always refreshing to be around as she seemed to always be in a bright humor, but she was usually rushing to her next appointment instead of making small talk with patients.

"I hope you do not get any ideas about procrastination from the doctor," Graham chimed in, sharing a smile with Jada.

"I know, I know," Jada confessed. "I'm stalling for time away from the office, but I can't help it. There are a few too many workers in the beehive of a medical wing I'm trying to hold together."

"Naturally," Graham agreed. "You are more than welcome to join me and my pupils for tea, should you need a quiet place to look over your charts this afternoon."

"I may take you up on that, Graham," said Jada. "That is, if I run out of busy work for myself. You would scarcely believe it, since Master Donovan's doctors took over my operation—" Jada pulled a face when she realized she had said something she shouldn't have. Graham tried to maintain his pleasant demeanor, but the dread in his eyes was unmistakable.

I looked to Kit and Armand with wide eyes and they both returned expressions of stunned excitement that plainly conveyed our shared sentiment: *What just happened?* I then realized that I'd forgotten to mention Donovan to either of them in my retelling of last night's tale of woe. It was strange that Donovan's swordsmen and doctors were all over the Aventine and yet we had not seen the young Master himself.

"I apologize," Jada said gravely to Graham, stealing me away from my ponderings about Donovan. "I've overstepped." She turned to us and said, "Allow me to explain—"

"Doctor," Graham interrupted quickly, "I should point out—"

"It's all right, Graham," Jada insisted. She fixed a very serene stare at him and took a deep breath. "Would you be good enough to get my coat from the other room?" she asked. Graham pursed his lips and bowed his head. He left the kitchen without another word, leaving me, Kit, and Armand alone and perplexed with Jada.

"It's been a long day," said Jada, crossing her arms. "And I forgot myself for a moment. I apologize for oversharing. I don't want to get the three of you into any trouble by telling you something I shouldn't."

"Doctor Jada," Kit asked meekly. "What's going on?"

Jada sighed. "You understand," she began, casting a wary glance over her shoulder, "that there are certain liberties I am entitled to that other members of staff are not?"

All three of us nodded in sync as we interpreted Jada's insinuation: Graham was not officially allowed to hear whatever she was about to say.

Jada made a point to look at each of us before she spoke again. "I must infringe upon your discretion, children, but the truth is, Master Donovan's doctors have come to the compound to assist with a recent inflation of injuries. Many guardsmen were fatally injured during rescue efforts, but many more suffered serious inflictions and frankly, I worried I wasn't capable of keeping up with it. Douglas was forced to make an executive call and request aid from Master Donovan." Jada hesitated for a moment, trying to decide how to phrase what came next with the most diplomacy.

"Such a drastic measure would not usually have been necessary, but due to the extent of Master James' injuries, we had to act fast." Jada was downright grim to report this. I let out a little moan at the news and Kit reached for my hand.

James had been hurt! That would explain why I hadn't been punished with severe prejudice when Liza wasn't found by morning. The gates of the compound had been shut to any who might carry that information out with them and spread it to other cities.

I was reeling. James had been hurt. Oh, no, James had been hurt....

"It's true," Graham said from the doorway. He held Jada's coat aloft as he gazed solemnly down at us. "Master James sustained serious injuries the night before last, and as a result, the compound has become temporary home to new doctors and guardsmen. Your safety is our concern, as always, I do not want you to worry—"

"How?" Armand blurted. "How was he injured?" He watched as Graham and Jada exchanged resigned shrugs.

"Master James went out with the swordsmen," Jada confessed quietly. "The men were attacked by a pack of volpines and his were among the more severe injuries—at least, among the survivors."

"And...Liza?" Kit croaked. His eyes were swimming with tears as he searched Jada's expression desperately.

"Search efforts are still underway," Jada said wanly. She held her hands up apologetically. "I'm sorry, children."

My head was pounding. James had been seriously hurt. Liza was still missing, after a deadly volpine attack....

Jada got to her feet and took her coat from Graham. "I'm sorry," she said again. She took up her satchel from the table. "For having said too much, and for troubling you with these things which you must never speak of to anyone. I should go."

"Doctor Jada," I moaned. Kit cried out when I keeled over in my chair. Armand leaped over to catch me but missed and I fell to the floor in a swoon. My head hit the floor with a loud crash and everything went dark.

When I came to, I saw through the skylight over my head that it was dusk outside. I could hear Armand's garbled voice through my door.

"Armie?" I called. Immediately, the door opened and Kit rushed in. Armand was on his heels and both of them were pale with worry.

"Daze," Kit sighed, relieved as he took my hand in both of his.

"Move over, Kit," Armand grouched. "She asked for me, remember?" He gazed down at me, smiling kindly. "How are you feeling, sweetheart?"

"My head hurts," I observed with a groan. The effort to sit up was painful.

"You fainted," Kit said.

"You've never done that before," Armand added.

"There she is!" said Jada, appearing behind the boys. Her smile was perfect and bright as she kneeled over me to feel my forehead. "You fainted in the kitchen, Daisy. Do you remember that?"

"Unfortunately," I replied. Armand grinned at my disdain.

"I take responsibility for the whole thing," Jada said sadly. "It was too much excitement for you, after everything you'd been through the day before. I shouldn't have told you all those morbid details."

"Will James be all right?" I asked. Jada frowned, disused to anyone other than the doctors referring to James without his title. We were allowed, James was firm about that, but it took some staff members longer than others to get comfortable hearing it.

"Master James will be right as rain in no time," Jada assured me. "I don't want you to worry about him, that's my job." She flashed another smile and asked the boys to wait outside.

"No, please," I begged. "I want them here."

"Suit yourself, honey," Jada said. "I'm going to give you a mild sedative to help you sleep. I'll be back to check on you in the morning, but you need to rest. I don't want you working or studying for three days, is that understood?"

"Yes, Doctor," I said immediately. Tears welled in my eyes when I saw Jada withdraw a small syringe from her satchel, attached to the top of which was a very long needle. I hated needles and I could never seem to brave them like Liza or the boys.

"It's all right, Daze," Kit said, squeezing my hand. "We're right here."

"Just a pinch, and it'll be over!" Jada encouraged. The needle pricked the inside of my arm and I gritted my teeth. The injection burned for a few moments before a heavy drowsiness clouded my mind.

"Get some rest now, Daisy," said Jada. "Boys, we need to give her some privacy."

"We'll be right outside!" Kit insisted.

"Shout if you need us!" Armand chimed in.

I was asleep as soon as the door shut. There were no sunny places in this slumber, just thoughtless, drifting darkness. I curled up and reveled to feel the throbbing on the side of my head subside. I was out for what felt like only a few hours but when I finally awoke to find Jada listening to my heart through a stethoscope, she told me that I'd been asleep for nearly a full day. She told me that the boys were keeping very busy, that the swelling on my head had gone down completely, just like the bruise on my cheek. Jada gave me a glass of water and a tiny pink pill to swallow. Apparently, it would help me feel stronger when I woke up the next morning, for I hadn't had a meal in a while and she didn't want me to faint again when I stood up.

I had another dreamless sleep after Jada left. My pillows were too comforting to abandon, so I stayed right where I was. I didn't even miss the sunny place in my dreams now that I'd gotten a few tries at the alternative. When morning arrived, I felt incredibly rested and ready to go back to my routine. After my bath and breakfast, which the boys nervously watched me eat as though they feared I'd faint all over again, I was dismayed when Graham turned me away from a lesson. I forgot that Jada had ordered me to abstain from work for the next two days. I read in the study until I finished my book, then I painted in the studio, missing Liza's loom as the loneliness of working alone made my shoulders sag. I wanted to put on my slippers and throw myself into some ballet, but Kit and Armand worried over me when I brought it up.

The boys waited until Graham left the Tribute wing to pull me into lingering hugs and hold me close to share gossip.

"We overheard Jada telling the tutors that James himself had assigned her to watch over you when we went to the tailor," Kit said.

"Apparently, he asked about your temperament and she told him you fainted because you overheard a servant talking about the volpine attack," Armand said. He rolled his eyes contemptuously. "At least she had the decency to not name which servant, and save Graham's reputation in the process."

"So he's all right?" I asked. "James is all right?"

Armand served me a patronizing frown. "Daisy," he said dryly. "Donovan's doctors are staying at the compound. Of course James is all right."

"But have you seen him?" I asked.

"No," Kit said. "No one's seen him around the compound, but dinner keeps going into the Masters' chambers and not coming out...."

"We've all seen Quinn's face, though," Armand said uneasily. When he saw me wait for him to elaborate, he explained, "His eyes are blackened and he's got stitches in his jaw."

I felt as though I'd been hit in the gut.

"James didn't hurt him enough to hinder his responsibilities," Kit swiftly reminded me.

"What makes you think James did it?" Armand asked. "He was injured. He probably had Douglas do it."

"I have to lie down," I decided wisely, for my head had begun to spin again. Kit and Armand followed me down the hall to my room and sat on the foot of my bed when I crawled under the covers. They watched me with such sorrowful expressions. I hated that I worried them like this. They'd never paid this much attention to me before.

"I'm sorry we upset you," Armand said. I was surprised to hear it, as he rarely apologized for anything.

"It's not you," I said forgivingly. "Quinn reminds me of the library. I don't like to think about it."

"Was it so terrible?" Kit wondered.

"It was." I wanted to tell them how much I hated myself for failing and how afraid I was for Liza, but words failed me. I looked at the boys for a long while, cherishing the warmth they instilled in me that wiped away the failure and the fright. "Liza is alive out there," I declared. "I know it. She got away from James and the others, and she escaped." I knew the Armand was bursting to disagree with me, to remind me how improbably it was that Liza somehow triumphed over James, a pack of volpines that even Donovan's swordsmen couldn't, and the harsh winter exposure. I almost reprimanded Armand prematurely for his blatant doubts, but then I remembered Liza had been barefoot when she leaped from the window.

"I miss her," Kit admitted softly.

Kit's visage became cloudy as tears brimmed my eyes. "Do you think she misses us?" I asked.

"If she's alive, she probably hasn't had the time to think of us," Armand said. There was my pessimistic friend. He got up from the bed and nudged Kit to accompany him.

"Let's leave Daisy alone," he said. "She should rest. Besides, with Jada and Graham dropping in unannounced, I don't want to be caught in here after dark." They left me on my own. I closed my eyes and sought the solace of sleep, finding it after a few minutes of tossing and turning.

The two days that followed were long. I lost interest in my studies which frustrated Graham to no end. He reminded me four times how important our education was, if not to myself than to James, but neither the promise of sugar nor the threat of vinegar could persuade me to regain my focus. Graham sent me to the ballet studio for an entire day. I was so exhausted by the end of it, I skipped dinner and collapsed on my bed in my tights. Kit began to really show how blue he was over Liza by picking at his food and quickly becoming impatient with Graham during his lessons. The only time he was moderately calm was when he sat at the piano after dinner, but he was weary of that sooner than usual and ended up halting mid-movement to shut the keys away and go to bed.

Armand stubbornly maintained his routine. He slaved away in the kitchen to make elegant and complicated dishes that he ended up throwing away. I could tell he was determined to set an example, if only to convince Graham that we weren't gradually losing our pleasant dispositions; we all knew that James had expressly ordered the staff to keep us happy to the best of their ability, and if our behavior reflected to the contrary, many of our favorite tutors would suffer for it.

On the fifth day since Liza had run away, a familiar rhythm began to beat in the compound. The tradesmen appeared more frequently than they had all week and we heard from Graham—discreetly, of course—that Jada's medical wing would soon be back in her capable hands with considerably less traffic. The boys and I took that as a signal of defeat on James' part, that despite the remaining presence of guardsmen, the search efforts were for the most part finished. Secretly, Kit and I agreed Liza must have truly found someplace safe, since she hadn't been found hurt or worse for nearly a week. Armand stopped reminding us of the unlikelihood that Liza, in spite of the terrible weather conditions, found a camp in which to hide that James couldn't reach with guardsmen, money, or influence. I wasn't sure if that meant Armand felt the same as Kit and me, but when he let up on the constant reality checks, I began to believe that a seed of hope might survive this dread.

I had just changed into my new linen garments and left the ballet studio when I noticed a commotion near the east gate of the compound. Curious, I tugged my hair out of the tight bun I'd tied it back into for dance and made my way over to see what the fuss was about.

The first time I met Donovan the Master was during his visit to the Aventine for the summer solstice celebration last year. Each time he visited the compound since (he made a point to come frequently to train new guardsmen for James), us four Tributes were treated to lavish dinners at the young Master's behest. All four of us loved his visits, even though Donovan's reputation was fearsome: he was lethal with a blade, a deadly soldier who fought with legendary strength and precision. He was also famous for his Adonis-like beauty and vivacious wit. When I emerged through the crowd enough to see what the tradesmen were congregated around, I saw Donovan standing with Douglas just inside the gate.

His thick, dark hair was clipped short but it was pushed back atop his head in a stylish wave that showed his hair was a little curly at the tips. He was laughing at something one of Douglas' guardsmen had said and his teeth were pristinely white and sharp looking, a lot like James'. His eyes were blazing and blue, and quite mesmerizing to behold; so much so that it took me more than a second to realize that he was staring right at me.

"Daisy!" he exclaimed delightedly. The tradesmen around me startled and parted immediately, making way for Donovan to approach. He took my hands in his and drank up the sight of me.

"Goodness, you're so tall! And so beautiful, too!" he professed gladly, flashing a winsome smile. "You are a welcome sight for sore eyes, my dear!"

"Thank you, Donovan," I said, smiling uncontrollably.

"Douglas, find Lorraine and kindly ask her to put the kitchen staff through their paces. I have been dreaming about that honey roasted ham the whole journey over—and Daisy, you must tell me what you and the boys have been up to!" Donovan took my ballet bag and shouldered it for me, then offered his arm to me. I didn't see a polite way to refuse him so I took it and tried to ignore every pair of eyes in the compound follow us down the hall. I told him I'd come from ballet and he spent the next minute extoling the virtues of dance, how graceful fighters were the most valuable, and that judging on the level of skill I'd achieved since the last time he saw me, he thought I was on the fast track to expert status. I couldn't help but smile and laugh when he joked sweetly, sharing quiet little bits of gossip he'd picked up from the tradesmen. He was as charming as he was handsome and it made my stomach feel fluttery to think of everyone in the compound seeing me escorted around by him.

"They may not be in," I said to Donovan about Kit and Armand as we approached the Tribute wing. Before Donovan and I reached the door, Armand emerged from inside, followed closely by Kit and Graham. Both of their eyes lit up—they adored Donovan.

"Donovan!" Armand cheered. Donovan politely slipped his arm away and walked forward to embrace Armand, who was grinning widely. Armand's dark hair made him look like he could be Donovan's brother.

"Well, this is a welcome surprise!" Kit said jovially, taking a turn at clasping Donovan on the back.

"Look at the two of you! You're grown men!" Donovan praised. "Before long I'll be trying to steal you away from James to come and train with me in the southern camps!"

"I wish," Armand remarked bitterly. He wore a smile to show Donovan he was kidding but Kit and I knew that he meant it.

"What brings you to the compound, Master Donovan?" Graham asked, giving Donovan's hand a firm shake.

"Apart from some rather stiff business of Masters, I've come to accompany some of my swordsmen back to the camps," said Donovan. I noticed that all four of us were staring at Donovan. It made me wonder how someone so magnetic ended up as a soldier and not the Master of his own compound, like James.

"The swordsmen are returning to the camps?" Kit asked, crossing his arms.

"Even the best swordsmen have homes and families, Kit," said Donovan. "It's a simple matter of rotation, nothing to worry about. Besides, some of the doctors are returning to the camps as well, and I like to make sure that fresh supplies of medicine are well protected on the way."

The answer seemed to satisfy Kit. "Would you like to come in?" he asked, gesturing to the door. "Armand and I were just going to visit the market to pick up a few things for dinner."

"Nonsense, I'll have some brought in," said Donovan. The three of us cheered. "After you, I insist! I'd so enjoy a chance to talk with each of you!" Graham excused himself and I followed Armand and Donovan inside.

"Best chance we'll get to hear about Liza," Kit whispered to me as I brushed past him. I shot him a wary glance as we walked through the study. Donovan was no fool; he'd pay attention to every question, sideways looks, and raised eyebrows as long as Liza was the subject. My stomach churned with uneasy dread as I wondered if Donovan had been summoned to the compound by James to determine whether we knew of a place Liza could go, or if we were planning to stage another escape.

If he was suspicious, though, Donovan did not show it. He wanted to know all about our studies: my ballet, Armand's artful cooking, Kit's music, and everything in between. He tested our languages too and doubled over laughing at my impeccable Italian accent. He said over and over how impressed he was with us. He even mindfully waited for us to permit the chefs and servants into our wing so that they could adorn the table with a succulent ham and about a dozen little salads and vegetable medleys. Donovan offered us some of the wine he brought in and Armand was the only one who indulged him. His more refined palate was able to detect what he described as a "perfect blend of earth and fruit," an observation which spurred even more lavishing praise from Donovan.

We asked him about his time in the southern camps. He spun exciting tales littered with awe-inspiring and often violent imagery. The way he spoke about swordplay was poetic, and I thought he might be more captivated by the subject than we were.

"You strike me as the type of young man who would excel at swordplay," Donovan said to Armand. "If James can't find a suitable tutor, I'd be happy to make an apprentice of you." Armand let out a hollow chuckle and tried not to look too disappointed.

"Have I embarrassed you?" Donovan asked, flashing a sort of secretive smile.

Kit's gaze fell. "You see, Donovan," he said, disguising awkwardness with shyness. "James does not allow us access to weapons. It would be—"

"Against the rules," Donovan recited, nodding in understanding. "How stupid of me, I forgot about that little clause of his." Donovan reached into his pocket and pulled out a shiny silver box, out of which he withdrew a thin white cigarette. I was a little appalled when he lit it without asking us whether or not he might smoke in our wing, but none of us would have said no to him anyway.

"He's very specific, isn't he? James, I mean." Donovan took a long drag of his cigarette. "He can be difficult, I know, but he is the Master of this place because of his ability to keep this place, and everyone in it, safe."

I almost scoffed. Since when did "difficult" equate with brutal? Or cruel?

"What about Liza?" Armand asked. I was moved by the smooth fervor in his voice and the way he said Liza's name.

Donovan sighed and took another pull from his cigarette. "It's complicated, Armand," he purred. "The situation as it stands—" Donovan broke off abruptly and turned sharply in his seat, looking to the front of the apartment.

The alarm wailed in the halls, though it was muffled through our door. My heart leaped to my throat. Kit and Armand looked at each other across the table, too stunned to speak. Donovan jumped up from the table and rushed to the door, the three of us sending our chairs tumbling backward as we ran after him. Donovan realized we were following him just as he made it to the front door of the wing.

"Stay close to me," he insisted, putting a hand on the hilt of a knife he had strapped to his waist—he knew there would be no convincing us to stay at home, as we'd never have listened. Kit and I clasped hands as the three of us ran after Donovan, following the troop of guardsmen who'd just jogged by toward the west gate. I saw Quinn up ahead, his face splotched with black and purple abrasions, yelling at the servants to stay in their dwellings. The west gate slammed shut just as we rounded the corner, a blast of winter air freezing the entire hall as flurries of snow soared in its wake.

"Out of the way!" shouted a guardsman as a cluster of four scouts bustled into the hall, bracing something between them that I couldn't see. Snow clung to their garments and their faces were bright red from the cold.

"Stop here," Donovan said, holding out his arm to keep the three of us behind him. Armand seized Donovan's shoulder as the scouts drew closer. His face went ashen. I craned my neck to see over the tall, broad shoulders of the surrounding guardsmen and finally saw the source of the commotion.

"Liza!" I wailed, bringing a hand up to cover my mouth. She was suspended between the four scouts, her hair and skin slick with melted snow and her lips tinged blue. Her eyelids were barely open but I could see her eyes swiveling back in their sockets as the scouts rushed her along the hallway.

"Liza!" Kit was frantic too. I released his hand and moved to run to Liza's side but Donovan caught me in his arms. I struggled to free myself but froze on the spot when I saw James cut through the crowd, his features sharp with concern.

"Is she alive?" he demanded of the lead scout.

"Only just," the scout panted. "We found her in the ravine—buried under almost a foot of snow."

"Get the doctor!" James thundered. He glanced around desperately, not stopping to wonder why Kit, Armand, and I were outside our wing after hours, or why Donovan was holding me.

"With me," James said earnestly to the scouts. He led them back the way he came, towards the Masters' chambers. Donovan took my hand and pulled me along with him and the boys hurried to keep up with us. My heart was racing as we thoughtlessly ran across the threshold into the Masters' chambers—none of us had ever set foot in this part of the Aventine without specific permission from James, and here I was being dragged inside, assumedly not to be taken to the Master library. The wide, dimly lit hallway led to an ornate archway through which James led us, its passage leading to two more long hallways and finally a proud pair of doors, on the other side of which was a grand bedchamber. I had never seen anything like this grand room but I didn't spare an instant fixating on the furnishings—not when Liza was barely clinging to life.

"Put her down," James ordered the scouts. They laid Liza out on the bed and hastily moved out of the way.

"She needs the medical staff, not a nap!" Armand criticized James churlishly.

"Shut your mouth or I'll have you removed," James snapped to Armand, pointing a warning finger at him. "Where the hell is the doctor?" he asked.

"Liza!" I called thickly, unabashedly crying in front of Donovan and James. "Liza, can you hear me?"

"I'm warning you, Daisy," James said severely. "Be silent or I will have you locked in your wing." Donovan held me bracingly by the shoulders, silently encouraging me to be quiet.

"Daze...Daisy...," Liza moaned in a thin, wavering voice. She heard me! The weakness of her voice seemed to startle James, as he gasped a little and forgot his temper. I could do nothing but weep to see Liza like this. Kit and Armand were beyond words.

"Master James!" gasped Jada, slowing from a run as she burst into the room past the mob of guards in the doorway. "They said you found her—" The doctor broke off when she looked at Liza. She rushed to the bedside and checked the pulse in Liza's neck. She grabbed at Liza's bare feet, which were an unnatural shade of violet, then her ice cold fingertips. She did not seem to be encouraged by any of her findings.

"All of you," James barked at the guardsmen standing astonished in the doorway. "Go wait outside, now." They wasted no time hanging around and shuffled in retreat until only Douglas and the frostbitten scouts remained.

"What were you thinking," uttered James, glaring at Donovan while Jada rapidly examined Liza's condition. "Bringing them in here like this?"

Donovan bristled under scrutiny. "There wasn't time to secure them."

"It takes two seconds to lock a door," James argued. A wink of defiance glittered in his eyes. "Perhaps I'll show you sometime."

"She's suffering from hypothermia," Jada observed seriously, standing once more at the bedside. "It's bad."

"Get whatever you need to save her," James commanded impatiently. "Do it fast, Jada!"

"She needs body heat," Jada pressed him. "I'll be back in two minutes with the portable—you four, come with me!" She disappeared down the hall with the scouts on her heels.

"Douglas," James said while stepping out of his boots. "Cut off her clothes." His fingertips flew down his front as he unbuttoned his shirt and my eyes bulged when he yanked the fabric aside, pulling his massive arms hastily out of its sleeves. James removed his clothing until he stood in nothing but a pair of sleek black shorts. I was stunned—I'd never seen a practically naked man in my life and the visage of James standing there as though he paid no mind to us bystanders had me speechless. A hideous contusion that marred James' side quickly stole my attention from his nudity, an injury so grisly that my jaw fell open. He'd obviously been nursing the gruesome bitemark, likely the work of a volpine he sustained in the attack during the rescue mission. I couldn't seem to tear my eyes away from it, or the deep scratches that laced over the very defined muscles of his bare shoulders.

We all watched aghast as Douglas carefully but quickly sliced the ruined linens off of Liza's body and tugged them away. Essentially naked, James climbed into bed beside Liza, whom Douglas had left in nothing but her underwear. I heard Armand grind his teeth in outrage at the sight of it; Kit's shoulders stiffened and my knees buckled, but thankfully Donovan was quick to catch me—it was blaringly shocking to see James wrap his arms around Liza, naked, and pull her close so that she was pressed against his chest.

"James?" Liza whimpered.

"Yes, Liza," James assured her. His lips twitched into the faintest of smiles. "I'm here."

"No...," Liza groaned. I saw her weakly brace her hands on his chest and try to push him away. James only wound his arms around her tighter, holding her possessively to his chest.

"Liza, you must be still," James insisted softly, gently.

"James," Liza sighed hoarsely. I heard Kit sob beside me as we saw Liza tremble in James' arms. Her fingers shook violently as she relented and curled into James—he was undoubtedly warm to the touch, and poor Liza was so cold, she was clutching at him like she couldn't get close enough to him.

"That's it," James praised. "Hold on to me, I'll warm you up. That's a good girl." James slid one of his legs between Liza's, determined to provide as much body heat as he could. Liza was mewling nonsensically through chattering teeth. James hushed her and bent his head so that his warm cheek rested on the crown of her head. Though I knew little about hypothermia, I imagined Liza was in an unimaginable amount of pain.

Jada swept into the room with a portable intravenous station in hand, and the three nurses behind her carried hot compresses and blankets that looked like silver, metallic paper.

"Apply the compresses to her hands and feet," Jada said blandly, her mind locked into emergency-mode. "I want this infusion started immediately so that we can get those blankets on her. I'm going to give you something for the pain, honey," she said to Liza in a clear voice.

"Where do you want me?" James asked Jada softy, so mindful of Liza.

"Right where you are," Jada replied errantly as she withdrew a syringe from a compartment in the intravenous station. She glanced over her shoulder at Douglas and added, "Get them out of here. They don't need to see this." She flicked the syringe in her grasp and stuck the needle in Liza's arm; Liza moaned in discomfort and I felt the floor beneath me begin to waver. I could have sworn I saw James press his lips to Liza's forehead.

My tear-blurred view of Liza and James was blocked suddenly as Douglas stood over me. "You heard the doctor," he said. "Let's go." I tried to take a step but in my woozy state, I couldn't hold my own weight. Donovan caught me, as he still had a hold on my arm, and seamlessly swung me into his arms. Crushed and mortified, I let him carry me out of James' room. My head lolled and limply sagged back when we turned the corner to the main hall and Donovan peered down at me.

"Are you going to faint, Daisy?" he asked.

"I don't know," I replied truthfully.

"Take some deep breaths," Donovan said, rubbing my arm as he carried me past the guardsmen assembled outside the Masters' rooms. "Try not to faint, Daisy. It'll be all right." I heard Armand make an angry exclamation followed by sounds of a scuffle behind us. Donovan stopped suddenly and turned on his heel. "Douglas, release him. He'll follow me, there's no need to man-handle him."

I perked up, concerned now that I needed to advocate for Armand, but I saw him fall in line behind Donovan with a sour look on his face. By the time we reached the Tribute wing, the alarms had been turned off and the servants had all returned to bed. Donovan let himself in through the front doors and walked me to the sofa in the front study. He set me down carefully, kneeling down on the carpet in front of me to peer up into my eyes.

"You've had a nasty shock," he said sadly. "Sit here. I'll get you something to settle your nerves." I nodded, dropping my hands in my lap after wiping my tears away. I'd grown so weary of crying yet I couldn't seem to stop it. I saw Armand pacing the short length of the study near the fireplace. His fists were balled at his sides and his jaw was clenched. Kit had taken a seat in the chair nearest to me. He laced his fingers together and braced them under his chin. He just stared forward, expressionless, saying nothing.

"I've sent for some servants to deal with dinner," Donovan announced, reemerging into the study. He held a little tray atop which four crystal glasses were arranged, filled halfway with a glittering amber fluid. He passed Armand a glass first and made a face when Armand swallowed the liquid in one gulp. Deciding he'd better leave him alone, Donovan handed Kit a glass in turn, who didn't even look up when he took it gently in his hand.

"You should probably sip this," Donovan said to me, pressing the glass into my hand and sitting beside me. I smelled it and frowned at the overwhelming scent of peat. Still, I sipped it and was pleasantly surprised to find the taste of it was smooth, and it carved a burning path of release down my throat when I swallowed it.

"Graham prefers us to abstain from drinking," Kit murmured, staring into his imbibement.

"When clearer heads are meant to prevail, I agree with your tutor," Donovan said. He sipped his own liquor and rested his back against the sofa cushion. "But not drinking whiskey after a shock would be inappropriate too. Drink up, Kit." Kit complied and grimaced at its potency.

"Don't you dare sit there and harp at us about what is and is not inappropriate," Armand growled. "Not after what James just did to Liza."

"What he did to her?" Donovan echoed quietly. "You mean, save her life?"

Incredulous, Armand rounded on him. "He cut off her clothes and put her in his bed!" he hollered. "Do you know what that was like for us to see? Daisy almost fainted!"

"It was shocking, yes," Donovan agreed. "Liza is very dear to you and seeing her in that condition must have been devastating—but if James had not sent men out to look for her, you never would have seen her again. If he did not do as Jada said, to share body heat with her, Liza could have died right in front of us."

I took another sip of whiskey, a larger one this time, and flinched when Armand kicked over the stack of books behind him.

"Armand, please," Donovan reasoned calmly. "Settle down."

"It's not right!" Armand insisted angrily. "He had no right to strip her dignity like that!"

"Armie," I sighed. "She was dying. There might not have been time to get her to the medical wing."

"Why didn't he let us do it, then?" Armand retorted, turning now on me. "There are three of us; we're bound to be warmer than just one man!" His question was rhetorical, I knew, so I didn't answer even though he paused for my response. "It's because it's against the rules for us to be in bed together," he said, revolted. "He's a gigantic hypocrite! Damn James and his damn rules—"

"You need to calm down," Donovan articulated sternly, getting to his feet. He reached into his jacket again and produced his cigarette case. He passed it to Armand, who took it without question and helped himself to a cigarette. I had no idea he smoked; I'd never seen him do it or even smelled it on him.

"You must trust that Liza is exactly where she needs to be right now," Donovan said after lighting Armand's cigarette. He placed a hand on Armand's shoulder and tightened his grip reassuringly. "Do you think Jada would have let Liza stay there if that weren't the case?"

"Of course not," I answered for Armand. I finished my whiskey and shivered. I felt warm and a little drowsy.

"She was gone," Kit said numbly, like he hadn't been listening to any of Armand's outburst.

"And now she's home," Donovan said. He was trying to lift Kit's spirits but he had grossly misunderstood what Kit had meant; Kit wasn't in awe that Liza had miraculously returned from certain death, he had believed that she'd achieved the thing we were all so hungry for—freedom. I knew that just like me, Kit was berating himself for being foolish enough to have hope. Armand was lucky to have spared himself this torment.

"Are we going to be in trouble?" I asked.

"No, Daisy," Donovan said. "You've done nothing wrong. I'll see to it that James understands how difficult this whole ordeal has been on you three; he will hear me out, and he'll agree that the best thing now is to take care of Liza and get everything back to the way it was."

Kit got to his feet and left the study without another word. Donovan looked sorry to see him go, but he turned back to Armand with devoted kindness in his eyes.

"Try to get some sleep," said Donovan. "And if you could refrain from mentioning any of these, ahem, *refreshments*, to Graham or James, I would appreciate it." Armand nodded and tossed his finished cigarette in the fireplace. He clapped Donovan on the shoulder and started off for his room. Donovan took up Kit's unfinished whiskey and swallowed the rest, taking a deep breath before turning back to me.

"Come along, I'd better walk you to your room." I took the hand he offered me and allowed him to help me off the sofa.

"I hope you'll sleep well, Daisy," Donovan said delicately, "now that Liza is home." I glanced into her empty room over his shoulder and shrugged.

"She's alive," I replied. "Thank you for helping me—I feel so silly, I've never been one to faint. And I don't think I've ever cried as often in my lifetime as I have this week."

"It pains me to see you so upset," Donovan admitted. He set a hand on my arm and for a moment, I thought he might draw me into his arms but he apparently decided better of it. He bade me goodnight and set off down the hall. I stood in my doorway until I heard the doors close behind him. Once I was sure I was alone, I swayed on my feet, a little drunk, and stepped into Liza's room. Her bed was unmade from almost a week ago when she'd last slept in it. I shut the door behind me and fell into Liza's blankets, sleep coiling around me in a hazy cloud.

I dreamed of snow: sunshine and snow, and the woman's voice calling me from somewhere I couldn't see.

"Daisy, my girl!" she called. "Come in from the cold!" I giggled and thought it was odd that my voice was so small. I spun around and fell in a mound of dusty snow with a *poof!* The chill of melting snowflakes on my cheeks stung and excited me. I rolled over onto my back to look toward where the woman's voice came from, but I was no longer in the sunshine. I was under that stark red canopy, floating in James' bed. I realized in horror that I was naked, and when I reached to grab a sheet to cover myself, I touched hot, bare flesh. James snaked his arms around my body, squeezing me tightly against him.

"That's it," he breathed in a hellish, sinister hiss. "There's a good girl—"

I awoke with a gasp, jerking myself into an upright position. I fumbled to untangle myself from Liza's sheet that had somehow wrapped around my chest in sleep, right where James had grabbed me in my dream.

That's it, I resolved. It was time to steady myself and gain control over this awful panic that was stealing my peace of mind. It was just a nightmare, nothing more. I let out a shuddering breath and rubbed my face with my hands before sliding out of Liza's bed. I forwent a bath and changed into a clean set of Liza's linens, too eager to meet the day to bother about presentation.

I breezed out of Liza's room with my long hair spilling over my shoulders. I smelled coffee in the kitchen, which was a bit strange as both the boys' bedroom doors were closed. No matter, I wrote it off. I entered the kitchen expecting to see Graham pouring himself his second cup of coffee but instead I saw James sitting at the table with a mug in hand.

"Good morning, Daisy," James said cordially. He was dressed today in a simple blue shirt and dark slacks. Looking at him now, I couldn't stop picturing him in yesterday's state of undress; worse yet, I noticed even more how strong his arms were even when he was relaxed because I knew exactly how buff he was under his clothes. It made me nervous.

"Have a seat, won't you?" James offered in the same pleasant tone. He gestured to the chair across from him, at which there was a full, steaming ceramic cup of coffee with a dash of cream already added.

Rigidly, I pulled the chair out and sat down. I took a sip of coffee and was hardly surprised yet very perturbed that he'd flavored it perfectly to my liking.

"I've dismissed Graham for the day. I think you and I should talk, Daisy," said James.

"As you say," I replied coolly.

James raised an eyebrow coyly, amused at my frostiness. "Jada told me you fainted," he said. "She was worried at first that you might be anemic, but after observing you for seventy-two hours, she attributed the episode to stress." He took a sip of coffee and sat perfectly still for a few beats. "Is there anything you would like to discuss with me, Daisy?" he asked. "More specifically, is there anything you can think of that might have caused you to overload from stress?"

I said nothing. I couldn't think to speak when I was totally focused on keeping my lips from quivering.

"Perhaps your ballet tutor has been pushing you too hard," James mused. "Should I find you a new teacher?"

"Helena is a wonderful instructor!" I blurted.

"I see," James said, chuckling. "Very well, I'll see to it that Helena remains at her post." His blue eyes were sparkling with mirth; he was enjoying this. "But I'm curious, Daisy. What could have upset you so badly? Graham says Armie and Kit have been worried sick—"

"I witnessed a girl I love like my own sister throw herself out of a window," I retorted firmly, interrupting James with vehement distaste. I did not like him using Armand's nickname.

"And that upset you?" James asked airily. "Hadn't I caught you about to do that very thing, seconds before?" His glare radiated smugness when tears sprang to my eyes and I quickly averted my gaze.

"That's not what happened," I murmured feebly. I had no choice but to deny it to his face.

"Don't lie to me, Daisy." James was not amused anymore. His features hardened and his voice lost its whimsical tone.

"I didn't!" I yelped. I flinched as James whacked the table with a flat palm.

"I've had enough of your antics," James told me caustically. "Within the span of a week, you staged a botched escape that was so ridiculously foolish that it might better be labeled a suicide attempt; you have flouted the rules of this compound by ignoring your studies, you cavorted with Donovan in the market for all to see, trespassed on a restricted area—*my own bedchamber*—and you got drunk on whiskey!" He was practically steaming.

"Did you think I wouldn't watch you every second of every day, after your little stunt in the library?" he demanded. "Did you think I wouldn't find out that Donovan plied you with liquor? Or that the boys continuously visit your room after hours?"

I was stunned. I'd always called Armand paranoid for lowering his voice to a whisper whenever James came up, even in our own wing, but it turned out he had been right to be so cautious. James was right—I'd been a righteous fool.

"I refuse to apologize for laying a hand on you the other night. You deserved it and we both know it," James said after taking a moment to gather his bearings. "Your actions prompted Liza to behave recklessly. She could have died that night, and as you well know she very well nearly did. As did I, by the way! A fact you know now too because of your intrusion on my privacy last night."

"I am sorry," I said. "I was so afraid for Liza, you can't imagine—"

"Can't I?" James interjected with umbrage. "Are you so arrogant in your assessment of me, that you don't think I lost several nights of sleep over this?"

"No, James," I admitted. I remembered how he hung out of the window after Liza, how completely terrified he was last night when those scouts carried her in from the outside.

"I did not come here to berate you," said James. "I meant what I said initially, I think we need to talk. After all, little girls do not suddenly decide to try to jump out of open windows." He searched my countenance with his blazing blue eyes. He almost looked disappointed. "Are you unhappy? Have I done something to upset you? Has a member of my staff caused you to feel helpless or despondent? I can't help you unless you talk to me, Daisy."

I chewed on my bottom lip as I felt sobs building up in my chest. I wanted so much to never cry again, especially in front of James. I hated him but I wanted to confide in him every overwhelming feeling of confusion and despair I felt. When I thought about how he clutched Liza to him in his bed last night, I wanted to hit him—but his gaze shone right through my icy contempt like hot sunlight.

I remembered what Liza had said, at the very beginning of this whole thing: We weren't born here, this is not our home. "I want to see Liza," I declared. I was so glad to hear myself sound much braver than I felt.

"You are bold just like her," James remarked. Bold like Liza, was that a good thing? "I am certain you would like nothing more than to see her, but

Liza is still recovering. You cannot see her today." The glimmer of satisfaction in his eyes was diabolical.

"I can assure you," I said, my nerve deflating, "that the staff has done nothing untoward or unkind to me, or to Liza." I swallowed the lump in my throat and tried to force the boldness back into my voice. "You did upset me, James, when you struck me."

"Daisy," groaned James, annoyed. "I've already told you, I refuse—"

"You told me not to lie to you," I reminded him hotly. "I'm only trying to answer your questions honestly."

James mulled this over with a stern expression. "Before the library, Daisy, have I ever done such a thing?" He waited for me to shake my head, knowing full well he'd never hit me before that night. He knew I was ducking the basis of his inquiry. "I am not Donovan, Daisy. I do not like violence. I will use force when I deem it necessary, which it was the other night in the library—the only reason you'd been allowed access to the library in the first place, in case you are wondering, is because I have come to reserve a certain fondness for you; you take your studies in stride, you are kind and polite to all with whom you interact, and up until recently you have been a very collected, obedient young woman. As was Liza," he remarked, mostly to himself. "But that is a different matter. I ask you, Daisy, what choice did I have other than to strike you, after you behaved in such a feckless manner?"

My insides burned with contempt for him. I would accept being slapped silly by James if it was because he was something of a bully—at least that way, he would be left accountable for it—but I would not be lectured about how my own actions left him with no other choice. I would not be convinced that it was really my fault he'd struck me.

"You are the Master of this compound, not I," I reminded him. "It's not my place to question when you choose to defer to violence. I'm only saying it upset me."

James let out a mirthless, metallic laugh. "Where did you pick up that viper's tongue?" he wondered. "If you continue to speak to me that way, I might just upset you again." The threat made my blood run cold. James pushed his coffee aside and leaned forward so that his elbows rested on the table.

"Would you care to know what I think has caused your consistent lapse in judgment—and dare I say, in manners?" asked James. "After I recused myself from the rescue efforts, I spent two nights racking my brain, trying to determine what possible reason Liza had had for risking her life and jumping like that; I exhausted all hypotheses of causation and arrived at the disturbing conclusion that our bold girl must have gotten the idea from you, Daisy, since you had tried and failed to do it first, right in front of her. And then I thought, why would my delicate, careful, sweet Daisy encourage such a brash idea?"

I didn't dare respond, lest James take it as a quip and upset me again, as he put it.

"My suspicions were confirmed when Donovan arrived yesterday to accompany his men back to the camps. You lit up like the sun when he spoke to you last summer, and he was not shy towards me about acclaiming your beauty in nearing womanhood; and when Quinn told me how he veritably scooped you up upon his arrival at the gate, I knew it must have been the whimsical folly of affection that made you forget your place in this compound." He smirked when he noticed my cheeks redden—I was so flustered by the false assumption that I didn't know what to say.

"Venus in her shell was never so lovely," James sneered darkly, making fun of my blush. "If it hadn't nearly cost Liza her life, or me mine, I'd say your desire to run away with Donovan was adorable."

"That's not—" I was fuming. "You are mistaken, James, I am not—"

"You should know," James smoothly interrupted me, "that Donovan is not stupid enough to breach the covenant of our partnership by interfering with you, a Tribute under my protection. I know it's he who inspired you to take such an incomprehensibly insane risk, but you have to take into account that whatever you think you know about him is only a shade of who he really is."

"James," I tried to explain. "Really, I—"

"I know things about Donovan that would straighten your hair," James said bluntly. "Ugly, repugnant things about him that you, my dear girl, couldn't imagine. More importantly, you know very well that there are strict rules regarding your conduct here. My job is to see that you abide by those rules, and I am not accustomed to doing a poor job in any respect. My advice to you is, put this silliness aside and forget whatever notion you may have about entangling yourself with Donovan."

I heard one of the boys' doors open and my gut sank in dread. If I were any more embarrassed, I'd burst into tears.

"We both know you're smarter than this, Daisy," James said. "For your sake, I hope you heed my advice." His glare was stone cold for a beat and then he softened his expression as he heard, like I did, the soft padding of bare feet down the hall. In an instant, his posture had gone from a snake poised to strike to a condoling, utterly non-threatening man.

"James!" blurted Kit from behind me. "I heard voices. I thought Graham was here?"

"Hello, Kit," James greeted him. His voice was much kinder than it had been a moment ago. "I've dismissed Graham for the day. I believe the three of you have earned a break."

"What is he doing here?" Armand asked, appearing in the doorway behind Kit. He spared no false air of propriety for James—he was clearly still furious about the way he'd handled Liza last night.

"I came to talk to Daisy," James said. "I will leave you to your breakfast presently. I would like to impart one final thing to you, Daisy, and I would like for you all to hear it: it is my sincere wish that you understand how seriously I take your safety here, and that I will be taking measures to ensure nothing like what happened to Liza will ever happen again." He waited to let the vaguely threatening words sink in.

"I hope that you will trust me," James said, staring directly into my eyes, "enough to keep you safe."

"Trust you?" I offered feebly. I tried to forget that the boys were standing behind me.

"That's a tall order," Armand remarked flippantly. James flickered his glare up to him and I could tell Armand likely bit his lip to hush himself.

"We want to," Kit insisted. "We saw what you did for Liza, and Daisy knows how bad it could have been. You couldn't possibly be any harder on her than she has been on herself." That wasn't true and we all knew it, but Kit was cleverly trying to express how apologetic we felt, though I wondered if Kit would be so quick to defect to James' good graces if he knew he had just accused me of having tried to run away with Donovan?

"I would find it easier to trust you," I said to James, "if I knew that the words I speak within the walls of this wing were only heard by the people to whom they're spoken, or if we would freely move about this wing without fear of being shadowed."

James leaned back in his chair and I jumped. He crossed his arms and stared at me with sheer disesteem in his blue eyes. "Privacy?" he questioned. "You're demanding privacy from me, after what you've done?"

"Not demanding," I begged. "*Asking*. Please, James. To be scrutinized like this—it wears on us, you have to understand. We haven't broken any rules, *major* rules," I added when his eyes widened to the contrary. I knew he was about to cite off the boys visiting my room, the whiskey, and the trespassing all over again so I quickly went on, "And if anyone deserves to be surveilled or punished, it's me. Not Armand and Kit."

"Trust must be earned," Kit said timidly.

"You're too right," James agreed slowly, still pondering whether or not he should agree to this.

"Please, James," I implored after almost a full minute of vibrant silence. James blinked his stormy blue eyes at me a few times before affording me a relenting sigh.

"Fine," he acquiesced, "but you two," he snapped suddenly at the boys, "I would like to remind you that it is expressly against the rules for you to visit each other's rooms after hours. I will temporarily relinquish my surveillance on this apartment, until I decide you can be trusted to behave in a more permanent setting, but if you keep up your nighttime visits, I will know about it." James pushed his chair back from the table and stood up, leaving his coffee unfinished.

"What about Liza?" Kit asked.

"As I told Daisy already, you cannot see her today," James said. He made to leave the kitchen on the heels of that edict, but neither of the boys would budge.

"You dismissed Graham today," said Armand as benignly as he could. "If we don't have work to do, all we'll do is worry about her. We must see her, please."

James planted his feet and groaned in consternation. "Very well," he huffed. "I don't want to be accused of harassing Liza when she's resting, so you must go through Jada first—she will brief you on the nature of Liza's recovery and decide whether or not you are allowed to see her." Kit and Armand cleared the path to the door and waited until the doors closed behind James.

"How long was he here?" Armand demanded as soon as we were comfortably alone.

"I'm not sure," I replied. "But he was sitting there when I came into the kitchen, less than an hour ago if I had to guess."

"I'm starving," decided Armand. He went to the refrigerator and pulled out whatever he could find that didn't require preparation—granola, apples, and a carafe of cold water.

"What did he say to you?" Kit asked. He poured himself some coffee and sat in James' chair.

"Well," I said hesitantly. I cleared my throat to rid my voice of its humiliated quiver. "He accused me of planting the idea of an escape because I'm in love with Donovan and planned to run away with him."

Kit spewed coffee into his own lap and Armand dropped his apples with a loud, "WHAT?"

"He can't be serious!" Kit yelped in a strangled voice. "How did he come up with that one?"

"Apparently, Donovan made a comment to James about my womanhood last summer," I said, blushing all over again—especially when Armand let out a hoot and muttered, "Womanhood, indeed!" under his breath. "He also noticed Donovan escort me back to the apartment yesterday after ballet."

Much to my offended shock, Kit did not immediately refute this claim. He dabbed at his clothes with a cloth napkin to get the spilled coffee off and pursed his lips while his eyes focused on the center of the table. It was the same face he'd made since he was a little boy, always when he was working out something in his head.

"It is *not* true," I said defensively. "I feel a little taken aback for having to say so!"

"Don't be ridiculous, Daze, of course it's not true," Kit said immediately. "But I can see how James would put two and two together...."

Incredulous, I turned to Armand, who just took a huge bite from an apple. "Would you mind explaining what he means by that?" I said.

"What?" Armand retorted, his mouth full of fruit. "You were practically *hanging* off Donovan yesterday, and you came clear across the compound in full view of the tradesmen while you did it."

"You hugged when you saw him—also in full view of the tradesmen! And Graham!" I cried angrily.

"Daisy, nobody cares about two men hugging!" Armand sniped back.

"I think," Kit interrupted loudly, "what Armie meant to say was, people tend to notice when a Master pays affection to a young woman, particularly a very—uh, comely young woman."

I glared at Kit. "What are you implying?" I asked, when at the same moment Armand wheezed in laughter.

"*Comely?* What are you, Graham's age?"

I ignored him.

"Part of your charm, Daze, is that you are so in tune with everyone except yourself," Kit said. "None of us are children anymore. It's the reason we aren't allowed to visit each other after hours. You're a beautiful young woman, everyone sees that but you, and it's only natural that James would believe that Donovan may have taken advantage—"

"Kit!" I cut him off shrilly. "How dare you!"

"Daisy, I'm not suggesting anything happened!" Kit exclaimed. "I know nothing did—"

"Or ever would!" I added, stung.

"But you have to realize," Kit said gently, "James noticed Donovan dote on you and made an assumption that is not as far-fetched as you might think. Donovan obviously enjoys spending time with you, and you can be quite alluring when you aren't paying any mind to yourself."

I was simply revolted. "I'm going to see Jada," I said, hastily leaving the table. I regretted not eating breakfast but I was so mad at Kit and Armand, I couldn't bear to be in their company. James I could understand misreading the situation, but the boys buying into such a notion was downright hurtful. As I breezed out of our wing, I saw that a number of servants and tradesmen were out and about, all of whom were trying not to look interested in the traffic coming out of our Tribute apartments. They must have seen James come out a few minutes before. I thought when I reached the medical ward of the compound to see Jada that I might have preferred to run into James a second time, as soon as I saw that she was already busy with a guest.

There was Donovan, dressed in a rich maroon shirt that was so different than his usual all-black attire. He had more than one knife strapped to his person today. When I appeared in the doorway, I distracted him from what looked like the deep conversation he was having with Jada.

"Good morning, Doctor Jada," I said, keen to greet Jada first. "Hello, Donovan," I added curtly.

"Hello, Daisy," Donovan said. "How did you sleep?"

"James visited this morning," I said, hoping to coolly give him a clue as to why I refused to return the happy grin he'd given me while also refusing to answer the question.

"I see," Donovan said knowingly. His posture slouched a bit, clearly not knowing why I was giving him the cold shoulder today. I turned to Jada and forced a pleasant expression.

"James said I should see you about Liza," I explained.

"Of course he did," Jada sighed. "Let me tell you, honey, it was a very long night. I'm exhausted."

"I'm sure it was," I said. "I can't thank you enough for all you did to help her." I excluded thanks on the boys' behalf purposefully if not spitefully. I leaned over and searched the gallery of hospital beds, looking for a closed curtain that would give away Liza's cubicle.

"You want to see her, is that right?" Jada asked. I nodded profusely and Jada crossed her arms. "Daisy, Liza has been through a great ordeal. I managed to stabilize her, but I'm wary...." She bit her lip and furrowed her brows.

"Jada, she was so worried about Liza last night that she was almost faint," Donovan chimed in to my aid. I only resented him for it a little bit; I really was keen to see Liza.

"If the boys had come, I'd say no way," said Jada. I suppressed a triumphant smile—the less the merrier. That would teach them to entertain such lewd ideas! "But it'll be a short visit," Jada insisted.

"I understand," I gushed. I started past her, hoping to lead the way to Liza's bedside, but Jada stopped me.

"This way," she said. "Donovan, I'll be sure to catch up with you as soon as I've finished this." Despite my contempt that he'd made a comment to James about me last summer, I couldn't help but look to him before I followed Jada out of the hospital.

"Thank you," I whispered genuinely.

"Give her my best," Donovan said, flashing a smile. "If she's awake!"

I followed Jada at a bustling pace down the halls of the compound as butterflies fluttered in my stomach. I was bursting to see Liza but terrified that I would see her wraithlike, frozen countenance and make a less than encouraging face. I grew even more tense when I realized that Jada was leading me to the Master wing. The line of guardsmen waiting outside was impressive; I recognized very few of them, which meant they were Donovan's men and much more dangerous than the guardsmen who usually patrolled the compound.

"Is she allowed to accompany you?" asked Quinn, stepping forward out of the line to confront Jada and me.

"Master James defers to my judgment when it comes to my patients," Jada said, fearlessly looking past Quinn's blackened eye. "She's here to see Liza and I'm authorized to escort her."

Quinn scowled and stepped aside, but before I passed, he said to me, "If you want to come back without the doctor, you'll have to get word from the Master."

"As you say," I said nervously. I did not like the mean, hungry way Quinn looked at me and the ensuing discomfort spurred me to catch up with Jada. Once again, I was sweeping over the threshold of the Masters' chambers. I was in awe of the décor of this part of the compound. In all the commotion last night, I hadn't noticed all the detailed carvings in the wooden kickboards or the breathtakingly beautiful painted ceilings. Jada led me along the same hallway we'd chased the night before but took a left turn down a hallway that led away from James' room.

"She is very weak," Jada whispered as we reached a grand set of dark wooden doors. "I know it has been so hard on you, honey, but I want you to try not to upset her." I nodded, suddenly jittery with anxiety. My palms felt clammy as Jada opened the doors and knocked softly. "Liza, honey," Jada announced in a low voice, "there's someone here to see you."

"Doctor," croaked Liza, who was tucked under blankets in a reclined position in a massive bed. The room was dimly lit, and curtains were pulled over the windows all around the room. When Liza saw me enter the room behind Jada, her violet eyes welled with twinkling tears.

"Daisy!" she cried. She hardly made a sound. She reached for me, despite the intravenous lead in her arm, with hands that were wrapped in thick bandages. I hurried to her side and wrapped my arms around her, overcome with sorrowful joy.

"Oh, Liza," I lamented. I stroked her beautiful blonde hair the way Kit always did when he comforted me. "I was so afraid...."

"Stop it," Liza rasped. She pulled away and was grinning through her tears at me. She touched my face, the wool of her bandages rough on my cheek. "I am so glad to see you, Daisy. My Daisy."

"I'll give you two a moment—Daisy, remember, Liza must rest," Jada said gently from the doorway. "Keep it short. I'll be right back." I didn't take my eyes off Liza for a second; I waited until I heard the doors close behind us before I spoke.

"Where are the boys?" Liza asked.

I bit my tongue and remembered that Jada had instructed me to refrain from upsetting her. "They'll be along later," I said. "Jada said you were only allowed one visitor at a time."

"Come up here," Liza urged hoarsely, patting the mattress beside her. I crawled into bed with her and we piled our hands on top of one another's, like we did when we were children.

"Are you hurt?" I wanted to know. "Jada said you had hypothermia."

"I'm all right, Daze," Liza assured me. I wanted so badly to ask her if she remembered anything from last night, but Jada's warning to not upset her rang in my ears. It gave way to a tumultuous emotion I wasn't sure had a name.

"Liza," I said, pulling myself into a sitting position on the bed beside her. My voice was now as froggy as Liza's as I tried to surmise the right words. "That night in the library...I was a fool to have been there in the first place. I failed us, and you especially, when I lost my resolve. I'm so sorry, Liza. I'm so ashamed."

"Listen to me," Liza insisted. "You have nothing to be ashamed of. I was there too, Daisy. Quinn would have caught you before you could make the window." I knew she was right, but I bowed my head to hide the tears that spilled past my eyelashes. Liza held my chin in her hand and gently lifted my face so that she could look at me. "I'm the fool, Daisy, not you. Even if you had made it, they would have caught you. I am living proof of it." She took my hands once more in hers and squeezed. "It's me who ought to be ashamed. Armie was right—no one escapes, not ever, and I was so eager to prove him wrong that I nearly died. And now...," Liza shivered as though a cold wind passed through her. "Now, I owe my life to James."

"What happened out there, Liza? I know that James was attacked, I saw the bite mark on his chest, and the scratches—"

"The volpines," Liza rasped. She closed her eyes for a moment as if that might erase the memory of them. "You wouldn't have believed it, Daisy. I scarcely do. I climbed down so fast, I don't remember...but then I was in the snow. I was so desperate, I barely felt the cold. I ran as fast as I'd ever run in my life." I could see the terror playing across her eyes as she recalled that night, her hands still clutching mine. "I heard a terrible racket through the trees. They'd brought something down, and it was screaming. I heard the guardsmen behind me, over the alarm, and I thought, *I've got to lose them!* I ran toward the dying animal, hoping the guardsmen would be spooked or distracted by them; but I ran smack into one of them, and Daisy, it was a beast like I've never seen, or even read about."

"But you didn't have a scratch on you!" I gasped. We'd seen Liza practically naked, and her body had not been marred with scratches and bites like James' had been.

"It's the most damnable thing," Liza said numbly. "I ran into a volpine— on all four legs, it was nearly taller than me—and it snarled when I touched it, but it just *stared* at me. I looked into its eyes, those awful yellow things almost glowing. And it looked right back at me! Then its pack turned from the kill and watched me. My hands," Liza said, choking up, "were bleeding from the scaffolding. They were full of splinters, I thought the beasts would smell the blood on me and tear me apart, if not also because I'd infringed on their hunt. I thought, *It's over,* and then the guardsmen called out behind me. I heard James among them and knew that I had to run."

I realized that my mouth was open in rapt shock. "And?" I prompted her in a hushed voice.

"The volpines sort of snapped to attention," Liza went on. "They looked past me, in the direction of the guardsmen. I heard James shout my name and then I saw flashes of their torches in the dark."

"They found you!"

"Yes," Liza said. "But they found the volpines too. The beasts then abandoned their kill and attacked the guardsmen. They ran right past me. I swear to you, Daisy, the ground shook when they ran."

Chills swept across the tops of my arms. I was amazed. "And then you ran?"

"I left the volpines and guardsmen to their brawl," Liza said, nodding. "I looked back only once: James had cut down a volpine and was gaining on me. He wasn't ten yards from me when one of them crashed into him from the side; the pack was so many in number, it felt like the forest itself was trembling, and that any place I sought to hide in the darkness would be home to even more of them."

I was speechless.

"I must have run for hours," Liza recalled. "I could no longer hear the roaring volpines or the guardsmen behind me. I ran in the dark, sure that any snapping branch or distant sound was a guard or a beast. By the time the sun rose, I was exhausted and freezing. The light barely shines through the treetops, the forest is so dense, but I glimpsed a cavern and ducked inside. I got as far away from the mouth of the cave as I could, away from the wind and snow, and rested. I pulled some of the splinters out of my hands and tried to sleep. I don't know how long I stayed there, but I could hear animals outside and didn't want to risk being discovered with blood on me."

"You were gone for five days," I said. Liza seemed disappointed by this.

"It felt like so much longer," she sighed. "I was in that cave for so long, I started to succumb to the cold. I knew I had to try my luck in the forest again, in the hopes of coming across a tradesman or someone with provisions—"

"Or shoes," I offered.

"Exactly," said Liza. "I realized when I left the cave that I was much weaker than I thought I would be. I walked where the snow wasn't so deep for a long time. I couldn't find the sun, I had no idea in which direction I was going. Before long, my feet hurt to walk on and I lost the feeling in my hands. I was so out of it, Daisy, I started to wonder if I was still in the cave, dreaming that I was wandering through the forest. I came to when I heard movement ahead, and I saw the green coats of Donovan's swordsmen. They saw me, shouted out, and I ran; I don't know where I found the energy, but it carried me into the denser part of the woods. The snow was deep now, up to my knees, but I forced myself to go on. I came to the precipice of a ravine and with the swordsmen behind me, I saw no other choice but to go down. I knew they wouldn't follow me to down such a path. A few tried to—I was worried Donovan himself was there and I had to count on that being true. I knew he would be the one to apprehend me, if the stories are true, so I decided to play my odds a second time and jump once more just to get away from the swordsmen...I never saw the bottom of the ravine, I only remember falling before I landed in a snow drift and passed out."

I reached up to wipe at my eyes. Liza looked as though she might cry, but her eyes were hopelessly dry. The end of her story was clear: the swordsmen sent for the scouts, who knew better than any how to navigate that terrain. It was there that they found her, half dead in the snow.

I couldn't bring myself to speak. I pulled Liza into my arms and held her tightly as I stifled a sob. What she described in a nearly indiscernibly hoarse voice was a living nightmare, out of which she had woken to find herself in the prison she had failed to escape—that we had both failed to escape. I remembered all the things we had said before, when we had planned this whole thing in the beginning, and how hopeful and bright the idea of leaving this place had been. After hearing what Liza had experienced, no sunlight, no beautiful visages, no happy and free people to be seen, I felt crushed under the weight that the idea I clung to about a world outside of the compound was nothing but an illusion.

"Jada told me that James struck you," Liza said after a while.

"He did," I confirmed stiffly.

"I'm sorry, Daze."

I shrugged a shoulder. "He also believes that the reason I tried to escape was because I had a love affair with Donovan and planned to run away with him."

Liza's guffaw was piteous since her voice was spent. "Preposterous," she said. "Leave it to James to concoct a fabrication like that; he wouldn't understand us wanting to be free for the sake of freedom."

The notion made me chuckle dryly, like Armand. "Perhaps not," I said. I was bothered by an unanswered question then, since an important detail had remained unrevealed after Liza had finished her tale of escape and consequent recapture. "You lost your voice…." I was reluctant to bring up the topic, since she had already shared so much of her pain with me. I assumed she hadn't explained her hoarse state because it was something she could not bring herself to speak of.

"Jada said I was dehydrated," Liza said. "And after I came to, when I had strength enough to speak, I spent the small hours in—" Her voice caught in her throat. She seemed to catch herself from saying something she oughtn't, like Jada had when she'd overstepped days ago and revealed details about James' health that she shouldn't have. "I was speaking with James," Liza decided after a moment. Her demeanor darkened drastically and I did not ask her any follow up questions regarding what that conversation had entailed. I could only imagine how upsetting it would have been to argue with James after such an ordeal—or even at all, because the closest I'd come to arguing with him was during our encounter this morning, and I'd been so intimidated by him that I'd shut down. I couldn't even think of what it would be like to raise my voice to him.

Liza turned to peer up at me, leaning against my arm. "Everything we said about him is right, Daisy," she told me. "His obsession with control—he wouldn't allow Jada to move me to the hospital, and I'd wager he posted an entire security squadron outside."

"He did," I said.

"Typical," Liza said, scowling. "The way he talks about us and this place, as if he knows better no matter what…." She cleared her throat. "Jada's so keen to keep him happy. You should have seen her try to shut me up last night! She threatened to sedate me, *twice*, if I didn't stop engaging him! She couldn't throw him out, so she had to turn on me…. I can't fathom how she expected me to keep my mouth shut after the things he said…."

I sensed a wave of anger build up in Liza, which seemed to warm her skin to the touch. "What a week it's been for arguing," I sighed in an effort to diffuse this temper-inciting topic.

"Has it been?" she asked. She caught me looking embarrassed and saw right through me. "That's really why the boys aren't here," she guessed. Before

I could tell Liza about my little spat with Kit and Armand, a soft knock sounded at the door. I expected to see Jada step through to tell me that my visit was now over, but James was there, looking stony as ever.

"Come along, Daisy," he said solemnly. "Liza needs to rest."

"I'll walk you to the door," Liza said. Her eyes were locked on James as she climbed out of bed. I tried to stop her, insisting that she should stay in bed. "Nonsense," she insisted. "I can manage!"

"No, you can't," James sighed. "Get back into bed, Liza."

"No!" Liza snapped.

"Liza!" I gasped. After everything she had been through, I couldn't believe she'd shout at him like that. And there went James, marching past me. He grappled onto Liza's arm and forcibly lifted her back into bed. I was shocked to see it but I knew that he wasn't using all his strength to move her—he didn't have to, she was still so weak.

"Get your hands off me!" Liza shrieked. She was putting up a feeble struggle and James was obviously bored by the minimal pressure he was applying to keep her in bed.

"Daisy," he said over his shoulder. "Go outside and get Jada, please."

I turned on the spot and went to get Jada without thinking. Liza called him names as I hurried out of the room, accusing him of being a "ruthless bastard" more than once. Jada met me outside, flanked by two nurses. I guessed by the sad look on her face and the readiness of her apprentices that she had been expecting this.

"I'm sorry," I hastily explained. "I tried not to upset her, but James—"

"It's not your fault," Jada assured me. She set her hand on my arm and smiled at me. "She's very troubled. I'm sure once she calms down, she'll feel better for having seen you." She and the nurses breezed past me into Liza's room and I wrapped my arms around my middle, tightly, to steady myself. I heard James murmuring quietly to Liza as she raged in her bed, shouting, "Why won't you tell me, then?" over and over until Jada's voice cut through the racket. Liza went silent. It was so sudden, I found myself holding my breath, waiting to hear anyone speak on the other side of the door.

I flinched when James slid through the double doors. He even had the decency to look apologetic for having startled me.

"She's been sedated," James said. "I think we should leave Jada to it, don't you?" I nodded, my eyes brimmed with tears. "Come with me, Daisy." I followed him slowly along the hall, likely headed to the door to the public compound.

"I hope that you can understand my position on this issue," James said as we rounded the corner in the dimly lit corridor. "I want more than anything to return Liza to the routine she shares with you, Armand, and Kit, but I'm concerned about her current state of mind. Did she share any details with you, regarding her time away from the compound?"

"She said it was very cold," I answered. I couldn't help but hear Armand nagging in my mind to keep my answers short and vague, while being truthful enough to avoid any scrutiny from the Masters. I could tell from the face James pulled that he knew I was holding back.

"It was," he said anyway. "She experienced trauma, and it's caused her to harbor a problematic attitude towards our way of life within these walls. I want you to know, I have posted extra security outside and have refrained from transferring Liza to the hospital because I am concerned for her safety." He cut me off, swerving in his path so that he was facing me, staring down at me with his knowing blue eyes. "I have never doubted nor worried about you, Daisy, until this week. I would like to ask you to keep in mind everything I have done for you before you tell me honestly—if I respect your wish to keep the Tribute wing private, will I live to regret it?" His eyes bore into mine and I found myself stuck in place.

All my years of staring up at him in fear and admiration melted away until I saw James, or at least a glimpse of him, for who he was: He was just a man responsible for making sure that life in the compound ran smoothly, and he was afraid to compromise the legalities that protected the four of us. I did not know how valuable we were to him, but I knew that we were crucial enough to him that he risked his own life and the lives of his men to bring the one of us who managed to escape back alive.

Everyone in this place feared James. Liza, the boldest of us, had been broken by him, that much was clear. I felt a spark of the wildness I saw in her eyes the night she leaped from the open library window course through me; if I wanted to salvage anything from our original cause, to be free of this place, then the answer I would give to James now must be careful and smart.

"No, James," I replied at last. "I know now more than ever, thanks to Liza, that the rules you have put in place are for my safety." I let my lower lip quiver. "I just want Liza to be all right."

"She will be, Daisy," James said. He frowned sadly down at me. "I'll make sure of it." He continued down the hall and I followed him. "Liza has learned a hard lesson," James said when we reached the doors leading out of the Masters' rooms. "But I fear it was a necessary one."

"As you say," I said to James. A biting pinch of defiance pricked my heart as I stared at him, my expression still the perfect mask of distress on behalf of Liza. It wasn't my worry for Liza that powered my resolution now; it was my loyalty to her that filled me with renewed strength. I swore to myself in that moment that James would live to regret his trial of trusting me with my own thoughts.

"Very good," James said. I could see that he was pleased with my performance.

"James," I said quietly as he led me out of the doors, behind the line of guardsmen assembled outside. "Quinn said that I will need your permission if I come back to visit Liza. I would like to see her again soon, but since she will not be moved to the hospital…." I left the suggestion open ended. James was clearly hesitant.

"I'll have to speak with the boys first," James said. "But I suppose it would be all right if you came back to see Liza—if Jada approves, of course. I'll let Quinn know."

I smiled genuinely, relieved that I would have access to Liza after the disastrous ending to our short visit. It would give me plenty of time to talk to Kit and Armand and devise a new plan, one that would leave behind the misbegotten recklessness of jumping through the first open window we could find. As frightened as I was of James, whose presence would always be a threat no matter how gentle or forgiving he pretended to be around me, I reminded myself what Liza, my poor sister, had said at the very start of this:

"There are four of us and only one of him," she had said with conviction. "And we're stronger when we're together."

Chapter Two

As the summit drew nearer, the Aventine was proving its worth as the jewel compound of the Master System. A veritable fortress capable of withstanding heavy siege and large enough to fit a city inside (a facet that would come in handy as Masters and their companions flooded in from all across the continent), the Aventine was not just a safe haven for the civilians, Tributes, and Masters who lived inside but their secrets too. Its fortified walls held in the secret scandal of Liza's brash escape and her humiliation of being dragged back alive. The structure contained not just Liza's shame, but James the Master's as well—never before had a Master cheated death so narrowly, certainly not this close to a summit.

Only a few were privy to the curious and appalling events that had transpired in just a week. The servants and tradesmen knew enough to keep their eyes down and ears closed to the rumors. Some of the charming denizens of the trade floor flirted fragments of the truth out of the more sociable swordsmen but they never dared to share anything they'd heard for fear of what James would do.

However, when it became clear that the revered Master was out of commission, careless whispers began to circulate as the speculations of what had really happened that night when the alarms had gone off became more wildly embellished by the hour. To help ease the public's perception, Donovan's soldiers took on the chore of integrating themselves with James' men, who in every way behaved differently when they were on duty. The swordsmen of the southern compound never hurried or hushed their voices when they spoke freely to one another, whereas the Aventine's guards maintained an air of careful control at all times. It was Donovan's opinion that a guard with nothing to hide should act as such, but James' fellows were trained to be stoic and discreet no matter what.

With so many new faces mingling with the old ones, the Aventine's halls lent a rare intimacy to its wanderers. James' Tributes had never seen so many people bustle through the common areas by day and were easily discouraged by the increase in foot traffic—at least, two of the three Tributes who were able to move about the halls were. When Kit and Daisy opted to take lessons in the study or kitchen to avoid the crowds, Armand propelled himself out into the market whenever he could to seek the detached proximity to the strangers swarming his familiar floors. It was his best chance to catch blips of conversation between guards and servants in the hopes of patching together some semblance of a report as to how James was recovering from the brutal animal attack detailed in Daisy's secondhand account.

Armand was not alone in feeling the thrill of James' absence. All around the Aventine, regardless of status, people seemed to be invigorated by the same buzz a roomful of students might experience when their teacher unexpectedly left his class. Some bent the rules by opening their shops or stands minutes before the allowed time, others found sordid excitement in trading those items that they might never have disclosed on their manifest had James been around to see them sell. With each successful, inconsequential act of rebellion by its residents, the Aventine's seemingly unsupervised atmosphere infected people with the sense of luckiness; everyone knew these days were numbered, but without James' aura permeating the market, it was difficult to shake the delightful ease that came with such miniscule freedom.

Donovan felt the boost of morale the most of anyone in the compound. When he made the morning rounds in the market and among the guards, he held himself with the air of a man who might be pretending that he was the Master of this place instead of James. He reveled in the smiles and genuinely glad greetings paid to him by most whom he passed. As he made his way to the Tribute wing, he wondered how James could be anything less than happy to have the job he did.

When he pressed the bell off to the side of the Tribute's front door, Donovan frowned and reminded himself that James had probably never been happy about anything, let alone the many perks that came with being Master of the Aventine.

"Donovan!" Daisy appeared in the suddenly open door, beaming.

"Just the girl I wanted to see!" Donovan smoothly caught her hand in his fingers and raised it ceremoniously to his lips. "Mind if I come in?"

"Of course," said Daisy, stepping aside to allow him inside.

"Would you prefer I remove my boots?" asked Donovan once he stood in the entryway of the Tribute apartments. He glanced down at Daisy's bare feet sheepishly and waited for her to reply.

"Leave them on, by all means." Daisy led the way into the study, where Kit was sitting opposite his kindly tutor Graham at a desk lined with papers and maps.

"Hello, Donovan!" Kit stood to shake Donovan's hand and give his arm a friendly clap. By the look of him, Donovan thought if he were to repay the gesture, Kit's arm would be just as firm as his own. He wondered what kind of fitness regimen James outlined for the boy that kept him in such fine condition.

"Master Donovan." Graham was tired but cheerful, as usual.

"Daisy was kind enough to offer me an oasis," said Donovan with a grin as he looked back at Daisy. "It's a madhouse out there."

"Armand finds it stimulating," said Kit with a shudder.

"I'll bet he does," said Donovan.

"How is Liza today?" asked Daisy. Donovan supposed she couldn't keep in the question any longer.

"I'm afraid I don't know, I haven't been that way this morning."

"We can only hope that she is resting," said Graham. His very fatherly approach to relating to his pupils was by far his most endearing quality, almost equal to his enduring optimism. "Doctor Jada will see to it that Liza recovers in no time, I'm sure."

"Though it's up to James whether or not she can come home to us," muttered Kit, sounding a lot like Armand. He tried his best to contain his critical tone but he was overpowered by his jealousy of Daisy to pull it off. After all, Daisy remained the only one of them James had allowed to see Liza yet.

"Patience pays off," Donovan told the young Tribute.

"You're too right, Master Donovan." Graham invited Kit to sit down and resume the lesson. As soon as Donovan caught on that it was all about southern geography, he happily joined Graham and Kit, and insisted Daisy follow suit. Graham described the climate of the region, as well as several of its more prominent cities, and Donovan peppered in personal accounts of his time in each place, tales which usually involved a flare of bravado and swordplay. Graham was not accustomed to so many interruptions during a lecture but he was pleased to see his pupils engaged in the subject rather than pretending to pay attention while really thinking desperately about Liza.

After a while of this, Graham declared it was time to conclude the lesson and move on to lunch. "I'm beginning to think Armand has washed his hands of his education and is committed to fending for himself out in the market all day," said Graham as he stacked the papers covering the desk into a neat pile.

"Maybe he went to see Liza?" Daisy hoped.

"I don't think so, Daisy." Graham frowned. He was just as worried as his pupil was about poor Liza but knew better than Daisy did, that pigs would fly before James ever let Armand in to see Liza by himself. As Graham suspected, Daisy and Kit looked expectantly to Donovan. Why he was their favorite he could deduce very easily, though it took most of the tutor's self-control and wisdom not to pass along some of the truths he had learned about the very young Master over the years to his students. After all, it was his job to instruct them, not give them a glimpse behind the System's curtain.

"Isn't there anything you can do?" Daisy was woefully unaware of how persuasive she really was—her ignorance of her soft features and bright eyes was a large part of that.

"I have to be very careful about how I spend my favors, Daisy. But...I'll tell you what," said Donovan who, even for a charmer, was powerless against Daisy's appeal. "Does Liza have a favorite book? A drawing tablet, perhaps? I can see to it that she receives something of hers from home, to keep her company while she recuperates."

Daisy stood and disappeared into the hallway, her long hair swishing over her shoulders in her wake. She returned a moment later with a felt-covered book clasped in her hands. She hugged it to her chest before offering it to Donovan. "My poems," she said. "All my favorites—most of them are Liza's, too. I copied down all of them from different books so I could commit them to memory."

Impressed, Donovan took the book and flipped through its contents. "*I must have been sleeping a hundred years in the world of the poets, and did not know about hell on earth,*" he read aloud. "I had no idea your taste in poetry was so Biblical, Daisy."

The girl reddened under Donovan's wry gaze. "Can you get them to Liza?"

"I'll do my utmost," said Donovan with a wink. He tucked the book under his arm. "Thank you for letting me enjoy my small reprieve from business that is much less enjoyable than your lesson." Kit and Daisy showed him to the door and thanked him in turn for helping them deliver such a small comfort to Liza. "It is my pleasure," Donovan assured them. "Give Armand my best; I'm sorry to have missed him."

"I'm sure he'll be cross about missing your visit," said Kit. "If you manage to see Liza, please tell her we are thinking of her."

"And we want her to come home," Daisy added.

"Of course," replied Donovan. He gestured to the book under his arm and smiled. "I'm sure this will help a great deal." After affording the Tributes one more heart-stopping grin, Donovan turned on the heel of his boot and delved back into the bustling hall where just about everyone was hurrying to do the work they wanted done before James was well enough to haunt the trade floor again.

Chapter Three

Armand

I woke up before sunrise for the sixth day in a row. Even in sleep, I could not escape the rushing, worried thoughts of Liza and what her escape and recapture would mean for the rest of us. Dreadful panic sank its hooks into my chest as I considered how serious our living situation had become in a matter of hours, for not just us Tributes would be accountable for Liza's brash escape; we weren't that lucky. Every person who lived out of this compound would be affected by Liza's actions, and worst of all, I was responsible for the whole thing…. I felt I could do nothing but grimace at the stitch in my chest as the rushing panic began to boil over. Desperate to quell it before I was sick, I took to the floor and assumed a plank position, braced by my toes and hands, and pushed up from the carpet in rapid motions. I kept at it until my arms burned and my back felt like it would give out. I lowered myself to the floor and rolled over onto my back, my chest heaving, to stare up at the tiny circular window over my head. I could tell by the dusty shade of lavender tinting the sky that daybreak was still a way off. I closed my eyes and cursed, for I could have used a much longer sleep.

Since early childhood, certainly since I came to live at the compound, I struggled with nerves. Jada's predecessor Doctor Gordon told me that physical exertion would help me regain control of my mind, which prompted James the Master to encourage me to practice an athletic variation of martial arts at age ten. He'd piously pointed out that he had been put to work at the same age, and if I were to apply myself with as much focus and commitment as he had, someday I could be a Master like him—as if that were something to strive to be.

"Master Armie does have a certain ring to it," Liza had teased me.

"Liza is strong," Daisy had said to James. "She could be a Master too!"

"Women procure the title of 'Mistress,' Daisy," James had corrected her. "There are many rules to follow as a Master, and I don't know if Liza would find the duties to her liking."

"More rules than we have?" Kit had asked, astonished.

"Yes, indeed," James had said. If I hadn't known better, I'd have thought James was proud of us that day. Part of the reason I never trusted James when I was a boy was because James always carried himself with the demeanor of a much older man, but I learned when I was ten just by butting my nose into servants' conversations in the market that James could not possibly have been a day over twenty-five. Graham had always taught me that there is no age minimum for the wise, but James had too much power for a young man, in my opinion, and therefore I rejected the idea that he could be so gifted in every attribute.

I never trusted James at all, really. Daisy, Liza, and Kit didn't know any different and to protect myself, I pretended to share their awe of him. The truth was, I remembered my life before the compound: if I closed my eyes, I could summon the memory of my mother and father with ease; I could recall the smell of my home, my real home, and the sound of my parents' voices…not that I often exercised that ability, for with those memories came the ache of yearning and the taunting illusion of hope that I might see them again someday.

Months ago, when Kit, Daisy, and Liza began to whisper to each other about finding a life outside the compound, I came very close to sharing with them my memories of home but stopped just before I could form the words. Not only was I certain that James was listening, but those moments were the only things I had left of my own. I never put pen to paper about those memories, never tried to draw the faces of my parents the way Liza had. The closest I came to sharing my grasp of our identity with the three of them was when I learned to cook and prepared us all a savory loaf of very grainy bread. I baked it from scent memory alone and when the four of us ate it together, I knew that somehow, we were all back home where we belonged, if only for a few moments.

I heaved myself off the carpeted floor of my bedroom and went immediately to the bath, hoping to scald away the impulse to kick myself for perpetuating by neutrality the girls' plan to escape. James was calling it an attempt—a botched suicide attempt, more specifically—but he was wrong on both counts. It didn't matter than Liza had run away and been found; she had succeeded in escaping the compound and royally pissed James off in the process... I honestly wasn't sure which feat made prouder of Liza.

I told myself as I sank underneath the surface of intensely hot bathwater that we were all fools to think we could get away from this place. Because of her commitment to ignoring my advice, Daisy was learning a difficult lesson about showing weakness in front of James. I knew better than the three of them that the only way to stay off James' radar was to maintain the appearance of a young man who genuinely enjoyed holding himself to the careful, practical standards of the very structured life James arduously mapped out for us. I learned how to hide behind my own eyes so that Graham and James, and even Jada, couldn't read my emotions. I followed the rules until they staunchly conflicted with my private values, like when James decreed that we weren't allowed to spend time in each other's rooms after dark or share a bed with one another. For several years in a row, the only comfort I could cleave to long enough to fall asleep were Kit and the girls—Kit was like a little brother to me, and Daisy was our precious baby sister; while Liza and I were just as close, our bond was different because we were the older pair among the four of us. We shared brief moments of intimacy as often as we could, especially on the days we felt the most alone in the world.

Liza could sense when I was at odds with my nerves, I was certain. The morning of the day she jumped, mere days ago, she'd come up behind me in the kitchen while I was washing up breakfast dishes and hugged me around the middle.

"Someday we'll be free, Armie," she'd whispered. Free to love one another, free of this compound, free of James—it was a dangerous notion and I knew it because of the hope it inspired in me.

"Forget about it, Liza," I'd told her. I'd turned around with her arms still around me, my hands still caked with soap suds from the sink, and returned the embrace. I squeezed her a little tighter to impress how serious I was.

"I want to be free too," I'd murmured softly, knowing that I only had a few seconds to spare before we had to step away from each other. "But I am begging you to be reasonable—no one escapes, Liza. We are powerless against James. He'll never let us go."

Liza shook her head and smoothed her hands up my back. "I'm not afraid of him, Armie." I'd frowned sadly down at her, searching her beautiful round violet eyes for a girl to whom I could get through but I couldn't find one.

"You should be," I'd said. It was the last thing I'd said to her before she'd followed Daisy to the library that night and leaped from the open window. It could have been the last thing I ever said to her, which made me wince to consider, but against the elements and James' ferocious will to catch her, I'd had to prepare myself for the likelihood that Liza would not survive the escape. I didn't sleep for a moment after Daisy came home to us and recounted the horrific tale; all I could do was hate myself for not trying to stop Liza. I resolved that I should have gone straight to James and confess the girls' conspiracy to escape the compound by any means necessary, despite it being an act of gross betrayal, because even though Liza and Daisy would hate me, and Kit would berate me relentlessly, I'd keep the three people I cared about close....

And I should have told Liza I loved her.

I was utterly desolate for the first two days. I tried to be patient when I could but I was too exhausted to keep a grip on my panic, so I disguised my impulse to weep by snapping at Kit and slandering Daisy. I couldn't think of a way out of this because I could only think about Liza, fighting for her life in the outside world. Then, Jada told us that James had been hurt in the rescue attempt. I reminded myself to be wary of an opportunity, for it was a rarity that James was ever out of commission; I was determined to be clever and wait, all the while keeping to my routine, until a circumstance from which I could benefit fell into my lap.

The chance came along soon after when Donovan arrived at the compound. Our significant past encounter had left me feeling anxious and a little flummoxed, but I had to be prepared to seize any opportunity Donovan might present, especially since Donovan's discretion assuaged any doubt I had about the possibility to pursue a sympathetic alliance.

And then came the second miracle, Liza—alive—and in Jada's capable hands. My eyesight had been washed over in a wave of furious crimson when I witnessed Jada turn Liza over into James' care. Seeing James take Liza in his arms, in his bed no less, was nearly enough to make me sick; thankfully, the morning after, as I nursed a minor hangover in the confines of my room, James the Bastard facilitated an epiphany so genius and unexpected that it brought a smile to my face.

It was that idea that compelled me to dress hastily after my bath and slip quietly out of my room, not-yet-daylight peeking through my lonely window overhead, and out of the Tribute wing. I headed straight to the gallery, an enclosed winding corridor in which the artistic tradesmen gathered in the late afternoon to barter handcrafted goods, which was empty of all pedestrian traffic at this time of day. Indeed there were many guardsmen about this morning, due to Liza's dramatic resurgence late last night, but none of them paid me any mind as I let myself into the gallery and closed the door behind me.

I made my way to the far end of the gallery hall, where stacks of artfully decorated crates lined the corners and obscured the door to the merchant office, where the tradesmen usually kept their personal items during market hours. I knew it was likely too early to expect Donovan, so I busied myself by rummaging carefully through the crates nearest to me. I found a collection of clay idols inside, modeled to resemble soldiers. The attention to detail was lacking, and I doubted these would ever make the trade floor. I wondered what other subpar trinkets were stored back here—Daisy was too old for dolls, but a dancer figurine might delight her.

"Up before the sun again, I see," sighed Donovan behind me. I smirked and turned around slowly. He was so catlike in the way he sauntered toward me, all the while watching me with piercingly teal, cunning eyes.

"What can I say," I said, "I'm a competitive early riser."

"Find anything that piques your interest?" Donovan asked, glancing to the crate of clay soldiers behind me.

"Nah," I said with a shrug. "I don't find swordsmen to be all that impressive." I grinned when Donovan's smirk twisted into a wry smile, revealing his glittering, sharp white teeth. I relented to him when he came forward and snaked his arms around me, his hands tracing along where my trousers fit snugly under my hips; in turn, I reached for him and let my hands roam across his firm chest.

"Where were you last night?" Donovan murmured, leaning in so that our noses nuzzled.

"Kit was up," I said, leaning into Donovan so that we stood even closer. "I couldn't get away." I smiled against Donovan's mouth when he brushed his lips over mine. "How long do we have?" I asked, thrilled to feel Donovan's erection against me.

"As long as you want," Donovan replied. He planted a slow, meandering row of kisses along the side of my throat. "What's the rush?" he asked between the tender, deliberate smooches.

"Just wondering, in case you're still planning to elope with Daisy," I chided, a little woozy when his lips suckled the pulse of my throat. Donovan hummed a laugh as he kissed me. The gentle vibrations sent chills down my spine delightfully.

"You heard about James' hilarious theory, did you?"

"Straight from the horse's mouth."

Donovan chuckled and smoothed his hands over my backside, giving my buttocks a rude squeeze. "Is this jealousy I detect, Armand?" He grazed his teeth over the curve of my neck where it meets my shoulder.

"Hardly," I said unevenly, tilting my head back a little to hide the roll of my eyes. "Daisy's a child."

"You *are* jealous," said Donovan, grinning at my expense. "Would you take her place as my bride, Armie?"

I stiffened at his use of my nickname—he knew it was only for Kit and the girls; he was just being snide. "White is not really my color," I said dryly.

"Don't I know it." He kissed me on the mouth, holding me against him. I curled my fingers into loose fists and tugged his collar, parting my lips for his tongue. It was remarkably easy to forget my nerves when I was kissing him, he was just so magnetic.

Last summer, during his brief visit over the solstice weekend, Donovan had gone to the studio to practice swordplay, expecting the room to be empty. He'd found me there, playing with the blunted sword I'd found in an unlocked supply cabinet. Donovan hadn't punished me for touching a weapon or being out of bounds after dark, like James would have. Instead he showed me how to hold the blade properly and how to move, and I'd been so completely enraptured by him that when he stood close to show me how to swing my arm, I'd dropped the sword to the floor with a clatter and threw my arms around his neck; I'd been so hungry for closeness, any scrap of intimacy I would get, that first sloppy entanglement was over before it had barely begun. Donovan had been so patient with me despite how urgently I'd taken him, making himself pliable to me as if he recognized something of himself in the frantic boy who was essentially forcing himself onto him. I took great pride in the groans he made low in his throat when I took him in my mouth or otherwise, for I felt a power over him and his status as a Master that filled me with satisfaction. He was just as eager to elicit pleasured vocal responses from me—sometimes I hated him for everything he was and everything he made me feel, but the sensations he lavished upon me were too wonderful to loathe.

Afterwards, he'd kissed me sweetly and told me that I was the most beautiful and sad boy he'd ever laid eyes on.

I was grateful to Donovan for giving me what I needed. We met up several more times over those two days, during which he was unrelenting and gratifying to a degree I'd never known. I came to find that there was an insurmountable giddiness that came with pleasing him that stole me away from my sense of captivity in bursts of released joy which resulted in a three-month-long depression when he left to return to his camps in the south. If it weren't for his many visits to the Aventine since then, I would have sworn off such entanglements for good just to protect my heart.

Donovan was the opportunity of feasible escape I'd been waiting nearly twenty years for. I was immensely fond of him, it was true, and yet I knew if I could cultivate his lustful adoration for me, I might persuade him to covet me away to the southern camps, far away from this compound. I could leave him long enough to reach Kit and the girls or maybe even convince Donovan to smuggle the three of them away from James one by one, not only succeeding in getting them away from James, but securing a safe place in which we could lie low until James relinquished his likely religiously furtive search efforts.

I felt slightly guilty for allowing Daisy to bear an accusation which embarrassed her—that farcical idea that she'd been bound to elope with Donovan when she'd tried to escape—but it was vital to my mechanisms to supply no suspicious or personal information regarding Donovan's proclivities in bodily delights to the others. I was rough with Donovan in anger when I realized that he likely would take advantage of Daisy if even the slightest chance presented itself, but he responded in kind and worked me with such invigoration that I forgot my frustration.

I was breathless and smiling like a fool when we were finished. We pulled ourselves up and propped our backs against the crates behind us, Donovan chuckling contentedly to himself while I mussed my hair and tugged my trousers back on.

"She pointed out that we're too friendly with each other, you know," I told Donovan, still out of breath.

"Daisy is a smart girl, but her naivety blinds her," said Donovan. "You worry too much, lover." He reached for his clothes too, rummaging through his pockets until he found his silver cigarette case. He withdrew one and lit it, then passed it to me. Breathing in the smoke reminded me just how deep a breath I could take and after another long drag, I felt a grounding calm wash over me. We passed the cigarette back and forth until it was finished. I wanted about ten more but I knew I would reek from sharing this one already. Donovan tucked away the silver case and slowly, reluctantly, dressed. We'd already gone twice, and as much as I wanted to stay to lose my worries a third time, I knew that we would risk being caught if we stayed put.

I shied away from Donovan's earlier endearment about how much I worried. "What can you do for Liza?" I asked.

"That remains to be seen." He stood up and pulled me to my feet beside him. "I can talk to James," he offered. "But it'll have to be just that. I can't push too hard, or he'll let on that I'm hiding something from him."

I knew he was right. He kissed me and I clasped his cheek with one hand. "Tomorrow?" I asked.

"I'll stop in later, to check on Kit and Daisy," said Donovan. "Maybe tonight?"

"Maybe," I agreed. Donovan smiled and left me in the gallery storeroom, where I waited the customary few minutes before leaving too. I didn't see him in the market when I emerged from the gallery entrance, which wasn't uncommon. I was relieved to see that bustling life had been breathed into the looming main halls since I'd met Donovan, even more so when a passing fruit merchant wished me a polite "Good morning!" and tossed me an orange, which I peeled and devoured right away. The artists wouldn't wake up before lunch, so the gallery would stay quiet for hours still, but the other tradesmen met the day when the sun did.

I smelled freshly baked bread and the wisps of spices as carts of food were wheeled past me as I made my way through the crowd to the medical ward of the compound. I hoped she'd allow me to see Liza despite the early hour—I keenly preferred mine to be the first face she saw today, not James' contemptuous mug.

"Good morning, Doctor," I announced, ducking into the medical ward as soon as I passed it. Jada was holding an enormous stack of papers in her arms, reading notes on a bright screen in front of her while holding a pencil between her teeth. Jada looked up at me, plopped the papers down on a desk to her left, snatched the pencil out of her mouth, and took my elbow in her hand.

"You want to visit Liza, is that right?" she asked, leading me out of the medical wing at a quick pace.

"I hoped I could," I said, confused by Jada's worried hurry. "Daisy said Liza was in a troubled state yesterday—"

"You could say that," Jada interjected quietly. "You need to talk some sense into that girl, Armand. I thought seeing Daisy might convince her to behave, but after Daisy left, I had to sedate Liza." The easygoing bliss I felt after seeing Donovan fizzled away into a burning anger.

"Did James hit her?"

"I don't believe he did," Jada said. I could see the line of guardsmen blocking the way to the Masters' chambers up ahead. "But I wouldn't strike it from the realm of possibility. He's speaking with her now, at least he said he would when he left my office a short while ago. She said the most outrageous things yesterday, Armand, you wouldn't believe it."

"Yes," I disagreed flatly, "I would." I knew better than Jada how tenacious and stubborn Liza could be when she was incensed, but I also knew as well as Jada that bickering with me or Kit was far different than provoking James.

"Is he permitted inside?" the brutish Quinn asked, his severely bruised face still serving as a cautionary tale to the other guardsmen.

"He's with me," Jada said curtly. Quinn stepped aside and allowed me to follow Jada through the doors to the Masters' chambers.

"You're the only person I can think of who can get through to her," Jada said to me in a hushed voice as she walked as fast as she could without jogging down the hall.

"I will try to," I said. The nauseous guilt in my gut churned as I thought once again, if I'd told her about my memory of home on the day she'd escaped, none of us would be in this conundrum.

"Stay out here," Jada instructed quietly, halting in front of a set of doors. "Until I call you in."

Chapter Four

I dreamed of falling no matter how heavily Jada sedated me. The memory of diving into the freezing-cold night air stole the breath from my lungs and jolted me out of sleep with a violent spasm. I sat up, careful not to put too much pressure on my sore hands, and took a few deep breaths. It took me a moment to assess my surroundings and recall that I was not in my room in the Tribute wing, but here in a guest suite in the Master chambers. I hated this room for how exquisite it was, down to the last detail. When Graham taught me about ancient monarchs and the regal quarters they lived in, I imagined bedrooms just like this one. It was fit for a queen but as I glanced around at the intricate carvings in the walls or curled up to find warmth underneath these sheets that were much finer than the ones that made up my bed in the Tribute wing, I found myself repulsed.

This was still a cage, no matter how prettily it was decorated, and through no fault but my own I'd be stuck here for good. I'd tasted the open air and gotten farther from the compound than I'd imagined I would, but here I was, not only back within these walls but sealed in the most secure part of the compound. My failure chilled me and made my palms sweat. I could all but smell it on these cream-colored silk sheets. Poor Daisy was punishing herself for what she believed to be a failure, but it was thanks to James and his dastardly timing that she hadn't succeeded.

Yet, what had going through with it really done for me, anyway? I'd landed myself back in James' clutches and I couldn't close my eyes without seeing how far down the ground was; so high up that the forest floor was hidden by its treetops, and then I couldn't stop the heated sting of adrenaline from burning behind my eyes or my rushing blood blaring in my ears as I fell, arms outstretched, impossibly down, down, down....

I shivered and shook my head. Jada told me that reliving a distressing event in vivid detail like this, consistently, is an unfortunate effect of trauma. I found her ability to bury human emotion for the sake of clinical appropriation to be ruthless and infuriating—I'd known Jada since I could remember, which was my entire life in this place, and I had grown to love her for her kindness and gentle manner. She was always so sweet, calling us "honey" all the time. I couldn't help but scorn myself for never having suspected how loyal to James she really was. So far, the only real lesson I'd learned from this whole thing was how hopelessly foolish I was. Even worse, the more I contemplated my situation, I realized that Armand had been right from the start.

My anger wilted as I thought of Armand. I wanted so much to see him and let him hold me like Daisy had, but I'd have to apologize for not listening to him and the mere idea of speaking those words brought tears to my eyes. Daisy had been so pale when she'd come to see me.... I knew she was frightened to be in this sector of the compound, and to be shown out by James no less; I felt guilty for the explosive outburst I unleashed on James in front of her. Armand would never have let his fear of James show. I craved his willful pride and his brutal honesty; I was sick of tormenting myself with thoughts of my mistakes. I wanted someone else to do it.

A soft knock sounded at the door. My entire body tensed—it was probably Lorraine with my breakfast, but on the off chance it was Jada or James, I had to be sure to wear my meanest glare. I was right to do it, for a moment later James let himself into the room. He was wearing his usual dark clothing but today he had an ice pack strapped to his side. I had never seen him display anything on his person that might impugn his unbreakable reputation, but I remembered that we were in his rooms now, and he was free to move about his ward dressed as he pleased.

"Hello, Liza," said James. I said nothing. "How are you feeling today?"

I clenched my jaw and blinked slowly. "Fantastic." My voice was much smoother than it had been when Daisy visited, but I sort of liked its roughness. It made it easier to convey how displeased I was to see him.

James didn't like sarcasm. "You really worried Daisy yesterday."

"Can't be helped." I crossed my arms and winced—I kept forgetting about the intravenous line stuck in the crook of my arm. "Daisy is a worrier. She gets it from Kit."

"All right," James remarked, his brows furrowing in consternation. "Let's try it this way—your behavior yesterday was totally unacceptable."

"You have a problem with how I acted *yesterday?* Did you miss the part where I jumped out the window the week before?"

"Should I send for Jada?" James was threatening me with more sedatives but I wasn't buying into it. I didn't care.

"I don't know, do you need someone to swap out that cold compress?" I was needling his temper and my success showed. James mirrored my cross-armed stance and pursed his lips.

"No," he replied. I don't know why he felt the need to keep up the pretense of conversation; until he snapped or left, I was going to keep at him.

"I hope it hurts!" I hissed.

"It does." We stared each other down for a few moments of tense silence. "How long do you want to keep this up?" he asked quietly.

"Do you think this is a game?" I demanded hotly. I uncrossed my arms because I couldn't bear the discomfort of the needle in my arm. "That I'm being impetuous to wage a battle of wills with you?"

James was obviously discouraged to find that I was picking up where we'd left off the day before. "You tell me, Liza. You have done nothing but caterwaul since you came to," he pushed back angrily. "I regret having to use drastic measures to keep you in place, but you broke the rules of this compound—"

"This is my life, James!" I shouted. "It's Daisy's life, and Kit's life, and Armand's life too! We are not blind cattle roaming around these halls day in and day out; we are people with minds of our own, and feelings! You insist on teaching us everything that'll fit in our heads but you won't give us windows and you refuse to answer our questions!" My breath was uneven and I was near tears, much to my bitter dismay.

"It is not my job to answer your questions," James said simply. "You can hate me for that all you want, but my most important responsibility is to ensure your safety and uphold the conditions under which you live here."

"I don't *live* here," I snapped. "You just keep me too busy to remember that I can't leave."

"Liza," sighed James. "Please, I've told you already—"

"Tell me why we cannot leave!" I urged shrilly, my voice breaking as I raised it. James dropped his crossed arms and looked at me with those horribly captivating and stormy blue eyes of his.

"No."

"At least tell me why you wouldn't let me die!" I pleaded. Hot tears burned in my eyes and I was too angry to feel embarrassed.

"It is my job to keep you safe," James repeated tonelessly. "It would be difficult to do that if you had frozen to death."

"But for what?" I cried, my breaths hitching on swelling sobs in my throat. "What does it matter if I can't leave this place anyway?" I began to feel the shakiness of very real panic set into my chest. "I wish I never would have caught that stupid beam," I said. "I'd be better off dead than trapped here—"

"Liza!" James exclaimed. "Don't say such things!" I was a little stunned by the pity emanating from his stare. "Your life has value," he said. Was this sympathy from him? I felt enraged by it.

"To whom?" I demanded.

"To Daisy!" James insisted. "And the boys, of course! You're their family, Liza."

"Oh, but they have James the Master to keep them safe," I said venomously. "They don't need me in this cage alongside them—"

"Liza, stop it," James warned.

"It's true!" I said. "What difference would it have made to them if I froze to death?"

"It would make a difference," James said with succinct frustration, "to me." I glared up at James coldly.

"Why?" I asked. My eyes were dry as I watched James carefully, waiting for the slightest twitch to betray any inclination of how he felt. "Tell me why, James!" I yelled when he remained silent and still. Kit always shut up whenever arguments became too heated. It made me appreciate his patience but it also inculcated in me a serious loathing of the silent treatment.

"I did not realize," James said after a long deliberation, "that you were so unhappy here."

"It never occurred to you that I might be unhappy, when the only things I know about the world beyond these walls came from books and a tiny circular pane of glass over my bed?" I shook my head. "I was a fool for thinking I could get away from this place, but you are more the fool if you ever thought that you could raise us to think for ourselves but would never question your precious rules—that you could pass off a windowless cage as some kind of deranged, privileged high-life!"

"You and the others have been given more than you could possibly understand," James said darkly. "The unwavering security I have provided for you is rare; the people outside of these walls that you hate so passionately would kill to have the life you have."

"And I suppose I'm to thank you for that?" I snapped. "You really think you can turn this back around on me? To say that I'm ungrateful simply I didn't know to refuse your brand of generosity and protection? I did not know any better! I was a child!"

"You still are a child," James said coolly. He noticed his remark had spurned me and he shrugged. "Only a child would behave the way you have been."

"You will say anything to provoke me," I growled, my own temper sizzling in my gut. "You don't know how to control me anymore and it terrifies you!" I sucked in a gasp when he came around to my bedside much faster than I thought him capable. He leaned over me with a glare so fierce that I actually averted my eyes and pinched my lips together to keep them from quivering.

"Let me make something perfectly clear," James said. "I am *not* afraid of you, Liza. Your brattish petulance is hideous to behold; you have been gifted with every luxury you could ever desire, educated more than anyone your age could be taught on the outside, and protected from very real horrors you cannot begin to imagine, yet you think this place is so unyielding and awful? You would not last one day out there on your own."

I met his glare with renewed defiance in my eyes. "I lasted *five*," I hissed, right to his face. I could tell he was itching to hit me. I was buzzing with fear that felt like ice water dripping down my back—his strength had leveled me before—I had a scar to prove it—but I was desperate to push him to show his ferocity and prove my point, that he was a bully and a brute.

Instead of striking me, James curled his lips into a sickeningly satisfied smirk. "Oh, yes," he said, chuckling. "You really made it far, didn't you?"

I lashed out to hit him with my bandaged hand. He reached out on impulse and caught my wrist in his hand, his grip like an iron manacle. He laughed when I struggled to pull my hand back and couldn't; he was just too strong.

"Let go of me!" I tried to tug my arm away and gritting my teeth against the pinching of the needle in my arm.

"You raised a hand to me and have the gall to make demands?" James asked, the glimmer of malicious delight in his eyes. "Liza, this is a new level of boldness, even for you."

The burn of humiliation scorched my cheeks. I was struggling to take my hand back with as much strength as I could and James was barely bothered. He held my wrist in a steady grip as though I were a doll wriggling in his grasp. I hated him, I decided; what kind of man would find joy in toying with someone whom he outranked in every capacity?

"Send for Jada if you mean to subdue me," I groaned, engaging the sore muscles in my arms to yank my hand free.

"Still tough enough to give me orders, Liza?" James tut-tutted me and shifted his grip on my wrist so that he could slowly twist my arm, causing the intravenous line in my arm to shift. It stung terribly and I could tell my vein had been cut.

"James," I gasped urgently. I grappled onto his forearm with my free hand to stop him from twisting my wrist. "Let go of me! It hurts!" Tears flooded my eyes and I let out a strangled cry. James relinquished his hold on me and stepped back from my bedside. I clutched my arm to my chest as I gulped down heaving breaths. I looked up at him as tears spilled past my eyelashes and I wanted to curse his name for what he'd done, but a hopeless sense of quiet washed over me and I could not summon any admonishing words to spit at him. I bowed my head and bit the inside of my cheek in an effort to force the sobs building up in my throat to quell.

"The next time you raise a hand to me, I will have no choice but to respond in kind, which will be extremely unpleasant for the both of us. Whether or not you are in a sickbed, I guarantee you will regret trying to hit me. Do you understand?"

Chapter Five

Armand

I heard James' low voice inside and I wanted to shove my way in past Jada, but I forced myself to remain calm. If I meant to get Liza to see sense, I had to lead by example. Jada let herself in and announced herself. I could tell she was uncomfortable.

"What is it, Jada?" James snapped. Jada subtly signaled for me to step into the room behind her. I looked past James and right to Liza, who was pale, grief-stricken, and on the brink of weeping. My heart leaped painfully to see the agony teeming in her eyes—I almost gasped, but I caught my breath and made myself stand still; Liza was clutching her arm protectively to her chest and I knew right away James had hurt her. I looked to him and wished him dead. I thought of Daisy's haunting retelling of the volpine attack Liza told her James had suffered and I felt a vicious sense of relish when I thought of a monstrous beast breaking his bones.

"Keep it short." James nearly barreled into me on his way out, the bastard.

"I'll be back in a few minutes," Jada said. "Please try not to upset her," she added knowingly. I waited until we were alone to rush to Liza's side and take her in my arms. She melted into a sobbing mess as soon as Jada had closed the door. She was trembling in fear and in pain, and I held her tightly to stop her from shaking. She felt so small, so frail.

"What has he done to you?" I sighed, my voice cracking in sorrow.

"Armie," Liza cried. My heart throbbed painfully in my chest as she hugged me.

"I'm here now," I assured her. I kissed the crown of her head. "I've got you."

"He's a monster!" Liza sobbed. I scorned myself for how tame I'd been moments ago—I ought to have spat in James' face for this.

"I hate him too." I held Liza's face delicately between my hands and kissed her lips, quelling the desperate urge coursing through me to comfort her. I tasted her tears on my lips and pulled away, grimacing. I berated her—I couldn't help it. "What were you thinking, jumping from an open window? Are you out of your mind?"

"I had to get away," Liza weakly defended herself. "I had to try."

"You're a fool. Jumping out the window was the stupidest thing you could have done," I said, crushing her excuse with contempt. It all came pouring out of me, how foolish an idea it had been in the first place, how much the three of us had suffered in her absence: "It was a selfish, idiotic thing to do. I haven't slept in a week, Daisy is falling to pieces, and Kit's nerves are shot. The only good thing to come of it was that James almost killed himself chasing after you—"

"Did Daisy tell you that?" Liza interrupted in a froggy voice.

"You're damn right she did," I grumbled. "That girl is a wreck. You wouldn't recognize her, Liza, she barely eats, hardly sleeps, and she fainted in front of Jada and cracked her head on the floor. Kit's beside himself about it all."

"I never meant for it to affect her like this," Liza whimpered apologetically. I kept in mind that I was meant to convince Liza to be sensical, and lobbing guilt-ridden allegations at her like I had been was an aggressive tactic even by my standards. I could see that Liza was suffering from what I described, mostly because of her somewhat maternal responsibility for Daisy's wellbeing. I sympathized with the compulsion to protect Daisy, who was the most fragile of the four of us—even I pulled my punches with Daisy when an argument arose, something I never did with Kit or Liza.

"Daisy has got it in her head," I said, forcibly affecting a calmer tone, "that she's convinced James, in his perceived pity, to trust her."

"You don't think she'll try to do it again?"

"After what happened to you? She'd have to be a lunatic." I remembered the tone of James' voice when I eavesdropped on him and Daisy yesterday morning. "Though apparently that's the growing trend of the week...."

"She said James accused her of trying to elope with Donovan," Liza remarked, picking up on the subtext. I laughed bitterly. I wanted so much to tell Liza that I was working on my own way to get us away from here, but it was neither the time nor the place.

"Too bad it didn't work out. She'd make a pretty little bride," I japed, thinking of how amused Donovan was to think I was jealous of the idea. Liza frowned and furrowed her brows.

"How could you say such a thing?" she retorted, pulling away from me. "It's clearly untrue—"

"Of course it's untrue," I insisted, repressing a smile. "If James actually believed for a second that it was, he'd have done a lot worse than tease Daisy about it. But really, Liza, you didn't see her when Donovan arrived yesterday. She was hanging off him and batting her eyelashes." That was the truth of their parade about the compound, after all. They put on enough of a spectacle to make James suspicious. Then, I couldn't help but snort as I thought of how offended Daisy had been when Kit and I hadn't immediately refuted the idea. "I wish you'd heard Kit try to explain to her that the idea isn't as wild as she thinks it is. He said she was *comely.*"

"Daisy is a beautiful girl!" Liza said crossly, leaping to Daisy's defense. "And she doesn't realize the effect she has on people's affections. She's too lost in her own imagination to realize how charming she is."

"You don't need to defend her to me, Liza," I reminded her.

"Well, I hope she'd speak up on my account if either of you raised an eyebrow at a rumor of *me* having an affair with one of the Masters," Liza replied stiffly.

As someone who *was* having an affair with a Master, I did not comment on that particular sentiment. "It's James who raised an eyebrow, not me or Kit," I said instead. "And it wasn't just James—the market was full of nosy tradesmen. They all saw Donovan carry her out of here—"

"Donovan carried her out of here?" Liza interjected, puzzled.

"He did."

"Why would he do such a thing?" Liza pressed me. I set my jaw in an effort to control my expression, for it became clear that Liza did not remember the night of her rescue. I felt crestfallen when I realized that I would have to break it to her, that James had stripped her of her clothing and her dignity that night.

"She was faint. You were hypothermic. Jada said it was serious and because there wasn't time to secure the hospital...well, James kept the compound on lockdown when you were gone to keep the scandal of an escape quiet, you see, so since he couldn't take you to the hospital, he brought you into his bedroom."

Liza was stunned. "I assumed James had pulled out every stop to protect the sanctity of his precious rules after he'd lost me in the forest, but bringing me into his own room?"

"It's a jarring idea," I agreed with a shudder. I heaved a sigh and fixed a passive expression. How would I put this? "Anyway, Jada went to fetch her staff and James...." The words turned to ashes in my mouth. I just couldn't say the words—it would break her, I knew it would. I felt foolish and hastily finished the recounting. "He sent us away. Daisy was weeping and Kit was upset. He resented the noise and had Douglas show us out. And now he's got a squadron of meatheads guarding the Masters' chambers. Jada had to get special permission from James in order to bring me to see you. I suspect Kit will be along next, but it's at James' discretion to allow it."

The information I volunteered seemed to spark something sinister in Liza. Sorrow possessed her, dulling the sharpness of her eyes and weighing on her shoulders. She took my hands in hers, the bandages wrapped around her slim fingers making it look like she was wearing thick gloves.

"You've got to watch Daisy," she told me. "Make sure she doesn't do anything stupid." I agreed at once, reaching with one hand to grasp her shoulder.

"I hate to say it, but I'm glad it's you this happened to, and not Daisy. She wouldn't be able to bear this like you can."

Liza was hurt by this, I could tell, but she shrugged anyway. "I can?"

"You're strong, Liza." I could scarcely believe that I had to tell her that myself. Her pain was palpable and it broke my heart. I pressed my lips to her forehead and frowned, for she was clearly running a fever. Feverish or not, though, she was alive—I would be thankful for it no matter what it meant for me. I wanted to carry her out of here like Donovan had Daisy and take her back to our wing. Instead, I released Liza smoothly and straightened my posture when her bedroom door opened. Through it came the head of James' kitchen staff, Lorraine, with a tray of food in her hands. Jada came in after her, along with James. I made a point to stand between James and Liza, blocking his view of her.

"How long until she can return to our wing?" I asked Jada firmly, ignoring James as much as I could.

"When I decide it's appropriate," said James.

"I was speaking to the doctor," I snapped. He knew full well I'd directed the question to Jada, but he just couldn't bear to be ignored, the villain.... James pulled a face at my cheek, checking about the room for an audience that was not there to corroborate my rude elucidation.

"What has Graham been teaching you these days?" James wondered to himself. "That kind of backtalk I would expect from Liza, but from you, Armand? I thought you were the smart one." He was mad and he wanted me to back down, but when he chided Liza like that, my eyes glazed over in hatred of him. Liza tensed behind me as Jada and Lorraine fussed over her to avoid James' attention.

"Kindly answer Armand, would you, Jada? He wants to know when Liza can go back to the Tribute wing with the other distastefully rude children!" He was baiting me.

"Liza has been through an ordeal, Armand," Jada said tersely. "I would like to keep her for observation for a while longer, you understand."

"Well, she looks fine to me!" I rounded on Jada. "She can sit up and eat without assistance—surely she's fit enough to be observed in her own room?" I silently begged Jada to agree with me, to grant Liza the security of being home with me, Kit, and Daisy. Jada was smart; she must know that Liza stood the best chance away from James.

But then Jada sided with James, not to my surprise in the slightest. She was obviously cross with me for setting a bad example for Liza—she'd only let me in to see her on the promise that I would convince her to play nicely, but James was too surly for me to bear, and I refused to submit to him when he turned his animosity on Liza.

"Don't look so *forlorn*, Armand," said James, the smug fiend. "It's for Liza's safety that she stays here, and yours too."

"Spoken like a true megalomaniac," I muttered. The next thing I knew, his fist smacked me in the chin and I went flying to the side. He packed a mean right hook. I toppled over a bedside table, Liza screaming as I fell, and I threw myself to my feet before he could kick me. I wasn't solid on my feet, though, for he'd hit me hard enough that I was seeing stars, and James didn't give me the chance to steady myself before he hit me again. This time, I heard a high-pitched ringing in my ears, along with Liza's tray clattering to the floor as she scrambled out of bed. Jada caught her and yelled at James, a risky interference, but he ignored her and hauled me to my feet as my mouth filled with blood.

"You're a man now," James sneered in my face. "You know the consequences of mouthing off to me like that. I ought to knock you senseless!"

I wanted to spit in his face. Instead, through bloody teeth, I snarled, "You can't keep her here. She doesn't belong to you—" I grunted as James socked me in the gut. He wouldn't let me fall to the floor and I was startled by his strength—for a man who'd suffered such a nasty bite to the chest, James barely seemed to struggle to hold me up.

"But she belongs to you, is that it?" Liza begged James to let go of me and then a strange ripping sound heralded a gasp of pain from Liza. We all looked over to her and saw Jada gripping her tightly, holding her back from me and James, and the intravenous lead taped to Liza's arm had been torn away in the struggle. The crook of Liza's elbow was gushing blood and we four just stood there for a moment, horrified.

James threw me to the ground, where I fell at Jada's feet in a pile. I winced at the ache in my stomach and the blood seeping through my clenched teeth. I tried to get up to help Liza but James took a half step toward me and demanded Jada do it herself. Jada glanced at Liza's arm and apparently decided it was safe to prioritize second, because she then stooped to haul me off the floor with gusto I never would have guessed she was capable. Jada sat me down on Liza's bed and inspected my face, trying as I might have to turn away and insist she focus on Liza. James hoisted Liza's arm over her head to slow the bleeding and rummaged through Jada's bag for a bandage.

"I'll do that, if you don't mind," Jada said coolly, before James could tend to Liza himself. Jada passed me a cold compress to hold on my face before applying pressure to the bleeding IV cut on Liza's arm. She dutifully and efficiently wrapped Liza's arm in a gauze bandage while I probed the inside of my mouth with my tongue to see where my gums had been cut on my teeth.

"Do you have anything to say for yourself?" James asked me. I glared at him and took a deep, slow breath as I summoned the most hateful curse words I could think of.

"Armie, don't!" Liza insisted desperately. Once again, she proved that she knew me as well as I knew her. I don't think I would have cared if James came after me a second time, but Liza wouldn't have been able to watch it.

"Stay out of this!" James barked at Liza, turning on her. "Or would you care to repeat the same thing I just told you about what will happen the next time one of you steps out of line, Liza?"

"Master James, I am aware that I must defer to your judgment in matters like this," Jada interjected quickly, raising her voice above us all. "But as your chief medical officer, I must inform you that if I *were* the Master of this compound, I would ask you to leave before any more of this leads to stitches! Liza is my patient and it is imperative that she rest, not jump out of bed and cause further harm to herself!"

I expected James to return with a gruesome threat to Jada's job, but he remained silent. He did, however, make knowing, angry eye contact with her. Jada seemed to understand what he was implying and nodded.

"Armand," she said to me, "I'll show you out. I'm afraid that you will not be allowed to visit Liza moving forward."

That was what really broke Liza. She visibly deflated and cringed away from James with tears in her eyes. I was close to crying too, seeing her so defeated, so I tried to make it as easy as I could for her while cursing myself for losing my temper in the first place. I didn't dare look back at her, which would only upset her further. I shifted my hold on the ice pack pressed to my cheek and stood up gingerly from the bed to follow Jada out. Before I got more than a few steps away, Liza slid out of bed and wrapped her arms around me from behind, like she had in the kitchen.

"I love you, Armie," she said, so quietly that I barely heard her. My breath left me in a shallow gust. Her proclamation stung like a papercut under a fingernail, for I'd tormented myself for never saying it to her and now I couldn't possibly make such a profession, not with James right behind us.

She deserved to be told "I love you" more than I ever did, but James had taken even this away from her.

"Don't tell Daze what happened," she added.

"I won't," I said, nodding.

"Enough," James commanded. "See him out, and notify Quinn that he is not permitted to return."

I blinked tears from my eyes and walked on, aching to feel her arms slip away from me. Jada slammed the door behind us but I barely heard it, my heart was pounding so loudly in my ears.

"I will make sure Liza is all right when Master James leaves to attend to his business," Jada said stiffly to me, once we were far down the hall.

"She would be, if she was in her own bed. She belongs with us," I said, my articulate speech dulled by my swollen lower lip.

"I agree with you, Armand, yet thanks to that stunt you just pulled, Master James will never allow her back to your wing!" hissed Jada. I recoiled from the ferocity of her words. She'd never spoken to me that way but worse still, she was absolutely right. She led on, steaming, right through the exit to the main hall.

"Armand," Jada sighed, taking my arm and stopping me. We were standing before the Masters' chambers door but behind the guardsmen blocking it from the public eye.

"What?" I asked bitterly, wondering what else she could say to hurt me.

"I'm sorry," she said. She bowed and shook her head. "It was unfair of me to ask you to reign her in, but it just...." She trailed off and quickly glanced skyward, as though she were trying to keep tears from her eyes. "It breaks my heart to see you kids mistreated like this...." She had barely whispered that aloud, knowing full well that if she were overheard, the blotchy-faced Quinn would happily turn her over to James for speaking ill of him behind his back.

The rush of adrenaline from the altercation had finally worn off. I felt numb now, and cynical, and tired. "Why don't you do something about it, then?" I asked, searching Jada's sympathetic, wide brown eyes.

"I can't," Jada replied sadly. "He's a Master."

I scoffed bitterly and scorned Jada's pity. "You're no better than he is." I wanted to put her as far behind me as possible. I stepped past the line of guardsmen, shouldering past Quinn purposefully, and glared down any passing merchant who looked my way. Most were shocked to see my bleeding face as I emerged, obviously upset, from the Masters' chambers.

"Armand!" Donovan's aghast exclamation caught my attention. He hurried toward me against the foot traffic of the busy market. His eyes narrowed with sharp concern as he stopped short in front of me and reached for my face. I pulled away with a sour expression.

"What happened, Armand?" Donovan asked at once.

I heaved a dismal chuckle. "Ask James." I veered out of his way and walked past him. I'd have shoved him away if he tried to come after me, but instead he marched straight for the Masters' chambers. I was glad that he left me alone, for as I reached the Tribute wing, I realized that I was much closer to tears than I knew. If Donovan had touched me, I'd have melted in his arms and ruined everything.

I tasted metallic anger on my tongue as I rejected the feeling of helplessness that was dragging me into a rush of anxiety. Rushing thoughts swarmed my mind, circling around Jada's words: "Thanks to the stunt you just pulled, Master James will never allow her back to your wing." If I hadn't been so eager to throw all that nastiness back in James' face, Liza wouldn't be locked behind a set of doors I wouldn't see again...though what was so much better about the cage I was locked in?

I reminded myself that I had Kit and Daisy, and Liza had no one. Yet James still held the key to both our cages.

Chapter Six

Jada slammed the door behind James and Armand and the sound of it made me flinch. My ears were ringing as the gauze binding around my elbow throbbed. I felt instantly hollow the moment Armand vanished from sight, and though I knew it was impossible, I imagined I could feel the impact of Armand's footsteps follow the hallway out of the Masters' chambers.

"I think it would be best," James said after a few moments, "for you to get back into bed." I felt grief swell in my breast and I forced myself to choke up to keep a sob from escaping my throat. I looked up at the ceiling to will my tears away.

"I'll send away for someone to clear away this mess," said James while I continued to stare hatefully at the beautifully painted ceiling landscape. "And Lorraine will bring you another meal," James added. I felt something within me crumble away as I recognized that deplorable, gentlemanly deflection that was his trademark after losing his temper. He'd just beaten Armand after twisting my arm and now it was back to business—well, I wouldn't have it, and I didn't care about the consequences of my resistance.

"I am not hungry," I told him in a brittle voice. I cultivated my own temper as I slowly turned to face the glare I knew was waiting for me.

"This afternoon has already been exceedingly difficult," said James. "Don't make it worse by refusing to eat."

"And what if I do? Will you tell Jada to force food down my throat?"

"Well," sighed James. "Thanks to you, I've had to compromise Jada's very precarious good graces, so I would have to do it myself."

I couldn't rush him—he'd see me coming and level me far worse than he had Armand. I watched him and remembered the way he'd looked at me that night in the library, and the way he had been capable of directing his alarm right at me while hiding it from Quinn and Daisy. The kind of prowess he had over the way people could perceive him was perhaps more frightening than his ugly temper and proclivity to violence. He'd hit me before; I knew what to expect. If I wasn't going to be allowed visitors, I might as well rack up some more bruises.

I turned on the spot and went for the door. Since I was no longer attached to the intravenous lead, I was as off-leash as I would be. I'd gotten four strides in before James caught me and wrenched me off my feet. I shrieked in outrage and fought in his arms, hoping I could bear him to the ground or at turn around enough to jam a knee into his side.

"Liza, damn it, stop this!" James roared. I whimpered frantically as James lost just a slight of his hold on me, just enough for me to get a foot on the floor. I kicked off the little footing I had and gained enough leverage to swivel in his arms. I jabbed an elbow into his side, right along the stitched ridge of where the volpine had bitten him. James cried out in pain and released me automatically, as though I'd been electrified. I pushed him away and ran to the door but crashed into Donovan, who stumbled back at the force of my body's impact.

"What the hell is going on here?" Donovan shouted. We were both surprised. I didn't move; I was between two Masters and by reputation alone, they could both kill me in ten seconds flat. Donovan blocked the doorway but didn't make a move to grapple me like James had.

I was broken. I froze in place, my eyes locked into Donovan's.

"Get back into that bed," James said in a scathing voice, holding his side and baring his teeth. I was shaking in fear. Truthfully, I meant to comply, but my legs would not relent to my will to move. James reached for me and without meaning to, I screamed; Donovan lunged past me and shoved James, hard, in the chest. James staggered back and told Donovan he was out of his mind. Donovan reached for me with a gentle expression on his face.

"Liza, are you all right?" I couldn't help but burst into tears. I keeled forward and Donovan caught me in his arms. I sobbed into his chest and wrapped my arms around his waist. "It's all right, Liza," Donovan purred, hushing me. "It's all right, just breathe."

"What do you think you're doing?" James demanded. "Unhand her right away, Donovan, or so help me—"

"Step outside, James." Donovan held me protectively to his chest. "Now." Never in my life had I seen James obey a direct order like that, but I had never seen another Master pull rank on his peer, either. James might have argued with Donovan, but he was still holding his side and perhaps decided it wasn't worth the fight. He breezed past Donovan without another word. Once I was alone with Donovan, he carefully slipped away from me and stood back.

"Liza, you can tell me," said Donovan gently. "What happened?" His gaze dropped to the bloody gauze wrapped around my elbow. "You're bleeding!" Very gracefully, he reached for my arm slowly enough so that I could pull away if I wanted.

"It's nothing," I said thickly. "I pulled the lead from my arm. Jada patched me up." I wiped the tears from my cheeks. I didn't know how Donovan had the sense to keep away from me but I was grateful for it.

"I saw Armand on his way back to the Tribute wing," Donovan explained in a soft voice. "He's got a bad cut on his chin, and when I asked him what happened, he just said, 'Ask James.'"

"Armie said something he shouldn't have. James hit him and I tried to stop it."

"You tried to get between James and Armand?" Donovan asked, his eyes wide with disbelief. "Liza, you could have been hurt! What were you thinking?"

I gestured to the gauze and shook my head. "I'm an idiot," I said. "I'm a hopeless idiot." I fell into a mess of tears again and Donovan sighed in despondence.

"Oh, Liza," was all he could say. When he came forward and took my hand, I didn't stop him. He led me back to my bed, around to the other side to avoid stepping in the spilled dinner. He helped me swing my feet back onto the bed and under the silk sheets.

"I'll make sure that someone sees to this mess straight away," he said.

"I don't care about the food."

"I wasn't talking about the food," said Donovan, smiling. He was so handsome I couldn't help but feel some elation when I looked into his eyes. "Listen, Liza, I know it's been a terrible day for you. James has seldom experienced the feeling of vulnerability so he cannot see it in others, and therefore he doesn't fully grasp how isolating it can be. This is his compound and therefore he has every right to behave how he likes, but it was inappropriate of him to handle this the way he did." Donovan laid a hand on my shoulder. "I will speak to him about this, rest assured."

"I don't want you to get in trouble...."

"Please," Donovan said, chuckling. "James and I have history. I know how to express myself without igniting his temper."

"Thank you." It was the only thing I could think of to say. Donovan gave my hand a squeeze before he turned to leave. When he opened the door, a line of servants filed in. Donovan asked them politely to see to the food on the floor, and to ask Lorraine to send another plate. They all seemed to like Donovan as they happily and efficiently saw to his requests. None of them looked at me either, which was a nice touch. Even when Donovan left the room, the servants finished their tasks quickly. I was hardly glad to be alone, but I found solace in the fact that I was not with James.

I replayed the memory of Donovan shoving James away from me over and over in my head. I'd hit James in the face once and James had hit me so hard that I'd blacked out for several moments. I'd felt the monstrous strength of his grip more than once, especially over the past few hours, and yet Donovan had been able to push James away with enough strength to make him nearly lose his footing. Why wasn't Donovan the Master of this compound, if he could outmatch James in brawn and strength? Perhaps there was more to being a Master than just brute strength. I wouldn't know, as I'd never seen James in the midst of his duties. I'd often see him visit the tradesmen and deal out instructions accordingly, but how much did I really know about his daily life? I had no idea what it really took to keep this place running. I'd told James that he'd kept me too busy to notice how controlling he was but I must have been too busy to consider what made him a better Master than Donovan, too.

My body begged me to close my eyes and rest after the tumultuous afternoon I'd just had. I nodded off before Lorraine brought another tray of food up, which was just as well because I was not hungry at all. Slumber pressed me down into the plush mattress beneath me and for a while, my sleep was dreamless.

Chapter Seven

Armand

I stormed right past Graham and Kit in the kitchen, who had by the looks of it been in deep conversation. I glimpsed Daisy through her open bedroom door on my way to my room and she looked up worriedly when I breezed past. She must have seen the blood on my face because she scrambled off her bed. To avoid her worried pestering, I rushed into my room and kicked the door shut behind me.

"Armie!" Daisy called, knocking on my door a moment later. "What happened? Are you bleeding?"

"Not now, Daisy!" I said roughly. I sat down on the edge of my bed and gingerly felt my chin. I groaned when I prodded the cut there too hard and clenched my teeth painfully, forgetting that I had to be careful there, too.

"Armand?" Graham's deep voice sounded from outside. "Are you hurt?"

"Open the door, Armie," Kit insisted after him.

"Go away, all of you!" The painful stitch in my chest was back. I gripped the edge of my mattress with both hands and squeezed my eyes shut to block out the rapping at my door. Graham tried to reason with me through my door, reminding me that he was bound to follow the rules of his job and ascertain any injuries I sustain, but as my heart pounded in my chest and tension set into my shoulders, I knew I couldn't face them now—not when I was struggling like this. I wrenched myself off my bed and into the bathroom. I immediately cranked the knob in the shower on as hot as it could be, and I left the curtain pulled back so that the room could fill with steam.

I cursed myself for my petulance. I had no right to turn Kit and Daisy away like this, especially when they'd seen blood on my face and would do nothing but worry until I let them in. I took advantage of their caring which was a crime in the face of what Liza had been through today—no one was pounding on her door to kindly or sweetly ask after her.

I sank down to the floor and curled my knees up to my chest. I hugged my legs and took slow, measured breaths in counts of ten. The rising heat and steam helped a little, but I could hear knocking on my bedroom door and Daisy's pleas from the hall. I crawled to the tub and turned on the bathwater, the added roar of water drowning out the noise outside. I sighed with relief to be surrounded in white noise and leaned against the side of the bathtub, the cool ceramic soothing my aching face.

I couldn't push thoughts of Liza or James out of my mind. I kept hearing Jada's voice, heavy with sympathy, as she admitted she couldn't help us. Tears of rage brimmed in my eyes when I realized that it wasn't as if she *could* not, but that she *would* not. What reason would Jada have to sacrifice the security of her livelihood for us? I didn't doubt that she suffered to see James batter Liza and me—she was a doctor after all—but how could I be stupid enough to think that witnessing firsthand the brutality we went through might spur Jada to stand up to James? To use her position of power in the compound to advocate for four people who had none?

After a while, when beads of sweat dotted my forehead and the steam was so dense in the bathroom that I couldn't see the shower anymore, the stitch in my chest had dulled and my mind had quieted. My arm was leaden when I reached over to turn the bathwater off. I slowly got up and felt weak on my feet; I was tired and very hungry, but the thought of cooking only made me feel more exhausted. I turned off the shower too, relieved when I could no longer hear anyone knocking on my bedroom door. I grabbed my washcloth from the inside of the shower and wiped the sweat from my forehead. I then went to the sink to wet the cloth with cold water. I didn't want to try the kitchen for any ice because I knew Daisy and Kit would converge on me the instant I left my room. I wrung out the cloth and winced when I held it to my sore chin, then headed back to my bedroom so that I could lie down.

A gust of steam clouded around me when I left the bathroom. I half expected Kit and Daisy to be sitting on my bed waiting for me and I was so tired, I don't think I would have cared. Still, I was glad to have the room to myself and the cool air was nice in contrast to the steamy bathroom I'd just sulked in. I fell onto my bed and adjusted the cold cloth on my chin.

My mother's far away voice haunted me. "*Duérmete mi niño, duérmete mi amor,*" she sang to me. "*Duérmete pedazo de mi corazón....*"

I forced my mother's song from my head. If I let myself recall any more of it, I might burst into tears.

"Armand?" called a voice from outside my door. I rolled my eyes and heaved myself off my bed, heavy heart and all, with a groan. I knew it was just plain mean to refuse Kit and Daisy now. I'd have to let them in and go over the whole thing for them in agonizing detail. Maybe I was being too stubborn. Maybe their closeness and their endearing whispers would lift my spirits.

I opened the door, expecting to see Kit and Daisy standing there. It wasn't them, but Donovan. My face fell and I bowed my head, still holding the cold cloth to my chin.

"I've asked Graham and the others to let me speak with you, alone, for a minute," he said evenly, in his best calm, charming-Donovan way. "May I come in, Armand?"

"I don't care," I sighed. I turned my back on him but left the door open behind him. I walked to the middle of my room and slouched over, too tired to bother acting presentable in front of him. Donovan lightly closed the door behind me and came up right behind me, a medical-grade cold compress in hand.

"Let me see," he murmured, his teal eyes bright as he turned me around and tilted my head back gently. I took the cloth away and Donovan studied the cut on my chin. "I've seen worse," he deduced, though his expression was sharp with distress. He pressed the compress to my jaw, not over the cut itself, and to my surprised relief, the throbbing in my chin began to subside.

"Have you?" I hated myself for the tears that welled in my eyes as I stared into Donovan's.

"Oh, beautiful boy," Donovan sighed. "What's he done to you?"

His pity was too much for me. Tears flooded past my eyelashes and trickled down my cheeks. I averted my gaze to hide the shame of being broken by James from him. Donovan then leaned over and kissed the side of my neck, sending warmth and shivers down my back. I sighed when he wound his arm around my waist and held me against him, swaying a little where he stood, like Kit always did when he hugged the girls.

"He's a damn maniac," I insisted furiously. "He's a monster," I added, echoing Liza.

"Stop," Donovan chided delicately. "No more worrying about James, not from you, all right? I pulled him off Liza, and I'm going to have a word with him."

I looked up at the mention of Liza. "Is she all right?" I asked desperately.

"Armand, she's fine. I got there just in time. I told her I would try to get James under control, but I had to come and see you first—"

"The others will find out, if you stay too long," I said brusquely, pulling away. Donovan dropped the cold compress he'd been pressing to my face and held onto me tightly in both of his arms.

"Don't worry about them. They suspect nothing. Calm down, Armand." He was reasoning so patiently with me—what a fool. Didn't he know that contrary to his affirmations there was plenty to worry about? I felt anxiety rack my chest and I crumbled in Donovan's arms, for I had nothing else to do. I bent my head to rest on his shoulder and held him even tighter as silent sobs ripped from my chest. Donovan stepped forward, walking me backwards to my bed. He smoothed his hands up my back and tenderly cupped my face, kissing me and smudging my tears on his cheeks as he did. I kissed him back ardently, wincing but not stopping when a sudden, biting pain flared from the cut on my chin. My fingertips were trembling when I reached to take Donovan's collar in my fists but he caught my hands in his, pressing his lips together in a wry, disapproving frown.

"Armand, lover, you must calm down...."

"I can't," I moaned, kissing him hungrily. He parted his lips for me and I thought of our first time together, when he patiently let me have my way with him as though he knew somehow that I needed to be in control. I was no longer crying, but my breaths were hitched and frantic. This wasn't like the first time anymore; I needed Donovan to take me away from this. I craved his direction, his passionate relentlessness.

"Hold me," I urged, pulling on his shirt. "Take me, Donovan. Please, take me."

"Not now," Donovan replied roughly, between deep kisses. "They suspect nothing, but if I stay so long...." I could see in his eyes that my begging was effective, despite his temperate refusal to take me to bed. I couldn't accept that—I kissed him slowly, sweetly, and held myself back long enough to lean my forehead against his.

"I need you," I begged again. *"Please...."*

Donovan sighed resignedly and wet his lips that were slightly puffy from my fervid kisses. He put his hands on my shoulders and pressed me down so that I was sitting on the bed. He sat beside me, crooking a knee up so that he could face me, though I was facing forward. Donovan slid one arm across my shoulders, gripping the side of my neck with his hand. With the other, he smoothed down my chest, down my abdomen, until his fingertips plunged underneath the waistband of my trousers. I moaned when he took hold of my organ and he quickly hushed me with a kiss.

"Quietly, lover," he insisted breathlessly. He worked me with his hand and went on kissing me, the snake of ecstasy coiling within as he brought me closer and closer to my end.

"That's it," he whispered, praising the gleeful, nervous giggle that sounded in my throat as I felt the finish coming on. I grasped his shirtfront when the moment came, my entire body relaxing in a shudder of release as Donovan's eager rhythm quickened in a burst, then slowed as I shuddered again. I smiled against his lips. Donovan hummed a little laugh of his own and trailed a string of proud, tarrying smooches along the side of my neck. I felt a lasting wave of steadiness wash over me as my heartbeat was no longer skipping at a frenetic speed, nor were my nerves needling me to the point of panic.

"Will that tide you over until tonight, Armand?" he whispered. I nodded, still smiling as I held onto him. "I would love to stay," he said, slipping his hand carefully out of my trousers. "But I must go talk to James. He's likely cooled off by now." He kissed me once more and hesitated before standing up from the bed. "I wish I could say the same." He stooped and picked up the cloth I'd dropped on the floor and wiped his hand clean.

"Thank you," I told him genuinely. "I know that I can be—well, I wouldn't have been able to—" I broke off, blushing, when I saw the hazy glint in Donovan's eyes as he looked down at me, still sitting with my legs splayed on the bed. I wasn't sure if there was anyone else who could make me stammer with a look like that.

"I'm sure we'll find a way for you to make it up to me," said Donovan with a wink. "You can start by not worrying about Liza. I'm going to speak to James. He'll be better."

"I hope you're right," I said, getting to my feet on jelly-legs. "He really was a beast earlier. I've seen him mad, but I don't think I've ever seen him this desperate."

"Nor have I," Donovan agreed. "But I have a way of getting through to him. Leave it to me, lover." He then knelt to pick up the cold compress and once more touched it to my jaw, taking up my hand to take the place of his. He kissed me then, a sweet farewell, and went to the door. "You ought to tell Kit and Daisy what happened," he advised. "They love you, Armand. It hurts us to see you suffer."

I raised my eyebrows and smirked at him. "Us?"

Donovan smiled wryly. "Goodbye for now, beautiful boy." He reached up to smooth his hair at the back before leaving me alone again in my room.

Chapter Eight

I woke up a time later, my forehead matted with sweat, and noticed someone had pulled the down coverlet up to my chin. I was roasting under the blankets and I sat up to feel the cooler air of the room on my face and neck. I took off the bandages wrapped around my hands and fingers, grimacing at the many scrapes and glued-up cuts on my palms and fingers. I found the dull ache in the crook of my elbow distracting, so I unraveled the gauze to alleviate the throbbing. The bruise was appalling and dark—in better lighting, I would likely see dark purple and indigo colors splotched on the inside of my arm, spreading up to my shoulder. But the bleeding had stopped, and with the pressure relieved, I felt a little more comfortable.

On the bedside table was a carafe of water, which I took up and drank without first pouring it into a glass. I didn't realize how parched I'd been until I drained the thing, which stimulated my appetite. With a rumbling stomach, I tried to guess what time it might be, but the darkness of the room hinted it was the small hours. There would be no calling Lorraine now, so I resigned myself to lie back down and go back to sleep.

I dreamed of water and the soothing, soft lapping sounds of waves massaging a riverbed. I heard birds singing and I felt sunlight on my skin as I ran, my bare feet sliding over wet blades of grass.

"Eliza!" I heard a man's voice call. "Where are you, my baby?" My blond hair bounced in curls about my shoulders. The warmth was sweeter than honey and the water was so close. I looked over and saw Daisy, a cherubic little girl not much older than a toddler, making her way to me.

"Daisy, Daisy, give me your answer do!" I sang. I took her pudgy little hands in mine and swung her around, giggling to see her eyes crinkle when she threw her head back and laughed.

"Eliza, my angel!" my father called from behind me.

"Daddy!" I grinned widely and turned around, putting my arms out so that he could lift me up and hold me. The moment I turned, I did not see my father behind me, but James. He caught me and lifted me off my feet.

"That's it," he whispered. I frantically tried to extricate myself from his cage-like grasp. My back crashed into something soft—a bed? I looked around and saw a red veil hang over us. James pulled me close to his chest, his bare skin searing hot against my naked breasts. This wasn't the comforting heat of the sun; this was a blistering, poisonous burning.

"James," I moaned. I pushed him away but my muscles had turned to lead. I couldn't take my eyes off him, his features sharp with fraught determination. He was smiling at me, not in that gleeful malevolent way he had before, but in easy relief. It was as close to happiness as I'd ever seen in him.

"That's a good girl," James said. "Hold on to me—"

"I don't want you!" Like an answered prayer, James was gone; I was in my father's arms again, clinging to him and begging him to save me, to catch me, for I was falling impossibly down, down, down—

Again, I tossed myself out of slumber, jolting into a sitting position with a throaty outcry. I pulled my knees up to my chest and hugged them, burying my tear-streaked face into the blanket. I was shaking too, jarred by the visage of my father in a dream for the first time in years. I rarely dreamed of my parents so it was startling enough to experience just that, but the transition of my father into James was the worst nightmare I could recall.

I let out a shuddering sigh that shook loose most of my fright and cleared my throat. I'd forgotten that my own name, Liza, was just the nickname Daisy called me when we were in swaddling clothes; I don't think James knew that my true name was *Eliza* by the time I was brought up in the compound. The other three Tributes knew, of course, but not even Kit ever called me Eliza—and he was one to use a full name to impress a serious point. Then I snorted to myself bitterly, remembering how Daisy used to call him "Kitty" when we were little; how lucky Kit had been that the nickname hadn't stuck.

I snapped my attention to the opening door of my room. Jada was there with a nurse, both in fresh mint green uniforms.

"Good morning, Liza," Jada said in her nicest voice.

"What time is it?" I asked, rudely withholding a return greeting.

"It's just after eight o'clock," Jada replied. She came around to my bedside and touched the back of her hand to my forehead. She seemed content with my temperature and then noticed the empty carafe on the table. "You were thirsty, huh? That's good, I'm glad you had some water. Are you hungry?"

I fixed a pointed stare at her. She knew full well I hadn't eaten yesterday and I wasn't about to let her pretend that nothing had happened. "No," I lied. I refused to allow her any satisfaction in helping me. I don't think Jada believed me, but she didn't press the matter.

"I think you're in need of a bath," Jada said after checking my blood pressure and pupils. She took my arm and studied the gross bruise there for a moment.

"Is Armand all right?"

"He's just fine, honey," Jada replied, flashing a smile. I supposed two could play at the lying-for-spite game. I pulled an equally sour face and tugged my arm away. Jada's nurse—I think her name was Violet—bustled in from the bathroom with a bright air about her.

"If you are too weak to get up, I can help you bathe in bed," she said. "Otherwise, I've run a bath for you in the next room."

"Thank you." I made a point to be much kinder to her than to Jada. "I can get up. I'd like to bathe myself."

"As you say," said the nurse. She stripped my bedding and collected the bandages I'd discarded during the night before leaving me alone with Jada. I heard the rushing water in the bathroom and remembered my dream of playing with Daisy near the river. I shivered as a pang of nausea twisted in my stomach.

"Liza," Jada said quietly. "I know you're cross with me about yesterday. I hope you understand that I was doing my job, which means that even when I'm not tending to a patient, I am doing my utmost to diffuse potentially harmful situations."

"There was nothing *potentially* harmful about it," I snapped.

"I will never condone Master James' use of violence," Jada assured me sternly. "If I didn't think speaking my mind about the matter would make it worse, I would have done so."

"You see what he is," I said, thrusting my arm under her nose, the bruise that showed James' handiwork gleaming up at her. "He did this, you know. Twisted my arm just to prove he could hurt me."

"Master James said you raised a hand to him," Jada said.

"Oh, is that what Master James said?" I retorted flippantly. "How can you defend him after everything he has done?"

"Because despite my disapproval of how he manages the compound, he is a Master!" I could tell Jada was a little hurt by my waspishness. "Master James provides me with a safe place to live and a good job—one that is meaningful and challenging. You don't know how difficult those things are to come by on the outside, Liza, so I will choose to not take your judgment to heart. I am grateful to Master James for what he has done and I do not expect you to understand that."

"Good, because I don't!" It wasn't my place to argue with Jada about how she chose to live her life, especially since her mind was clearly made up about it. I would not, however, abide her lecturing me on James' alleged generosity and I told Jada as such. "Just remember that every good thing James gives you is something he has taken away from me. You justify the way he batters us because you like your job, because at the end of the day you could leave this place if you wanted to. I cannot do that, Jada. Daisy, Armand, Kit, and I do not have that luxury, and no amount of elite tutoring or privileged activities can disguise that truth." I slid off the bed and went to the bathroom without another word. If Jada had been offended by what I said, she didn't show it. She didn't call after me or offer some biting last word, she just sighed.

"Oh, come on," I groaned as soon as I set foot in the bathroom and shut the door behind me. This was undoubtedly the most lavish bathroom I'd ever beheld: There was a separate shower the size of my bedroom in the Tribute wing surrounded by pristinely clean glass walls. The rapidly filling bathtub in the center of the room was more aptly a small pool, halfway built into the floor. The marble sides of it were carved so smoothly that the tub itself looked as though it was made of clouds. The walls were painted to resemble a lofty, heavenly garden landscape. The bright yellows of the flowers drew my eyes along the details. I spotted a few daisies painted among the daffodils and I smiled, thinking of my Daisy.

I quickly forced the smile off my face. There was no room for contentedness in this sordidly blissful bathroom; not if I could help it. I stripped off my clothes quickly and tossed them behind me. I reached down to turn the crystal knobs and stop the flow of water before stepping into the bath. I hissed at the scalding heat of the water but forced myself to submerge my body until the water came up to my chin. The water seared my skin but in comparison to the burn of hypothermia, I preferred this sensation. I soaked for a long time, corralling my thoughts away from Armand's bleeding chin and the sound of James' fist when it smacked Armand's face. When it became nearly impossible to do that, I took a deep breath and slipped under the surface of the water. The tub was so enormous, I could lie down on my back fully stretched out on the bottom of the tub. I stayed under for as long as I could, forcing myself to be still while listening to my heartbeat.

I resurfaced and reached over the side of the tub for a bar of soap. The lavender scent was too strong but by the time I noticed, I'd already worked the suds through my hair. I rinsed the soap out quickly and climbed out of the tub and paused when I caught my reflection in the mirror.

I hardly recognized myself. My skin was bright red from the too-hot water but my face was so sallow and my eyelids were puffy, making me look like I was stuck in a perpetual daydream. With the mural as my backdrop in the mirror, I looked like I was standing in a field of flora, my wet hair hanging down past my shoulders and covering my breasts. I turned away from the peaceful visage of myself surrounded by nature and grabbed the clean clothes that were folded on the vanity. The undergarments were mine, fetched from my room, but the shirt and pants were much different than my usual linen frock. The shirt was made of weathered, dark heather fleece and the pants were a rich emerald green. The pigments were a welcome change from the cream-colored linens I normally donned, and I loved the feel of the fabric on my skin. I pulled on a pair of thick, soft woolen socks that matched the pants and was not surprised that I had not been given shoes. We never wore them around the compound, and it rarely occurred to us that we ever should.

I left the steamy bathroom, pulling my fingers through my hair to work out the tangles as I padded into the bedroom. I looked up expecting to see Jada waiting to finish our conversation but stopped in my tracks when I saw James sitting in the chair across the room.

"Relax," he said right away. He lifted a hand and showed me his palm as a sign of peace. "I came to talk." I swiped my damp hair over one shoulder and crossed my arms. I waited for him to speak, if that's what he came to do. The only words I had for him were fighting ones and the bath had made me feel shaky and weak.

"Donovan spoke to me on your behalf."

"That was kind of him," I offered stiffly. "Though I asked him not to."

"We discussed a number of topics," said James. "Namely your treatment. He made several strong arguments against my methods—something about catching flies with vinegar—and I must confess, I believe I owe you an apology."

I almost scoffed. I didn't believe it for a second—James *never* apologized for anything, because it would imply that he had a lapse in judgment.

"I'm disused to showing mercy; I was never shown any, and I don't believe that people who break the rules should be," James added. This was even harder to believe, that he would explain himself! "But," he sighed, "regardless of your own fault, you suffered a trauma. I understand that being removed from the others is probably making your situation worse, but staying here in my wing is a consequence of the dangerous choice you made. Now, I realize that acclimating to this new environment has been rough. Honestly, it has been daunting for me, too. I hope that we can move forward from this and seize the only opportunity before us, which is you healing and returning to your routine."

I pursed my lips and waited for him to go on. When he didn't, I realized that he was waiting for me to accept his apology.

"Is that all?"

James frowned and narrowed his stormy gaze. "Liza," he said. "I am trying to be reasonable and apologize for upsetting you." He seemed to struggle to say it aloud a second time.

"Did you apologize to Armand?"

"No." James took a deep breath and mirrored my crossed arms. "I do not intend to. I'm here to talk to you about *your* situation."

"Let's talk about my situation, then!" I exclaimed, forcing a falsely cheerful tone. "I would like to leave this place with Daisy and the boys and never return! Has your stance on refusing me changed since yesterday?"

James was furious but he remained seated. "It hasn't," he said. I wanted to laugh at the strain of his good manners.

"Then we have nothing to discuss."

"Liza," sighed James. He pinched the bridge of his nose and closed his eyes. "Your insufferable stubbornness is not going to get us anywhere."

"Get us anywhere?" I repeated churlishly. "I don't want to go anywhere with you!"

"Stop this," James demanded. He was visibly repressing his own temper and I felt a surge of pride to see him squirm.

"If your hope was to get through to me, you should have just sent Donovan to recite this speech himself. I don't want to watch you stumble through trying to catch me with sugar instead of vinegar because you've already caught me! It doesn't matter now how you treat me, this is your world and you have made it very clear that I am merely a foolish girl who lives in it!" My breath hitched in my chest and I was surprised at how fast tears welled in my eyes. I refused to cry in front of him—I could do a better job of maintaining my composure than James could and I was determined to prove it.

"It matters to me how you're treated," said James. "At the risk of rehashing a stale argument, I would like to remind you that I have always put your safety and happiness first. If I'd known how unhappy you truly are, I would have done something to change that. But, Liza, I am not a mind reader. I cannot help you if you do not tell me that you need help in the first place."

"If you really wanted to help, you would tell me how I got from out *there*," I said, thrusting a pointed finger at the closed curtains behind him, "to in *here!*"

James uncrossed his arms and let them fall dejectedly in his lap. "Fine!" He stood up from the desk and I braced myself for him to approach. Instead, he turned and went to the corner and pressed a switch. The curtains lifted from the windows automatically, slowly rolling up to reveal a breathtaking view of the treetops below the compound.

My jaw dropped—I couldn't help it. The sun was low in the sky, embellished with vibrant streaks of fiery orange and exotic red which provided a stunning contrast to the snow-capped trees. I rushed to the window right past James and put my hands and forehead against the glass, drinking up the glory of the winter afternoon. On the horizon, I could see birds flying low over the trees, swooping in majestic dives and pumping their wings to gain altitude. The window was thick-plated glass but the warmth of the sun penetrated its sturdiness. I felt the sun on my face and smiled broadly. I was frantic to look everywhere I could, to memorize every detail below the looming window.

"You want to know how you got from there to here?" James asked. I hadn't realized he was standing right beside me for I couldn't take my eyes off the awesome view. James pointed my attention away from the sun. "You came from all the way over there," he said. "You'd have to follow the curve of the earth for days to find your birthplace."

"Were the others born there too?" I uttered, too enraptured by the distant sight of home to put any disdain behind my voice.

"Yes," James replied. He spaded his hands in his pockets and looked out at the world with me.

"What is the place called?" I asked. "Do I have a family there—a *real* family?"

"Your parents are still there, yes. The place used to be called Kingsfield Township but now it's simply known as the Village. Just like this place used to be Martin's Ferry, but it's usually just 'the compound' to everyone now. Your room here looks over the east forests. The sea is on the other side, but you can't see it from here."

"It's wonderful," I murmured in awe. I drew back from the window to try to focus myself. "But how did I get from the Village to this place?" The words sounded so foreign to me, as if saying it aloud was like learning a new language.

"Almost twenty years ago now, the Masters and I were there to barter with the heads of the community," said James softly. "We ended up taking the four of you back to the compound with us. I carried you in myself."

I was stunned. He'd given so much but not nearly enough. How much older than I was he? James today might be in his thirties; if I was turning twenty-two years old in the spring, and James himself had been big enough to carry me here when I was two years old, he must be older than I thought.

"But you—how could that—why did you bring us back here?" I blurted, trying to articulate dozens of questions at once.

"Your parents wanted a better life for you," said James. "It's as I have said, the world outside these walls is a volatile, unforgiving place."

I was growing more and more impatient, yet I turned back to the window. I wanted more answers from him, but every time he gave me one, it only spurred more questions.

"But why can't we go back?"

James didn't answer me for a while. When I turned to look at him, I was startled to see that he was already peering down at me with inscrutable curiosity in his eyes. "It's the same reason I have built your lives around the rules of this place. They are the conditions your families set forth when we brought you back with us. You cannot go back because they wish for you to stay here."

Once more, I found myself stumbling at a mile per minute, trying to ask all the questions that arose from this new information. Was the outside world truly so horrendous that our parents would send us to live with the Masters? Why would they put into place all those awful rules that dictate our free will? And why would my parents leave me, their daughter, with a monster like James?

"You sent swordsmen after me the night I escaped," I said slowly. "Not gunmen."

"I couldn't risk one of them shooting you by accident," James explained. "The conditions clearly state that you must come to no harm."

I was inexplicably furious to hear this. "Bodily harm to me by one of your men would violate the conditions my own parents put into place, but you yourself are permitted to strike us?"

James shrugged. "It is at my discretion how I choose to enforce those rules, Liza," he said. "I made the rules and I still have to follow them, but I am tasked with ensuring that everyone in this compound follows them too." I wanted to hit him for it but I was too overwhelmed to start another fight. James knew it too. "You should eat. If you like, you may eat with me this afternoon."

I gaped up at James. "Eat—with you?"

"You are hardly in need of a sickbed anymore," James noticed. "Unless you would prefer to eat alone?" I knew that he was trying to prove that his newfound approach at handling me was working and I certainly did not want to dine across from him as though I were an esteemed guest of his…but if I played along and supped nicely, I might get him talking.

Without really meaning to, I glanced back to the window. "I don't want to miss this," I said wistfully. I planted my feet at the window and waited for him to say something threatening.

"Don't be foolish. You want to stay to look out the window? The view isn't going anywhere. I'll leave it open all day if you wish."

"Is this your attempt at catching flies with sugar?"

"A modicum of sugar, Liza," James said. "I will go back to vinegar if you push me to it."

It was strange to dine with James. His dining room was modest compared to the other rooms in this wing of the compound. The table was much larger than the one Kit, Daisy, Armand, and I had back in the Tribute wing, with eight chairs around it instead of four. Lorraine sent up a prepared a dish of roast beef, cabbage, and potatoes, which I wolfed down within minutes. James pointed out that my table manners left something to be desired, but he abstained from berating me because he knew I hadn't eaten in a day.

"What are those?" I asked him, when he pulled a tiny bottle of pill capsules from his jacket pocket and shook a few into his hand.

"Supplements." He popped the pills into his mouth and swallowed them down with a swish of water. "For my ligaments and bones," James explained. "And they help with the pain." I couldn't help but feel a little glad to think of him in pain from the volpine bite, but when my memory replayed the savage snarl of the beast and James screaming out when it barreled into him, my blood ran cold. We did not engage in any further small talk for, from what I gathered, James was hungry too. I didn't get another word from him about my family in Kingsfield Township. It frustrated me to no end but I had to reign in my temper if I was to keep up the appearance of respecting him so he'd tell me more down the line.

After I had my fill, James said he would have to see to his devices. I was free to go back to my room on my own time, but I must not leave the Masters' chambers—if I did, he reminded me, it would not bode well for me.

I asked him if I could have some supplies from my room, my sketchbook and pencils, and he said he would send away for them. He asked if I wanted my clothes and chuckled when I told him that I liked my new ones better.

"I thought you might," he said. "I'll see to it that your things are brought to your room."

"James?" I asked, taking my napkin off my lap and plopping it onto my plate. "When can I go back to my own room? Or see the others?"

"I'll have to determine that for myself," James answered curtly. "Daisy may visit you here, but until I'm certain that you can be trusted to move about the compound on your own, you will stay where you are."

I expected him to say it but I still felt crushed when he did. He left without a second glance, the heels of his shoes clicking in his wake as he left the dining room. I did return to my room after James left. My mind was buzzing with all I'd learned from James today. I'd asked for my sketchbook because drawing helped me to focus and calm my nerves, but truthfully, I just wanted to jot down the information I'd learned so that I could get it to Daisy; she and the boys would be thrilled to have these answers, and between the three of them, maybe they could get a word to the people in the Village.

I padded wearily down the hall to my room. With a full belly and an overwhelmed new sense of purpose, I felt as though I would drop like a stone, as Kit might put it. Once I got to my room, I was spellbound by the setting sun I saw through the open window. I pulled the pillows and blankets off my bed and made a nest for myself in front of the window. I curled up and hugged a cushion while my view of the outside tilted sideways. I watched the daylight fade from the sky while I thought of Kingsfield Township and the old river that ran through the woods there, where my dreams had taken me the night before in a strange sort of premonition about the knowledge to come. I wanted to tell all this to Daisy and the boys while it was still fresh in my mind. I drifted off to sleep murmuring the names out loud:

"Kingsfield...Township...Village...Martin's Ferry...James...carried...."

In my dreams, I was in James' arms. Icy wind howled around me and he held me tightly against him. I could hear my father calling my name, agonized and terrified.

"Eliza!" he cried. "Eliza! Come to me, baby!"

"Daddy!" I cried. I twisted in James' arms to try to break free and go to my father. I raged at James, "Let go of me!" The Master clutched me even tighter and dug his fingertips into my back to keep me from getting away. I managed to slip away from him after jamming a knee in his side, but instead of finding my footing and chasing after my father, I was swallowed by the cold air and fell down into the snow—

For a third time since I'd returned to the compound, I awoke startled, pitching myself into an upright position. I was still in my bundle of blankets by the window, a cold sweat beaded on my forehead and the tops of my arms. I let out a whooshing sigh and slicked the sweat off my forehead with the back of my hand. The stars in the night sky were twinkling brilliantly overhead as a strong wind blew snow flurries over the treetops. I keeled over in my heap of blankets once more and tried to go back to sleep, but I only tossed and turned until the morning sun rose and I sat up to watch it peek over the horizon. After a while, I resigned to get up and splash cold water on my face.

I heard a double knock on the bedroom door while I rinsed my mouth out with water. "Liza, may I come in?" called Graham from the other room. I wiped my chin on a towel and hurried into the bedroom.

"Graham!" He stepped through the door and bestowed his trademark kindly, knowing countenance on me.

"Good morning, Liza," he said. He extended his hand to me and I took it. "It's so nice to see you up and about. You don't know how worried I've been about you, my dear."

"It's good to see you!" I didn't mean for my voice to crack but it did, for I realized how sad I was to have to acknowledge my failure to escape to someone like Graham.

"Master James has asked me to bring you some supplies from home. I was hoping to resume your lessons today, but Master James believes you are in need of an academic hiatus. Therefore, I've brought some additional instruments which I hope you will make use of." Graham stepped aside and widened the gap in the door. A pair of servants brought in an enormous cherry wood easel.

"Oh, Graham!" I gushed. "It's beautiful!"

"I thought you might like it," Graham said, beaming. "Where would you like it, Liza?"

"By the window," I said automatically. The servants both eyed me curiously when they glimpsed the makeshift bed I'd made on the floor. I waved it away and insisted they set up the easel there anyway.

"Did you sleep there?" Graham asked, bemused.

"I can't get enough of this view," I confessed.

"Indeed it is a fine view, Liza." He pointed out the stack of books another servant carried in. "Those are a couple of volumes about expressionism, and one of them is a manual describing the various ways of mixing oil paints."

"Thank you so much. Really, you don't know how much this means to me."

Graham smiled and shrugged. "The paints came in this morning from the south. The tradesmen brought in the most beautiful selection of fabrics—but I digress, Liza. I sincerely hope I am not infringing on your recovery, but I did hire help to deliver your things from home…." With a knowing smile on his face, Graham turned to reveal Kit, who was standing in the doorway with my sketchbook in hand.

"Kit!" I barely had enough time to throw my arms up before Kit dropped my sketchbook to the floor and lifted me off my feet into a rib-crushing embrace.

"I was so afraid," Kit said, his voice muffled in my hair. "Daisy was sick from it, and then Armie came back bleeding and said you'd been hurt in a fight—"

"It's nothing," I assured him, squeezing him tightly. Kit was so warm and steady; he was a true source of comfort. I didn't fully know how badly I had missed him until he was swinging me in his arms.

"Kit has led an admirable example in the face of this trying circumstance," Graham announced to no one in particular. I knew he wasn't allowed to leave us alone together and was trying to be respectful of our limited reunion.

"Listen, Kit," I said. I pulled away from him but he kept his arms around my waist. "There isn't time," I told him in a private voice. "I have so much to tell you—"

"Excuse me, what is going on?"

Kit jumped and whirled around, stoically keeping me behind him as James joined us in the bedroom. The servants continued to work in the background behind us, but they noticeably slowed when they realized James was here.

"Master James," Graham greeted him. "I hope I have not overstepped but I asked Kit to help me deliver Liza's supplies—"

"I gave Quinn very express orders to bar anyone but my staff from entering this wing," James interrupted curtly. He looked to me and seemed disappointed. "Say goodbye to Kit, Liza. It's not appropriate for him to be here; I did not permit this interaction."

"James," I implored, a hair's width from bursting into tears. "If I could just speak to him for a moment longer—"

"It's all right, Liza," said Kit hastily. He turned around and held my hands. "I don't want to make things worse. I'll go. Just please, be good."

"There's a good fellow," said James. He seemed pleased that Kit obeyed him without having to repeat himself. James noticed the pile of blankets near the window. "Did you sleep on the floor, Liza?"

"Yes," I replied awkwardly. James laughed, which confused Graham and Kit.

"The easel is a nice touch," he remarked. Then he looked back to Kit. "Come along, Kit. I'll walk you out."

"I know the way," Kit offered. "If you have better things to do—"

"I have to speak with Quinn anyway," James batted Kit's objections aside. "Come on."

"Next time will be longer," Kit assured me. He looked down at me sadly and I could tell he wanted to hug me again but he was reluctant to test James' patience. I took the liberty and quickly put my arms around him.

"I love you," I whispered.

"Me too," Kit said. He stepped away from me and followed James to the entrance of the Masters' chambers. I did not envy Quinn, for I was sure James would have nothing but harsh criticism for letting Kit past the doors.

"I hope you get some rest," Graham said with an aura of farewell about him. He stooped to pick up the sketchbook Kit dropped earlier and handed it to me.

"Thank you for the easel and the books," I said. I knew that Graham was as culpable as Jada with respect to his loyalty to James, but he was so thoughtful and kind, I couldn't be angry with him—not after he sneaked Kit in under false pretenses just to comfort me. It was the kindest thing anyone had done for me in years. I waited for Graham to leave before opening my sketchbook; upon opening the leather cover, I discovered right away that it wasn't my sketchbook at all, but Kit's. He had simply swapped the covers. Tears came to my eyes as I flipped through the pages, my gaze lingering on the many detailed pencil portraits of Daisy, Armand, Graham, and myself. My heart swelled with adoration for Kit as I noticed the nuances of his style and how perfectly he'd captured the freckles on Daisy's face, Armand's long eyelashes and secretive smile, and the crinkles at the corners of Graham's eyes when he smiled. Kit had even lent the scar on my lip subtle captivation, for which I loved him even more. I flipped to the bookmarked page and at once began to cry, for the three of them had written a short inscription to me:

Armand's was the first, an excerpt from my favorite *Annabel Lee* penned in his carefully intrepid handwriting. The words broke my heart as the poetry rang in devastating truth, "*I* was a child, and *she* was a child, in this kingdom by the sea—" I sat down right there on the floor and read the rest of the stanza through tear-blurred eyes. The poem was all he'd written. There was no addendum or personalized message, but the poetry said everything he couldn't articulate and it meant the world to me.

Daisy's was the second note, written in her eager cursive: "Play along and we'll get you back in no time. We're only strong when we're together." That was something I'd said to her months ago, when we'd first breached the subject of escaping the compound. I felt proud of her for her surety but ultimately guilty for inspiring her to harbor such a dangerous resolve.

Kit's inscription was the last. His penmanship was rushed and difficult to read, since he was more accustomed to hastily scribbling musical notes in his compositions than letters. He wrote: "I hope you like the drawings. Now you can keep us close while being far away. You are with us always no matter where you go. J.T.M. may try to keep us apart, but he can't. Be strong. Love always, K."

I hugged the book to my chest as my shoulders shook in silent sobs. I was so moved by their solidarity and Graham's show of support that I couldn't get off the floor. Even out in the wintry wilderness, I hadn't felt so isolated or so small. After a while, I found the strength to drag myself over to the window and curl up in the blankets still piled there. I flipped through Kit's sketchbook again, pausing over each drawing for minutes at a time. I touched my lips errantly when I found my favorite sketch of Armand's countenance. Kit had seamlessly captured the light in Armand's eyes whenever he made a rare, genuine smile instead of his usual scowl. I missed him, all three of them, so terribly, that the grief of being kept from them crushed me.

I deserved this, I told myself. If I hadn't jumped out of the library window, I'd be with them now; Kit might be playing the piano while Daisy distracted Armand, who might have been simmering something over the stove, by practicing her ballet positions. I might have been pointing out Daisy's posture or sitting on the bench beside Kit, watching his fingers work the keys with easy grace.

Someone rapped at the door in a quick triple knock. I hastily wiped the tears on my cheeks away in time for Donovan to poke his head through the door.

"Hi, Liza," he said. "Is it all right if I come in?"

I shrugged. "We aren't in the Tribute wing, so you don't need my permission to enter," I said. "James certainly doesn't bother to ask for it."

"Yes, well, even James the Master sometimes forgets his manners," Donovan said, slipping all the way into the room. He shut the door behind him and leaned against it. How he managed to look so alluring and sorrowful at the same time was beyond my fathom, but he frowned when he looked from my stripped bed across the room and the pile of blankets amid which I was sitting.

"I see you got the easel I procured for you," he remarked. I was relieved that he didn't mention anything about the blankets. If I had to admit that I had a childish need to be near the windows one more time I would pull my hair, but I was surprised when Donovan said he'd sent the easel over.

"*You* procured?" I asked. "I thought Graham—?"

"I thought you could use something to keep you busy," said Donovan. "When Armand told me you enjoyed painting, I spoke to some tradesmen about incoming art supplies and the easel jumped out on the manifest."

"Thank you," I said. "For the easel, and for speaking to James on my behalf."

"You're welcome, Liza. Honestly, I believed it was necessary. Armand told me about the unfortunate display the other night, and Daisy has been so unlike herself lately. I think James needed to be reminded of a few things."

"I appreciate you visiting, Donovan, but did you come to tell me something? I don't mean to be rude, it's just that I really…." I trailed off so that I could swallow the lump in my throat. "I need to be alone right now."

"I understand," said Donovan. I looked him up and down and felt a surge of angry protectiveness wash over me; I owed Donovan for calling off James, but when I imagined Daisy hanging off him and how easy it would be for him to take advantage of her, I wanted to throw the easel at him.

"Listen, Liza," Donovan said, conscious of my steady gaze on him. "I wanted to talk to you about your position here. I know that James has been much stricter than usual and I've asked him to be more considerate of you before he metes out his laws. I came to ask you to be more considerate of James—" I set my jaw in anger immediately and Donovan hurried to finish his sentence, "—for your own sake, if only for the next few days."

"How could you say that to me," I wondered in furious disbelief, "after what he's done? You saw him in action with your own eyes, and you want me to be considerate of him?"

"Not unlike Daisy, James has not been himself," Donovan explained carefully. "You may notice that he has been forgetful of his tact and quick to anger? Have you ever known him to be so frequently violent? Or have you wondered why I'm still here, despite the fact that you've already been recovered?"

"I try not to wonder too much about James," I said stiffly. "The last place I want to be—besides where I am right now—is in James' head."

"There's to be a summit of us Masters," said Donovan. "It will take place in a few days and James is under a lot of pressure at the moment to keep the excitement of this week undisclosed."

Now *that* was something—a summit of Masters, here at this compound, and none of them knew about my escape; as frightened as I was of the prospect of a hall full of men like James, I was immensely satisfied to now have something worse than an elbow to the volpine bite with which to hurt James. If the other Masters knew he'd failed to keep me confined to the compound and that he'd almost been killed trying to bring me back, no less, James would be a laughingstock.

As if he could read my mind, Donovan took a seat on the edge of my bed and peered sternly into my eyes. "Don't go thinking you can spread around the scandalous tale of your escape attempt. Because that's what it was, Liza—an *attempt*. You and James both risked your lives and you're both back here now."

"Why are you speaking to me about this? Why tell me that the other Masters don't know about what happened if you want me to keep my mouth shut?"

"Liza," Donovan said quietly, knowingly. "There is an opportunity before you, if you are smart enough to play this out properly."

This unexpected conspiracy astounded me. I didn't know what to say in response to that, for I was too focused on unpacking that statement. An opportunity for what? Donovan spoke of using information like it was a game. What was he trying to play out?

"I want you to think about what you really want," Donovan said. He stood up from the bed and took a step closer to my spot on the floor. "And please, be smart. Otherwise any life you might attain outside of this place will not include the people who love you." He pointedly glanced to the sketchbook in my hands and then turned to the door, leaving me alone in the room with nothing but questions buzzing in my head. My mind felt like a whirlpool of torment and curiosity: Donovan had just given me something real to cling to and I'd snapped at him for bothering me while I wallowed in despondency, and now that I was alone again, I was so overwhelmed by it all that I wanted to curl up and sleep.

Instead, I opened Kit's sketchbook again and reread the three messages from my friends. I lingered over Armand's *Annabel Lee* stanzas and felt compelled to redirect my focus. I stashed the sketchbook under my pillow and stood up, bundling my hair into a knot at the back of my head as I made my way to the door. Just as I reached for the knob, the door opened and in stepped James, who seemed surprised to see me so near the doors.

"Liza," he greeted me. "I just met Donovan in the hall, I wanted to speak with you—"

"I was just coming to find you," I interrupted smoothly. James hated to be interrupted but he withheld whatever politely veiled threat he'd usually have offered.

"Is that so? I assume to appeal to my pathos and bargain for a longer visit from Kit?"

"On the contrary," I replied. Donovan's reminder to be smart was hanging over me. "I need to visit the gallery to get a canvas for my easel."

James was doubly taken aback. "You need a canvas?" He glanced once more to the blankets piled near the window, in front of which sat the empty easel.

"Is that acceptable to you?" I asked. I was tempted to cross my arms but I kept them hanging at my sides to keep from passing off as prickly.

James agreed too quickly. "Certainly." I could tell he was surprised that I hadn't come after him for separating me and Kit this morning. He seemed relieved, almost pleased, with my demeanor, but I wasn't going to let him off the hook so easily. I was too freshly angry that I hadn't had the chance to spend more time with Kit. Just because Donovan had told me to be smart about James didn't mean I couldn't draw on my boldness. I only hoped it would be effective.

"I thought it would be prudent to gather all the tools I'll need for painting before you lock me in my room," I said, holding my chin up high. "Before the summit, I mean." It was a huge risk and I knew he'd probably hit me for it, but when all he did was smirk and glower down at me, it was my turn to look relieved.

"I'm starting to wonder if the four of you have always been this quippy, and have only just lately lost your sense of respectability?" James rolled his eyes. "So Donovan told you about the summit, did he? I suppose it's just as well, though I would have told you myself when the time was right. I'm curious, Liza, what else did Donovan tell you?"

"He said that the other Masters don't know about what happened," I said, deciding to double down.

"Did he? And do you really believe that?"

"I don't know why Donovan would lie to me," I replied hotly. "I hear he can cut through a line of twenty armed guardsmen by himself. I doubt he would have a good reason to lie to a girl who will just be shut away anyway when the Masters arrive."

James chuckled. "Twenty armed guardsmen! Where did you hear such a preposterous thing? As good as he is with a blade, Donovan is not a god, Liza."

"So you'd agree, then?" I pressed. "He wouldn't have a reason to lie to me?"

"Donovan probably has a thousand reasons to lie to anyone on any given day," James sighed. "But due to his singularly redeeming character trait, I doubt very much that he would lie—"

"Which character trait would that be?"

James sighed and pursed his lips firmly. I knew I'd spent all the interruptions I'd get tonight, so I'd have to be careful not to do it again. "Donovan," James said succinctly, "has always been unambitious; as it happens, he was not lying to you, the others do not know about the fiasco that was your escape attempt. And before you ask, I have carefully kept the entire event under wraps to protect both of us—for which I'm sure you'd thank me by not behaving like an animal if you knew what is at stake."

I stayed quiet, waiting for him to finish speaking. He eyed me expectantly and I blurted, "Is that a purposefully vague and rhetorical statement, or...?"

"Come with me," said James abruptly, turning on his heel to pull the door open.

"Where are we going?" I asked, my cheeks hot as I felt a quiver of panic strum in my chest. Had I offended him?

"I'm taking you to the market to pick up a canvas," said James, as if annoyed that I was nervous about being led away without explanation. I was relieved, but still keen to keep up with his swift clipping pace. "When I told you about your family and the reason behind the rules in this compound," said James in a soft voice as he led me down the hall, "I did so against the wishes of my peers. It's inappropriate to discuss matters like that with Tributes, but as you are into your twenties, you are bound to find out soon enough on your own; more to the point, given the situation, I thought you might find some rooting solace in hearing about your birthplace." We rounded the corner to the wide double doors and James slipped his hand into the pocket of his slacks to retrieve a key. He unlocked the door to the Masters' chambers and revealed a line of armed guardsmen, standing at attention with their backs to us. They moved out of the way when James and I came through the doors, but they did not let me pass until James had locked the doors behind us and pocketed the key once more.

"I know you have your reservations about the life I have given you here," said James to me privately, as though every eye in the compound wasn't on us as he led me through the common halls to the trade market. "But for all your qualms with your inability to leave, you have not considered how different your life would be without the effected rules that keep you and the others happy, or well fed, or unharmed. There are places within the compound that are very accurately defined as prison cells. I'd have hoped you would be grateful for never having seen one; instead, you are trained in music and art and athletics by the tops of their fields. You are given your own apartments through which you may move about as you wish. I never asked you to think that you lead a charmed life, Liza, just one that might be better than the lives of those people outside of these walls."

Armand would have said something inflammatory to convey his disbelief in that sentiment, but I wasn't as unable to separate myself from it like he could. James didn't seem to be utterly self-serving when he described the aspects of my life that I apparently took for granted. And then there was that dreadful comment about actual prisons within the compound. I had never imagined this place, with its wide halls and cheery looking denizens of the market, to have prisons; largely because I thought of the Tribute wing I called home to be a prison of a sort.

"I know I'm privileged," I said quietly, wary of all the obvious averted gazes passing me by. "I didn't even think to wear shoes when I—" I cut myself off the moment I saw James tense, knowing I was about to speak publicly about the escape. "When I did what I did," I corrected myself. "But you said that my next birthday meant that I could know something real about my life—would you have told me about my parents sending me here after my birthday?"

"Despite my peers' insistence that I withhold it from you?" said James. "Yes, Liza. I would have."

The tears that sprang to my eyes couldn't have come at a more inopportune moment. I was not only being escorted through the most peopled part of the market during its busiest hour by James, but everyone we passed was pretending not to notice me walking around as though I hadn't just jumped out a window a week before and caused a major scandal—and it was all for nothing, as proved by what James had just said.

"If you'd told me anything true about my life just a day sooner, I never would have done what I did."

That caught James' attention. He slowed his pace and looked at me with a deflated sense of pity in his eyes.

"Liza, you look peaky. Are you going to faint?"

"Don't patronize me," I growled, my flaring temper making the heavy sadness hanging over me dissipate.

"I beg your pardon," said James, shaking off my brusqueness. "I'm inclined to be cautious when I notice your color pale like it did. Daisy fainted and hit her head; I would like to spare you the extra excitement if I can." We kept walking but James was watching me carefully—had I really paled so severely? I tried to force a more relaxed expression but I probably just looked even more pallid and fraught.

"I'll need a large easel," I offered, attempting to convince him that I wasn't as unwell as I looked.

"Very well, then." James led us to a trade station near the gallery and told me to take a look around. I resolved to be much pickier than usual, not only to annoy him but to spur him to barter with the merchant long enough for me to look around. I hoped to spot Kit and Armand, who usually haunted the gallery during the busy hour. I also wanted to glimpse any proof of heightened security that might prove a Master summit was in the works. I checked the scene for minutes and didn't see any trace of the boys, or Daisy.

With James' permission, while crestfallen that I couldn't find Daisy or the boys, I selected the largest possible canvas that would fit my easel and watched James pay for it. I marveled to see him engage with the merchants here, for he was never cruel, but polite and firm. I was certain that his reputation affected how the tradesmen spoke to him, but many of them seemed comfortable enough to tease him about the travel regulations or the taxes on their top-notch supplies, which is what drove their high prices. James didn't shut them down like he would have if Armand or I had japed at him—he even played along with a few merchants.

By the time James had arranged to have my canvas sent to the Masters' chambers, I hadn't seen anything noteworthy to recall for later and resigned to fiddle with the sleeves of my fleece shirt while the servants arriving for the shift change filed in and took notice of me, out and about with James. Before he led us back to the Masters' chambers, James asked me if there was anything else I wanted to see to in the market and I was so caught off-guard by the casual ease with which he asked the question, I said no.

The line of armed guardsmen waiting outside the Masters' chambers was much more intimidating than it had been on the way out. I had to remind myself of Daisy's inscription in Kit's sketchbook, to play nice, and not beg James to take me back to my own room in the Tribute wing as he reached into his pocket for the key to the most secure ward of the compound. My gaze flickered up to meet Quinn's as I followed James past the guardsmen and I couldn't control the appalled expression I must have pulled, to see the stitches in his cheeks amid the ghastly purple and black bruises around his eyes. I looked away almost immediately, but not before he cast a brutally visceral glare at me.

"What happened to him?" I asked James the moment he'd locked the doors behind us.

"To whom?" asked James, leading the way back to my room.

"Quinn—he looks terrible."

James sighed as a stoic expression fell over him. "He failed to uphold his duty as a guardsman of this compound." I felt sick just imagining how that punishment must have occurred. James' knuckles were absent of cuts of bruises that would have been sustained doling out the beating himself. It made me wonder to whom the responsibility fell.

"When is the summit?" I asked once James had opened the door to my room.

"The Masters will arrive in two days," replied James. He sounded weary of the subject, but I couldn't hold back the questions burning in my mind.

"Will you lock me in here, when they come?" I asked feebly.

"I haven't decided." James spaded his hands in his pockets. "I'm disheartened by your behavior over the past few days, to say the least. I suppose how you spend the two weeks over which the summit will take place is, in a way, up to you." He studied my expression furtively. "Do you want to be locked in your room when the Masters arrive?"

"No!" I crossed my arms to hide my shaking fingertips. "I don't want that. I want to be with the others—"

"Tell me, then," James interrupted, raising his voice over my pleading. "Can I trust you to maintain an air of normalcy and follow the rules, if I allow you to spend the summit with the others?" His stare bore into mine as if he were peering into my mind. I heard Donovan remind me about an opportunity and remembered Daisy's encouragement to play along, and then I felt like I was buried beneath a foot of snow all over again. My heart ached with loneliness and contempt for James. If I were faced with the opportunity to call James out in front of the other Masters, would I truly be able to hold my tongue? After raising a hand to Daisy, Armand, and even Quinn, for whom I reserved only the basest level of compassion?

Hating myself for it, I responded honestly. "No." I clenched my jaw to keep my teeth from chattering.

"Well," James huffed. "There you have it. Thank you for your honesty, Liza, it's a nice change." He turned and left me alone in my room. Tears welled in my eyes as my resolve to keep from weeping crumbled. I slipped my hair out of its knot at the back of my head and retreated to the nest of blankets, pulling Kit's sketchbook out from under my pillow to hold it close to my heart. When servants came to deliver the massive canvas, I pretended to be asleep. They set the canvas down and shuffled out hastily, not keen at all to interact with me. I waited until I was alone again to inspect the canvas. The servants hadn't set it on the easel at all, just leaned it on the inside wall and piled the paints that came with it on the floor beside it.

I don't know what drove me to drag myself to my feet and go to the canvas. I was despairing again, unable to quell the tears in my eyes, but I still took up the canvas in my hands—it was deceptively heavy—and lifted it up so that it sat on the easel. I faced the open window and saw the sinking afternoon sun hang in the sky, casting beautiful rays of golden light across the redwood tree-tops. I went to the boxes of paints and ripped into them, taking up a pallet of bright acrylics and an assortment of brushes. I attacked the canvas with ferocious passion, reciting *Annabel Lee* out loud and humming the tunes Kit had composed on his violin that I'd memorized over the years. Paint droplets flung up and flecked across my arms, face, neck, and hair. My eyes flickered back and forth between the landscape in the distance so often that I started to get a headache, but I couldn't tear myself away from the art.

I turned away food. I turned away Jada when she came to check on me. I was so entranced in my own head that I didn't even hear what Jada had said when she'd stuck her head in the doorway, but the noncommittal responses I gave her, while clearly distracted, seemed to satisfy her enough to make her leave. My arms began to ache after hours of lashing broad, long strokes of paint across the canvas. I forced myself to go on until my knees were weak from standing for so long and my wrist became too unsteady to hold the brush. I had clarity enough to close the paints but I dropped the brushes, still covered in amber and lavender paints, to the floor. I didn't take a step back to admire my work; I just staggered away from the easel and keeled over into the blankets by the window, not bothering to wipe off the paint smeared on my face and arms. I could even smell it in my hair.

Too tired to get back up and flip the switch that would lower the curtains, I rolled away from the glaring setting sunshine and fell asleep almost immediately. I did not dream of my father or of playing by the river with Baby Daisy, or even of falling. Instead I dreamed that I was huddled up in that cave, freezing to death as the winter winds outside howled and roared. There was a muffled silence to the outside, caused by the heavy snowfall, that brought on the sensation of being covered by a blanket. I had the vague sense of gravity, a pull in my gut as though I were being lifted, and then even the snow drifted away into heavy blackness.

I opened my eyes to see the sun rising over the trees. The inside of my mouth felt dry, and I tried to wet my lips but I was too parched to do it. I sat up in bed, not the pile of blankets on the floor I'd curled up in; the blankets on the floor had been cleared away, likely because I'd gotten paint on them, but Kit's sketchbook was on my bedside table, apparently undisturbed. The canvas I'd painted yesterday was gone, but leaning against the wall by the easel were three more blank ones. I ran my fingers through my hair and winced when I caught a glob of dried paint near the ends of my hair and almost yanked it out altogether. Scowling, I swung my legs out of bed and made my way to the bathroom. I ran the water as hot as I could stand it and stripped off my clothes, barely unnerved to see a fresh set folded and stacked near the vanity.

I checked my reflection in the mirror while the tub filled with water. I couldn't help but smile as the paint smudged on my face and arms blended in with the floral mural painted on the bathroom wall behind me. I didn't necessarily like for inspiration to have come from this place, but I'd worked so hard yesterday that I'd been too tired to have nightmares. I frowned when I noticed the bruise on the inside of my arm. It looked to be in its ugliest phase of healing, a mess of purple, green, and yellow, so I turned away and stepped into the bathtub. After scrubbing the dried paint off with that strong lavender soap, I sank to the bottom of the tub again and held my breath for as long as I could. My skin was stinging from the heat by the time I emerged and toweled off, but the hot water chased away the memory of being under the snow.

After the steam cleared from my bath and my hair dried, I plaited it over my shoulder and pulled on the thick socks that matched the fleece pants. I believed them to be a sort of wool blend, because my fingers and toes were still sore from contracting hypothermia and these new clothes were so comfortable and made it easier for me to maintain my body heat. I didn't want to pick up my paint brushes, which I noticed had been cleaned and neatly arranged on a small table beside the easel for me, mostly because my appetite was rearing. I was surprised to find that my door was unlocked. I let myself out into the hall and tried to recall the way to the dining room, all the while thinking of Daisy and the boys.

Our mornings together had been sacred in their normalcy; Graham always had coffee brewing, Armand was always bright-eyed and whisking eggs and sliced peppers together in a bowl bound for the skillet, Daisy was always fiddling with the tail of a teabag hanging over the side of a mug while reading a book, and Kit was usually the last one up, sleepy-faced and slow moving, greeting us with a tired smile when he meandered into our little kitchen.

I smiled just thinking of them, and of Daisy's warm "Good morning, Liza!" that I could count on every day. I forgot to pay attention to where I was going and resolved to try the first unlocked door I could find in hopes of scrounging up some semblance of breakfast. It took me three tries before I found an open door. Inside was a richly green, humid greenhouse, so lush and expanse that I let out a small exclamation of wonder. I didn't think twice about delving further inside, down a grated footpath in the middle of looming, enormous leafy plants. I grazed my fingertips along the leaves as I slowly passed, a smile spreading on my face as I heard birds singing overhead. The scent of fresh turf and flora distracted me from my rumbling belly—I was simply enchanted. There were plants all over the compound, as some of the main halls were home to indoor birch saplings and vegetable gardens nourished by synthetic sunlight, but this place was like something out of a fantasy.

I must have plodded along the path for several minutes before I heard voices up ahead. They were both distinctly male voices and though they were hushed, they seemed aggravated.

"The last thing I want to be is a nuisance," said a voice I immediately recognized as Donovan's. "I'd have left with my men the next morning, had the girl not been found—"

"And yet here you stand," said the second voice, unmistakably belonging to James.

"In the interest of frankness, my dear uncle, I think it's best for me to stay and advise you on how best to deal with Liza," said Donovan in an eagerly sardonic tone.

Uncle? Had my hearing failed me?

"I know how to handle Liza."

"Right—because you'd been doing such a marvelous job when I had to physically separate the two of you!" Donovan hissed a mocking laugh. "You can't whip her into shape with brutality like your infidels, James. You need to be gentle, kind—and a little charm wouldn't hurt, if you can manage it."

"You speak out of place, Donovan."

"So treating her like an adult hasn't been effective so far? You haven't noticed a stark difference between how she reacts when you treat her like a human being instead of like a butterfly whose wings you constantly threaten to pull off?"

"In this life you excel at two things, Donovan," James returned flatly. He was obviously stepping around having to admit that Donovan was in the right. "The mastery of swordplay and the seduction of whatever foolish, alluring specimen you come across. Why don't you spare me your diatribe and leave the mastery of this compound, and that includes how Liza is dealt with, to me, eh?"

"Aha! So you *are* sore about me paying attention to little Daisy—"

"Not as sore as you're about to be, if you keep acting like this is a joke."

I couldn't see either of them, too stunned by what they were saying to get any closer.

"The conditions are very clear," said James. "I will not allow you to compromise our already very delicate balance with Lorena and the others in the Village by interfering with that girl."

"Honestly, James," sighed Donovan. "It was just a bit of harmless flirtation—you've got to stop taking things so seriously!"

"Taking things seriously is why I am the Master of this compound and you are not," James said, his voice like low thunder. I imagined his eyes were an intense, angry blue by now. "And don't think for a second I wouldn't have taken serious action if I thought for even a moment that the repulsive rumors about you and my Tribute were true."

The conversation culminated in a few moments of silent tension; I imagined James was standing over Donovan in a threatening show of dominance.

"There's no sense in you returning to the camps now, with the summit just a day away," James uttered menacingly. "But you will stay out of my way if you know what's best for you. I hope you don't force me to do something I'd regret."

"Are you sure it's such a good idea to threaten me, James? I might not be the big, bad Master of this place, but I'm still a Master—I have more than enough pull to make your life hell."

"Would you like to put that to the test?"

Someone grabbed my arm and I cried out shrilly; I whipped around to face who'd grabbed me and saw Quinn, his visage still gruesome as ever, scowling down at me.

"What are you doing in here, little girl?" he demanded roughly. He seized my other arm and jerked me close to him, almost wrenching me off my feet. I heard the grates of the greenhouse walk clang as James and Donovan stormed over.

"What is the meaning of this?" James exclaimed, appearing behind Quinn with Donovan at his heels.

"She was out of bounds, Master James," Quinn snapped, not taking his glare off me for a second.

"The door was unlocked!" I gasped. "I was looking for the kitchen!"

"Or maybe you were looking for another open window?" Quinn retorted. His fingers dug into my arms and I worried he would throttle me. James ordered Quinn to immediately unhand me and the guardsman released me roughly at once. I careened into the guardrail on the other side of the footpath; if I hadn't, I'd have spilled into the plants head over heels. Donovan caught me before my knees gave out and held my arm, standing between me and Quinn.

"Donovan," said James. "Please take Liza to the kitchen and see that she's fed and taken care of. I would like to have a word with Quinn."

"Of course," Donovan complied. The acidity between them from their heated conversation moments ago had vanished. I didn't spare a glance to either James or Quinn as Donovan led me back down the footpath. "Are you all right, Liza?" We bustled out of the greenhouse fast and Donovan released my arm, taking my hand instead.

"I'm fine," I insisted breathlessly. I was shaken by it, I had to admit to myself. I was glad Donovan had lent me his hand enough to feel no embarrassment about gripping it so tightly. Once we reached the door, Donovan pulled me over the threshold into the main hall of the Masters' chambers and shut the greenhouse door, locking it behind us.

"James has a key," Donovan assured me. "He won't want to be disturbed, believe me. Are you sure you're all right?"

"Yes," I said, though I shook my head to the contrary.

"Come on, let's get you some breakfast. You're shaking like a leaf." He offered me his arm and I took it. I was grateful in a way for Quinn to have surprised me, for now it would be easy to hide the fact that I was reeling from all I'd overheard in the greenhouse.

James was Donovan's uncle. Daisy and the boys would be amazed to hear it.

"I've seen your painting," Donovan said, rousing me from what he perceived to be a rush of panicked thoughts. "It's beautiful work, Liza. You've got real talent."

"Thank you," I replied automatically. "I didn't get the chance to see it this morning when I woke up, as it had been taken from the easel."

"I had it sent to Daisy," Donovan confessed. "I replaced the canvas three-fold, however, in case you might be offended that I took the liberty."

"Daisy will love it." It warmed me to think of her waking up to a window to the outside world captured in a painting. I wished I could show her the view from my room; if James would truly allow her to visit me in this part of the compound, I would sit with her in front of it and tell her all about Kingsfield Township and the things James told me about our parents.

Donovan escorted me to the dining room, where a full breakfast spread was laid out elegantly on the table. An impressive amount of fresh fruit was piled high on a platter surrounded by expertly cooked meats and sweet breads.

"I can call someone to serve you," Donovan offered. "But you are free to build your own plate." That was all the go-ahead I needed—I was starving, especially after the excitement in the greenhouse. I must have devoured four lemon-blueberry muffins and twice as many rations of bacon before Donovan pointed out that I should slow down; instead of heeding his polite reminder to apply my table manners, I took several gulps of orange juice and helped myself to even more food.

"I'm sorry," I sighed, once I'd had my fill. "I didn't eat a scrap of food yesterday. I never eat when I work."

"Frankly, I wouldn't blame you for a lack of appetite." Donovan locked his teal blue eyes into mine and cocked his head slightly. "I believe it's safe to assume, you overheard me speaking with James this morning?"

I blushed without meaning to. "I honestly was looking for the kitchen, but then I saw all that green…the garden was unlike anything I've ever seen, and I got carried away—"

"My dear Liza," Donovan chided softly. "There's no need to explain. I'm not angry with you for being curious. I'm not my uncle." He blinked a few times, watching me knowingly. "I know you heard me point out our relation. It's nothing to be nervous about, Liza, don't worry. You've proven to be a worthy confidante. I know you'll be discreet."

"James will address it with me, regardless," I worried.

"Oh, I wouldn't worry over it. James didn't know you were there to hear us; otherwise, he would have chosen his words a lot more carefully. Believe me, you have nothing to fuss about. Now, Quinn, on the other hand…." He was clearly less optimistic about Quinn getting caught red-handed than me. "Look, Liza, James and I have always butted heads. With the summit so soon, both our tempers are a little hard pressed. Trust me, he'll deal with Quinn and likely behave as though the incident in the greenhouse never happened."

"Are you sure?"

"I would be shocked if he brought it up with you. James does not like to talk about my mother, his sister—addressing what you overheard would bring him too close to that subject."

I decided to trust Donovan's judgment. He knew James better than I did, or ever would apparently, since they were family. Pondering their relation reminded me of what I'd been upset about, before Quinn had grabbed me.

"I don't like the things you said about Daisy."

"It's regrettable that you had to hear it," Donovan said. I frowned, thinking it was a very poor attempt to sidestep an apology. I wasn't sure what I wanted him to say about it, really.

"I like what James said about her even less. The way he put it, when he said you weren't allowed to *interfere* with *his* Tribute." My cheeks burned as I recalled James' dark, keen words, *I know how to deal with Liza.*

"It's not the most romantic turn of phrases, is it? *Interfere.* James can be so clinical about his rules, and you know he likes to remind us as often as he can that he alone holds the fates of everyone in this compound," Donovan said simply. "Incidentally, he's right; it would be against the rules for me to pursue any kind of relationship with Daisy beyond the platonic, regardless of how fond I am of her. Which I am, Liza, and I'm sure you will agree with me about why: Daisy is a beautiful young woman and utterly charming because of her ignorance of it. In fact, as I see it, you are both beautiful now that you've reached maturity, if you'll permit me to say."

"She certainly will not." James had emerged into the dining room in time to hear Donovan's compliments. I gulped when I saw blood on his knuckles which gleamed in the overhead lighting. Donovan straightened his posture and swallowed what was left of his coffee—it was apparent that neither of us knew James had been within earshot.

James grabbed a cloth napkin from the table and carefully wiped his knuckles clean, glancing balefully at Donovan. "Liza, the next time Donovan makes a comment about your appearance, in fact, about anything beyond the confines of small talk, I give you permission to tell him to shut his mouth."

"As you say," I agreed stiffly.

"James, there's no reason to be so severe," Donovan reasoned. I raised my eyebrows; this was as close to sheepish as I'd ever seen him.

"Go ask Quinn if I am in the mood today for backtalk." He glared at Donovan until Donovan averted his gaze. I'd heard him threaten James that he could make his life miserable, but even he seemed to feel the need to back down.

"Excuse me," Donovan said, rising from his chair. "I have some errands to see to." He quit the dining room in graceful haste, leaving me alone with James in ringing silence.

"If I could," James said quietly, "I'd have given you permission to hit him. Of all the inappropriate things to say…well, he ought to be slapped. It doesn't seem to have any effect when I do it, so maybe he'll heed a rebuke from you."

To that, I had nothing to say. "I'm sorry to have disturbed you in the greenhouse."

"Don't be. The greenhouse is unlocked for a reason." James pinched the bridge of his nose. "To be honest, Liza, the debacle this morning ranks very low on my list of things I need to worry about." He set the bloodied napkin down and helped himself to coffee and a piece of toast from the rack in front of him. "I apologize for Quinn's behavior. He had no right to put his hands on you."

I nodded in acknowledgment but couldn't seem to summon any words. I watched James eat his breakfast, my eyes glued to the bruises on his knuckles. I almost mentioned the new canvasses I found in my room this morning, but I didn't want the conversation to lead back to Donovan after their disgruntling interaction earlier.

"I spoke to Graham this morning," said James after he'd finished chewing his toast. "Daisy would like to visit you this afternoon. I told her she would be allowed as long as she finishes her work for the day."

"I would like that," I said, teeming with enthusiasm.

"Depending on how your visit goes," said James, "and whether or not you apply some discretion regarding how the nature between Donovan and I stands, I may consider allowing you to return to the Tribute wing after the summit."

The implication behind his statement was overt: Keep what I've learned to myself and I might be able to go home.

"One more thing, Liza," said James when I tried to excuse myself from breakfast. "If there is anything you need from the market, or you wish to leave your room to walk the halls of this ward, Douglas or I will accompany you." He noticed my features wilt and explained, "You are free to visit the greenhouse again, if you're so inclined, but I would rather avoid another incident like the one today by ensuring you do not move about these halls alone."

I supposed that was fair. I nodded and left the dining room to find that Douglas was waiting outside the door for me. I guessed he was the only guardsman in James' service allowed to sport facial hair, for his dark beard was always clipped short but very noticeable.

"Hello, Liza," he said. His demeanor was a mix of sternness and pleasantness, and I found it difficult to harbor any disdain for him. "Are you going back to your room?"

"Yes," I replied. "I'd like to wait there for Daisy."

"As you say," Douglas said easily. "Master James has asked—"

"For you to accompany me, I know," I said. I let him lead the way, noticing the kind smiles the servants gave Douglas when he passed. He'd been hand selected by James to lead the guardsmen of the compound, which meant Douglas was just as dangerous as Donovan with a weapon in-hand, but much less threatening than the Masters. I'd known Douglas for five years now, and I knew him to be an unimposing, gentlemanly servant to James. Without a doubt, I preferred him to Quinn as an escort.

"I'll be just outside, Liza," said Douglas, planting the heel of his boot on the floor outside my room. "If you need anything, let me know and I'll send someone to take care of it."

"Thank you, Douglas." I chewed on my lower lip in hesitation before I went into my room. "Is Quinn all right?"

Douglas' expression didn't darken for an instant. "I wouldn't worry about Quinn if I were you, Liza. We guardsmen have a brotherhood of sorts, but when you earn as many slights with the Masters like Quinn has, there's not much to do but keep an eye out for someone to take up the job in his place."

"He's no longer a guardsman?" I asked with a gasp.

"It's a matter of time, Liza. At this point, it might be better for his health to find work elsewhere, maybe someplace with a more patient Master." Douglas could be candid about James unlike the other guardsmen, since his station was so prominent. Perhaps Douglas was right about that. I had to imagine that on the spectrum of Masters, James must fall on the more astringent end. I'd seen the nasty side of James' temper but he'd never blackened my eye or given me stitches like he had Quinn; maybe he deserved a post outside of James the Master's control, where there were no Tributes like me to get him into trouble?

"Maybe," I said to Douglas. I closed the door behind myself and crawled back into bed, eager to snooze a little while my full belly digested the overabundance of breakfast I'd consumed. I looked forward to waking in time to see Daisy, which only keyed me up too much to sleep. I loaded one of the new, blank canvases onto the easel and raised the curtains from the window to take in the view, which I would paint again in this different light. I must have painted for hours before my door opened—I expected Daisy to be there, but it was Douglas, informing me that lunch was being served in the dining room. I dismissed Douglas, telling him that I was not hungry but he was free to go and eat. I assured him I would stay in my room, in case Daisy visited, and he seemed to think that was an agreeable compromise.

Disappointed still, I returned to my painting and covered my anxiety in vivid brushstrokes. I was too distracted to make anything noteworthy, already knowing I wouldn't be satisfied with this piece. I put the brushes down and sat cross-legged in front of the window. I knew it was foolish to get worked up like this, but I was eager to see Daisy and tell her about everything I'd learned from inside the Masters' chambers. The more I thought about it, though, the more I realized I would have to be more careful than just spilling it all to Daisy. If James was listening, which I had reason to believe he would be, he'd never let me return to the Tribute wing, and he might punish Daisy for conspiring with me.

Quickly, as though Daisy might be on her way here any moment, I got up and snatched Kit's sketchbook from my bedside table. I thumbed the book open to the next empty page, just past the three inscriptions from Daisy and the boys, and slipped the pencil from its place in the binding. I tapped the page a few times with the graphite tip, thinking fast about how best to describe the information I needed to pass on. The most pertinent point was our origin—Kingsfield Township. I drew a large square in the middle of the page and penciled in some trees, sketching out an overhead map to the best of my estimation. I labeled the square "Martin's Ferry, Aventine" and then a little volpine face below it. I glanced out the window, my eyes fixed on the distant point James had said Kingsfield Township could be found. I scribbled a bullet point far from the compound square and wrote "Kingsfield Township, The Village" beside it.

How would I tell them that we came from Kingsfield Township? I chewed on my lip and added the river from my dreams near the Kingsfield Township dot. Daisy was just a little thing when we were there; I doubted she would recall the river from our childhood, but Armand might. Still, to make it crystal clear, I wrote in tiny letters "home" underneath the river. I smudged it with the side of my pinky finger in case James or anyone else intercepted the makeshift map.

Now, how to break the news of the family bond between James and Donovan? I thought of writing a message as though it was a journal entry, hiding a code within the words, but it would be too transparent. Armand had known how to perfectly encapsulate how he felt in poetry…maybe I should find a literary tool to disguise the truth of what I meant to tell them.

It took me just a moment to decide the perfect medium. I began to sketch a portrait of James and was eventually perturbed by how well I was able to capture his stoic expression. On the page opposite James, I drew Donovan. His face was meant to be drawn, his features flawlessly angular and symmetrical. I didn't mean to make him look so satisfied with himself, but when I thought of Donovan, I always imagined him smirking. Lastly, I drew a portrait of Daisy. I drew her with her hair pulled back, like it was when she practiced her ballet. Her eyes were kind in this likeness, which was as close to Daisy's resting expression as I could get.

Underneath James, I wrote, *J.T.M. as Claudius*. Under Donovan, I wrote, *D.T.M. as Hamlet*. Finally, as a warning to Daisy that both James and Donovan were paying careful attention to her, I labeled hers as *my Daisy is Ophelia*. I knew that all three of them would refuse to believe that James and Donovan were uncle and nephew, but they would have to take my word for it until I could see them in person to divulge the details. I tucked the pencil away into the binding of the sketchbook and closed it. I wrapped the thin, attached leather cord tightly around it and set it on the bed. When Daisy came, *if* Daisy came, I would keep the conversation whimsical but insist she take the sketchbook home with her to look over with the boys. Until then, I decided to return to my painting and wait impatiently for Daisy to arrive.

Hours later, when the sun began to sink low in the sky, I knew Daisy was not going to visit. I almost cried as I accepted it, but being woeful wouldn't solve anything. Dejected, I put down my paintbrush and swept my hair back from my face. I groaned when I realized I'd just smeared wet, green paint on my forehead and went to the bathroom to wash my face and hands.

"Liza?" called Douglas from the other room.

"Yes?" I asked, my face still pressed into a towel.

"Dinner is about to be served."

I left the towel beside the sink basin and went back to the bedroom. "I don't think I'm in the mood," I told him.

Douglas stepped away from my unfinished painting and frowned. "You should eat...." He gestured to the painting and back to me. "You paint with such fervor," he remarked. "You must have worked up an appetite?"

"It's not that I'm not hungry," I admitted with a sigh. "I just don't want to sit at the table with James and pretend to be pleasant."

"I understand," Douglas said. "I'd be happy to have food send here so you can eat in your room. I'm certain Master James would be agreeable to that."

"Thank you." Graham would have pressured me to join James at the table so that I wouldn't forget how to behave at a proper dinner setting and I was glad Douglas did not. "May I ask you something, Douglas?" I asked just before Douglas left the room.

"Of course, Liza."

I went to the bed and took up Kit's sketchbook. "Daisy was supposed to visit today and I drew her some portraits. Would you please take this to her? Or at least see that she receives it?"

"Master James did tell me to expect her.... I can't imagine what could have kept her away. Of course, I'd be happy to deliver this to her. I'll see to it after I arrange for your dinner to be brought up."

"Thank you, Douglas," I enthused. "I appreciate your kindness."

"It's no problem, Liza," said Douglas. "I'll be back presently." He shut the door behind him and I heaved a sigh. I might as well bathe as long as I knew Daisy wouldn't be along. Just as the plodding of Douglas' boots dissipated, I heard a hissing crinkle as a slip of paper slid under my door. A little alarmed, I stood still and listened for approaching or receding footsteps. When I heard nothing, I tiptoed over to the doors and quickly picked up the paper, folded in half, from the floor. It was a note!

Liza, it read, *I couldn't visit today. There is to be a gathering of Masters and James said there was too much going on, and that I should wait until the Masters have left. The boys and I must see you! We have arranged with Donovan to stay late in the studio. The guardsmen will leave the doors for just under five minutes before the midnight shift change. If you can, please slip away and come to us. Love, Daisy.*

My heart was racing. A clandestine meeting with all three of them tonight? I could hardly wait! And Donovan agreed to let them all stay in the studio to facilitate it. Their timing could not be better, for Douglas would see to it that Daisy would get the sketchbook, she would share it with the boys, and we could all discuss it together tonight.

I refolded the note carefully and rolled it tightly around the handle of my favorite paintbrush. I bundled them all together and put them away, concealing the note amid my art supplies. I'd have burned it, but I doubted James would leave matches or the like lying around in my room.

The rest of the evening dragged by unbearably slow. Douglas returned with my supper and I ate it as slowly as I could. After I finished, I bathed and braided my hair into an intricate plait. I couldn't seem to find enough tasks with which to busy myself; I even picked up my paintbrush again, but no matter how hard I tried, I could not draw focus to my work. Eventually, I sprawled across the floor and stretched my arms, legs, and back while I measured my breathing in counts of twenty seconds. Time poured into those breaths and I slowly floated away from the frantic anticipation of sneaking out of my room to meet Daisy, Kit, and Armand.

My mind was guilty. I kept expecting James to stop in unannounced and foil my plans to slip away in the night. I flinched at the slightest sound, even if I made it. I even shut the curtains so that I wouldn't measure time by the slowly darkening sky outside. When the clock on my bedside table read eleven-thirty, I was so exhausted from worrying all evening that I worried I'd fall asleep and miss my chance. I got up and paced the floor, maybe two dozen times in ten minutes, when I decided that I couldn't wait any longer. I went to the door and opened it slowly—if Douglas was standing guard, I'd tell him to send Jada with a headache pill or some such excuse.

He was gone! With my heart in my throat, I shut my bedroom door behind me and followed the corridor on the balls of my feet to the main doors. I knew how to slip between the merchant booths to avoid being seen in the main hall, but I'd have to reach the Masters' chambers entrance first. I prayed it would be unlocked when I got there, that I wouldn't encounter a servant, or guardsman, or James—and by some miracle, my path was wide open. My fingertips were shaking as I reached for the doorknob of the main doors. I gave it a turn as dread coiled in my stomach like a searing hot snake.

"Yes!" I hissed. The door was open. I flitted through and shut it carefully behind me and ran for the closest merchant post. Not only was I risking James' cruelty by sneaking away from my room, but I'd never been in the marketplace at this hour before, ever. It was spooky, almost surreal, to see the hall closed for business. Without the lively voices echoing in the hall or the bustle of boots on the floor, it felt like a museum or an empty dreamscape. I did, however, hear the heavy footfalls of guardsmen coming down the way once I reached the east wing entrance. It was easy to move about here unseen because so many of the tapestries and rugs for sale were still hung up behind the merchant stands. I hid for a few seconds behind a larger rug before slipping around the corner, the studio dead ahead. I could see a dim light beyond the frosted glass windows and grinned as I let myself into the studio.

"It's me!" I whispered gleefully. "I made it!" I beamed, searching the studio floor for my friends. "Psst! It's Liza!" I peered around the support beams near the back of the studio and checked behind the shelves of rolled-up sponge mats and ballet slippers.

"Daisy?" I called, daring to raise my voice a little louder. I knitted my eyebrows and frowned. I was alone, as far as I could tell. I checked the clock hanging over the shelves; it was six minutes to midnight. Daisy's note had said I should come to them before midnight—if I was late, perhaps the plan had changed?

"You look lost, little girl," sneered a low voice from behind me. I whirled around with a sucking gasp and saw Quinn standing in the doorway. The swelling of his cheek was gruesome to behold but it was nothing compared to the sheer malice glinting in his eyes.

"What's the matter, Liza?" Quinn took a step toward me and I realized in horror that there was no doorway leading out of the studio behind me. "Can't find your friends?"

"What have you done to them?"

"I'll tell you," Quinn replied. "I put their lives before mine, just like I did yours, and for what?" His speech was staggered, as if he'd bitten his tongue.

James must have hit him in the mouth and cut his knuckles on Quinn's teeth. He took another two steps toward me and I took one back—I was in real trouble, that much was clear.

"Don't worry, Liza, your Tribute friends aren't here. They're safely locked away in their pretty little prison for the night—and why shouldn't they be? I stopped that sweet little thing from jumping out the window, only to be beaten within an inch of my sanity by James the Master," Quinn drawled. "Too bad you didn't die, Liza. It would have been better if you had." The hate radiating from him was rancid, like the smell of rotten meat. I took another step back as he advanced once more, slowly, baring his bloody gums at me.

"Stay away from me." I was terrified of him. I wanted to scream but I feared it would enrage him.

"You want to be free, is that it?" Quinn wet his lips. "You want to get away from the Masters, Liza?"

I shook my head. I didn't dare reply, lest I aggravate him.

"Well, it's not too late for that," offered Quinn. "The Masters will be here in a few short hours but maybe there's a way you can escape after all?" He snorted bitterly. "No one escapes," he rasped, taking one more step forward. We were now just a few feet apart. My nerves were buzzing, the hairs across my arms and on the back of my neck standing up.

Quinn reached behind him and withdrew a shining silver blade from his belt. My eyes locked on it as my racing heartbeat thundered in my ears.

"I should have slit your pretty throat the day I met you, and spared us all this trouble."

"Please," I whimpered. "Don't hurt me!"

"I'm not going to hurt you, Liza," Quinn replied with a cruel smile. "I'm going to set you free." I had just a second to react when I saw Quinn tighten his grip on his knife.

"JAMES!" I screamed for the only person I could think of who could stop this. I flung myself away from Quinn as he lunged for me, the blade missing my body by an inch. I ran for the only way out, screaming for James again. "HELP!" I bellowed as loudly as I could. The thick socks on my feet did not grip the polished wooden floor as well as Quinn's boots did, for just as I was about to make the exit, Quinn caught me and bore me down. I crashed to the floor, my cheek knocking against the cold wood as Quinn crushed my legs underneath him.

"Stop fighting, you stupid little bitch!" Quinn roared. I shrieked as he grabbed my arm and turned me over. He reached back with the knife and I threw my arms up to shield my face; the blade cut deep lesions in my forearms, slicing through my flesh like butter. I wailed as my own blood spilled over my chest in a great gush, the cuts stinging as they bled. I wriggled bodily to try to get out from under Quinn, but he was too huge and far too cumbersome for me to even budge. With his free hand, he tried to grapple onto one of my wrists, but they were slick with blood and I would not—*could* not—keep still.

Quinn tried to gash my throat open despite my raised arms in the way. I struggled to avoid it entirely, but I felt the stinging kiss of the blade tear into my shoulder all the same and I screamed in pain. I kicked my legs and pushed at Quinn with my bloody hands, but my restraint only seemed to egg him on and make him stronger. I couldn't breathe with his weight pressing down on my chest.

"Shut up!" Quinn thundered over my screaming. He drove a knee into my side and I gagged on my own voice, my breath left me all at once in a rushing groan. I couldn't move. I couldn't think. My heart skittered as my lungs convulsed, desperate for more air, but Quinn was on top of me and my chest couldn't hold his weight.

I'd begun to see spots before my eyes right as Quinn was suddenly heaved off of me. I sucked in a gasping, guttural breath and rolled to the side. My shoulder and arms were in agony and my blood was spilling in throbs, spreading across the wooden floor beneath me. I was huddled, helpless, in a bloody ball on the floor when I blinked a few times and tried to focus my vision. I saw James and Quinn struggling on the floor, the knife having been knocked from Quinn's hand. James had his arm locked around Quinn's throat. The acrid smell of copper suffocated me as I watched, unable to look away, as Quinn desperately rasped for breath.

A strangled, choking sob ripped from my throat as James shifted his weight, giving a heavy yank, and then Quinn's neck made a sickening, wet snap. The rest of his body went slack and I pinched my eyes closed to block out the view.

"Liza!" James was there, his hands on me, carefully turning me onto my back. "Liza, look at me," he pleaded urgently. I could do nothing but cry. I reached for James with bloody hands and he pulled me into his lap.

"You're going to be all right," James insisted. "You're safe now."

"I can't—" I sobbed. I was dizzy and breathing too fast. "James, please—" my breath hitched on another sob. The lesion cut into my shoulder was raw with awful pain, and I felt like my entire chest had been hacked open. It hurt to even hold my head up.

"I've got you," James reminded me. He lifted me from the floor effortlessly, swinging my legs over his other arm, and carried me away. I cried into his chest, shivering in seizing terror.

Quinn had been seconds away from killing me. He was dead; I'd watched him die. But still I felt that he was on me, forcing the air from my lungs, his blade carving away at my arms as it searched furiously for my throat.

This living, waking nightmare world passed in a blur. James shouted commands over his shoulder and I could hear the loud rush of swarming guardsmen, but my own heartbeat was so loud in my ears that it sounded like thunderous drumming in my head. Stranger still, I felt James' heart pounding faster than mine as I buried my face in his chest. I heard him holler to clear the hall moments before I was set down on a bed.

"Liza, honey," Jada said. Her voice sounded so far away and I couldn't even see her. "You're going to be fine, sweetheart." Was that a crack in her voice? Was Jada afraid?

James pulled away from me and I lashed out with my left arm, since I couldn't feel my right arm anymore. I clenched my fingers around James' wrist as tight as I could.

"No," I begged. "Please!" I held on to keep him from leaving my side. I felt a burning in the crook of my arm before the lights above me faded into darkness.

I opened my eyes in a haze. I stared up into a red canopy and faintly heard voices around me.

"I've told you, Master James," I heard Jada iterate. "Quinn is dead and you won't get any answers from him—"

"I *told* you," Donovan insisted. "You should have let me escort Quinn from the premises!"

"I should have sent him away a week ago," James said darkly.

"I take full responsibility, James," Douglas declared.

"You're mistaken. The fault is mine." No one tried to argue with James. The room fell silent.

"James," I moaned, trying to sit up. He and Jada rushed to my side, their worried faces hovering over me amid the red curtain overhead.

"Lie very still," Jada said in a steady, careful voice. "You've been concussed, and if you sit up like that you could pull your stitches."

Stitches? I began to weep softly. My head was spinning. "James, I need to see them," I begged. "I need to see Armie and Kit, and Daisy. Please. I need to know they're all right...."

"They're perfectly safe, still in bed," said James. "You must rest." He frowned sadly as I started to really bawl and then he nodded to Jada, who went for something in her bag.

Before I knew it, I was drifting away again. I found no dreams of falling or fathers in sleep, just frigid darkness. Sometimes I smelled blood or my shoulder gave a sharp twinge that made me gasp, but I couldn't find the strength to open my eyes or even shift positions in slumber. Once, I thought I heard James speaking with someone whose voice I did not recognize, but my tired mind pushed the noise away and I fell back into the void of sleep.

I came to a while later, hours or days later I wasn't sure, and found that my right arm was fastened in a snug sleeve that made me hug my torso. My mouth was dry but I swallowed anyway and pushed myself up to a sitting position with my left arm, wincing sharply when a red-hot pain seared across my forearm. I looked at my arm and saw it had been wrapped with gauze, likely stitched up cleanly underneath. I groaned and swayed as my head throbbed.

"Easy," encouraged Jada, bustling over from the other side of the bed to place a hand on my uninjured shoulder. "I want you to take it very slow, Liza."

"I feel sick," I mumbled, gritting my teeth against the dull pain in my arm.

"Nausea is a common side effect to some of the more potent painkillers," Jada explained. "It'll pass, especially if you get some food in you."

The idea of eating made me feel even queasier. "What's wrong with my arm?"

"You have about twenty stitches in your right shoulder. You sustained a deep lesion on your *levator scapulae* and I put you in a sling to keep you from tearing the muscle while it heals."

I wished I hadn't asked. "And my arms?"

"Those defensive wounds are the deepest," Jada said gravely. "But they're all stitched up and on the mend." Jada fixed a wistfully proud stare at me. "The cuts on your arms will hurt for a while, Liza, but if you hadn't put your hands up…." She blinked a few times and rubbed my shoulder. "Well, I'm just glad that you're awake now. It was a very close call."

"I expect James will punish me."

"Oh, no, honey," Jada insisted. "Don't think like that. You need to rest—"

"I broke the rules!" I blurted, my eyes welling with tears. "I left my room without Douglas and left the Masters' chambers. I broke the rules, Jada!"

"Liza, calm down. There's nothing to fear. I know that *you* know that what you did was against the rules, but in light of what happened—I don't think there's anything Master James can do to address that. He and I both want you to recover."

I didn't believe her. For all I knew, Jada was nursing me back to health so that I'd be fit enough to be beaten within an inch of my sanity—like Quinn had been.

"I see you're awake," said James, standing in the doorway of whatever enormous room we were in. He looked world weary but relieved to see me up. "How are you feeling?" I clamped my mouth shut and pursed my lips together to stop them from quivering. I couldn't look at him, so I fixed my eyes on the white gauze wrapped around my left forearm. Tears dropped down into my lap as my shoulders shook, which made me grit my teeth in pain.

"Oh, Liza," sighed Jada. "You poor thing…."

"I'm so sorry," I cried. I covered my eyes with my left hand and surrendered to this fresh bout of weeping. Jada put her hand on my shoulder and hushed me. She stroked my hair when I cried even harder.

"You've been through so much," Jada said. "It's okay to cry, just let it out." I didn't see any way to stop, so I did as I was told. I sat and cried, and relived the whole thing twice over in my mind. I recoiled from Jada when I thought of Quinn on top of me. I flinched from her reassuring touch when I thought of Quinn's knife slicing open my arms.

"Jada, will you please give me a moment alone with Liza?" asked James, after a few minutes of this. Jada petted my hair one more time and assured me that, if I needed anything, she would be right outside. I tried to sit up straight and calm myself, wiping my tears and trying not to squint too drastically as my head throbbed.

"I told you to take Douglas with you whenever you left your room," said James as soon as we were alone.

"I know."

"I have postponed the summit of my peers, an unprecedented action in the short history of these meetings, but scandalous nevertheless; all because after what happened last night, I am utterly unprepared to socialize with any of them or even devote a fraction of my attention to affairs that cannot afford to be put off."

"I'm sorry…."

James crossed his arms and stared into my eyes as a forlorn frustration set in his features. "Quinn almost killed you! What the hell were you thinking? Don't answer that," he spat, his face animated in rapt discontent. "Truthfully, I don't give a damn what you were thinking, but do tell me how you managed to get from your room to the studio—all the way across the compound—without coming across a single guardsman?"

"I just did," I confessed. "I left my room and Douglas wasn't there, and the doors to the hall were unlocked. The guards must have been changing their shift, as there were none outside."

James uncrossed his arms and shook his hands at his sides as if tension was droplets of water on his sleeves and he was trying to flick it off. "You expect me to believe that?"

"I'm telling the truth!"

James scowled and turned his back on me for a moment. "And you were just, what? Going for a midnight stroll?"

"I was—going to the Tribute wing." It was a stumbling lie by my standards. I was fragile enough to pass it off, apparently, because James seemed to believe me.

"No doubt to whisper to the others about all you've seen behind the curtain? To try to formulate some new, equally idiotic escape plan?" When I did not respond, James stepped closer until he stood at the foot of the bed. "I want you to look at me so that I can see if you are telling the truth when you answer this question."

I did as he said.

"Were you having sex with Quinn?"

"No!" I blurted at once, my cheeks flushing and bile rising in my throat at the thought of it.

"Don't you dare snap at me, Liza. The studio is hardly on the way to the Tribute wing, which is where you claimed you were going. You made a point of slipping into the studio unnoticed: I've got Donovan telling me I need to consider an affair between you and Quinn as a motive for you sneaking off to meet him in secret, while at the same time, Jada assures me that it's impossible. I have every right to demand the truth from you in this regard, however radical the question may seem to you."

"You forbid such acts," I reminded James, disgusted. "You told me so when I came of age."

"I also forbid acts such as the jumping out of windows, but that didn't stop you, did it?"

I took a breath to tell him that I'd received a note from Daisy to absolve myself of James' vile accusation, but I stopped myself short. He would make straight for Daisy if I told him about the summons to meet in private and when I thought about Daisy being dragged out of bed for questioning, I shivered.

"I am at a loss, Liza. I cannot fathom why you would risk your safety and your place here by once again breaking compound laws and running around after hours. Did you think you could escape by walking out of the front door? You've seen it for yourself, how unforgiving it is out there. When we found you and brought you back here, it was challenging and frustrating, but I thought you learned something valuable in your failure; and now I find out, you're still harboring an agenda, still scratching around for a way out like a wild animal. And you were almost killed in the process."

James searched my expression for some tell of cognition. He crossed his arms again. "I feel as though I'm at the end of reason with you, Liza. I don't know how else to convince you that what you are doing is the purest definition of foolish? Imagine what this is doing to Daisy, and Armand, and Kit. Quinn was inches away from cutting your throat—how would you feel if it were Daisy he'd gone after? And even so, you were nearly killed. If that isn't enough to make you see sense…." He came around and sat beside me on the bed.

"Is your dream of freedom really worth your life, Liza?"

I pondered the question for a moment as I sat cut up, bruised, and broken in bed. All those weeks ago when Daisy, Kit, and I began to discuss life outside of the compound—eventually dragging Armand into talks with us—we merely described a dream, like James had said: There was no sunlight in the trees below and instead of loving parents, I found a pack of volpines and nearly froze to death. My choice to risk my life and escape led to Quinn's punishment and subsequent murderous hatred of me. If I'd never gone near that window, none of this would have happened.

"No," I told James numbly. "It isn't."

"Your life has meaning here," James said. I failed to see how but I did not ask him to elaborate. "I'm going to send away for some food. You should eat and get your strength back."

"Will you ever let me see them again?" I asked, thinking of Daisy, Kit, and Armand.

"You'll need to get well first," James said in perhaps the kindest tone I'd ever heard him use. "And you will not see them here. The only people allowed in this room are Jada and myself."

"Am I not returning to my old room?"

"Not for the time being. Your things will remain there, undisturbed, in case that changes." I peered around this new bedroom, at the crushed velvet canopy over my head and the stunning, looming paintings hung on the walls. I noticed the intravenous station and several other monitors I hadn't seen before were plugged into the floor.

"Is this a hospital room?" Why else would it be wired to support medical equipment like this?

"This is my room," said James. "Now, you need to rest. Drink that water and I'll return with some food."

I gingerly reached for the cup of water to my left and sipped it. I was tucked into James the Master's bed thinking, *Oh, I've done it this time!* as the nagging feeling of dissent that had spurred me to move forward for weeks slowly vanished. I couldn't think of a single reason to leave this room, so I sat back and waited for James to return.

Chapter Nine

Kit

"They're saying *that girl* is dead."

The phrase made my blood run cold and my gut lurch with dread. "Excuse me!" I called, catching the attention of the two women in servant garb I'd overheard up ahead. I jogged over and excused myself again. "What are you talking about? Has someone died?"

The women exchanged knowing glances. "Young man, it may be best for you to return to your wing. One of the Masters will be along soon enough, I expect." They were both embarrassed to have been overheard but I was overwhelmed with worry now and couldn't let them go without explaining.

"Wait a minute," I insisted. I disliked using my status as a Tribute to make demands like that, but between the commotion earlier and all these gossiped whispers passing around the market, I had to know what was going on.

"Yes, sir?" the other woman asked.

"Please," I said. "Tell me—is someone dead?"

"That movement instructor, Helena, had to arrange for the guardsmen to carry a body out of her studio this morning," one woman explained quietly.

"It was a bloody mess," the other elaborated. "There was some talk of excitement from the Masters' chambers, and then in the night a body is found in the compound?" She shook her head. "They didn't even raise the alarm— they're saying it was that Tribute girl."

"Liza?" I gasped. Without a second glance, I pushed past the women and hurried toward the studio. A crowd had gathered outside the studio and I weaved through people, trying to keep my wits about me as I went.

"It's a scandal," a tradesman muttered behind me, clicking his tongue.

"That poor girl," another woman remarked.

I shouldered my way through to the front of the crowd and when I saw that there were no guardsmen blocking the entrance to the studio, I held my chin up and strode in. A wave of nausea hit me as I smelled something off, a coppery, meaty smell; I rounded the corner and cried out when I saw smeared pools of sticky, dried blood on the wooden floor.

"Kit, you shouldn't be here!" Douglas insisted from beside me.

"What happened?" I asked in a strangled voice, unable to tear my eyes from the blood. "People said—Liza isn't dead, Douglas, please tell me she's not dead!"

"Come with me," Douglas said brusquely, taking me by the arm and pulling me away from the mess inside.

I was a stammering mess. "Douglas, please—you must tell me, is Liza—?"

"She's alive," said Douglas, once we were outside of the studio. I was so relieved I actually clapped Douglas on the arm.

"Thank goodness," I sighed. "But there was so much blood—what on earth happened?"

"Master James has asked me not to divulge the details," said Douglas. The man was following orders, I knew, but still I glared at him.

"I'm not interested in what Master James said to you. I am her family, Douglas. You must tell me what happened!"

"I'm sorry, Kit," Douglas said with a shrug. "You'll have to wait for Master James to find you and explain." It would be pointless to argue with him, so I checked my temper and nodded. My hands were shaking so I hastened my pace as I went back to our apartment. I was so focused on pushing away the images of that blood that I almost ran squarely into Donovan.

"Kit!" he exclaimed, reaching to steady me. "What's wrong? We've been looking for you." I looked up to see Armand standing beside Donovan. Of course he was; they were always roaming the compound together these days.

"Something happened in the studio," I said in a wavering voice. I looked right at Armand, whom I'd rarely seen so concerned.

"Who told you about this?" Donovan asked, pulling my focus back to him.

"I heard two servants saying a girl had died," I said. "Then I went to the studio, and there was so much blood...."

"What?" snapped Armand, rounding on Donovan. "There was blood?"

"All right," Donovan declared. "Both of you, come with me. Now." He led us back to the Tribute wing hastily and took up Armand's chair by the fire.

"You didn't say there was blood!" Armand barked at Donovan as soon as we were inside the den.

My patience was rapidly thinning. "Will one of you please tell me what is going on?"

"Last night, there was an attempt on Liza's life," said Donovan. I dropped into my own armchair and covered my gaping mouth with my hand.

"What kind of an attempt?" Armand demanded. "By whom?"

Donovan hesitated. He leaned forward to rest his elbows on his knees, deliberating his words carefully. "Quinn attacked her with a knife," he said finally. "It was a very close call, but Liza is alive."

"And Quinn?" Armand asked, the fervor ever rampant in his voice.

"He's dead," said Donovan.

My mind raced as a dozen emotions flooded my heart at once. Twice in two weeks, I'd felt this insidious shock take over my body and leave me helpless against it, and both times Liza's life had been at stake. Armand and Donovan traded terse words as I tried not to imagine Liza, crying for help and bleeding, at the mercy of a murderous brute like Quinn.

"Where is she?" I asked Donovan, interrupting whatever he was saying to Armand. "Can we see her?"

"James won't let us," sneered Armand. He folded his arms and paced between me and Donovan. "Two near-death scrapes for her in two damn weeks? Liza will never see outside of the Masters' chambers again—"

"You've got to be rational and patient," Donovan insisted. "Two things I know that are difficult for you," he added tersely. I glanced nervously between Donovan and Armand—clearly there was some understanding between them of which I was not privy, because if I'd said something like that to Armand, he would have retaliated at once and eviscerated me whereas Donovan only earned a warning glare from him. I could think of no reason Armand would have let a comment like that slide.

"Liza must recover from her injuries before James will even think about letting you three in to see her," said Donovan.

I knew he was right. "Does Daisy know?" I asked. Donovan shook his head. "Would you mind staying here, when I tell her?"

"Certainly, Kit," said Donovan. Without waiting for any further bitter proclamations from Armand, I went to wake Daisy, who I knew was still in her room. Liza had sent my sketchbook back to us yesterday afternoon and Daisy had spent every hour since holed up in bed, poring over it. It fazed me a little because I was sure Daisy didn't know just how many drawings I'd done of her, but in light of all that had happened, perhaps it would bring her comfort to know that I was so fond of her smile.

I knocked once on her door before letting myself in. "Daze?" I cracked the door open and saw she had fallen asleep sitting up in bed, the sketchbook in her lap, and her blonde hair spilling down her shoulders.

"Daisy," I roused her gently, going to the bedside and reaching down to touch her knee.

"Kit," she sighed, smiling sleepily. "What time is it?"

"You've got to get up and come out to the study," I said somberly. "Donovan's here."

"What happened?" Daisy was immediately alert as she slid out of bed, putting the sketchbook aside. "Kit, tell me," she said, swiping at her hair until she had enough of it to pull back into a slapdash bun.

"It's about Liza," I obliged her. "Come on." I took Daisy's hand and led her out to the den, where Armand and Donovan were seated across from each other. I took it upon myself to steer Daisy to the sofa before breaking the news of the attempt on Liza's life. Daisy went pale as a sheet when I told her about it, and when Donovan detailed the incident, Daisy's features twisted into a mask of sheer horror.

"She's alive," I reminded Daisy, holding tightly to her hand.

"We have to see her," Daisy croaked, sniffling. Donovan passed her a handkerchief and she seized it swiftly, dabbing at her eyes and tip of her nose.

"James won't allow it," Donovan said, apparently having conceded to Armand's sentiment. "Not until she's had time to recover, anyway."

"No." Daisy glared at Donovan with a ferocity I didn't realize she was capable of. "You're a Master. You can get us in to see her. I don't care if she's unconscious or if we can't stay for more than a minute. We must see her, Donovan."

Even Armand seemed impressed by Daisy's intensity.

"I'll see what I can do," Donovan said finally. "I'll be in touch soon."

I waited until Donovan was gone before looking to Daisy. "Please tell me you didn't have anything to do with this."

"What do you mean by that?" Daisy asked, a little defensively.

"You know damn well what he means," Armand snapped, unexpectedly taking my side.

"Armand, please don't curse at her...," I blandly admonished him.

"Ever since you blinked your pretty doe-eyes at Donovan, you've been uncharacteristically quiet," Armand went on, shrugging off my chastisement. "You went from a radical escapist to a docile, model prisoner—am I supposed to turn a blind eye to such a laughable act? Well, I refuse to do it. I see right through you, Daisy. You're trying to escape again!"

"So what if I am?" Daisy asked hotly. She turned to me and softened her tone as she said, "How does that make you think I had something to do with what Quinn did to Liza?"

"Liza sent us back the sketchbook, with some portraits filled in, and you holed up with it for hours; the next thing we hear is she was nearly murdered," Armand supposed, answering for me while leaving the insinuation open-ended. Daisy shrugged in a way that clearly expressed, 'so what?'

"She wasn't attacked in the Masters' chambers, Daisy," I explained. "She was in the gallery, alone. Did she send you a message about meeting up to escape?"

"No," Daisy said deliberately. "Both of you must believe me: I have no idea how Liza could have gotten away from James like that, or what she was doing in the gallery. She could have been hiding, or going to meet someone—"

"Who would she possibly have been going to meet, unless you sent her a message to arrange it?" Armand asked.

"I don't know, Armie," said Daisy. "I swear to you—both of you—I didn't send her a message. Truly, I was too focused on trying to figure out what her message to us means!"

"The portraits she drew in my sketchbook?" I asked. Daisy nodded. "She drew you, James, and Donovan as leading Hamlet characters. Unless she's trying to tell us that James is Donovan's uncle, I don't know what it could mean."

"James? Donovan's uncle?" Armand chuckled and shook his head. "That's ridiculous. There must be something else buried in that message."

"I think she drew me as Ophelia to warn me," Daisy said in a small voice. I could see despair hanging over Daisy like a sepulchral cloud and I took her hand again to comfort her.

"She doesn't want you to do anything foolish," said Armand with an air of confessional to his words. "She asked me to protect you from yourself, Daisy. She doesn't want you to make anything worse."

"Maybe Quinn thought she was me?" Daisy postulated sadly. "I've seen the way he looks—*looked* at me—and I'm the reason James beat his face black and blue."

"And you do practice your ballet in the gallery, sometimes very late...," Armand surmised. He crossed his arms as he contemplated the dark notion. "If one of us were killed, James would be humiliated," he went on. "The scrutiny would ruin him if he couldn't control what went on in his own compound; and with the summit of Masters just a day away, he might have been stripped of his rank."

The three of us sat back for a minute to imagine what it would be like if James were stripped of power. We seemed to share the same sense of gravitas about it. My palms went clammy when I considered how very possible it would be for Quinn to have conspired to murder Liza—or Daisy—in seeking revenge against James. A mere demotion would never justify such violent means, but if James was removed as Master, would his rules go with him?

"We must see Liza," I said aloud, mostly to snap myself out of my reverie. "We need to confirm the meaning of her message."

"What if James doesn't let us in to see her all together?" Daisy asked.

"Easy," Armand replied at once. "He'll let you in to see her. You'll have to field the visit and make sure we get as much information from Liza before James cuts it short."

"Easy?" Daisy and I wondered simultaneously.

"We can't know how Liza will be," I told Armand. "I agree with you, however; he'll allow Daisy to see her."

"So, Daze, it'll be up to you to gauge her state of mind and find out what she meant by those drawings," Armand said decisively, promptly wrapping up the conversation.

Daisy tugged on my hand and chewed on her lip. "What if I can't?"

"Forget about the message," I said. "Liza has been through an inconceivably awful ordeal and she needs someone to tell her that she's not alone."

"I'm sure Jada is with her," Daisy hoped.

"Jada is a liar," Armand refuted. "She doesn't care about Liza, not really."

"How could you say such a thing? Jada adores us!" Daisy exclaimed, stung. Even I made a face at Armand for suggesting that Jada, who has been nothing but kind to us since we'd met her, was a liar.

"She doesn't," Armand insisted vehemently. "She acts like she does, but it's James she cares about. Jada would sell each of us out if it meant gaining approval from James."

"She has to demonstrate blind loyalty to him, just like the rest of them," Daisy pushed back. "But it doesn't mean she's pretending to care about us."

"Keep telling yourself that, sweetheart."

"Enough, Armie," I sighed, frowning up at him. "We shouldn't be bickering like this, not when we came so close to losing Liza again." Armand backed off, seeming to agree with me, and took a seat opposite me and Daisy. The den fell quiet as we all retreated to flicker through the dreary thoughts in our minds.

"Things are so different now," I said after a while. "When have we ever been at odds with each other like this? When have we ever been separated for this long, or seen James this severe?" I looked to Daisy, whose delicate features softened with a very gentle, mournful grace. I felt compelled to tell her how much I regretted partaking in conversations that led to such a disastrous escape attempt, but when the words arranged themselves, a lump rose in my throat.

"You're right, Kit. Things *are* different," Daisy agreed. Tears brimmed in her warm, umber eyes. "The truth is, we are all different, we just didn't know it until Liza jumped out of that window: we're no longer Graham's four perfect little pupils, so caught up in being the brightest and pleasing the instructors that we mistook this place as an incubator of excellence, never seeing it as the cage it really is."

"I would give anything," I said, deftly disguising the quiver of my voice, "to remember even a second of life before we came here."

"Sometimes I dream about my mother," Daisy said, smiling though a tear trickled down her cheek. "I can't ever see her, only hear her voice. She calls me when I'm playing outside." She released my hand to wipe her tear away and sniffed. "It might not be a real memory," she admitted. "Maybe it's just a dream in which I hear a woman's voice, but it feels warm to think of my mother."

My heart sank. I longed for any recollection of even one of my parents, even in dreams, but it was like reaching for a light switch in the darkness and never finding it. Sometimes a certain scent would trigger a sense of recognition, but it never brought on a real memory. I knew Daisy and I were the younger pair, and because we'd been brought to live here when we were still in swaddling clothes, it wasn't my fault that I couldn't remember home; still, jealousy left an unpleasant taste in my mouth. Daisy took my hand again and squeezed it between hers.

"Do you remember anything from home, Armie?" Daisy asked. Armand was no longer crossing his arms, but hugging himself across his chest. His face was stamped with the most peculiar expression: he looked frightened and on the brink of tears himself, but there was a brightness to his eyes that made him look peaceful.

"*Daisy, Daisy, give me your answer do,*" he sang softly. The playful tune was hauntingly familiar; a shudder passed through Daisy's whole body and her eyes widened, more tears spilling down her cheeks.

"What is it?" I asked Daisy. She went rigid and clutched my hand tightly. She was beyond words.

"Her mother used to sing it to her," Armand said, making knowing eye contact with Daisy. "Liza used to sing it, too, when we played together by the river." Daisy took a shaky breath and cried silently.

"My mother used to sing to me too," said Armand. "She'd sing to me in Spanish, not just when she'd put me to sleep, but all the time. In the kitchen when she baked bread, in the yard when I played with Liza. I called her 'mama' but her name is Edita. Papa is Angelo, and I have his eyes."

I was moved almost to pieces by the endearing innocence of Armand's voice, apart from being shocked that he'd kept this trove of memories about our lives outside the compound to himself all this time. I barely recognized the vulnerable boy sitting across from me and Daisy, whose expression was somehow both elated and grief-stricken at once.

"You remember?" I asked as Daisy wept beside me.

"If I close my eyes, I can still see them as vividly as though I'd seen them yesterday," said Armand thickly.

"You never told us?" Daisy sobbed. I reached for her and though she did not recoil when I slipped an arm across her shoulders, she did not relax or take her eyes off Armand.

"Those memories are the only thing I had that were really mine," Armand said. When tears spilled from his eyes, he hastily wiped them away.

"Except they aren't just yours, Armand!" Daisy cried angrily. "They never were, those memories belong to us, too! That song—" She broke off as a sob hitched in her chest. She held the back of her hand against her lips, shielding her trembling, childlike frown from Armand for the sake of her dignity.

"I am sorry," Armand professed. "Daisy, Kit, I am so sorry that I've hurt you by keeping this from you all these years. I was going to tell you—"

"When, Armie?" Daisy demanded roughly. "Which moment were you carefully waiting for to remind us that we used to have families? To prove that we aren't dreaming of falsehoods and ghosts we never really knew?"

"I was afraid of what it would do to you," Armand replied desperately. "You were so fixed on the path of getting out of here, I worried that if I told you I remembered our childhood, it would push you to a reckless escape attempt!"

"More reckless than jumping out of a damn window?" Daisy retorted. She was really angry—she never cursed.

"I couldn't bear the thought of losing the three of you," said Armand, now crying as profusely as Daisy. "Please, you have to know that I wanted to tell you for so long—I *was* going to tell you, but then this escape business took hold of you and I didn't know what to do."

"Maybe if I knew that my mother really loved me, that she used to sing to me and hold me, that she hadn't just given birth to me and sent me here without so much as a second thought, I wouldn't have risked my life trying to escape in the first place!" Daisy cried.

"It would have been too great a risk to tell you," said Armand.

"How dare you?" Daisy fired back in tearful frustration. "How dare you make that decision for us!" She pushed herself off the sofa and quit the room, burying her face in her hands and sobbing as she ran for her bedroom. Armand cursed and bowed his head, smearing his hands across his face. I could see anxiety rack his body as he smacked himself on the side of the head in awful self-resentment.

"Don't, Armand."

"You were right, Kit. I'm a scoundrel," Armand moaned. "This is all my fault. I should have stopped it from the start. I should have told you…." I stood up and went to Armand. I didn't have the heart to agree with him, to tell him *yes*, he should have told me everything he'd remembered from childhood; I just sat beside him and put my arm around him. What could I do, but forgive him? He was my brother and my friend, and I knew better than the girls how he relentlessly tormented himself over this.

"I'll speak to Daisy," I told him. "She's not angry with you, Armie. She'll hurt for a while over it but she loves you."

"You said it yourself, things are different now. She has every right to hate me for this and she knows full well that she doesn't have to forgive me."

"But she will, you'll see. Anyway, why did you keep it from us all this time? We only got it in our heads to try to leave a few months ago. What about when we were kids?"

"I was too convinced that James would find out," Armand confessed. "I wanted to share what I can remember so much, but when I thought about James hearing us sing to Daisy, or hear me talk about my mother…. I couldn't risk it, Kit. I refuse to share the last intrinsic valuable we have—the memory of home—for it's the one thing he hasn't taken from us."

"So you made yourself the protector of our identities? That's a lot of pressure to put on yourself, Armand. Especially when you and I both know that Liza wouldn't have jumped if she'd known—"

"I know that, Kit!" Armand snapped, slipping out of my grasp and getting to his feet. "What do you want me to say? If I'd shared with Liza a sliver of what I know, none of us would be in this position? Well, I already know that it's my own fault everything went awry!"

"No one but you has said that it's your fault," I calmly pointed out. "You've got to stop shouldering everything on your own, Armand. You could have told me and I would have helped leverage some of that burden; who knows, I could have even helped you tell the girls, if you'd just trusted me."

"But do you trust me, Kit?" Armand asked. "Would you trust my judgment if I told you that I *can* shoulder everything on my own?"

His careful syntax perplexed me and there was an urgency in his eyes that hadn't been there a moment ago. "I don't believe anyone can shoulder everything on his own," I replied. "Nor do I believe that he should have to. I'm always going to support you, Armie, you know that."

"I do," Armand replied in a small voice.

"Armand," I said slowly. I locked my features into the most benign expression I could muster and peered up at him. "Is there something else you're holding back?"

"Don't be absurd," Armand said at once. He spoke quickly when he was nervous, so I didn't believe him and I was discouraged that he'd lied to my face.

"Because if there is something you need to get off your chest, you can talk to me." I had to be careful to be gentle when trying to pry the truth from him. "We're only strong when we're together."

"I am not Daisy," Armand said angrily. "You can't feed me that line to make everything rosy; I know better. Maybe if we'd been kept apart, we never would have cooked up the idiotic scheme in the first place."

It was my turn to be stung and angry. "How could you say that, Armand? We have only one thing to cling to in here and it's each other. Liza has been separated from us for a little over a week and she was almost murdered. Do you honestly think we'd be better off apart?"

"Time will tell, I expect," said Armand, shrugging. "We're not likely to get Liza back after what happened. Maybe now we'll have the chance to find out if we're better off apart; maybe we'll all be murdered, and we can have done with this whole damn thing."

I could not tolerate Armand when he focused his turmoil and bitterness outward to protect himself from feeling the extent of his anguish; it made him so unbearably cruel. I'd already seen him throw it in Daisy's face about Liza and now he'd done it to me one time too many. I got to my feet once more and glared into his eyes as all my sorrow and frustration flooded mine.

"If you wanted to be alone, all you had to do was ask, instead of showing your teeth and snapping at me like an animal." Collected as I could muster, I turned from him and made for the door of the apartments, eager to put space between us until I could reign in my temper.

"Where are you going?" Armand asked after me.

"To fetch the guardsmen," I snapped over my shoulder. "Someone should tell them there's a whining volpine in the Tribute wing, wearing Armand's clothes." It was mean but I didn't care. The way he talked about our lives revealed how bitterly savage he was when he was low and I couldn't help but think sometimes that he enjoyed slinging out cruel remarks that would drag the rest of us down to his miserable state.

I wasn't brave enough to tell him to his face that he reminded me of James when he behaved as such. It would both break his heart and enrage him, and while he and I both were trained extensively in self-defense, Armand was stronger than me and he knew it. I wasn't interested in earning a scar on my lip like Liza had from James and more importantly, I refused to lend any input toward Armand's heartlessness. He could sink to a James-like level of brutishness all he wanted but I would rise above it, if only for the sake of keeping us united. Graham was always praising the example I set for the others and admittedly, it did help to pull on his kindly encouragements at times like this. I had to hold out hope to see my parents again someday, however slim the chance was. I would be ashamed to return to them a hand-crafted model of James the Master's making, in manner and of mind.

I set out from the Tribute wing at a good pace. Walking would help me organize my thoughts. I'd walk as many laps around the halls of the compound until the urge to hit something subsided. I didn't realize how grimly I'd been glaring until I rounded the corner and collided with an old man, the force of it practically knocking the stony expression off my face and I hurried to steady the man while frantically apologizing.

"I am so terribly sorry!"

"Watch it, boy!" the old man griped. "It's nearly high noon! The foot traffic is at its busiest and you ought to pay closer attention!"

"Yes, of course." I held out my hand for the old man to take. He scoffed at my hand before looking at me with scornful pale blue eyes. He glanced at my fawn linen shirt and almost immediately, his expression washed over with faint recognition.

"You're a Tribute?" He took my hand and shook it with a forceful grip, much stronger than I would have expected. Now that he wasn't eyeing me balefully, I liked the look of this old man. His features were proud, his eyes were sharp and clear, and his posture denoted good health. He was clearly scores older than me but he hardly looked ancient. His skin wasn't waxy or lined with veins like most elderly people I'd seen around the compound—on the contrary, his complexion was a natural caramel color and the only thing that gave away his age were the streaks of grey and silver in his dark hair. He wore the simple forest green garments of a tradesman and black boots that were scuffed and flecked with mud.

"My name is Kit," I introduced myself.

"Kit, eh?" the old man said. "Never met a clumsy Kit before, but if I've learned one thing in this life, it's that surprises wait around every corner. Would you help an old man like me along the hall?"

"I would be glad to," I said, slightly off balanced by his rapid change in demeanor. "Sir," I added quickly, remembering my manners.

"You have a Master's manners, Kit," the old man said with a chuckle. I controlled my expression carefully so that I did not convey disgust at the old man's try at a compliment. He reached down to pick up a deerskin sack that he'd dropped when I'd bumped into him.

"Be a good fellow and carry this for me, would you?"

"Certainly," I said. I was surprised by how heavy it was and I wondered how he'd carried it this far by himself, though I guessed he might be deceptively strong based on his firm handshake. "Have you come to trade in the market, sir? Maybe I'm familiar with your goods," I said, making polite conversation as I walked beside him down the market hall.

"You would have been a little child the last time I visited this place," the man said. "And besides, what you're carrying for me is not for trade. It's a gift for James the Master—you know where his rooms are, don't you, Kit?"

"I do," I answered uneasily. A gift for James? I felt unsafe and nervous suddenly. I looked around for the guardsmen, hoping to catch one of their gazes and indicate that they needed to alert James, but then I recalled that a line of armed guards would be waiting outside the Masters' rooms anyway.

"It's just this way, sir," I said, turning down the market lane that led to the Masters' rooms. No one seemed to look twice at us, for it wasn't unusual in the slightest for me to walk about the trade floors with a merchant. For all anyone knew, I was arranging to have sheet music brought in for my piano lessons, or exotic spices for Armand's culinary practices. I stole sideways glances at my strange old companion and, based on his bearings, couldn't help but feel that he did not actually need me to show him the way to the Masters' rooms. I debated whether or not I should make an excuse to depart his company, but as the strap of the heavy sack dug into my shoulder, I couldn't think of a polite way to do it.

"Well, sir," I said, slowing my pace just a few yards from the steps up to the Masters' rooms. "James' quarters are that way. You'll need to speak with the guards before entering—"

"Don't pay any mind to those guards, Kit," the old man said. He reached up and put a hand on my shoulder, bracing himself as he started up the steps. I couldn't very well leave him to struggle up the stairs on his own, so I went along with him. We were both a little out of breath when we reached the landing at the top of the stairs, facing a line of confused and annoyed guardsmen.

"These rooms are closed to tradesmen, sir," said a tall guard at the middle of the line.

"As well they should be," said the old man. "One can never know what a tradesmen might track into the hallowed halls of the Masters. Now, *you* must be Quinn's replacement," he said after taking a beat to size up the guard who had addressed us. I balked, as did the guard. How could this man know Quinn, let alone that he had been replaced overnight?

"I am, sir," said the guard.

"Would you care to know how I made such an easy guess of it?" the old man asked, a hint of amused malice in his voice. Without waiting for an answer, he said, "You look nervous, that's how. I could read it on your face from the bottom of the steps."

The new guard did not have anything to say to that. The guard standing beside him, a seasoned soldier of James' named Nathan, stepped in to cover his comrade's fluster.

"It's as he said, these rooms are closed to you, sir," said Nathan sternly. "Kindly move along."

"He said the way is closed to tradesmen, if I recall correctly. I am not a tradesman, and I have business with James the Master," said the old man. He gave my shoulder a pat. "The boy said he'd take me to see him, so let us through."

"Look, Old Timer," said Nathan. "I don't care what the Tribute promised you, we've got express orders from Master James to bar entrance to these rooms to anyone but him and the doctor." Nathan looked to me and glared. "Who is this person, Kit? What business does he have with Master James?"

Before I could respond with a very clear "I don't know," the old man groaned in impatience. "My business with James the Master is none of yours," he growled. "I do not like to be kept waiting. If you won't let us through, I'll have to ask you to send for him at once." I tensed as Nathan and the two guardsmen flanking him came forward—I could tell they did not appreciate taking orders from such a pedantic, snide old man.

"Whom should we say is requesting to see him?" Nathan asked through teeth gritted in annoyance. The old man clapped me on the back and startled me.

"Tell him Kit is here to see him," said the old man, almost cheerfully. "Tell him Kit's here with a gift. That ought to be enough to get us through the doors, eh?" He was baiting Nathan, to my appalled surprise.

"Who should I tell Master James has been escorted here by his Tribute?" Nathan asked, glowering at the old man. The old man raised an eyebrow and smirked. He removed his hand from my shoulder and straightened his posture. He was barely taller than me but his aura towered over us all. A chilly air seemed to radiate from him and it triggered a nauseous sense of recognition in me, but I couldn't place it.

"Tell him Kit has brought Haitham here to see him," said the old man. I saw two guardsmen standing at the end of the line pale immediately.

"Right. Wait here," said Nathan brusquely, rolling his eyes while turning to go and pass along the message to James. I watched the nervous guardsmen hesitate to get Nathan's attention, but they remained frozen in their posts. They looked away from Haitham, the old man, and stared straight ahead.

"Thank you for carrying that all the way up here for me," said Haitham softly to me. I didn't say anything, I just nodded. I was clearly missing something and I was too nervous to see James to respond. Not more than a minute passed before Nathan reappeared, his cheeks flushed with embarrassment.

"Master Haitham," Nathan announced in a thin voice. "Please, come in."

I completely locked up. This man was *Master?*

"Come along, Kit," Haitham the Master said with a grisly satisfied smile. I practically skipped forward when I realized that he'd already taken several steps toward the open door. I'd instinctively gone totally compliant by this startling development and I was not about to test the patience of a Master who could inspire such an instantaneous response from James, whose reputation alone was enough to frighten me.

For the third time in a week, I found myself anxiously making my way down the hall of the Masters' rooms. The walls and ceilings in here were so different than the rest of the compound—even our little apartments—but I couldn't focus long enough to notice each ornate detail of the wood carvings lining the wood paneling of the walls. I kept in stride with Haitham, who was walking down the hall with the careless air of someone who might be sauntering through a dreamscape, not a man going to meet with arguably one of the most unpleasant people on the planet.

Haitham did not halt at the door to knock when he let himself in through a set of ceiling-high wooden doors. I followed him over the threshold but when Nathan closed the door behind me and Haitham, I retreated so that I stood with my back against it. I didn't dare drop the heavy sack to the floor but the strap was really biting into my shoulder, so I gathered it in my hands to alleviate some of the weight.

When I was situated as comfortably as I could be against the door, I looked up and saw that we were in a vast room that resembled some famous old cathedrals I'd seen in books. The ceiling was looming and domed, painted with impossibly beautiful scenes of nature. There were benches lining the walls, placed under stained glass windows whose scenes depicted ferocious-looking beasts in vivid colors. James stood a way down the long room with his arms folded.

He'd just removed his reading spectacles when I caught his eye—he gave a quick shake of his head and narrowed his blue eyes at me before turning his gaze to Haitham.

"I didn't expect to see you this week," James said stiffly.

"I will not be told when to come and go as though I'm one of your staff," said Haitham, crossing the room to a table under one of the many stained glass windows. On top of it sat a silver water basin and a stack of white linens. Haitham washed his hands in the basin and dried his hands with a scrap of linen, not bothering to turn to James when he spoke.

"When I make arrangements to visit another's compound, I like to keep my appointment," said Haitham. "I take abrupt cancellations as a prominent offense, James. Imagine my disappointment when you, my favorite and the most capable of all the Masters, sent word that you decided to postpone the summit?" He shook his head and clicked his tongue, swiveling on the spot so that he could finally look upon James.

"I apologize for the inconvenience," James said. "There was a pressing matter that required my sole attention." This shocked me—James never volunteered an apology, whether or not he was at fault, nor did he ever explain himself. It made me wonder if Haitham outranked James, but I'd never been led to believe that there was such a thing as a hierarchy of Masters.

"I don't give a damn about your apology," Haitham said severely. He glanced at me over his shoulder and chuckled. "And I don't give a damn if the boy hears this—you deserve the embarrassment. Do you know how easy it was for me to get in here? Your guardsmen at the outer gates were impressive, but the ones at the door are downright twitchy. And the way you let your Tributes move around the compound as if they own the place...," He sighed, clicking his tongue.

"I have my methods," James replied dryly. "It's at my discretion to decide how they conduct themselves here."

"You have your methods, and I have mine." Haitham dropped the linen towel to the floor and pushed his sleeves back to his elbows as he went to James. I gasped and clapped a hand over my mouth when Haitham hit James in the side, sinking his fist into his abdomen with a pointed *thud!* and dropping him to the floor. James gritted his teeth and held his breath, not daring to make a sound as he clutched his ribs gingerly. I recalled the volpine bite I'd glimpsed the night Liza had been found. I wondered sickeningly how Haitham would have known about its placement, and subsequently where to aim his punch.

"Do you have any idea the problems you have created for me by postponing the summit?" Haitham asked, standing over James in a gross display of dominance. I didn't dare make a move, as much as I wanted to scrabble for the doorknob behind me and run from the room. "Because of your lack of devotion to our work and inability to control what goes on in this compound, the Village leaders have threatened to defy our accords!"

"Lorena would never allow such a thing," James grunted, keeping his eyes averted. He let out a guttural cry when Haitham kicked him in the side.

"Are you all-knowing, James?" Haitham thundered. "Is that why you can claim for certain that the structural integrity of our system isn't compromised because of you?"

"I am not," James groaned, climbing slowly to his feet. He favored his side as he stood and forced an even expression as he looked at Haitham. "But if I had not postponed the summit, and thereby closed the gates of this compound to outsiders, word of the internal issues I've faced would have gotten out. You must take my word for it, sir. What I did was necessary for the good of us all."

"You've become arrogant." Haitham turned away from James in disgust.

"As you say," James supposed. "But while I am not all-knowing as you suggest, I *can* say for certain that if Lorena's daughter had died, the accords would be nullified and the system would have died in the subsequent revolt."

As Haitham considered this, I carefully let out the breath I'd been holding. I had no idea what they were fighting about—I did not know anything about the crucial accords Haitham mentioned, but I could definitely connect his comment about Lorena's daughter almost dying. It was Liza he'd been talking about, whose mother's name must be Lorena. I wondered if Armand remembered that, too; my anger at him melted away to fear, for I now only hoped I would be able to get out of this room in one piece so I could tell him all this.

"Tell me about the incident," Haitham said, going once more to the basin. He cupped his hands together and dipped them into the water so that he could rinse his face.

"My guardsman, Quinn, stalked the girl to one of her lessons." James glanced at me with a warning glint in his eyes—he knew as well as I did that Liza hadn't been to a lesson in over a week. He was lying to Haitham and urging me to corroborate whatever tale he was about to spin. "He attacked her in the studio with a knife and I dealt with it."

Armand would have commended the lie for having so few details while looping in the true events that transpired. It would be easy for me to confirm the story, for as far as I knew, that had been the case.

"Was she raped?" Haitham asked after he dried his face with a fresh linen towel. Hearing the word forced me to imagine the very action in kind, making my mouth go dry. I despised the casual air with which Haitham said it and it made me queasy.

"No," James returned with similar matter-of-factness. "I got to her before he could try it, but from what I gathered, he was solely interested in cutting her throat."

"Good," Haitham sighed. "Lorena's conditions are very specific in that regard. It would have been a disaster if he'd tampered with the girl."

Tampered? His rude candor stunned me. My cheeks felt hot and I forced myself to keep quiet, for the sentiment behind Haitham's words were utterly despicable and I felt the urge to express my horror out loud. How could he be relieved about keeping to conditions instead of being grateful that a girl had not been so invasively attacked?

"He did cause her serious injuries, with the blade," James reminded Haitham. He eyed me knowingly, reading the scowl on my face as a sign that I was about to speak up. "The lesions on her arms and shoulder needed dozens of stitches—"

"Minor details," Haitham interjected, waving away James' elaboration. "Let the doctors worry about that kind of thing. How long will it take until she's presentable?"

"It's difficult to say," James replied. "I'd have to consult the doctors about those minor details you won't be bothered by in order to put together an accurate time table." I could hardly believe the salty tone of his voice. James had never strayed off the path of strict politeness in front of me like this.

"Ah, there's your spine," Haitham drawled. "I was wondering when I'd see it."

Both James and Haitham turned sharply to face me when I dropped the bag to the floor at my feet. I'd had enough of this. "Excuse me," I said, succinctly emphasizing my manners though my tone was highly inflammatory. "My presence during whatever *this* is—" I gestured between the two of them, "—is clearly unnecessary. I'd like to leave now." James shook his head, discouraging me from speaking, while Haitham let out a mirthless hoot.

"There's nothing quite like the fire of youth, eh, James?" Haitham said. He looked back to me with veiled eyes and a smirk on his face. "It's far too early in the conversation for you to leave us, Kit. I'd like you to stay. I'm interested in your take on a few matters." He took slow steps toward me and I immediately regretted standing with my back to the door, for there was nowhere for me to run. Though it made me frantic, a daring spark of contempt bloomed in my gut. Perhaps it was too reckless of me to take a lead from James, but Haitham's smugness revolted me, especially in the face of how he had just spoken of Liza.

"You've done a marvelous job of being patient so far—was it hearing about Quinn attacking your Tribute friend Liza that got you all fed up? Or like myself, have you heard enough out of James?" Haitham's smirk curled into a grin and he waited for me to reply.

"I believe I've heard enough on all counts, *sir*," I said, perfectly mimicking James' quippy tone from a moment ago.

"You remind me of James, when he was your age," Haitham remarked. "He never knew when to hold his tongue either, but I suppose it's the mark of great potential in a young man to be flippant to his elders." He folded his hands behind his back and stopped short of me, looking me up and down slowly. "If I were your Master," he said, all the brightness gone from his amused expression, "I would take great joy in marring that pretty face of yours for speaking to me like that." He took a step forward so that we were standing nearly nose-to-nose.

"Haitham," James declared. "I must ask you to step away from him." Haitham didn't budge; he just glared into my eyes. I didn't dare blink or look to James, who was carefully approaching us behind Haitham's back.

"They don't have *rape* here at the compound, do they, Kit?" Haitham uttered, articulating the ugly word with a sneer. "I always forget that you Tributes are protected from the hideous truths of the outside world. Do you ever thank your lucky stars that it was the four of you chosen to be here, not some other fortunate children? If you haven't, perhaps you ought to—you might have been all too familiar with the revolting concept, otherwise."

I felt a rush of rage wash over me and I clenched my jaw tightly. I wasn't even sure if I'd be able to summon words with which to describe how much I despised Haitham, not just for writing off the notion that Liza could have been raped, but because in addition to that, here he was trying to frighten me into believing that James had somehow saved us all from that prospect by keeping us from our families.

"Haitham," James said again, spurring him to back away from me.

"Before I forget," Haitham said after a moment, pulling his gaze from me and stooping to pick up the sack I'd dropped at my feet, "I brought you a gift, James." Haitham reached into the bag and withdrew a bundle of tawny fur, flecked with patches of umber and copper. He passed it to James, who took it without question yet made a face as he recognized the material for what it was.

"A volpine skin," he said, turning it over in his hands.

"You think I'd let a monster get away with attacking my only son?" Haitham wondered. James and I both blanched—he was Haitham's *son*?

"You shouldn't have," James gawped uneasily. Whether he meant Haitham shouldn't have gone through the trouble, or said in front of me that James was his son was unclear.

"Every action has consequences, even for beasts," Haitham insisted, clapping James on his bad shoulder. James grimaced and Haitham just laughed. "I couldn't possibly determine which of those foul creatures was the one that got you, so I had them all killed and collected the skin of the biggest one. I thought it might go nicely in your library?"

James, seemingly detached from his own body, nodded. "Of course," he said dully. "Thank you, sir."

"As if I'd ever arrive emptyhanded to a summit." Haitham chuckled to himself. "Now, back to business. I want to see the girl when she's presentable." This latest shift in demeanor befuddled me. I could hardly keep up with

Haitham's violent mood swings, and even James looked to be slightly motion-sick from it.

"It's as I said, I will have to confer with the doctors," said James. "I will be sure to inform you when she is well enough to receive visitors."

"Fine," sighed Haitham, whose current temperament seemed to be an all-consuming impatience. "Go and confer with them, then. Take that skin with you, and tell Donovan that I'll be speaking to both of you after I've had some lunch."

"Would you like to go to your room?" James asked, lingering in place un-easily.

"Later," Haitham said. "I'd like to meditate for a while here, first." He turned and looked expectantly at James. "Excused," he permitted. James hoisted the volpine skin into his arms and immediately quit the long hall.

"Come on," he muttered to me as he reached for the doorknob. I did not need telling twice; I was on James' heels as we left Haitham alone. We bustled into the hallway where Douglas was waiting for us. James dropped the volpine skin and gritted his teeth as he leaned on Douglas, clutching his side.

"My medicine," James groaned to Douglas urgently. Douglas hastily pulled out a small bottle of pill capsules and emptied a few into his hand for James to take.

"Master James, what happened?" Douglas asked in a hushed voice.

"It's nothing, don't fret over me," James hissed. "Get that *thing*," he said, pointing to the skin on the floor beside him, "out of my sight."

"What would you like me to do with it?" Douglas asked, stooping at once to collect the bundle of fur in his arms.

"Burn it."

"Are you sure that's a good idea?" I asked, my eyes wide. I shuddered to think what Haitham might to if he went to the library and did not find that volpine fur. James peered down at me with a somewhat stricken expression on his face, as though he was trying to convince himself that I hadn't just ques-tioned him. Douglas didn't wait for James to affirm his wishes; he just turned and hurried away with the volpine skin in his arms.

"Come with me, Kit," James said quietly, beckoning me to follow him. He took two steps before wincing and holding his side again.

"Are you all right?" I blurted, before I could stop myself.

"To be honest, Kit, I am feeling very put out. As you can see, I have a—*precarious* relationship with Haitham. I do not care for surprise visits from anyone, least of all Haitham; nor do I relish an audience during our encounters."

"I understand why," I said, candidly conveying my consternation. I didn't know where to start, Haitham's violence or the things he said about Liza. And then, there was the whole matter of all I'd heard about Liza's mother Lorena and the accords she evidently had with the Masters. "What exactly are 'the accords'?" I asked. "Lorena is Liza's mother, am I right? What are the conditions of hers that Haitham was so concerned about?"

"Never call him by his first name, not even in conversation," James said, leading me around the corner to another extravagant hallway of closed doors. "To you, he must always be 'sir' or 'Master,' and this is hardly the place to discuss those matters; moreover, you should not have been privy to that conversation in the first place." He checked behind us briefly before opening a door to his left and slipping inside, pulling me in behind him. I was astonished by the enormous and lush greenhouse inside. I hadn't imagined anything this beautiful and peaceful could be within the Masters' rooms. The air was dewy and warm, and over the sound of James locking the door behind us, I could hear birds chirping.

"Now, Kit, listen to me very closely," said James, taking hold of my forearm and looking very seriously into my eyes. "Yes, Haitham is my father," he confessed at once, before I even had the chance to bring it up. "As you know, Masters maintain a status of equality as far as rank goes, but Haitham likes to rely on nepotism to secure his alliance with me. Unfortunately for me, it is not only mutually beneficial, but a very effective way to govern our compounds. It is imperative that you keep everything you overheard between us to yourself—as much as you may be tempted to share the details of what went on to the others, you must not divulge *any* of it to *anyone*."

"He doesn't know about Liza's escape," I concluded. The fear in James' eyes was too telling.

"He does not," James admitted. "Kit, I am not telling you this to frighten you, but if he were to ever discover that I did not sustain my injuries during a hunting accident, that I was hurt trying to find Liza after she escaped, he would not hesitate to take her into his custody."

"What would he do to her?"

"You don't want to know, Kit. But I'm sure you might guess how Liza would be treated under his care, based on what you've seen. Haitham's deciduous temper is nothing compared to the fury of his influence scorned."

I felt sick: Haitham was unequivocally a terror of a man, far worse than James, which was a harrowing realization in itself. My mind immediately went to Armand and Daisy, from whom I resolved I could not keep this development, though it might devastate Daisy irreparably to hear about this. I lingered on Daisy and arrived at an even more risky conclusion—that I now had information at my disposal that would humiliate James, which I would have to use to our benefit. For all Armand's prickly comments, he was right to warn me to be clever about dealing with James.

"I've got to tell them at least a part of this, James," I said. "They've got to know to lie, if pressed about your injury."

James cursed. "Very well."

"But if it helps Liza, I won't tell them anything else. I'll do anything you want if you keep him away from her." That performance would have pleased Armand, for it was a totally truthful mechanism to elicit the same sympathetic trust from James that Daisy had. I was unprepared for the inscrutable glimmer of admiration that shined in James' tempestuous blue eyes. He even frowned sadly, as if he was caught off guard by what he felt.

"You really love her, don't you?"

"I do," I professed. "She's my family, James." I wished his pity wasn't so evident. Maybe if I were Armand, I could have conjured some biting quip to remind him that I was not interested in his compassion.

James shook his head. "I envy you for the freedom you have to love like that. You must take my word for it, Kit, you're a fool to love anyone in this place."

"You're wrong," I said after heaving a nettled scoff at him, speaking for Armand and the girls. "It's the only real thing we have."

"It's compunction like that, Kit, which makes me wonder whether Haitham was right—perhaps I have coddled the four of you." With a renewed fervor to his voice, he added convincingly, "Everything inside these walls is a commodity to be traded or taken, including love. If you harbor it and are foolish enough to think you can keep it to yourself, it is not I who is wrong, but you."

"My love for the others doesn't endanger them, James," I insisted gently, as though I were speaking to Daisy. "It protects them."

"There was a time once when I would say that I hope you're right about that," said James. "But I've been proven wrong myself, many times over." The medicine he took seemed to kick in just then, for he let out a long breath and seemed to loosen some of the tension in his shoulders. "I won't thank you for keeping what happened just now to yourself, you understand? This is a deal, a fair exchange: You keep your mouth shut and I will do everything in my power to protect Liza from Haitham." He offered me his hand.

"And the others—Daisy and Armand?" I added. James took a moment to consider my addendum before nodding.

"Daisy and Armand, too," he relented. I shook James' hand, pumping it twice as we sealed our agreement. James suggested I should head back to the Tribute wing and I nodded, eager to avoid a second run-in with Haitham. He unlocked the greenhouse door and peered out before leading me down the hall to the exit. I thought about all the things I wanted him to tell Liza for us, but I knew he'd just agreed to much more than he liked bargaining for, and any further requests I would make would be shot down.

"Kit," James whispered when we reached the doors that led to the main halls. "About Liza's attack—during the day, did any you receive a message from her about meeting you after hours in the studio?"

"No," I replied.

"Don't lie to me, Kit...."

"It's true, we didn't; Armand and I thought Daisy might have sought to see her, but she swore to us that she knew nothing about Liza leaving the Masters' rooms," I insisted. I watched James closely, wondering what he was getting at.

"Go straight back to your wing," James instructed sharply, noticing my deliberate studying of his features. "Don't stop to trade with anyone, don't engage any of your instructors, just get back to your apartment. And do not, under any circumstance, utter Haitham's name to anyone, do you understand?"

"Yes." I did as I was told and returned to the Tribute wing, hoping no one would notice my unusually serene expression and slow, measured strides. When I entered our wing, I heard Graham's voice coming from the kitchen. I followed his voice and the smell of fresh coffee and saw that Daisy and Armand were sitting across from each other at the table, their faces masks of solemn contempt.

"Hello, Kit," Graham said gravely. "I was just discussing the very upsetting incident that has happened, with regard to Liza." I took a seat between Armand and Daisy, both of whom shot accusatory glances at one another, completely ignoring the discerning look I was trying to pass along. "Liza is being taken care of by the best doctors at Master James' disposal," Graham assured us. "In fact, I would not be surprised if—"

"I went on a walk in the market," I blurted, interrupting Graham. Armand and Daisy peered curiously at me at my off-kilter exclamation. "To clear my head, you know. After hearing about Liza." Graham nodded understandingly while Armand and Daisy slowly began to realize that I was trying to tell them something. "I kept thinking about Hamlet." At once, the aggression was wiped off Armand and Daisy's faces. Their eyes widened fractionally and they paid close, furtive attention.

"About *Hamlet*?" Graham repeated. "The play, by William Shakespeare? That *Hamlet*?"

"Yes!" I replied. "The very one. I was thinking about how much *Liza* reminds me of Ophelia," I said, practically tapping out my true message in Morse Code, that it was Liza who was in danger now, not Daisy as Liza had tried to warn us.

"That is a very grim observation, Kit," Graham scolded. "Especially in light of what's happened to poor Liza—"

"You'll have to forgive Kit," Armand spoke up, hushing Graham. His eyes remained locked onto me. "He has the tendency to be melancholy during trying times. What's on your mind, Kit?"

"Well, I couldn't recall—maybe you can help me, Graham, but was there ever any mention of Claudius's father in the play?" I asked. Armand and Daisy looked puzzled.

"I don't believe there was, Kit," Graham said after a moment's reflection.

"It's been quite a time since I read the play myself. I would have to give the manuscript a glance again to be certain."

"It's just, I wonder, how differently the story would have played out if Claudius and Hamlet's father the king had a living parent," I went on in a measured pace, looking between Daisy and Armand. "A father, for instance. His presence in the court of Denmark would have affected everyone, especially Ophelia."

"Claudius's...*father?*" Daisy echoed, her expression both horrified and still bewildered.

"Yes," I insisted. "That's what I'm saying."

"I'm afraid I don't follow you," Graham admitted, warily eyeing the three of us. The seasoned polyhistor could tell that I was putting weight to my words for a reason but as far as I could tell, he couldn't make out what my message might be. There had been a handful of times when we'd traded secrets under the guise of our subjects in front of Graham, but never under such pressing circumstances. I had to remind myself that as much as I wanted to give Armand and Daisy the true name of whom I spoke, there was too great a chance that Graham would recognize Haitham's name, and then my deal with James would be compromised.

"It seems to be that Ophelia would indeed have been affected by such a character," Graham declared. "Likely for the worse, in my opinion."

"Hamlet would protect her," Armand said with conviction.

"He would," Daisy agreed.

"And what if Claudius promised to?" I asked. Armand and Daisy looked to each other now in addled awe.

"Did he, really?" Daisy asked. I nodded at her, then to Armand. None of us was sure how to react or what to say next. They were clearly reeling from my affirmation that James had promised to protect Liza: in Armand's eyes, I saw disbelief and unease, and in Daisy's I saw fright and relief.

"All right, you three," Graham interrupted with a sigh. "I would leave you alone to speak outside the realm of coded literary metaphors, but Master James has asked me to resume your lessons full time; despite my objections, I think it may be best for you to have an outlet for productive focus."

"He wants us to sit here and study cartography, when Liza is lying in a hospital bed?" Daisy complained. I began to suspect that her forlorn look when I'd come in earlier was not because of her proximity to Armand, but at Graham's announcement that James wanted us put back to work.

"We should listen to him, Daze," I said softly, before Graham could lend a patronizing remark about the importance of pursuing academia. After all I'd seen between James and Haitham this morning, the last thing I wanted was for Daisy to push to visit Liza and put herself in Haitham's path. I had to hold up my end of the bargain and keep Armand and Daisy in line so that James could keep them safe. I deduced it would be far easier to do that within the confines of our wing than risk encountering Haitham out in the marketplace.

"Liza would want us to keep working and stay safe," I added. I reached for Daisy's hand and she let me take it. I peered into her eyes knowingly and smiled gently. "Trust me," I murmured. Daisy returned my smile when I gave her fingers a squeeze.

"Fine," she relented wryly.

"Do we have to study cartography?" was Armand's dry remark.

"Very good!" Graham enthused. He drained his coffee mug and turned to set it in the sink, then back to us to clap his hands together. "And no, Armand, I thought today we would explore a subject involving more arithmetic."

"Even better," Armand sighed with sarcasm.

"In the study, then," Graham declared brightly, leading the way to the study. Armand and Daisy jumped up, both of them setting their hands on my shoulders to whisper in my ears.

"James' father is here?" hissed Daisy.

"What the hell happened, Kit?" Armand whispered urgently.

"Later," I placated them. I didn't realize how badly I'd needed their bracing grasps on my shoulders until I was between them. I wanted to spill it all right there but I knew that we had to play along with Graham, at James' request, if I was to do my part.

"The hell with Graham!" Armand whispered urgently. "He'll wait, and so will the lesson! What happened? Did you see Liza?"

"No," I replied quietly. "I didn't see Liza. But I talked to James, and—"

"Pupils, come along!" Graham called.

"We're just refilling the pot for tea!" Daisy sang, reaching behind her to flip the sink on. "You spoke to James?" she asked, her voice muffled by the rushing water in the sink.

"I did," I said. "He's going to keep Liza safe, but we have to keep our noses down. His father is a Master too, and he's here for the summit."

"I thought James cancelled the summit?" said Armand, folding his arms across his chest.

"He tried to but Haitham wouldn't hear of it." I was so nervous to be overheard that I barely spoke audibly. I doubted very much that either of them could make out Haitham's name clearly.

"We need to talk to Donovan," Armand decided blatantly. I looked to Daisy, who was very pale and chewing on her lip as she leaned against the sink.

"Daisy," I said, reaching for her. "Are you all right?"

"I'm fine," she assured me, welcoming my arms around her. "I'm just trying to imagine what James' father would be like, and I'm at a loss."

"I will tell you more later," I promised. "Come on now, before Graham gets even more suspicious." Armand and Daisy followed me into the study reluctantly. Each of us was fixating on the seemingly insurmountable task ahead, which was pretending to focus on our studies instead of thinking only of James, Liza, and Haitham.

I wondered what might happen tomorrow. The thought of seeing Haitham again filled me with dreadful anticipation, but as I was the only one among the four of us to have seen James, our formidable Master, beaten to the floor—a feat that I never would have believed unless I'd seen it myself—I knew that I would have to remain steady no matter what. I could not unleash my temper like Armand, I could not bottle up my fear until I fainted like Daisy, no—to keep them all safe, I would have to be ready to make the right decisions on all our behalf. It was hardly a comforting resolution, but it gave me strength to think on how crucial keeping to my agreement with James was; and yet, I could not shake the feeling that there was a finality to this deal, that when I had shaken hands with James the Master, I'd somehow sealed my fate.

Chapter Ten

I was curled up in bed, alone, when I awoke from a hazy slumber because of a raw ache in my shoulder. My temples throbbed and I was parched. With every beat of my heart, the pain in my shoulder ebbed, sending flares of discomfort up the side of my neck in dull bites. I didn't even try to move, as adjusting my position might make the pain even worse. I glanced around the wide room at the art on the walls and the portable station set up beside me, then at a sizeable cot set up by the corner where I assumed Jada would move me at some point today. Even looking around worsened my headache, so I decided to lie still and take slow, careful breaths while I stared up at the red canopy hanging over me.

I closed my eyes and saw my blood spilling from the gashes in my arms, spurting in hot gushes all over my chest. I opened my eyes at once and told myself, *stop, breathe,* but my lungs arrested and I was back in the studio, Quinn on top of me, pinning me to the floor, raging at me to stop fighting....

The bedroom door opened and I expelled the strangled breath I'd been holding. James was here, scowling and glaring. He shut the door behind him and leaned against it for a moment. He wasn't looking at me. Perhaps he thought I was asleep, but I watched as his features fell the instant the door shut, giving way to a look so desolate and anguished, it filled me with curiosity. James reached for his side and glanced up, now realizing that I was awake and staring at him.

"How do you feel?" he asked, his voice strained.

"Everything hurts," I croaked, my throat dry and sore. James stepped away from the door, still holding his side, and came over to my side of his massive bed. He reached for the carafe of water on the bedside table and poured me a splash. I winced as I sat up to take the glass from him with my good hand, the one not strapped to my chest, and James put his hand on my back to support my weight as I gulped the water down.

"Easy," he said, helping me slowly lie back down.

"What time is it?" I asked, sounding a little less raspy.

"I don't know," James sighed. He went to the other side of the bed and my gaze followed him. He was almost limping across the room, gingerly favoring his injury. He sat down on the bed and lowered himself into a recumbent position. I tried not to focus too intently on the fact that he was laying an arm's reach away from me.

"I'll take the cot tonight if you wish to sleep in the bed, but I just need to lie down right now," James said after a while.

"As you say." It hurt my neck to turn to look at him but there was something disarmingly gentle about his disposition, which fascinated me. I was underneath the coverlet, but he was apparently too exhausted to pull it back. He covered his face with his hands after heavily exhaling. He then reached into his pocket for the little bottle I'd seen before, and after he twisted the cap off, he rattled two small pills out of the top.

"Here," he said, offering me one of the capsules. "For the pain."

"Thank you." I took it with my left hand, placed the tiny pill on my tongue, and swallowed it. James followed suit, taking a pill before pocketing the bottle. I couldn't help but look back to James, who was staring straight up at the canopy overhead, blinking slowly as he ground his teeth. I didn't want to arouse his temper by questioning him (or by nagging him to stop grinding his teeth) but I'd never seen him so subdued and obviously distressed. The curiosity was almost as unbearable as the ache in my shoulder.

"What happened?" I asked James softly.

"I don't want to discuss it," murmured James. I frowned and did not accept his answer. He was downright shaken and I was so taken aback to see a sliver of vulnerability in him that I had to press him.

"Did you tell the others about last night?"

"Yes," James sighed. "Of course I did."

"And are they all right? Are they safe?"

"They're safe," James assured me. "Liza, please. I really need a few minutes of quiet." I let him have his quiet, which he'd requested at an opportune time, for the pill I'd taken took effect then. The pain in my shoulder receded and my limbs felt pleasantly floaty. My eyelids grew heavy and I relished the lofty buzz that was setting into my body.

I didn't remember falling asleep, but when I rolled my head to the side after waking from a nap, I saw that James was asleep beside me. He was utterly still and on his side with his arm crooked up under his head. How remarkable it was to see him asleep, for when his features weren't guarded and stern, or even glaring at me, James looked peaceful and actually much younger than I perceived him to be.

A soft triplet of knocks sounded at the door. I waited for James to notice and stir, but when he didn't, more knocks came, though they were more like respectful taps than anything.

"James."

"What is it?" he murmured, his eyes still closed. I doubted he was really even awake.

"James," I said again, "Wake up. Someone's at the door." He stirred a little, blinking his eyes a few times. The knocks sounded at the door again and then he was wide awake, surprised as though he'd forgotten that I was in his room to begin with.

"Shit." Suddenly he was sliding out of bed, mussing his hair as he hurried to the door. He cleared his throat to rid his voice of its drowsy slur and pulled the door open. "What is it?" he said brusquely.

"Master Donovan is waiting for you in the library, sir," said Douglas, whom I could not see past James through the narrow opening of the door.

"Very well," James said. "I'll be along shortly." He shut the door and turned back to me. "I have work to see to," he explained, going to the looming wooden wardrobe on the other side of the room. He pulled it open and yanked out a fresh shirt, then proceeded to hastily change out of the one he was wearing. I looked away hastily upon seeing his bare chest, though the awful bruises on his ribs drew my eyes.

"I'll return with dinner. Until then, I'll send Jada along to check on you. I'll see if she'd be willing to bring you some books or something to pass the time—do not get out of bed without her here and do not leave this room."

"As you say," I replied. James shut the door of the wardrobe and turned back to me.

"I have matters to discuss with you when I return," he said. "Please try to rest, Liza."

After he left, I was alone with nothing to distract me from the nagging memories of Quinn's assault. I felt much better after the drowsiness of the pain pill wore off because I felt rested and it still kept the pain at bay. I dared to sit up and was relieved that the pain in my arm did not flare at the shift in position. My headache was still there, but sitting up seemed to be all right. James told me not to get out of bed without Jada present: if I got dizzy, I would fall again and either hit my head or pull my stitches trying to catch myself, so instead of getting up, I swung my legs off the side of the bed and reached for the carafe of water. I drank until every last drop was gone and felt incredibly full.

The doorknob to James' room turned but remained closed. Whoever was trying to open it bumped against it, startling me on their impact. My heart galloped into a sprint and my mind whispered hateful, panicked assumptions in my ear that promised the return of an assailant with a blade, who had just been waiting for James to step away to try once more to kill me.

Several knocks sounded on the door. "Master James, it's the doctor!" called Jada in a muffled voice. I audibly sighed and put my hand to my racing heart. She must have forgotten her key and tried to push the door open while it was locked. I got out of bed, technically disobeying James even though Jada was just outside. I reached the door and twisted the lock underneath the knob. I opened the door to see Jada standing there, looking puzzled.

"Liza, you shouldn't be out of bed. Where is Master James?"

"He said he had work to do," I replied. "The door was locked. I thought he said you were the only one allowed in here besides himself. Is there something wrong with your key?"

"I suppose so," said Jada, after trying her key again on the open door. "He must have changed the locks and neglected to give me a new key. Come on, let's get you back into bed." She helped me back to bed even though I insisted I'd gotten to the door by myself. "You've got some color back in your cheeks," she noticed, flashing a smile. "You sound tired, though. Have you gotten any sleep today, honey?"

"Some," I supposed. "I was thirsty when I woke up but I'm not hungry."

"You may not be for a time. The painkillers in your system will interfere with your appetite," explained Jada. She took my pulse, carefully checked my blood pressure, listened to my heart, and pressed against the right side of my ribcage with a gentle hand. When I winced, she withdrew at once and gave my good shoulder a reassuring pat.

"I'm sorry, honey," she said. "I had to check your ribs for bruising, but I think they're just a little sore. That's a relief, huh? One less thing to worry about!" She went to her bag and withdrew a small metallic square with a screen and a few buttons on it. "Master James asked me to bring you something to keep you busy, and since you might find holding a book with one hand to be something of a struggle, I brought you some music." Jada set the little device in my lap and pulled a long black cord out of her pocket that forked almost at the end, with two little buds on the tips.

"I asked Graham to program it," Jada told me. "He put on all of Kit's piano pieces and dozens of other tracks that he thought you would enjoy."

"Thank you, Jada," I mumbled, turning over the metal square in my hand.

"Listen, Liza," Jada said softly, sitting on the edge of the bed. "I wanted to say how sorry I am that you've suffered so much, in just a week. As someone who has devoted her life to helping others, it breaks my heart to see you in pain like this. What Quinn did was just...." She shook her head and gesticulated helplessly. "He was not a bad man, but sometimes, in the minds of men, that lifeline which holds them back from inhumanity just snaps."

"Or they're pushed to it," I offered bitterly. "James beat him senseless because of what I did."

"What happened to Quinn was not your fault, Liza. Quinn knew the responsibilities and risks of his job when he signed on to work for Master James. He was aware of what would happen if he failed to uphold his duty, and that as a Master, James must deal out the punishment in accordance with the severity of his misgivings—"

"Could you please stop talking about it like that? You don't have to outline his contract to me, Jada, I know exactly what happened. I ran away, Quinn couldn't catch me, and James took it out on his face. Of course Quinn hated me after that! He hated me enough to try to kill me, and the prize at the end of it would be humiliating James for being an inadequate Master!"

Jada sat back and pursed her lips sheepishly. "I didn't mean to upset you," she said. "Sometimes it helps to look at a situation with clinical eyes; it leaves less room for troublesome emotions. If I look at what Quinn did to you in terms of his role here at the compound and the consequences of his actions, it makes it possible for me to remain calm and move forward. It's a method of coping that you might find helpful, Liza."

"It doesn't seem all that simple to me," I said, still vexed. I took a moment to consider Jada's advice all the same, though her method of coping, as she put it, seemed to strip Quinn of his humanity. I remembered with a shiver how heavy he was on top of me, how he'd gritted his teeth in the struggle, how he'd sweated and cursed me, and then the wet snap of his neck—Quinn was not the product of an occupational mishap, he was a living, breathing, mad dog beaten by his owner, who attacked the object of his rage the first chance he could get off his leash.

"What were you doing in the studio, Liza?" Jada asked. "How did you end up there, with Quinn?"

"I already told James, I wasn't sleeping with Quinn." If the topic wasn't such an inflammatory one and if Jada wasn't the person asking me about it, I would have felt guilty about being so waspishly defensive.

"I didn't think you were," Jada replied. I could tell my biting remark had ruffled her feathers but at the same time, I got the impression that she was smug to have my validation about what she'd assured James. She waited for me to answer her question all the same. I nervously weighed my options and remembered that a large part of Jada's success as the Aventine's head doctor was her dependable discretion. I decided to confide in Jada in the hopes that she might share what I was about to say to James in a way that would at least somewhat lessen his furious reaction.

"A note was slipped under my door. It was from Daisy, saying she wanted to meet me in the studio at midnight." I felt sick again when I remembered how worried I'd been that Quinn had hurt Daisy or the boys before me.

"What happened to the note, Liza?" Jada asked.

"I—oh," I had begun to say, but I realized that I couldn't recall. Had I burned it? Ripped it up? "I don't remember."

"Liza, are you certain?" asked Jada. "The note said, specifically, that you were to get to the studio at midnight?"

"Yes," I said. "I told you, I don't remember what I did with it. If you let me out of my room, I suppose I could search for it—"

"You leave that to me," Jada said sternly. "Master James would have my hide if I let you out of here, regardless of whether or not I escorted you. No, you just rest and let me handle this."

"I have had it with you talking to me like a child, Jada!"

"I apologize for that, and assure you it's not my intention to coddle you, far from it. You have had two brushes with near-death in less than ten days, Liza, and that requires a level of patience and practicality on my part. Your place is right here, where you can be safe while you recuperate. I promise you, I will go to Master James and see to this note business, but you need to stay put and rest."

I wanted to bite back at her but I kept my mouth shut. She was no better than James; she only wanted to maintain her position of power and use it to control the people below her. I didn't have the strength to fight with her. I just laid back in bed and looked away from Jada, back to the canopy overhead.

"I am sorry, Liza," Jada said again. She stood up from the bed and touched my arm. "Would you like me to help you bathe?" I wanted to reject her peace offer but I craved the hot water of a bath and stubbornly agreed. Around the gauze on my forearms, Jada wrapped a bright green, translucent plastic film that she said would keep water from soaking the bandages. She took the sling off my right arm and helped me undress. The joint in my elbow creaked as I carefully extended my arm, but the pain in my shoulder was still manageable. When I was naked, I looked at myself in the mirror of James' bathroom and saw a dark spot on my side where Quinn had jammed his knee. There were still bandages dressed over the contusion on my shoulder, so I couldn't see how bad it was.

The hot water felt wonderful on my tired limbs. Jada sponged my back and washed my hair for me, thankfully not with the strong lavender soap that my guest room in the Masters' chambers had been stocked with. I liked the minty citrus scent of it, which helped me relax and let the tension out of my shoulders. Once I was out of the tub and dry, Jada helped me dress in a clean set of pajama-like garments, comfortable fleece pants and a short-sleeved cotton shirt that exposed the bruises in the crooks of my arms from the needles Jada likely stuck me with last night.

Jada helped me put my sling back on and explained that she was less worried about me ripping my stitches now and more concerned that I might hurt the muscle in my shoulder that had been cut. She told me that if I was careful and restful over the next three days, she would allow me to take it off for sleep. She steered me to the cot she'd rolled in from the hospital, but I remembered that James had offered to take the cot tonight. I was hardly being spiteful, but I liked to have the canopy over me. Jada tucked me in and gave me another dose of pain medicine for the evening.

"If there's anything you need, you can page me by pressing the blue button on the portable station," said Jada. "Though you may need to get up to let me in, until Master James gets me a new key."

"Thank you, Jada," I said, though it took some effort to contrive graciousness. She left and I busied myself with the handheld music device she'd left me. I found solace in the soft piano tunes that played through the earbuds, recognizing the ones Kit favored and always played in the den of the Tribute wing. The medicine Jada had given me was effective and did not bring on the rush of drowsiness like the pill James had given me. Without the bother of pain digging into my shoulder, I felt restless. I spent several minutes trying to detangle the cord of the earbuds, becoming frustrated after just a few seconds to only have one clumsy hand at my disposal. With dark thoughts in mind, I left the cord how it was and got out of bed, turning up the volume so that I was drowning in the melodies of Brahms and Bach. I took a turn around James' room, peering up at the paintings on his walls, pushing away all the recognizable styles and artists from my studies so that I was only noticing the blend of colors and the sense of isolation conveyed on each canvas.

There were bold streaks of reds and blues in the large painting I found to be particularly evocative, between two shrouded windows by the bed. The painting depicted a sunset over the ocean from a high vantage point, which made me wonder, was this like the landscape I'd painted in my Master suite? I glanced around, finally finding a switch near one of the windows. I flipped it and triggered the curtains to automatically rise.

Once again, my breath left me in an awed whoosh. I was looking over an ocean so bright by the reflected sunlight that I had to squint my eyes to see out. I pressed my hand to the thick glass of the window and drank up the sight of it—the water stretched out all the way to the horizon, the entirety of its vast body glittering in waves of light. The sky was brilliantly blue and through the glass of the window, I could feel the warmth of the sun on my skin, if only slightly.

I went to the cot on the other side of the room and picked up the pillow and top coverlet, dragging them across the floor to make a new blanket nest under the window. I carefully lowered myself down, mindful of my sore shoulder and forearms, until I was lying on my side. The music playing lent the view a majesty that moved me to tears. I cried softly and stared out at the ocean until I fell asleep, despite the blazing light showering me.

I woke up what must have been hours later, I knew because the sunlight was gone; I was not on the pile of blankets by the window, but back in James' bed. I sat up and looked to the windows, frowning to see that the curtains had been lowered.

"I told you to stay in bed," James said, emerging from the bathroom. He was wearing fresh clothes and his hair was wet; he must have just bathed.

"Jada came by earlier," I explained. "You gave her the wrong key, so I had to get up to let her in." James pointed to the blankets on the floor and gave me a look that seemed to say, "Try again." I glared right back at him. "I was restless. I didn't have anything to do, so I got up to look at your paintings."

"That you could have done in bed. If Jada couldn't get into the room, she should have come to me."

"I'm glad I got up to let her in," I said defiantly. He was making me explain myself and I finally felt rested enough to argue with him. "She patronizes me worse than you do, but at least she gave me music to occupy myself—"

"Another activity you could have done in bed," James interrupted in laconic agitation. "Liza, I do not dole out orders for my own enjoyment—"

I muttered, "Could have fooled me...."

"Liza," James snapped, his features hard. "Stop it. I simply do not want to risk you hurting yourself, so I will remind you again, you are not to be out of bed without Jada's supervision."

"Then why not move me to the hospital ward?" There was no grievance backing my words, it was an honest question. "Post a battalion of guardsmen there, where Jada and her staff can supervise me from sunup to sundown!"

"Because, Liza," said James shortly, "you have already proven that I could post a squadron of guardsmen outside your door and you would find a way to disregard your safety and almost get yourself killed. You have made it abundantly clear that the only way I can ensure you will not do something like that again is if you are literally within my reach."

"It's because of your guardsman that I'm in this condition in the first place," I said with a scowl, despising the very domineering sense he was making.

"Had you not slipped out from under Douglas' watch, perhaps you wouldn't be."

"Did Jada tell you about the note? The one from Daisy that was slipped under my door, asking me to meet her in the studio?"

"She did," James replied. "I spoke to Kit earlier, he denied any involvement."

"But have you asked Daisy?" While I did not want him harassing Daisy, it would prove that I was not delusional.

"No, Liza, I did not," James said. "I had your room searched for a message and none was found, and I don't believe Daisy would be foolish enough to pull off a stunt like sneaking out after hours—there is evidence in spades to prove that's more your style."

"I'm telling you," I said angrily, "I did not imagine it!"

"Quinn must have written it! He was a churlish brute at the worst of times but he was not an idiot. He could have easily figured out that the best way to lure you away from protection and into the open would be to pose as Daisy and arrange a clandestine meeting!"

"And you think Quinn's sausage fingers could hold a pen deftly enough to copy Daisy's handwriting perfectly? Down to the last letter?"

"Clearly, I underestimated him," said James bitterly.

"You have an answer for everything, don't you?" I retorted, becoming shrill as my contempt for him burned in my stomach.

"I suppose I do!" James sniped back. I considered getting out of bed just to provoke him but instead I took up the music device that was on the bedside table. I ripped the cord out of the port and thrust the bundle at James.

"If I had the use of both my hands, I swear I would strangle myself with these just to spare myself another poisonous word from you!" Tears of frustration brimmed my eyes to their lashes. James crossed the room in a few sweeping strides and snatched them out of my hand.

"You must never speak of such a thing, Liza," he demanded, tossing the tangled cord behind him and grabbing my upper arm. "*Never*—do you understand?"

In an act of unprecedented boldness, I reached up and seized a fistful of his shirt tightly in my hand. I yanked him toward me, straining the sore stitches in my arm. "Why do you care so much about my life?" I shouted, in tears and a ragged voice that did not belong to me. James was plainly startled, so much so that he forgot to threaten me into releasing him. He did not glare when he looked into my eyes, he just stared sadly at me, speechless. I wanted to scream at him, to dare him against pitying me, but I too was beyond words. All my strength failed me as I sobbed, keeling forward so that my face was buried in his chest.

I asked him, "Why?" over and over, inconsolable. James put his arms around me but did not say a word. He was mindful of my shoulder, so he did not hold me tightly, like I wanted him to. Armand would have squeezed me until this torrent of grief passed. Thinking of him made my heart ache and I cried even harder.

"Liza," sighed James after a while of this. "Please don't cry." I gasped for breath and loosened my grip on his shirtfront, but I couldn't seem to stop. "Liza," James said again. "I'm sorry." He held me a little tighter, suspending the sinking feeling in the pit of my stomach. His arms were bracing and strong, and I didn't feel like I was fading away when they were around me. My weeping subsided after a time. James gently withdrew his arms and reached into his pocket for the bottle of pills, taking one out and handing it to me. I was still shaking from unevenly breathing, but I took it and popped it into my mouth. I took the glass of water James offered me and swallowed the little capsule, forcing myself to finish the rest of the water, too. I laid down and James helped me arrange a pillow under my slung shoulder.

Not another word was spoken between us. I laid very still in bed for a long time, managing the hitched breaths that slowly became sparse as I calmed down. James dimmed the lights so that only the light on his side of the bed was on, and he sat up beside me with a book in his lap. He ignored the knocks at the door, Jada first and later the servants with dinner. Neither of us were hungry. He didn't bother trying to convince me to eat, not when he knew he wouldn't touch a scrap of food himself.

The only warning I had that the medicine had taken effect was the sudden regulation of my breathing and a deep calm that set in to every muscle. I fell asleep and was relieved to find the dreamless void of drugged slumber. Everything melted away into it until I was blissfully alone in a heavy, warm state of mind.

When I woke up, the room was still dark and there was no daylight peeking out from behind the curtains. I guessed that it must have been the small hours, but James' bedside light was still dim. I turned to look for him and was surprised to see he was watching me with glistening eyes.

"How is your pain?" James asked softly, in an impossibly small voice.

"Dull," I replied in a murmur. I studied his expression, the body language portrayed in his posture. "And how is your pain, James?" It wasn't cheek, it was a real question. Every perceptible detail indicated he was in anguish, but what was the cause?

"I don't think I've ever been so perpetually surprised as I have been over the past two weeks," said James. He was almost wistful when he spoke, but his eyes were teeming with sorrow as he looked into my eyes. "This circumstance—" he gestured to me, and the very short space between us, "it's unorthodox, even by my standards. This whole ordeal has me at a loss: I find it frustrating and exhausting. After all the years I've maintained my status as a Master successfully, because of my ability to foresee problems before they arise and orchestrate preventative solutions…yet now, consistently, I find myself floundering to stabilize us all."

"You pride yourself in your work," I offered.

"No, Liza," James was quick to correct me. "I am careful to never take pride in what I do. Pride leads to carelessness, and that is an unacceptable trait in a Master."

"That sounds like rather a harsh edict."

"Something my father taught me," murmured James. "It's because of him that I am in this position. And consequently, so are you." He crossed his arms and cleared his throat. "Because of my father, I know how to deal with pain. I know how to deal with many ugly facets of life in this place, but guilt...."

I grew more and more anxious. I wondered if he'd taken one too many painkilling capsules? He was hardly unhinged, but seeing him so vulnerable was downright chilling, and I'd heard enough from the tradespeople in the market to know that it was never a good sign for a man to sit up late at night and talk in dark, vague, broken sentences of his father.

"We've fought over your life so many times over the past week, I've lost count. Believe it or not, Liza, over each passing day when I have to arrange for a new drastic safety measure, it wears on me in a way I didn't think it could. Then after you were brought back from the forest, you asked me why I had bothered to save your life; I did not bother to answer your question. After Quinn tried to kill you, I didn't know how else to guarantee your safety than to keep you with me." James looked into my eyes for a long moment before looking away. "I can see in your eyes that you're in pain far worse than I am, and it's got little to do with the wounds in your arms," he said, sparing the bandages around my arms a glance. "Guilt is something that cuts deeper than any blade ever could."

"What has guilt got to do with it?" His speech had captivated me and I found myself hungry to hear him finally explain himself.

"You said you wanted to strangle yourself," James reminded me bitterly. "I can do everything in my power to stop you from jumping out another window, or be attacked by a guardsman, but I'm afraid I don't have a protocol for stopping you from surrendering your will to live. I've told you many times that your life has value, but it's apparent that my word isn't enough to convince you that your survival is crucial. Only the truth can do that, I see it now." His words were strings tied to me that pulled me upright like I was a puppet. I bit the inside of my cheek when the sutures in my shoulder strained painfully as I sat up, making my eyes water, but I would not break eye contact with James. As he held me in his gaze, for the first time, he was just as vulnerable as I was. I could scarcely breathe, I was so terrified for what he was about to say.

"I lied to you," he confessed. "When I told you about your parents sending you to live here: they did not send you, you were brought here. I was just fifteen years old, a kid, when I went with the Masters to campaign in the outer territories nineteen years ago. You were just a toddler, only three years old, when we went to the Village to negotiate with the leaders of the Free Factions."

I didn't dare interrupt. What if he lost his nerve and fell silent? James noticed the lost look in my eyes and explained, "After the Quake, those who staked a claim on the wild northwest region of the Masterlands came together and called themselves the Free Factions. They pledged themselves to be vessels of liberty instead of preservation and peace, the pillars on which the Masters built their standing. When the Masters held the very first summit almost fifty years ago, it was to take the responsibility of regulating the continent. The Free Factions rejected the proposed new system because of how they valued freedom and refused to partake. Even outside of the system, the Free Factions continued to outnumber the Masters by a landslide, which gave them majority advantage in their resistance. For thirty or so years, we lived separately by our own systems, on very brittle functioning terms. Both sides began to waver, as the Free Factions fell victim to invading colonies and the Masters' essential supplies diminished. The Masters of the time knew that the only way to survive was to unify the population as a whole—they came up with a creative solution to the problem by looking past the masses of the Free Factions and instead focused on winning over their leaders, your parents."

"My parents?" I echoed in stunned disbelief.

"Yes," said James. "Officially, they were eight of the audacious, most persuasive yet upstanding members of the Free Factions, but it was widely known that only two within the group were able to pull rank among the others: Your mother Lorena and her brother—Kit's father—Marshall. The other leaders are the di Felces and the Blackburns, Armand's and Daisy's parents."

"Kit is my cousin?" I yelped.

"He is," said James, nodding.

I was speechless—I almost killed myself to get back to my relatives and one had been sleeping across the hall from me this whole time.

"The Masters knew that the best chance they stood of swaying the Free Factions to agree to the new system was to go directly to Lorena and Marshall and make their case. They sent an envoy of their best diplomats and their lead negotiator, a promising Mistress named Petra. My sister." James paused and reached up to touch the bridge of his nose, an action I always associated with the levies of his temper breaking, but in light of the current subject matter, perhaps it was more to do with a deeper emotional qualm of his.

"She's Donovan's mother," I said. James hardly seemed surprised to hear that I knew about their relation.

"Indeed," he said. "She was my older sister. I was fifteen when we lost her; Donovan was only eight."

"You lost her?" I asked. "She died?"

"You see," James explained further, "the Free Factions are even more protective over their land than I am of mine. The Masters waited for Petra to send word from within the Kingsfield Township, the seat of your parents' compound, but none came. She was gone for almost a year before we heard she had been arrested by the Factions for trespassing on their land and was being held in the Village—their laws were clear: Masters were not permitted on their lands, let alone anywhere near their compound. The Masters reached out to treaty peace with your parents, not only to bargain for Petra's release but to settle the discontent between them.

"It was the first summit held away from here and the only one since. I was too young to take part in the summit, as decreed by the system's laws, but one of the Masters, my own father, convinced the others to take me along; I heard him extol my intelligence and capability, assuring them that I would be a Master someday and should participate in this pivotal negotiation, but I knew he only wanted me along because I would obey any and all orders he would give me. My father was always one to break his own rules, in the sense that he condemned pride in Masters but he himself was too proud to let his daughter be held by his rivals, people whom he believed to be savage and liberal to a fault. So, my father made me his failsafe in getting Petra back from your parents— to what end, I did not know at the time.

"We were reluctantly allowed into the Village for the summit. The compound in Kingsfield was a crude one back then, swarming with armed guards and volpines they'd trained to guard the grounds. Your parents were young ones, just ten years my seniors, when I met them. They treated me with much less severity than they did the Masters because I was young enough to show no threat to them. I was able to move about as I pleased, unlike the Masters, who were watched with fastidious care. The negotiations went on for days, until one night my father came to me with a task.

"'It's time to crush the dissent of these people,' he said to me. He told me what to do and I obeyed him, as I always did."

I watched James in horror as he swallowed a lump in his throat and forced himself to look into my eyes.

"While the Masters and the Factions leaders sat across from each other, debating the new system, I stole four sleeping little ones from their beds and took them in haste with a company of Master guardsmen out of the Village, to this compound."

"You carried me in yourself." Tears spilled over my lashes and down my cheeks. I felt sick. I could hardly breathe.

"I did," James said. "As soon as the summit concluded that day, my father and the Masters left what belongings they'd brought and hastily followed my trail back to this compound, the location of which was kept secret from the Factions. Minutes after the Masters escaped, your parents found the empty nursery. They rallied their forces to chase us down and get you back, but they found a final offer fixed to the gate of their compound: 'Pledge to the system or your children will die.' Your mother, Lorena, sent word that she would agree to our terms on the spot while, in a rage, Marshall went to my sister's detention quarters and murdered her.

"Despite the gross treachery that took place on both sides, the decision to fold to the Masters was unanimous. Your parents would not risk the lives of their children, and no one in the Factions would ask them to. So, they sent conditions under which the Masters must keep the four of you. Should any of the conditions go by the wayside, the treaty would be nullified and they would wage war on the Masters. Even Lorena vowed she would raze the new system to ashes if any harm ever came to you children, regardless of how much innocent blood would be shed in the process.

"My father refused to accept the conditions, in light of what Marshall had done to Petra, but the Masters overruled him and made me Master of this compound as a reward for what I'd done to secure the Free Factions' forbearance."

Ringing silence deafened me. Heartbroken, I wept silently. The grand truth of our life here was more hideous than I could have imagined. I was sitting beside the very man who had stolen me from my crib as my parents were in talks with the Masters for peace. I was dizzy and in pain. I could not bring myself to speak a syllable.

"If you'd fallen to your death, if you'd died in the woods, if Quinn had killed you…if you even tried to kill yourself, it would all be undone." James was fighting himself to keep from succumbing to my contagious grief, to the point that he was raspy. "That's why I care so much about your life, Liza. Because it is my responsibility to keep you alive, for the sake of everyone in this compound and outside it."

"And they call us 'Tributes'?" I asked, gutted. "As though we're equal to the volunteers whose cities send to work for the Masters every year? As though we're not living, breathing expiations that enforce our parents' obedience?" James did nothing but shake his head. I reached up to wipe the tears from my cheek with consternation. "I suppose calling us what we are—*hostages*—would send the wrong message to the blindly ignorant people who pass through here every day?" The fires of anger burned deep within me and I scrambled out from under the covers to get to my feet.

"Does Jada know?" I demanded desperately, glaring at James as I continued to cry. "Does Graham? Does everyone know that you earned your title *James the Master* because you followed orders that took babies away from their parents?"

"Of course they know."

"So every time they look at us, they see the bargaining chips you stole?" I paced away from him, holding tension in my abdomen to keep from doubling over. I was on the edge of hysterics—I could not stop imagining James creeping into my nursery and lifting me into his arms, a child coveting another child, for the sake of resolving a governmental squabble. Worse yet, it was not for fear of James that his laws were followed, it was because every person who traded in the marketplace and lived under his protection was devoted to the very system that put him in place.

"Liza, I am so sorry." James got to his feet slowly and started to come around the bed.

"Stay away from me!"

James froze on the spot and held up his hands, just like he had that night in the library. "Liza, please, I know this has hurt you terribly, but you must calm down—"

"Go to hell!" I snarled.

"I'm already there, Liza," said James, derelict and somber as he looked into my eyes. "This is not the life I would have chosen for myself. I know you won't believe me but I know what it feels like to be trapped and helpless. Do you think I don't wake each morning to regret the things I did all those years ago?"

"No," I snapped. "I don't believe it for a second!"

"I do, Liza," James said gently. "But regret cannot undo the past. This is not the life I wanted, but it's the only one I have. The only thing I can do is my job—protect the innocent people that depend on this compound and its security to survive."

"I want to leave," I said simply. I was shaking with fury and anguish. I felt wild when I looked at James, far more wild than I had the night I'd leaped from the open library window.

"You know I can't let you go."

"You can! You took me away, you can let me go! Let me go, James!"

"No," said James. "I cannot. I will not."

Wailing, I went for the door. I caught the doorknob in my hand and turned it, but the door would not budge. Through tear-blurred eyes I looked up and saw James had his hand braced against the door, stopping me from pulling it open. With my one good arm, I tried to shove him away. He was even sturdier than the door.

"I hate you!" I screamed. "Let me out!" I hit him in the face and he winced when my nails scratched his cheek. He didn't stop me from hitting him a second time but when he saw my eyes seek out the spot on his chest where the volpine bite was, he grabbed my arm and held me back.

"Let go of me!" I struggled to free myself from his grasp but with one arm pinned to my chest in a sling, I was once again helpless against him. I kicked at him, lost my balance, and fell; James bent to catch me and effortlessly hoisted me into his arms.

194

"Stop, Liza, you'll pull your stitches," he said loudly, over my baleful crying.

"I don't care!" I sobbed. "I want my mother!"

"And she wants you," James said, straining to hold me as I wriggled in his arms. "She wants you whole, Liza. You've got to stop this or you're going to hurt yourself!" He shifted his hold on me so that he could swing my legs up and carry me.

I kicked and screamed in his arms. "Hurt me! Hurt me so you break the rules too! Hurt me so you can send me back!"

"No, Liza. I won't." James carried me back to the bed, but as he hushed me, I realized that my efforts to get him to drop me were futile. Where would I go if James let me out of this room? The hall only led to another set of locked doors, through which I would not get far. I'd learned already that I was just a little bird in this vast, labyrinth of a cage, whose feet were bare, whose wing was broken—I was a bird who had no chance of getting back to her mother's nest.

Panic as raw as the winter snow that had almost frozen me to death set into my limbs. I suffocated on the realization—there truly was no way out. James set me on the bed and I laid there, limp, broken by the things he'd told me. I put my head back and covered my face with my hand, sobbing in mournful, ebbing waves to try to expel the sorrow pooling in my heart. I cried until I couldn't hear myself anymore. I rolled to my side when my breaths became too hitched for me to lie still and slowly, the pain faded away into sleep.

I tossed in a fitful sleep for hours. Twice, I woke up covered in sweat, crying out as Quinn hunted me in my dreams. I was vocal enough in escaping my nightmares that I roused James, who reached out to touch my back and murmur to me until I came to long enough to realize that I'd been dreaming. By the time I opened my eyes and saw sunlight dimly shining through the cracks in the curtains, my face was swollen from crying and my throat was dry like sandpaper. I sat up with a groan, the stiffness in my shoulder surging painfully as I moved to get out of bed.

I took the carafe of water and drank directly from it, downing its entire contents before setting it back down with a loud clang. I looked around the room and saw that I was alone. Just as well, I thought, for I wasn't sure what I would do if James tried to apologize again.

I got up and slowly padded to the bathroom. The mirror was steamy; James had clearly showered recently. I wiped away so that I could see my reflection and was not surprised in the least to see a wan, puffy-eyed shell of a girl staring back at me. I wondered if I looked like my mother, Lorena, and was crestfallen when I realized that I would never see her myself to determine the extent of my likeness to her. The sling fitted across my chest felt too tight and I yanked on the straps until it was slack enough to pull off. I dropped it to the floor of the bathroom and touched very carefully the bandages taped over my shoulder.

I heard the door shut from the next room. "Liza?" James called loudly with alarm. Something was set down with a loud clatter. I heaved a sigh and left the bathroom in time to almost walk right into James.

"Oh! There you are," he said. He seemed to be relieved to see me but when he noticed my absent sling, he frowned. "You shouldn't be out of bed. What happened to your shoulder brace?"

What was this? Was he being *fragile* with me?

"Don't worry," I offered brusquely in a nasal voice, "I got up to wash my face and take a drink of water, not drown myself in the tub—I would hate to violate one of those *conditions*." I'd tried to sound menacing but I just sounded tired. I addressed the missing sling callously. "It was too tight. My elbow got stiff. Anything else you want to pick apart?"

"No," James replied tonelessly. I was too tired to fight with him but part of me was dying to engage him, especially when he was trying so intently to avoid an altercation. "I brought you breakfast," he said, gesturing to the table near the cot in the corner, atop which sat a tray of covered food.

"I don't want to eat in bed."

"Liza," James sighed. "Can we please not do this? You must eat—"

"Can I not sit at a table?" I demanded, my voice getting rougher by the minute. "Or is that luxury solely reserved for those who are not hostages of yours?"

James airily cleared his throat in a show of clumsy restraint. I could see in his eyes that he was just about to snap back at me but hastily stopped himself—if I wasn't so exhausted, I would have found it hilarious.

"I'll arrange to have a table brought in," James said in a brittle tone. "I can put it by the window?" I almost told him that I'd prefer he put the table *through* the window, but he might have actually gotten me back for that one. I shook my head as I rolled my eyes in aggressive apathy.

"Fine," I replied. James raised an eyebrow at my attitude and I blushed. "I suppose I would appreciate that," I tried again. My thanks, however hollow they were, seemed to satisfy him. He turned on his heel to leave the room, likely to send for servants to carry in a table, but I stopped him.

"I realize that I will never see outside of this compound," I said curtly. James turned to look at me with a pitying curiosity in his gaze that made me feel pathetic. "As long as you mean to control my parents and keep me here, I'll never leave—I understand that now. What I want to know is, will I ever see outside of this room? Will you ever let me see the others again?" I hated myself for the lump in my throat that made my speech even froggier.

"It remains to be seen, Liza."

"Are you worried that I'll tell them the truth?" I asked, once more in tears and unable to suppress them.

"Yes."

"Well, you shouldn't be," I retorted, reaching up with both hands to dry my cheeks, causing a searing pain to tug under the gauze covering my shoulder.

"I shouldn't be?" James asked. He crossed his arms and I mirrored him, if only to alleviate the pain in my shoulder.

"I wouldn't know where to start! Look at me—I can't even speak of it without falling to pieces! I couldn't bear to break their hearts the way you broke mine. You said it yourself—guilt cuts deeper than any blade could, and I would know! I can't even begin to think of what I'd say to them to lessen the pain of hearing the truth!"

To this, James said nothing.

"I am telling you now, if you don't let me see them, I will lose my mind. After last night, I am happy to drop any and all pretense that I am not hopelessly at your mercy. You say you cannot and will not let me go? Fine—I accept that! You are at odds to come up with a solution to this crisis? Offer me the only thing you can afford to give me: give me back my old life. I beg of you, James, *please* let me get back to the others!"

The few moments that passed next dragged on in slow agony. James was staring at me as though I were some inhuman siren whom he could not understand and I was hanging on by a thread, waiting for him to deny me and cut away the last shred of hope I had left.

"All right, Liza." James uncrossed his arms in a shrug. "I don't know what else to do with you, otherwise. I've never seen another person in so much pain, except—" He broke off with a sigh. "Well, there you have it. I'll arrange for the others to be brought in to visit you, but not here. And you won't be left alone with them, I'm afraid."

"Thank you." I closed my eyes, knowing I might have praised the skies if I hadn't been so breathlessly relieved. I had no use for privacy with the others. All that mattered was that I would see them, hold them, and be with them.

Chapter Eleven

Armand

"Armand," Graham grumbled admonishingly. "You have been pretending to read the same page for fifteen minutes!"

"Has it only been fifteen minutes?" I was haughty but I couldn't help it—here we were, sitting down to read about the history of serf culture, as though our lives were completely on track! As though Liza weren't laid up somewhere hidden away with stitches holding her together!

"Armand," Graham said again, "I know you are suffering because of everything that's gone on with Liza, but you cannot sit with your head in the storm clouds of worry, wringing your hands while you wait for news."

"Can I not? It seems to be more useful than poring over Renaissance social structure...."

"Armie," Kit chided from his place on the sofa beside me. "Don't...."

"What?" I snapped. I slammed my book in a huff and got to my feet, dropping the book on the couch behind me. "Is it so unusual that I would be disinterested in resuming our studies after everything that happened? Do you seriously expect us to ignore the compound falling apart around us while you preach the merits of an archaic system of government?"

"It's not so archaic, Armand," Graham mused. "Everything in history, however long ago it occurred, has context in our present lives; imagine for a moment how different our lives here would be, if the systems of the past had never been formed?"

Now I was *really* fuming. His patience when I was so frustrated was unbearable. Kit was just like him—so determined to go the other way when I exposed just a sliver of the hypocrisy of this place, he bordered on spiteful.

"We might be slaves to James' whim right alongside you," I supposed smartly. Behind me, Kit groaned and massaged his temples. Across from me, in her armchair, Daisy glared at me with outrage in her eyes for daring to offend Graham, whom she often regarded as our sort-of father figure. I did not harbor her fondness for the staff James paid handsomely to keep us busy, so I did not show her any sense of remorse for my biting comment. Instead, I looked back to Graham, who was annoyingly passive as ever.

"Do you need to take a break, Armand?" he asked calmly.

"Yes, I think I do," I replied, trying in vain to match the evenness of his voice.

"All right, Armand," Graham sighed. "Why don't you take a walk and return to us when you're feeling less argumentative?"

"He might never come back, you realize?" Kit chimed in under his breath. That was all the permission I needed—I side-stepped Graham and bustled out of the study, my jaw clenched and my gut aflutter with heated restlessness.

As soon as I left our wing, I was taken aback by the crowds in the marketplace today. There was hardly space to pass between pedestrians as tradesmen buzzed around the wide halls of the compound like frantic drone bees. They shouted offers every few seconds, baiting any passerby who would hear them to come look at their goods. I was eager to lose my thoughts among the deafening chatter of the busy market, so I slipped into the crowd and opened my ears, catching a new voice with every step I took. Someone bumped my shoulder and I turned to offer a disgruntled "excuse me" but then I saw it was only Donovan.

"You shouldn't be out and about," he murmured, shrouding his voice under the cover of the din in the marketplace.

"It's nice to see you too," I returned, my feelings sore.

Donovan rolled his eyes and flashed a secretive smirk. "Don't be a brat. This place is crawling with Masters—more to the point, it's the busiest it's been all year, and you aren't wearing any shoes."

"Are you offering to carry me back to my room?" I was crestfallen when Donovan's features hardened, instead of warming at such a flirtatious suggestion.

"What's gotten into you?" he hissed with incredulity, scanning the crowd around us for a sign of someone having overheard me. There I was, thinking I had no more good will to be burned away, when Donovan of all people would scorn a harmless, whispered tease! My face flushed as the last of my esteem fizzled into a poisonous bitterness. The hell with him, then!

"Pardon my cheek, Master Donovan," I said flatly. "I'll leave you to your summit." Donovan's eyebrows shot up, as though I'd just told him to go defile himself in whatever fashion he saw fit. I turned on my heel and dove into the current of foot traffic that took me toward the west hall. I didn't dare to check behind me, to see if Donovan was following me, but even if he was hot on my heels, I would have done my best to lose him. I wanted to be alone to rage into this mood that had befallen me. I felt more and more pathetic as I stormed down the hall, glaring intently enough to cause earnest tradespeople to veer out of my way.

I wanted to shove them all out of my way but I forced my arms to hang at my sides. I stiffly balled my fists when I thought, *Oh, yes, Armand, you've really shown Donovan—you've left him to go sulk alone, and you'll really get far in bare feet!*

When I realized I was utterly helpless, I wanted to cry. I was in real danger of losing face in public, so I glanced around for the first diversion into a private place I could find. I cut across the crowd to the studio, which was dark inside, probably because the instructor who operated out of it was still shaken by Quinn's messy attack on Liza. The doors were shut but thankfully unlocked. I slipped inside swiftly and shut the door behind me, exasperatedly losing my breath when the cacophony outside was abruptly muffled, leaving me alone with my hateful thoughts.

Spurned by Donovan, berated by Graham, written off by Kit—I felt like a worthless, impetuous child. I left the lights off in the studio and crossed the wide room to the other side, hoping Helena's office would be an unlocked hideout for me, but when I looked down and saw the bloodstained floor underneath my feet, I came to a staggering halt. Terror coiled around my heart like barbed wire. I felt haunted as the ringing silence stifled the room. I could hear sounds that were not there: Liza's screams, the tempered whine of Quinn's blade as it sliced through the air.

I wanted to leave but I could not move. I was standing in what remained of Liza's latest brush with death, which had clearly been scrubbed away as much as it could. I was grateful for the darkness around me, for the stain was only discernible as a dark spot on the floor. Had the room been lit properly, had I been able to see the dark red pigment of it, I would have taken lead from Daisy and fainted where I stood.

"Hey," said Donovan, suddenly standing behind me. Every follicle on my body stood up as I flinched, electrified, by this surprise. My heart was galloping as I gasped, turning to see Donovan already approaching me sheepishly.

"How could you sneak up on me, here, of all places?" I whispered furiously, both hands clutching the front of my tunic. Donovan whimpered a sad chuckle and reached for me.

"I'm sorry, lover," he professed. "I didn't realize—I didn't mean to frighten you. I came in and you were standing so still, I thought you could hear me."

"Well, you've successfully infuriated me and scared the hell out of me in the span of ten minutes," I snapped, pulling away from him. "Congratulations. You can go now."

"Don't be that way," Donovan implored. He reached for me again and I took two steps back.

"I'm serious," I insisted. "I don't want you here. Leave me alone."

"Armand," sighed Donovan. He crossed his arms. "I'm sorry I snapped at you, but you were coming on very strong, and with so much attention on James' Tributes lately, we could have been seen—"

"*James' Tributes*," I echoed. I laughed mirthlessly. "Don't waste an apology on me, Donovan. Those are for real people, and as I'm just one of *James' Tributes*...."

"Spare me your waspishness, Armand." Donovan maintained an air of contrition but I could tell he was growing impatient.

"You're pathetic," I spat. "You've come to me in my fishbowl of a bedroom, right under James' nose before! But the second there might be other Masters around, you tuck your tail between your legs and reject me?"

"Reject—what are you talking about?" Donovan demanded, flustered as he uncrossed his arms. "Armand, you came on to me in full view of the marketplace! What was I to do, throw you down in the middle of the hall and take you in front of everyone? Try to be reasonable!"

"What do you care, anyway? You're a Master. You're free to bed down whomever you choose!"

"Bed down!" Donovan exclaimed in a hushed, scandalized voice. "Armand, what the hell has gotten into you?"

"I know what being a puppet looks like," I uttered angrily. "I've watched Jada and Graham for years. I know what it looks like when someone pretends that they aren't completely controlled by the Masters. You are using me just like James uses the rest of them! I suppose I never thought you were capable of doing it to me."

Donovan looked up at the ceiling and muttered in apparent disbelief a truly impressive string of curse words. "Listen to me, please, my beautiful, foolish lover," he said quietly, advancing slowly toward me. "Whatever motive you believe I have for keeping our tryst a secret is misconstrued; I am protecting *you*, Armand, by keeping you at arm's length during this summit. There are very clear rules regarding the treatment of Tributes—"

"Those only pertain to the girls," I interjected hotly. "Even Kit knows that." He was trying to foist the accountability for his behavior onto James' rules and I refused to hear it.

"No, Armand," Donovan corrected me with succinct irritation. "The rules apply to you all. The consequences of breaking those rules are more severe than you realize—"

"And you're protecting me from those consequences, is that right?" I heaved another metallic, cruel guffaw. "You can't even pull rank to keep James from batting me around like a training dummy, how could you possibly think shutting me down when I whisper to you in jest would somehow protect me?"

"You have not the *faintest* idea of what you speak, no idea of the risks I've taken by making you my lover. And worse yet, you think I could reject you after the bond we've formed? You really don't understand." The look of disappointment that fell over his face critically wounded my angry resolve. He had masterfully deflected my accusation that he was pathetic—it hit me hard, in the chest, after it bounced off of him.

"You repel me," I said. I had to make him leave before I burst into tears in front of him. It would break me if I fell at his feet. "You want to keep me at arm's length? Fine—I don't want you near me, either!"

"I never said I didn't want you near." He'd been hurt by my words, which admittedly pleased me in a brattish sense, but now I could see that he was going to try to make up. To be kind. I didn't deserve any of that from him; I couldn't handle it. I crossed my arms against him and fixed my meanest glare.

"Leave me alone, Donovan."

"Come on, Armie…," he urged, trying to sway me by using my nickname. It just reminded me of Liza.

"Get out!" I uncrossed my arms to hold my fists at my sides. I did not expect Donovan to plant his feet and purse his lips in defiance.

"Is that an order? *You* don't give *me* orders, Armand."

"I just did! Go. I don't want you here." Donovan glanced down at my clenched fists and cocked his head.

"You want to hit me, Armand?" he asked. He came forward until he was standing within reach. His lips parted in a sneer, his sharp teeth grimacing at me. "Go ahead. Hit me. That's an order." There was dark satisfaction in his eyes as he stared into mine. Did he really want me to hit him?

I hesitated, though in that moment I wanted nothing more than to hit him. "I would hate to mark your face before your summit with the other Masters," I offered snidely.

"Your concern is touching," Donovan said. "Come on, Armand—you said it yourself, you think I'm too pathetic to pull rank. I'm ordering you to hit me. You clearly want to!"

Before I had the chance to hesitate for another instant, I drew upon the anger welling in my chest and hit Donovan. I cracked my palm across his face and barely felt the throbbing stinging on my hand afterward, my body buzzing too intensely in the aftershock. My heartbeat was a deafening drum in my ears. Donovan looked back to me with a wild glint of joy in his teal eyes.

"Was that the best you could do?"

I slapped him in the face again, harder this time. He barely staggered from the force of it and when he looked back to me, he was grinning. "Oh, please, *Daisy* could hit harder than that!" The son of a bitch was baiting me! I reached back to hit him again, this time with my closed fist, but in a snap, Donovan lashed out and caught my arm; he twisted in place and kicked my legs out from under me, and before I knew it, he was pinning me to the floor.

"Get off me!" I urged, fighting to tear myself out of his grasp.

"This is what you wanted, isn't it?" Donovan asked breathlessly. A dark blotch covered his left cheek like a shadow, marking where I'd smacked him. "You want me to play your deep, dark mind games with you?" He bent his head and kissed my neck slowly, lightly. I shivered when his teeth grazed over my earlobe.

"They're not games," I growled unevenly. "And you're a cad. A real bastard."

"Scoundrel," Donovan rebutted.

"Villain!"

"Louse!"

"Quim!" I hissed, struggling to get out from under him. Donovan laughed at the insult, though his eyes betrayed how angry he'd become. His lips curled into a menacing smirk as he glared down at me while holding me down with apparently more effort than he thought he'd need to apply.

"*Tribute!*" It was the cruelest insult he could surmise. It was effective too—I felt stronger than I ever had, thanks to the hot sun of rage that had risen in me, and I used it to shove Donovan off me. The second I was free, I scrambled to my feet and started for the door; Donovan caught me, yanked me around, and kissed me roughly, trapping me in his arms. I grunted when he tugged the hair at the back of my head and pulled my head back so that he could drag his teeth over the tender flesh covering my throat.

"Is this what you wanted?" he whispered urgently, his breath hot on my ear, as he held me tightly against him.

"Yes," I moaned. I couldn't help it. I surrendered to him as he kissed me again with desperation that almost leveled us both. Donovan pulled me around and led me to the little office behind him. It was windowless inside, much darker than the rest of the studio. He bent me over the desk and yanked my trousers away before I had time to steady myself; he grasped me by the hips and thrust forward, spilling me bodily over the top of the desk.

I was a mess of gasps and outcries.

"Keep it up, Armand! You want them all to hear? Is that it?" I clung to the edges of the desk as though for dear life, praising Donovan as he worked me with the tireless expertise I'd come to crave so dearly. He showered me with terse praise too, breaking off into delighted groans of pleasure when I began begging him not to stop. Before I knew it, we were rolling in satisfied waves away from the savage animosity that had sparked our violent entanglement. On the floor of the studio office, we laid side by side, breathless, chuckling tiredly at one another.

"I'm sorry about earlier," I sighed into the darkness. Donovan put a hand on my heaving chest and I reached to take his hand in mine. I lifted his hand to my lips and brushed them across his knuckles. "I really don't know what's the matter with me...."

"I do," Donovan said, rolling over so that his front was pressed to my side. "You're a very smart, healthy young man, Armand. You need more than academic stimulation to suit your needs. You need rigorous action, a routine that challenges both your body and your mind."

"A routine that I might find in the southern camps?" I wondered wryly. The bottom dropped out of my stomach immediately after I suggested it, for fear of arousing his temper again by being childish.

Donovan shrugged. "Sure." He planted a kiss on my shoulder and sat up to slip into his trousers. His response stunned me—*sure?* I'd been waiting months for this moment and now that it was upon me, I didn't know what to say.

"What is it?" Donovan asked softly, noticing my awestruck expression.

"You've surprised me, is all," I managed to say. I laughed at how ridiculously smitten I sounded, a tone that Donovan found endearing, for he stole another kiss.

"Beautiful boy," he murmured against my lips. "I should go. I regrettably have a very long afternoon ahead of me. Oh, and Armand, I can't bear it when we argue; the next time you want a rough go of it, just say so."

I was glad to be in a dark room, otherwise, he would have seen me turn a vibrant shade of red. I got up with him and dressed. Donovan fussed with my hair for a minute, insisting that I must have the studio looking like I hadn't just stepped out of a tornado.

"Promise me you won't wander around by yourself," Donovan said abruptly as we made our way out of the studio. "Not with all this trouble with guardsmen, and with so many Masters about...."

"As you say," I agreed. "But why would you worry about me going around alone around the Masters?" As much as I hated to admit it, I was protected by James as long as I was here. I couldn't fathom why Donovan would caution me to avoid others like him, for as far as I knew, none of them could be as bad as James.

"I don't mean to impugn the others' reputations," Donovan said, tiptoeing around his words. He took a moment to smooth his hands down his front, and another to reach up and smooth my hair back in front. He flashed a brief smile before opening the door to the main hall but was sure to correct his expression into a benignly pleasant one before exiting the studio before me.

"There is one Master in particular of whom you should be mindfully wary," Donovan began to say in a secretive tone.

"There you are, Armand," came James' curt voice from behind us. I turned to see him emerge from the crowd of rowdy tradespeople, looking surly as ever, with Daisy and Kit on his heels. "Armand," said James, frowning as he looked from me to the door of the studio. "What were you doing in the studio?"

My mouth went dry. Thankfully, Donovan clapped me on the shoulder and stepped in. "He asked me to see the place where Liza was attacked," he explained gravely to James. "He's been struggling with the incident, I thought it would help him to see that the space has been cleaned."

"Very well," James permitted. I stared past him at Kit, whose eyes were sharply dubious as he noticed the dread in mine. I shrugged my shoulders as if to say, "So what?"

"James is taking us to see Liza," Daisy prompted.

"Really?" My heart leaped to my throat. I whirled around to look at Donovan, who smiled in encouragement.

"Please let her know I am thinking of her," he said to me. After nodding politely to James, Donovan turned and set off toward the east hall. I looked back to James with bright eyes.

"I take it, it won't be a long visit?" I asked.

"It might be, if you come now," James replied impatiently. I moved out of his way and fell hastily into stride with Kit and Daisy, who looped her arm through mine as we hurried along the hall in James' wake.

"I don't know how you could bear to be in that place," Daisy muttered to me disapprovingly.

"I had to see it for myself," I murmured to her. I was glad that she kept her eyes forward, lest she see the flush bloom in my cheeks.

"I'm so nervous," Daisy said to me once the steps to the Masters' rooms were in sight.

"Kit and I are with you," I reminded her.

"We'll need to be brave," Kit said to Daisy. "For Liza."

"Indeed," said James, whom we had all forgotten was within earshot. He led the way up the steps and waved at his armed guardsmen to step aside for us. "Liza has been through a terrible trauma," James said to us once we were within the quiet, grandiose halls of the Masters' rooms. "I ought to prepare you, it shows; Doctor Miles has outdone herself yet again to make sure Liza's health improves, but she is still very weak, very rattled, and very tired." James led us around several more corners until we came to a set of double doors in the middle of a wide hall. He reached into his trousers for a key and unlocked one of the doors, revealing an indescribably gorgeous greenhouse, misty with dew with domed ceilings of painted glass overhead. Kit was the first to follow James over the threshold. I was glad to have Daisy to hold onto, for we were both speechless to see so many exotic-looking plants looming over us.

"Your visit will not be cut short for any other reason except Liza's stamina," James said, his heavy footsteps causing the grates of the footpath to clatter slightly. "She's taken a dose of medicine for her pain which may render her unable to stay awake for very long. I will remind you, however, that you will not be alone with her; I have guards posted in the greenhouse just a few yards down each path, and if they determine that Liza is upset or in need of rest, they will show you out. Understood?"

The three of us blurted "Yes" in agreement. I imagined Kit and Daisy felt the same as I did—queasy with anticipation to see the extent of the damage done to our Liza.

"You'll find her up ahead," said James, stopping abruptly as the grated footpath began to curve around a grove of thick ferns.

"Thank you for this," Kit said to him. James nodded, gesturing for us to step around him. I let Daisy go first. Once we were rid of James, Daisy reached for Kit's hand and we went together down the path until we came to a clearing in the flora.

There was Liza, looking impossibly small as she sat huddled on a cushioned bench. Her long blonde hair was damp and braided over her shoulder and I could see a strip of stark white bandaging peeking out of the collar of her loose clothing. One of her arms was secured to her chest by a dark sleeve attached to several thick straps. Her violet eyes were swimming in tears as she looked up and saw us coming at her, and with her free arm she reached for us.

She was so pale and so wan, so fragile, I stopped in my tracks. Daisy went to her knees and hugged Liza around the middle, bursting into tears as Liza held her in her lap and sang her name over and over. Kit sat beside Liza on the bench and gently smoothed his hand over her head, tears trickling down his cheeks as he looked into her eyes.

"I'm all right," she wept, the corners of her eyes crinkling as she tried to keep from crying even harder.

"Look at what he did to you!" Kit said thickly, carefully cupping Liza's face to wipe her tears away with the sides of his thumbs. "Is your arm broken?"

"No," Liza assured him, still holding Daisy close as her shoulders shook with sobs. "The sling is so I won't pull the stitches in my shoulder. Really— I'm all right, Kit, please don't cry. You don't know how happy I am to be with the three of you." She bowed her head as more sobs welled in her chest. "You'll never know how badly I've missed you...."

"When Donovan told us what had happened," Daisy chimed in, her voice froggier than I'd ever heard it, "I thought I was losing my mind. I was so afraid for you, Liza...."

"Stop that," Liza said, smiling sadly down into Daisy's face. "I'm all right." She turned her glittering eyes on me, then, and the teeming agony in her eyes stole my breath. "Armie," she sighed. She wiped her own tears away with the back of her hand. "Armie, what is it?"

I couldn't bring myself to speak. Liza had wasted away in the few short days since I'd seen her, since our last dramatic and violent visit. I didn't know how Kit and Daisy could cry tears of joy to hold her in their arms or smile to see her sitting up. The light in her eyes was flickering; she was barely clinging to any semblance of purpose. I could see it as plainly as I could see the bruise on the side of her face: Her spirit was utterly broken.

Liza saw me glimpse the shattered spark of hope in her eyes and stood up, Kit and Daisy protesting as gently as they could. Liza ignored their insistence that she stay put, to save her strength, and came to me at once. She wrapped her arm around my neck and buried her face in the hollow of my throat. I wound my arms around her waist and lifted her off her feet, heedful not to jostle the arm strapped to her chest. A mournful whimper ripped from my chest when she pressed her lips to my neck.

I wanted to demand of her, what has James done? For Quinn's attempt on her life wouldn't have shaken Liza to the core like this—not my Liza. She would have fought for her fire, become even more brash and certain of herself. The girl I held in my arms was something less now, stripped of an innocence I could only recognize from its absence. I squeezed her even tighter and didn't even stop when she winced in discomfort. I would hold her together myself if I had to.

"I'm all right, Armie," Liza assured me in a raspy voice. I set her down immediately and held her around the waist far enough so that I could glare frantically into her eyes.

"Liar," I blubbered. "You're *alive*, not all right!"

"Armand, please," Liza implored. "Don't make me say it...."

"Look at yourself!" I urged her. I turned my gaze to Kit and Daisy, who were both still in tears as they watched me harp at Liza. "Look at her! Does she look all right to you?"

"She's been through hell, Armie," Daisy said angrily. "For goodness' sake, will you stop manhandling her?"

"Armie's right, Liza," Kit declared. I was shocked that he'd taken my side, but I was glad to have him beside me.

"I'm as all right as I will be," Liza said to us.

"Quinn nearly murdered you!"

"I know," sighed Liza. She reached up and touched my face. "Armand, I know you don't do well with this sort of thing—"

"Liza, you don't need to be our balm," I told her. I took her hand in mine and pressed a kiss into her palm before holding it against my chest. "You sent Kit's book back with those portraits, and that map. Why would you send secrets to us if you weren't planning to do something drastic again?"

Liza's features darkened. "I did not mean to end up cut to ribbons at Quinn's mercy, suffice to say." She cleared her throat and gave my chest a little push. "I want you to forget about those portraits," she said softly. She was clearly speaking to the three of us but I knew she mostly meant me.

"How can you say that?" I asked. I pondered for a moment, remembering that there were unfriendly ears all around us. "The message underneath the portraits—is it as obvious as the labels suggest?"

"It doesn't matter anymore," Liza said, shaking her head. "None of it matters."

I let go of Liza's hand and took a step back from her. "You spent weeks trying to convince me to come around to your side," I uttered, looking to all three of them. "Now you're telling me none of it matters? That it's over?"

"Yes, Armie." Liza did not sound happy to say it out loud and the admission did not appear to cut her as deeply as it did me.

"What about the map, Liza?" Daisy asked in a trembling voice. She came forward and stood beside me, her golden eyes ablaze with confoundment. "The village by the river—it's a real place, Liza. It's where we came from. Armand remembers everything." She didn't spare me the sideways glare I knew she wanted to. Despite my contempt for Daisy's driving motivation to escape this place, which had caused all this upset in the first place, I was undeniably supportive of her line of reasoning. Liza risked her life to try to get back to our real home, and now she expected us to disavow the entire notion because of what Quinn had done?

"You remember?" Liza blurted, rounding on me.

"Everything," I admitted shamelessly.

"He remembers the song about me, the one you and my mom would sing to me when I was little," Daisy told Liza desperately. "He remembers our parents, their voices, their faces, everything!" She shivered and took a gulp of air past the lump in her throat, reaching to take Liza's hand. "Liza, now more than ever, we've got to get back to them!"

"It'll never happen," Liza muttered, taking her hand back from Daisy. "Whether or not you remember them, Armand, we'll never get back to them."

But Liza had no idea about my relationship with Donovan. This very morning, he'd agreed in no uncertain terms that he would take me with him to the southern camps, away from James and this rotten cage of his. Liza's nihilism was understandable, given all she'd been through, but it was ill-founded all the same.

"I know you're tired," Kit said, coming around to join the circle we'd formed in the greenhouse clearing. "You're traumatized by the awful things you've seen in such a short time, but you can't give up now, Liza." His lips curled into a tragic smirk and he shrugged as more tears spilled down his face. "We're only strong when we're together, remember?"

"This compound is the only place we'll ever be together," Liza said, returning Kit's pitying smile. "I'm the only one who's seen the outside world—believe me, I would much rather settle for the sacrifices we make to survive here than be out there, especially if it means I get to keep the three of you close."

"But what will we *do*, Liza?" Daisy implored tearfully.

"What we should have been doing all along," Liza replied. "Study, dance, play piano. Follow the rules. It'll be worth it because we'll be together. You'll see." She let out a lamenting sigh and peered into Daisy's woeful brown eyes. "We're all each other has."

Her words pricked my heart like thorns. Daisy was soon beside herself. She turned away to gather her bearings and Kit put his arms around her to hasten this process. With the two of them facing away from me and Liza, I considered kissing her. Looking into her eyes was like looking in a mirror of the past: I had been hopeless and desolate and broken once, just like Liza was now, and that first time with Donovan breathed life into me when I thought there was nothing left to pull me back from the pain. I wanted to breathe life back into Liza, for it hurt me to see the emptiness in her eyes, but I couldn't bring myself to do it.

"Will you sit with me?" Liza asked. "This medicine makes me so drowsy, and I don't have much time before it takes effect. All I want is to be close to you."

I would not refuse Liza the comfort of closeness. I put my arms around her and walked us back to the bench, closely followed by Kit and Daisy. Daisy sat at Liza's feet and laid her head in Liza's lap. Kit and I propped Liza up by sitting closely beside her. The four of us sat together in silence, listening to birds sing up high in the treetops.

"I've disappointed you," Liza said after a while.

"That's not true," Kit said. "We love you, Liza. We just want you to get better."

I hadn't even considered feeling disappointed until Liza said it. Resolve consumed me—Liza was too broken to instill hope in Daisy and Kit, and though I was too weak to take up the job myself, what I had to offer the three of them was even more crucial. I couldn't tell them that I meant to convince Donovan to take us away from this place; I would just have to pull it off and put it to them when the time came.

After a few minutes, Liza drifted away into the void of the painkiller medication. She slumped over slowly until her head was resting on my shoulder. I nudged Daisy lightly and she picked her head up to see what I wanted. When she saw that Liza was asleep, Daisy shamelessly studied Liza's features with a sad, longing glint in her eyes. I knew she was drinking up the sight of Liza because we weren't sure when we would see her next. Kit noticed Daisy's searching stare and carefully shifted his position so that he could face Liza. He took her hand in his and softly stroked the back of it.

"We'll get her back," I whispered to the others.

"How?" Daisy wondered. I didn't answer her. Instead, I slipped my arm behind Liza and delicately pulled her into my lap and she curled into my chest. I stood up with her in my arms and carried her slowly along the greenhouse path, Kit and Daisy flanking us protectively. I saw Douglas up ahead and he instantly snapped to attention and approached us concernedly.

"What happened to her?" he asked.

"She's fine," Kit hissed, cautioning Douglas to be quiet by holding a finger to his lips. "She's asleep." Douglas was visibly relieved and looked to me.

"Would you like me to take her?" he asked. I glared at him for assuming she was too heavy for me to carry myself—Douglas wasn't much bigger than me, and regardless, I could carry Liza around the clock without faltering if I had to.

"Show us to her room, Douglas," I said. He afforded the slumbering Liza in my arms a final look and decided not to argue with me. He led us out of the greenhouse and back into the Masters' halls, where five guardsmen were waiting outside the door. Jada was there too, with a cot and a ready portable. Like Douglas, Jada showed urgent concern when she saw me emerge from the greenhouse with Liza in my arms. Kit told her gently that Liza had succumbed to the effects of the medicine, which seemed to placate Jada.

"You may set her here, Armand," Jada said in a hushed voice, pulling up the rolling cot in front of me. I bent to lay Liza down on the cot and I felt like crying. I simply did not want to let her go. But since I knew there would be nothing else to do than let Jada make Liza better, I let Liza slip out of my grasp. Daisy pulled a cover over her and smoothed the hair back from her forehead.

"I'm going to take her someplace quiet," Jada told us, taking hold of the cot's rail. Daisy sniffled and quickly bowed her head to hide her tears. "Oh, honey," Jada sighed, clicking her tongue. "I know it's hard to see her like this. I promise you, she'll be back to her old self before you know it."

"When will we see her again?" Kit asked. He boldly reached down and laced his fingers between Daisy's as she continued to cry. Even I was surprised to see him show affection like this in front of Jada and James' guards.

"Likely very soon," Jada said brightly, cheerfully ignoring Kit's action. "Master James agrees with me, for Liza to fully recover, she will need to rejoin your routine as soon as possible." It was hard for me to be relieved to hear this, as it was hard for me to believe that James would agree to a recuperation tactic that would involve letting Liza anywhere near us.

"In any case," Jada said, "I will be sure to keep Graham apprised of Liza's wellbeing so that he can ease your worry." She wheeled Liza away, disappearing around the corner with her. As soon as Liza was out of sight, the three of us wilted in place.

"Come along," Douglas volunteered, stepping forward. "I'll show you out."

I was glad that he would escort us out of these halls instead of James. Kit and Daisy followed Douglas, though they released each other's hand. I think they worried James might be around any one of these corners; while they were comfortable enough to comfort each other in front of Jada, James would have no qualm addressing the display of affection.

It wasn't James we ran into as we left the Masters' rooms, but Donovan. He warmly greeted us all, saving a lingering hug for Daisy. I wanted to roll my eyes when he put his arms around her but I forced myself to abide by the warning he'd given me earlier, that we needed to be more careful.

"I can't thank you enough for convincing James to let us see her," Daisy enthused, touching her hand to her heart. "It meant so much to us."

"Please, Daisy." Donovan waved away her gratitude. "I'm happy to advocate for you, you know that. How was Liza?"

"She was in an amount of pain," Kit sighed. He was clearly troubled by it, like I was.

"She's been through a lot," I added. "Jada tells us she'll be better soon, maybe even ready to come back to us."

"Is that so?" Donovan mused. "That's wonderful news! The sooner she can return to the comfort of a more familiar place, the better." I noticed how much rosier his left cheek was than his right and I couldn't suppress a knowing smile.

"Have dinner with us tonight, won't you, Donovan?" I suggested. Donovan eyed me with an astute sparkle to his eyes.

"Oh, yes!" Daisy agreed fervently. "You must!"

"I'll cook," I offered, wondering how humble I could possibly come across while smirking at Donovan like I was. "As a thank you, for speaking to James on Liza's behalf." Titillation washed over his countenance. He grinned slyly right back at me, likely wondering what possible ulterior angle I was working by getting him into my kitchen.

"I would be honored to join you for dinner," he said, flashing a smile.

"Good," I said. "We'll see you tonight." We said our goodbyes after assuring Donovan we could make our way back to our wing alone, as he probably had much more important affairs to see to. Daisy was so weary by the time we got back to our apartments, she flopped over onto the sofa in the study and laid her arm across her face, shielding her eyes from the lamplight. Kit also excused himself to his room for a bit, citing a nasty headache. I was exhausted by all that had transpired this morning as much as they were, if not more, thanks to the rigorous exertion I'd taken after quitting my studies, but I had to visit the marketplace and procure everything I'd need for dinner. I threw myself into the preparation, downing cup after cup of coffee as I worked in the kitchen. I heard Kit's door open and close; I guessed he'd gotten up to dote on Daisy in some form or another, but immediately focused back to my work.

Dinnertime came faster than I thought it would, thanks to the nonstop flurry of preparations I'd seen to. The table was set and I'd just put two freshly baked loaves of bread out to cool on the countertop when Donovan arrived. Kit and Daisy were wearing fresh garments when they went to let Donovan in. Daisy had plaited her hair and draped it over her shoulder, beautifully accentuating the curve of her neck. Even Kit had combed his hair, which made me worry that Donovan might find my visage to be frazzled, for my sleeves were still pushed back and wearing an apron around my waist when he came into the kitchen.

"Look at you," he remarked, looking me up and down as he leaned against the kitchen doorway.

"Yes, well," I said wryly, wiping my hands on my apron before hastily undoing it. "May I plate you some bruschetta? I have fresh bread, and caprese too—"

"My appetite is plenty whetted, thank you," Donovan interrupted, pointedly watching me stuff my crumpled apron into the nearest drawer. Kit and Daisy took up their plates and began to serve themselves. Daisy glanced up at me and tapped her chin indicatively.

"You have flour smudged on your face, Armie," she said. I reached for a napkin and smeared it across my face, hoping to clean off the flour and whatever else I might have touched to it. Donovan was grinning at me as I did, which instilled a fluttery sensation in my gut. I insisted he sit and make himself comfortable. He obliged me and sat between me and Daisy while I served him dinner and once we were all ready to eat, we lifted our glasses of sparkling water and toasted to him in thanks; Donovan toasted to Liza's health, and then the three of them took turns complimenting the cuisine and making satisfied noises as they ate.

It was the most normal meal we'd had in weeks. We made pleasant small talk, careful to avoid subjects that were too close to Liza, Quinn, or even James. The closest we got to James was when I asked Donovan how the summit was going: His response was, "Let's just say I was looking forward to having an excuse to not join the others for supper; and really, I'd rather not sully this lovely gathering with you all by discussing business."

When we were all finished, we sat back with full bellies and enjoyed a few beats of content silence, during which I imagined for just a moment what it would be like if we were all having dinner together someplace else. The only person missing was Liza, but even still, it was easier than I thought to imagine us sitting together, enjoying each other's company, far off in the southern camps; perhaps in a room with windows we might open to let in the nighttime air.

Kit and Daisy insisted I stay seated when it was time to clear the table, as the chef should not clean up after his guests, but I wanted all of this to be over with so that I could steal Donovan away—or let him steal me, whichever option arose first. I settled for drying the dishes and Donovan even helped put plates away. Daisy dried her hands and came over to put her arms around me.

"Thank you for cooking, Armie," she said.

"You're welcome, sweetheart," I replied, using my pet name just to see her make the adorably annoyed, crinkled frown she did every time I said it.

"Would you think me terribly rude for turning in?" Daisy asked Donovan, after pulling a face at me. "These days, I get so tired after dinner…." She was tired, I knew, but really she just wanted to shut herself in her room so she could stare at that painting of Liza's until she fell asleep.

"Of course not," Donovan assured her. "It's been a long day for all of us. Thank you, all of you, for having me." I couldn't help but purse my lips when Daisy put her hand on Donovan's chest as she breezed out of the kitchen. Kit clapped Donovan's shoulder and assured him that the pleasure was all ours.

"You're going to bed?" I asked quizzically. Kit was a night owl; more than once, I'd given up trying to meet Donovan because Kit would be up in the study until after midnight.

"I hardly slept last night," Kit told me softly. He seemed to be wary of Daisy overhearing him.

"Oh," I said. "Here I thought you might be tuckered out from today's gripping delve into serfs and their impact on renaissance social structure…." Kit smiled wryly at my sardonic comment and Donovan seemed surprised that Kit found it so amusing rather than offensive.

"Maybe a little," Kit suggested. He afforded me a warm smile and felt compelled to follow Daisy's suit. He stepped over and hugged me, not for more than a few seconds, but very tightly. "Goodnight, brother," he said.

"Goodnight, Kit." I was a little in awe—Kit could be sentimental at the best of times, but something about the nonchalance of with which he'd called me "brother" tugged at my heartstrings. It moved me enough to distract me from Donovan's admiring stare from across the kitchen. By the time I caught him watching me, I realized that he hadn't ever looked at me like this before.

"What is it?" I asked softly. Donovan pursed his lips and shrugged.

"You've surprised me, is all," he said, in a near-perfect imitation of that very same phrase I'd articulated earlier.

"They're both in bed by now," I murmured, nodding my head after Kit and Daisy. "Are you going back to the summit?"

"I ought to," Donovan sighed.

"I was hoping you would stay," I said. Donovan returned my longing glance and grinned.

"I was hoping you would say that," he said. I flipped the lights off in the kitchen and took Donovan's hand in mine; I lingered in the hall for a moment, keeping Donovan behind me, until I was sure Kit and Daisy wouldn't poke their heads out of their bedrooms. Quietly, I led Donovan down the hall to my room. Just before I went into my room, Donovan tugged my arm.

"Not there," he whispered. He took me instead to Liza's empty room and swiftly pulled me inside after him, closing the door softly behind us.

"Here?" I raised my eyebrows and glanced around Liza's dark room. Donovan tapped the switch on the wall to turn on the dim light on her bedside table.

"This room won't be monitored," he explained.

"Mine won't be either," I replied. "James said he put a stop to it, as a show of good faith."

"You really believe he'd be so kind?" Donovan asked with an arched eyebrow. I hissed a little laugh.

"No, I suppose not," I acknowledged. Donovan pulled me into his arms and kissed my lips tenderly.

"I could have dined all night on the sight of you with your sleeves up, all mussed and rugged in the kitchen," he whispered in my ear. He kissed down the side of my neck as I smoothed my fingers over his chest. Donovan caught the hem of my linen shirt and swiftly pulled it up, and I raised my arms to ease it off completely. Donovan brushed his lips across my clavicle, holding me against him as I leaned back a little so that he could better plant kisses across my chest.

This was it—this was the moment when I would go for broke. It wasn't just Donovan's earnest, adoring touch that sent a wave of gooseflesh over my body; it was also a feverish anticipation that I didn't expect to take such a strong hold in me. Donovan was nuzzling my neck when I felt brave enough to say it, though it was as gentle as a whisper and just as quiet:

"I love you."

Donovan stilled at once. Very slowly, he straightened his posture to look me keenly in the eyes. His expression was almost wild, his teal eyes searching for any inkling of affirmation in my features.

"What did you say?" he asked. His voice was hungry in excited disbelief.

"I love you, Donovan," I said. My lips twitched into a nervous smile as I went on, "I think I have since last summer, when we were together for the first time. I know it's stupid, and insane—"

"Oh, it is," Donovan blurted. "Stupid *and* insane." He was smiling back at me now.

"You saved my life when you kissed me that day. And now, with everything that's gone on…I love you. I have no choice but to tell you, I love you."

Donovan swooped in and kissed me with ready glee etched into every line of his face. He smiled against my lips and hummed a laugh before he broke away.

"Armand," he said, practically gushing. "You're making me blush…." He kissed me again, tightening his hold on me. He held back after a minute or so of this, just enough to rest his forehead against mine. "You must know," he murmured, "I do love you too, beautiful boy."

I hopped off my feet to wind my legs around his waist, kissing him joyously. I was matched to his stature but Donovan caught me all the same and spun us around twice before taking me to the bed behind us. We came together amid the unmade sheets, grasping at each other and kissing messily as we went. By the time it was finished, we were still coiled into a knot of limbs that only lovers could tie.

"You are extraordinary," Donovan professed breathlessly, holding me to him as both our chests heaved in the tired aftermath.

"I had an excellent teacher," I praised him.

"You hardly needed encouragement, let alone instruction," Donovan said, smiling wickedly at me. I wanted to return the sentiment, but I frowned instead, which prompted Donovan to catch my chin between his fingers, just next to the fresh scar from the cut James had given me there.

"What is it, Armand?"

"I'm afraid," I admitted. "For the future. *Our* future."

"What do you mean?" Donovan shifted his position in bed so that I was held snugly to his side. I extricated myself from his arms and propped myself up on my elbow so I could better look into his eyes.

"When this summit is over, you will return to the south, won't you?" I didn't wait for him to reply; I could tell he was concocting some vague, diplomatic but quelling response. "I understand that there are rules," I went on, "but when I think of you going away for another nine months...." I shook my head. "None of us know how bad it's going to be when the pressure of the summit is gone; we have no idea what James might do, in light of everything with Liza...what if he never permits you to return?"

"I am a Master, the same as James," Donovan reminded me. "He cannot bar me from his compound as long as I have business here—"

"Business you can justify," I pointed out. "And you know how cruel he can be. It's not just me you protect when you're here, Donovan, but Kit, Daisy, and Liza too. You have shown such compassion for us all by speaking up for us to James. No one here will take up that courageous a job when you leave, Donovan. They're all too afraid of him."

Donovan went silent as my words sank in. He stroked my arm absentmindedly with the backs of his fingers as he considered all I'd said. "Lover, it's so much more complicated than you realize...."

"Allow me to uncomplicate it for you: I love you. You love me. We cannot be together here, not in this place. Not while James the Master operates every puppet string from on high."

"What would you have me do?" Donovan was so serene yet cold when he spoke, as though this talk of James was turning his stomach.

"Use your position to help us get out of here! When the summit ends, and it's time for you to return to the camps in the south, take us with you!"

"*Us?*" Donovan was incredulous. "As in, all four of you?"

"I love you," I repeated. "I want nothing more than to be with you, and I do not want to put an ultimatum to you like this, but if being together means leaving Kit and the girls behind, to suffer James' wrath...."

"Armand, stop." He smoothed my hair back and held my face. "I hear your concerns. I have my own, too. But the things in motion, as far as the summit goes...." He broke off to wet his lips. "It would be risk enough to steal you away, let alone all four of you. I do love you, Armand, and I am very moved by your devotion to the others…." He was deep in consideration now. "I don't even think I could make arrangements in time for the summit's end, just two weeks away. It would be too dangerous." He puffed a contemptuous sigh, in spite of himself, it seemed, before peering into my eyes.

"But for you, my love, I will try." I was so relieved when he agreed I kissed him and climbed into his lap. Donovan laughed and indulged me for a time, but he was sliding out of my grasp before long. "Armand, if I'm to get any semblance of a plan together, I can't stay a minute longer," he said regrettably. He climbed out of bed and dressed quickly, before I'd have the chance to pull him back in with me; though, upon reflection, he was probably right to move on. We'd been quiet enough, but it would be disastrous if Kit caught a spell of insomnia and came looking for me. So, with great care, we slipped out of Liza's room and down the hall, halting before the door to the main hall to make our farewells.

"As long as I am busy with the summit, I need you to promise that you won't go poking around the studio by yourself again," said Donovan. "I'd rather you avoid walking around the compound alone altogether."

"That Master you tried to warn me about," I recalled. "Before James found me, to take us to Liza. Is that what this is about?"

"At the risk of worrying you, I won't get into too much detail, but suffice to say, James did not devise his extreme methods of mastery on his own—just like the best of them, he was taught. I do not want you to meet the only Master I know of who is more volatile than James, especially if you're on your own." Donovan's gravitas was contagious. I felt dread pile like stones in my stomach at the thought of someone who was worse than James.

"You will have nothing to fear as long as you keep to your routine," Donovan added, in a forcibly cheerier tone. "Even James doesn't want you to have any run-ins with Haitham." He kissed me quickly on the lips and smiled when I touched his face.

"We both know I'm going to worry anyway," I said. "Just as you will."

"You're probably right. Goodnight, Armand."

"Goodnight, Donovan. Remember," I added, just as he was walking through the double doors, "we're only strong when we're together." He smiled over his shoulder and left, and I shut the doors behind him. The apartment was desolately still and quiet in his absence. I was electrified with the thrilling feeling of accomplishment. I started for my room, probably to take a shower before bed to quiet my nerves, but I hesitated.

I remembered how hurt Daisy had been by me harboring memories of our childhood. Kit had encouraged me to confide in him, and while I knew that uttering aloud the words "I'm going to get us out of here and Donovan is going to help" was a risk in itself, I couldn't shake the guilt that came with being the only one in this apartment who would fall asleep tonight with hope in his heart.

Daisy was likely already asleep. She also might press me to divulge just how and why Donovan agreed to help us escape and I was so excited by the concept, I might tell her. Until I was certain she wouldn't cast judgment on me for the means about which I had just secured our exit strategy, I decided Kit was the better bet. He might criticize me for being a hypocrite, inculcating in them for weeks about how foolish it was to try to get away from James, but he'd shut up if I told him to. He may not even take offense to such an edict, in light of our triumph.

I went to Kit's closed bedroom door and quietly tapped my fingertips to the polished wood.

"Kit," I whispered. "It's me." He didn't answer. He had probably fallen asleep reading in bed, as he was wont to do, so I carefully opened his door a crack and peered inside. His bedside lamp was on, but his bed was empty.

"Kit?" I whispered again. I let myself into his room, checking around the frame of his bathroom door. Where the hell was he? Had he gone to the study to read, while I was in Liza's room with Donovan? I paled—had he heard us together?

I breezed out of Kit's room without bothering to shut the door behind me. I started for the dark study, anxious to find Kit sitting there, waiting with caustic words to confront me about the vastly inappropriate farewell he may have seen me bestow on Donovan, but I froze when I passed the door to Daisy's room. I glanced down and through the crack between the door and the carpet, I glimpsed the faintest glow of light. With meticulous caution, I leaned against Daisy's door and pressed my ear to the wood.

Two voices, lowered so much so that I couldn't decipher what they spoke of. One of them followed the cadence of Daisy's chime-like voice, the other one was low, almost sorrowful, undeniably Kit's. I considered bursting into the room, to tease them for holing up in Daisy's room after hours—but what would I find?

I chided myself for guessing they would be in any form of mutual compromise, but who was I to say? And when their hushed conversation came to an abrupt halt, I felt even more like an intruder in my own home. How curious it was that my resolve dissipated so quickly. Could Kit and Daisy really be— *together?*

This would be a mystery to mull over tomorrow, and it was a telling sign that I was meant to keep the promise of our escape to myself. I continued to chastise myself as I stepped away from Daisy's door to go to bed, not before catching Kit's doorknob and quietly pulling his door shut before I went to my room. I may as well let him think that I was none the wiser to his late night visit to Daisy's room, whatever its purpose was.

By the time I stepped out of the shower, I was finally exhausted. I fell into my bed, too lazy to crawl under the covers. I wondered if I would be able to keep from making comments to Kit and Daisy tomorrow, or if I would be able to keep my plan with Donovan to myself. I thought about our farewell earlier and smiled faintly. I didn't think Donovan would have bought such a phrase, the one Kit used to rally us together, but perhaps love softened his usual aversion to sentimentality?

I drifted off to sleep, my mother's lullaby humming in my head, wondering how we all came to be such sneaky little hypocrites.

Chapter Twelve

Time passed in slow, grueling stretches. I had fallen asleep between Kit and Armand in the greenhouse and woken up not underneath that looming red curtain, but in the corner cot on the other side of the room. I was sore, less so than I was the day before and yet I found myself wishing I could go back to sleep to avoid the interminable sense that I was bound in my own body. My waking thoughts were even less welcome.

I had broken something in Armand by striking down the very escapist propaganda I had helped cultivate. I saw it with my own eyes when he looked at me in the greenhouse: When I told Armand to his face that none of it mattered anymore, not only did his heart break to hear it, but I knew that he saw right through me. Had he so much as raised an eyebrow to question what had really caused my change of mind, I'd have told them all the terrible truth behind how we came to live in the summit compound even though it would be like pressing hard on a bruise. I then wondered how Armand could be so perceptive while Kit and Daisy were so caught up by my damaged appearance, but perhaps that was the nature of my separate bond with him. I recalled how Armand had admitted to remembering our childhoods and I cringed as my affection for him was replaced with bitterness. I ventured that if I'd had the stamina to confront him about it, he would cite some stoic reason as to why he kept such valuable memories to himself.

I didn't want to think about it anymore. It was bad enough that my dreams were haunted by Quinn and his knife, let alone the voices of my parents, specifically my father as of late, calling out to me in warning. I meant what I told the others, that it was all over, that none of it mattered anymore. I resigned that I wouldn't see my parents again and strangely, it comforted me to know I would not have to worry about what their voices sounded like now. What difference would it make to imagine how they sounded or looked twenty years after I, their daughter, had been abducted?

James opened the door and slipped swiftly through, pulling it closed behind him. He spared me one look before crossing the room to his desk, where he took a seat and after putting on his reading spectacles, began to shuffle through the stack of letters.

"What time is it?" I asked, sitting up and swinging my legs over the side of the cot.

"Late," James replied softly, not looking up from his work.

"After dinner?" I was slightly loath to acknowledge my rumbling stomach.

"Yes. Are you hungry? I can have food brought up." He marked his spot on the letter with his thumb and turned in his chair to look at me. "Well?"

"Very hungry," I said wryly. James set the letter he was holding on the desk and breezed across the room to the portable. He pressed one of the buttons on top of the machine twice, then went to the bedroom door. "Douglas," said James, though Douglas wasn't visible through the slender crack in the door, "Liza has paged for some dinner. See to it that it's brought up and that Violet is properly seen out." James shut the door again and returned to his desk.

"Thank you," I said after a while.

"It's nothing." He sounded sullen. "It's not your fault you slept through dinner, with the painkillers Jada's been giving you—"

"Not for dinner," I explained. "For letting me see them. Thank you." James seemed to be pleasantly caught off guard. He smirked briefly and returned to his work.

"You're welcome." His manners were truly automatic. Dinner was shortly delivered thereafter. I ate in bed, wolfing down my meal to satiate my voracious appetite, and set the empty tray on the floor when I was finished, the plates still practically spinning. I plugged in the headphones to the music device Jada had given me and curled up in the cot, facing away from James so that his brightly burning desk lamp wouldn't bother me. Kit's piano playing lulled me to sleep, chasing the dark thoughts from my mind long enough for me to relax.

I woke up because James was rousing me in a hushed voice. My cheeks were wet with tears and I jerked upright, momentarily disoriented when I looked up and didn't see the red curtain hanging overhead.

"It was Quinn," I said, shaking.

"It was only a nightmare," James assured me. "He's not here. You're safe." He gently laid his hand on my arm and my shoulders relaxed, though my eyes were still wide and searching when I looked up at him. I could see plainly that he'd been sleeping, though his desk lamp was still on. I buried my face in my hands and groaned out of dismay.

"I'm sorry," I said. I felt silly for having startled him awake, but even more ridiculous for having calmed almost instantly at his touch on my arm.

"Don't be," James replied, stifling a yawn. "Go back to sleep." Only when I laid back down did he turn to pad back to the bed. I shivered under my covers, sweaty from the chilling nightmare. I watched James flip the desktop lamp off and throw the covers back so that he could groggily climb into bed. Though it was now totally dark in the room, and I could not see his face, I was certain he had fallen asleep the moment his head touched the pillow.

The next morning, James suggested I return to my studies with Graham and the others. He seemed to think after talking with Jada that a return to my routine might help me recover from the emotional trauma of Quinn's attack. I readily agreed, excited to see the three people I loved the most so soon after our last visit. James was wary about me moving freely about the compound, though. With so much work piling up around the summit, he couldn't risk becoming distracted with arranging a new security detail that would pass for subtle under the noses of the other Masters, so he decided to move group schooling sessions to the vastly more secured room within the Masters' chambers, the one I had been staying in before the attack.

Daisy, Armand, Kit, and Graham joined me there after they breakfasted in the Tribute wing. Daisy brought me a quilt from my old bedroom, which we laid out on the floor near the window for lessons. Kit and Armand spent the first group school day peering in wonderment out the window and Graham didn't even fuss; he seemed to be so glad to have the four of us back together under his tutelage that he just praised the boys for having such keen focus for the first time in weeks.

I really was fond of Graham. In a way I loved him for his unwavering patience and practicality, especially after everything I'd been through. Armand was a lot like him in that respect, for while he was even-tempered and a perfectionist to a near fault, he was an excellent judge of others around him. He had become uncharacteristically upbeat overnight. He seemed to regard Kit and Daisy with a proud fondness, calling Daisy "sweetheart" more than ever and happily studying alongside Kit, not once rolling his eyes when Kit checked his facts or corrected his rhetoric. Armand was even happier to sit beside me, to brush his fingers across my cheek to tuck stray locks of my hair behind my ear when I couldn't reach them with my good arm. In silence or in conversation, Armand paid close attention to me, which brought me great comfort; yet he did not ask me once about life in the Masters' chambers, nor did he show any disdain when I excused myself to go and rest—unlike Kit or Daisy, who would uneasily point out, "But Liza, we're in your room, where will you go to lie down?"

I don't think Graham knew that I slept in James' room. I wondered constantly if Jada had told him about it, since they were usually very friendly with one another and often took advantage of the little liberties they could take as higher ranking members of staff. I doubted it, as James likely forbade Jada from mentioning the arrangement to anyone in the compound besides Douglas. If Graham did know, or even suspect, I was inclined to think he would let on by affecting an air of disapproval. Either way, this fractionally adjusted old routine was suitable.

Four days later, I still had my arm in a sling, and Jada was constantly reminding me to take pills to sleep at night, but I only needed those when I was alone. I was not welcome in my own dreams, where Quinn always seemed to be waiting with a blade in hand, but as long as James was there to rouse me from sleep and remind me where I was, I could roll over and fall back asleep easily enough. And after I fought through the nights, I got to spend each day with my three favorite people, though I wasn't able to draw, paint, or practice gymnastics. Graham suggested I learn to draw with my left hand, which I tried one afternoon and the picture I made was so sloppy, Armand keeled over in laughter.

"Ambidexterity is a very useful skill," Graham said over Armand's howling. "Master Donovan can fight expertly with a sword in either hand, you know."

"Sometimes he holds a sword in each hand," Kit remarked. Armand eyed him quizzically and Kit expressed defensively, "He told me so himself!"

"When did he do that?" Armand asked.

"Yesterday afternoon," Daisy answered for Kit, a little errantly as she was still skimming the pages of the book in her lap. "He came to our wing to measure Liza's painting for a frame."

"When, yesterday?" Armand pressed Daisy. "I didn't see him when he stopped by."

"You weren't in," Daisy replied smartly. "And anyway, I didn't realize you were the Master of the Tribute wing and insist on knowing all the comings and goings...."

"Keep it up, sweetheart," Armand retorted. Under his breath, he added, "Would that I *did* know...." I couldn't tell if he was legitimately bitter or just being quippy for the sake of normalcy.

"I would prefer the three of you to debate, not bicker," Graham chastised.

"Who's bickering?" Armand asked. "Daisy, look, Liza's picture looks like your early work!" We all burst out laughing, even Daisy, at whose expense Armand's jab had been. Feeling more like myself than I had in days, I tugged on the straps of my sling until it was loose enough for me to slip off. Graham frowned to see me loose of my medical shackle, but he did not voice his disapproval when I reached for the sketchpad and took up a charcoal pencil with my good hand. I barely noticed the stiffness in my arm as I worked on my sketch, a busy, hasty drawing of Daisy in a dramatic ballerina's pose. Her arms and legs were extended gracefully to near perfection, at least in my eyes. I made sure to capture the proud angle she always held her chin when she danced. When I turned it over, Daisy beamed and hugged the sketch to her chest.

"I'd rather Donovan expend his free time having *this* framed," she told me. "I haven't danced since—" she broke off and self-consciously blushed. "I haven't felt like dancing, anyway," she confessed sheepishly.

"I hear Helena is going to reopen the studio as soon as the floors are replaced," Armand told me. He gave Kit a very brotherly nudge when he caught Kit frowning and staring straight ahead while he pondered some grave idea, instead of noticing Daisy fidget beside him. Kit took Daisy's hand in his, startling her out of her worried reverie.

"You don't have to hide from Liza, Daze," Kit told her. I couldn't help but nod in agreement.

"I'm okay, Daisy," I said, reaching for her. "I know you're a ballerina, but you don't have to tiptoe around what happened."

"You're so brave, Liza," Daisy said, smiling sadly. "I wish I could be as brave as you have been." I felt compelled to correct Daisy, to assure her that despite what she perceived, she had been carrying herself very bravely over the past few weeks. When I opened my mouth to speak, I found myself stuck at the threshold. Even trying to extol her bravery made me feel small, like I might fade away before I could get two words in.

"Bravery is a high target to aim for, Daisy," Graham said, uncomfortably regaining his control over the conversation. "When we look at our influences, whether it is within the parameters of art, history, science, what have you, bravery is a fairly common trait among the most prominent in their fields...."

I locked eyes with Armand. We shared a bored eye roll—we could sense a lecture coming on.

"...what very few people forget when they idolize those prominent figures is that, historically, many of these men and women were not brave at all, but merely possessed a self-imposed sense of duty to either their craft or the factions depending on them—" Graham was cut off abruptly as the door to our bedroom-and-classroom opened. Donovan fluidly stepped over the threshold with a crazed expression, his blazing blue eyes were wide as he closed the door softly behind him and held a finger to his lips, gesturing for silence. Disturbed and curious, we all fell quiet and waited for him to explain.

"Sorry!" gushed Donovan in a whisper. His smile was dazzling as he sauntered toward us, which masked his apparent out-of-breath fluster. "I hate to duck in during a lesson, but I was hoping to avoid—"

"Donovan, there you are," said an old man, who flung the door open behind Donovan. He wore dark vestments and an even darker smirk. In his hands, he held a crude paring knife and an apple, into which several thin slices had been cut. Donovan's back was to him, so we all saw how his features contorted into an expression of pure discomfort while the old man behind him could not. I furrowed my brows along with Armand and Daisy. Kit and Graham, contrary to our confused reactions, immediately sat straight up to keep stiff postures.

Who was this man?

"Master Haitham," Graham spoke up. He stood up from his chair to greet the old Master, who seemed genuinely intrigued to see Graham surrounded by the four of us. Armand and Daisy seemed to be stunned—what did they know about him that I did not?

"Graham Keating?" Haitham the Master was apparently glad to receive Graham's extended hand after stabbing his knife into his apple to free his hand. "All these years, and you're still in the teaching profession. If I had your credentials, I'd have retired years ago!" His voice was like Graham's, mellow and measured. I got the feeling that if he raised his voice, it would be thunderous and frightening. He was past his middle age, I could tell, but he held himself with the composure of a much younger man.

"As long as there are earnest pupils, I will remain at my post," Graham said proudly. "Master Haitham, these are Master James' Tributes, Liza, Daisy, Armand, and—"

"Kit," Haitham declared. "We've met before."

I looked at once to Kit to convey through a nervously flabbergasted expression my confusion and worry. Kit avoided my eyes and instead kept his gaze locked onto Haitham.

"So this is James' rescue, Liza the Tribute," Haitham said, looking me up and down. He cut into his apple and placed the freshly cut piece between his teeth before taking a step toward me.

"We were just in the middle of a lecture, sir," Kit piped up quickly, moving into Haitham's path. A white hot surge of protectiveness swelled within me when Haitham fixed a menacing glare on Kit. I went to stand beside Kit but Graham cut in front of me.

"I wasn't expecting you this week, Master Haitham," Graham said, conjuring up his most bumbling and innocent tone. The more I saw of this strange behavior, the more I dreaded the presence of this old man. Graham was the sturdiest man I knew in this place; I'd never seen him shaken.

"This is an atypical summit, to say the least," Haitham said to Graham, obviously in distaste. "I wouldn't be bothered to linger, only James has insisted that our business is both urgent and fragile, and therefore must be handled very carefully over as much time as the Masters see fit." The old man turned his attention to me once again and I felt uncomfortably self-conscious, as though the air around me had suddenly thickened.

"I was looking for Graham in the hopes he would remember the name of that sensei James had hired for the boys a few years ago," Donovan lied smoothly, expertly applying his legendary charm to dissipate the tension around us. "If I'd known you were seeking a sympathetic ear, I'd have gladly met you in the library. Why don't we walk there together?" Anyone else would have come across as desperate, but Donovan's ingenuity sold the false innocence seamlessly—or so I thought, for Haitham appeared to be immune to Donovan's spell. He edged around Kit and Graham, staring at me and tilting his head curiously.

"Remarkable," Haitham said. "She looks just like her mother."

A mixture of fury and grief strummed in my chest as Haitham's observation rendered me speechless.

"His name was Yuki," Graham said to Donovan, shamelessly propping up Donovan's false reason for intruding on our lesson. "A great sensei in his time, to be sure, though I believe he's long since retired."

"Yes, I believe he is," Donovan said in a cheerfully hollow tone.

"He taught you a thing or two, did he not?" Haitham asked me, ignoring Graham and Donovan's banter on either side of us.

"Yes," I replied curtly. "Years ago, now."

"Yes, I remember the scandalous story that came of it," Haitham recalled. "You're the very same Liza who raised a hand to James in front of his staff, aren't you?"

"If memory serves, he raised a hand to me in kind," I said. Beside Haitham, Graham blanched and narrowed his disapproving, worried gaze at me. Haitham merely shook his head as a sinister chuckle sounded in his throat.

"You sound like your mother, too," Haitham told me. "You'll want to keep that biting wit of yours in check before it gets you into even more trouble." He stared pointedly at the bandages on my arms. "Kit was foggy on the details of your little excitement but I'd wager you mouthed off to Quinn one too many times. Is that why he tried to kill you?"

It was as though Haitham had pressed a hot iron to the lesion on my shoulder. My face burned with humiliation, my eyes filling at once with tears. I felt the need to spit in his face for saying such a thing. I was so overcome with rushing anger and embarrassment...and what did he mean, that Kit had been "foggy" on the details of the attack? How could Kit divulge such private affairs to a man like Haitham?

"Master Haitham, I should tell you that Liza has suffered no little trauma at Quinn's hands," Graham said right away. Besides Donovan, Graham was the only one in the room able to speak freely to a Master. "I feel I ought to remind you, sir, that kind of remark is in extremely poor taste!" Even Graham was flustered. I dared to steal a glance at the others and I saw Daisy had clapped a hand over her mouth. Armand's fists were balled at his sides and Kit was holding one of his arms in a tight grip to keep him from stepping forward.

"Is it?" Haitham asked. He smiled to see me upset before shrugging and turning from me, shining his hateful gaze of phony contrition at Graham. "No matter. It's James' job to treat her traumatic slights, not mine."

He was pure evil, I decided. A despicable bastard whom I hated intensely.

"And James has made a stellar job of it," Donovan offered, quickly moving between Haitham and Armand, who seemed just a hair away from losing his temper. "Tribute affairs can be tricky at the best of times, but James has had the good sense to collaborate with me on heightening security, the guardsmen rotations for example—"

"So I have seen," Haitham interrupted, sounding bored. "Though it hardly takes a logic professor to point out that if James had really done his job, that guardsman wouldn't have set foot on this compound in the first place."

"Is it considered polite for one Master to openly criticize another like that?" I blurted, my face hot. "Where are your Master's manners?" I refused to let Haitham's offense stand like that, not after James had saved my life just moments before Quinn would have taken it. Apparently, everyone was surprised when I defended James to Haitham, especially Daisy and the boys.

"I think what Liza is trying to point out," Donovan interjected quickly, "is that unfortunate incidents like her attack can happen in even the safest environments, that even the greatest of Masters let things slip through the cracks every now and then."

Haitham fixed an unimpressed glare at Donovan. "No," he said. "They do not."

"Excuse me?" said James, standing now in the open doorway of the room. His blue eyes were ablaze with fury—he was practically vibrating with anger. "What is going on here?"

"James," Haitham said pleasantly, as though James wasn't looking at him as though he was about to commit murder. "Good of you to intrude. I was looking for Donovan earlier and I stumbled in to find him chatting with your Tributes!"

James turned his glare on Donovan and I felt the small hairs on the back of my neck stand up.

"Graham, it was nice to see you after all these years," Haitham said, apparently he'd had enough of this charade. He turned from me to once more take in Daisy, Kit, and Armand with careful, crooked deliberation. "It has been very interesting to meet you. Kit, a rare pleasure to see you again; Donovan, I'm sure I'll remember what it was I wanted to speak with you about—for now, it seems to have escaped me."

All of us cringed in Haitham's wake when he quit the room. He strolled right past James as though he hadn't a care in the world, blissfully ignorant of the viscous rage permeating the room around James. I couldn't help but look to Kit, who was clenching his jaw and staring at James in disgust.

"Graham!" James thundered abruptly. Daisy and I both flinched. "Take them back to the Tribute wing at once!"

"Come along, pupils," Graham agreed lowly, ushering us out of the room. For a jarring moment, I thought James was seeing red too intensely to see that I was following Graham and the others back to our wing. Kit held us back for a moment, stopping short in the doorway to lean close to James.

"You promised!" he hissed bitterly.

"Kit, I am in no mood," James cautioned him. "Go back to your wing. I'll deal with this."

"Oh, I've heard that before!" Kit fired back in a hushed, venomous tone, not budging an inch. I made to slip around him and follow Armand into the hall, but in a snap, James braced his hand on the doorway, blocking my way with his arm.

"This is not the time or place, Kit," said James, all the while flashing a warning look at me. "You will wait in the hall for Douglas, Liza. You are not to set foot outside these chambers."

"As you say," I said immediately. James dropped his arm and let us through. Kit was steaming as he bustled out of the room. Daisy slipped her fingers between mine and Armand followed closely behind me. We all jumped—Daisy whimpered—when the doors to my old room slammed behind us. Donovan had not emerged after Graham; I did not want to think about the lashing he was receiving behind those doors.

"What the hell was that about?" Armand whispered in my ear.

"Who was that man, Kit?" I asked.

"Haitham the Master," Kit begrudgingly mumbled through gritted teeth.

"Yeah, we gathered," Armand retorted dryly as we rounded the corner, clipping fast toward the exit of the Masters' rooms.

"You met him before?" I asked. "When?"

Kit came to a sudden halt, turning to peer at me with an angry, strained expression. "A few days ago," he said quietly. "He's James' father."

"What!" I yelped. Armand and Daisy were hardly surprised. I wanted to beg them to explain but I couldn't seem to find the words. It was all I could do not to double over from the queasy, sucker-punched feeling that slammed into me.

James' father, the one who gave the order to steal us from our parents during their summit for rapprochement; the old man who grinned to see me squirm after he made snide remarks about Quinn nearly murdering me. Someone so vile had confirmed what I had been wondering since James told me the truth about how we came to be here, that I did in fact resemble my mother. Even worse, according to Haitham, I embodied her boldness. I was sick from this, utterly revolted.

"We need to keep moving," Graham insisted, gently pushing Armand and Daisy along. "Master James has ordered me to take you back to your apartments and I intend to do that before we get into any more trouble!"

"We're in trouble?" Armand asked. "But why?" I wished I could tell him all the horrible things Haitham had done but the words failed me.

"Armand," Graham sighed, visibly becoming vexed when none of us moved at his insistence. "This is serious. Master Haitham's radar is not the place we want to be. I implore you, all of you, to return with me to your wing of the compound."

"I'll explain everything once we get back," Kit assured me, eager to assuage my pale and shaken demeanor.

"James said I have to stay here," I said slowly, once we reached the hallway leading to the exit.

"You should hear what I have to say, Liza," Kit said gravely, "especially since you run a greater risk of running into him than we do." Little did Kit know, however, I knew exactly what kind of stuff Haitham was made of.

"There will be other lessons," Graham urged, now bordering on desperate to leave the Masters' rooms. "Other times to discuss this. We must leave now."

"It's all right," I said airily. "Go. I'll be fine." Once again, I could see that Armand was the only one who did not believe me. I set my hand on his chest and peered into his eyes. "Go, Armie. Take care of them."

"Come to us later if you can," he said. "Tell James it's for dinner if you must."

"I will." I knew James would never allow it but I said it anyway. I stayed down the hall while Graham hurried them out. I stood still for a few minutes after the doors opened and shut, just listening to the quiet ringing through the halls. I looked over when I heard footsteps and saw Douglas approaching at a quicker pace than usual.

"Douglas," I greeted him.

"You'd better come with me," said Douglas, not returning a salutation. He led me back to James' room and told me to stay put. When he advised me to wait a while before paging the kitchens for dinner, I wondered how the tense situation could have escalated. Still, I did as I was told. I hadn't seen James that angry before, at least without an exposure that culminated in violence, and I was not keen on catching him at his worst. I wondered if Douglas had—maybe he hadn't, which was why he wanted me safely removed from the warpath leading from my old room.

I wasn't hungry and the ache in my shoulder was still relatively dull. In all the excitement, I'd left my sling in my old room so I couldn't bind my arm comfortably to my chest. With a sigh, I took up the sketchbook I kept tucked into the portable by my cot. I opened the curtains and pulled up James' desk chair, with my good arm, right in front of the wide window. I folded my legs under me, so close to the window that my knees touched the glass, and set the pad in my lap. With a charcoal pencil in hand, I stared out at the crashing waves and dark grey sky overhead. Raindrops splattered against the window as a howling wind raged outside, whipping across the treetops below. I began to draw waves, pages of them, wearing the charcoal down as I dragged the tip across the paper in jagged, wild lines. I poured my anger, my humiliation, and my sorrow into the waves, stopping only when the door to James' room closed with a soft thud.

I looked up to see James leaning against the doors, looking down at his feet with a pained expression twisting his features into the face of a much younger, almost vulnerable man. I almost got up but hesitated.

"James?" I said, simply to alert him of my presence. He sighed and wiped his mouth with the back of his hand. It came away bloody and I stood up. "What happened?"

"It's nothing." I could see when I took a few steps closer that his lip had been cut. He looked up at me quizzically when he didn't see my arm strapped to my chest. "Where's the sling?"

"I left it in the classroom," I said. I bit the inside of my cheek before nervously asking, "Are you all right?"

James snorted, as though I'd just asked him a silly question—perhaps I had. "It's nothing, Liza. I hit Donovan. He hit me back. It wasn't the first time we've scuffled, and it won't be the last." He crossed the room to his desk and yanked open a drawer to take out a clean handkerchief, which he then folded and held to his lip. I crossed my arms as I watched him pull the tiny bottle of painkiller capsules out of his pocket and fumble with the cap.

"He said I looked like my mother."

"Who, Donovan?"

"Haitham." The word stung us both. The vindication I felt to see James recoil when I brought up his father boiled away to shame, as I remembered the sickly eager look in Haitham's eyes when he saw he'd gotten to me. "He said I sounded just like her, too," I added. "How did he know Kit, James? How could you have let a man like that anywhere near him, knowing the truth about how we were brought here?"

James shook his head and sighed, dejected. "This is what he does," he said. "This is his game: how few strings can he pull at once to inflict the most damage." He winced and touched the cloth to his lip again.

"Kit isn't a string!" I exclaimed, the lump in my throat breaking apart my stony resolve.

"I know he isn't," James said. "I didn't mean to say he was. He was wrong to speak to you about your mother."

"He knew about Quinn." James took a second handkerchief out of his desk drawer and offered it to me. I took it to dab at my eyes, glaring at him all the same. "He said Kit told him about it. Is that true?"

"No, I'm afraid I did. Haitham's idea of a fun is turning people against each other, as proven by my latest scrap with Donovan. I'm sure his goal is to make you angry with Kit. Did it work?"

"Of course not! Why would I be angry with Kit? He was likely bullied into talking to Haitham in the first place!"

"Haitham is hardly past his prime, but it doesn't mean he isn't likely to switch tactics every now and then just to make it interesting for himself," James said, a darkness falling over his features. "This is precisely what I was talking about, Liza. The measures I've taken to protect you, all four of you, include keeping you as far from Haitham's reach as I can. You wouldn't have found out about him at all if it hadn't been for—"

"For my botched suicide attempt, as you call it?" I cut in angrily. "Your father has already humiliated me today, I don't need any further comments from you!"

"I was going to say, if it hadn't been for Donovan, who led him right to you." I resented him for his patience, for it weighted my already despondent shoulders down with guilt over my displaced outburst. James chuckled in spite of himself and dropped his folded kerchief on his desk. "He has a penchant for humiliation, my father. I haven't seen him in almost ten years, by prejudiced choice on my part, but still he can waltz right in and deconstruct the foundation I've been fortifying against him since I was a child."

I did not expect James to be so forthcoming. I felt strangely self-conscious when he crossed his arms and began to slowly pace across the room before me. I'd seen him ready to rip Donovan to shreds earlier, but now he was introspective, cynical, and unable to sit still? I was struck by his resemblance to Armand, so much so that I couldn't think of a single thing to say.

"I imagine you are struggling with the things he said to you, about your mother," James said. I nodded, biting down on my lower lip to keep it from trembling. "You should know—at the risk of further upsetting you, in case you are searching for some sense of comfort—that I have met your mother many times over the years, during summits like this ongoing one. I won't pretend to know her well, though I probably know Lorena better than my own mother, considering she died when I was an infant." James caught himself digressing. "The similarities Haitham pointed out between you and Lorena are true. You look so much like her and you've inherited many of her strongest traits...she would likely deck me worse than Donovan did today for presuming so, but I believe she would be proud of the parts of her that shine through you."

I was incredibly moved—startled, even, to see James express himself with such soft, almost poetic cadence. My heart swelled as I recognized in his eyes the same loneliness I saw in my reflection after every scalding bath I took. Outside, a clap of thunder cut through the sky. Like a frightened child who wanted to hide under the covers during a storm like this, I wanted Armand, Daisy, and Kit for comfort, for as quelling as James' words had been, they left me feeling lonelier than ever.

"I want to see Daisy and the boys," I told James.

"Liza," he sighed. "Not today."

"Please?" I tried again. "You can take me yourself if you feel you have to. I just...." I sniffed and wiped my cheeks dry. "I need to be with them."

James refused me. "Tomorrow." I knew he would say it but I dreaded the disappointment that set in after I was forced to accept that I would have to bear these tormenting thoughts alone. I turned from James and went back to my seat, from which I could see branchlike bolts of lightning strike the sea. I put charcoal to paper incessantly, flipping over the sketchpad with desperation every few minutes after I'd filled each page. I didn't bother to listen for James. I knew he would take another pill and lie down, or if I was lucky, he would see that I had his desk chair and leave to work somewhere else.

I paused my drawing for a moment when I heard a door shut. I wasn't sure if James had gone to bathe or if he'd actually left the room. Either way, I was determined to prove to him that I could bear my isolation better than he could, that as much as I wanted to page Jada for a dose of painkilling medicine to stifle the awful bite of humiliation and loneliness, I could take my sadness and put it all into the stormy ocean outside.

James was gone for a long time. I must have filled over half the sketchpad with my captures of the dark, tossing sea outside in the span of an hour. I set the book down and went to my cot to retrieve my music device. I went right back to the chair by the window and turned up the volume of the music as loud as I could stand it. Armand used to tell me about how he would measure his breathing to settle his nerves. I tried to do it, remembering little about the process, before I decided it was pointless to try to stop myself from chasing my thoughts down a spiraling, tumultuous shaft, at the bottom of which was the writhing ache of companionless seclusion.

One of the budlike headphones was yanked out of my ear. I started, surprised to see James standing over me.

"You scared me!" I yelped, clutching at my racing heart.

"I didn't mean to," James said, holding his hands up. He waited for me to shut off my music and wind the cord around the little device. "I did try to get your attention," he offered. I winced and touched the bandages covering my shoulder.

"My back was to the door," I said. "What is it?"

"I spoke to Graham just now, after the summit affairs concluded down the hall," said James. I noticed his furrowed brow and pursed lips—he was cross, for the second time today, but what had I done to merit him frightening me like that? "He said that you—Liza, earlier today, after Donovan interrupted your lesson with the others, did you...defend me, to Haitham?" James was studying my expression meticulously.

"No," I replied nervously.

"Graham said you did. He said you became defiant and accused Haitham of forgetting his manners."

"Everything that came out of his mouth was repugnant!" I had probably never flipped on one of my own lies so fast, I was that furious about Haitham. I wondered why James would ask me about this at all if Graham had already told him about the incident. James let out a shaky breath and braced his hands on the arms of my chair.

"Listen to me, Liza," he said roughly. "However horrendously Haitham behaves around you, no matter what he says, you must never—I repeat *never*—do anything like that again!"

"Why shouldn't I?" It was no little outrage that James would rebuke me for defending him and then tack on this latest addendum, that Haitham could use Quinn's attack against me and demand I abstain from defending myself.

"Haitham is not like other Masters, Liza," James insisted in a pained voice. "He views things like compassion and kindness as grotesque weaknesses. If you give him even the slightest glimpse of altruism, he will go out of his way to make sure you live to regret it."

"How can you stand to work with him? If he's so terrible, why haven't the other Masters sent him away?"

"He is cunning and connected in ways even I couldn't guess." The way he spoke made me believe he'd made this argument before. "The only thing he's better at than maximizing the benefits of the system is protecting himself. You cannot push back on him like you did today, not ever! He is happy to play the non-threatening old man he looks like but he is not that person, I assure you. I do not want you to ever meet the true version of himself." He withdrew his grasp on the arms of my chair but stood over me still to impress his seriousness.

I said nothing to James for a while. Instead I stared up at him, sifting past the defensiveness and anger glowering from his eyes. I hoped to recognize something truthful there, something beyond his need to be obeyed, or feared, or respected. Maybe James did not know the difference between the latter two; it would explain a lot. I wanted so much to ask James, "What happened? What did Haitham do to you?" but I was too worried that he would tell me something that would leave a scar much uglier than the ones Quinn had given me.

"What happened to him to make him like this?" I asked instead, about Haitham. James appeared perturbed. "I've read that grief takes hold of some people in strange ways," I prompted him, remembering that he'd said his mother had died when he was an infant, and that his sister Petra had been murdered in his adolescence.

"I don't believe that anything happened to him," said James, who suddenly sounded very hollow. "He may not have been a hateful child but the shadow of the monster he is now was always there. *He* happened, plain and simple.

And then a cluster of like-minded individuals put him in power. Combined with the arrogance of youth and the nurturing environment of being comfortable enough to display his repugnance, as you described it, in front of his peers—that's how the monster came to be."

If I were to point out to James that he'd essentially just described himself, would it wound him? Would he hit me? I didn't find Haitham and his son to be identical by any means, but I couldn't help but be fascinated by James' phrasing. I couldn't imagine any child being cruel or hateful, even James; nor could I imagine an adolescent arrogant enough to successfully abuse the trust of those who politically opposed him. Furthermore, I could not make sense of a group of people's decision to reward such a person's obedience with a position of power simply to serve their system.

I had a scar on my lip to prove that James was comfortable enough to display his own brand of repugnance in front of his peers. James and Haitham were undeniably similar, and yet when I lingered on the memory that day on the training floor, I could still recall the way James had almost laughed when I'd hit him. The look in his eyes when he'd paid me back resonated with a certain mindlessness, as though punishing me for striking him was merely a reflex.

Haitham's jabs about Quinn and my mother had been calculated. It was obvious that he was present and engaged when he spoke, making sure every deplorable thing he said ring with an iniquitous purpose.

I shuddered involuntarily when I thought about the attack and how James had dragged Quinn away from me. How he killed him for me. How panicked his voice had been when he pulled me, bleeding and suffering, into his arms. How he had stayed with me until I succumbed to the painkillers. How he woke up each night since to quiet my frightened cries from the nightmares in which I relived the whole thing, and how he remained at my side until I fell back asleep.

There was a difference, if I could only name one, between father and son. Despite James' mean streak and consistent efforts to hide it from all of us, he possessed the very thing Haitham perceived as a weakness: it was compassion. He just kept it buried under ugly mood swings and violent outbursts so that no one could see it was there.

"Are you worried that Haitham will do something, because I defended you to him?" I asked.

"Yes," James said without reservation. "In fact, I am certain he will. It's not you he'll blame for that show of loyalty, or whatever it was that made you speak up to him—it's me."

"You're a Master, same as he is. What could he possibly do to you?"

"Haitham knows very well that the lives of the people in this compound and its very stability rests on my shoulders. He doesn't have to lay a finger on me to compromise my authority; that would be too direct for him. He'd target everyone around me, down to the last tradesman, to make his point." James sighed bitterly. "It's my duty, Liza. I will put myself between him and this compound because it is my job to do so—that includes protecting the conditions your parents laid out."

"You really hate him," I said, reading his darkened expression carefully.

"That is irrelevant," said James. "I learned a long time ago that I do not have a choice between doing what I want and fulfilling what I must do. I despise my father, I have no qualms about telling you so, but if I turn my back on him in the middle of this summit, the peace we've kept between Masters and Free Factions for all these years will crumble. That's what I've been trying to tell you all along, Liza, that your actions have immense consequences for everyone around you. You perceive the motive behind the measures I've taken to keep you safe to be nothing more than controlling, for the sake of my status as a Master? Far from it. I'm trying to make sure that everyone you pass in these halls has a place to live, eat, and trade safely—and I didn't ask to serve the system like this any more than you asked to be brought up in it."

Guilt trickled down my face as though someone had cracked an egg over my head. It was not for James' sake that I felt ashamed now but for the people I put at risk when I leaped from the library window, namely the only three people I loved in the world. I leaned forward in my seat and hugged my middle, awkwardly balancing my elbows on the tops of my thighs as I looked up at James.

"You almost jumped out of that library window right after me," I recalled, detaching my voice from the quiver in my chest. "You must have spent hundreds of nights before that, sitting before that very window with a book in your lap. Tell me, did you ever look out over the trees and imagine slipping away into the night, telling no one, to leave everything behind, and save yourself? Don't you ever think about escaping this place?"

More human as I'd ever seen him, James smirked sadly down at me with understanding shining in his blue eyes. "I consider it often," he admitted.

"What stops you?"

"You." He cleared his throat and crossed his arms. "The four of you. I brought you here. I can't abjure my responsibility to you and everyone else in this compound. After all, no one escapes—Armand reminds you often enough, I'm surprised the idea never stuck." Saying aloud his own edict brought forth a dulcet sigh. "Contrary to popular belief, being a Master does not mean that I am exempt from that law."

When I looked up at him, I recognized a raw sheen of isolation in his eyes. "I didn't realize you had so much in common with us."

"Maybe I do," said James with a shrug. "It's the things you have in common with *me* that I worry about."

I couldn't help but agree with that. "Me too," I said. James noticed then just how much of his guard was down and checked himself. The sorrow vanished from his countenance behind a wall of neutrality before my eyes. James pushed his sleeve back and checked his wristwatch.

"It's late, Liza. It's inappropriate of me to engage you in a conversation of this nature, especially such a long one when you are meant to be resting." There was James the Master, persistently reserved as he hid behind his practiced manners. He may as well have walked out of the room and reentered as an entirely different person.

Still, I took his cue. I got to my feet and pushed the desk chair back to its place. I took up my nearly full sketchpad and retreated to my cot, unable to shake the feeling that I was wrong to have spoken to James at all about his private life. Worse yet, the more I pondered the things he'd said, the less angry I was with him. James interrupted my reverie to tell me he had to step out shortly to make arrangements for his summit gathering tomorrow morning. I went to bathe, to wash away the conflicting ideas I had about who James really was. I'd come to like the lavender soap that had at first been too strong for my liking, and then after a relatively short soak, I redressed and crawled back into bed before James returned from his late-night errand.

Maybe it was the candor with which James and I finally applied when we talked, or the way he removed his usual pretense and shared his tribulations earnestly, but as I drifted off, I was confident that I might be the only soul under this roof who had ever seen that side of him. I fell asleep feeling less alone than I had in months.

It was not Quinn who haunted my unconscious mind, but Haitham: I dreamed once more of falling, down, down, down—it was not a support beam that I caught, but Haitham's outstretched hand. He pulled my arm and I was no longer suspended over the floor underneath the compound, but inside the movement studio. The scent of blood was all around but I could not feel its warmth on me. Haitham drew me further within the studio, grinning widely to show off a row of horrifically sharp teeth. He shoved me before the mirror and yanked my arms up over my head.

"Turn!" he cawed, twisting me around as though I were a doll. In the mirror, I could see myself, aghast and miserable, dancing along with Haitham's rough direction. I looked like myself but an insidious dread, the kind that only exists in dreams, welled in my stomach. I was looking at my mother, not my reflection. She was frantic to keep up with my movements, matching each forced twirl.

"Keep going, baby," my mother said in my voice. "You've got to keep going."

I turned away from myself-as-my-mother to look at Haitham, who had morphed somehow into Quinn midway through one of my turns. I screamed as he spun me into his arms; once I was held against his chest, he jammed a blade into the side of my neck—

I let out a strangled cry and woke myself up by painfully swiping at my neck to deflect a blade that was not there and in the process, I thwacked the strip of gauze taped over my shoulder with the heel of my hand. I kicked out from under my sheets and struggled to steady my breathing. With the curtains open, I could only see the outline of James as he rushed over to me from his bed. I burst into tears, in pain and in fright, just as James set his hand on my arm.

"Liza, you're all right," he assured me. "It was only a dream. You're safe."

"I hurt myself!" I whined, groaning as I reached to tenderly touch my shoulder.

"Do you want something for the pain?"

"No, I just need to sit for a minute." I gulped a deep breath and shivered. James sighed groggily and nodded.

"I'll get you some water." He went to the bedside table and brought back a glass of water, which he told me to drink slowly instead of downing it at once. He must have been exhausted, for he went back to sleep before I laid back down.

I tried to settle my nerves but found it to be impossible. When I curled up on the cot to close my eyes, I felt as though Haitham was hovering over me. I got up and went to James' bed, seeking the solace of the looming canopy overhead. James did not stir when I slid under the covers—his bed was so wide, we were over an arm's reach apart. At least this way, if I had another nightmare, James would be close. With the canopy hanging over me and the sound of the crashing sea outside, I slowly fell back asleep.

Chapter Thirteen

James the Master must have laid awake for a full hour before even a hint of drowsiness pooled behind his tired, tempestuous eyes. He had gone to bed late and would rise early, just a few hours from now, to face another day of systemic debate. Why not call it a circus instead of a summit, he wondered as he tried in vain to force the pressing matters from his exhausted mind. After a rotten day like this one, James was prepared to beg for a restful night's sleep.

Liza had long since departed the land of the wakeful; James could hear her steady sighs across the room as she slept in her cot, curled up to favor her injured arm. It took her no time to drift off after her evening dose of medication, a luxury James could not afford since the girl had suffered such a violent near-death encounter. Each night since the attack, the moment Liza's pain-dulling drugs wore off, she would shriek and toss as though her sheets through some cruel alchemy had become the man who would have killed her. These nightmares usually arrived the moment James was able to close his eyes and doze. He began to anticipate them according to how desperate he was for sleep—tonight's episode might be moments away, James was so keen to shut the world away for just a few hours....

It was a knock at the Master's door, not a cry or moan from Liza, that caught his attention and summoned him away from the solace of slumber. James heaved himself out of his bed, a furnishing fit for a king, and padded over to answer the door.

"Master James," Douglas whispered, nodding curtly. "It's late, I know."

"You didn't wake me." James couldn't complain even if he tried. "What is it?"

Douglas frowned. "There's been a—disturbance." He tucked his thumbs into his belt. "At the east gate."

"What manner of disturbance?" Since the other Masters had arrived for the summit, his desk had been flooded every morning with reports of entry control problems, curfew disruptions, and various other misdemeanors that he didn't care to deal with.

"A lethal one, sir. Two of ours were found outside the gate." Douglas anticipated his Master's response, a menacing curse and a sub-zero degree glare. James shut his door for a minute and emerged after, fully dressed down to his boots. After locking the doors tightly, James turned on his heel and marched down the hall with Douglas at his side. He knew the Master well enough to get the crucial details of his report out now, within the privacy of the Master wing, as James would berate him unrelentingly for uttering a precious phrase in the common areas. "It's a mess, sir. The doctor isn't sure if the scouts attacked each other—"

"Which scouts?"

"Mars and Dominic," Douglas replied at once. "There are no witnesses who can attest to Doctor Miles' theory that they killed each other. She isn't sure what to make of it beyond that."

"Who else knows?"

"Just me, Nathan, David, Doctor Miles, and a handful of Donovan's men," said Douglas. He followed James down the steps leading away from the Masters' wing.

"So Donovan, too." James wanted to hit something. By the time he reached the east gate, he was practically jogging. Two of his guardsmen opened the doors for him and before the Master knew it, he was swallowed up in a gust of winter air—just the thing he needed to jar himself out of his exhaustion. James saw Jada, bundled in a heap of downy, standing over two heaps of unmoving scout uniforms. Beside her was Nathan, his hands crammed in his pockets to save his fingers from the biting cold. When he saw James approach, he straightened his posture and tried his best to look tolerant of the weather.

"Who found them?" James went straight to Nathan for this report.

"Donovan's three, over there," said Nathan, pointing out each soldier as they shuffled close together to keep warm. Even in their heavy green cloaks and fur-lined boots, they were chilled to the bone from standing outside for so long. Nathan's nose was bright red and his speech was slurred, his lips numb from the cold. "They called me and David right away." Nathan warned James as the Master went to kneel over the dead scouts, "It's gruesome, sir...."

James' heart sank as he glimpsed up close the ribbons of bloody flesh that used to be Dominic the Scout's throat. The scout's chest was sliced up too. Mars' fatal wounds were similar. Upon closer inspection, James noticed defensive cuts on the backs of Mars' arms—cuts so deep, the man's ulna was visible at the bases of each gash.

"It must have been a terrible brawl," said Jada. James stood to face her and could tell by the many shades she'd paled, this grisly scene would haunt her for a long time.

"You three!" James raised his voice to catch the attention of Donovan's scouts. He beckoned for them to come over and they obeyed hastily. "Did you find them here or were they moved?"

"They were moved, Master James," said the tallest of the three scouts. "We were concerned the blood would draw unwanted attention from anything that might be sniffing around the forest."

James supposed moving the bodies was an acceptable reason as to how Donovan's scouts came to be covered in blood. "Describe the scene. Were they dead upon your arrival?"

"Yes, sir." The brawniest of the scouts was the only one of the three who managed to hold James' eye contact without wavering. He also seemed to be the least affected by the cold. "The only tracks we could see were those of your guardsmen, sir, so as far as we can tell—"

"I'll be the judge of that," said James. "Take me to where you found them."

"Sir, the tracks will have been swept up in the snow by now," said the brawny scout. "There's a fierce wind building up from the south. We were coming in from a patrol for shelter when we found the bodies."

Biting back a curse, James swiveled back to frown over his dead scouts. Both of these men had been well liked among the guards. James found them to be capable and obedient, not rowdy and violent as the manner of their demise would impose. There was a slender chance that his two scouts had imbibed themselves with spirits and argued violently while making their rounds but it was far more likely that Mars and Dominic had stumbled into something treacherous that they, as proved by Mars' defensive wounds, did not expect to find. Reluctant as he was to imagine who might be trespassing on the grounds below, James had to pursue that avenue of deduction—his men had not killed each other, he was certain.

"As far as you know, these men killed each other." It was his prerogative as Master of the Aventine to dictate which truths he would have the residents of his compound believe. The summit had everyone on edge and to keep up the appearance of peace in the Aventine, James would have to keep these murders hidden behind a veil of secrecy if he could. He would have to play out solving this mystery by keeping his suspicions to himself.

"Oh, don't tell me you actually believe that?" scoffed Haitham, who had slipped through the gate while James glowered over his scouts. The older man was bundled in a cloak that more resembled a thick woolen blanket, black to match his heart. He watched James dole out orders to his guards, instructing them brusquely to move the bodies as soon as possible and just as discreetly. "This isn't just a mess, James. It's a calling card, and you know exactly who sent it."

"As long as there is an abundance of staff at your disposal in the medical wing, I'd like full autopsies on both Mars and Dominic," James said to Jada. At his dismissal, the doctor took leave of the bitter cold to trade the sleepwear under her coat for work clothes. For Jada, this long night had just become even longer.

"Are you really going to ignore her?" Haitham asked with a cock of his head.

"I'm not ignoring Harriet," muttered James. "I'm ignoring you."

"She is not a cat leaving dead birds on your doorstep for the fun of it," Haitham said in a louder voice. He wanted the scouts and guards to hear every syllable spoken between him and their Master. "Do you think it's an accident that the Free Factions have been particularly feisty over the past seventy-two hours? Or that your scouts turned up slaughtered in the midst of this summit?"

James spared his father a scathing glance before chuffing a tired, sardonic chuckle. "I was wondering when you would cry wolf," he said.

"Proof that a wolf is on the prowl lies there." Haitham pointed to the dead bodies at James' feet. "Harriet and her radicals are under your proud nose, James. It's not merely a threat, it's a message. She's close, ready to strike—"

"You're paranoid," spat James. Haitham challenging his authority behind closed doors was one thing, but the Aventine's Master was too tired to tolerate this pushback in front of his guards. He raised his pitch in kind to make sure he was heard by all who stood outside. "There has never been a breach in this compound, structurally or otherwise. I will investigate the deaths of my scouts and deal with the findings as I see fit, not jump to hysterical conclusions about Free Agents roaming the forest under our feet!"

Haitham merely smiled. "You are underestimating the gravity of this situation, James."

"Perhaps you're right," James retorted. "I'll defer to your judgment, sir, since it is you—not I—that has a history of underestimating Harriet."

"Keep it up," growled Haitham, lowering his voice as his temper surged to the surface. He would not be engaged nor bested in a contest of stubborn wills by his own son, regardless of his superior status. "There could easily be a third body found outside by morning."

James bared his teeth and glared back at his father. The old man's threat was not an empty one but James was hardly intimidated, as such a bold claim proved how frightened Haitham was. "Try me," said James, who savored his father's dread above all else. Without having to summon them, the guards flanked James with their hands set on the hilts of their blades. Haitham held his ground for a moment before shrinking where he stood and looking away first from his son's provocative stare.

"Let it be known that James the Master turned away the valuable counsel of his elder in a time of crisis," Haitham declared, drawing his cloak tighter around his chest.

"I'll make sure to have that put in a history book," replied James dryly.

"You'll remember this moment, when all of this comes crashing down around you."

Now *that* was an empty threat, thought James. "Essential staff members are not permitted to leave the Aventine until further notice," he said. He turned to his guards, mindful to raise his voice so that Haitham could hear him even as he marched back to the gate. "No one sets foot outside the gates without my express consent."

By the time James retuned to the Master wing, the night had devolved from the mere small hours to the onset of dawn. His edict had already circulated the Aventine's halls thanks to the earnestly dutiful night guards and the order of lockdown was already setting a stringent tone for the new day. With leaden muscles and a nagging headache, James reached his bedchamber with just enough stamina to unlock the doors, push one open, and shut it behind him. He could have fallen where he stood and slept quite soundly on the floor, but he willed himself to drag his feet over to the bed.

No sooner had he flopped down on the mattress than Liza began to stir, murmuring in distress.

"Please," sighed James. "Not again." He was not one to pray but he found himself pleading to the sliver of night that remained. He would give anything for Liza's nightmare to subside. The girl began to struggle frantically amid her bedding. She cried out and James heaved himself out of bed, rushing with energy he did not have to her side. He touched her arm gently and shushed her woeful outbursts. Her eyelids lifted enough for James to see the whites of her eyes in the dark.

"Quinn—" She gasped for breath. She was not truly awake but caught in the demimonde, between reality and her terrible memories of the attack.

"He's gone," James assured Liza. "It's all right. You're safe." The Tribute let out a whimper and laid her head back on her pillow. Sleep took mercy on her and lulled her away from reliving the assault. Once James was sure the girl would stay still, he fell into his bed once more. Lying on his stomach with his face buried in his pillow, James shut his eyes and waited for sleep to take him like it had Liza. Instead, lurid visions of cut throats and dead men in the snow flashed across the backs of James' eyelids. Words of condolence that would have to be penned to the families of his murdered scouts began to take form in James' mind, too, pushing sleep farther and farther away.

James rolled over onto his back and stared up into the canopy hanging over him. Between Haitham's sulfurous presence in the Aventine, the matters that would be argued at the summit meetings in just a few short hours, and the knowledge of the autopsies taking place at that moment, James surrendered his defeat. He would not sleep a wink tonight.

"To hell with it," he sighed. He heaved himself out of bed, knowing that dawn was approaching swiftly, and went to bathe. He would need a head start on the day despite his aversion to taking part in a single aspect of it.

Irrelevant, James coached himself as he pondered how badly he did not want to be a Master today. His was a grueling and thankless job. If he could not prove that he was up to the task, how could he expect others to do their jobs too?

Chapter Fourteen

These days, I craved the breaks I had from thinking so hard about how I was supposed to move forward after everything that had happened. Returning to my ballet lessons was more than just a much needed break though; it was a way for me to live by Armand's jaded practices and protect myself by pretending to play the Masters' game. If I were to be seen dancing again, acting as though there were nothing weighing on my mind, no one would think twice about the private machinations I contemplated.

James had seen to it that no evidence of Liza's attack remained here in the studio. I didn't know whether to be thankful that he'd restored my safe place or insulted that he'd so hastily covered up the only proof of his incompetence as a Master so that he could save face under the noses of the visiting ones. I hated to think of James now, for it brought to mind the awful mental image of Liza, eyes dulled by pain medicine and spirit drained by his tyrannical influence. Perhaps the most painful collateral damage was Armand's change of heart, for after Liza had insisted that everything we'd built our hopes on was out of reach, that the shocking relations between James, Donovan, and Haitham suddenly meant nothing, Armand had retreated within himself.

Armand was distracted and downright mean at times, now only calling me "sweetheart" in bitterness. It was as though he resented me, but for what?

Kit's fire had been stamped out too by all we had been through over the past few weeks. I took careful pride in rousing his attitude, my most recent success, and it brought a smile to my face as I tied on my pointe shoes and went to the center of the studio. Truthfully, I was more relieved than ever to be back in this studio, so much so that I spent every spare moment I could scrounge up voluntarily being criticized by my very strict but graceful instructor, Helena.

"What's become of your posture, girl?" Helena asked sharply. Her hands came down on my shoulders and I winced when she squeezed me tightly. "Are you a dancer or an overcooked noodle? What is this loose form? Tighten up. I won't tell you again."

"Yes, Miss Helena," I replied quickly, badly suppressing my smile as I thought of Kit. I amended my poise once she took her hands away. I repeated the form exercises, mindful of Helena's laser-like gaze on me as I moved. I couldn't help but lend every extension of my arm a longer curl or farther reach. I felt a new appreciation for my body today and I could see no point in trying to hold myself back.

"It's this ridiculous summit that's got you off balance, isn't it, Daisy?" Helena murmured, circling me slowly as I hopped up on tiptoe, my toenails screaming in pain after weeks of being out of my pointe shoes. I breathed through it, eager to impress my teacher. "Everyone under this roof is on edge. I know you children are especially under scrutiny, but as for the rest of us?" She clicked her tongue. "You'd think these tradesfolk would be accustomed to a gathering of Masters—they act like it is the end of society as we know it, but I've seen how these summits go." She tapped my arm and I slumped out of my held position, gritting my teeth as my toes and ankles throbbed. All the delight that had carried me on a cloud into the lesson had dissipated.

"How do they go?"

"Oh, you know, the Masters gather under the pretense of settling affairs or expanding their reach, maybe argue for a few days about their conflict with the Free Factions, but it's really all so they can throw a great big party and congratulate each other on being king of the hill," Helena said. She never tried to hide her gripes and I appreciated that about her.

"But do they usually take so long?" I asked. "I've never seen a summit. I wouldn't know." Helena's dark eyes were shiny with contemptuous hilarity as she laughed to herself.

"If a man's job for two weeks is to get his balls fondled, would you expect him to be quick to conclude his business?" she asked with a smile.

I blushed at her crass language and Helena chuckled. "You worked hard today, Daisy. After a messy few weeks, I'm glad to be working with you again." She came over to me and laid her hand on my arm before narrowing her eyes and saying, "Your form was loose, your turns sloppy. We'll work on those tomorrow—don't come in here with that sad face, girl, you know I'm only making you better."

I nodded and thanked her, then went to gingerly change out of my pointe shoes and gather my things. Helena went to her office and shut the door, likely to smoke one of those reeking hand-rolled cigarettes she was famous for passing around on solstice holidays, leaving me alone in the studio.

My legs hurt and I was starving but the rigorous practicing felt good. I pulled my socks on over my aching, bruised feet, staring all the while at the freshly polished wooden floor. I left the studio with my clothes stuffed in my shoulder bag, grateful for the short walk from the studio to our wing as I'd worked too strenuously to put on clean clothes without showering first. Beads of sweat made loose hairs that had fallen out of my bun cling to the back of my neck. I kept a slow pace as I walked back to the Tribute wing, both to be gentle on my sore feet and to relish the cool air of the main hall.

"My, my, look at you," said Donovan, falling fluidly into step with me. "I see the studio has been reopened."

"It has been," I replied with a grin. "Though over two weeks have passed since my last lesson and according to Helena, I'm already extremely lazy."

"By Helena's standards, maybe," Donovan surmised. "You've dealt with a lot in two weeks." He wore a green tunic today with dark slacks and shiny black boots. The chiseled muscles of his chest were accentuated by the cling of his shirt's fabric and the blade strapped to his back. I wondered if there was a singular color that would be uncomplimentary on him—he even looked good in all black.

"Not as much as Liza," I murmured.

"Of course," Donovan agreed. "How has she been, Daisy? I saw her the other day when I interrupted your lesson."

"With Master Haitham," I said, pointedly watching Donovan to reveal any knowing sign that would confirm his relation to the old man. Donovan's expression never faltered. "She seems to be better," I added quickly so Donovan wouldn't notice I'd brought Haitham up to try to put him off balance.

"She's unbreakable, that one," Donovan remarked appreciatively.

"Liza?" I shook my head. "Maybe so, given everything she's overcome. I can't help but think if it weren't for the summit, she'd be home with us."

"Daisy," Donovan assured me, "Liza is under James' and Jada's careful watch. I know being apart from her is hard on you three, but it really is for the best."

"You don't know her like we do," I told him, daring to correct him without carefully lacing my words with manners. "If she weren't so much like Armand, I wouldn't be so keen to get her back with us."

Donovan lightly touched my arm, slowing me to a stop. He came around to face me, wearing a soft frown etched with concern. "What do you mean?"

"It's silly," I murmured, shaking my head. It was hard for me to hold Donovan's gaze, for when I stared up into his blue eyes, my cheeks felt hot. "Just an observation, something I can't really explain...."

"You can tell me anything, Daisy," Donovan said, as though he did not care in the slightest that we were surrounded by passing tradesfolk. I hated to think of being seen fidgeting with my ballet satchel while conversing with Donovan, especially after the heinous theory James had concocted. I decided to be bold, like Liza, and match Donovan's confidence.

"Liza can hide behind her eyes," I explained. "She shuts down and forces the calmest, most neutral expression she can. No matter how angry or upset she might be, if she wants to, she can hide it. It keeps tutors from guessing what she's thinking."

"And this little trick is something she picked up from Armand?" Donovan asked. I couldn't tell if he was disturbed or fascinated by this idea.

"Since we were nine or ten," I said. "Kit and I pretend not to notice when Armand does it, but we're so close, we can read the signs. And I read them on Liza whenever we meet for lessons. She's hiding, but it's not to keep Graham from perceiving her moods. It's to keep us from seeing how much pain she's in...." I broke off as a lump came to my throat. Donovan frowned and touched my shoulder.

"You're in pain too, Daisy," he said sadly. "Hiding in plain sight can be a dangerous endeavor, especially if it's a prolonged habit. I'd hate for you to lose touch with the ability to honestly show how you feel…." Donovan cut his sympathies short as something caught his eye behind me. I turned to see Graham, standing close to three armed guardsmen who were pointedly detaining him. It was not so much of a commotion as it was a tense exchange, but I could tell that Graham was nearing outrage, and I was suddenly very aware that the passersby in the hall were slowing to watch just like Donovan and me.

I followed Donovan closely over to the guardsmen, keeping with his sweeping strides.

"What is going on here?" he asked smoothly. If only James had ever bothered to affect a kinder tone when asking after his staff like Donovan had.

"I am simply trying to exit the main hall," Graham said stiffly to Donovan. "These guards are refusing to let me pass."

"Why?" Donovan asked curtly, looking expectantly to the center guardsman. I recognized him as Nathan, as he was famous for being one of the best fighters in James' service.

"Just following orders, Master Donovan," Nathan replied.

"What orders are those?"

"Keating is not cleared to leave the compound," Nathan said. In his voice was an agitation that suggested he'd already stated his orders multiple times already.

"But that is preposterous!" Graham exclaimed in heated disbelief. "I am a tenured tutor in the service of James the Master; I have been for nearly ten years! Why would he decree such a thing?"

"It is not our practice to question Master James' orders," Nathan said flatly. He looked to Donovan for support, sparing me an uncomfortable glare as he shifted his planted feet.

"Is there an inclement weather warning in the area?" Donovan asked. I could tell that he was trying to smooth over the rising tension, as he was apparently now aware of how many people were now blatantly watching this scene.

"It's an issue of staff safety, sir," Nathan said. "I have instructed Keating to return to his quarters, and unless he obeys, we will have to escort him—"

"Escort me?" Graham repeated hotly. "As if I would refuse to go quietly and make a spectacle in front of my pupil!"

"Well. then, Mister Keating," Nathan said, stretching out his syllables in a very patronizing manner, "I suggest you move along. I wouldn't worry about your wife reprimanding you for missing lunch." I glared at Nathan to see him sneer at Graham like that.

"You are a hateful bastard!" Graham thundered, his cheeks darkening. I sucked in a little gasp to hear him use language like this—this behavior was unprecedented.

"Now, Graham," Donovan tried to reason.

"How dare you mention my wife!" Graham's temper was explosive now. "You have added a flagrant insult to an egregiously misplaced injury, and I guarantee you that Master James will hear about this!" He turned on his heel away from the guardsmen and stormed back through the crowd, still in his coat with his bag over his shoulder. I crossed my arms and laid my palm flat over my clavicle, watching worriedly after him.

"We have guests for the summit, Nathan," I heard Donovan remind the guardsman behind me in a quiet, measured tone. "I think we both know you could have handled that more discreetly than you did."

"Master James permits me to enforce his orders as I see fit," Nathan offered with a shrug. It was the closest he could get to telling Donovan to mind his own business, for even he wouldn't dare contradicting a Master so blatantly.

"I don't believe James would approve of you making a jab at Keating's wife," Donovan replied coolly. "Especially if your defense is to claim he does." I noticed the color in Nathan's face pale indiscernibly, for it was common knowledge that James did not tolerate being spoken for.

"As you say," Nathan mumbled. Donovan eyed him knowingly and Nathan quickly added, "Sir!" in a much clearer voice. Donovan seemed pleased by his show of respect and turned his back on Nathan, looking now to me with a sympathetic frown.

"I'm sure Graham will apologize for using such brash language in front of you. It was unfairly provoked, you understand."

"Why did the mention of his wife upset him so badly?" I asked. "What happened to her?"

"It's not my place to tell you, Daisy," Donovan answered somberly. "If I were you, I would be careful not to address it with Graham, especially after the little scene a very insensitive Nathan prompted today."

"Of course not. I only wonder…well, he seemed more heartbroken than angry with Nathan. With everything that's happened to us over the past few weeks, if my tutor is in need of a kind word, I would want to offer him some comfort." Donovan stopped short when I expressed my sentiment. He gazed down at me with something of an awestruck sheen to his eyes.

"Daisy," he remarked with a smile. "That's so thoughtful. I'm so impressed by you."

I bowed my head and fidgeted with the strap of my ballet satchel. "Graham has been so good to us," I said. "If I never mention this again, if it's what he needs, it's the least I could do." Donovan reached out to push a lock of my loose hair from my forehead.

"You know, Daisy," he said softly. "Sometimes I think—"

"Oh, I hope I'm interrupting!" chimed a sweet, wry voice. Annoyed, I looked over expecting to see a teasing tradesperson, perhaps dispatched to deliver a message from James to Donovan. Instead, I laid eyes on the most beautiful young woman I'd ever seen, a sight which took me by surprise. The shiny, loose garment she donned was cut to show off her smooth, rich caramel skin—not to mention her voluptuous figure which was expressly defined by her garment's plunging neckline. When she reached for Donovan, the thin golden bracelets dangling from her wrists clinked together and lent her movements an almost mystical quality.

"Dulce!" Donovan enthused, his greeting accompanied by a broad smile. He returned the girl's hug warmly, squeezing her tightly around her waist.

"*Hola, primo!*" the girl, Dulce, cheered. She pulled away from Donovan and smiled brightly up at him. "I've been looking for you all over! This compound is like a maze but I can't get enough of it! All the people, the food, oh, and the shopping—" She cut herself off as her eyes fell on me. I was taken aback by her gorgeously dark eyes. They sent a jolt through me, for I truly felt like looking at her was like glimpsing the sun through my bedroom skylight.

"Hello, lovely!" she sang, reaching to pull me into a similar embrace.

"Hello," I said, eyeing Donovan somewhat nervously over Dulce's shoulder. He only grinned wider.

"I'd like you to meet my cousin Dulce," Donovan said to me once Dulce stepped away. Her long hair spilled loosely over her shoulders in coils of fragrant chestnut locks and I immediately felt the pull of envy, for I was certain her tresses needed no styling. Even Liza, whose hair was so beautiful, took time to brush it out until it shone.

"It's a pleasure to meet you," I said, forming a courteous smile. Donovan took a breath to introduce me but Dulce held up a hand quickly to hush him.

"A girl wearing Tribute colors with a dancer's body and such impeccable manners? You must be James' Daisy," she said brightly. I fought the impulse to knit my brows together—I had never been introduced as someone belonging to James before—so I twisted my frown into a begrudging smile. Donovan said this girl was his cousin; I could not be rude to a future Mistress.

"I don't think my reputation has ever preceded me," I said, a little stiff. Dulce seemed to be studying me with fervid curiosity and for the first time since I could remember, I didn't have my etiquette to lean back on. Holding eye contact was polite, but would she consider it a challenge? Looking at Donovan seemed to be the safer bet but I reminded myself to be bold, like Liza.

"Are you attending the summit?" I asked.

"You mean, have I elected to sit around with those serious old people and let hot air out of my head all day? No thank you," Dulce said, brushing her hair over her left shoulder.

"Excuse Dulce's flippancy, Daisy," Donovan teased. "She doesn't reserve much reverence for the important progress we've gathered to achieve. Besides, her head is big enough without being invested in the prestige of the summit."

Dulce gave Donovan's arm a playfully indignant swat. "Don't listen to him, Daisy," Dulce said with a wicked smile as she looped her arm through mine. "Any disdain I have for those boring old Master details is something I get from him! Now, you must tell me all the ins and outs of this place! I want to know everything about this compound. I've been dreaming of visiting for years!"

"Daisy has responsibilities to see to," Donovan said, turning to walk with me and Dulce as she led me along the trade floor. I appreciated Donovan's attempt to relieve me of his cousin's company, for though she was nice enough, I was getting hungrier by the second and Dulce seemed to be siphoning what was left of my energy. Keeping up with manners at a time like this was exhausting.

"I didn't know Tributes worked!" Dulce wondered excitedly.

"Not in the market," I told her. "The boys and I mostly work with our tutor during the day—"

Dulce interrupted with an eager gasp. "Boys? How exciting! My schooling is all-girls and has been since I was twelve. My tutors think the boys my age would be too distracted by me and my classmates." I nodded knowingly. If Dulce's classmates were of her caliber, I couldn't say I would blame the boys in her class for focusing on her over their studies. "So," Dulce went on, "when you aren't studying or dancing, what do you do? Do you go with any of these dashing tradesmen I've seen around here?" She flashed a daring smile while color rushed to my cheeks.

"James wouldn't permit such a thing," I said outright, as though James were standing behind me. Dulce giggled.

"Listen to you, calling him by his first name!" She tugged on my arm so that our shoulders touched.

"He insists that we do," I said, a little defensive.

"I hear James the Master insists on every facet of daily life around here," Dulce told me in a secretive voice. She noticed my features harden and reached across my shoulders with her arm to hold me in a cherishing embrace as we continued along the market hall. "I didn't mean to belittle you by laughing, Daisy. This whole place is just so charming and I love the way you speak about Master James."

I supposed I didn't mind. I knew that "dulce" in Spanish meant "sweet" and by that translation, the girl was certainly aptly named. I looked to Donovan and found that he was waiting with a knowing glance, as if to say, "I know how she is."

"This is my first ever visit to the summit compound," Dulce went on earnestly. I was tempted to point out that I'd not seen outside of these walls in almost twenty years, but I thought better of it.

"Was it a long journey?" I asked instead.

"Almost three days!" Dulce sighed. "It felt like the car seat was crawling with fire ants by the time we arrived, so that's why I'm set to walk the halls of this place until I learn my way around."

"If it's a tour you want, I'm happy to show you around until your heart is content," Donovan said.

"I'd prefer Daisy show me around," Dulce said flatly. "You'll only take me to the fencing arenas or the sparring floors and go on for hours about the innovative designs and how 'swordplay is an art' and all that." Donovan rolled his eyes as we rounded the corner, landing just outside the Tribute apartments.

I was exhausted but I knew that if I had Dulce to myself for even an hour, I could learn more about what went on outside of this place than I ever could by chatting with Donovan. I was about to offer myself as a tour guide when the doors to the Tribute wing opened and out came Kit and Armand, who was holding a small parcel under his arm.

My heart leaped when Kit set his warm gaze on me and smiled, though it only lasted a moment because Kit then noticed Dulce on my arm. Armand had emerged with a scowl but was visibly taken aback by Dulce's beauty, as I had been, or because he had almost walked straight into Donovan. Both of the boys stared at Dulce in astonishment that I couldn't help notice was different than mine had been—I hoped it was because they were surprised to see me cleaved to a stranger.

"Well, hello there!" Dulce said with a grin.

"Hello," both boys said in wary unison.

"This is Dulce," I said pointedly to jar them out of their stares. "Donovan's cousin. She's here visiting for the summit."

Kit's manners kicked in immediately. He stepped forward with his hand extended. "Pleasure to meet you. I'm Kit, this is Armand."

Dulce smiled pleasantly enough at Kit, who quickly flickered his eyes to meet mine to convey a flash of his bemusement, but she let her eyes settle on Armand for a moment or two longer.

"It's very nice to meet you," she said, heaving a dreamy sigh that even puzzled Donovan. Armand returned the salutation dryly, then turned to me with renewed contempt in his eyes.

"Where have you been?" he asked. He transferred the parcel under his arm to the other impatiently.

"The studio," I said. I did not hide how his snappiness had offended me.

"I met Donovan outside, then I met Dulce. They were kind enough to walk with me back to the apartment—"

"You have us running very late for our afternoon lesson," Armand said, stomping on my attempt at niceness. My heart sank; I'd completely forgotten about our lesson with Liza!

"I'm sorry, Armie," I blurted at once. "I forgot. I didn't realize we were going today." I turned to Dulce and politely extracted her arm from mine. "I apologize, I have a very important lesson this afternoon. I have to go."

"Are you tackling any particular subject?" Dulce asked. "I would love to accompany you, if you'll have me!"

"I'm afraid that's out of the question," Armand said. He very rudely did not explain himself further, he simply stood by, ignoring Donovan's searching eyes, and waited for me to say farewell. Dulce bristled; I was under the impression that she was not used to being turned down.

"Have you eaten, Daisy?" Kit asked, breaking up Armand's brusqueness with the light question. My stomach grumbled as I shook my head.

"We just packed up leftovers from lunch," Kit said.

"Are those for me?" Donovan suggested, eyeing the parcel under Armand's arm.

"They're for Liza," said Armand, correcting his frown for Donovan's sake.

Kit came forward and took my ballet bag from me, shouldering it himself. "I'll fix you a plate, then you can change before we head out."

"We're already fifteen minutes late!" Armand growled. I pursed my lips to see him in such a remarkably awful mood.

"For goodness' sake, Armand!" At last Kit was fed up with Armand's caustic attitude. "Go ahead, then, if you're in such a hurry!" Armand took Kit's direction without stopping to mutter something mean under his breath. Donovan excused himself from us and trailed after him. I was glad to see it, for perhaps Donovan could give Armand a decent talking to and convince him not to behave so roughly when it came time for us to see Liza.

"I am terribly sorry about him," Kit said to Dulce, still looking after Armand.

"Is he always so rude?" Dulce asked. I could tell Kit was about to assure her otherwise, but he caught himself and breathed a little chuckle.

"Actually, yes," he said. He winked at me and I couldn't help but mirror his smile. "It's been a trying time for us," Kit elaborated gently. "Our friend Liza—well, she's been ill lately. It's put a strain on Armand, and with all the activity around the summit…." He glanced at me knowingly, still wearing a soft smile. He really could effortlessly smooth over any situation; I would never be as graceful in pointe shoes as Kit was in his social etiquette.

"I really should go inside and change for my lesson," I said to Dulce. "But I would like to make it up to you, for Armand's behavior. Would you like to join us for dinner?" My proposal seemed to surprise Kit while it obviously delighted Dulce.

"You want to entertain me for dinner?" she said, clasping her hands wistfully.

"Armand is an excellent cook," Kit said, to sweeten the prospect. It was so like him to pay Armand a compliment as long as he wasn't there to hear it. "It actually lifts his spirits to do it, and I'm sure he would like the opportunity to make a better second impression. If it's entertainment you're keen on, you know Daisy dances. And I play piano. I'm sure we can find something to suit your liking."

"I would be honored!" Before Kit or I could brace ourselves, Dulce was on us for very familiar, tight hugs. Kit grimaced modestly over the girl's shoulder at her brash display of affection and I realized I'd pulled a rather stony face to see it. Thankfully, she released Kit almost as quick as she'd grabbed him. "As much as I would like to insist on joining you for this lesson of yours, I think I'd rather give your Tribute friend time to cool off. I'll see you for dinner later!"

Kit and I said goodbye to her as she turned on the high heels of her boots as she marched away, her bracelets chiming together as she went toward the marketplace. Without another word, I turned to take Kit's arm in mine and pulled him into the apartment after me. Kit closed the door behind us and leaned his back against them. The second the door closed, I turned and pressed my lips to Kit's. He sighed through his nose and dropped my ballet bag at our feet. He set his hands on my waist, smoothing them then up my back to hold me closer against him. I wrapped my arms around his neck as my lips curled into a smile against his. We kissed for a few moments before both of us broke apart with a secretive laugh.

"What was that about?" Kit murmured, touching his forehead to mine.

"I'm happy to see you," I said. "Happier that I have you alone for a few minutes."

"No," Kit said, chuckling. "Back there, with Donovan's cousin."

"Oh," I said. I stepped back from Kit, still keeping my hands on him. "She's quite a girl, isn't she?"

"I'll say," Kit remarked somberly. He shook his head as his lips twitched into a reluctant grin. "She pressed her breasts into my chest just now."

"Ahem," I said, bolstering the nerve to be a little garish. "That was me." Kit reddened beautifully and laughed, leaning over to kiss me again.

"I meant outside," he corrected me wryly. There was regret in his eyes now, and I could guess what he was about to say. "We really are late to see Liza," he said—I was right.

"I'll change," I said. I slipped away from him, deliberately smoothing my hands down his front and catching his hand in mine as I backed slowly toward my room. When only our fingertips were touching, I dropped my arm and let Kit go to the kitchen to fix me a plate of leftovers. I hardly felt hungry anymore, my stomach full of fluttering wings. I went into my room and stripped off my clothes, humming to myself as I thought of the other night, when I had first kissed Kit and let him kiss me back.

The feeling was still very fresh in my heart: we had come home from seeing Liza in the greenhouse utterly heartbroken, the boys especially so, and it was the lowest I had felt since the night Liza had jumped from the library window. I had known in my miserable bones that I was alone now in my mission to get away from James and the compound. It was a notion so daunting that it sent me into shock, for which I was grateful, because otherwise I would have completely fallen apart.

That night, after a funereal supper with Donovan, I'd hugged poor Armie and excused myself. I'd been so close to tears, I knew if I'd hung around the kitchen, I would have made a fool of myself in front of Donovan. When Kit excused himself too, it dawned on me that if I was going to push through the setback Liza had laid out, I would need Kit. I'd taken his hand in the hallway and pulled him into my room and asked him to sit in front of Liza's painting.

I hadn't the slightest idea of how I could kindle a spark again within Kit, but I knew Liza's passionate glimpse of the outside world would help. For a while, we looked at the painting without saying anything to each other. I couldn't surmise a thing to say that didn't start with "Liza would want us to keep going" so I stayed quiet, until at last, I looked at the horizon in the painting and said to Kit, "Somewhere out there are people who would never do to Liza what the Masters have done. You and Armie might think I am a fool for thinking it, after everything we've seen, but I still believe that we are meant to be out there. We are meant to be free. We are meant to stand under the sun together, meant to feel the wind on our skin and live in a home with windows, and doors through which we can come and go as we see fit."

Kit had bowed his head and heaved a heavy sigh. It had pained him to look at Liza's painting; it had hurt him to feel hope. "I just don't see how, Daze," he'd muttered. I could see him purse his lips to keep them from quivering.

"I'll tell you how," I had said. I'd let the tears run down my cheeks and the roughness of my voice come through. I'd wanted Kit to see that I was in despair too. I'd wanted him to know he didn't have to hide it from me. I'd caught his chin delicately in my fingers and turned him to look at me. "We have lived by James' rules for our entire lives but here we are, together, after hours. Inside each of us is a truth that no Master can suppress with his edicts or closed fist: We may play along with the Master's game, but they cannot extinguish our purpose to be free."

"Daze," Kit had said, trying to ground me. "You saw Liza. You heard what she said. Trying to escape this place almost got her murdered—it's a miracle James didn't leave her out there to die just to teach us a lesson. Instead, we got her back in one piece. If that isn't a sign that this whole thing is pointless...."

"Liza's pain may hide the truth from her, but we are her family," I had insisted. "I believe it's still there, it's just buried under James' influence and all the terrible things she's seen. We just have to remind her." I had peered deep into Kit's glistening brown eyes, elated to see that he was hearing me.

"You have a resilience I have not noticed before," Kit had said. He had clasped my hands in his and swallowed past the lump in his throat. "I hear you say all these things about hope, truth, and freedom, and it only makes me think of how much I really care about you. Maybe all those weeks ago when Liza came to us with the idea, I held your candle of hope too, but Daisy...I just don't have it anymore. When I think about getting away from this place, I want to so badly, but then I remember what happened to Liza. If we move forward on this path, and something were to happen to you, I couldn't bear it."

It had been crystal clear to me in that moment: a flicker of purpose remained in Kit, but just like Liza, I had to remind him. So I had resolved to pull him close, perhaps with too much vigor. I'd brought his lips crashing down on mine and for many moments as my heart swelled, we embraced; we took gasping breaths in between, clung to each other, tasted each other's tears on our lips. After we had held each other at arm's length for some time but before either of us had gone to sleep, cuddled together in my bed, I'd promised Kit that we would be smarter and more careful than last time, no matter how long it took.

I had nurtured a wildfire in us both that night. As I quickly dressed into fresh linens, eager to get to Liza, I wondered if she would be proud of me for pulling Kit back from the precipice of defeat as I had. I took my hair out of its messy bun and ran my fingers through it, twisting it into a braid that hung down my back.

"Dulce is the daughter of a Mistress," I told Kit when I emerged into the kitchen. Kit set a plate of bread, cheeses, and fruit before me and took a seat beside me at the table.

"Do you think she'd help us?" he asked. We were alone enough to share kisses but still, Kit lowered his voice.

"She might," I said, still chewing. "At the very least, she can tell us a lot."

"She's close to Donovan," Kit warned. "We'll have to be discreet."

"The way she carries herself," I mused, taking into account Kit's observation about Dulce and Donovan's relationship. "It's as though she finds us *cute*. I think we can use that to our advantage, if we indulge her a little." I thought for a minute longer, scarfing down my lunch as I thought of the vital points I must share with Kit before we left the apartment.

"What is it?" Kit asked, noticing my discouraged frown.

"I'm thinking about her social standing," I said. "She uses James' title when she speaks of him. She was tickled when I didn't, and she seemed jealous of us having lessons together."

"How do you mean?" Kit asked.

"Apparently, Dulce's lessons are girls-only," I explained. Kit's eyebrows went up in an "aha" moment and he contemplated for a moment, folding his hands together like he always did when he worked out problems in his head. I told him furthermore about the interaction with Dulce, mentioning how insistent she was that I show her around instead of Donovan.

"We can work with that," Kit said. "There's an intersection of privilege we have in common, but clearly there are liberties we can take that she can't. At dinner, we must be sure to talk her through all the things we can do as James' Tributes that she can't—but it must be done so in a way that isn't boastful. We must remain totally modest, as though we've never given it much thought that we can refer to James without his title, or give orders to his servants."

"I agree," I said, a little out of breath after wolfing down so much food. "Based on what I could tell about her from our limited exposure, I think that's the best way to approach her."

"Just for information," Kit reminded me.

"Of course," I said, pushing my chair back so that I could deposit my plate in the kitchen sink.

"And we'll have to talk to Armand," said Kit. He noticed my shoulders sag and stood up to pull me into his arms. "Let's go see Liza first, eh?" he said. I smiled and followed him out of the apartments. We saw Dulce being shown a Mistress' courtesy by several of the apparel vendors in the market on our way to the Masters' rooms and decided we were glad that Tributes did not work on the trade floor.

The guardsmen let us through easily enough, though they expressly told us to come as a group next time. Kit whispered to me once we were making our way to Liza's room, "I wonder if Armand incited Donovan to give them a hard time about letting him in alone?" I shrugged, knowing that Nathan might have cause to do whatever Donovan told him without question after the altercation with Graham. I wondered if Graham would even be present for this lesson, after the upsetting scene in the entrance hall earlier.

We saw Douglas stationed outside of Liza's room and he was kind enough to greet Kit and me with a fleeting smile when we approached. "Did you two get lost?" he asked.

"I was working with Miss Helena in the studio," I explained. "I was running late. Armand was anxious to get some of the lunch he made to Liza before it went cold."

"I see," Douglas replied. "It might be best for the three of you to travel together next time. The traffic in the marketplace is heavy with all the summit guests, and Master James might prefer you to keep to yourselves." I dreaded to think of what that really meant as Douglas turned and unlocked the door with his key. Kit and I let ourselves in and Liza was on us at once.

"Your sling is gone!" I cheerfully observed as she threw her arms around me. When Liza stepped back and I saw her brows knit with concern, I instantly felt guilty.

"You didn't come with Armand," she said. "I was so worried. He said you were separated?"

"Liza, we're all right," Kit assured her. He returned her embrace, swaying gently with her in his arms. "We were hardly *separated*," he said, his teeth clenched as he shot Armand a stern look over Liza's shoulder. Armand glared right back at him and went back to paging through the book in his lap.

"We met Donovan's cousin," I told Liza, taking her hand between both of mine once Kit had let her go. "She made me late, but I was already behind coming back from the st—from ballet," I hastily altered my choice of words so as not to trigger Liza's trauma by mentioning the studio. Succinctly agitated, I went on, "Armand was in a decidedly rotten mood, so Kit and I told him to go ahead while I changed and ate something."

Liza rolled her eyes and pulled me further into the room, down on the lavish cushion beside her. "You could have eaten here," she said. "I can send away for anything I want, you know." I could see she was cross with us for making her worry but I couldn't help but smile to hear some fervor back in her voice.

"How are you?" I asked her. Liza dropped her gaze to our stacked hands in her lap and wet her lips.

"I'm fine," was all she had to say.

"You seem much better," Kit offered, pulling up a chair so that he could sit near Liza's knees. "Your color is back, I think."

"Liza has refused her afternoon dose of pain medicine," Graham said from his seat at the desk. I was somewhat startled by him, as he'd been so still and quiet when we came in.

"That medicine dulls my mind," Liza rebutted. Her tone was stale, like she'd just been arguing with him about it. "I only really take them before bed now." I frowned to think of Liza bearing with pain but I was distracted by Graham's docile tone. I looked at him and was hardly surprised when he raised a hand to stop me asking after him, as if he was just waiting for me to bring up the scene earlier.

"I owe you an apology, Daisy," Graham said, sounding world weary. Kit, Liza, and Armand all turned to me.

"Sir, you don't have to say anything—" I tried to interject, attempting to spare him the indignity of explaining himself to me in front of the others. I'd meant what I said to Donovan about wanting to respect Graham after all the kindness he had shown us.

"Please," Graham hushed me. "My behavior earlier was reprehensible, regardless of whether or not I set a very poor example."

I felt chilled. *I fear Daisy has set a very poor example*, I heard James say to Liza in my mind.

"What is he talking about?" Kit asked. I was still too disturbed by the likeness of Graham's words to James' and I shivered a little.

"Master James' guardsman, Nathan, and I had a disagreement in the entrance hall this afternoon," Graham said. "Regrettably, I spoke profanely in front of Daisy."

The others blanched, loath to picture what Graham losing his temper must have looked like.

"It was inappropriate of me, and very unprofessional of me to have forgotten myself as I did." Graham unfolded his hands and removed his spectacles so that he could rub the flat of his hand on his forehead.

"There's no need to apologize," I said to Graham. "After being my tutor all this time, I think you know that I understand how stressful this summit has been on us all. I take no offense to you forgetting yourself to a snide bully like Nathan."

"Daze!" Kit hissed, urging me not to follow Graham's lead and forget myself. I didn't take my eyes off Graham, and was pleased to see that my gamble had paid off. I could see Graham was proud of me for slinging such insults at Nathan.

"You are astute as ever, Daisy," Graham replied.

"What on earth caused this 'disagreement' as you call it?" Armand asked at once. He couldn't resist begging for details.

"Nathan wouldn't let him leave the compound," I said after Graham nodded in approval. "He said it was a matter of safety? What did he mean by that?"

The four of us waited on baited breath for Graham to go on. We knew he wasn't allowed to share security details like that with us and likely wouldn't, and unless he had spoken to James about it since then, he probably didn't know himself.

"Evidently the bodies of two scouts were found this morning," Graham said after a few tense moments of deliberation. "Master James has closed the compound gates while an investigation is conducted."

"Were they killed?" Armand wanted to know.

"I'm afraid so," Graham said. "As of today, it is unclear whether they engaged in a deadly dispute, or if a more sinister event occurred."

"I've heard enough," Liza said thinly. I came to my senses as though I'd been jolted by a static shock. Of course it was distasteful to talk about murder in front of her, while she was still in a fragile state.

"I am sorry, my dear children." He shook his head and put his spectacles away in his jacket's breast pocket. "These have been dark days. It's my job to teach you your lessons and guide you through your daily lives here, and lately I find myself wishing that so much of the latter were different." He spared a sorrowful glance for Liza then, and she looked back to him with curiosity twinkling in her violet eyes.

"Is it true you have a daughter my age?" she asked. Graham covered his mouth with his hand and cleared his throat to hide the tremble of his usually steady voice.

"I used to," Graham said. "She's been gone for years now."

Liza's room was filled with deafening silence for what felt like minutes.

"I'm sorry," Liza said. I felt tears rush past my eyelashes before I realized I was overcome with secondhand grief. I left Liza's side, went to Graham's, and set my hand on his shoulder—an unprecedented move on my part, for such personal contact with a tutor was generally frowned upon. We had been brought closer together by the lurid events of the past two weeks and I thought that now, more than ever, was the time to show it.

Graham very sweetly laid his hand over mine and patted it a few times. "I appreciate your kindness, Daisy. Thank you." I kept my hand on his shoulder for a few more moments while Graham gathered his bearing. Once I relinquished my touch, Graham seemed to revert to his old self. "It seems unfair that I am not permitted to grant the four of you any privacy," he said. "I know you would value even the briefest semblance of your typical routine…in light of Kit and Daisy's tardiness, I don't see why we can't turn this lesson into an informal gathering of sorts. In fact, if you'll excuse me, I think I'll have a word with Douglas outside about retrieving some books from the Master library."

We were all stunned but warmed to our toes at Graham's gesture. Armand scrambled to his feet to meet Graham at Liza's bedchamber door, where he offered Graham his hand. Graham shook it and showed his trademark guarded smile.

"Just a minute," he said, disappearing outside. The second the door shut behind Graham, the four of us rushed together. Armand's bitterness crumbled away when Liza put her arm around him; for a blissful two minutes, we stood as a family again.

"That was surreal," Armand said, the first of us to speak up.

"I had no idea he had a family," Kit added.

"You should have heard Graham, when Nathan made a comment about his wife," I said. We moved our little conspiratorial circle to the floor at the foot of Liza's bed. We sat facing each other, close enough that our knees were touching, so that we could keep our voices down.

"I can't even imagine Graham using profanity," Armand said in disbelief. "In front of you, no less!"

"He called Nathan a 'hateful bastard,'" I recounted gravely. Liza touched her fingers to her mouth.

"Speaking of family," Kit chimed in, prompting me with wide eyes. "Donovan's cousin Dulce is joining us for dinner tonight."

"She's not!" Armand balked. "Whose brilliant idea was that?"

"Mine," I owned up to his criticism.

"Before you go off on her," Kit warned Armand, as Armand was assuredly working out a few choice phrases for me, "remember moments ago, Graham told us that scouts were found outside this compound. This young woman might be the only way to learn what's going on around here without arousing suspicion."

"He's right, Armie," I insisted. "She's the daughter of a Mistress who made it clear from the moment I met her that she intends to ingratiate herself to us. We can get an idea of what's really happening if we can earn her trust—you're lucky she agreed to it, after how rude you were to her."

I saw Armand bite his tongue. I could tell he wanted nothing more than to fire back at me for picking on his manners. Instead of telling me off, he looked to Liza, who was peering urgently into his eyes. I knew that look; I'd seen her turn it on him more than once, to encourage him to set aside whatever stubborn stance he was about to take and fold to me, or Kit.

"I suppose that would be smart of us," he agreed.

"Is there anything you want us to find out?" I asked Liza, sadly realizing that she wouldn't be there. Before she could answer, the door behind us opened. Evidently Graham had given us all the time he was able to. I looked up to greet him and the smile fell off my face and crashed to the floor as I saw James standing there instead of Graham. Kit and I stood up right away.

"Don't get up on my account," James said. I couldn't tell if he was scoffing or sincere. "Graham tells me the lesson is over for today. It's time for you all to let Liza rest." His gaze narrowed when he stared past me at Liza, who winced in pain as she pushed herself to her feet. Armand reached to help her up and very brazenly kept his hold on Liza's waist, even though Liza was steady on her feet.

"I would like eat dinner in the Tribute wing tonight," Liza said to James. I looked back at her in veiled amazement, as I wouldn't have expected her to address him so outright, let alone in such a calm, almost familiar manner.

"I'm afraid not," James said. "This compound is packed almost to capacity with guests."

"So?" Liza replied. I tensed, waiting for her to start yelling or lunge at him.

"So," James sighed matter-of-factly, "I'm not comfortable escorting you through a crowd like that. You're not well enough."

"I feel fine," Liza pushed back. "Please. Armand is cooking." Now I was really surprised—her tone didn't waver toward threatening or aggression in the slightest.

"You don't look fine," James said. Apparently he reserved no inhibitions about offending Liza. "Do you really want to be scrutinized by every passerby?"

"I don't care about that," Liza professed. "I just want to have dinner with my family."

"Too many questions might be raised if you were seen in less-than-top shape," James said. "You will have to join them another time." That was his final word.

"We're expecting a guest," I blurted. "We were hoping to introduce her to Liza." I regretted speaking immediately, for James then turned his laser stare down at me.

"What's this?"

"Donovan's charming cousin Dulce," Kit answered, taking a small side step toward me.

I raised an eyebrow. Charming?

"Daisy met her in the market today. She seemed very interested in being shown around the compound, and very curious to see the inside of our apartments."

"You know full well that no one apart from myself, your tutor, and the doctor are permitted inside the wing," James reminded me coolly.

"Unless they're invited," Armand added. "Daisy invited her." James looked between the three of us for a minute, his suspicion aroused.

"Absolutely not," he said at last. I let out an outraged huff.

"That's *your* rule, James!" I exclaimed.

"I know it is, and therefore it's my prerogative to have the final say," he retorted. "Donovan visiting you for an odd meal is one thing—at least he's of official Master status. I will not allow you to parade guests of my compound around your living space. It was inappropriate of Dulce to accept in the first place."

"Then we'll have dinner here," Liza declared over our feeble-at-best arguments. James crossed his arms and stared her down.

"Excuse me?"

"You can sit Douglas right beside me if you wish," Liza said. "I assume that you would afford a future Mistress the courtesy of dining in the Masters' rooms, and since you've already allowed Daisy and the boys in to have lessons with me here, you wouldn't object to them joining us for dinner."

I hardly dared look at James. Liza had him there, and he knew it. And he wasn't happy about it.

"In fact, if you don't have a summit meeting to attend, you're welcome to join us," Liza said bravely, striking down any remaining sliver of hesitation James might have. He had to agree to this—he just had to, otherwise he would be opening himself up to the very scrutiny to which he advised Liza not subject herself, for what reason could he have to refuse us? Other than for the sake of it, I could practically hear Armand mutter under his breath.

"Fine." I saw a notch in James' jaw click after he gave his consent.

"Thank you," said Liza. It was the softest voice I'd ever heard her use with James.

"It will be an early dinner," James said crossly. "Liza still needs her rest." He left the lingering impression that he was still in control of this, which we all knew anyway. Graham slipped through the door after James had gone with an appalled look on his face.

"I think we'd better leave Liza to rest," he said. "Before James comes back and changes his mind" was the unspoken sentiment. We each gave Liza a long hug, Armand's the last and longest, before we left. I was electrified as we walked back to our wing. I felt possessed by this little victory, so much so that I struggled to keep the spring from my step. It was even harder to suppress the urge to reach for Kit's hand as we edged our way through the crowded hall.

Once inside our apartment, though, Kit jumped up and pulled me into his arms. Armand punched a fist into the air and grinned widely, showing all his teeth.

"So James the Master *does* negotiate!" Armand cheered.

"Liza did the negotiating," I observed, unable to stop smiling.

"So she did, sweetheart," Armand said. There wasn't a hint of bitterness to the nickname this time, for which I was overjoyed. I hugged him for it. "Now we have to break bread with—what did you call her, Kit? *Charming Cousin Dulce?*"

"It bothered James to hear me say it," Kit defended himself, dropping onto the sofa in the study. "That's the only reason I did."

"She's interesting," I said, sitting beside Kit. "You can't deny that."

"If by 'interesting' you mean good-looking and foolish, you're right," Armand said. He took a seat in his chair by the fire and folded his arms. "I didn't like the way she was all over you, Daze."

"It's got to be a good sign that James disapproves of her," I said. Armand had no choice but to agree with me. Then, a harrowing thought clouded my optimism. I looked to Kit. "We're not going to be able to talk to her," I said. "Not like we want to."

"Why not?" Kit asked.

"We'll be in James' dining room," I explained, leaving a pregnant pause to prompt Kit to understand my meaning. Neither he nor Armand seemed to follow. "He'll be listening to our every word!" While Kit pondered this discouraging development, Armand sat forward in his chair and set his elbows on his knees.

"What do you mean, Daisy?" he asked. I almost squirmed at the tone of his voice because he sounded so much like James then, as though he knew fully well what I meant and was only asking to make me fumble over my words. "Not like we want to? How were you planning on talking to her?" I could tell Kit was about to speak up for me so I sat forward too, matching Armand's posture, to show both of them that I was not about to shy from my convictions.

"We were hoping," I said to Armand, mindful of my volume, "that Dulce might help us."

"Help us," Armand echoed, his tone empty.

"Yes," I said. "To leave this place, once and for all." I felt Kit tense beside me, preparing for an incredulous outburst to occur across the room. Instead of immediately berating me and raising his voice, Armand sat back in his chair and folded his arms again. He heaved a very saturnine sigh and shook his head, all the while staring at me with a strange glint in his eyes. Was he scoffing at me? Was he about to commend my persistence or call me an idiot and leave? I couldn't guess. He cracked a sardonic smile and chuckled.

"*We*," he whispered to himself. "Of course." He gracefully rose from his chair and turned his back to me and Kit to lean with his palms on the hearth mantle. Kit was tapping his heel and I was growing steadily nervous too. "You two have continued talking about this escape-the-compound business, after everything that happened to Liza?"

"Just because you stormed out...well, it doesn't mean the conversation was over," I said. Armand turned around angrily, holding his arms rigidly at his sides.

"Were you going to tell me what you had planned?" Armand demanded. "Or do I have the sheer happenstance of being in the room to thank for my inclusion?"

"Of course we were going to tell you!"

"So that's the truth of it!" Armand fired back. "The two of you are a 'we' now, is that right?" Kit got up wordlessly and retreated to the kitchen, making sure to give Armand a wide berth on his way out of the room.

"We—you and I—have not spoken more than two words to each other in days, Armand," I said. "You have been sulking ever since we saw Liza in the greenhouse—"

"This has nothing to do with Liza!" Armand snapped. Kit reappeared with glass stemware in hand, filled generously with dark red wine. I'd forgotten Donovan had left it here, the night Liza was found. The servants he sent to clean up the meal must have thoughtlessly put it away in a cupboard. I silently praised Kit for bearing the foresight to dull Armand's anger as he passed the glass over, then return to his seat beside me. Armand took it thanklessly and took a gulp of wine, then set the glass on the mantle. He looked so annoyed, almost tormented as he began to pace. If he were Kit, he would have folded his hands together and rested his chin on the tips of his thumbs.

"That's wrong of me to say," Armand said after issuing a groaning sigh. "This is *entirely* to do with Liza. I ought to wring her neck for giving you the idea in the first place...."

"Armand!" Kit yelped furiously. "How dare you say such a thing!"

"Though it may come as a shock to you," I uttered roughly, grinding my teeth to keep my composure, "I am capable of having thoughts all on my own. Liza didn't need to give it to me; I know well enough that I hate this forsaken place. Is my own desire to leave so outlandish a concept?"

"No, but your commitment to fulfilling that desire has proved to be life-threatening more than once," Armand said with vehement contempt.

"Don't you see how terrible this place really is? That Liza would rather have leapt from an open window to her death than stay here another day? For goodness' sake, maybe she's right!"

"Daisy, listen to yourself!" Armand bellowed.

"Don't yell at her!" Kit warned.

"No, you listen to me!" I leaped to my feet and glared at Armand. "I will not let James the Master punish us for being who we are anymore. He can force us to conform to his precious routine or beat us into obeying his every last rule, but he cannot tell us how to think and it's his own fault for thinking he ever could!" I was breathless. I'd stunned Armand to silence. "I never wanted Liza to get hurt—I never wanted any of this to happen, but I'm glad it did because we know just how careful we have to be now."

"'We' means all of us, Armie," Kit said. Armand chewed on his lower lip. It was plain that he was struggling with his words, but when it looked like he was about to confess, he seemed to remember where he was and looked almost afraid. He took up his wine glass and drank.

"We can do this," I told him. I rested my hands on his shoulders. "Don't you want to leave this place?"

"I do," he murmured. "I just—Daisy, Kit, you have to know…." He was quiet for a moment. I was afraid of what he might say next because of how fragile he'd become under my touch. "All right," he said at last. "We'll talk to Dulce. You have my support."

I saw defeat in his eyes. I didn't know what to say to him, so I pulled him close and put my arms around him. "We can do this," I said again. "You'll see."

"I suppose I will," he said, sounding a little lighter. He stepped back from me and smiled down at me sadly. "I'm going to shower before dinner," he said. "You two…well, come get me when it's time to go. Or more likely, when James stops by to tell us it's off." There was my Armie, cynical and teasing. He downed the remaining wine and left me and Kit alone in the study.

"Something's the matter with him," Kit whispered, staring after Armand.

"He's just hurt that we didn't include him from the start," I said. Kit nodded but I could tell he didn't really agree. I sat back down next to him and leaned over, resting my head on Kit's shoulder. He put his arm around me and we sat together in silence for a while, each of us thinking about the precarious evening to come.

Chapter Fifteen

Kit

At every Winter Solstice feast, James would line tables down the center of the main halls in the compound so that everyone under its roof could dine together in celebration. Those dinners were extravagant beyond imagination: Whole roasted pigs and lambs were decorated and displayed as succulent centerpieces of the feast, flowers and lights filled the halls and were strung up in tresses overhead, transforming the compound into an awe-inspiring palace from one of the fantasy stories Daisy used to read as a child. Over all these years at the compound, I had been more or less content in my day-to-day life, but whenever those decorations went up, I was filled with wonder and a sense of belonging. Daisy would pretend to be a princess underneath the twinkling lights in the halls and hum waltzes to herself as she twirled down the corridors between lessons. I loved to watch her stare up at the lights and take deep breaths to smell the evergreen branches.

For our dinner together in the Masters' chambers, Dulce had spared no expense in setting the mood. She had created an island out of my happy memories of festival season from an ordinary dinner table, piled high with roasted meats and freshly baked breads underneath a swirling chandelier and hanging ropes of luscious flowers. I was so astonished at first sight that I halted in the dining room's doorway and made Armand bump into me from behind.

"Come in, come in!" Dulce greeted us. She had changed into another revealing garment, a rich violet gown, and braided flowers into her thick, curly hair. Dulce swept around the table to put her arms around each of us, a gesture which I was glad to see discomforted Armand enough to stop him from harping at me for lingering in the doorway.

"What a beautiful table," Daisy remarked, the hint of a smile playing across her face.

"It was the most I could do with short notice," Dulce said, returning to her seat. "When Master James sent word that we were having dinner here— well, I was disappointed that I would not see the inside of your wing, but I know how he is about his rules."

"Yes, he is unyielding," Armand sighed. His features brightened up when Liza entered the room behind Dulce's chair at the head of the table. I was nearest to her so I greeted her with a hug.

"Do you think she overdid the décor?" Liza whispered to me.

"Not even a little bit," I said with a wink after pulling away.

"I count seven place settings," Dulce said with a frown, after the four of us sat down in pairs on either side of her. "This isn't going to be just us, then?"

"You say that like it's a bad thing," said Donovan, entering the dining room. He didn't take a second look at the lavish decorations before swooping in to kiss Dulce's cheek and take a seat beside Armand across from me.

"You can't blame me for wanting the four of you to myself," Dulce said. Her smile as she shared the conceit of the moment with us was dazzling.

"Of course not," Donovan agreed, nudging Armand playfully with his shoulder. "But you ought to learn, *chipil,* to hide your disappointment better." I laughed nervously when Dulce lifted a fork and mock-threatened to poke Donovan with it. Most girls wouldn't take kindly to being called "spoiled" but Dulce seemed to have a soft spot for Donovan. I wondered if there was anyone who wasn't at the mercy of Donovan's charms.

As if on cue, James entered the room behind Dulce. Dulce did not stand to greet him; instead, she offered a very pleasant "Good evening, Master James!" James took her hand and kissed the top of it, affording Dulce the briefest of smiles.

"*Hola, sobrina,*" he said in casual Spanish. He glanced to each of us and nodded. "Good evening."

"Thank you for accommodating us," Liza said to him, once he sat down at the other end of the table. Daisy pushed her ankle against mine under the table, prompting me to join her in thanking James. Armand murmured some thanks too, but he said them to his plate instead of anywhere in James' direction.

James was amused by this. "I hope you didn't rehearse that," he said, laying his cloth napkin in his lap. "It was incomprehensible at best." We all smiled uncomfortably, unsure whether or not James was joking. I realized that I was stiffly sitting up, my back zipped to my seat. We had never had such an intimate dinner with James before.

Dulce eagerly called in the servants to serve us and began to ask us about life in the compound. While heaps of rice and vegetables were spooned onto our plates with quiet aplomb by James' staff, Daisy engaged Dulce in the beginning of a conversation about how our days typically went. I jumped in when I could, offering details about my piano lessons and anecdotes about Liza's gymnastics. We were careful not to mention martial arts, lest the infamous hit-heard-round-the-world story come up, but as the dinner went on, James seemed to be enjoying himself.

"Tell us about yourself, Dulce," I said after helping myself to a second portion of steak.

"You're entering a minefield, Kit," Donovan warned me with a mischievous grin. "*Prinesa vandiosa* over here will keep us here talking until curfew."

"*Seriamente, barbero?*" Dulce replied daringly, glaring at Donovan. "You'll have to excuse him, *mi nuevos amigos*, he forgets that any show of vanity I portray is one I learned from him first!" Donovan laughed and I saw that he was proud of her wit. I was glad of their closeness, for I would have found it difficult to navigate the conversation around so much name-calling otherwise.

"I don't have much to say about myself, really," Dulce sighed, waving a servant over to pour her a glass of wine. "I go to school just like you. I have my dance lessons and I ride horses after lunch when I don't feel like studying philosophy. Lately, the girls and I have taken to entertaining the older man who works in the sweet shop in town—"

"And I'm sure by 'entertaining' you mean 'harassing'?" Donovan interjected.

Dulce fixed a wry glare his way and went on, "After our lesson, we run all the way from the classroom to the middle of town and sing to him until he gives us sweets. We're very good; we always sing at gatherings and parties. Sometimes we dance too."

"I don't think I could ever dance in front of an audience," Daisy said gravely. She looked to me and asked, "Do you think you could play in front of so many people?"

"I suppose I could," I said with a shrug. "At a certain point, I'm not sure I would notice an audience."

"Perhaps you ought to consider it," Dulce said. "Or are there no such platforms here at the summit compound?"

"I don't think Kit is as open to making a spectacle of himself as you are, Dulce," Donovan teased.

"On the contrary, I wouldn't be adverse to arranging a recital if you were interested, Kit. You play exceptionally well," James remarked. The compliment warmed me. I found it easier to relax my posture, even though part of me still distrusted any kindness from James.

"You ought to count yourself lucky, Kit," Dulce said. "My mother has yet to praise a performance of mine."

"Your mother is a Mistress, is she not?" asked Armand.

"Donovan lives out of her compound in the south, yes," James answered for Dulce.

"Selenis reserves little appreciation for the arts," Donovan said secretively to us, as though he were shielding James from overhearing him.

"If you were responsible for such an extensive operation, you might not have the time to enjoy song and dance either," said James. Camaraderie amongst the Masters was unbreakable. If witnessing the violent exchange between Haitham and James had taught me one thing, it was that Masters may behave how they like behind closed doors, but in public, they must appear to be united always.

"Mama says that too," Dulce concurred somberly. "You know how it is, Doni," she said to Donovan. "It's a very serious place to live, with all the soldiers coming and going, and Mama's staff. It's mostly to do with the convenience of its geography, but our compound is one of the busiest." I'd grown up in these halls surrounded by bustling tradesmen, scholars, instructors, and soldiers; it was hard to imagine a busier place than this one.

"How many compounds are there?" Daisy asked, pointedly turning from James to address Dulce alone.

"Seven," Dulce replied. "Including Master James' summit compound. That's hardly any, I know, but things do get very crowded." Seven was not a number at which any of us could balk—that was far greater than what the others and I had thought. With a Master at the helm of each, excluding Haitham for he was of his own ilk, that meant there were six others like James. How many other Tributes were there between six other compounds?

"Change the subject," James said to Daisy. I felt the residual sting of embarrassment from Daisy, followed by stark disappointment. She'd skirted too close to Master business and James wasn't having it.

"As you say," she said. "I apologize, James." I shifted my leg under the table so that it touched Daisy's. She still wilted under James' gaze but she seemed comforted.

"For what?" Dulce asked. She was disturbed by the very tame display of James' influence over us.

"The affairs of Masters is a topic I do not generally explore with my Tributes," James explained. "There are too many more appropriate subjects I would rather discuss." Dulce relented but when she looked to Daisy, she caught my eye in turn and expressed with a subtlety I didn't expect her to convey an obvious distaste for what James had said. I sent her a look that plainly said, "Leave it alone."

Once again, Dulce surprised me. She did the opposite. "May I ask out of genuine curiosity, Master James, if it's not too closely entangled with the affairs of the Masters, why your Tributes are permitted to call you by your first name while I am not?"

She'd scored major points with Armand then, I knew. James had sent others before reeling from the mere look he was giving Dulce now, but she squared up to it as though she took it as a challenge. She folded her hands together and rested her chin on them, balancing her elbows on the table—another thing James would have chastised anyone else for.

James set his knife and fork down. As gratifying as it was to see Dulce push back on James in a way Armand, the girls, and I never could, I knew that James was the heavy hitter in proving his dominance. "It is directly categorized into Master affairs, but as you are so persistent, I will clarify the matter for you." I looked to Liza, who seemed to be feeling the tension worse than the rest of us. "The reason the four of them may refer to me by my first name alone is because of their unique status in this compound. They are permitted to exercise our familiarity, as we have lived and worked together for nineteen years. They are still held to my rules, despite the fact that you and everyone else are expected to show me the respect of using my title."

I couldn't help but look at Dulce, who seemed to absorb this with a curious look of defiance in her eyes. She seemed disappointed, too, and she struck me then as the type of person who knew when to pick her battles because she waved it off.

"Does that answer your question?" James insisted on driving his point home.

"It does," Dulce said benignly. She reached for a bushel of grapes in a dish beside mine and popped one into her mouth. She seemed bored now. I had to say something quickly, before James decided he was fed up and put an end to this interaction.

"I thought for sure you were going to ask us why we don't wear shoes," I said, daring to smile. Dulce laughed with renewed delight and touched my arm.

"I almost forgot about that! Why don't you?" she asked. "I would imagine your feet would freeze out in the snow without boots."

"It's simple," I replied, forcing a careless tone. "We don't leave the compound." I could practically feel James swelling with frustration, as he had just vetoed the subject moments before.

"Never?" Dulce asked, scandalized. "Why not?"

Because James is a tyrant, I thought, but Liza offered an interesting excuse.

"Haven't you heard? The region is practically overrun with volpines," she said. Dulce gave a very theatrical gasp and immediately went on about the monstrous creatures and the stories she'd heard. Donovan chimed in, eagerly steering the conversation away from volpines. I stole a glance at Liza and saw her looking knowingly at James, who to my bewilderment was ashen. It was as though he was haunted by the creature's bite, the mark of which I had seen in its gruesome glory.

Dulce called for dinner to be cleared, then dessert. I was practically counting the minutes until James would decide he'd had enough. Armand appeared to have recognized some of himself in Dulce after her stare-down with James and was engaging her with politesse he hadn't shown me or Daisy in weeks over a platter of brightly colored *pan dulce* knots—apparently, these were Dulce's favorite. For some time, the conversation bounced between him, Dulce, and Donovan only. As much as I was certain Armand shared many traits with her, I felt I had plenty in common with Dulce. The way she talked about art and her love of movement resonated with me. Though she had many, many friends, she was so earnest in expressing herself. I got the feeling she was dis-used to being listened to so intently.

I looked again to Liza and a sharp pain pricked my heart to see her fad-ing before my eyes. She realized I was staring and blinked slowly, lovingly, at me to assure me she was just tired. Her eyelashes were so thick that they always made her eyelids look a little heavy but there was something dark behind her eyes.

"We're the same age, aren't we, Daisy?" Dulce asked, jolting me out of my reverie.

"Yes," Daisy said. She took a sip of the dessert espresso in front of her and crinkled her nose at its bitterness.

"Daisy and I are both eighteen as of this year," I elaborated. It kept Dulce from teasing Daisy about her tolerance of strong coffee.

"Perfect," Dulce said, beaming. "Doni, I told you, they're not too young at all!" When we looked to her in confusion, Dulce giggled and explained, "The summit falls on my birthday this week so I couldn't have a party at our compound. Donovan helped me convince Mama to throw me a party at the Aventine! Lucky for me, Mama thinks it would be the perfect opportunity to impress the other Masters, and what better place to celebrate than here? What do you think?"

"If it's anything like dinner tonight, I'm sure it'll be very elegant," I said. Dulce tossed her head in laughter.

"No, I mean, I want you to come! All four of you!" she exclaimed. "You would be my guests of honor! How about it?" I was about to say, "I don't think James would allow it," but with him at the table, I couldn't speak for him with-out risking his temper. Liza was speechless too and eyed Dulce in disbelief.

"It's very kind of you to invite us," I said finally, after checking Armand's expression for a clue that he might know what to say. "Really, it is. But I don't think we could...." Out of options, I looked to James. He was tapping his index finger on the table and looking right at me. There was no hint of malice, no threat of anger. He was simply waiting.

"Why not?" Dulce whined. "You would have so much fun, I promise!"

"Why not, indeed?" Donovan asked. He sat back in his chair and crossed his arms, gazing down the table at James. "Can you think of a reason they shouldn't accept Dulce's invitation?" The question was rank with blatant pretense, and all I knew was that we had suddenly been thrust in the middle of a power play between James and Donovan, and I had no idea what the stakes were on either side. Truthfully, I would rather have been offered something as simple as dinner alone with Liza, Daisy, and Armand, but perhaps Dulce's birthday party would advance our progress toward learning something from Dulce which we could use to our advantage? We were on the spot, same as James was, and I perceived that he was cautious of Donovan watching him. Did he want us to refuse? If so, did that mean we should accept, regardless of whether or not we wanted to?

"Not at all," James said at last. He took the napkin from his lap and plopped it on his plate to cover his untouched dessert.

"Wonderful! It's settled, then, you'll come!" Dulce clapped her hands and took a bite of *pan dulce*. Donovan lifted his glass of wine at James, offering a wordless toast with a look of pure smugness stamped onto his features.

"I think I need to lie down," Liza said after taking in the silent exchange between James and Donovan. James looked relieved.

"Very well," he said, standing up from the table. "I'll have the doctor take you to your room. You three," he said to me, Armand, and Daisy, "it's time for you to wrap things up. Nathan will see you back to your wing. Donovan and I ought to return to the summit, don't you agree?" He did not wait for Donovan to reply before breezing out of the room. He did not say goodnight to Dulce, which seemed to wound her as though she had personally offended James—and maybe she had.

"Excuse me," I said, abruptly tossing my napkin on my seat. I rushed out of the door after James, glimpsing him storming down the hall. I jogged to catch up with him and surprised him when I fell into stride beside him.

"I don't think I need to remind you how I feel about you wandering around the Masters' rooms without an escort," James said through clenched teeth.

"Who better to escort me than you?" I said. James stopped then and turned to face me, crossing his arms across his chest.

"What do you want, Kit?" he asked. His impatience was contagious.

"You don't want us anywhere near Dulce or her party," I said, watching James' expression go sour right away.

"No," he said. "I do not."

"Why?" I implored, mindful to keep my voice down.

"That is not your concern," James said. His words rang with finality and I knew he was trying to get rid of me.

"I meant, why did you give us permission to accept her invitation?" I asked. The pause during which James contemplated a response felt constricting and heated around my throat, because I knew questioning any decision of his was a risk in itself. "I agreed to do whatever you ask of me, to protect the others," I reminded him. I thought about Haitham finding Daisy in the midst of Dulce's celebration and my mouth went dry. "If there is a reason you don't want us there, tell me what it is and I can convince the others not to attend." I knew it would not be easy to persuade Armand, but if James had legitimate cause to disapprove, I would fight him on this if I had to. I expected James to pinch the bridge of his nose and berate me for expecting him to explain himself, but he checked down the hall over my shoulder and then behind himself.

"As the Master of this compound, every move I make is criticized. Whether or not you know—or care—that same scrutiny is applied to all demonyms of this place, as long as the summit is going on. I am vehemently against the idea of you socializing with my peers not only because it would violate your privacy, but because there is a very real risk that you four might be perceived by them to be—well, comfortable."

"Would that be so terrible?" I wondered. "You always say that the reason you've put so many rules in place is to ensure our safety and overall happiness."

"True, but this is different," James explained quietly. "It is also now irrelevant—you agreed to this farcical spectacle in front of Donovan, who will know right away that I interfered if you rescind your acceptance." I couldn't believe what I was hearing! James was surrendering his ironclad hold over us to save face in front of Donovan? I felt the beginnings of a panic seize my heart to think of what kind of sinister politics were at play, and I had made them worse by chasing after James; I would be watched now, because of this public aside.

"What should I do?" I asked him. I folded my arms to keep from fidgeting nervously and tried not to kick myself. My nerves stood on edge when James sighed dejectedly and bowed his head.

"Let me worry about it," he said softly. "If currying favor with my niece is truly what comes naturally to you, so be it." He had officially confounded me.

"As you say," I said stiffly. I left him standing in the hall to return to the dining room and made sure to check my expression before entering the room again. If I plainly revealed even a sliver of how perturbed I was, Armand and the girls would be on me in a minute and I wouldn't risk it in front of Donovan.

"Is everything all right?" Dulce asked me once I hastily took my seat.

"Of course," I said. "I just had to ask James…well, I thought I would take advantage of his generous mood and ask him if we could move you back in with us, Liza." Lying to her was unkind of me and I felt crushed by the sorry smile Liza made at me.

"You shouldn't have bothered him, Kit," she said. "I assume he didn't go for it?"

"He didn't."

"Well, thank you for trying." Liza folded her napkin beside her plate and tweaked her smile into a happy one for Dulce. "And thank you for eating with us. As you have heard, I have not been well. It's nice to have friends with whom I can pass the time." She stood up slowly, careful of the stitches concealed by the high collar of her green frock. She kissed the top of Daisy's head and gave Armand's shoulder a lingering grasp. He leaned toward her enough for her fingers to brush the side of his face when she walked away. Douglas was waiting for her outside to lead her back to her bedroom, where I had no doubt she would pile her blankets in front of the huge window and fall asleep.

"I believe James was right about getting back to business," Donovan said, looking rather pleased with himself. He stood up and kissed Dulce's cheek after saying farewell to us all, and then Nathan appeared in the doorway to tell us it was time to move along.

"This was spectacular," Dulce said after giving me a stifling hug. "I'm so excited! I'll see you all tomorrow!"

The walk back to the Tribute wing was quiet. I knew to expect a barrage of questions from Daisy and Armand once we were alone—they were practically buzzing while we made our way through the marketplace. I kept my eyes forward and ignored the watchful pedestrians along the way. Nathan must have had his own dinner waiting for him because when we were merely within sight of our front door, he offered a very brusque "I'm sure you three can manage the rest of the way. Be sure to stay put and send away for an escort if you need to step out before curfew" before turning on his heel and setting off for the Masters' chambers.

"Out with it," Armand said, the instant I'd closed the door behind us.

"What did you say to James?" Daisy joined in urgently. I held my hands up for quiet and led them into the sitting room.

"I asked James why he didn't want us to go to Dulce's birthday party," I explained.

"Are you insane?" Armand hissed. "You just ran after him and questioned him to his face? You could have been knocked senseless!"

"He might catch onto us, Kit!" Daisy exclaimed crossly. "What were you thinking?"

"Both of you, be quiet," I said, sitting down in Armand's chair by the fireplace. The two of them dropped onto the couch and sat forward with their hands clasped together, elbows on knees. "Yes, I chased after James to ask him why he was adverse to us attending the party. I thought I'd stand a chance of getting the truth out of him. After all, I've never seen him leave a decision like that up to us, especially when Donovan was staring right at him like the whole thing was some kind of test—or did neither of you notice that?"

"But, Kit," Armand said gravely, his dark eyes wide with concern, "asking him outright like that...."

"It wasn't a reach for me," I defended myself. "I think he trusts me, in his way." In a low voice, I proceeded to tell them about the harrowing altercation I had witnessed between James and Haitham—I didn't bother excusing why I hadn't told them until now and as I described the shocking violence and disturbing warning James had given me in the greenhouse afterward, I guessed I wouldn't have to; Armand and Daisy were both wan and appalled by the time I finished the tale.

"I don't believe it," Armand uttered. "I just don't believe it. He *struck* James?"

"He is worse than James in every conceivable way," I said.

"What kind of man pretends to be a harmless old tradesman for no reason?" Daisy wondered in a strained voice.

"Oh, he had a reason," I said. "I believe he did it to gauge my character. Had he introduced himself as Haitham the Master, I would never have spoken to him like I did—I don't know, maybe I would have sent for James right away? He enjoyed making Nathan squirm in front of the other guardsmen, and I know that everything he said to Liza on the day you all met him was strategic in nature, to get in her head the way he'd gotten into mine. Regardless, from what I contrived of James' summation of his father, the old fiend has a mechanism for everything he does."

"And you think this makes James trust you?" Armand wanted to know.

"Well, there is one more thing," I said. My cheeks felt hot as I mustered the nerve to tell them everything I said to James right up until the moment I'd shaken his hand. Daisy covered her mouth with her hand when I was done and Armand sat back on the sofa looking utterly perplexed.

"So...you're James' man?" he said softly.

"I wouldn't say it like that," I said. "Either way, he saw fit to answer my question."

"Did he?" Armand gushed. "Damn it, Kit, what did he say?"

"He said no, he did not approve of us accepting Dulce's invitation," I recalled carefully. "He didn't want us to be seen as comfortable around his peers, but it didn't matter what he thought because Donovan was there."

Armand's lips curled into a smile. "Good," he said.

"Is it?" Daisy asked. I could see she shared my reservations about going against James' wishes.

"Absolutely," Armand declared. "We're going to go to that party and make a point to enjoy ourselves at all costs. The only reason he's relinquished his control is because Haitham's mere presence here puts him off. The second this summit is over, he'll revert to his usual, cruel self and punish us with maximum prejudice for departing from his whims."

Maybe Armand was right. "But is acting purely to spite him the right thing to do? He might not find any footing on punishing us for being pressured by his niece to go to a 'farcical spectacle' as he put it, but if we flout him in front of his peers...." I broke off with a shudder, not wanting to go into any detail so that Daisy might be spared visualizing such an upsetting prospect.

"You think James trusts you," Armand said. "You could be right. Maybe he does, and he told you why he doesn't want us to go because he trusts you will follow his implicit instructions; or maybe it's *you* who trusts *him* to live up to his end of the deal you made? Let me remind you, Kit, that James has already defaulted on his part. He didn't keep Haitham away from Liza, or me, or Daisy. He doesn't give a damn about us because he only cares about himself. As long as the other Masters kiss his ring when this summit is over, he couldn't care less about what we do or if we trust him."

"What would you have me do?" I asked. He was painting me to be a fool and if there was one thing I could not stand from Armand, it was condescension.

"Trust the only person who has proved time and time again that he's actually trustworthy! Trust Donovan!" Armand insisted. "If the only reason James deferred to us about Dulce's ridiculous party invitation was that Donovan was sitting right next to him, don't you think that means we should go? That we should be as comfortable as we damn well like for a change? Daisy, you were just saying to me that we need to stop letting James control who we are. Well, you're right—tomorrow night, we have the chance to make a stand and show him that he can't keep us in line anymore."

I'd never seen Armand so possessed by an idea. For me to put my faith in Donovan...well, I never would have thought Armand would have been so incensed to convince me. Consequently, it gave me great pause to go along with it.

"Donovan's been a friend to us," Daisy agreed. "He never treats us as though we were...." She trailed off, searching for the right word.

"Commodities," I said. I thought of what James had said to me about love and the risk at which it put the people to whom I gave it.

"I think we should go," Daisy said. "And I think we should indulge Dulce's every fancy." She couldn't help but smile when Armand put his arm around her and planted an overzealous smooch on her cheek. They really looked like a brother and sister then: Armand snickering and squeezing Daisy closer as she wiped her cheek off with her sleeve.

"It's going to make a difference," Armand assured me. "A last hurrah of sorts—you'll see, Kit. Maybe now that we're all in agreement...." He cracked a warm smile. "I get it now," he said. "We're only strong when we're together." He stood up and rubbed his hands together earnestly. "I think I'll stop at the market to get us something special for breakfast tomorrow." Beaming, Daisy reminded him to send away for an escort and Armand yelled, "The hell with Nathan!" over his shoulder as he left the Tribute wing.

I was on my feet at once, reaching for Daisy as soon as Armand had left. I took her hands, pulled her to her feet, and kissed her lips as the excitement instilled by Armand's spirited speech electrified my every nerve. Daisy was overwhelmed by it too and giggled as we kissed. She curled her fingers in my hair and sighed when I hugged her around the waist.

"Is this real?" I murmured against her lips. Daisy ran her fingertips through the hair at the back of my head and sent a wave of tingles down to my toes.

"It has to be," whispered Daisy. "But I feel like I would float away if you let go." I held her closer to me and bent to kiss the side of her neck. The cord of desire I felt for her strummed within me when she let out a little moan. I felt unsteady on my feet suddenly, woozy even, when Daisy peered up at me with a hazy, sultry glimmer in her eyes, the likes of which I had never seen before. That look inspired a tension in me, a driving unease that made me clench my teeth and lose my train of thought when I stared back at her. Holding Daisy in my arms, I keeled forward and settled her underneath me on the sofa. A voice in the back of my mind was incessantly interrupting, insisting in an annoying manner that this was not appropriate.

I expressly did not care to listen to that voice, the one prudently warning me that Armand might reappear at any moment. I wanted to keep feeling Daisy underneath me, the warmth of her body against mine. The petal soft brushes of her lips on mine stole my breath and took me worlds away, to a place where there was only the two of us and an eager pressure building between our bodies. Defying still my nagging conscience, I smoothed one of my hands down the slope of her satin smooth neck and down the side of her torso. Apparently, I'd tickled her a little because she giggled and kissed me with delighted fervor. My senses sharpened and I held her to me covetously—my Daisy, my sweet, beautiful, soft Daisy. I wanted any part of her body I could reach.

When I slipped my fingers behind the crook of her knee and hitched her leg over my hip, Daisy stilled beneath me.

"Kit," she murmured. "Wait." I pressed kisses into the side of her throat and nuzzled her ear, loving the feel of her shiver under my touch. With each breath I took, I reveled in the perfume of her hair and smiled to think of how fitting it was that a girl named after a flower would smell like one.

"Kit," Daisy said again. Her hands were on my shoulders, gentle as ever, but she was holding me still. "Not here." She wanted me to stop, and now the voice that had been bothering me to restrain myself was begging me to persist—to change her mind with more kisses, more whispers of adoration....

I wrenched myself away. *Don't be a scoundrel,* I told myself. I was off Daisy in a second and sliding away from her, to sit at the other end of the sofa and be very still while my heartbeats slowed to a normal pace.

"I'm sorry," Daisy sighed. She sat up too and swung her legs over the edge of the couch.

"No," I blurted. "That's all right, Daze." Speech felt sloppy and my hands felt shaky. Unbelievable! I was practically slap-happy.

"It's not that—well, I didn't want to stop, I just...." Daisy breathed an airy laugh and hid her eyes behind her hands. "I didn't want Armie to come home and find us...*like that.*"

"No," I agreed. I had to laugh out loud when I imagined Armand coming in to find Daisy and me entangled on the sofa. I would have clobbered him for interrupting. I then made the mistake of looking back at Daisy and when I saw the rosy tint to her cheeks and the sort of dazed look in her eyes—the dazed look I had put there—I felt more compelled than ever to take her into my arms again and obey every instinct I had to keep her close.

That settled it—I pushed myself to my feet and started for my room for a shower. Daisy asked after me but I did not stop to respond. To err on the side of caution, I locked my bedroom door behind me before stripping down and hurrying to the shower. I didn't bother tweaking the hot water faucet before backing into the rushing, cold water. I forced myself to stay under the water until I could think straight. The annoying voice in the back of my mind was back and much louder, reminding me how lucky I was that I hadn't been caught, that I should never be so reckless again. What had I been thinking?

I smiled when Daisy came to mind again, that bashful smirk on her face and her radiant blush. I was admittedly nervous about Dulce's party, knowing that I would have to police my behavior twice as forcefully than today. We would be socializing with Masters and Mistresses alike and they would be watching us, making note of every move we made. I worried too about what James had refused to tell me, especially because it meant that one wrong step could spell disaster for us. And for Liza, who was isolated from us.

I exited the shower and dressed. I left my room when I was positive I'd regained my sea legs and heard Daisy in the kitchen with Armand, no doubt helping him put away groceries for breakfast. I was proud of Armand for finding reason and standing with us finally. It made the plan to leave this place feel more real than ever. I imagined us living in a house, surrounded by light and plants like James' greenhouse; Armand would cook and Liza would be at her easel every morning, and by their lead I would fill my days with only hobbies and hours spent outside in the open air, under the sun. Maybe Daisy and I would dwell together, where we could share kisses without fear of being discovered. We could sit together by a river and sing like we did when we were little children, before we came to the compound—and none of us would ever think of James the Master ever again.

Consumed by excited anticipation, I sat down at the piano and began to play. I knew Armand and Daisy had gone from the kitchen to the study to read while I played, like they always did. I poured all my hope into my music, letting it slowly flow through me in waves of release. Only when my back hurt from sitting up and my eyelids felt heavy did I close the keys and stand up from the bench. It signaled bedtime for us all, because as soon as the music stopped, I saw the study light switch off.

"Goodnight," I said to Armand and Daisy.

"Right behind you," Armand yawned.

"Goodnight, Kit," called Daisy softly. I loved them both. I felt lucky for the first time in my life as I crawled into bed and I fell asleep the moment my head touched my pillow.

Chapter Sixteen

I guessed James had gone long before I'd woken up. His bed was already made by the time I noticed the strip of daylight blazing through the tiny opening in the curtains and sat up in my cot. I was less sore today than I had been since the attack—so much so that I stretched with my arms over my head without thinking to mind my stitches. My forearms throbbed when I put my arms back down but the discomfort didn't consume me as it usually did. As I slid out of the cot and padded toward the bathroom, I let my mind wander and was relieved when it took me away from Quinn to a morning back in my familiar Tribute rooms.

It was last spring and I had been sore from being broken in by my new gymnastics instructor. I had woken up late, petrified that I had missed my lesson and would face severe ramifications from James, only to find Armand, Daisy, and Kit cooking lunch in the kitchen. Stifling anguish had left me in a gust—it was our day off, and I'd forgotten all about it. Daisy had looked up to see smiling at the slapdash ponytail I'd frantically pulled my hair into as I rushed down the hallway. Armand smiled crookedly at me and winked, making my heart leap. I was bursting with happiness to see him dutifully standing over Kit, who was busy at the stove with his back to me.

"What's on the menu?"

"There you are, Liza!" Kit had exclaimed. "Armie is showing me how to make *cassoulet.*"

I'd hummed supportively and my stomach had grumbled. "Is it coming along well?"

"Well, it's not your banana bread," Armand had sighed. I pursed my lips and crinkled my nose at him for teasing me. "It's virtually impossible to mess up stew." Still, he stayed close to Kit, looking over his shoulder.

"Only because you made the stock," Kit had murmured. Despite Armand's lingering over him, he still seemed proud of himself.

"Please. All I did was add the beans." Armand had grinned then, fixing a knowing, mischievous stare at me.

I felt his love so warmly that day. It was like standing in the sunlight. The Masters' rooms could have windows on all sides and an open roof, and it would still be empty of a light like that. I wondered with tears in my eyes if the three of them were cooking breakfast now, trading japes and smiles over coffee and Daisy's tea. The cool tiled floor of the bathroom soothed me a little but then, when I leaned over the sink to rinse my mouth out, I made the mistake of looking at my reflection. I was wan and fragile-looking, my eyes teeming with tears. A little whimper escaped me and I clamped a hand over my mouth as sobs welled in my chest.

I missed my family.

I cranked the sink knob and caught cold water in my hands as it flowed from the faucet. I splashed it on my face to try to snap myself out of this melancholy spell, which sort of worked. I wanted a bath then—as hot as I could stand it, to quell the overwhelming anxiety that was racking my body. I filled the tub with hot water and crawled in after unceremoniously stripping down. The stitches gashes on my arms screamed when they hit the water—I hissed a dozen curse words as I stilled immediately from the piercing pain of it, mostly at myself for forgetting to wrap them in the green plastic tape Jada had left somewhere in here for me. The tears came at once and I let them fall down my cheeks. I couldn't help but feel sorry for myself and I sobbed earnestly, letting the crushing loneliness I felt break down every careful wall of control I had built since the attack.

"Idiot," I growled through clenched teeth. If I hadn't jumped out the library window, I could be at home with Daisy, Armand, and Kit right now. I wished I had never learned anything of the truth—my kidnapping, Petra's murder, Haitham's treachery, James' unwilling devotion to him, none of it. I gripped the edges of the tub in each hand and took a deep breath before pushing myself under the surface of the hot bathwater.

Even when Quinn had cut my flesh open, it hadn't hurt like this. I forced myself to stay under water as the sutures in my shoulder, and every nerve surrounding them, wailed in agony. I screamed, my voice leaving me in a garbled flood of air bubbles underwater. I took an involuntary gasp for breath after and shot out of the tub, coughing on the water I'd accidentally swallowed. Water pooled around me as I sat naked on the floor, my knees drawn to my chest. I was shaking and gritting my teeth while my shoulder throbbed. I leaned my head back, against the cold ceramic of the sink, and took a shuddering breath.

This place was worse than a prison, I thought. It was hell. And I was all alone.

I dried off and frowned at my tangled, damp hair. Getting it wet for a few seconds was hardly washing it, but I couldn't be bothered to go for the lavender soap sitting beside the bath. I brushed it out and let it hang down my back while I peeled off the wet bandages covering my arms and shoulder. I immediately knew I shouldn't have because when I took one look at the stitches poking out of my skin, I swayed on my feet.

"Easy," I coached myself. I felt as though I might throw up when I saw the sutured gash on my shoulder. I blinked and saw blood in my mind's eye, then found myself grasping at the sink basin to keep myself standing. I shook my head and suppressed the reflex to gag, pulling on fresh clothes as fast as I could. The stitches were itchy underneath the fleece sleeves so I rolled the sleeves back—carefully, so I wouldn't pull one of them on the fabric. I knew if even one of those tiny notches were to be displaced, I would pass out and probably hit my head.

I held the wall as I made for my cot. I crawled on top of the blankets, feeling dizzy and very cold. I curled into a ball and hid my face behind my hands. A cyclone of guilt, shame, and grief twisted through me as I tried to force myself back to sleep. It became clear to me after a minute of this that I was very close to breaking down again. My throat hurt from strangling the sobs down, so I resolved to imagine the only things that I knew would make me calm.

Armand roaring with laughter after the fire I'd started while trying to bake bread had triggered the kitchen's sprinkler system, Daisy shrieking and slipping on the wet floor as she'd tried to escape the downpour in the kitchen, but catching Kit on her way down and dragging him comically to the floor beside her. James had vehemently scorned our irresponsible behavior, of course. We had all laughed ourselves hoarse already, and seeing him standing so furious and serious in a puddle of fire-preventative water in the kitchen pushed us to almost hysteria.

"You little maniacs," James had remarked crossly. "You could have burned the place down!"

"Imagine!" Armand had wheezed. "Your stately summit compound—burned down by a loaf of banana bread!" How had he been brave enough to look James in the eye and laugh? He'd paid for it, naturally; James had yanked him to his feet and thrown him in his room for the rest of the day, without meals, but the memory was unspoiled by the show of brute force. It had made the rest of us shut up at once, but even so, in the throes of my crippling isolation, the joy and hilarity I'd felt that day was palpable now. My shivering subsided and I drifted off into a floating, lucid slumber.

I woke up to the bedroom door slamming shut. I shot upright as though I'd had a nightmare and looked wildly at James, who was grimacing and holding his hands into fists at his sides. His eyes were pinched closed as he breathed heavily—obviously he was trying to manage his temper. I made no sound. I didn't even move, lest I trigger his rage and summon him to me. James turned to the wall next to him and punched a wooden panel so hard that it cracked. I clapped my hands to my mouth and watched him lean into the wall, bracing his looming frame by setting his hands flat on either side of the cracked panel.

"What happened?" I dared to question him.

"Liza...." He was warning me to be quiet.

"You're bleeding," I said, noticing the shiny red line forming along his knuckle.

"It's nothing." James stepped away from the wall and turned to face me, his striking blue eyes were ablaze with anger and something that looked like suffering. I climbed out of my cot, slowly, and made my way across the room to him. The slightest sign of reproach on his part would have sent me backing away, but he merely stood still as I came close. With a very annoyed roll of his eyes, he held up his hand to display the cut on his knuckle. It wasn't nothing. Drops of blood were rolling down the back of his hand to his wrist, and I couldn't believe he wasn't showing signs of distress or being in pain. When I reached for his arm, he pulled away and eyed me warily.

"May I ask what you think you're doing?" His tone was brittle but his glare showed some surprise.

"You split your hand open," I said. "It looks deep."

"I said it was nothing." Truly, he was intractable through and through.

"I'll send for the doctor anyway," I said. "We both could use a little patching up." I showed him my arms, stitches side up under my rolled-up sleeves.

"Liza!" James' irritation stole his attention from his likely throbbing right hand. He carefully took my wrists and scanned my arms for signs of damage or infection—or at least, I assumed that's what he was looking for. "Why did you remove the gauze?"

"I forgot to cover them when I bathed," I admitted. James let go of my hands and heaved an annoyed groan.

"You are making me regret leaving you unattended for even an hour, Liza," James said angrily. "Do I have to stand over you day in and day out to ensure you don't do anything foolish?"

"I'm sorry!" I didn't mean to shout and I quickly bowed my head, averting my eyes. My defensiveness seemed to have startled James, for instead of snarling something menacing at me, he folded his arms across his chest and shook his head.

"Of course. Come over here, I'll do it myself."

I looked up curiously. "You will?"

"It's a simple patch job," James sighed. "Sit." I did as I was told and held my arms out. James went to the portable by my cot and pulled out a roll of stark white gauze and tape from the small drawer underneath. He then went to his desk and pulled out a small pair of scissors from a locked drawer at the top.

I guessed that James hadn't kept his scissors locked away *before* I'd moved into his room. Whether he thought I might hurt him or myself was unclear. As I tried to ignore the offensive idea that he didn't trust me with sharp objects, James sat beside me and began to unravel the gauze. He then cursed when a smudge of scarlet dotted the clean bandage—his hand was really bleeding a lot. He tore the bloodstained stuff off and then handed the roll to me.

"Really?" I asked.

"If you're squeamish, I can send for Jada," James said. He raised an eyebrow as if to question my sensibilities.

"I'll do it," I said, taking the gauze from him. I was a woman grown, after all. "Honestly, until everything with Quinn, blood has never bothered me. It's surprising, but...."

"Yes?" James prompted me. I pointedly took his hand in mine so that I could wipe the blood on his hand off.

"This is exactly the kind of thing you would declare to be inappropriate conduct," I said. Nervously, I smiled and quickly focused my gaze on the task at hand.

"I think medical necessities call for the occasional breach of social boundaries," James said. I supposed he was right as I tore off a small square of gauze and folded it into a smaller piece, then pressed it gently over the cut on his hand. Keeping it in place with my thumb, I spun the roll around his hand and noticed how strong it was, even while it was relaxed and held between mine. I finished and handed the gauze back to James so that he could wrap my arms.

"The abrasions seem to be healing well." His fingers were clearly more deft than mine, as it took him only seconds to wrap each arm.

"They'll leave awful scars," I remarked glumly.

"I don't think so," James disagreed. "Noticeable maybe, but not gruesome." He reached for his side, where I knew the volpine bite had left a scar best described by the latter of his supposition. I flushed when I thought of his grim expression at my mention of it at dinner with Dulce the night before, highlighted by a pang of guilt. James stood from the side of the cot.

"James?" He turned back to face me expectantly, gauze still in hand. I reached up to undo the button at my collar and shrugged my shoulder gingerly free of my blouse. James took a lingering look at the ghastly line of sutures tracing along my skin, just inches away from my throat.

"Certainly," he decided, snapping into a composed, clinical version of himself. He went to the portable and retrieved a packet of white bandaging, then took his seat again beside me. The heft of him made the rail of the little bed creak. I was very aware of our strange posture: I was leaning toward him with my chin turned away, and James was so close to me, I could feel his breath on my neck. When his thumb brushed the pulse on my throat, I shivered. James whispered something to himself.

"What is it? Did I pull a stitch?"

"No," James replied. He finished carefully taping the bandage over my shoulder and quickly stood from the cot. I tugged my blouse back over my exposed skin and fastened the button. "It's remarkable you survived, Liza. I didn't realize how close the blade was to your neck."

I could do nothing but stare back at him and try not to cry. For a moment, I thought he was rearing up to say something important but a triplet of knocks at the door interrupted him. James went to the door and opened it, and was passed a large cream-colored box by a woman in servant dress. I furrowed my brow as I studied the box, which was enormous even in James' arms—specifically the bright green ribbon wrapped around it. James scoffed and tugged a card from the top of the parcel, awkwardly prying it open with his freshly bandaged hand. Evidently, he found the inscription to be preposterous.

"I'm afraid that even two near-death experiences cannot prepare you for the ordeal that awaits you," James said with a bitter sneer, delivering the box to the foot of my cot. Aghast, I rigidly reached to lift the top off of the package away, expecting to find something horrible inside. What I saw instead was a dusty rose-colored garment, into which were sewn dozens of tiny, sparkling gems.

"It's a dress," I gasped, pulling the slinky gown out of the box. I had never seen anything so beautiful in my life. The sparkling bodice of it was spellbinding and the skirt fell to the floor in an elegant sweep as it unfurled in my hands. Unmistakably, I found a long slit up the side, which would show off the wearer's legs in a daring, seductive display.

"From my niece," James said, his voice dripping with venom. He stuck the card out to me and I took it from him, reading quickly the loopy scrawl inside:

Beautiful Liza,

I asked around and apparently you Tributes don't own anything suitable to wear to my birthday party. I hope you like this gown. I think it will make you feel like a princess! The shoes are mine, one of my favorite pairs, and I was assured they would fit you. Enjoy! I'm excited for tonight!

Besos,

Dulce

I gulped upon finishing the note. James was really steaming and glared at the dress Dulce had sent me worse than he ever had at a living adversary.

"It was very thoughtful of her," I said after a while.

"Don't say a word to me about it," James snapped. "It's bad enough you're going along with this in the first place—"

"*I'm* going along with it? What about you, James the Master? If you're so opposed to the idea, put a stop to it!"

"If you interrupt me again, I will do more than that." James turned his back on me and my new dress and I could see the muscles in his back rippling as his entire body tensed.

"I can't wear this," I moaned, looking back to the dress. "I've never worn a dress in my life, let alone something so fine."

"Then don't," James offered spitefully. "Truthfully, I don't care if you show up in your pajamas, but you agreed to attend in front of Donovan, and I can't have him thinking I've had any kind of hand in it if you don't go."

I set the dress aside and stood up, daring to question James a second time. "You have battered people in front of me for doing much less than this—tell me what has happened between you and Donovan so that I can understand why you're folding to him now, and taking it out on me in turn!"

James' temper was in full swing now. "How dare you say such a thing! You have no right to make any such demands!"

"I'm not going to play dress up for your niece's sake, when you're going around punching holes in the walls to cope with whatever has happened," I assured him. "Just because you saved my life doesn't mean I'm any less immune to your brand of punishment. Quinn's knife may have cut me to ribbons but you put a scar on my face long before he marked my arms—I'm not interested in earning another one from you."

James let his held breath out in a steady stream of muttered curses, most of which described his disbelief of my gall. "You think after what that beast did to you, I would cause you any more strife?" His voice was pained.

Had my words wounded him?

"All I'm saying is, please don't give me leave to attend Dulce's party if you're just going to punish me for it later." I crossed my arms to hide how meek I felt to see James struggle between his temper and his manners.

"You will never understand the world of pressure I am under," said James. "I cannot put it more plainly than that. This summit is unlike any other, no thanks to you, and the measures I have had to undertake to ensure it runs smoothly have caused me to overextend my capacity to handle the other Masters. Dulce's ridiculous party is not a glamorous celebration, as the costume she sent you might suggest."

"Then tell me what it is."

"It is a test, Liza," James said. He always chose his words carefully; I could tell he was trying to make it sound threatening without prompting me to ask him to explain further.

"I see," I said. His tactic didn't work with me. "And the four of us attending would ensure you fail, is that right?" James did not answer me. "Is it Haitham? Will he do something to us, if we go?"

"I would not allow him to do such a thing," James assured me in a hard voice. "I am in a very bad position among my peers right now, Liza. This spectacle will not make things easier for me—or what I'm trying to accomplish."

I knew that would be the end of it. No matter how hard I pressed him to explain himself, he would never give in. He'd chosen his vague closing statement precisely, like he did everything. I looked to the dress laid out on my bed and resigned myself to compromise.

"Even if it fits, my bandages will show. I won't wear it."

James swallowed hard. "I will find Dulce and let her know the style was not to your liking; she will undoubtedly send another, which I am sure will be a better fit." This was the first time he had ever met me in the middle on an issue and I let it show on my face that I was impressed. James held his hands out in a gesture of surrender. "It's done, Liza. You don't have any repercussions to fear from me. But if you feel unwell at any point this evening—"

"You'll have me escorted back here, right away." I was two-for-two, for interrupting him. James' lips became a very thin line and his eyes smoldered down at me. "I'd better hold on to the shoes, don't you think?" I wondered.

"Don't push it," said James.

Wisely, I kept my mouth shut. I breezed past him and took up my sketchpad from the corner of his desk, where I'd left it the night before. I found Douglas waiting outside for me and asked him to take me to the greenhouse for a while, as there would be no lessons today. I found the humidity to be relaxing as I took my usual spot on the bench, in the farthest corner of the would-be jungle. I didn't work for long before Douglas came to retrieve me, saying I had a visitor in my bedroom.

"Not Daisy or the boys, I'm afraid," he said, noticing the way my features lit up at the prospect of seeing the others.

"It couldn't be Talisa?" I asked, thinking that my gymnastics instructor might be worried enough to call on me in the Masters' chambers. Douglas pulled a curiously grim expression.

"If you would like me to interrupt in five minutes with an excuse, tell me now," he said. He paused with his hand on the doorknob, waiting for my response, and I nodded hastily even though I had no idea what he was so apprehensive over. Once Douglas swung the door open, I understood. Dulce sat amid the pile of fluffy pillows at the head of my old bed and beamed when she laid eyes on me.

"Liza!" she greeted me sweetly. How anyone could be so graceful in high-heeled shoes like hers was baffling. I opened my arms just in time for Dulce to pull me into a familiar embrace, though she was not in enough of a hurry to deprive me the chance to admire her amber-colored dress. Her hair smelled of spicy sugarplums and after she pulled away, I knew her scent would linger on me for a while. I could hardly complain—she was scrumptious to behold and even lovelier to listen to.

"Master James passed a message to me through my mother," she explained in her honeysuckle sweet voice, her Spanish accent lending her cadence an exotic allure. "Not surprisingly, he is old fashioned; he hated the dress I sent you for tonight, but fortunately I brought dozens with me. You look about my size." She flickered her dark eyes up and down my figure and grinned. "Did you try the shoes? They'll match just about everything I have."

"I didn't see them," I admitted. "James made such a fuss over the dress…." It did not bother me to paint James as a villain to save face in front of Dulce.

"I asked around to make sure they would fit you," Dulce assured me.

"If they're as tall as those," I said, pointedly glancing at the shoes on Dulce's feet, "I should warn you, I'll embarrass us both. I don't think I could walk in them without someone to hold me up."

"You were made for those shoes, Liza," Dulce purred. Her hands affectionately braced me and I noticed how warm she was. She blinked her long eyelashes at me and pursed her full lips in a smirk. "Besides, heels are excellent excuses to hold onto men—especially ones with arms like Armand. It's a shame I learned how to walk in shoes like these when I was twelve, otherwise I'm sure I would find an excuse to hang off his arm…though, I'm not above faking a twisted ankle." Dulce giggled secretively and gave my arm a playful nudge. She said Armand's name hungrily and I bristled with jealousy as gooseflesh sweep up my spine.

"As you say," I said, forcing a cheery tone to match Dulce's. Maybe I was emulating James a little just then, by using politesse to disguise my disdain for the subject matter.

"Your manners are adorable," Dulce said. "You'll fit right in with us—well, after we do something about your hair."

"My hair?" My cheeks burned.

"You have the most beautiful blonde hair, Liza," Dulce gushed, reaching to sweep aside a few loose strands. "But I'm curious to see what it would look like with a bit of styling." She had hardly asked my permission to toy with my hair—I certainly hadn't given it—before Dulce was gently pulling my long tresses through dainty fingers, mussing it this way and that. She lavished me with generous compliments, mostly to do with how she "would kill" to have hair that laid so smoothly. I returned an honest observation about how much I admired her wild curls and immediately thereafter appreciated how cunning this girl was—I'd walked unsuspecting into a coy trap.

"You like curls?" Dulce winked at me. "I thought you'd never ask." She led me by the hand into the bathroom and sat me down on a settee she'd dragged in before I'd set foot in my old room. I had to smile even though I rolled my eyes at the obvious setup, which only seemed to further delight Dulce. She took up a heated ceramic wand in one hand and went about coiling slender ribbons of my hair around its length, forming gorgeous, thick curls that bounced down my shoulders once she pulled the wand away.

"Are you sure…?" I stammered, nervously watching myself start to resemble a portrait of an aristocrat.

"Trust me, *bonita*, you'll love it when I'm finished." Dulce did not seem the type to break a promise, especially one laid at the altar of vanity, so I re-signed to keep my eyes averted from the mirror until she was finished. Her fingertips grazed the collar of my shirt and she pulled it aside, exposing the white gauze underneath.

"What happened here?" Dulce asked in a worried, hushed tone.

"An accident," I said. Dulce touched my shoulder with her free hand and frowned down at me. I could tell she wasn't likely to drop the subject without getting a few extra details but I wasn't keen to divulge the horror of Quinn's attack. I steeled my features and blinked up innocently at her reflection. "Is something wrong?" I asked, my voice too high.

"No." Apparently, Dulce was content to let it go—at least for now. She went back to curling my hair, telling me errantly about her friends back at her mother's compound. "Last summer, my girl Josefina went out to the orange grove with Gerardo, one of Donovan's swordsmen. When she came back, she had a scarlet love mark on her neck. She actually touched one of these to it so her mother wouldn't see it for what it was," Dulce said, brandishing the curling wand with wide, scandalized eyes. My jaw dropped to hear such a thing. Burning myself with a hot ceramic rod to cover the evidence of a fervent embrace seemed a preposterous notion.

"Could her mother's punishment really be worse than a burn blister?" I wondered. Dulce narrowed her gaze and stuck out her hip.

"*Seriamente*, Liza?" Dulce shook her head and set the curling wand aside. "Had Señora Agueda found out one of Doni's men gave her only daughter a *coso*, she would have raised high hell!"

"So the rules are the same there as they are here? You aren't allowed to fraternize with anyone?"

Dulce let out a bubbly trill of a laugh. "Thankfully, we do not share that very bleak rule! No, you misunderstand me. It's just that everybody knows Doni's men are off-limits. The things they get up to...I think Master James would say they were 'unsavory' at best. Señora Agueda is always telling us to keep away from them. I don't blame Fina for covering it up, because her mother would insist on having him flogged, but no one except Doni can dole out punishment on the men in his service." I chewed on my lip as I pondered the likeness between Donovan and James in that regard. Dulce delicately pulled apart the curls she'd just fashioned, humming a laugh under her breath as she tucked my hair into place.

"Not that I blame Fina for chasing after him in the first place. Gerardo has this look in his eyes...." Dulce sighed and I could see her dazzling brown eyes glaze over at the thought of this man. "And he cuts a very handsome figure. *And* he dances. He's like a perfect daydream."

"I think I understand why your instructors insist on separating you from the boys," I remarked. Dulce hooted and gave my arm a harmless swat. I smiled at her, glad to have someone whom I could taunt in jest.

"I'd be worse than Fina, believe me, if it weren't for my responsibility to live up to my mother's reputation. And I'll tell you something, Liza, the boys would trip over themselves lining up to whisper nothings in your ear," Dulce declared, sweeping a curl back from where it fell over my cheek. She affected an eager air of secrecy, as though she was going to whisper something rude. "Were you serious? You aren't allowed to—what did you call it? Fraternize?"

"Very serious," I said gravely. It felt awkward having to explain how rigidly we were expected to keep to our codes of conduct after Dulce had painted such a rosy picture of her life in the southern compound. Dulce pulled a face, horrified by the notion of such a stringent lifestyle.

"If it's any consolation, I think we just made it a little tougher for those good-looking tradesmen to keep to that law." She gestured to the mirror and I peered nervously at my reflection.

My worries had all been in vain. I'd expected those curls to make me look ridiculous but the way Dulce had settled them in shining blonde cascades down my shoulders was simply stunning. I was shocked by how refined I looked— so much so, all thoughts of my sore shoulder flew from my mind and I carefully swiveled my head from side to side to take in each meticulously arranged wave.

"This has to be your finest work," I raved.

"Hardly," Dulce waved away the compliment. "I can do so much more, but your eyes demand attention. I wouldn't dream of stealing it away with a braided crown or even a knot." I could tell she had been toying with the idea earlier from the way she'd arranged my hair at the back. "I'd say you need a touch of something else, but your lashes are already so thick. And your lips—

well, I don't have any shades that would go with your color, and I doubt Master James lets you keep any makeup."

"He expressly forbids it," I agreed. I turned to Dulce and laid my hand on her arm. "Thank you for this."

"It's been my pleasure." She smiled beautifully down at me, keenly proud of her handiwork. "Now, come along—I want you to help me choose which earrings to wear tonight!" I was happy to follow Dulce out of my room and, with Douglas at my heels, to her chamber, which had been decorated down to the wainscoting with ropes of shiny silks and flowers that she had likely brought from home. I had never known anyone as glamorous as Dulce and I thought I genuinely liked her company. When I'd first met her just a day ago, I thought she was the silliest girl I'd ever met and was happy to share James' bland contempt for her. I learned fast that she was simply teeming with vibrant energy and eager to share her thoughts with anyone who would linger long enough to hear them. There was a forgivable vanity to Dulce too, a trait which I wrestled with as she dragged out not only a selection of priceless jewel earrings, but pendants on gold chains and assortments of gilded wristbands. I often condemned girls like Dulce, who fussed over clothing and superficial garnishing like she did, but she was kind and bright.

Perhaps she even reminded me a little of Daisy.

After we'd picked out several jewelry options, Dulce paraded dress after dress out of her closet and with each one came a story: "I wore this to the solstice pageant last year"; "This was the third dress I wore the night of my quinceañera"; and the most intriguing one, "This *azul* gown from my mother, for when I take my induction oath."

"You traveled with all these?" I asked, staring awestruck at the mountain of garments piled on her bed.

Dulce shrugged. "My mother always says, a woman of status must be prepared for every occasion when visiting another master's compound."

"I think you'd be plenty prepared with the first six," I pointed out.

Dulce clicked her tongue at me. "Are you even a real girl, Liza?"

A servant interrupted the show and tell to inform Miss Dulce that it would soon be time to join the Masters in the south wing for the festivities. Dulce really went into a flurry then, diving into her closet for the one dress she intended to wear that wasn't among the stack on her bed. She bustled toward the dressing screen at the corner of the room with a royal violet dress in hand, but not before she reached into the array of gowns and pulled out a midnight blue sheath and tossed it to me.

"Dulce, I couldn't possibly—"

"Oh, yes, you possibly *could*, and you will!" Dulce insisted airily, disappearing behind the screen. "When I come out, I want to see it on you!" I held the dress up with a groan and felt a little prickly to be corralled like this, as though I were a doll Dulce was dressing up. As I inspected the garment, I couldn't help but chuckle at the realization that I was very much a plaything for Dulce—she'd already done my hair, tied a slender silver chain around my neck, and watched me walk around in high-heeled shoes she'd put on my feet herself.

What was the harm in indulging her after all that?

I resolved to change quickly, as I was eager to hide the bandages on my arms from her. Thankfully, the crushed velvet dress she'd pitched at me had long sleeves, tapered at the ends to form gothic points that draped across the backs of each hand. The fabric covered my shoulders and concealed the evidence of Quinn's violent deed, which filled me with relief, and the skirt fell in a loose swoop just past my knees. I gave my hair a careful tousle and smoothed my hands down my front.

Fluttering wings took flight in my belly when I glanced down and noticed the gown's low neckline. James would never allow this, not for one moment. I tugged at the v-line, trying to pull it up so that the tops of my breasts and the cleft between them would stay hidden, but the expert tailoring of the dress held fast to its design. Maybe if I took off the silver chain around my neck, the attention would not be drawn to my chest? I reached up to fuddle with the clasp right as Dulce emerged from behind the dressing screen with a felicitous gasp.

"Liza, look at you!" She actually clapped her hands together as she swept over to me, as though she didn't look like a sun-kissed goddess in her satin gown.

"I don't think dresses are meant for me," I confessed, crestfallen.

"Oh, Liza." Dulce's curls shimmered as she shook her head, a wild grin twisting across her face. "That dress was made for you. You look good enough to eat!"

"Is that a good thing?" I wondered, paling.

Dulce rolled her eyes and clicked her tongue. "Don't be so modest, Liza. You look perfect!"

"Really?" I blushed and hid my nervous smile behind my fingers. Dulce seized my arm and pulled me in front of the full-length mirror across the room. I barely recognized the woman standing there in the blue dress, whose eyes were wide with pleasant surprise and whose body seemed to be much curvier than I recalled. The snugness of the velvety garment hugged every graceful slope of my figure without suffocating me. The skirt swayed when I turned to the side, taking in every visage of myself in this getup as I could.

"You are beautiful and touchable," Dulce crooned proudly. "Do you see now, how perfect you are?"

"I don't know what to say." I stifled a giggle by letting my breath go in a cool stream of air.

"Say you'll have fun tonight and stop being so stiff. Relax a little! Move around; let the dress guide your body language." She sidled close to me, joining my reflection in the mirror. Of course, she was satisfied with her own visage. She adorned the glimmering pieces of jewelry laid out and smirked as she planted her hand on her hip and held her chin up, as if she were challenging her reflection.

"I'm not sure about the chain," I said, returning to my worried inhibitions about my plunging neckline. Dulce merely sighed and swiveled to face me.

"I promise, you can pull it off. You'll have to trust me on this—if you're worried about whether or not Master James will approve, just stand beside me all night and I'll bat him off." I couldn't think of anything less likely to occur than Dulce managing to intimidate James, but still, I considered her suggestion for a moment and decided to take her up on it—besides, if I stood next to Dulce, whose own neckline might have showed off her navel had it fallen any lower, no one would notice the cut of my gown.

"Now for shoes, and the finishing touches!" Dulce retrieved a little red bottle from her bedside table and dabbed a touch of shiny oil to her fingertip, then applied the fragrant liquid to the soft spots underneath both of my ears. I smelled citrus with a wisp of almonds. Dulce then gracefully applied her own perfume by withdrawing a tiny glass stylus from a teardrop shaped vial and lightly swiped it across her wrists, then touching her wrists to her throat before rubbing them together. She stepped into her impossibly tall, sharp-looking heels and led me out of the room.

"I was worried you'd never come out," Douglas murmured to me as he followed me and Dulce along the hall to the south wing.

"Should I be worried?" I whispered to Douglas, glancing at my dress as my heels clacked in Dulce's wake.

Before Douglas could answer, Dulce put her arm across my shoulders and hugged me to her side. "You've got to stop worrying," she whined. "You aren't going to stick out like a sore thumb. You're perfectly suited for an evening like tonight. And besides, wait until you see Daisy and the boys...."

My heart pounded in my chest. I had been so worried about the firestorm James would rain on me to see me gussied up by his niece that I hadn't spared a second thought to what Daisy and Kit would think. And Armand....

Dulce traipsed us along to the south wing entrance. I could hear a pulsing rhythm throbbing on the other side of the heavy, reinforced doors. Had I been any more steady on my feet in these shoes, I would have dug my heels in. Instead, I clenched my jaw and leaned into Dulce. The servants posted at the doors swung them open upon our approach—I wondered if they even recognized me—and the scene inside the south wing took my breath away.

It had been transformed into a place other than the south wing altogether. Round tables that seated six guests circled the looming walls, down which hung tapestries of vibrant landscapes and forest scenes. Emerald, ruby, and white gold bulbs of light twinkled down in elegant ropes from the ceiling, which made the entire room feel like something out of a fantasy. If I were a star, I would have felt right at home. At the back of the room sat a dozen musicians, dressed to the nines in flashy waistcoats and ties. They played swaying, lively music at a volume that encouraged pleasant salutatory conversation but not dancing...at least, not yet; I supposed there would be time for that later, judging by the enormous open space in the center of the room.

The guests themselves were pristinely outfitted to match the décor. I saw more sweeping ball gowns and tapered tuxedo jackets than I ever had in a vast array of daring colors. Servants moved like worker bees through the clusters of guests, balancing polished trays of crystal stemware on nimble fingertips.

One of them, an older man I recognized from his service in the Masters' chambers, breezed by me and Dulce with a tray and pushed a flute filled to the brim with fizzing, golden fluid into my hand.

"Oh, no. Thank you," I blurted, trying to pass the glass back to him. Even I wasn't keen to test James' patience by wearing a dress like this *and* imbibe myself, no matter how much I wanted to exercise a little freedom as Dulce's companion.

"Don't turn your nose up at good champagne!" Dulce hissed, clinking the rim of her glass against mine before helping herself to a generous swallow of the stuff. She caught me glance around warily and sighed haughtily. "Remember, Liza, you're *my* guest at *my* party. My mother has seen to it that every refreshment provided falls within the parameters of Master James' ridiculous rules."

I took a sip of the bubbling champagne and felt a glorious warmth spread from my throat all the way to my toes. I was in no sense an aficionado of the stuff, but I knew enough about my host to determine that this was the best money could buy. Dulce looked around expectantly and apparently she spotted someone she knew across the room. She looped my arm through hers and led me over to a voluptuous, dark-haired woman in a long black dress.

"There you are, *mija*," the woman said, affording Dulce a radiant smile and a kiss on both her cheeks. She turned her sparkling eyes on me and I was struck by their secondhand familiarity.

"Mama, this is James' Tribute, Liza," Dulce introduced me. "Liza, this is my mother."

"Mistress Selenis García de Solana," said Mistress Selenis. She extended her hand with polite ease but the way she shook my hand made it clear that such pleasantries were a mere reflex for her.

"It's very nice to meet you," I said. I couldn't quite take my eyes off of Selenis. Her skin was smooth and rich, though her hand was chilly to the touch. Her lips were heart shaped like Dulce's…actually, most of Selenis' features had clearly been passed down to her daughter. Jada would probably comment on how Dulce would never worry about where age would take her, because while Selenis had to be in her fifties, I wouldn't have placed her a day over thirty-five. The only trace of a flaw in the woman's features was a notched scar on her chin that seemed to be hidden partially by a subtle dab of makeup. The scar was thick—the injury, whatever it had been, must have been deep.

"I see Dulce gave you the grand tour of her closet," remarked Selenis coolly, flickering her gaze down my figure.

I snapped my gaze back to meet Selenis' eyes. "She's been very generous," I said.

"It's you who has been generous. Most girls find Dulce to be overly frivolous, yet my daughter tells me you have kindly shared a meal and lots of your time with her." Something else about Selenis was familiar in the way her stare went right through me. It took me but a moment to recognize that it was the same countenance James often sported around the compound, though where James always paired that stare with malice or the threat of violence, Selenis maintained a mask of perfectly passive patience instead. Still, I found the effect of the contradicting elements to be daunting. I was on the edge of fidgeting with my hands when I remembered that I held a glass of champagne, so I took a sip to buy myself time to reconcile with my nerves.

Selenis turned to Dulce, who appeared to have let her mother's harsh observation roll off her. "Have you seen Donovan?" Selenis asked. If I didn't know any better, I would have said she sounded bored.

"Ma, it's Doni," Dulce said. Her voice sounded different when she spoke in front of her mother. "Look for the group of fawning *mininos* and he'll be at the center." Selenis pursed her lips in wry agreement and glanced calmly around the massive hall.

"Tell me, young lady, how do you like the room?" I doubted Selenis actually cared about my opinion of her daughter's birthday party decorations.

"Everything is so beautiful," I said anyway. "It's like an enchanted painting come to life. I've never seen a place like this."

"Do you paint?" Selenis asked.

"I do."

"It's hard to imagine my little brother sponsoring such a costly pastime that doesn't involve punching something," Selenis replied. She flashed a teasing, conspiratorial smile my way and I felt my need to drink more champagne lessen.

"Then again, Selenis, you were never very imaginative." James appeared beside me in a crisply pressed black suit that somehow slimmed down his massive frame while accentuating his silhouette. He looked quite trim, I was surprised to see, as I peered up at him nervously and braced myself for the worst. If James had any reservations for my presentation, he did not show them. In fact, he almost looked intrigued, but then his eyes trailed down. He was too much of a gentleman (in public, at least) to let his gaze anywhere near the neckline of my borrowed dress as his eye fell on the stemware of champagne in my hand. I considered handing it over to him, but thought better of it.

I would not let him scare me in front of Dulce and Selenis. I raised the crystal flute to my lips, sipped, and was amazed to see no actual fire spark from his flint angry glare.

"You may be right about that, James," said Selenis. She remained unphased by his presence, the first Mistress or Master I had ever seen not shrink in proximity to James. I caught myself before I became too rattled by it, for I would probably never think of Kit as anything less than my brother no matter how fearsome his reputation.

"*Hola, tío,*" Dulce chimed, perhaps too cheerfully.

"Happy Birthday, *niña,*" James said. He leaned over to kiss Dulce on the cheek first, then Selenis.

"Everything looks wonderful! Thank you for arranging all of this." Dulce fixed her sweetest smile at James, who was of course immune to its residual charm.

"It's gratuitous for my taste, but I suppose one only reaches induction age once." James took up a glass of champagne as a servant passed carrying a tray full of them and downed half the contents in one gulp.

"It's nice to see you've lightened up over the years," Selenis remarked dryly. My eyes widened.

"I'm not in the habit of being mocked in front of my Tribute," James said to her. His tone was absent of a threat but his sister's jab clearly left a bitter taste in his mouth.

Whereas any other individual might stammer and backpedal over her words, Selenis merely smiled. "If memory serves, your attitude was far worse when you were this young lady's age. If only you had her charm, you might have gotten away with some of it." I got the sense that Selenis, much like Armand, felt no greater satisfaction than playing the eldest sibling card. Still, she was the first to back off. "Oh, James, put your hackles down. This is a family celebration."

"Indeed." James' posture stiffening was the only warning any of us had before Haitham the Master approached us. He held no drink in his long fingers and his suit was hardly a formal one, but he wore his silver-streaked dark hair combed back from his prominent forehead. I did not disguise my hatred of him when those miserable blue-stained pits he called eyes found me.

"What a curious evening this has turned out to be," Haitham said, showing his teeth in a poor attempt at a smile.

"Thank you for coming. And for your very generous donation," Dulce said, though her tone did not inflect the slightest shred of hospitality or gratitude. So, she hated Haitham as much as I did? We could be the best of friends alone based on that one commonality....

"Now that you're of induction age, will you pursue a fellowship here at the Aventine?" Haitham asked Dulce. "You appear to make friends fast." Haitham returned his sinister stare to me and I was glad to let James step in front of me, cutting off the other Master's view of me before my blood truly ran cold.

"Sure as I am that Dulce learned a Mistress' manner from her mother, I doubt she wants to pass the time discussing politics with you at her own birthday celebration." Hateful heat radiated from James, palpable as sulfur. My wrist trembled and I raised my other hand to hold up my glass of champagne steady.

The music in the background transitioned smoothly into a faster, robust symphony.

"Have I touched a nerve?" Haitham wondered. The sardonic bastard.

"You've made an appearance," Selenis said in a perfect imitation of James. "Dulce has thanked you for your contribution to her induction fund. You know fully well that James and I have nothing to say to you."

"Am I unwelcome at my granddaughter's birthday celebration?" Haitham's voice dropped an octave, lending his tone a surly, much less amused air. I watched Selenis smooth back a thick tendril of her dark hair and fix a stare at her father that might have transformed her classically beauteous features into those of a vicious wolf. A frigid presence tumbled down Selenis' shoulders as she adopted the same look in her eyes as the volpine in the woods.

"Get away from me." It was decidedly not a suggestion. Dulce instinctively edged close to her mother but Selenis never took her eyes off Haitham. In the end—minutes or an hour later, I couldn't be sure—the old man turned from us and made his retreat through the crowd of visiting Masters and their guests.

"Help yourself to anything that catches your eye, young lady," Selenis said to me, turning on a dime to become once more the diplomatic, politely aloof woman she'd been moments before. "I trust you will remember to tend to your duties as the guest of honor, *mija?*"

Dulce must have felt she had a choice in the matter but the reality was, she would obey the gentle suggestion her mother had given without failing. "*Sí,* Mama." Dulce kissed her mother and, like me, was a little hypnotized when Selenis walked away. Her skirt flared when she left me, Dulce, and James in her wake to greet the newest guests. Like a light, Dulce switched on her bubbly demeanor and turned back to face me.

"Family drama," she sighed apologetically. She was pointedly ignoring James. "Can't be helped! Are you hungry?"

"Yes," James answered for me. "I wonder if you should track down Lorraine about those empanadas you requested—the staff seemed to be running behind schedule when I arrived." Dulce hesitated to leave me but her mother's words were hanging over us still and she excused herself quickly to go and make sure the guests would not go hungry any longer than necessary. As soon as Dulce's back was turned, James took the glass of champagne from me. I put up a weak protest but cut myself off when he downed the contents of his glass, then mine. He set the two empty glasses on a serving tray as one was carried past.

"You get one more of those," he sternly told me. "I expect you to politely decline any such imbibements after that."

"As you say," I said automatically.

"If you so much as hiccup, I'll have Douglas take you out of here." He still wore a strip of white gauze across the knuckles on his right hand, which he hastily spaded in his pocket just as someone touched the small of my back.

"Is that really you, Liza?" Donovan was radiant as ever in a sharp black tuxedo and dark green tie. When I turned to greet him, mostly to get his hand off my back, I noticed he sported a smartly folded pocket square that perfectly matched his tie. "You look like a queen." Donovan took my hand in his and brushed his lips across my knuckles.

"Thank you," I said. "Dulce lent me the dress."

"Of course she did," Donovan said with a grin. He spared James a sideways glance. "That's a nasty paper cut you have there, James...."

"Don't be cute," James muttered.

"I'm glad to see you up and about," Donovan said to me. He still held my hand in his and, when I made to withdraw it, he clasped it between both of his and held tight. Daring to wink at me in front of James, he asked, "May I get a better look at you?" His trademark smile aroused a very excited curiosity in me. Donovan took his usual liberty and spun me around by the hand, like we'd been dancing and was now making a show of the end pose. Mystified, I followed his lead, and when my feet found a solid mark and my skirt settled around my legs again, I was staring into three pairs of familiar eyes that looked at me as if we were a mirage.

Daisy was a picture of purity in a soft pink dress that hugged her petite waist and spilled down along her long legs. She was a midsummer night's dream, a daisy in a tulip gown. Her hair spilled over her shoulders in wild curls and her lips were tinged red as she beamed at me. I went to her and caught her up in my arms, smiling like I never had, so overjoyed to see her and be near her. I'd never seen her so perfectly outfitted to match the natural beauty I knew was inside her.

"I didn't recognize you," Daisy said into my hair. It was like hugging sunlight. She wouldn't let go and my heart broke from happiness.

The sensation inspired the most startling revelation I'd come to since I jumped out the window and turned my life inside out—that it is not tragedy or loneliness that breaks the heart, but love. Love so big it consumes every ventricle and spreads with each heartbeat until the body is saturated with it, until there's so much that it can't go anywhere and it all just seeps through every shared glance and smile. I had attributed my isolation and strife to my heartbreak but I knew the second I laid eyes on the three of them that those circumstances were merely reminders of the love I felt, the love that I was desperately cleaving to every second I spent apart from them.

"Look at you!" Kit exclaimed. Daisy released me, letting Kit fold me into his arms. I was hardly surprised to see how august and refined Kit looked with his hair combed high over his forehead and the sleeves of his shirt pushed up to his elbows, a stylistic choice that showed off the definition of his arms and shoulders that I never knew was there. He reached around my waist and hugged me close like he always did, appreciating the velvet of my dress just as I smoothed my fingers across the back of his satin vest.

"Kit, you're so *dashing*...." I couldn't keep from smiling ear to ear when Kit laughed. It felt like we were old friends meeting for the first time in years, drinking up the sight of one another and the sound of each other's voice.

"You look lovely," Kit said. "I think we all clean up nicely, don't you agree?"

And then I was reminded all over again what love was when Kit stepped aside and made way for Armand. I looked up into the face of a man, not the boy alongside whom I had been brought up in the compound. The connection between us was practically vibrating. When I looked into his eyes with such a full heart, I wagered I could have trusted that thread that bound us together enough to lead me through a pitch-dark forest. He wore a fitted shirt and a collar, long trousers, and a tapered waistcoat that was nearly the same shade of green as Donovan's tie. He wore shoes that I was sure fit him perfectly, but I was so disused to seeing them on that I thought his feet looked huge. In a twist of hilarious coincidence, I glimpsed Armand staring down at my feet too!

"I thought you'd gotten taller!" he said. I raised my arms and he swept me into his, whirling me around once and setting me down carefully on my high shoes. "You look surprised to see me," he said after standing back, though he held my hands in his.

"I wouldn't say I'm surprised," I said. Kit and Daisy stood on either side and I knew that we must have had an audience by now—for all I cared, though, the four of us were alone under the lights in the south wing.

"What would you say you are, then?" Armand wanted to know, his voice dropping low so that only we three—or maybe just me—could hear him.

"The words 'incandescently happy' come to mind...." I burst out laughing when Armand rolled his eyes, for I'd just quoted one of his least favorite storybooks to him under the pretense of returning an intimate sentiment.

"There you all are!" Dulce had reappeared in a flurry of perfume and purple silk. She was slender enough to slip between me and Kit without having to push either of us aside. The three of them plied Dulce with sincerities and compliments, on both her gown and the arrangement of the south wing, until she was fully satiated on niceties. "Come on, let's get some food in you! I want all of you out dancing with me!"

James' frosty shadow barged in on our circle once more. "If you show any sign of dizziness, I'll send for Jada on the spot." He made sure I locked eyes with him and acknowledged him before standing down. Dulce led Kit and Daisy away in haste and Armand took my hand in his, staring James down as he did.

"Did you hear something, Liza?" he asked. James seethed as Armand pulled me along after him. My hand went clammy in his, for I knew how close Armand had come to getting throttled in public. But I had spent day after day craving Armand's bold defiance of James and seeing him blatantly insulted, knowing fully well that he would never cause a scene in the presence of his peers, was invigorating. It made each *pan dulce* knot taste that much sweeter. The guests seemed content to keep their distance from us—not spatially, but in manner. The south wing was packed with bodies, and we were constantly having to excuse ourselves as we strived to keep up with Dulce. And yet, if we shouldered past a Master or a Mistress from another compound, none made any formal introductions.

"We have our Kit to thank for that," Daisy assured me in a hushed voice. I offered a more pragmatic assumption, that it was James who must have said something to the others to keep them from approaching us, but then Daisy said, "One in the same, Liza. I'll explain everything later."

We did just as Dulce urged as the evening passed: We ate, we laughed, we engaged in pleasant small talk, all while following her as she made several laps around the room. If James was keeping an eye on me, I did not notice. At one point, I glimpsed Jada in a navy gown and a demure pair of gloves. She smiled warmly my way, though I did not return the gesture. As I began to wonder if Graham were here too, Armand pinched my waist and urged me to "stop looking over my shoulder for James' sourpuss!" He had blossomed into somewhat of a social butterfly as Dulce imbibed him with champagne. Then, a servant came around with a tray full of tiny glasses filled with clear fluid that smelled like fuel and Dulce insisted we all join her in tossing one back with her.

"I'm sure I'll hate it," Daisy said to Dulce, making a face.

"It's best to take a little lick of salt first, then nibble on something sour after," Dulce explained. Daisy hung back and stayed next to Kit, who had drunk the least out of us all. Donovan and Armand were the only two who actually partook in the challenge with Dulce, and when Selenis saw Donovan bite into a lime wedge afterward, she waved at the musicians and declared that it was time for "the *real* party" to start!

"First, a toast!" Donovan took up a fresh glass of champagne and the room full of Masters, Mistresses, their guests, and privileged tradesmen joined him. "To my sweet cousin, I am overjoyed to celebrate such a momentous birthday with you! To Dulce, the most beautiful girl on earth, and to James the Master for making all of this possible!"

"Cheers!" rang out in the south wing, followed by a pause as the guests sipped their drinks. My stomach turned at Donovan's final words—by the look on James' face, his had too. But his sourpuss (as Armand had called it) went unnoticed. The musicians struck up a much louder and exotic song, the rhythm of which was impossible not to move to. Dulce grabbed Armand and insisted he dance with her. My shoulder had begun to ache so I told Armand with a look to go ahead and placate Dulce. After all, it was her birthday.

"Don't go far," Armand whispered to me before following Dulce out to the floor. His breath was laced with smokiness from the gulp of clear stuff he'd tossed back earlier. There was something so liberated about him, besides the fact that he was probably very drunk. I checked the crowd across the dance floor for James, to gauge just how displeased he was to see Armand like this, but he was deep in conversation with Selenis and a slender woman wearing a sleeveless red gown.

"This is going to be a rare treat," Donovan whispered, appearing at my side. He smiled as he looked after Armand, who was a good dancer even under the influence of champagne.

"He's celebrating," I said, joining Donovan in staring at Armand. Kit and Daisy joined them out in the middle of the dance floor along with several other couples. The swaying music was spellbinding, especially when everyone moved in graceful synchronicity.

"It seems a shame to let them have all the fun," said Donovan. He held out his hand to me. "Shall we?" I bit the inside of my cheek to suppress a whine as the ache in my shoulder dug in and gave him my left hand. The man was utterly irresistible at the worst of times; I could hardly refuse him when I knew Dulce's friends in the southern compound would pay a king's ransom to have a chance like this. In fact, I was relieved to follow Donovan through the crowd of onlookers to the dance floor because between him and Armand, Donovan had more practice at this and was therefore more likely to hold me up while I got used to moving in these shoes.

Before we reached the open floor, a hand caught my arm and tugged me almost off my feet. I sucked in a gasp of pain at the sutures in my shoulder pinched sharply and whirled around frantically to see who'd grabbed me.

"So hell *has* frozen over!" A man no taller than James but twice as broad stared down at me. His face was bright red and his eyes were wide with alarm as he clutched my arm in one hand and a snifter of what smelled like rubbing alcohol in the other.

"Excuse me?" I demanded.

"What are you doing here, Lorena?" the man asked in a booming, frantic voice. My heart leaped into my throat and furious tears welled in my eyes. Donovan locked his hand around the man's wrist and immediately pried his grip off my arm.

"Diego, you're drunk." Donovan glared daggers at the man and made a point to stand between us. "For goodness' sake, the party's barely started. Go sleep it off."

"But she—Donovan, look at her, I could have sworn she was—" Diego stammered. Donovan silenced him with just a look. The man hadn't tacked on any variation of Donovan's title when he addressed him, so he was either utterly drunk or he was a Master himself.

"Go." Donovan's voice was low, to spare the guests around us the scandal of an altercation on top of the man seizing me like a rag doll, but his tone was no less menacing than Selenis' had been when she'd squared off with Haitham. Diego turned on an unsteady heel and retreated. Donovan carefully took my elbow and peered into my eyes as soon as he was gone. "Are you all right, Liza?"

"I need a moment," I said. In my mind, I ran fast to take cover behind a mask of self-control. If I started to cry now, I would start sobbing and James would swoop in.

"Of course." Donovan took my hand in his and led me swiftly away from the dance floor toward a set of doors that were mostly hidden by an enormous curtain. Donovan slipped through a door without closing it after himself and pulled me through behind him. We were in an empty servant's passage which was quiet except for the thumping of the music beating through the doors. I buried my face in my hands and groaned to keep a sob from tearing out of my throat.

"I'm so sorry, Liza," said Donovan. He crossed his arms and stayed within arm's reach as his teal eyes searched my face in sorrow. "He had no right to touch you. Are you hurt?"

"I'm all right," I insisted. My heart was racing and I felt sweat break out on my forehead. I was nauseous, I was so shaken and angry. "Did you hear what he said?"

"I did. He's a famous lush, so it doesn't surprise me that he thought you were—well, that he thought you were someone else." Donovan sighed. "I don't think the rest of us would put up with him if it weren't for the mountain of money he's got hidden away."

So Diego was a Master, Donovan had just confirmed. Another fiend like Haitham, another brute like James.

"He's lucky James didn't witness that little display," Donovan mused darkly, mostly to himself. "Still, I'm sure being manhandled like that brought back terrible memories for you."

"It's not that," I explained. I felt so shaky that I began to pace.

"You can talk to me, Liza," Donovan reminded me in a voice that was smoother than my velvet dress.

I supposed this would be the moment to test how heavily I could rely on Donovan. "He didn't think I was just anybody else, Donovan. He mistook me for my mother. That's why he grabbed me." I watched Donovan's concern evolve into astonishment in a snap.

"How do you know that?"

"I know everything." I stared hard into Donovan's eyes, unblinking, for a few moments. He broke eye contact and copied my pacing.

"I don't know what to say." Donovan must have been stunned, for he'd never met a crisis he hadn't been able to smooth over with an alluring turn of phrase.

"So Haitham wasn't lying? I look just like my mother?" I could see Donovan's cheeks go ashen at the mention of his grandfather.

"Liza, you must understand," Donovan blurted. "It simply isn't my place to tell you such things. I've known you your whole life, and you and the others are very dear to me. It wouldn't be fair to you if I were to feed you morsels of truth about your parents, no matter how much I think you deserve a little transparency."

"But it *is* true? I look enough like my mother that I'm mistaken for her by other Masters?" I had to know.

"Your likeness to her is uncanny. Twenty years ago, you could be her," Donovan admitted sadly. Strangely, I felt better to hear it. Days ago, James had said something similar to me. Somehow, it was different coming from Donovan...comforting, maybe.

"I haven't told the others." I wasn't sure why I was offering such details to Donovan but I began to feel less sickened by Diego's disturbing mishap.

"No?" Donovan raised an impeccable eyebrow.

"I wouldn't know where to start," I sighed. "And I gave my word that I wouldn't, anyway."

"You sound like James," said Donovan.

"As you say." I felt exhausted as the adrenaline burned itself out of my system. Donovan and I were quiet for a minute and were both probably thinking that we should return to the party before we were missed—though, I seriously doubted Donovan would face the kind of grim reception I would if I caused any alarm by disappearing for a few minutes.

"You met my aunt Selenis, right?" Donovan asked. He surprised me by not cutting our excursion short but I still nodded, curious to see what he was getting at. "I see. And, if I may ask, did she call you 'young lady' or did she defer to James instead of speaking directly to you?"

"She addressed me only as 'young lady,'" I replied. I hadn't paid attention to the fact that Selenis did not use my name even once. "But Dulce introduced me by name."

Donovan was grinning. "I'm sure she did. Did you happen to notice the scar on Selenis' chin?" He waited for me to nod before closing the short distance between us, keeping his foxlike crooked smile intact as he did. "Your mother put it there, years ago. I saw the whole ordeal myself. She and the other Faction head Marshall Danvers came to the village up north to arrange for supplies to be delivered to the outer compound—for which Diego paid handsomely, keep in mind—and Selenis chose a bad time to remind Lorena what was at stake if any foul play were to arise during their visit."

"They fought?" I balked.

"It was hardly a fight," Donovan corrected me as a lurid sheen of reminiscence glazed over his eyes. "It's common knowledge among the Masters to watch out for Lorena's temper. Goodness knows James was always warning Selenis to watch her tone…alas, my aunt was neither tactful nor did she maintain a safe distance. She said what she said, and Lorena struck her with the handle of a farm tool and told her to keep her daughter's name out of her mouth if she wanted to keep her tongue."

I surged with pride while a deep longing bit painfully into my chest. That Lorena would be so protective of my name alone enough to strike a Mistress—James' sister, no less—was a feat so daring, only a mother could have done it. I couldn't imagine what she would do if she knew what I'd been through, how much worse it had been than a venomous Mistress uttering my name out of spite.

"I've told you this because I want you to embrace the boldness you have so obviously inherited from Lorena." Donovan took my hand in his and I had to tilt my chin up to look him in the eyes. "Don't let an old rummy like Diego spoil the evening for you. After everything you've been through, after carrying such a heavy burden of truth on your own, you deserve to experience joy and fun, Liza. Why shouldn't you cash in on the little privilege you have?"

He was absolutely right. Here I was, inexplicably alive after nearly dying twice in two weeks, hiding out in a dismal hallway while the three people I loved most in the world were on the other side of the doors, dancing and reveling in each other's company?

"Everyone out there knows the truth about how we came to be here," I croaked. "They either see me, see my mother and hate me, or they see the hostage James stole to bring my parents to heel."

"Liza, my darling, allow me to share a very valuable perspective with you about the people out there: it does not matter in the slightest what they think of you. Believe me, it doesn't. I know things about the Masters that would repulse you; do not let their reputations or status distract you from who they truly are. They are some of the most conniving and savage individuals alive. The only reason they run the system is because they were vicious enough to fight their way to the top and are wealthy enough to keep everyone else down."

"You speak so highly of your peers," I remarked dryly.

"How do you think I came to be a Master, Liza?" Donovan released my hand but his imploring gaze held me very still. "Moreover, why do you think I bothered? I'll tell you—because if we don't like the way a system works, it is our duty to become a part of it and change it until we do. You might think yourself helpless, Liza, but you aren't. I learned from a very young age that the only strengths I had to propel me to where I am today were what made me different from everyone else. Any fool could have been born with good looks into a family like mine, but had I not been clever enough to make myself indispensable to the people dancing and gossiping out there, I would not be standing here with you."

"But I already am indispensable to them, Donovan. Without me, or Daisy, or the boys, the Masters you so freely condemn would have nothing to hold over our parents' heads. There's nothing left to do for us but do as we're told."

"I refuse to believe that." Donovan reached for his pocket square, withdrew it from the breast pocket of his jacket with a flick, and handed it to me. Only then did I realize I had let a tear slip from my eye.

"Thank you," I said. "It feels impossible to face them even though I love them so much…. It feels like I'm betraying them by lying."

"You don't want them to feel the pain that learning the truth caused you."

"No. It would kill me if I hurt them." As I dabbed at my cheek, Donovan looked to me with renewed vigor in his eyes.

"Sometimes we have to lie to protect the people we love," Donovan said, his lips forming a solemn frown. "But you must find the strength within to make tonight count, Liza. If you can't do it for yourself, do it for them. You think of them as your family? Why not prove to them that you're strong enough to come back to them? Go out there and show the Masters that you are not just James' Tribute. Heed no glances or whispers from anyone. Show them you are Lorena's daughter, whether they think you know so or not."

My eyes were dry and my heart was full. If there was one thing I could manage to do tonight, it was make my mother proud of me. I passed the handkerchief back to Donovan and he grinned as he stuffed it back in his pocket.

"Good girl." He offered me his elbow and led me back through the doors behind us, toward the thrilling tempo of the music playing louder than ever. I held my head up as though my dress were made of courage itself.

"There you are!" Daisy was there right away, flanked by the boys. "You missed the first dance, you know."

"Where did you go?" James demanded, advancing on us. I knew it would only be a matter of seconds before James found us, though I couldn't have guessed that he would look so outwardly rattled. He actually looked relieved to see me. "You were standing there one minute and gone the next."

"There was a brief encounter with Diego," Donovan explained quietly.

James' attention snapped to Donovan. "Oh?" was all he said.

"Liza was upset," said Donovan. "I put her in the servants' corridor to give her a few moments' privacy." He did not think twice before reaching for Armand's wrist and placing my hand in Armand's. The message between them was clear—"Get her out of here." I didn't have the chance to thank Donovan for staying behind to explain the sordid ordeal to James before Armand led me away from the two Masters.

"Encounter? Who the hell is Diego?" Armand put his arm around me as we followed Kit, Daisy, and Dulce over to the table piled high with exotic desserts and fruits.

"A drunk old Master," I murmured. Armand was so warm. "Donovan sent him away. I'm fine."

"Good of him," Armand sighed. He took a moment to study my expression which meant it took him less than that to determine that I was far from fine. "Liza...."

"Armie." The thick eyelashes framing his shining eyes made his eyelids seem heavy. I flushed when I saw him take a long look at my lips. The music was suddenly very loud and I slipped easily out from under his arm.

"Come on and dance with me," I urged him. I couldn't describe the look that befell him—had he a drink in hand, I was certain he would have dropped it. He obeyed me as though I'd hypnotized him, only he was smirking like a devil as he escorted me out to the crowded dance floor and spun me around. Armand was among the few people in attendance tonight who knew about my injuries but he did not lead with fragile hands. I knew Daisy and Kit would find us but for now, I had Armand all to myself and I cherished each tilt, sway, and step with him.

Three songs had started and ended by the time Armand and I touched back down to reality. He spun me into Kit's arms so that we could dance together and in turn took up Daisy as his partner, but not before teasing her. "Remember, sweetheart, you're the dancer—it's time to make good on your years of lessons and show me a thing or two!" Daisy threw her head back and laughed, and proceeded to flawlessly and professionally follow Armand's lead.

"We might be the only sober ones here, besides James," Kit said to me with a rare judgmental raise of his eyebrows. I could only laugh and hug Kit close. Just like he was one to sneeze with his whole body, Kit's smile took up his entire face. He moved with a sunny energy he must have borrowed from Daisy. When I eventually did tire of dancing, Kit took me to sit down at a table nearest the dancers so that we could watch Armand and Daisy trade partners with Dulce and whichever handsome tradesman she'd dragged onto the floor with her. We laughed and sipped on ice water (which we suspected James had instructed a servant to bring over to us) and simply enjoyed the music. Once the evening crossed the threshold into later hours, Dulce was regularly summoned to the sidelines by Selenis so that she could properly farewell the guests who kept traditionally early hours.

Once we noticed Armand and Donovan twirl Daisy dizzyingly between them, Kit and I agreed that she needed a reprieve. The music compelled us to keep moving and after a while, we had all separately shared an entire song with each other. Dulce had not resurfaced from her latest aside to farewell her guests, so I took it upon myself to excuse myself and find her—if only for a reason to sit down for a few minutes. I passed James on my meandering path to find Dulce. He was in absent conversation with the woman in the red dress I had seen him with earlier.

With a jolt, I recognized the woman as Daisy's ballet instructor, Helena.

From where I was standing, even from a short glance, I could see that the crushing bodice of Helena's gown garishly pushed her breasts up in a decidedly less-than-subtle style. I had always admired Helena's sharp eyes but otherwise soft features, as she was a top dance instructor and innately carried herself gracefully around the compound. Looking at her now, though, I felt much less self-conscious for the cut of *my* dress left a lot more to the imagination than Helena's did. I hastily looked away from the scene.

I caught a glimpse of Dulce's skirt flaring and looked up in time to see Selenis take her into the same servant corridor Donovan and I had ducked into earlier. I slowed my determined steps, reminding myself not to be nosy…but it was not mere curiosity that drove me to pursue Dulce and her mother. An insidious nagging filled my gut like black smoke. I had only the raised hairs on the backs of my arms and the foul sense that something was wrong to carry me after them, shrouded by a nonchalant pretense and calm movements.

The door was left slightly ajar. I suspected it was to discourage any onlookers from having any notion that they had disappeared into a servant gully other than to adjust their clothing or briefly trade casual remarks away from the noise of the party. I piled my hair on top of my head and fanned the back of my neck, feigning exhaust as my reason to be loitering at the back of the south wing.

I did not know what to expect, just that I should expect something I might not like. The first thing I heard was an exchange between mother and daughter in rapid Spanish. It took me a few moments to catch up with the translation: Selenis was speaking passionately about success, about progress, and how proud she was of Dulce.

"*Estoy orgullosa de mí misma y espero que tú también lo estés,*" Dulce assured her mother that she should be proud, and that Dulce herself was proud. The two went back and forth for a time: Selenis said a lot about how fruitful this year would be for Dulce because of how well she had done tonight. Dulce agreed and offered little else.

"You have done so well," Selenis said. For the first time all night, she sounded sincere. "You would have made your father so happy tonight, *mija.*"

"I had hoped you would say that," Dulce replied. Was she tearful? "I only ask that you tell me someday why you tasked me with buttering up *tío's*

Tributes. I hope the nature of the task is not a reflection of how you see my skill set."

"What makes you say that, *mi preciosa?*" asked Selenis.

"Because earning their trust was so *easy*," enthused Dulce, her tone lofty and proud.

My blood boiling, I slipped through the crevice of the open door and slammed it behind me. Dulce and Selenis startled. "I would apologize for the intrusion but I am *not* sorry," I said. My heartbeat thundered in my ears so loudly, I could barely hear myself.

"Liza!" Dulce yelped. "What are you doing here?"

"I slipped through the doorway on all the butter slicked to my heels," I offered coolly.

"Young lady," Selenis intervened, applying her best tricks to intimidate me. "You ought to remember where you are, and to whom you are speaking." Every time I looked at the scar on her chin, I imagined my mother clobbering her for merely saying my name aloud and felt totally immune to the Mistress's methods.

I decided to ignore Selenis. "You have done so well," I said to Dulce, echoing her mother's praise from moments ago. "You are an empty-headed little doll of your mother's design, I see that now. I can't even blame you for doing as you're told without so much as a second thought, because you *have* no thoughts at all, do you?"

"Liza!" Dulce gasped.

"It never occurred to you to ask what your mother's true purpose was, I suppose! You never thought far enough ahead to think of how this would affect us. All you could think about were the rewards you might reap by sowing the seed she told you to plant!" It was not my shoulder or the lesions on my forearms that burned now, but my eyes. "What was your game, Dulce? To get close to us and feed information back to your mother? To poison us against each other, like Haitham would?"

"Liza, don't be ridiculous," Dulce tried to interject. Her usually kiss-ready lips went slack when I took three sweeping steps toward her. I had caught her in the act and she just realized that she may not emerge unscathed from her play at being a Mistress.

"To think I ever trusted you," I said. I shook my head, scorning the both of us bitterly. "You used kindness to insert yourself in our lives. You *lied.*"

"Liza," Dulce pleaded once again. "Please, it's not as you say—"

"You don't get it, Dulce!" My hurt feelings had bubbled to the surface, conjoined in a dangerous chemical reaction with the rage searing my veins. "You blindly agreed to be a cheap little tool for them!"

"Them?" Dulce repeated tearfully.

"Don't pretend you think of us as equals! From the beginning, ever since you arrived, you have classified everyone in this forsaken place—us and them!" I had become shrill, almost hysterical. "I am a Tribute, same as Daisy, Kit, and Armand! There are Tributes, and there are Masters, and you know damn well which side you serve!"

"You will watch your language in my presence, young lady," Selenis warned me.

"Or what? You may be Mistress Selenis García de Solana," I said, emulating the cold fury I imagined my mother had, "but this is James the Master's house. You cannot touch me."

For an instant, my body was not my own. Selenis lashed out to slap me with her free hand and I caught her wrist; in the time it took for Dulce to throw her hands up to cover her gasping mouth, I relinquished my hold on Selenis and smacked the crystal flute out of her hand. It shattered on the hardwood floor at Dulce's feet, expensive wine and shards of priceless stone exploded everywhere.

I was bloodthirsty. I wanted nothing more than to rake my nails across Selenis' cheek and send her spilling to the floor amid the broken crystal fragments everywhere. Selenis hardly cowered to behold my threatening glare, which made the impulse all the more appealing. I realized she was looking at me as though I were a manic, growling beast...then, when I remembered to breathe, the aggression I felt triggered the scent memory of my own blood. Somewhere in the back of my mind, I was right back in the studio with Quinn on top of me, screaming at me to stop fighting....

Did Selenis see Haitham or James standing across from her instead of me? Or was she remembering the moment my own mother gave her the scar at which, even now, I couldn't stop staring?

"I would give that scar of yours a twin," I said, brandishing my fiercest glare. "The only thing keeping me from doing it is the fact that I would never see the look on your face when you next see Lorena to tell her that her daughter put it there." I turned to Dulce then, who was weeping silently to see me threaten her mother as I had. I yanked the chain she had given me from my neck and dropped it at her feet. "I swear, if I thought I could get out of here naked, I would tear this dress off right here and throw it at you!"

I ripped away from the pair of them, deafening myself to anything they might have said as I stormed out of the double doors and kicked them shut behind me. I was overcome with exhilaration and shame. I had not felt so alive since I had faced James in the Master library but I knew that I had grossly overstepped my boundaries to both Selenis and Dulce, and would probably suffer for it later. Before either of them could take retaliating action, I needed to get out of here.

Leaving without saying goodbye to Daisy, Kit, and Armand would make for a sorry finish to their evenings, but I would rather them blame James for plucking me out of this horrible party than have them scorn me and worry them over making a hasty getaway without explaining myself. I marched right up to James. He was right where I left him with Helena at his side.

"I want to go to bed," I said in my best try at a calm request. "Right now."

James stood up at once and buttoned his open jacket. "Are you well?"

I shook my head. I was prepared to offer a list of excuses about my sore shoulder, spent nerves, et cetera, but James did not ask for a single one before excusing himself from Helena and guiding me out of the south wing.

"I'll ask Douglas to take you back," James said. He slowed as we neared the exit in out of character hesitation. "Would you like to say goodnight to Daisy and the boys?"

"I don't want to worry them."

James was taken aback by my stiffness but he did not question me. He opened the doors and said briefly to the servant attending the entrance, "Get me Douglas." James then peered down at me, his blue eyes searching mine for a tell of my abrupt distress. "You aren't dizzy, are you?" Again, I shook my head. James seemed relieved and accepted my nonverbal answer without scrutiny. "Jada would be cross with me if you got sick from that champagne, after the medicine you've taken."

"Master James," Douglas announced himself, slipping through the doors to the south wing without waiting for a servant to open them for him. He took one look at James and quickly reached into his pocket for a little case of rattling pill capsules. James took them graciously and popped one into his mouth as I paid Douglas an impressed nod for being able to ascertain James' need of his own medicine so fast.

"Take Liza back to the room," James instructed. He seemed to feel relief from the pill he'd taken already.

Douglas nodded. "It's late, sir. Would you rather I stay and keep an eye on things?"

"No. Armand is drunk. I can't let them out of my sight until they're escorted back to the Tribute wing. See to it that Liza is returned to the room, then make sure Nathan is sent upstairs." James returned to the party, leaving Douglas to follow his orders.

I looked back once, as Douglas held open the door to the main hall for me. I did not see Selenis or Dulce, which meant I had chosen my moment to leave well; but when I saw Armand, Kit, and Daisy congregated at the supper table looking tired and happy, I felt a fissure split my heart into thirds.

I could not put them in the middle of this. Without so much as blowing them a kiss but wishing I could cry out to them, I turned my back on my family and the entire south wing. Once the servants stationed at the main doors had closed them behind me and Douglas, I reached back and removed from my feet the shoes Dulce had lent me. I passed them to the man standing watch over the left door and asked him to make sure they found Mistress Dulce by tomorrow morning.

"I take it something happened between the two of you?" Douglas asked quietly as he led me down the hall. He took my silence as a telling answer. "Rubbing elbows with little Mistresses is a risk, Liza. Between you and me, I think you're smart to quit while you're ahead." I wasn't sure why I felt better to have Douglas' approval of my disavowal of all things Dulce but it quieted my nerves some as I walked with him down the hall. The floor was freezing but it was soothing on the soles of my bare feet.

"She's deplorable," I muttered. "She and her mother, both."

Douglas made wide eyes at me as we climbed the stairs to the Master chambers' entrance. "I'll try to remember not to repeat that to Master James," he said.

"Tell him what you like," I said flippantly. "All you can do is your job, like the doctor and everybody else. I don't expect you to care about what James does to me for insulting his family."

"Dulce really got under your skin, didn't she?" Douglas asked. He opened the door to the Master chambers for me and followed me toward James' room. "It's not your fault. The people in that room were raised to play people like fiddles. You weren't the first to fall for their act, and you won't be the last. That's the truth of parties like this—any gathering of Masters, really. Even summits. It's all a circus to them and we are the animals."

I said nothing in response because there was nothing to say. He was right and we both knew it. All I could do was rake my fingers through my hair in the hopes of destroying any sign that Dulce had ever touched me.

"Goodnight, Liza," Douglas said. "Before I lock you in, would you like to send away for some food? I believe the kitchens are still in a frenzy but I'm sure they would find time to send up a plate—"

"No, thank you," I said. "But wait outside for just a minute." I marched into the bathroom, shut the door behind me, and promptly tugged the dress off over my head. I stepped into my familiar heather grey sleeping pants and dark green shirt, feeling very much at home in the loose garments. My hair was uncooperatively still set despite my efforts to muss it up, which made for an uneven style of glamorous above the neck and lazily casual below it. I did not bother to fold the dress as I brought it to Douglas, who hung it over his arm as if it were a fine linen dining napkin.

"Please see that it gets back to its Mistress," I said.

"As you say," said Douglas. He shut the bedroom door and I waited to move until the bolt clicked into place. I went back to the bathroom to brush my teeth and attack my hair with a brush. I knew it would kill the curls if I showered, but I didn't want to bother with the waterproof bandage wraps on my own. After a few minutes, I had brushed my hair until a barely perceivable wave took shape near the tips.

I was so tired now that the grating excitement had worn out of my muscles. I opened all the window shades and saw the moon shining bright over the tumultuous ocean far down below. I then bypassed my cot entirely and went for the bed, sliding under the covers swiftly after switching the lights off. I stared up into the red canopy, illuminated in dramatic folds by the moonlight. I still smelled the perfume Dulce had applied to my neck but I was too dismayed to get up again to wash it off.

Daisy, by far the most beguiling guest in attendance all night, was probably so disappointed that I'd gone without saying goodbye. I imagined Kit consoling her with gentle reminders that we would see each other again soon, like he always did. My heart sank when I thought of Armand making a scene, driven by contempt for James while an excess of champagne had stripped away any compunction he had to control himself. I rolled over to my good side and shut the idea out of my head. Instead, I let my mind linger on how much I loved his hands at my waist, guiding me across the dance floor after him. All that wine and merriment had made him so warm to the touch. Had I ever looked at his lips the same way he had mine? I fell asleep thinking of him.

Chapter Seventeen

Kit

I was the least surprised of the three of us to hear James had sent Liza to bed without letting her say goodnight to us. Part of me had guessed when Liza, a vision of starlight in a radiant blue gown, left us to find Dulce, I could imagine too easily James pouncing on the opportunity to send her away without risking Armand making a scene. By the time we caught up with Dulce under the luminous, colorful wisps overhead, she was less than her unerringly charming self.

"I may have had a splash more tequila than I should have," Dulce excused herself. "My mother asked me to make the rounds. I'll catch up to you in just a few minutes!" In a whirl of purple and strong perfume, she was gone. I was about to go after her—there was something in her eyes I didn't like—when Daisy wrapped her arms around me from the side. She rested her chin on my shoulder and smiled up at me, her cheeks rosier than ever.

"Excuse me, have we met before?" I teased her. I couldn't take my eyes off her.

"No, but you were standing over here looking lonely as a cloud," said Daisy, teasing me right back. "I had to come introduce myself to such an *incredibly* handsome stranger...." I chuckled nervously and put my arm across her shoulders, walking us over to a table topped with elegant glasses that were filled with what I hoped was just water.

"How many glasses of that champagne have you had?" I asked, handing Daisy a glass of water. She shrugged and downed the entire thing.

"It's delicious stuff, Kit," Daisy said defensively. Then she giggled and said, "About half as many as Armie, so about...a hundred?" She laughed at herself and looped her arm through mine.

That's what I was afraid of. "Very funny," I murmured to Daisy. I looked over to Armand, who was seated at our dinner table next to Donovan, leaning in close so that the other man could hear him over the music. I couldn't help but notice that Donovan had drunk as much as Armand, if not more, but seemed to be infinitely more collected.

"Do you think Liza's in trouble?" Daisy asked.

"No." I was still watching the room warily when I replied to Daisy's worried question. As sorry as I was not to have hugged Liza goodbye, I trusted that she was safer back in her suite within the Masters' chambers, where Haitham was not permitted to wander freely like he was in the south wing. I'd spotted him a few times over the course of the night and he had given me a significant and dreadful wink each time our eyes had met. Dulce's mother Selenis had a chill about her that set my teeth on edge as I watched her tend to each guest in measured beats that guaranteed time to exchange pleasantries but not enough to spark a conversation. I hesitated to approach Selenis, or anyone else for that matter.

Now and then James would appear in the corner of my eye and I pretended not to see him. I wanted him to see me keeping my eyes on Daisy and Armand to show him I was doing my part and that I trusted him to look after us. The only downside was, it meant that James caught every tender moment I shared with Daisy. I resolved to worry about that later though, for as soon as I started to frown at a fixed point across the room, pretending to listen to Daisy while I worked our situation out in my head, Graham stepped in front of me with a very tall, slim woman at his side.

"Kit," Graham greeted me. I held my hand out to him at once. Daisy said hello to Graham too but she anchored herself on my arm while she gave the woman next to him a savory glance.

"I didn't expect to see you here," I said to Graham. He wore the same jacket he typically did to teach lessons but he had swapped the tired taupe shirt underneath for a clean white one.

"I wouldn't be, but I was hoping to speak with Master James. He is otherwise occupied but it gave me the chance to reconnect with a former pupil of mine. Kit, Daisy, this is Mistress Magdalene."

"It's a rare pleasure to meet the two of you," Magdalene said. Her voice was syrup sweet and just as smooth, and when she held out her hand to me and Daisy, she made sure to hold each of ours between hers for a few moments while maintaining keen eye contact. Her eyes were brilliantly green with warm brown halos around her irises. Combined with her height, long face, and sharp nose, I found her to be a very peculiar looking if unconventionally beautiful woman.

"Graham was your instructor?" Daisy asked.

"Once upon a time," Magdalene said. "It's thanks to his instruction that I have my own compound now, far up north."

"Magdalene is a doctor of environmental sciences," Graham explained. "Her mastery of biology and organic chemistry are of particular interest to the other Masters."

"It must be terribly fascinating work," I remarked.

"He means the Masters find my specialties to be valuable, not interesting," Magdalene corrected with a dazzling smile. "He tells me you two are exceptional students, very talented in the arts? I hear Helena Kovachev is the best ballet mentor in all the continents. You must be quite something if you're able to keep up with her." Daisy beamed at the compliment but of course would not take it without foisting the attention away from herself.

"You should hear Kit play piano," she said. "He's a genius."

"I would like that," Magdalene said. I could tell she genuinely meant it. "Still, I know how protective James is over his Tributes. I won't keep you from the festivities. It was lovely to meet you charming young people." Magdalene excused herself and gave Graham's arm a friendly squeeze before sauntering away.

"She is very beautiful," Daisy muttered to me.

"I didn't realize you had friends in such high places," I said to Graham. A servant came by with a tray of champagne to offer us but Graham and I sent him away with a politely negating wave.

"Many of my former students went on to achieve prestige after leaving my tutelage," Graham said. "Mistress Magdalene is certainly the most congenial of my graduates, but I wouldn't say outright that we are friends. Speaking of my students, I saw Liza earlier but I did not get the chance to say hello."

"James sent her to bed early," I explained.

"Goodness gracious, does this count as early?" Graham grimaced as he checked his wristwatch. "She looked well. I'm sorry I didn't get a chance to tell her so."

"I'll pass along your well wishes if you like," offered Daisy. Graham thanked her but declined politely, not wanting to trouble her. "As you say, sir. Kit, I'm going to freshen up."

"Do you want me to go with you?" I asked right away. Daisy giggled and shook her head, her curly hair shimmering as it caught the orbs of light over us.

"I'll be right back." She breezed away and I reminded myself that James would watch her, but I was prepared to run after her if I so much as suspected Haitham was in Daisy's vicinity.

"You three look like you're enjoying yourselves," Graham noticed with an air of disapproval.

"This party is unlike anything we've ever seen," I said in our collective defense. I knew Graham wasn't really criticizing us so I kept my tone respectful. "Besides, I don't think Armand's ever met a rule he didn't bend if he could…."

"Where did he get to, I wonder?" Graham looked over his shoulder over the wide hall in search of Armand.

I shrugged. "He was with Donovan just a minute ago," I said. I checked back to our table to see that Armand and Donovan had gone. Instinctively, I then searched for Daisy and saw her speaking to Selenis, the older woman seeming even more passively reserved standing opposite Daisy.

"You shouldn't leave him alone with Master Donovan."

I was jarred enough by what Graham just said to snap my eyes forward. "What?"

"Excuse me, Kit," Graham said abruptly. I turned to follow his gaze and saw James making his way alone to the water table.

"Sir, wait," I tried to keep him with me long enough to explain his vague and very troubling remark but he merely patted my shoulder and went after James. He made it a few paces before Jada, whom I did not recognize at first in such elegant attire, stopped him with a question.

"You look awfully serious for someone so fancy," drawled Armand, sidling up to me with a dubious grin on his face. I rolled my eyes.

"As you say," I relented.

"Have a drink, Kitty," Armand encouraged me, snatching a full flute of champagne off a passing tray. I had no strong feelings one way or the other about the invocation of my childhood nickname, but when Armand said it just to make fun, I bristled.

"I'm surprised there's any left," I said, checking his inappropriate cheek with a carping rejoinder.

"Don't be an ass," said Armand. "I'm only teasing. What's got you looking so professorial?" He barely managed to get through that sentence without stumbling over his words and apparently decided more champagne might help.

"Graham," I said. "He just said the strangest thing...."

"He's a strange gentleman," Armand declared. He took a large gulp of champagne and clapped me on the back. "Tonight is a good night, brother. I wish you'd have the decency to at least *pretend* to have fun...."

"I *am* having fun," I said crossly. "At least I was—"

"When Liza was here," Armand sighed. "I know. I wish she hadn't gone."

"She looked beautiful," I said, knowing it was too early to reminisce.

"Like a whole woman." Armand's shoulders sagged. He was suddenly too morose to finish his champagne.

"Chin up, Armie," I insisted, jabbing him playfully with my elbow. "It's still a party." Daisy returned with a bright smile, though she pulled a face when she noticed the sway in Armand's stance.

"Are you ready for bed, Armie?" she asked.

"Hell no," Armand replied. The musicians struck up another dance tune and it stirred up something in Armand to hear it. "It's still a party, like Kit said!" He downed the rest of his champagne and set the stemware down on the table behind him. He stooped quickly and lifted Daisy up in to his arms. Daisy squealed as Armand carried her toward the dance floor, where many other guests had flocked upon hearing the first few notes of this particular melody—apparently, it was a crowd favorite.

I saw a dark suit jacket zip fast through the crowd and I tried to warn Armand, but James was faster than my attempt to catch Armand's attention. James took hold of my brother so hard that Armand nearly dropped Daisy. He set her down as carefully as anyone in his state could have and gritted his teeth against the discomforting grip James had on his elbow.

"Put her down," James growled. "You are completely inebriated and you are making a fool of yourself!"

"You ought to try it sometime; you might not be so constantly insufferable!" Armand snarled at James. Daisy's face went white so fast, I worried she would faint.

"If you say one more word, I will drop you in front of everyone in this room. You think I won't?" James planted his feet and formed a fist with his right hand as Armand took a breath to speak. "You are about to be sorely mistaken—and *very* sore."

"Armand," I said quickly. "He'll do it. Say nothing."

"You'll take orders from Kit, but not me?" James clicked his tongue and shook his head. For him to bait Armand like this, especially while he was intoxicated, was a very risky game even for James. I knew for a fact that there were many reasons Armand had to want to take a swing at James—starting with repaying the scar he'd put on Liza's lip when they were teenagers and ending with his current rotten attitude. I prayed that Armand would remember Daisy was standing right beside him and behave.

"I think it's time to go," I said. I stared straight at Armand, begging him with my eyes to look at me and not James. He turned his angry attention to me and in a split second, when he saw how desperately I was pleading with him, he relented. I could see that he resented me for it but he went along anyway. Daisy practically fell into Armand, though it was unclear whether or not she was supporting herself or trying to weigh Armand down so he couldn't lunge at James.

James beckoned behind him for Nathan and gave specific instructions about how we were to be escorted to the threshold of our apartments and locked in for the night.

Good, I thought. As Nathan led us away, I said to James, "I think Graham was looking for you." It was a night of not saying farewell to friends apparently, as we left Dulce in the south wing to her own devices without so much as a "Thank you for inviting us." Daisy removed her shoes as soon as the double doors closed behind us and blocked out the thumping of the music roaring inside. I was tempted to follow her suit, but between holding Daisy herself on my arm and her shoes in my other hand, I thought it would be sloppy to stop and take off my own shoes.

The walk back was quiet. I didn't dare say anything to Armand, for fear that he would weave a tapestry of acerbic expletives about James, which Nathan would be duty-bound to report, yielding disastrous results. Daisy was exhausted and leaned her head against my shoulder as we made our way back to the Tribute wing. I saw servants passing out trays of leftovers from the party, pressing them into the hands of their friends and insisting the food would not keep overnight, for there was no room to refrigerate all of it. Some of them were sipping champagne out of tiny ceramic teacups and laughing, dancing together to the echoing music they could barely hear from down the hall.

"Look," Daisy whispered with a giggle. A young man and woman were embracing off in the corner of the market, lips locked passionately.

"Don't disturb them," I told her softly.

Daisy sighed and picked her head up. "What were you and Donovan talking about, Armie?" she asked Armand, who was keeping up with Nathan's brisk pace.

"Physics," Armand placated her bitterly. Facing off with James had called to the surface a very nasty mood that I could tell would only get worse as the minutes ticked by. Nathan was elated when we reached the Tribute wing (I guessed he had a plate of food waiting for him somewhere) and he locked the door behind us as soon as it sealed shut. As soon as the three of us were inside, I touched the light switch and illuminated the entryway in a pool of soft light. Armand and I kicked off our shoes, I dropped Daisy's on mine, and we all let out a collective sigh.

"We should turn in," I said. Armand ignored me and made a beeline for the kitchen. Daisy turned to me and batted her eyelashes, her pink lips curling into a winsome smirk. I reached for her but flinched when a cupboard door slammed from the kitchen. Daisy frowned.

"Go to bed," I whispered. *I'll be right along,* I mouthed silently. Daisy nodded and padded down the hallway. I went into the kitchen and found Armand sitting at the table, shirt unbuttoned to the waist, vest discarded and hung over the dish rack, with a loaf of bread in his hands. He was tearing off large chunks and biting off smaller pieces with his teeth. I was inclined to push a bread knife toward him but thought better of it.

"Go to bed, Kit," Armand said, his mouth full of bread. "I know you want to. I've spoiled our evening; you can't bear to look at me."

"Don't be an idiot. You didn't ruin anything, James did." I sat down across from him at the table. "As usual."

"He's such a bastard," Armand muttered. He offered me a hunk of bread and I took it. He'd baked a sweet cinnamon loaf the day before and I couldn't refuse it even though I knew it was a sugary snack to eat so soon before bed.

"There's nothing to be done about it," I resigned.

Armand snorted. "Oh, no?" He shook his head and chuckled darkly to himself. "I can think of a few things...." He took one last bite of bread and devoured it, rolling the rest of the loaf across the table. He wasn't passing it to me so much as he was trying to send it to the floor. "It doesn't matter anyway. In a couple of days, we won't have to worry about James anymore."

"We can only hope things with Dulce pull through so quickly," I said. Armand crossed his arms, elbows on the table, and put his head down.

"I wasn't talking about Dulce," he said, his voice muffled through the cage his arms formed around his face.

"What do you mean, then?" I asked. A dreaded sigh escaped me when I heard Armand begin to snore. "Armie, don't go to sleep. What do you mean?" I waited for him to stir but he let out a deep sigh, signaling a rapidly incoming slumber. I got up and went around the table to him and hooked my arms underneath his. It would have been an easier job to haul a sack of bricks out of a chair and down the hall, but I managed as best I could on my own. Armand muttered to me incomprehensively, talking about how thrilled he would be to "see the look on his face when this is all over," and I grew steadily more nervous about the vague assurances he was making. I dropped Armand on his bed in a heap and took up his ankles so I could set his legs on the mattress too.

I was beginning to understand how Armand must have felt when the girls were off planning their initial escape. If this was even close to that anxious dread, then we all owed him an apology in the morning. "Get some rest, Armand," I said.

"It'll be all right, Kit," Armand sighed, settling into his pillow. "As soon as Donovan gets us out of here, everything will be different. You'll see."

I froze. "Donovan?" I was perplexed. "Why did you say that?" I knew I had mere seconds before Armand succumbed to his exhaustion. I wondered if I was prepared to slap him awake if he nodded off before he answered me.

"Because he promised."

I narrowed my gaze and folded my arms across my chest. "And why would Donovan promise such a thing?"

"Because," said Armand. His lips twitched into a smile. "He loves me."

"Armand." He went silent. I kicked the corner of his bed to jostle him awake but it was no use. He was out cold. Meanwhile, in the land of the living, my mind was buzzing. I knew on one hand *exactly* what Armand was getting at when he said that Donovan "loved" him, but on the other very rational hand, I refused to believe it. I stared down at my sleeping friend, a man I loved like my brother and knew better than he did himself. No, it was not possible. How could it be?

The pit of my stomach dropped out when I recalled the morning James had taken us to see Liza after the attack. Donovan and Armand had come out of the vacant studio just seconds before we found them in the main hall. Could they have been…?

No. No, I insisted, because Dulce had told no less than a dozen anecdotes about Donovan's conquests in the south where women flung themselves at him left and right. Did that mean anything, though? Cursing my education, from which I had learned that pretty much everybody might do just about anything with practically anyone within the realm of intimacy, I flipped the lights off in Armand's room and shut the door behind me as I bolted into the hallway. Where had this panic I felt come from? I racked my brains for any reasonable threat I could pull at that would steady my nerves.

Just this evening, Graham had said Armand should not be alone with Donovan. I covered my open, aghast mouth as the epiphany truly sank in: if Graham, the cleverest man in the entire compound—whose acclaim as a tutor had helped his former student acquire her own compound and title—had figured out Armand's scheme, it must be true.

Worse still, it meant that he knew about my accord with James. Why else would he warn me to keep Armand and Donovan from being alone together if not for the sake of upholding James' conditions? If Armand was telling the truth, that Donovan promised to get us out of here…well, I would have to make my peace with that somehow before the summit of Masters came to its conclusion.

If James found out before then, it would be bloody. What he would do to Armand would be worse than anything that had happened over the past few weeks. The two men already hated each other's innards and this would make the perfect excuse for James to execute a punishment on Armand that I feared would border on attempted murder. I gulped past the worried lump in my throat and made my way to my room down the hall. I imagined I looked grey when I closed my bedroom door and leaned my forehead against the wood of it for a few moments.

"Are you all right?" asked Daisy. I jumped around, startled by her unexpected presence. The shock doubled as I realized Daisy was at the very least topless—probably fully naked—and under my sheets. Her long wavy hair was draped over one bare shoulder, drawing my wide-eyed gaze to her breasts and their tiny, pink nipples peeking out like rosebuds just over the bunched-up duvet cover around her waist.

"Daisy!" I turned around to face the door again, my voice strangled and my mouth very dry. Once again, my mind was at odds. That nagging voice was back again, warning the curious response my body seemed to be having to stay with my back turned to the naked girl in my bed, no matter how much I relished the sight of her there.

"Relax, Kit," Daisy said. "Come here."

"I really shouldn't," I said, more to myself than to Daisy.

"Would you just come over and sit?" Daisy asked softly. "You look awful." I closed my eyes and shook my head. As much as I wanted to stay, I knew the right thing to do was to leave Daisy in my bed and go barricade myself in Liza's room. "Kit," Daisy sighed. "Please?"

I bit down hard on my bottom lip and gently banged my forehead against the door a few times. *Don't be a scoundrel,* I cautioned myself as I turned around to face her—I couldn't say no to her. I took measured steps around to the side of the bed Daisy was not occupying and sat on the edge of the mattress, well over an arm's reach within Daisy. I forced myself to hold eye contact with Daisy, knowing that if I took one look at her body, I would launch myself across the bed and….

No. I wouldn't allow myself to entertain such an idea. My willpower was shoddy at best even now as I sat away from her but it would take the space of just a wink from her to ruin me.

"Is Armie all right?" Daisy asked. All the strife I had felt moments ago in the hallway washed away completely the instant I'd laid eyes on Daisy's breasts—Armie who?

Yes, the nagging voice hissed. *Think of Armand. That'll kill the insects fluttering in your stomach.*

"He's asleep," I replied. "I put him in bed. He was saying…." I trailed off, mystified by the alluring glow coming off Daisy like a heat lamp. She cocked her head and made the river of curls flowing over her shoulder wave undoubtedly across her breasts. I swallowed hard, reminding myself forcefully that if I let my gaze fall below her throat, I was a goner. "It doesn't matter what he was saying," I muttered, my mouth full of marbles.

"No," Daisy agreed. "Come over here." She patted the spot on the bed beside her.

"Daisy," I tried to reason with her. "I really don't think—"

"If you aren't going to come over here, could you at least not say my name like that?" she asked, taunting me with a magnetic, daring smile.

"I can't help it." I could do nothing more than mumble.

"Tonight is special. We took great strides with Dulce and her mother. The majesty of that party and all the champagne and dancing aside, I finally feel like we're close to getting out of here. Even if we're a step farther than we were yesterday, it's progress." She sat up straighter and folded her legs under my blankets, dropping her hands in her lap. "When you held me in your arms tonight, it felt as though I were flying. I am so safe with you, Kit. I always have been. You are the circle of light over my head, my little window of sunshine when I am awake and when I'm asleep. You make me feel hopeful. You make me feel loved."

I was moved almost beyond words. "You know that I love you, Daze."

"I love you too, Kit." She reached for my hand and I did not try to pull away. Her floral scent smothered me and I closed my eyes when she walked her fingers up to the crook of my arm, where she held onto my arm to keep me still while she brushed my hair back on the side of my head. My arms broke out in gooseflesh at her touch and the nagging voice was drowned by my heart-beat pounding in my ears. My eyelids felt heavy and a tightness was gathering in my stomach.

"You understand what I'm asking, Kit?" Daisy said in a voice barely louder than a whisper. I nodded, keeping my eyes closed. "Kit, look at me."

Ridiculous though it was, I felt frightened. But again, I could not say no to her. I opened my eyes to see her imploring smile that warmed me to my toes, her lovely breasts brushing the duvet as she leaned forward.

"I want you to make love to me." She pulled at my arm and I followed her across the bed. She set my hand over her right breast and my resolve crumbled away to feel the heat of her soft body burning into my palm.

"Daisy...." It was a poor attempt to cling onto my fleeing willpower. Daisy answered me with a long kiss.

"Make me fly again," she whispered against my lips. She pressed her body into me as I lowered her down to the bed with a kiss, shedding my vest and shirt as we reclined. My fingers shook like branches in a storm as I reached for the clasp of my trousers. I was thrilled by the idea of the sensations I was about to discover and more than anything, I wanted to match Daisy's offer and give myself to her entirely. I would be hers as much as she would be mine, but wasn't that always how it was between us anyway? We'd exercised every facet of intimacy together but this one. This new yet final frontier was irresistible and right underneath me. As I propped myself up over Daisy's body, she pulled the duvet away and opened her legs so that I could settle between them. She wrapped her arms around my neck and breathed in deeply as we kissed again, exhilarated by the anticipation of what would come next.

"Daisy," I said when she ran her hands down the length of my back. She peered up at me with a dreamy glaze over her brown eyes.

"Kit, what's wrong?" she asked, stilling under me. I couldn't say it but she knew—all physical evidence to the contrary, she knew what I was going to say. She smiled sadly and tucked some strands of my longer hair behind my ear. "You can't."

"I want to," I said, keeping my rigid pose over her. My voice was thick and I was terrified I would start to cry. "Daisy, I want to show you how much I love you...."

"But you won't," she said. How could she look so at ease, in the position she was in? If I'd been courageous enough to lie naked in wait to present myself to an intended lover and been refused, however gently, I would have thrown something.

"Is it because we're not married?" she asked in the timid tone I'd expected her to take on.

"No," I said at once. "Of course not." I bent my head to kiss her, to assure her that it was not because I didn't find her desirable—nothing could be farther from the truth. "I just don't want it to be like this. Not under *his* roof." That was the second thing I could not bring myself to do—mention James by name when I was with Daisy in this way.

"Kit," Daisy sighed. "He can't control us. He can't say whether or not I can give myself to you. I love you. It's our decision to make."

"Is it not enough for me to promise that I love you?" I asked. "I swear to you now, Daisy, I want nothing more than to devote the rest of this night to you, to prove to you how much I love you…but in a matter of days, if we really will be free, I do not want each following union we share to remind us of this place. I don't want *his* influence over us to sully this experience for you. You deserve so much more."

Daisy absorbed all of this with a much braver face than I'd made while saying my piece. She stroked the hair at the back of my head, her arms still around me. "That's all you want, is to wait until we're free?" Daisy cupped my face in her hands and kissed me.

"Not by far," I said. It really did pain me to withhold myself. I could see how much she wanted this to happen and how disappointed she was that I'd denied her.

Even I couldn't believe I'd denied her. I hated myself for it.

"Oh, Kit." She sighed and touched my lips with her delicate, porcelain fingertips.

"I'm so sorry."

Daisy hushed me with a little shake of her head. "I understand," she murmured. I rolled to the side and Daisy sat up in bed to reach over and lift her discarded pajama shirt from the floor. She pulled it over her head with a sad air of sobriety about her and it made me feel like the lowest man alive. I slipped underneath the covers beside her and was pleasantly surprised when she put the light out and joined me once more. She pushed at my shoulder so that I turned over with my back to her and then hugged me against her front, her arm snugly holding me around the waist. I could feel the tip of her nose at the back of my neck. I shivered when she let out a sleepy sigh and sent a whisper of cool air over my shoulder. She kissed me sweetly and cuddled me even tighter.

"Worlds away," she whispered as we lay, fit together like two spoons, in my bed. What had I ever done in my life to deserve a girl like Daisy?

"Soon we will be," I told her. "I promise."

Chapter Eighteen

I twisted restlessly in my slumber. I was sweating when I woke up to the feel of arms around me and then the soothing coolness of a fresh pillow under my face. I settled under much lighter covers and stretched my legs out, sighing in glad relief to have achieved a mellower temperature. I opened my eyes later, blinking slow like a cat, and saw that I had been moved to my cot.

So much for letting me take the bed, I thought with a scowl when I turned over to see James' sleeping silhouette, where it always was at this time of night, in his own bed. At least he hadn't closed the window shades. I set my head back on my pillow and fell back to sleep in a drowsy swoon.

When I came to a while later, it was still pitch black outside. A choking sensation had woken me—I was crying, I realized, when I wiped at my cheek and in the shying moonlight I saw a glistening of tears on my fingers. Whatever I had been dreaming of was not Quinn's attempt on my life; otherwise, I would have woken up with a shout. I remembered the feel of arms around me, which had been James moving me, but....

Armand. I had been dreaming of Armand.

I'd felt the touch of his lips, his breath against my ear, his possessive whispering of my name as his arms held me tightly against him. It felt like I was suffocating, I wanted him so much that I wanted to cry even more. Like I had done days ago in the throes of a similar emotional state, I climbed quietly out of my cot and crawled into the larger bed. Whatever I was feeling was harder to bear when I was across the room, alone, under cold sheets, so I dried my eyes and rolled over to force myself back to sleep. The problem was, I couldn't keep my eyes closed. I could tell by the position of the moon that the night had passed well into the small hours but dawn's approach was still far away.

The sea outside was calm now and through a thin veil of clouds, I could see stars glittering all the way to the horizon.

Go to sleep, I urged myself. I rolled over away from the window, closed my eyes, and suddenly that drunk Master Diego was grabbing onto my arm. I clenched my jaw at the effort to force the incident out of my mind; then, Donovan's face was looming over mine, encouraging me to remember my place in all this. The words were dead on my tongue but they were sharp in my imagination: I would live out the rest of my days here behind a closed door, whether I was to be isolated in the Masters' chambers, or thrown in the mix with Daisy, Kit, Armand, and every Master of the system, I would be alone. Knowing the truth meant that even if I was allowed to move back to my old room, Daisy and the boys would never really have me back.

And Lorena would never see me, her daughter, again.

Even gussied up like a baby Mistress, like Dulce, I was an outsider. No amount of dancing or drinking would let me forget it, just as no amount of punishment or threats could keep me from trying to change any of it. After all, I have lived on both sides of my reality and even straddled the line that separates them. Donovan might have convinced anyone else in my position that she was not helpless and it might have worked, but it would not be true for me any more than my dream of Armand had been.

I banished all thoughts from my head and laid on my back. *Stare up at that red canopy until you fall asleep*, I ordered myself. I sighed when I realized that it was impossible. I would have to accept that there was no more sleep to be had tonight. Then I turned my head and saw James asleep on his back and thought, how strange that we were mirroring positions—his head was turned to face me too. If he opened his eyes, he'd find mine staring right back at him.

I found myself captivated by the sight of him sleeping. All signs of torment and frustration were wiped clean from his features. Without his glower and set jaw, James looked somehow younger. Utterly peaceful. Mindful of disrupting his sleep or twinging my shoulder, I edged closer to him. We were lying just an arm's reach across and I was so fascinated by his serene countenance that I rolled over and reached slowly to lay my hand on his cheek. I expected him to wake at my touch but he did not budge. He didn't even stir. He was warm like Armand had been but his skin was rough from the shadow of a beard he would probably shave off in the morning.

I lifted my hand from his face and set it on his chest, my palm covering the spot over his heart. I could feel the muscle working beneath my hand, its beat steady and calm and in sync with his slow, slumbering breathing. I smoothed my hand over his chest with fastidious care, knowing that if I reached just an inch too far, I would find the spot where that volpine had bitten him. I couldn't bear the idea of spurring him awake in pain, so I curled to his side and put my hand back over his heart. I closed my eyes and focused on James as I tried to match my breathing to his.

Synchronizing our breathing was much easier for me than dancing had been. As soon as our hearts were beating as one, I felt a heavy calm wash over me. The warmth of another body beside mine after so many weeks of hopeless isolation instilled a sensation in me that was sunnier and lovelier than hugging Daisy or even dancing with Armand.

I snuggled closer to James, my chest flush against his arm, and put my lips to his shoulder.

"Hmm?" James murmured, conscious enough to flutter an eyelid. I suspected he thought he was dreaming because he fell back asleep right away. I shivered a little and shifted my knee over so that one of my legs touched his. I breathed in, the scent of his spiced citrus soap and warm bed filled my nostrils. I remembered how many times he'd woken up to hush me out of my nightmares and gone back to bed so fast. He really was a deep sleeper.

I pressed my lips to his shoulder again in a gentle but unmistakably rousing gesture.

"What is it?" mumbled James, now somewhat lucid as he reached up to lay his hand on the arm I had slung across his chest. The moment his hand rested over mine, a waking jolt seemed to pass through him and his eyes opened wide. He took one look at me, nestled beside him in his bed, and immediately sat up. Heaving an exasperated sigh, James slipped away from me and swung his legs over the side of the bed.

"Liza," he grumbled. He tried to rouse himself more awake by mussing his face in his hands. "What are you doing?" I sat up too and crawled over in pursuit of him to the side of the bed where he sat. I propped myself up on my knees, my legs folded under me.

"Feeling you," I whispered. "You looked so peaceful." I touched James on his back, skimming my fingertips up between his shoulder blades until my knuckles brushed the hair at the nape of his neck.

"Liza, what are you *doing?*"

I sifted slowly through the thick, dark hair at the back of his head as if he were made of precious glass. I smiled softly when I felt tingles chase down his neck and touched my lips to the slope of his shoulder to seal the smile there.

"I'm feeling you," I told James. I took my hand from his head and grasped his tense right shoulder, tracing his clavicle with my left hand until the edge of my thumb reached his throat.

"Liza…."

I felt the reverberation of his voice echo in his chest. James sat very still as I caressed the backs of my fingers along the front of his throat until they touched the underside of his jaw, where I could feel his pulse was much quicker than it had been a minute ago—perhaps he worried I would give chase if he got up from bed and left my side? I then took his chin between my thumb and my forefinger so that I could tilt his head just enough to the side. The tip of my nose stroked the exposed side of this neck as I decidedly kissed him there.

"Liza," James groaned unevenly, "you can't…."

"Why?" I wondered. I kissed his throat again and very slowly traced my fingernails lightly down his strong back. James fought to maintain his rigid posture but he couldn't hide from me the resonating sigh he made in relief or the shudder I felt him give in response. I craned my neck up so that the slope of my nose touched his earlobe. "Is it because of those *conditions?*" I asked in a whisper. He tensed when I released his chin like he was going to get up from the bed. To ground him, I clasped the other side of his neck, cleaving him to me. He stayed put when I kissed his throat again.

No, James wasn't going anywhere.

"It is," I guessed, based on his lack of response. "Well, I don't care about them." I moved even closer to him, trapping him in my arms. "They're my mother's conditions, not mine." I put my lips against his ear. "Certainly not now."

Renouncing those conditions felt utterly liberating for me but I could only imagine how it felt for James to be free of them now, how stifling it had been for him to live with them. Upholding them had been killing him—I knew it to be true as he melted slowly under my touch—slowly and cruelly, by ensuring his isolation from everyone close to him. Just like me, James had been living behind closed doors. It was his inherited duty to maintain the sanctity of those damn conditions and my attempts to escape them, even Quinn's attempt to forcibly break them, had chained me to James' fate.

Was it right that we should both be held hostage by those conditions?

"Liza," James offered in vague protest. I felt gratified right down to my toes when he said my name as though it was the breath of fresh, nighttime air he needed so badly.

"James," I sighed. "Hold me. I say you can, that's all I care about." I let my hand wander down his front until I caught the hem of his shirt.

"Liza," James said again when I slipped my hand beneath the sheath of cotton and let my fingertips glide across his abdomen and up to the light, soft hair that dusted his chest. "Please...."

"Please," I echoed in a whispered tone, kissing his shoulder once more. My eyes welled with desperate tears as I nuzzled into his throat, brushing my lips in brief strokes against the tender spot just under his jaw.

We were both trembling. I could have burst into tears or laughter but all I wanted was for him to touch me back.

"You let me see you," I said urgently. My lips twisted into a frown as I fought to keep from giving into the overwhelming ache in my heart. I painfully sat back from him so that I could lose myself in the waves tossing amid his blue eyes. "And I see you now, James. You're so alone. You hurt so much from it, you can barely stand it. I feel it too, James. We don't have to be alone."

James tore his gaze from mine and leaned forward, putting his elbows on his knees so that he could bury his face in his hands. He was doing his damnedest to live up to his indelible reputation but he did not once try to push me away. When I kissed his shoulder I felt the hard muscles in his back relax, relenting to my touch. I had felt woozy a minute ago but now I was wide awake, eager for him to turn to me. I glanced down to where I could see my knee rest against his thigh. I slid my hand over the inside of his leg and let it stay there while I braced my other hand on his shoulder, pushing him suggestively back down to the bed.

James reacted in a flash, snatching both of my wrists in his hands. He held me still and just far away from him so that I wasn't touching him. He looked desperately hungry when his eyes bore into mine.

"Please, Liza," he implored. "I am being as gentle with you as I know how."

"Don't be." I'd never begged James for something like this before.

"I cannot do this."

"I want you to."

"Liza." His voice sounded rough. "Please understand, but I cannot share your bed." I took a long breath and found it impossible not to relish the spiced scent of him—my pupils might have dilated, I liked it so much. I did not try to extricate my arms from his grasp for James was stronger than me and we both knew it, but my submission to him meant he would continue to hold onto me. As I looked into his eyes, ones that I had countless times glared into in defiance, and felt the drumming of my own heart coaxing me to show him just how stubborn I could be too.

"This isn't my bed," I reminded him, never once breaking eye contact. James heaved one final embittered sigh as his restraint melted away and he gave into me. Still holding my wrists, he swooped forward and kissed me, molding his lips to fit mine. He let my wrists go after pulling me close and I slid my arms around his neck as a roaring fire ignited in the pit of my stomach. James snaked his arms around my waist and constricted, sealing us together. We swayed for a moment as the embrace tested our balance but then James pulled me into his lap where I could squeeze his middle between my bent knees. He reached up to cradle my face between his hands, waiting to kiss me again long enough to see my smile and return it, happily bemused, in kind.

James kissed me tenderly at first, curling his fingers in the hair at the back of my head. I freely explored his chest with my hands and thought, *Oh, he is good at this....*

I grabbed at his shirt in my fists when James tightened his hold and tugged on my hair, craning my head back so that he could better kiss my throat. My eyelashes fluttered and I hummed appreciatively at the warm sensations blooming under every brush of his lips on my skin. James smoothed his hands down until he grasped the small of my back and then he let himself fall backward onto the bed, guiding me to hover over him.

I could have sang, I was so glad to have swayed him my way for a change. I wanted to say, now that wasn't so difficult, was it?

James' fingers lightly grazed up my thighs until they disappeared under the hem of my shirt. He waited, staring up at me with a dazed look in his eyes, until I understood with a quiver what he wanted me to do. Straddling him, I pulled my shirt off over my head and threw the garment aside. I bent down to press my breasts to his chest, my lips searching for his. I felt him smile as I kissed him and couldn't stop myself from giggling airily against his mouth. I expected him to say something but I knew that now was not the time for words.

Instead, James let his hands roam over my bare back, down my backside, and along the sides of my legs. I kissed him some more, deeper this time, with enough fervor that my hair fell like a blonde curtain around his face. I dipped my hands under the hem of his shirt and he helped me ease it off. The bruises and squares of white bandages did not distract me from the chiseled muscles of his chest like he perhaps worried they would. I leaned down to plant soft, adoring kisses down his chest as a rising stiffness arose underneath where my legs were spread, in James' lap.

"Say the word," James said, smoothing my hair out of my face as I made my way back up to his lips.

"Yes," I breathed. "Yes, please."

James grinned. "Good girl," he praised me wryly. He grasped me by the waist and lithely rolled, capsizing me and settling himself snugly on top of my body. I parted my lips for him while fighting the impulse to bring my teeth down on his lip. I hitched a knee over his hip to push him closer, which he found to be thrilling enough to let out a low groan as we tasted each other. He pulled away, taking his lips with him so that he could nuzzle the soft spot under my ear.

It was like turning a magic key. Shivers rippled across my entire body from that spot, especially when James picked his head up and dragged his teeth lightly over my earlobe. I became putty in his hands, which was apparently his goal. James took his time lavishing slow smooches along the side of my throat, along the ridge of my jaw, and then down to my clavicle, and then lower, between my breasts, and lower…until his lips brushed under my navel and I realized I'd been holding my breath. James stopped moving and looked to me for his cue to keep going.

"It's good," I blurted, flushing brilliantly.

"Good?" James seemed dissatisfied. He floated back over me so that his bare chest pressed into my breasts and kissed me. He slid his hands up my sides and kissed the side of my neck again. I felt as though I could envelope James into me or be swallowed by the mattress I was sinking into.

"*Very* good," I sighed. When I became once again malleable in his hands, James hooked his fingertips around the waistband of my pants and in a singular, fluid motion, he pulled my legs free of any clothing. I propped myself up on my elbows and willed myself to stay still for the few seconds it took for James to level himself to my state of undress. He found himself in a pool of moonlight just as I caught sight of him fully naked. It was both the previously undiscovered proximity of a man with whom I intended to join in bed and the size of his organ that sent my heart leaping to my throat. I bit down on my lip to keep from grinning out of sheer nervous excitement. I couldn't take my eyes off him and I became suddenly aware and embarrassed of my staring. Part of me wanted to hide behind my hands and curl into the sheets underneath us, but then I would miss his touch, his attention, his desire….

Instead, I raised my gaze to his eyes for just a moment or two. James swooped in and kissed me so thoroughly that I closed my eyes and let him lay me beneath him on the bed. He patiently trained his focus to my throat, as he had quickly figured out that it was my favorite place to be kissed while I gradually responded to his every movement. He used his hands to prime the rest of my body for the elevation of intimacy I craved most of all, starting with brief, softly teasing touches to my breasts and working up to rocking his hips slowly, tantalizingly, against me. Combined with every other curiously electric sensation James aroused in me, I quickly became enraptured and moaned.

"*Wonderful.*"

That was all the go-ahead James needed to kiss me again and reach between our bodies. His initial touch between my legs made me gasp in excitement. I held tightly onto James by the shoulders as I stared pleadingly into his eyes.

"You're trembling," he remarked, his voice splendidly ragged.

"Yes," I agreed breathlessly.

"Should I stop?" he asked, stilling over me.

"Don't you dare!"

I lost the capacity to speak after that. After the briefest shock of something other than pain but just as thrilling, I was suspended by a tight cord of lust knotted in my belly and pulled into a new world of ecstasy. It got worse when James let out a guttural groan—he liked this as much as I did, it seemed. Still, this head splitting pleasure was too much but not enough: I dug my nails into his back and urged him to stop being so careful in very few words. James showered my lips and throat with searching, ravenous kisses as I clung to him tighter and tighter with every thrust of his hips.

Before long I dragged his lips back to mine. James indulged me for a while but he broke away to let his forehead rest on mine as his breath left him in quick, heavy beats. This was ravishing, worshipping, unbearable pleasure....

"James!" I gasped. I wanted to scream.

"Let go," he encouraged me. "Just let it all go." It was good advice: I did, and my arrival was extraordinary. It was leaping and falling out of the library window, but instead of freezing night air biting into my flesh, it was a curling, gorgeous heat that welled underneath my skin. I was soaring up and yet somehow within my body....

And James was there to catch me. My jaw dropped as my back arched, forcing a low scream from my lungs. James said my name so many times, easing me through my arrival as he held tight to me and fought off his own. I could not force the broad smile off my face as we rocked together, especially when it came time for James to meet the same felicitous end I had. He bent his head and tested the hollow of my throat with his teeth just as his body gave a great tremor of release.

Moonlight bathed us as our desperate breaths quelled. James rolled to his back and I curled into his chest, bestowing unto him gracious kisses as I drifted off to sleep in his arms. Not only did I feel so whole with him near, but I felt a consuming sense of accomplishment that warmed me to my bones.

That night, James and I had finally escaped the compound, if only for a while.

Sometime later, when it must have been morning, I awoke to the errant caressing of fingertips at my temple. It was a soft gesture which soothed me out of a bottomless, peaceful slumber that was for the first time in weeks free of nightmares. I slowly blinked my eyes open, glad to see the warm, umber sunlight seeping into the bedroom to enrich the bold red of the canopy hanging over me. My head was cradled in the crook of James' arm and I turned to look at him. He was staring up at the canopy, stroking the soft hair just over my ear.

"I thought you might be gone by now." I had come to know from sharing a room with him for even a short time that he was usually up and out before the sun rose. I was glad to feel his body against mine upon waking, in a haze of golden light, and even gladder when he peered into my eyes with his impossibly blue ones as his lips curled into a soft, wry smile.

"I would not have left this room for anything," he said.

"But the summit," I reminded him in a temperate tone of the duties we both knew he ought to see to. James merely traced a swirl in my hair with the tip of his finger and kept smiling.

"I am exactly where I am needed the most." He found the curve of my waist with his other hand and pulled me in close, sealing our bodies together as our lips met. "How do you feel?" he murmured, our noses still touching.

"Weightless," I replied. "Warm. And very safe." James kissed my forehead and then the bridge of my nose. I should have expected the question—he knew details about my body that no other man I might have taken as my lover would know, such as that there had been no one before him. But I still blushed, which James seemed to find charming.

"You are extraordinary," he said. "What possessed you last night, Liza?"

"I was out of my mind," I told James. I snaked the top of my foot up his calf and his gaze sharpened.

"So was I." He ran his hand down my side and gripped my thigh, pulling my leg up so that my knee rested over his hip. I leaned my head back, baring my throat to him. He nibbled, very gently, the tender flesh there, taking my cue without hesitation and making me melt in his arms all over again. We fluidly rearranged our limbs so that he was on me, his head bowed while he kissed my neck. A low chuckle sounded in his throat when I smoothed my hands down his back until I could palm his buttocks and tighten my grip possessively, all the while flashing a satisfied grin.

I told him what I wanted, leaving no room for interpretation on his part.

"Was that an order?" James asked, pressing a gossamer, whispered kiss into the shell of my ear. My skin surged with heat as a boldness in me reared its head, likely turning my cheeks scarlet.

"You heard me." I did not need to repeat myself—James was all too imposed to oblige. Perhaps it was the daylight that heightened my senses or the thrill of James' affections, but every move of his performance had me enthralled and gasping. Before long, I was biting down on my lip to stifle a praising outcry. I felt myself begin to go off the deep end and I grasped at the sheets on either side in anticipation of the release I knew was coming.

"Not the sheets," James coaxed breathlessly, "hold on to me." With the remnant of a smile on my face, as I was too consumed with mounting delight to maintain one, I obliged James and grasped his shoulders as he worked our bodies toward culmination. Whatever revitalizing effect the daylight had on me was clearly showing in James too and we achieved that wordless but not soundless finish together, both a little shakier in the aftermath this morning than we had been last night.

"Who are you, and what have you done with James the Master?" I panted, breathlessly teasing him once he fell onto the pillow to my left—after all, he had technically just taken an order from his own Tribute.

"It is not what *I* have done, but you." He too was eagerly catching his breath. He noticed me staring at him and reached to push the hair out of my eyes. "What is it?" he asked.

"I am an entirely new woman today," I said. "And you, an entirely new man." I couldn't form the words to say how odd it was to lay feasting, ardent eyes on him and have my heart go to war with my head about the colliding emotions welling in me. I had only known the man lying in bed beside me now for a few short hours, even though I barely had a memory of my life at this compound in which James the Master was not present. Denial whispered in my ear, hissing in a dark voice about a man whose hands had threatened me, restrained me, and once struck me; these were the same hands that had just last night held me close in sleep and closer before in sex. Daunting was the prospect of reconciling the conflicting ideas, but as I laid beside James in the wake of our latest dizzying entanglement, I thought about all the foolish decisions I had made in a few short weeks and realized that the result of my latest was the only one that yielded a sense of belonging.

Even my daringly confident old self would not know what to do with such a feeling.

James could tell I was buttoning up my inhibitions. He reached for me but winced at a sudden stitch in his side and he clapped a hand to the thickest bandage covering the volpine bite on his ribcage. I sat up right away, worried by his sharp gasp of pain. I rolled over and grabbed the case of pills I knew he kept on his bedside table, ignoring the twinge in my shoulder as I passed them to him. James took a capsule out but hesitated before popping it into his mouth.

"I should eat," he said. "Are you hungry?" At the mention of food, my stomach rumbled—of course, I remembered that neither of us had eaten more than a scrap of food at Dulce's birthday party. It had been at least a day since either of us had eaten.

"Can we eat in bed?" I asked, raising an eyebrow. James forsook the pain he felt and pulled me into his arms, apparently unable to help himself in his famished state, at least for a few minutes. He sat up before long, prying my searching lips from his, and declared we must get up to bathe before any food could be sent up. I got up to follow him to the bathroom and my knees turned to jelly, sending me wobbling back down to the bed. This time, I went along with the impulse to hide behind my hands. James was sore and must have been as jelly-legged as I was, but he doubled back and lifted me into his arms with a dignified smirk, carrying me to the bathroom. After carefully wrapping the bandages around my forearms with that waterproof green tape, securing a square over the patch covering my shoulder, and covering the tiny squares of gauze stuck to his side, James took me by the hand and led me under the hot water that fell from the ceiling like rain. I loved the look of him, buff, nude, and slick with water so much that I threw my arms around his neck and kissed him, not stopping until his back bumped the wall of the shower.

"Liza," James said, his voice muffled by my lips. "We can't both be punch drunk...."

He was probably right but I kept my hands on him as often as I could anyway. It took me a lot longer to suds my hair from root to tip than it did for James and he stepped out of the shower before I finished rinsing.

"Stay," I implored.

"I'm not going far," James said. "I have to shave." By the time I wrung my hair out and turned the water off, James was halfway through shaving. This was the second vulnerable look I'd witnessed him in the middle of— he was focused entirely on guiding the straight razor carefully down his cheek, then over his throat. I dressed slowly, aware now of some sore muscles in my abdomen as I bent over to step into my soft trousers. As soon as I had my socks and top on, I went to the drawer near James for a hairbrush and he stilled, wary of me making a sudden movement and spurring him to cut himself.

"Don't stop on my account." We stood side by side for a few minutes, James shaving while I brushed through my wet hair. He'd just put his razor away when I glimpsed with a gasp a dark red spot on the side of his neck that had been covered a moment ago by his fragrant shaving cream.

"What?" he asked, alarmed.

"Your neck!" I dropped the hairbrush on the counter and went to inspect it. Not only was there flagrant evidence of my clearly overzealous intimate avidity—Dulce would have called it for what it was, a *coso*—but I could make out several red spots on James' shoulders where I'd dug my nails in.

James checked his reflection, regarded the mark, and merely shrugged. "It doesn't bother me," he wrote off my frantic reaction. "It's a very favorable token of your esteem, I think."

"What if someone sees it?" I asked, knowing that the real question was what would he do *when* someone noticed the mark?

"We woke up in a new world this morning," James told me, stepping forward so he could wind his arms around my waist. "But outside of that room—" he flickered his gaze toward the bedroom, "—I am still very much the Master of this compound. Even if it isn't hidden by my collar, which I'm certain it will be, I'm not interested in the questions of my peers, nor their criticisms." His gaze transformed into a glare at the thought of anyone addressing such a thing with him.

There he was, the indelible James the Master. I felt foolish for fussing over what was obviously a very trivial thing to him, but then again, I never thought the revered James the Master would be holding me preciously in his arms.

"Furthermore," James mused slowly, as though navigating this next topic would be like endeavoring to cross a choppy river over a thin layer of ice. "I have every intention of preserving your safety, now more than ever." He didn't just mean my physical safety, but the warm security I'd told him I felt in his presence in our waking moments. "That means that when we are not alone together, we will have to maintain relating to one another as though nothing has ever happened between us—at least, for the time being." It was hard not to become instantly discouraged. I bowed my head and rested my forehead against James' chest as I slowly felt crushed by the implications he had introduced.

I had not given a single thought about what the possible future of an affair like this would entail. Not only was James thinking twelve steps ahead of me, however true to his nature it was, he had also just warned me that he would likely be his cruel, unrelenting self as long as we were outside of his bedroom.

The truth was, I did not know how long I would remain at this compound. I had accepted that I would not return to Kingsfield Township, likely ever, to be reunited with my family. Now that I had given myself to James, I faced the idea of what committing to him would be like and he had already spelled out that for himself:

Whatever our bond was now had just been declared something to be kept behind yet another closed door, just like any other facet of his private life.

"Liza." James lightly tilted my chin up so that he could peer down into my eyes. "It will not be easy for me, I hope you know that. This experience has been...well, suffice to say, these are somewhat uncharted waters for me."

"And for me." I made my voice hard and channeled a little of my old self by meeting his stare with a spark of defiance in my eyes.

"Of course," James agreed. "I thought this morning, what happened between us...." He broke off; was he bashful? "What I mean to say is, I thought our continuation of last night was enough to show you that I do not regret a single moment of any of it. Though I may live to, knowing you."

First he was bashful, now he was cracking a joke? And a very dry joke, at that?

"If what we achieve together physically is not enough, if you need other reassurances that I am completely spellbound by you, I will give you as many as you need." He stroked my cheeks with the soft sides of his thumbs. "If it will earn me your grace and your patience, I will fill every private silence we share with professions of how lovely your lips are to kiss...." He brushed his lips across mine. "How the hue of your irises is rarer than any treasure I have ever seen...." He planted two more kisses across each of my eyelids. "How your legs are smooth and graceful, and I might never again know a moment's peace again after finding out how they fit so perfectly wrapped around me...."

"James." He had reduced me almost to a crumbling ruin in his arms, the fiend.

"You know the truth about me, the things I've done in my past, and despite the pain I have caused you, you still seduced me with a determination that has truly humbled me. Despite what lies we must tell through our actions in public, I will do whatever I must to show you how truly in awe I am of your enduring heart and your boldness—a trait that somehow, I'd wager, will get us both into trouble." A distinct roughness overtook James when he spoke, just like the night he had confessed to me the truth of how I'd come to the compound. If there was one thing I'd learned about keeping such close quarters with him recently, it was that he might be quick to anger, but his other emotions were also equally close to the surface. He'd just learned to hide them with the one that would keep people the farthest away—his gruesome temper.

I wondered if it was true, that he had been humbled by me (although, I would have described my behavior last night as "desperate" if anything, not "determined" as he had put it) or if he was simply assuaging the trepidation he'd sensed in me moments ago. When he held me by the small of my back and lowered his lips over mine, I was inclined to believe it was the former.

"I need you to trust me, trust that I know what I am doing what's right for both of us." He brushed his thumb over the pulse in my neck and held my gaze in sincerity. He smelled superbly of fresh cedar from his shaving lotion and with my hands on his chest, I felt that his heartbeat was utterly steady.

"I trust you," I admitted, a little more wistfully than I would have liked to sound. I might have been one of the fanciful girls in Daisy's storybooks for a moment.

"Thank you." James gathered my hands in his and pressed the backs of my fingers to his lips. "Go and page the kitchen to send something up—the switch on my desk, not the portable. Flip it twice so that Lorraine will know to send two servings." I sighed and let my eyes roll a little as I slipped from his grasp. When I reached the threshold to the bedroom, I paused and looked back at James.

"As you say, lover."

"Go." James was grinning. If I didn't send for some food, he might actually devour me. I flipped the switch on James' desk, as directed, which would signal the kitchen to prepare what I prayed would be an enormous breakfast. It was still very early in the morning, despite how bright the sun shone over the ocean outside. I took it upon myself to drag the considerably disheveled covers of the bed up, tugging them this way and that until it looked somewhat presentable.

James had emerged dressed in his usual dark-collared shirt and dark trousers when a knock at the door sounded.

"That was fast," I remarked. My stomach rumbled again and I sat on the edge of my cot to keep out of the delivery cart's way. James unlocked the door and answered it.

"Sir." It was Douglas, not Lorraine and her assistants with breakfast.

"What is it?" James asked promptly. Douglas glanced past him, at me, and kept his mouth shut tight. When I saw how pale Douglas was, I stood up from my cot, my ears perked up so that I would not miss a syllable said between them. James noticed Douglas' apparent aversion to sharing his report in front of me so he slipped outside and closed the door behind him.

It had been ten minutes since James decreed we must keep up an act and already I was cursing his commitment to his role as my grouchy, authoritative guardian. I wasn't too bitter about it to ignore the dread pooling in my stomach though—if I didn't know any better, Douglas was veritably upset. Each second that passed as I waited for James to reappear was grueling. The ache in my shoulder had begun to resurface and I could practically feel my blood sugar dropping, the stress of not knowing what possible bad news Douglas had come to deliver depleting the rest of my already low stamina.

James reappeared through the door and shut it behind him carefully. He was ashen and kept his wide eyes fixed on the floor.

"What happened?" I asked. James crossed an arm across his chest while clamping his other hand over his mouth. He was shocked. "James," I insisted. "What—?"

"Liza," James said. The next words that came out of his mouth leveled me like a violent punch to the chest. A whistling sound like a ready tea kettle screamed in my ears as a whooshing sensation made me feel like I was about to be sick. James lunged forward just as my knees buckled and he caught me as the room went hazy and dim.

Sometime later, I woke up to the smell of bacon. My eyes shot open and I sat up fast in my cot, which made my head spin. James launched out of his desk chair and crossed the room in hasty strides.

"Sit still for a moment," he insisted. I ignored him and grabbed a slice of bacon off the plate, cramming into my mouth with unladylike fervor. James let me finish it before pressing a glass of orange juice into my hand, insisting I drink it all. He passed me two pieces of toast and I finished them before either of us said a word.

"Tell me it isn't true," I begged him.

"I'm sorry to say that it is," James said, bowing his head gravely for a beat. "Jada sent word confirming it just a minute ago." He stooped and collected a pair of boots from underneath my cot and set them on the foot of the bed. "I need you to finish eating and make yourself presentable."

"What are you going to do?"

"Several things," James replied. "But first, after you have eaten and regained the strength you need to accompany me, I'm going to take you with me to the Tribute wing. I think it would be best to have you there when I break the news to the others."

I nodded, tears brimming my eyes. James frowned and leaned in to kiss me. I closed my eyes and tears spilled down my cheeks, only to be wiped away tenderly by James as he straightened up.

"I need you to be brave, Liza. Just for a little while. Can you manage it?" His sympathy was breaking my heart.

"Yes," I said at once. For Daisy and the boys, I would face Quinn again if I had to. Without shedding another tear, I cleared my plate even though my stomach was knotted with anguish as I wolfed down what was left of my food.

I got out of bed with James at my side in case I fainted again. When he was satisfied with my steadiness, I went to the bathroom to rinse out my mouth and braid my hair back. Slipping the boots on was strange but I did so with haste, as I knew that I would only edge closer breaking down the longer it took me to get ready.

James waited for me at the door. I took his hand and squeezed it just before he led us into the hall. "Are you ready?" he asked, squeezing my hand back.

I nodded and let my hand fall away from his. "Lead the way."

Chapter Nineteen

Kit

I was not worlds away when I woke up the next morning, but still in my bed, underneath a halo of daylight in James the Master's compound. For the first time in as long as I could remember, my bedroom did not feel like home. Perhaps it was my heart that had relocated to a sunny, airy, and open place outside of these walls so that the rest of me felt like a tourist here. When I looked over at Daisy, asleep on her left side but with her right arm extended behind her so that she could touch my hand, my heart swelled with a love for her that warmed me to my bones.

It was the best sleep I'd had in months. I would fill our apartment with music today to celebrate that feat as well as the happiness Daisy had instilled in me, and of course the increasingly affirming promise that we would soon be free of this place—and I could finally give Daisy the intimacy she wanted and deserved. I rolled to my side and toyed with a lock of Daisy's hair, eager to touch her but not to wake her. In sleep, she was especially precious. I wondered if our door to the main hall would be unlocked if I tried to go out and fetch her some semblance of breakfast—perhaps even a flower to set on the pillow beside her, so that the first thing she would see when she woke would make her smile.

My bedroom door swung open. I shot up in bed, utterly terrified in a snap that the two of us were about to be dragged out of bed and flogged.

"Liza!" I yelped, for there she was in my bedroom doorway. My heart leaped to see her at home, though my stomach clenched when I realized even though it was not a Master or a guardsman, Daisy and I had still been caught together.

To my astonishment, Liza did not blink twice to see Daisy beside me like

I thought she would. I glimpsed a bundle of clothes—Daisy's—under her arm as she quickly closed the door behind herself and turned to face me, her expression pale and fraught.

"Get up right away," she insisted in an urgent whisper.

"Daisy," I said, reaching over to rouse Daisy out of her slumber. She was disgruntled by how roughly I'd shaken her awake but hushed when Liza came over to us and dropped Daisy's clothes on the foot of the bed.

"You've got to hurry," she said. "Get dressed, both of you. James thinks I've already woken you up, Daze, and that we're waking you now, Kit." There was no trace of reproach nor praise in Liza's voice as Daisy and I threw back my covers and stripped fast out of our sleeping clothes and into fresh ones.

"James is here?" I said, yanking a shirt over my head.

"Something has happened," Liza said. At once, her lips quivered into a frown and her eyes welled with tears.

"Liza, what is it?" Daisy asked, jumping into a pair of trousers. Liza seemed to catch herself before bursting into tears, for she was obviously on the brink of doing so, and spared one lingering look for me and Daisy. She held out her hands for us and we each took one, desperate for some hint or explanation. Liza merely smiled, though tears rolled down her cheeks.

"I won't say a word," she promised, looking knowingly between us. The way she was smiling made me think she might be happy to see Daisy and me together but the pain in her violet eyes was just too alarming for me to worry about how she felt about this revelation. "Come on," she urged us. We swept from my room and down the hall, past Armand's open bedroom door to the kitchen.

James stood leaning against the countertop by the sink with his arms crossed, looking morose and exhausted but still intimidating and imposing as ever. Armand sat at the table, looking significantly worse for the wear. My upper lip broke out in sweat when I locked eyes with James and recognized the darkness of ill tidings there.

"Sit down," he said. Helpless but to obey him, Daisy, Liza, and I dropped into the empty chairs circling the table. Liza laced her fingers together and squeezed her own hands. It took everything in me to stop from taking Daisy's hands in a similarly tight hold.

"Will you please tell us what is going on?" Armand asked, his gaze trained to the mask of grief that was Liza's expression.

"I'm afraid I must inform you that Graham Keating was found dead this morning." James held a stony resolve as we sucked in gasps and then immediately hurled panicked demands at him.

"Found dead? By whom?" I shouted without meaning to.

"How?" Daisy choked. She clutched at Liza's hands for dear life.

"The morning guardsmen were performing their duties and came across his body, in his suite here in the compound," James said evenly, though I could tell he was tormented and had to force himself to hold our bewildered and devastated stares.

"*How?*" Daisy repeated desperately. "How did he die, James?" I couldn't look at Daisy or I would bawl like a child right along with her, I was certain.

"It appears to have been a suicide."

Tears blurred my vision. My chest was suddenly hollow—totally absent of my heart and lungs. I simply could not move, could not breathe. Daisy moaned and sobbed, putting her head down on the table and giving way to sobbing, the likes of which I had never heard before. Liza reached up to cover her face with a hand, still keeping a hold of Daisy with the other. Armand smacked the table with both hands as he pushed himself urgently to his feet. He rushed past James to the sink and promptly lost his stomach contents.

I pinched my eyes shut. Graham—killed himself? Graham, dead, by his own hand? I repeated the words over and over in my head but it still did not make sense.

"Easy," I heard James say. Armand had vomited again. I opened my eyes, the tears that had clouded my vision now rolling down my cheeks. I saw James grasp Armand's arm to steady him as he lowered to the floor. "Breathe, Kit," James said to me. A sob strangled me as I took a breath at James' command. Armand was white as a sheet and sweating on the kitchen floor. Daisy was hysterical.

"I'm going to pass out," Armand murmured.

"All right," James said. "Liza, his head." Liza scooted her chair back and joined Armand on the floor. She took his head in her lap as James took my brother's ankles and held his legs up high—an awkward display, but I remembered errantly that it would help the blood flow to his head, where it was needed most. After a minute or so of this, James carefully lowered Armand's legs back to the floor and told him very firmly to stay there. James then flipped on the sink, not only to wash the sick away but to fill a glass of water. He set it in front of me and told me to drink.

"Why?" I asked. James just repeated himself and I took a drink to appease him. "He wanted to see you last night," I said numbly.

"I did not speak with him," James replied thinly.

"No," I sighed. I took another drink of water. "Of course. It doesn't matter anyway." James left the kitchen for a moment, leaving the four of us alone in our bereaved stupor.

"It can't be!" Daisy sobbed. "He—he—can't be...."

I looked at Liza cradling Armand's head in her lap. She smoothed his hair back with her fingers and whispered something to him that seemed to calm him—at least enough to make him close his eyes. James reappeared with a blanket from the study and draped it over Daisy's shoulders.

"I am very sorry for your loss," James said after standing over us for a while.

Graham would have said, "I am so sorry, my dear pupils."

Instead of reaching to cover the stitch in my chest, I laid my hand on Daisy's back and smoothed the blanket between her shoulders.

"How was it done?" I asked in a voice that did not belong to me.

"Kit." James sighed. "It doesn't matter how it was done. This is a terrible shock for you all and the details would only—"

"James," I said, interrupting him coolly. I looked up at him. James frowned and stared at the back of Daisy's head for a moment. "The truth, if you please," I prompted him. Daisy was already traumatized—we all were, so what was the harm?

"I would rather you hear it from me and not someone in the market," James relented. "As you are all well aware, I maintain very strict rules regarding the handling of firearms in this compound. Sometime last night—I don't know the precise hour—Graham apparently procured a firearm from one of my off-duty guardsmen who had attended Dulce's event and...." James left the rest to our imaginations and a dismal gravitas sank into my limbs.

I had lost sleep for weeks, thinking of how isolated Liza has been while being kept away from us but no grim scenario I had concocted and agonized over could compare to the idea of Graham feeling so alone that the only conceivable way to escape it was a bullet—that he not only felt so hopelessly alone, but he violently tore himself free of his life alone, too.

"He shot himself?" Armand sat up, swaying a little. Liza steadied him though she seemed shakier than he was. They were both in tears.

"He did," said James. "Jada confirmed it just a while ago."

Armand swore but James did not scold him. Daisy slowly suppressed her sobs. Armand looked as though he wanted to stand but decided to stay low, with Liza, for comfort. When Daisy picked her head up, I expected her to turn to me with an expression so woeful it would reduce me to the pile she had been moments before; instead, there was a cold indignance in her eyes that stilled me and for a moment, I did not recognize her. Daisy pushed her chair back and stood, turning on James slowly as though she were a viper coiling to lock eyes on its prey and the blanket he'd draped over her shoulders fell to the floor behind us.

"This is your fault!"

James recoiled as though Daisy had slapped him.

"You trained those damnable brutes whom you call guardsmen to be cruel, *evil* bullies—just like you! When you barred Graham from leaving this place, Nathan went after him with no regard for his humanity. He threw Graham's dead wife and child in his face and sneered as he did it! And all because he wanted to make you proud of his heinous manners when he spurned Graham simply for exercising his right to leave!" Daisy was transformed. Her words cut into James like daggers, stunning him speechless.

"It was for his own safety that I did not allow him to leave." James rarely explained himself. I had only ever witnessed him do such a thing to Haitham, but I had never seen him balk in the face of one of us, least of all Daisy. And she'd cussed at him.

"Oh, how safe he is now, in death!" Daisy's clipped tone was venomous. She took a step close to James, uncharacteristically squaring up to him. "You think you have any control over our safety, James? Quinn nearly murdered Liza! Nathan's cruelty pushed a kind, suffering man to murder himself with the gun he took from another guard! Those men are *yours*, James. You taught them to behave that way, you alpha male of a pack of rabid beasts. You are a failure of a Master!"

"Daisy!" Liza shrieked. She scrambled to her feet just as James reached back to level Daisy to the floor. I tried to step in front of her but Daisy pushed me away with a strength I did not ever suspect she had and she kept her eyes fixed on James as he held his hand back—it was a miracle that he had hesitated at all.

"Do it." Daisy was inhuman. "Prove me right, Master James." James was so furious, his lips were pressed together in a thin white line and his breathing was ragged. Liza stood by Daisy's side, eyes wild and pleading for mercy, but even she did not dare to cross between the two. She and I both froze in place and held our breath when James lashed out quick as lightning to seize Daisy by the roots of her hair at the back of her head, the muscles of his arm bulging as his grip tightened.

"Let go of her!" I couldn't believe Liza would speak to him when he looked as murderous as I'd ever seen him.

James ignored her, keeping his glare fixed on my poor Daisy. "I have put more on the line for you, you impertinent little idiot, than you could possibly comprehend."

"James," Liza implored tearfully. She saw as well as I could that Daisy's eyes were watering from the likely excruciating pull James had on her hair. "Please, let go of her."

"Shut up, Liza." James gave Daisy a wrench and she whimpered. To see her jerked around filled me with such panic and rage, it was as though my pupils swallowed my irises as the entire kitchen seemed to shrink into a tunnel in the breadth of an instant—still, I could not move. "You have no idea the kind of turmoil you would be drowning in had I not put an end to it, nor the faintest clue of how many times I have put myself between you and strife you could not fathom. If I were the failure of a Master you think I am, so help me, I would take leave of my duty, drag you back to the library, and throw you out of that damn window!" He relinquished his hold on Daisy roughly, sending her to the floor in a heap. Liza and I took to the floor at Daisy's side, though she seemed to be lost somewhere in her mind and her eyes stared ahead blankly as though the kitchen were empty.

"Suicide inspires a wide range of reactions in even the most level-headed individuals," James said stiffly. "In light of the personal tragedy you have just suffered, I will overlook the very ugly manner in which you forgot yourself, Daisy, but just this once. If you ever speak to me that way again, I promise you, the consequences will be even uglier."

If Daisy had heard James, she made no sign of it. Thankfully, James did not ask for one.

"I have Graham's affairs to see to," he said, looking to Liza. "I'll see you back to my rooms before I attend to them."

Liza shook her head. "I'm staying here."

I expected James to haul Liza to her feet and make good on the threat he made to Daisy at least in part, to drag Liza out of here by her hair, but instead he just sighed and glared sternly. "Fine. For the day. But I'm locking the door when I leave, and I will return for you after supper."

The four of us listened for the sound of the front door shut, and for the bolt to lock into place, before so much as blinking.

"Are you all right, Daisy?" Liza was the first to ask. She peered into Daisy's eyes to search for unspoken permission before reaching to check the back of her head. Daisy flinched when Liza touched the spot where James had nearly ripped the hair out by the roots and Liza withdrew her careful inspection at once.

"That was something, sweetheart," Armand said, sitting on the floor like the rest of us but across the kitchen. I looked to him and saw tears streaming down his cheeks. He was pale, sweating, and trembling. It must have killed him to sit by and watch, as I had, knowing that any attempt to get between James and Daisy would have made things much worse.

"He could have snapped my neck." Daisy's voice was lofty, like she was dreaming. "I knew he was strong, he's hit me before, but he could have—in that instant, I swear—"

"Daisy," I hushed her. She was rambling and in shock. I needed to get her into bed or indeed anywhere that was not this forsaken kitchen. A laugh bubbled up in Daisy's throat and she sat giggling in a haze between me and Liza, who were perched at her side like nervous parents.

"Did I really say he was a failure, to his face?" Daisy kept laughing.

"You made me proud." Armand was still weeping but he heaved a chuckle, apparently infected by the hysteria that had spellbound Daisy.

"Would he really throw me out the window?" Daisy wondered.

"No." Liza dropped a kiss on the top of Daisy's head. "Of course not. Come on now, Kit and I will take you out of here." I helped Liza lift Daisy to her feet and took her to her room. Putting her to bed was easy, for Daisy was suffering some kind of nervous episode that was rapidly draining her of energy and even the capacity to speak. She was muttering about—well, I didn't even know what, when she started to tremble and nod off. I started to back out of the room after making sure Daisy was tucked in but Liza stopped me.

"Stay with her," she whispered.

"She should rest," I worried.

"Kit. She needs you." I took Liza's word, as she was probably the only one among us who knew for a fact how difficult it was to sleep alone in the wake of a trauma. Unafraid of Liza bearing witness to the breach of proximity I was committing, I climbed over Daisy's covers and settled beside her on the bed, holding her close against my front. Sure enough, as soon as I hugged her, I could feel tension melt from Daisy's frame and she slowly drifted off.

A tear trickled sideways from the bridge of my nose as I laid beside Daisy. I did not know if she had frightened herself into this state by drawing upon a boldness even Liza had never exposed to us and challenging James' authority to his face, or if James had scared her silly. And I thought of Graham through-out, wondering in anguish how truly desolate he must have felt in order to turn to such violent means…

Sometime later, I realized I must have fallen asleep. It made sense, as my nerves were shot. Daisy was still snoozing in my arms and the window over her bed told me that it was still daylight. Carefully, I slipped off the bed and padded out of her room in search of Liza and Armand. I found them in the study, sitting on the sofa together; they sat shoulder to shoulder with Liza's leg draped over Armand's knee, their heads resting against each other's. I did not disturb the utter silence when I joined them on the couch, lowering myself lightly at Liza's other side. She reached over and held my hand.

"I had no idea." Liza was talking about me and Daisy. I put my arm around Liza and ended up clasping Armand's other shoulder.

"It wouldn't have happened if it weren't for you." My words sounded accusatory by accident so I quickly amended my sentiment, "I was spiraling after you jumped and then everything with Quinn.... She could see I was losing myself, and she kissed me to bring me back down to earth."

"I'm glad she did," said Liza. "I'd never forgive myself if you lost yourself because of me."

"I wouldn't have, Liza. I couldn't leave her." A lump rose in my throat and I held on to Liza's hand for bravery. "I love her."

"You always have." Armand's addition was surprisingly soft. "As I have, too. She is our heart."

The three of us cried quietly together for a while, reflecting on the overwhelming protectiveness and care we shared for Daisy, the youngest of us, who had proven today that she was the most delicate but somehow undoubtedly the bravest of us all.

We began to talk of Graham even though it pained us. We remembered his patience when we were too rowdy or argumentative during lessons, his passion for history, his pride when he watched Daisy dance or heard me play piano, and his unwaveringly kind brand of pragmatism. We wondered about his other students and if they would come to the compound to pay last respects to him, or if he would be sent home. These musings came with a heavy sadness, for we realized how little we actually knew about Graham—where was his home? Would he be laid to rest near his wife? Would such a custom be something Graham, whom we guessed was not religious, have even desired?

Worst of all, I wrestled with something else as we talked in low voices about our departed tutor, the matter of the last time I had seen him alive.

"He was quiet when I saw him at Dulce's party," I said. "He introduced me to Mistress Magdalene and left suddenly to find James. But he said...." I hesitated, not wanting to put Armand on the spot when he was so vulnerable. Liza and Armand were waiting for me to say something. My stamina was already forfeit, so I told them what Graham said, a warning about not being alone with Donovan.

"I wonder why he would have said such a thing," Armand wondered thinly. I did not have the heart to dive into the troubling things he said to me last night, when he was quite drunk in his bedroom.

"I don't know about Donovan, or why Graham would have said something so ominous without explanation, but I do know Dulce is not one to be trusted." Darkness passed over Liza's features as she went into sullen detail about catching Mistress Selenis praising Dulce for "buttering up" the four of us. My jaw dropped when Liza said she raised a hand to the Mistress. Armand clicked his tongue once the tale was over and shook his head.

"Well, if she isn't a conniving little witch after all," he mused.

"I'm not surprised," I confessed with a sigh. "Though I am disappointed."

"Any girl that beautiful would be foolish not to use her charms to her advantage," said Daisy, appearing in the study threshold. It was unlike her to be cynical, but in light of all that had happened today I supposed it was fitting. Her hair was mussed from sleeping but she did not look rested in the slightest.

"Then I guess that makes you a fool, sweetheart," Armand teased her, cracking a guilty grin. Daisy chimed a tired laugh and raised her hands only to let them fall dejectedly onto her thighs.

"I don't pretend to be anything other than what I am, Armie," Daisy said.

"You should have told me you were in love," Armand retorted in a much more serious voice. I glimpsed Daisy make a barely discernible flick of her gaze toward Liza before batting her lashes at Armand once more.

"I could say the same to you," Daisy said. Apparently, Armand did not have a waiting quip in response to that. Daisy accepted the stalemate and curled up next to me on the sofa, dragging a quilt over her lap. She kissed my cheek and seemed to be very happy that she could do so in front of Liza and Armand.

"I've been thinking…," said Liza. She stood from the couch and went to the middle of the room, facing us as she laced her fingers together and held them in front of her. "You see, all I have time to do these days is think. Sometimes I think about how much I miss the three of you and it hurts worse than anything. Now that poor Graham has—well, I can't help but think of something I said to James, a few weeks ago." She took a deep breath before continuing.

"In the heat of one of our near-brawls—"

"*One* of them?" Armand was disturbed. "How many near-brawls were there?"

Liza ignored him. "I told James I'd strangle myself with a cord if I had use of both my hands." Liza's admission confirmed my worst fear and Daisy felt me tense. True to the brave streak she had ever since she was a child, Liza went on. "It frightened him to hear it—it sounds implausible, that he would ever be afraid of anything, but I've seen fragments of what his life is like in the Masters' rooms. You must believe me when I tell you that what I said to him in anger and pain truly did shake him. It inspired him to tell me something— something I promised him I would not repeat to anyone, but I cannot keep this to myself any longer."

Daisy, Armand, and I were hanging on her every word. A new light of energy had been kindled in us at the prospect of Liza sharing something confidential she had discovered in the Master wing, that finally our weeks of waiting and sneaking around might amount to something. The roof of my mouth turned to cotton when Liza slowly sat down on the floor of the study, folding her legs under her, and steady herself with a sighing, whooshing breath.

"Far away from the Aventine Compound lies a village formerly known as Kingsfield Township," she said. "It's where our parents preside as leading members of the Free Factions. Nineteen years ago, while our parents were treating peace with the Masters, we were stolen in the night as hostages so that our parents would bend to the Master System."

"Stolen?" Daisy whimpered. "James said our parents *sent* us here!"

"No," Liza replied gently. "They did not. In fact, the arrangement is so hated, it causes friction between the Masters and the Free Factions even now." Liza told us the story Donovan had shared with her the night before, about how Liza's mother savagely attacked Mistress Selenis years ago for just mentioning her daughter's name.

I felt a hunger unlike anything I'd experienced before as I watched Liza patiently wait for I'm sure what she expected would be an interminable barrage of questions.

"Tell us everything you know." Armand sat forward and rested his elbows on his knees. "We were stolen? By whom?"

Liza's expression darkened. "Haitham the Master."

Chapter Twenty

Armand

My head was spinning by the time Liza had concluded her tale. More than once, she had to stop to keep herself from getting too emotional to speak. Welcome was the news that she and Kit were relatives by blood—I'd always suspected as such, since they looked so alike as children. What shocked me the most was imagining Kit's father Marshall committing such a gruesome act, a murder for revenge. How could such a man produce a boy like Kit, who had never harmed so much as an insect? Maybe a man whose only son, a gentle lamb of a child like Kit, had been stolen from him in his infancy was enough to infuriate Marshall into divorcing himself from his humanity. I could remember a man with sunny hair and blue eyes with a strong jaw—maybe I had called him "uncle" as a toddler? I did not like to think on it, especially since recalling the faces of family only brought forth my own mother and father, the sound of their voices....

Liza had made it clear that all Masters knew of this story. It made me wonder how Donovan could ever have embraced Kit, knowing his father had murdered Petra the Mistress, his mother. I did not know how I would ever address it with Donovan either, without at the very least giving away that I knew the truth at last.

Kit was plainly broken to hear what his father had done. Daisy had fallen silent when Liza said Lorena had agreed to the terms on the spot and that the thousands of people that made up the Free Factions had vowed to obey the Master System in order to protect children they had never even met. Truthfully, the very sentimental fact had moved me to tears, too. An old sense of belonging seeped into my heart to hear about Lorena's fierce protectiveness and the other members heeling to James and the others just to spare us harm.

A radiant idea occurred to me. "The son of a bitch didn't keep what Quinn did to you a secret because of the other Masters!" I exclaimed, my cheeks hot. "He knew if your mother heard about an attack, their agreement would be nullified!"

"How do they keep track of us?" Kit wondered. "They must at least receive proof that we're alive at certain intervals—there's no way they would take James at his word that we were safe."

"That I do not know," Liza said. "I didn't think to ask James."

"If we could get word to them, that would be the end of this." My mind was racing as I thought of how many tradesmen flitted in and out of this place, how easy it would be to plant a message in a crate of goods bound for Kingsfield or whatever the hell our parents called the place now. I could even persuade Donovan to send a messenger there, or at least try.

"It's not so simple," said Liza. "The accords protect everyone who lives here, and countless other villages who rely on the Aventine for food and protection."

"Forgive me, Liza, but I cannot find any sympathy for people who freely agree to accept help from a kidnapper's violent dictator of a son," I snapped with a scowl.

"You sound like James when you talk like that," Liza said, glaring at me. I immediately softened my gaze—I was far from embracing her in the open, like Kit did Daisy, but I was not about to spoil Liza's homecoming with picking a fight.

"But, Liza," Kit chimed in, "think of all the people who have gone along with this from the beginning to protect us. Don't those people deserve to be free of the leverage Haitham and James hold over them?"

"I believe that a reprieve is in called for," Liza agreed. "But we are still saddled in the same trap we have been ever since we were carried through the main gate as infants—we cannot leave. Dulce is not trustworthy and the only member of James' staff who ever defended us is dead." Ringing silence followed her words. She was right on all counts, though she didn't know about the card I had up my sleeve.

"Can we not manipulate Dulce right back?" Daisy asked. "She is a pawn of her mother's but at least we know where we stand with her."

"I'm afraid my temper may have permanently erased that option, moving forward," Liza said, turning sheepish.

The three of them weighed other options for a while, though Kit was offering considerably less than the girls. I struggled to find the right opportunity to jump in and take Liza's lead, to courageously confess my own working designs of getting us away from James, but the longer I waited, the less likely it seemed to go over well.

And my head was pounding.

"There's also the matter of the dead guardsmen," Kit pointed out, pulling me back into the conversation at hand.

"Graham said they were scouts," Daisy errantly corrected him.

"Fine," Kit conceded with a wave. "He said they were murdered, though the guards aren't sure if it was a dispute or something else."

"What else could it be?" Daisy asked. I was too tired to roll my eyes, for though I loved the girl especially today, her naiveté could be staggering at times.

"James has been twitchy about security and not just because of the summit. You saw with your own eyes, Daze, that he barred Graham from leaving the compound. Suppose there are meant to be scheduled exchanges between James and our parents, updates or photographs of us that prove our wellbeing. When Liza tried to escape, James would not have been able to prove she was not only safe but alive for almost a week. What if our parents sent Free Faction scouts to look for us?" My words fell heavily on the others' ears. A clash of awe and horror seemed to hang over each of them.

"Do you think the scouts they found were sent by the Free Factions?" Kit asked, turning to me.

"Maybe?" I shrugged. "Liza, James told you that they trained volpines to guard the Kingsfield compound. You encountered some when you escaped—"

Daisy interjected with a gasp, "Do you think the reason they didn't attack you was because they had been trained by our parents? That they might have recognized you as a person who wasn't a threat to them?"

"That's highly unlikely," Kit argued, channeling some of Graham's pragmatism. "They're enough like foxes to bear the intelligence they would need to differentiate between humans, but too much like wolves to not defend their kill. Liza said she barreled into one just after they'd brought something down—"

"My mother." Liza's mutter was barely audible. I saw tears spring to her eyes as a revelation dawned on her. "I look just like my mother. If those beasts were truly from the compound, they might have seen me and thought I was her."

"Liza," Kit reasoned gently, "creatures like volpines favor scent recognition over the visual. Even if you look similar to your mother...."

"That old, drunk Master at Dulce's party thought I *was* her," Liza retorted. "He was stunned. He addressed me by her name even."

"I don't know it matters now," said Kit. "I heard Haitham himself say that he had all the volpines in the area rounded up and slaughtered. He brought James a skin to prove it." That deflated the traction of our imaginations just enough to call another weighted silence to the study. I decided to take up his role as the positive instigator, since Kit had apparently taken up mine as the naysayer.

"You might be right, Liza," I said. "Think about it—our parents could have been searching for us for years. After all, what mother or father would sit idly by while their child was raised by his abductors? We know that they trained volpines to guard their compound, but what if they sent them as preliminary scouts? Time goes by, they eliminate areas on a map where James could be living with us but still, there is too much ground to cover while maintaining the secrecy needed to track us down without arousing the Masters' suspicion. Imagine, then, that you are Liza's mother and suddenly there is no word on your daughter, about whom you were promised regular updates: days pass and when you try to reach James the Master, you are greeted only with radio silence, then days turn to weeks and the pack of creatures you sent to find your children do not return—the scouts who likely accompanied them have not sent word."

I let the supposition sink in for a moment before adding the finishing, life-altering idea. "While you three have been plotting an escape all this time, our parents have probably been trying to free us. If that's the truth...Liza, you may have come closer to escaping than you thought."

The concept stunned Liza. "I might have been found by a Free Faction scout, had I stayed in that cave a day longer."

"Or you could have succumbed to the cold." As much as I liked trying on Kit's hat and inspiring the girls with altruistic and almost lofty imagery, I couldn't seem to let go of my cynicism. "Liza," I urged, "whatever happened, you are alive now and home with us. If there is a sliver of truth to what we've discussed here today, then all we have to do is exactly what I have been saying from the start—follow the rules, keep our heads down, and don't give James any reason to fly off the handle like he did today."

"Given everything that has happened with Dulce, and now poor Graham...." Daisy shuddered. "It seems like we can do nothing else but trust in our parents to find us." Her smile was nervous. I think she found saying "our parents" aloud and in such an active tense was odd to her.

"James will let me come home soon, for good." Liza was insistent on this. "I know this morning was brutal but the fact that he let me stay today is promising. When the summit is over, life will go back to normal for us."

Now was the time to tell them that Donovan had agreed to at least try to make arrangements for us to make an escape by the end of the summit. All our hopes to leave the Aventine were finally synchronized and riding on a timeline much shorter than any of us could have planned for—if I needed them to be ready to go at a moment's notice, they would need the few days remaining of the summit to prepare.

"Now, when the summit is over...," I said, swallowing my nerves and facing the three people I now trusted more than anyone in my life. "I want you to know—" I shut my mouth as soon as I heard the apartment front door slide open. Daisy and Kit, who had been huddled together for hours now, shot two feet apart and then not a second later, James was standing in the doorway and looking expectantly to Liza.

"Let's go." He spared no greeting for us. He waved at Liza impatiently, beckoning her to her feet. She obliged him but only to come to each of us for a farewell hug. I got up to hold her in my arms, gritting my teeth against the threat of a migraine that throbbed in my head.

"Be good," I whispered.

"Get some sleep," she murmured. I refused to be the first to let go.

"Liza. Now." James hated to see us take advantage of the small margin of physical contact we were allowed, so naturally I had to linger as long as I could with Liza. I smoothed my hand down her braid to the small of her back as she slipped away from me and I looked up in time to catch James glaring furiously at me. We said our goodbyes and watched Liza leave the wing but then I turned my head and the room rolled. I dropped back onto the couch without warning, startling Daisy and Kit, who seemed to think I was going to faint.

"I'm all right," I said. "We should have asked *him* if we might go into the market, as we're out of groceries and I need to eat something before my skull splits down the middle…." From the epic hangover I experienced this morning to the tragic news of Graham, and the terribly stressful grappling between James and Daisy to the story of our kidnapping, every ounce of my energy was spent. I knew I must have looked horrible, otherwise Daisy wouldn't be making such a fuss.

"I didn't hear him lock the door," Kit said, going to the front hall to check the door. He poked his head in a moment later with some good news, finally. "It's open. What do you need?"

"I can't stand to cook anything," I said. "Something hot, and a lot of it." Kit dug around the laundry sacks kept in the front closet near the door until he found a pair of thick socks to pull on. "For goodness' sake, Daze, do I look that poorly? Kit looked like he was going to call a doctor just now."

Daisy frowned at me. Apparently, I was too tired to effectively make a joke. "I'll get you some water," she said. I watched her walk away, noticing the graceful sway of her hips and floaty swing of her arms in a new light. Now that I knew she and Kit had bundled together, I couldn't help but see her as a woman and not solely the girl I'd grown up with and thought of as my little sister. I wanted to tease her but when I thought about it, nothing about it was funny.

"It makes sense now," I said loud enough for my voice to carry through to the kitchen. "Why Kit made a deal with James, to keep Haitham away from us."

"I don't like to think about that horrible old man." Daisy returned with a glass of cool water and pressed it carefully into my hands. "Besides, Kit didn't know Haitham was responsible for our being here when he made an agreement with James."

"That's our Kit," I said, a little breathless after gulping down the water. "Always looking ahead." I knew I was right to trust Kit when he returned moments later with a whole roasted chicken, a pile of potatoes, and a jug of opaque liquid.

"That was a quick trip," I remarked.

"You need to eat." I smirked because Kit rarely worried over me. It was all too endearing to see him rush into the kitchen with dinner for me. I heard the clatter of plates and cutlery, a few choice mutterings from Kit, and glasses clink together on the table before the slosh of fluid leaving a bottle. Kit bustled into the study with two tall glasses of the misty liquid in his hands. He gave one to me and set the other on the end table next to Daisy.

"Drink up," he said. I took a sip of the drink and almost gagged.

"What the hell is that?" I sputtered, trying to pass the glass back to him. "It's rancid!"

"The tradesman who gave it to me said it would be good for you," said Kit. "It's mostly coconut water, but it's got lots of other vitamins in it—"

"It's awful," I insisted. Kit wouldn't take it back. Instead, he folded his arms across his chest and stared sternly down at me.

"Pinch your nose if you have to," he said. "Armie, you look terrible. Drink all of it now so you can eat, otherwise I'll call for Jada and I really don't think—"

"Oh, all right, Master Kit." I downed the contents of the glass, as I was still a grown man, without complaint. I ate too—a lot. Kit and Daisy witnessed me ripping into the roasted chicken and shoveling potatoes into my mouth with a sort of disturbed curiosity and I half expected Kit to make another jab at me and my occasional likeness to a volpine. When they were satisfied with how much I'd eaten, they helped themselves to dinner. We sat in silence for a long time, each of us contemplating how absurd it seemed that our lives had just been changed forever. Kit decided it was time to turn in and I eyed the two of them with teasing scorn.

"I suppose you two are going to share a room from now on?" Daisy shrugged and her cheeks turned pink. She was pretending she hadn't heard me so that she wouldn't have to answer.

"Could you blame us, after the day we've had?" Kit asked me, lending his tone an air of defensive flippancy.

"I couldn't." I met his gaze and smiled to show I meant no harm. "It's just...I don't know, a little strange to think of you two sleeping together." Daisy got to her feet as she held our stacked dinner plates and took them to the kitchen much quicker than she probably would have if the subject matter had been something else.

"We have been through hell today, Armand. I don't think either of us could sleep if we didn't have the comfort of another body close by—"

"Relax, Kit," I assured him. "I said sleeping together, not…oh, how did Doctor Christian put it when he spelled everything out for us? 'Entwine yourselves in the physical bliss of one another'?"

"We haven't." Daisy was in the doorway, her arms folded and her eyes narrowed. "And we won't. I don't want to, not under James' roof."

"I'm sorry, Daze." Her frankness made me feel guilty to have teased them. Where did a scoundrel like me find the conceit to cast judgment on them for lying together, in whatever capacity they have been? "Get some rest, both of you. I'll turn in myself. I just need to sit and think for a while."

"Should I leave the light on?" Kit asked, pausing by the switch near the hallway as he followed Daisy to her room. I shook my head. My headache was mostly gone but I wanted a few moments in the dark to myself. "If you want to sit with us…." Kit's features were suddenly very sad. "It could be like old times. What do you say?"

"Kit, don't be silly. Go to bed. Make sure Daisy gets some sleep." If there was one place in this entire compound where I would feel the most invasive, it would be cozied up between Kit and Daisy.

"Try not to stay up all night," said Kit after he turned the light off. "Your pallor has improved after having some food but you still look like you've been chewed up and spit out."

I waited for his soft footfalls to retreat down the hall before replying softly, "Thank you for getting me used to the feeling of having parents to fuss over me, Kit." I smiled in the darkness, then carefully got to my feet. I felt unbelievably steadier standing up and scowled when I thought of the utterly disgusting stuff Kit had made me drink earlier, knowing it was probably to thank for my renewed vigor. I could see the lights from the market shining dimly through the clouded plexiglass window of the front door as I was certain the trade floor was still very much open for business.

I made sure Daisy's bedroom door was shut before shadowing past her room to close mine. In case they emerged before I returned, they would think I was in bed. I slipped out of the front door and out into the main hall, careful to keep my pace and posture casual. I wanted to find Donovan because I had no intention of being the only one in Tribute wing to sleep alone tonight.

I found Dulce before I did my lover. I debated not stopping to save the poor tradesman she was hanging off of but it occurred to me that the best way to attract Donovan's attention might be to linger near a little Mistress for a while. And admittedly, part of me wanted to engage Dulce and get a few jabs in as recompense for manipulating us at her mother's behest.

"Mister Kittaka?" I said earnestly, catching the eye of the silken good salesmen. By the looks of his goods, Dulce was probably trying to sweet talk her way into a free bolt of the stuff which she would no doubt fashion into some kind of revealing garment.

"Hello, young man," the tradesman greeted me, relieved enough to flash a generous smile. "As you can see I am currently helping a customer, but if you would be kind enough to wait—"

"That won't be necessary." Dulce turned to me and I saw heat flare under her cheeks as something more robust than sheer happiness to see me glazed over her eyes. I offered her my arm. "Walk with me, won't you?"

"Armand, this is a very nice surprise!" Dulce took mercy on Kittaka and looped her arm through mine. "Such a gentleman. How nice of Master James to teach you such fine manners." She smelled deliciously of fresh bread and sugar.

I chuckled as I imagined how fast the smile would slip off her face had she seen "fine-mannered" James in action this morning. Kittaka folded his hands in praising thanks to me as I led Dulce away from his stand and I nodded to him in return.

"By the looks of you, I can tell you had fun last night," said Dulce as she pursed her lips.

"Really?" I shrugged. "Kit told me I look like hell." The darkness of Graham's death still hung over me and thinking of him made my stomach flop, so I shoved it as far out of my mind as I could.

"You are a rose on parade compared to some of the Masters," Dulce whispered, giggling. "We brought that tequila from home. It's famous for turning parties into ragers—"

"It's a pity Liza couldn't stay," I interrupted coolly. I swelled with pride to see Dulce go grey but I was not surprised when she recovered without missing a beat.

"I was told she wasn't feeling well." She gave what I suspected to be a purposeful sway of her hips as she walked so that she brushed against my side. "And you must consider, your Master James is so strict about his rules."

"He's the devil," I agreed dryly. Dulce burst out laughing as we rounded the corner into the busiest sector of the market. Scents of cooking food laced the air along with the unmistakable aroma of Dulce's perfume. "Between the two of us," I said to Dulce, pitching my voice so that it would not carry beyond our conspiracy, "I know you caught a glimpse of Liza's temper last night. She told me about it."

Dulce gave every sign that she was not used to being called out for her manipulations. She stopped walking suddenly and stammered, "Armand, I—I didn't...." I had to hang on to her to keep her arm from slipping out of mine.

"*No hay necesidad de tener miedo,*" I coaxed in Spanish. "*No voy a morder, cariño.*" A visible shiver possessed Dulce for a beat. She gaped up at me with intrigued surprise and I couldn't help but grin to see her speechless for once. It took her a moment to collect herself, to realize that she had stopped short in the middle of a busy market to moon up at me.

"Is James the devil, or are you?" she asked. "Anyway, I'm not half as worried about your bite as I was about Liza's bark." She relaxed and allowed me to continue to escort her down the hall, though we kept a slow pace.

"I know what you mean," I said. "She and I grew up together. I've seen her angry—she doesn't like being lied to, is all."

"She made that abundantly clear." Dulce swallowed hard. She stole a sheepish glance up at me and heaved a sorry sigh. "You don't understand what it's like," she went on. "I have no choice but to be complicit with my mother, no matter how much I like the four of you. When she asks someone to do something, it's not so much a question as *un edicto*. No one says no to Selenis—not if she knows what's good for her, not even her own daughter."

"I have spent nineteen years within the walls of this place with James as my keeper, and you don't think I understand what it feels like to have no choice of my own?" I shook my head.

"We have more in common than I thought," Dulce pointed out. "Our lives are the same, just in different places." I was the one who stopped walking then. I even dropped Dulce's arm.

"*Escúchame bien*, Dulce," I said to the selfish girl in front of me. "Our lives are *not* the same. I understand why you lied to us and did your mother's bidding without question—but where you are limited by a sense of familial obligation, I am oppressed by the laws of the Masters. You might say no to your mother and face a couple of harsh words, maybe suffer some embarrassment or be sent to bed without supper; when I say no to James, I am *beaten*. Daisy did not guard her words around him this very morning and had he been inclined, he could have broken her neck. And let me remind you, you are free to leave this compound and any other at will and when you decide you want to go home, you will join your parents there and they will welcome you happily, whereas I would be forcibly detained if I even strayed too close to the main doors—and have not seen my parents since I was three years old. To you, liberty is a burden! And you don't even care that the people you tricked into befriending you would give *anything* to have that freedom!"

My breath was spent. Despite my fervor, I had not spoken any louder than I needed to for Dulce to hear me but my throat was raw as though I had shouted. I had wielded my words as weapons and cut the fanciful tapestry of Dulce's reality to shreds. I could see it in her eyes that were glassy with tears that she was wounded by all I had told her and as I stood over her, shaking with something that felt like hysteria but much, much angrier, I feared that, had I blue eyes, I might be mistaken for James.

A hand touched my back. "Enough." Donovan's careful directive was magnetic. I could not step away from him nor summon anything else to say to his cousin. I felt Donovan's fingers wrap around my upper arm. "Let's go. You can't be here."

I glared at Dulce. "*¿Ver? Siempre siguiendo ordenes.*" Dulce clapped her hand over her trembling lips to stifle a sob and hastily looked away. She was plainly afraid of me, or more likely afraid of the truth I had just laid at her feet.

"Now." I let Donovan lead me away through the crowd, all of them averting their eyes as though they weren't dying to see the drama unfold for themselves: James' Tribute arguing with Mistress Selenis' daughter? And in public? It was a scandal and would make for sensational gossip.

When the din of the main hall died down and the rushing bodies were no longer swarming in every direction, I realized Donovan had taken me into the medical wing. It was deserted at this time of night, as Jada and her worker bees were through with their practice hours and were likely dining with the summit crowd. Donovan turned me around once we were sufficiently secluded and cupped my face in his hands.

"What did you say to that poor little girl, huh?" He frowned when I unraveled before his eyes. "She was scared stiff of you, lover." I couldn't help it, I cried like a little boy.

"I told her what she didn't want to hear, that she doesn't really care," I wept. "It's a joke to her, to everyone! They just come and go! And no one sees the suffering because no one wants to!"

"Armand...." Donovan pulled me into his arms, squeezing me tightly to still the sobs that shook my body.

"Graham is dead." I clutched at Donovan as if he were a stopper to the sinkhole of grief collapsing in my chest. I closed my eyes and on the backs of my eyelids, I could only envision my tutor's final moments and imagine the all-encompassing desperation he must have felt to escape this place.

"I know. I'm so sorry." Donovan's voice hitched, as though he felt an acute heartache that matched mine. He held me still for a while longer, until my sobbing ebbed. When he sweetly cradled my face once more in his hands and peered into my eyes, I saw that his were also glistening with sadness.

"Take me away from here," I begged him. I took hold of his shirt and leaned into his front. "Please, Donovan. I'm going to die here. I don't want to die here—"

"Don't say that." Donovan hushed me with a lingering kiss. Just when I tilted my head back, inviting him to deepen our embrace, Donovan pulled away fast and took my hand. He pulled me out of the quiet ward of empty cots and through a door that was deliberately made to look like part of the wall. I knew these passages existed from exploring the main halls as a child. Graham used to call them "squirrel stashes" because the servants would duck into these secret passes to share rich goods they'd sneaked out of the Master kitchens or markets (or for lovers' trysts) but I never could map out the exact locations of them all—or where the narrow halls let out. Still, I would have followed Donovan anywhere, especially in my current state.

"In here." Donovan felt along the barely lit hallway and opened another door, through which I could see the amber glow of candlelight. These must be the emergency passages, in case the Master of the Aventine were to find himself host to unwelcome guests and wanted to hide away, out of danger. I was grateful in the moment for James' paranoia and militant preparedness, for where else would Donovan have found such a hasty nook in which to hide me?

All thoughts of James and danger vanished as soon as Donovan took me in his arms again. His hands pulled me close, for comfort and assurance, as his lips found mine. His attention quenched my desire of intimacy and escape. For the first time, his shirt was off before mine. I barely had the chance to lift my arms before Donovan pulled me loose of my shirt and for a few precious, not totally silent moments, warm skin-on-skin contact was the only balm to soothe me.

"It breaks my heart to see you like this," whispered Donovan. "Ask me for anything, anything to make you happy again, and I'll do it. Just don't cry." He fluidly went to his knees, catching the waist of my trousers so that he lowered them to the floor. His lips were on me again as he planted a crescent moon of kisses underneath my navel.

"I just want to be free," I confessed. He rose up to meet my gaze again, his lips touching mine delicately as though he were suddenly afraid that he would break me.

"I've taken care of everything," he said, the wisp of a smile visible in the dim candlelight. "No more worrying about that, lover." He kissed me, tasting me without hurry. "Now, again, ask me for anything, Armand. Let me turn this terrible day around for you."

I was out of my head with exhaustion, grief, and desire for him. It was the ghost of the anger when I had spoken to Dulce that answered for me now, in Spanish, knowing Donovan would understand me.

"*Voltéate.*"

Chapter Twenty-one

Every pretense that James was nothing to me but my Master dissolved the moment we were alone together. I turned on him the second the door to his bedroom shut behind us, furious and immediately in tears.

"I ought to slap you for what you did to Daisy!"

"I have had a very long day, Liza," said James. "But do not think I am not fit to go a few rounds with you."

I had no choice but to refute that claim and got in one good thwack on his chest before James caught my arm in his grip. I hit him again with my other hand, hard, and I might have really hurt him but James did not show it. He let out an annoyed huff and shoved me away from him.

"You bastard!" He'd almost pushed me off my feet!

"Back off, Liza." James relied on my many years of watching him lose his temper, only revealing through his thin pressed lips and tensed shoulders that he was not in a joking mood. Well, I wasn't having it—I felt hot all over and seeing how patiently he expected me to obey him only made me angrier. I unfurled the fist I held at my side and moved toward him, only for James to retreat four steps away from me.

"I mean it—don't come close to me if you're going to hit me. I don't have the stomach for an outburst right now and if you take your claws out with me, damn it, I'll treat you like an animal."

"You're the animal," I snarled. "You are twice Daisy's size and ten times stronger than she is! You almost ripped her hair out! She was afraid you were going to break her neck—and so was I!"

"You know, Liza," James remarked in an cutting wistfulness, "I had half a mind to do just that. You heard what she said to me. If you were me, would you have let that disgusting behavior go unchecked?"

"I wouldn't have jerked her around like a doll just to prove I could! We just lost our teacher; he was important to us. Especially to Daisy." I gritted my teeth and stifled my argument, knowing James would only overpower me with relish the more I fought him. We locked eyes and I found pain in his—Daisy's words had really gotten to him. "I didn't think you would listen to Daisy, of all people."

"Why wouldn't I?" James said quietly. "How couldn't I? I listen to every criticism doled out, whether or not I asked for it. Just because I don't act on what you think I ought to doesn't mean I don't take it to heart." James waited a full two minutes before he spoke again and I realized he had been holding the tension in the room with a puppeteer's expertise. I raked my hands through my hair, releasing the nervous energy still buzzing through my fingertips.

"You of all people should know what it feels like," James said. He was pacing near his desk, not looking at me at all. "You lose your temper easier than I do mine. Daisy provoked me. I had every right to address the hateful things she said as I saw fit."

"Maybe. I don't want to think about what you would have done if I hadn't been there to call you off." Like a wary predator might look after a creature of her ilk, I studied James' every movement with precision, gauging his posture and breathing to determine whether or not I was in danger of the very lapse in temper control he spoke of. James sensed my caution and slowed his pacing to a deliberate halt, to show me that he was cooled off. I was inclined to test him, to perhaps confess that I had told the others the truth about how we came to Aventine, but even I was too tired to imagine how I might have to untangle myself from a poor reaction on James' part.

"Thank you," I said instead, "for letting me stay with them today."

James snorted a caustic laugh. "What was I to do?" he wondered aloud. "Lock you in this room like a spoil of war, or keep you at my side while I carried Graham's body out of his room?"

I blanched. "You did *what?*"

"I did my job, Liza." James pinched the bridge of his nose, signaling his worn down patience and impending headache. "Heavens help me, Daisy is right about my guardsmen. They are brawlers and keen to follow orders, but they are not suitable in matters like undertaking a man like Graham Keating."

Carefully, I chided him. "Jada would have seen to it, had you asked her."

"Jada did not hire him, I did. He is my responsibility, just like every other staff member who works under my roof." James dropped into his desk chair and rubbed his chin, lost in apparent guilty anguish. I thought about how he carried me, bleeding and hysterical, out of the studio after I'd been attacked. He could have waited for the doctors to arrive and move me but he had, I supposed, refused. Once again, I wrestled with what I knew of James, his monstrous proclivity to enraged violence, and the man who sat before me who may have been as close to tears as I was.

Could I go to a man and comfort him after he had been so terrible to Daisy today? Furthermore, I had to wonder, had I been protecting James by telling the others it had been Haitham who had abducted us? Or had I been selfishly protecting myself? I knew it was wrong to spare James when it came to telling Daisy, Kit, and Armand the truth, but when the time had come to honestly answer Armand's question, who had stolen us as young children, I simply could not sell James out to them.

"Tell me what's going on, James," I said. "You hit the wall so hard it cracked yesterday, you flew off the handle with Daisy this morning...." I shrugged in innocence when James turned his glower on me. "I have shared everything with you. You said it yourself: I showed unprecedented determination to get you to share yourself with me. Why would I stop now, when you're clearly in pain?" James mulled over his conflict some more and I felt the irritating heat of frustration build up in me as I considered how hypocritically he was behaving. We'd explored each other's bodies with desperation and lust more than once in just the span of one day and yet he still had to fight himself to be honest with me.

"I wouldn't know where to start, Liza." James was weary but I wasn't going to let him cite exhaustion to get out of this.

"How about you tell me more about the unfathomable turmoil you hung over Daisy's head this morning," I prompted him. "You stand between us and something terrible. What is it?"

James was quiet for a while. He dropped his hand from propping up his chin so that he could absently strum the edge of a stack of papers with the side of his thumb. "The summit," he said. "I am very much alone among my peers when it comes to the question of what is to be done about the four of you… maybe not isolated, if I'm going to be perfectly honest, but grossly outnumbered. If you really think about it," James said softly, "you might realize what the problem is without me having to spell it out."

I sat on the edge of the bed, choking on the fear of what he might say next. I held my breath without meaning to. "For the sake of time, James, please just tell me." I suddenly felt and sounded very small.

"It will be twenty years in the spring, Liza," replied James, sounding even smaller. "You four have been raised apart from your parents for so long…the Factions decided recently that it no longer makes sense to keep up their end of an agreement that was made without their consent. Even ten years ago, it was difficult to keep relations between Masters and the Free Factions from boiling over. It's become harder and harder for your parents to convince their constituents that they must stay subservient to us in order to spare the lives of estranged children who are being, in the eyes of the Factions, pampered by their enemies."

I gulped. "They've forfeited the conditions?"

"Of course not," James said. "Your parents have made it clear that they will go to war with the Masters before the promised safety of their children is put aside. But you and I both know how laughable my attempt to keep up my end of that bargain has been." James sighed and flattened his hand on the desk, refusing to look at me. "In short, the time has come for us to meet again with your parents to try to reach some kind of agreement," he elaborated in a dull tone.

"But why?" I wondered, my voice cracking.

"I keep trying to tell you, things outside of Aventine are far from safe. Dissent and violence outside of compounds are growing more and more common." James softened his sentiment but still would not look at me. "The Masters believe another look into the Tribute system might be the best way to bring the Free Factions to heel."

"Tribute law is the most clinical and thought out branch of the Master system," I recited nervously. "You told us that when we were kids. Villages send Tributes to serve the Masters in exchange for goods and protection—it's worked for as long as I can remember, Graham said almost all the way back to when the system was forged. What aspect of it begs revisiting?"

James looked at me as though I had charmed him with a very morose joke. "I am not talking about rehashing the claiming of voluntary Tributes, Liza. Even if every village, city, and farming cluster sent one Tribute per family, it would still not be enough to keep the peace. The Masters want to take more children from the Free Factions."

"No!" I was on my feet, my palms clammy as my mouth went dry. "You cannot let them do it, James, you can't—"

"I am doing everything in my power to keep that from happening," James interjected, scooting his chair back by just an inch. "But I am one of many and we each have a vote…and even that doesn't make it as simple as counting opinions. The system was devised in order to keep the Masterlands safe and the laws about how we make decisions were written to avoid overriding of any kind. Matters like this are ones that require a unanimous vote to move forward, so you can see how it might be difficult for me to stake my case. Ever since the others arrived for the summit, I have been professing an argument against displacing more young children to use against their parents day in and day out—"

"There is no argument," I insisted. "They cannot take babies from their parents to keep hostage."

"Except that we have already done it," James replied firmly. "And it bought us nearly twenty years of unwavering obedience."

I couldn't comprehend what I was hearing. I felt sick all over again, like when James had first told me about how we came to the Aventine.

"You must believe me when I say I have left no room for speculation with regard to my stance on the matter," said James. "I am vehemently against the notion. However, the four of you, by some awful karmic affront, only prove the contrary point to my stance."

"I don't even know what that means," I admitted helplessly.

"I cannot stake a valid claim against the virtues of raising Tributes away from their Free parents, not when the four of you turned out to be such exceptional individuals."

"We went to that party," I said mutely, reeling with humiliation.

"The second the others saw how comfortably you fit in at that damn birthday fiasco, they reached an almost unanimous decision. I could smell it on them. They like the idea of you remaining here, especially now that you are all old enough to raise the children they want to take."

I let out a furious wail and threw myself to my feet. I paced between the bed and the window, certain that I would scream and cry if I didn't get up and move around. *Us?* The Masters want *us* to raise the next generation of kidnapped infants? I scorned James for not at least appearing as disgusted by the idea as I imagined I did.

"Remember, I never wanted you to set foot near Dulce or my sister," James added. I felt ready to hit him again for adding insult to injury.

"And you didn't see the point of arguing with them anymore, so you spent the morning in bed with me instead." I liked being an excuse for James to ignore his job even less than I liked being his Tribute.

"I have been fighting with the others for weeks," James said. "I do not want to see another wave of children carried in any more than I want to watch you raise them. I believe there are other ways to resolve the tension between us and the Free Factions, but too many are unwilling to part with the funds necessary to pursue those alternatives. Even less are willing to give it the time it needs."

"Alternatives?" I asked, even though I did not want to know what heinous options could possibly be in the shadow of such an unthinkable initial proposal.

"To separate you, for a start," said James. "You and Armand are old enough to take an induction oath. Even a very traditional Master or Mistress would arrange for you to understudy the system for no longer than a year, given your unique backgrounds."

I swayed on my feet at the prospect of becoming a Mistress while feeling as though I had been socked in the gut—which I actually might have preferred. I could imagine Selenis saying something like "That ought to teach Lorena a lesson" if she were to mentor her enemy's daughter by sponsoring my Mistress education. Because we grew up under James, whose reputation as a fearsome and powerful Master reached every corner of the continent, Armand and I might even be inducted sooner, under special circumstances. The idea was so unnatural and so devastating to imagine, I could not speak to or look at James for a long while.

"The situation as it stands is a precarious one," James said, standing warily as he noticed my steadiness falter. "I don't want to put you through the trauma of separation after everything you've been through. Even if I have to put in an extension to this ridiculous summit, I will do whatever I have to in order to ensure you are not sent away."

Clouds of dismay parted to make way for the cold moon of contempt that rose in my heart. "And what about the others?" I demanded. "You made a very nasty point to Daisy that you are putting your reputation on the line for *all of us*, remember?"

James fixed his gaze to show that he would not be scared off by my rapidly growing upset. "I don't expect you to understand the risk involved in being the singular voice speaking against the will of the Masters."

"So you would agree to keep me here and send them away, separating us, to become one of you?"

James held his ground. "Without question."

"You—" I was so angry that I could not even think of a curse to sling at him. "James! How could you say that?"

"It is the lesser of two evils! This is the only way I can see to keep you all alive and moving forward that does not make things worse for all parties—including the innocent children who would suffer without their parents, just as you have! For goodness' sake, what would you have me do?"

"Say no to it all, you coward!" I hated the hot tears welling in my eyes. "Make them listen to you!"

"Would that I alone could make decisions for the Masters, Liza," sighed James. He was barely tolerating my outbursts and all the while, his mighty reputation was crumbling away before my eyes. "It doesn't make me a coward to go along with what's best for you."

"And you think what's best for me is to stay here? With you?" My vocal chords twisted together uncomfortably as I forced myself not to cry while staying rooted in place. Even though I knew he would have no qualms about rising up to meet me, the thought of lunging at James seemed more and more marvelous.

"Yes, I do," said James. "Especially after last night. I don't even want to think about you going outside of this room."

"Well, you're about to!" I stormed around the desk, far out of his reach, to the door. I yanked on the doorknobs but they room was locked up tight. I swiveled around slowly, checking the anger gnawing at my stomach like a ravenous wolf, to glare at James. He had not taken a step to go after me. "Unlock the door," I growled. "Now."

James actually chuckled. "No."

"I am deadly serious," I warned him. "I want out of here. I want my old room back."

"No," James said again.

"So you do intend to keep me locked up in here," I supposed. "Your very own spoil of war." If looks could kill, James would be choking to death on the floor.

"Are we at war, Liza?" he asked, folding his arms and cocking his head.

"We will be, if you don't let me out of here…," *before I come at you and aim for that bite*, was the unspoken finish to my very real threat.

"I see." James took a measured step toward me. His easy prowl did not fool me, his eyes glued to my body. He would react in a flash to the first sign of attack he could catch and probably level me as recompense for questioning him, shouting at him, and trying to hit him. "As I have no intention of letting you out of here, especially now that you look like a murderous harpy and are therefore unfit to be seen in public, consider us at war. Allow me to be the first to offer my terms for armistice."

I shook my head. "I refuse your terms." I wanted to call him a bastard a hundred more times.

"For the first time in my life, I stand to lose much more than just my reputation," James said, taking another slow sweep toward me. "I am too used to being the Master of this compound to be told what to do and I have little patience when it comes to abstaining selfish impulses. I do not want to be steamrolled by the others in any matter, but it looks like I am going to have to compromise in order to save us all from a very unsavory future. I will do what I can to uphold my own oath and do what's best for the four of you but if I cannot, I will keep you here with me."

"You're not compromising," I spat. "You're giving up. There is a world of difference between the two."

James was resolute. "I will not lose you," he said, stating his hard limit.

"And I will not lose the others!" I was shrill but I didn't care. James could be as unyielding as he wanted but he would never match my drive to protect my family.

"Did it ever occur to you that as a Mistress, you would finally have the vagility you are so desperate to attain?" James asked. "You would no longer be bound by Tribute law! You would be able to have a real life!"

"I'm surprised you are in support of such a thing. After all, it would mean that you would no longer be my Master. Who would you order around if I become your peer and you are no longer permitted to speak down to me?" I held my chin up and tried to keep my voice as even as possible. "You can forget it, James. I will not be part of a system that deals in the leasing of human beings or the abduction of innocent children."

James groaned in bitter frustration. "You haven't seen your mother in nineteen years! How the hell have you become her?"

I erupted in anger, giving in gloriously to the provocation. I knew James would guard his volpine bite or ensnare me in his arms before I got the chance to hit him there, so I aimed a kick at his knee. I let out a triumphant "Ha!" when my foot nailed his shin and he cursed sharply. I swung an elbow at his jaw but severely underestimated how much angrier I'd made him by kicking him. He caught my arm and spun me around, my limbs flailing as I lost my balance.

Had I been a spectator of this particular altercation, I would have thought that I was much easier to manhandle than Daisy had been for him earlier. James flung me on the bed and climbed on top of me, pinning me down while I struggled underneath him.

"Stop this!" he commanded. The whites of his eyes lent a stark contrast to his blue irises that were dark and beyond irritated.

My heart skipped a beat as I was transported back to the dark studio. James became Quinn and in a snap, all of my fury morphed into icy, gripping terror. My pulse throbbed in my neck and I was hyperaware of how open my throat was to him. Now I was fighting to escape his unbreakable grip but not so that I could try to land another strike on him. I was helpless to reason with every buzzing cell in my body that was screaming at me to get away, get away, don't let him cut your throat....

"No!" My voice was strangled by that same stinging fear. I was an animal caught in a trap and my heart was beating so fast, I thought it would burst. "Let go of me—please! Stop!"

James saw the panic in my eyes for what it truly was. He went rigid for a moment and then let go of my arms. I frantically scrambled out from under him and across the bed until my back hit the headboard. I hastily curled my knees to my chest and buried my face in my hands. I was sobbing uncontrollably in seconds, unable to wipe the image of Quinn's bared teeth as he sliced at my arms out of my mind.

"I'm sorry, Liza." James did not move from the foot of the bed and though I could not see him, I knew he was being careful from making even the slightest move. My breaths hitched in my chest as I pushed my hair back from my face to stave off the sensation that I could not take in enough air. "I'm so sorry," he said again. He crawled closer to me but stayed far enough away so that I could not reach him.

The stench of metallic blood burned in my nostrils. I flinched as though Quinn were right in front of me.

"He's gone," James reminded me. "He's not here. You're all right." He inched closer as my bawling went on. "I'll never scare you like that again. You have my word." I gulped and took a shuddering, deep breath. I let the air out in a stream, slowly regaining control of myself. I forced myself to look away from James and to the uncovered window, to the sea down below. I watched the tossing water as my panic ebbed and my heart rate slowed.

When I looked back to James, he was holding his hand out to me.

"You have to promise me that you will never do what you did to Daisy this morning, ever again." My frayed nerves borrowed me a hysterical ferocity that I hadn't expected to utilize. "Don't ever raise a hand to Kit, Armand, or Daisy. I cannot touch you again if I know you might hurt them."

"You have my word," James repeated, nodding. Without question. Still trembling, I crawled into James' lap and wrapped my arms around him. He held me in a similar embrace and I pressed my lips to the crook of his neck just under his ear in thanks. Unbridled, I then kissed his lips, begging him with my body to take us both out of the compound, like we had the night before. I would do anything to forget my pain for just a little while.

James handled me delicately, laying me down on the bed under him with a cautious grace he hadn't employed previously. He kept himself propped up with one arm so that he was not nearly as close as I wanted him. With a dutiful air about him, bordering on apologetic, James bent his head and kissed my throat tenderly. In gossamer brushes of his lips, James planted kisses along the bandage covering my shoulder. He let me tug at his shirt but stopped me when I pushed away at the waistband of his trousers.

"Liza." James was being so soft and patient but I was still shaking.

"I'm all right," I insisted. James frowned and kissed my lips. We remained recumbent and kissing for a while, James laying over me and plying me with soft touches. Heat flared under my skin wherever his mouth or his fingers touched me. After a while of this, when my shaking had subsided to make way for a restless stirring of another sort, James slipped a hand around my waist and guided me to roll over so that I was lying on my front. I let out a great sigh as James pressed adoring kisses down my back, sending my panicked nerves from earlier packing. My gracious lover seemed to be satisfied with me, or maybe just himself for successfully calming me down, and ran his hands along the backs of my arms, stroking softly with the side of his thumb the place he might have bruised me when he stopped me from elbowing his face mere minutes ago. He settled down behind me, holding me to his front. Tears sprang to my eyes again when I realized he was content to stay there.

"Won't you do it to me again?"

"Liza," James murmured, his lips touching my ear. "You're should rest." It was the kindest "no" he'd probably ever offered anyone in his life.

"Don't you want to?" I was confused by his gentle refusal after the long, unhurried time he'd just spent lying on top of me, kissing all the places he hadn't reached last night.

"Yes, I do." James left his explanation at that and dropped a careful kiss onto my shoulder. I was worried right away that his guilt over upsetting me was now carrying him away from me. I turned in his arms until I was facing him. He saw me wince at the twinge in my shoulder and blinked across the pillow at me in sorrow, disapproving of my efforts to convince him to do what I wanted.

"Kiss me," I said. I laid my hand on his neck and waited for him to lean forward to touch his lips to my waiting ones. I loved to stroke his dark hair back with the edges of my nails simply to reap the reward of feeling him melt under my touch as I did under his. I tilted my chin back and guided James to kiss me there again. I moaned in gratitude when he nibbled the side of my neck and smoothed his hands up my back.

"James," I begged. I was behaving like a cat, purring his name and sliding my leg over his body so that my knee rested on his waist. I pulled him closer to me, the insides of my thighs burning as I gave a slight rock of my pelvis against his.

"Liza," James interrupted our kiss to say in an uneven voice. "Don't."

I froze. I could feel his breath on my lips as his heart beat steadily against mine. There were tears in my eyes again. "Why?" My own voice was still ragged but rejection lent it a rather pathetic high pitch. James tried to pull away but I trapped him in my arms to keep him close.

"I triggered a panic attack in you," he said, his face reddening in shame.

"It was Quinn who hurt me," I corrected him. "It's him I'm afraid of, not you—"

"No, Liza. I can't accept that." James rolled away from me and sat at the edge of the bed with his back to me.

I protested his action at once. "Stop making everything about yourself. If there is anything I need to help me feel safe right now, it's being held by you. I'm—" my voice caught unexpectedly in my throat. Apologies were difficult—no wonder James hated to make them. "I'm sorry we fought," I said. "I shouldn't have hit you or kicked you. I just got so angry, and I'm so upset by everything you said about the others taking more children...." All of my anger washed over me again just thinking about it.

"You came after me like a wildcat because of what I said about your mother," James pointed out. He still would not look at me.

"All the same," I said, supposing I could not argue with him on that point. Just like last night, I crawled after him and settled behind him on my knees so that I could touch his back. Heeding my own advice, I quieted my frustration and tried to guess a reason James was so resolute in refusing me that had nothing to do with me. "Is it grief that's making you turn me away?" I asked. I could not blame a man who had earlier today carried the dead body of his tutor to the mortuary for not wanting to engage my whims.

"No," James said. I was beginning to despise the word.

"Then tell me why."

James heaved a sigh. "I scared you almost to death, Liza."

"You apologized." And he promised not to hurt the others ever again. "I don't know how else to convince you that I do not hate you for what happened."

I peered over his shoulder and saw James smiled sadly. "It's for both our sakes that I insist I join you only in sleep tonight, Liza." He bowed his head as he searched within himself for words I dreaded to hear. "Sex cannot be the balm for a hurt I inflicted," he said. "Causing you pain is a terrible way to repay the trust you put in me to give you pleasure and I don't want to confuse you by taking you to bed every time I lose my temper and upset you. I used to be that man, Liza, and I don't ever want to be him again. That kind of relationship costs more than anyone involved can afford to pay in the end."

I was reminded by his stoic affirmations that he was far more experienced in this avenue of intimacy than I was. I did not like how easy it was to imagine James, young and handsome, as the cruel lover of a faceless beauty to whom he had been committed. Based on the torment he expressed to me, I had to assume that the affair had ended in disaster.

I got up off the bed, came around to face him, and kneeled before him so that I could marvel up into those blue eyes of his. I blinked up at him purposefully, making sure he was focused on me before asking him, "Then, you don't want me?" It was a silly question, for I knew fully well that he did. I only wanted to hear him say it.

James cupped my face delicately in his hands. "It is not a question of whether or not I *want* you, Liza," he assured me. I noticed a miniscule dilation in his pupils which made me wet my lips. "Between last night and this morning…." I felt how hot his palms were on my cheeks. I turned my head just enough to press a kiss to his wrist. James smiled. "It is tempting to lose myself in you for the rest of the night. But I am not a Neanderthal. I can show restraint where it is needed."

I wanted to ask him what he planned to do about *my* restraint but one look from him silenced me. So he was going to make me seduce him all over again?

"Very well," I resolved. What was I to do other than go along with his wish? I knew the more I pushed him, the more he would ask me to think of all that had happened today and erode away at my determination until I was as sullen as he was. Perhaps he even had a salient point in his abstinence: I was so eager to forget the tribulations of the day that I might overlook what continuing our affair would mean for us in the future? Soon, I was just as peppered with weighing thoughts as James was.

Neither of us had any semblance of a carnal appetite now, I was positive. Slowly, I rose to my feet, pausing to touch my lips to his briefly, sweetly. I took his hand and slid back into bed, pulling him reluctantly in under the covers beside me. He put his arms around me and I curled into his chest. I thought about Kit and his ability to soothe Daisy merely by his presence. If I could show James that he had been doing just that for me ever since Quinn's attack, he would understand that I could never see him as the horrible past-version of himself that he seemed to think still lingered in him.

"Sleep," I said. I could feel James worrying as he held me and I wanted him to relax, if he could, without me kissing him out of his spiral.

"Thank you," he murmured. My lips formed a sleepy smile—I hadn't realized how tired I'd been, which meant James had been right all along. I could be right too; I would have to show him. There was always the morning.

Chapter Twenty-two

Armand

At first, I felt alarmed to wake naturally in darkness and worried that I had grossly overslept, but then I remembered that I had fallen asleep in this cozy windowless cupboard, for lack of a better term. I felt Donovan beside me and his warmth triggered a tired, wry smile that I showed to the dark room; we must have done this dozens of times but this was the first time we had been able to sleep together afterwards. Now that the candlelight that had illuminated our amorous congress last night was out, there was just quiet, blackness, myself, and Donovan.

"Are you awake?" I whispered. Donovan hummed affirmatively.

"I was sure I would be dead to the world after last night," he said. He shifted in the little bed so that he could nuzzle the side of my neck. I felt his lips twist into a grin. "I barely slept. I'm too worked up."

"I feel good." I meant it, which was odd because I hadn't felt good in weeks—maybe longer than that. I beamed in the darkness when Donovan's hand glided like silk down my front until his fingertips brushed the tuft of soft hair underneath my navel and beyond. He teased the length of my organ with his hand and kissed me.

"You feel better than good," he remarked. It was a testament to his good looks that I could tell exactly which mischievous expression his handsome features had taken on even in the dark. I had never felt so relaxed to be naked with him, to touch him and let him touch me. We usually had to take such great care in avoiding detection, so much so that our affair had been constituted on spur of the moment, fast, passionate trysts whenever we could get at each other discreetly. To be enveloped by privacy and the safety of darkness allowed an urgent sense of intimacy I'd never experienced to swell in me with every breath.

"Again?" I smiled wryly as Donovan rolled over and settled on top of me. "I couldn't possibly...."

Donovan nipped my lip and took me by the hips. "Oh, yes, you can," he insisted. His nails dragged across the sides of my thighs when I wrapped my legs around his waist. As much as I had enjoyed doing the driving last night, we both seemed to prefer when Donovan took charge of our pace. I was shaky from all the exertion amid the previous several hours and Donovan was so possessed with determined elation, I was helpless to do anything but hold onto him while we made love.

The little room was hot when arrivals found us both. Donovan settled down at my side and held me close while his rugged breaths slowed. He pressed a secretive kiss to the side of my face and rested his chin on my shoulder.

"I don't want to let go of you," he murmured. My mind floated away from the compound for a while, finding imaginary sunny hills beyond the walls around me. As I contemplated bliss, a pang of guilt pricked my heart and that old stitch was back in my chest. It seized my postcoital joy and strangled it until it withered into something ugly.

"What is it?" Donovan asked. Even in darkness, he could detect my sudden change in demeanor.

"For just a few hours," I replied in a tiny voice. "I forgot he was dead."

"Armand, don't torture yourself." He was a fighter and had been since he was a teenager; he must have lost soldiers over the years, maybe even to suicide. I got the feeling he'd given this speech before. "What happened to Graham is regrettable, but you can't let such unfortunate things like sudden death stop you from appreciating your life."

"The moment I turn a blind eye to the suffering of others, I will become like James." Sharing my secret fear in the dark, with Donovan's arms around me, made me feel even lower.

"I've told you, lover, I don't want you to worry about James anymore." He was urging me away from unfavorable subject matter and I supposed I couldn't blame him—not many men would want to discuss the complexities of life and death, not to mention his uncle, while lying in bed with his lover.

"You said you've taken care of everything," I said, taking Donovan's lead to change the subject to something a little less morose. What could be more hopeful than the notion of leaving this place, once and for all?

"Yes," said Donovan. "In a few days, when the summit is concluded, everything will be different."

"Really?" From the stitch in my chest bloomed a warm, buzzing excitement. I turned my head so that my nose almost touched Donovan's. "You found a way to get us out of here?"

"Better." The blossom of hope in my chest wilted. Without meaning to, I snuggled close to Donovan to hide the dread that was rapidly needling down my spine.

"What could be better than being rid of this place?" I asked uncertainly, cloaking the doubt in my voice by barely whispering.

"I was having a hard time coming up with an effective way of smuggling four of James' most protected commodities out of his fortress of a compound," Donovan explained with a sigh. "Then I thought, it would be much easier to deal with the actual problem than risk my status and yours by staging an escape more reckless and dramatic than Liza's."

"The actual problem?" I was beginning to feel like a confused child, repeating Donovan's words in earnest.

Donovan chuckled. "James, of course," he said. "At the risk of divulging too much sensitive information, when I ought to be whispering poetic nothings in your ear, lover, the solution was clear as day; it dawned on me when Liza made such a brash stance against him. The other Masters agree with me: James' time as Master of the Aventine has come to an end."

My blood ran cold. I did not know how I'd be able to hide my blatant distaste from Donovan this time.

"He's had a good run," Donovan assured me. "It's best for everyone to have him moved to a less high-profile compound. Once he is gone, I will take his place here." Pride radiated from him as nausea stirred in my stomach.

"What will happen to us?" I nervously wondered.

"We can discuss it together if you like," Donovan supposed. "Since you and Liza are of age, I imagine we could induct you both and cut ties with those pesky Tribute rules. You and I could stay here together—once you achieve Mastery, you'll find that there is nothing out of reach. But it's like I said, we can discuss it later. There's no sense in tangling ourselves up in the details at a time like this."

To put it plainly, I was dumbfounded. All thoughts and processing of emotions ceased. Shock gripped me in its awful clutches and it took every ounce of self-control not to recoil from Donovan's touch. He expected us to *stay* here? To take oaths and become Masters? And *stay* here? He had no intention of leaving or taking us away. Why would he, when he was convinced the point of the whole plan was to get away from James? I realized at once that I was an idiot. Liza had nearly jumped to her death but I had just taken the cake—because of course Donovan would decide to supplant James in order to spare himself the hassle of facing his wrath, should he succeed in stealing us out from under him.

"Of course." I sounded detached and panicked when Donovan sat up quickly, leaning over me in concern.

"Are you all right, Armand?" he asked. "I thought you would be happy… ." My doubt was contagious. I snapped myself out of it and urged myself to lie—lie *very well*—to him.

"I am," I said. I let tears fill my eyes, though he could not see them. Crying roughed my tone and disguised the horror that burned like a hot poker in my throat.

"You are?"

"Yes." I kissed him. "Thank you." The words were an acrid curse on my lips.

Relieved, Donovan returned a precious, lingering kiss. "I only want to make you happy," he promised. I surrendered myself to him for fear of betraying my true reaction. We kissed for a while longer, Donovan absorbing every moment alone with me that he could.

"I don't want to check the time," he said, affecting a mopey tone as he pulled just enough away from me to reach for his belongings. He rummaged around until he found his wristwatch, tapped a button on the side so that its face illuminated, and read the time. He hung his head and sighed. "So much for getting a head start on breakfast," he said. He bent his head so that he could kiss my lips once more.

"I could eat," I offered.

"And so you will," said Donovan. "I'll have something sent to your wing. I'm afraid I can't join you. I've delayed as long as I can but I have lots to see to today."

"The summit isn't finished," I agreed. I gulped and added, "And you aren't the Aventine's Master yet."

Donovan laughed a little and got up from the bed. "No, not yet." I could tell he was grinning as he stepped into his trousers. "But I am still a Master, and therefore I order you not to worry for another moment about any of this. Don't even think about Dulce—I'll smooth things over for you, as far as she and Selenis are concerned."

I reached for his hand and kissed the inside of his wrist. "What would I do without you?" I said. I wondered how I hadn't been sick, I had offered the nicety so forcefully.

"Don't think about that either," Donovan added the addendum onto his playful order with a chuckle.

"As you say," I replied. We dressed quickly even though I felt unsteady on my feet more than I had in the past few troubling weeks. Donovan led me out of our lover's nook and down the imposing corridor. He assured me that my exit would be hidden by the busy morning activity in the main hall.

"I'll arrange for some breakfast to be sent over right away," Donovan told me, catching my hands and pulling me close for a farewell embrace.

"Thank you." I didn't know what else to say.

"You ought to get some rest," he said. "I'll see you later." He was pleasantly surprised by the exuberance with which I kissed him then, but I was really just overcompensating for how tight-lipped I'd been for the last fifteen minutes.

"Later," I rasped in concurrence against his lips. Donovan seemed to have a hard time stepping away from me but in a moment, he disappeared down the dark hallway and left me alone. I pushed the wall open, letting in a pool of bright light and the flurried din of the main hall. As far as I could tell, no one had noticed me emerge from the secret doorway. Everyone was rushing to get to the trade floor and procure their breakfasts.

I floated through the crowd, wondering when this lot had become so surreal. I was not Armand anymore, just a body carrying a head down the wide hall. I tried to imagine this precise scene, every morning, for the rest of my sorry future and came to the conclusion that I was too in shock to cry. I was beyond panic; disassociating was a necessary response, because if I could actually feel how terrified and ashamed I was, I would most certainly unravel on the spot.

You are in over your head, I told myself. Thoughts rushed me as though I were standing underneath a waterfall. I wouldn't move to avoid the crashing waves, there was no point. I was afraid for Liza, for Daisy and Kit. For myself. It was happening all over again, the library scheming, the search for open windows, the teeming secrets that connected Kit and the girls and isolated me from them; then it was all worry and fright, Liza was gone, then there was blood on the floor of the studio....

I saw my mother and father in my mind. I wished more than anything as I wandered the main hall that I could be their little *Armandito* and small enough to scoop up into their arms. I was drowning in the truth—there was no one to take responsibility for me now, no unconditional patience or understanding. I had undertaken one job, to convince Donovan to take me and my family out of here, and I had royally loused it up. I wanted to kick myself for thinking I'd been clever. Had I a brain in my head, I would have stopped this all before it began, I would have—

The epiphany stopped me in my tracks. I had said it from the start, when Liza had jumped out of the library window. I had raked myself over the hot coals of regret for not doing the very thing I knew I must do now, in order to extinguish this plan of Donovan's that would keep us all prisoners of the system for the rest of our lives.

I would have to go to James.

My bearing returned as I accepted the notion as a necessary one. The guilt and shame in me did not care that James would probably kill me for my part in this; perhaps it's what I deserved. The rationality and determination creeping into my slowly-turning present mind pointed out that if there was any person capable of turning this around, James was him. With him as the Master of the compound, we stood a chance of escaping. Maybe it would take some time, but the odds were better than if Donovan were to preside over us.

As my sense returned to me, my shoulders sagged and I felt like crying. There really was no other way, yet I couldn't push away the whining question, how did I get here? How was this my life? Well, it wouldn't ever be mine if I stayed here. I tightened my abdomen to force tall posture. I looked around and noticed that I was already almost back to the Tribute wing. I spent the few minutes it took to find our front door thinking of how I would do it. It was reasonable to assume I was being watched—if I went to find James in the Masters' chambers, Donovan might hear that his lover made a beeline for his enemy just after hearing about a plot to remove him from his seat of power.

I would not condemn myself any further than I was about to. Kit and Daisy would have to leave the apartment, for I would not endanger them in this. After all, I would have to call James to our wing.

I breezed through the front doors and was greeted by the calm silence of an empty apartment. I found a note on the kitchen table, elegantly penned in Daisy's loopy hand:

> *We went to track down some breakfast and some paint for Liza. Be back soon. —Daze*

I pocketed the note as though keeping Daisy's signature close to me would make this easier. I went to the sink, gulped an amount of water from the faucet, and rummaged around the cupboards for anything that would pass for breakfast. I found some of that awful coconut concoction Kit had brought me yesterday and resigned to chugging what was left of it, knowing that I would need my strength for what was next.

Near the front door, on the wall opposite the light switches, were three buttons. All of them had been installed to page the emergency channels that we'd never had to use: one called a guardsmen detail, James had explained years ago, in the event of an interloper or some other very urgent threat to our immediate safety; One called the doctor, in case of illness or at-home injury; The last called James himself and was only to be used in the most dire circumstances—a curious edict, for until today, I had never been able to surmise a reason to push it that wouldn't require the guardsmen or the doctor instead.

I stared at the button for a few moments in jittery anticipation before reaching up and pushing the damn thing. As soon as I withdrew, the face of the button lit up in a little blue glow. It must mean my page had gone through successfully, which meant I did not need to linger near the door for James to arrive. He would let himself in, I was sure. Knowing him, he would be prickly as ever to be summoned as though he were some common Tribute like myself.

I paced in the study, eager to get away from the door. I rubbed my hands together and let each breath out in a whooshing stream, eager to steady my nerves. Even though I was not the type to do it, I prayed for Daisy and Kit to take their sweet time in the market and not beat James here.

Maybe a minute later, I heard the door slide open. My heart leaped to my throat and I turned to see James stride down the hall. When he peered into the study and saw me standing there, he entered the room with an air of puzzled caution about him.

"Armand?" He seemed to be scanning me from head to toe for some sense of distress. "Did you mean to call for the doctor?"

"No," I said. "I paged you myself. On purpose." He crossed his arms and his biceps bulged. I tried not to think of how terrible his strength could be when backed by his temper.

"Is something the matter?" There was no baleful glint in his blue eyes now, only intrigue and worry.

My mouth went dry as I cleared my throat. "Would you lock the door, please?" I asked. James' eyes narrowed fractionally. He was now not only worried but very suspicious. "Please," I repeated. "Kit and Daisy aren't here. I would like to speak to you alone." James warily obliged me. It took him just a moment to go back into the entryway and punch in the five-digit code only he could use to bar anyone from entering the wing. When he reappeared, I could tell his apprehension was growing by the second.

"Won't you sit down?" I invited him to take the chair I most often sat in near the fire.

James the Master did not budge. "What's going on, Armand?"

A whimper slipped from my throat as I sighed. "I have to tell you...." I swallowed hard and steeled myself. Maybe if I showed a pinch of courage, James might think twice before beating me senseless. "It's about the summit."

"The summit," James echoed dryly.

"Yes," I insisted. "Well, after the summit, really."

"Get to the point, Armand."

I took a long, deep breath. I imagined that I was outside of myself in order to summon the strength needed to say what must be said now. "When the summit is over," I said as tension gripped my stomach in its fist, "the others will inform you that you are no longer the Master of the Aventine compound. Donovan will take your place as Master and while induction oaths will be put to me and Liza, you will be transferred to a less reputable compound—"

"No!" James dropped his folded arms and took a step back as though I'd knocked the wind out of him. "Who told you this?"

"Donovan." I thought surely my heart would burst out of my chest.

James clenched his fists and took measured, pacing steps toward the hearth of the study while his eyes flickered back and forth as he frantically and furiously worked it out in his head. I could tell by the aghast sheen that coated his eyes that a particularly shocking thought had just occurred to him. He paused and slowly peered over to me. "This is very sensitive information," James said in a voice that was so murderously low, it could have belonged to an animal. "Why would Donovan tell *you* this? Of all people?"

"Because I asked him to help us escape this place and he agreed, only he couldn't find a way to get us all out. He seems to think this would be a better solution." Viscous silence permeated the study. James' blood was boiling. He was so angry that he looked away from me for a while.

"I wonder," said James, his features transformed by dark curiosity, "why Donovan would agree to such a thing?"

"Because," I said weakly, "I made him my lover." I saw James coming for me and I pinched my eyes closed just as he took hold of my shirt and slammed me against the bookshelf behind us. I was careful not to make a sound, even when my head cracked hard against a wooden shelf. I kept my eyes shut too, though I could feel James' breath on my face.

"You conniving little bastard!" he hissed. "Do you have any idea what you've done?"

"I'm sorry!" I dared to open my eyes and I was caught in his ensnaring glare. "You have to believe me, I had no idea he would do this, James! I swear it! When he told me this morning what he and the Masters planned to do, I knew I'd made a mistake. I knew I had to tell you—"

"This morning?" James shook with rage. "You were together *this very morning?*"

"Yes!" I whispered my reply desperately. The floodgate of frightened honesty had opened. James could ask me anything now and I would describe the truth of it in detail.

"I don't believe this!" James insisted, glaring holes through my soul with his black eyes.

"I'm sorry," I whimpered again. "I made a mistake—"

"This is no ordinary mistake! This is a blunder of epic proportions!"

"I know!" I was shaking too as he held me with increasing pressure against the bookshelf. "Tell me what to do, James. Tell me how fix this—"

James wrenched himself away and spun an awesome rope of curse words. "You have no idea how lucky you are, that I am a man of my word…." He shook his head and buried his face in his hands. He groaned angrily and clasped the back of his neck with his hands so that he could stare up at the ceiling. "To think, all this time I was convinced he would make a play for Daisy. I watched that girl like a hawk for weeks, for nothing! What a thundering moron am I!"

My head throbbed where it had hit the bookshelf. I did not dare to move or say another word. James was unraveling before my eyes, laughing bitterly to himself and muttering poisonous sentence fragments under his breath. At one point, he stopped speaking and moving altogether. He stayed that way for a moment or two, then he let out a rageful roar and kicked the chair by the hearth across the room.

"What the hell am I going to do?" I wasn't sure if he was asking me or himself—I said nothing, just to be safe. I was surprised to see pain in his eyes instead of the frightening thirst for violence I thought I would recognize there. "How do you suppose we extricate ourselves from this mess?" he asked. "I am honestly at a loss." James the Master had never surrendered, not in my memories or in the stories I'd heard of him. He had never so much as inferred that he might crave advice, least of all from me, but as I stared back at him, I could tell that he was waiting for me to reply.

"You can't let him do it. I don't know how, but you've got to stop him from fulfilling this plan."

"*I've* got to stop him? You mean you expect me to clean up this mess on my own? Oh, no, Armand." James came toward me, menacing as ever. "You contributed to this disaster, you're going to play your part in undoing it."

"I will do whatever you ask of me." I might have felt foolish to throw myself at his mercy if I had any semblance of pride left. James took my assurance into account and once more turned his back on me, his mind likely frantically hurtling toward a solution.

"What did you think would happen?" he asked, defeated. "Did you think he would throw a hood over your head, smuggle you away from here, and then what? You would live out the rest of your days together on a beach somewhere?"

"I had hoped to make our way back to our parents." James heaved a throaty laugh to hear this.

"You would risk my life, and Kit's, and the girls'—indeed, every person who resides in this compound by assisting a Master coup, and your grand design's endgame was to end up with your parents?" James was in awe of my apparent stupidity.

"I haven't seen them in nineteen years," I said, trying and failing to not sound pathetic, "but I am still Angelo and Edita di Felce's son. They still want me to come home."

That put a stop to James' cruel laughter. "So you got Donovan to tell you everything?" He showed his teeth in a mean smile. "I've known some snakes in my time, Armand, but you really put them to shame—"

"Donovan didn't tell me about what happened," I interrupted him as he insulted me. "I remember everything about being a child in my parents' home, Kit and Daisy as babies, even Liza's parents. And anyway, I didn't need Donovan to tell me everything. Liza did."

James' complexion paled but his eyes remained alive in anger. "She did?"

"Yes. We know all about your father, Haitham the Master, and how the old scoundrel stole us from our cribs. I won't be ridiculed by you for wanting to do whatever I could to get myself, Kit, and the girls back to our parents." Even I had to wonder where the bold streak had come from. "I know about the conditions, too." I reminded him of those rules set forth by Liza's mother in case James had a mind to punish her for betraying his trust later.

"So you know that you've broken them."

"*I* broke them?" I leaned into the surprising embrace of bravery and stood up to him. "You broke them that day you hit Liza so hard that you split her lip! From what I gathered from Liza's recounting, you were charged with ensuring no harm came to us!"

"I am permitted to enforce the rules of this compound as I see fit. Liza's past act of revolt aside, you deliberately disobeyed my rules—I don't even want to know how many times," James replied coldly.

"Well, I can count on one hand the number of times you've directly harmed us," I pointed out. "And I think my parents, the ones who set forth those conditions in the first place, would rather I took a Master as a lover than be beaten by one."

"Had you put any thought to what will happen when—let's say, by some miracle—I am able to stop Donovan from taking my place here?" James decided to come at me from a different angle and ignore my latest remark. "If Donovan comes forward with the details of your affair, the already very arbitrary treaty between us and the Free Factions is nullified. The fallout will be even messier than you could contemplate."

I folded my arms and returned James' glare. "Had you told us about the conditions in the first place, I might never have involved Donovan."

"Don't even try to foist the accountability off yourself," James snapped. "Was I to trust a bunch of reckless, emotional children with the truth in case one of them might seduce one of my many adversaries?"

"He's your nephew!" I exclaimed, aghast that anyone could think of his much younger relative as his adversary.

"Our relation is irrelevant! If you had known about the conditions, you would have done whatever you could to nullify them at the first opportunity— which, at this point, I might have preferred; seeing as how you botched my life as well as yours, all so that you could run back to your parents."

"I had no idea what Donovan was planning to do until this morning," I said, forcing myself to save my breath by not addressing how psychopathic his choice of words proved he was.

"That I believe," said James. "You have no idea who Donovan is, nor *what* he is." I challenged James to enlighten me and he was all too happy to oblige me. "I imagine your lover has convinced you that he is in every sense your saving grace? That his mastery of violence only means he is that much more in tune with his patience and delicate manners? You must believe me when I tell you, Donovan has been an expert liar since he learned how to talk. He is a very prettily packaged product of everything that makes this system thrive: He is cunning, wealthy, strong, and vicious."

"Why, then, would you allow him anywhere near your compound?"

"If I had realized how ambitious he really is, I never would have," James answered honestly. "He is as dangerous as they come, Armand." James barred himself against any follow-up remark I might've had by crossing his arms. "Tempted as I am to let you live in the sordid nest of lies you've build for yourself, I refuse to be made a fool out of by Donovan, of all people."

We were at the beginning again. "Tell me what to do," I implored.

James bowed his head in thought. "Every move we make from now on must be made with surgical precision. Until I can work out exactly how we're going to move forward, you're going to have to maintain as though everything between the two of you…." He broke off to shake his head, as though he were struggling to reconcile his disdain with his enduring commitment to his own preservation. "You must not give him the slightest sign that anything is amiss. You can be uncanny at the best of times and if I am going to get us out of this, you're going to have to be better than Donovan at playing innocent. And when I do give you directions, you must follow them to the letter."

"I will," I promised.

"You must do whatever he wants, as any hesitation on your part will only arouse his suspicion," said James. "Until I figure out what I'm going to do with you, I will make excuses to visit you here, at your apartment, to hear from you everything he's said in your confidence. At least you weren't stupid enough to try to visit me in the Masters' rooms." A curious look befell him then and he crossed his arms again. "Kit and Daisy don't know about your affair, do they?"

"No," I assured him. "I almost told them so many times—" Loud banging on the apartment front door disrupted my explanation. James turned to look after the sound and seemed to reach a conclusion as to who was pounding on the door at the same time I did.

"That'll be Kit?" he assumed. I nodded. "I posted Nathan outside," James added. "He's supposed to deter this sort of thing."

I thought of Daisy's blatant contempt for the guardsman outside and chewed on my lip. "Douglas may have been a better choice?" I may as well question James now that he'd refrained from murdering me over my treachery with Donovan.

"You'd rather Nathan stand guard over Liza's door?" James asked, raising an eyebrow. He didn't wait for me to respond before going to the entryway. I heard the chirps of his five-digit code and then the whoosh of the front door sliding open. I blushed furiously on the spot, knowing that I was seconds away from facing Kit and Daisy in the midst of my confession to James. He'd let them in, I had to assume he would out me to them now if only to make an example of me.

"What's going on?" Kit demanded, making his way swiftly into the study. Daisy was joined to his hip, eyeing me worriedly over Kit's shoulder.

"Have a seat," James offered the two of them.

Kit planted his feet and rounded on him. "What happened? Why wouldn't Nathan let us in?"

"Are you in trouble?" Daisy asked me quietly. I was practically folding in on myself in front of them. I couldn't blame her for assuming right away that I'd done something wrong.

"Yes," James answered for me. Kit and Daisy looked to me expectantly and I withered under their stares, hating how accustomed I'd grown to seeing the signs they exhibited when bracing for bad news. I looked to James, waiting for him to speak for me in no kind verses about what I'd done. Instead, James squared his shoulders and cleared his throat. I could see him fighting a smirk. "I'll leave you to it," he said. The bastard. Of course, he was going to make me divulge the whole thing all over again. "Don't look at me like that, Armand. This is your doing, not mine. I'm going to try to figure out a way out of this while the three of you practice not breathing a word of this outside of this room at your evening lesson."

"Evening lesson?" I yelped. I was in no state to attend such a thing; I was ready to drop from exhaustion as it was.

"That's right," James declared. "You'll meet with a tutor in the gallery after dinner. We must maintain an air of normalcy if we're to have a chance of reversing the chain of events you have activated."

"Will one of you please tell us what is going on?" Kit implored, his brows furrowed in consternation.

James left without another word. Once he was gone from my sight, I crumpled to the floor and leaned against the bookshelf, head still throbbing, and hid my face behind my hands.

"Armand, you're scaring me," Daisy said breathlessly. Her gentle hands were on me in the span of a heartbeat.

"Did he hurt you?" Kit asked. "What happened?"

"We came back from the market and saw Nathan standing outside," Daisy told me. "When he said James was in there and the door was locked...." She shivered.

"I've ruined everything," I gasped as panic threatened to wring my stomach out.

"You haven't," Daisy assured me. "Why would you say such a thing?"

"You're going to hyperventilate if you don't calm down," Kit said severely. I was hopeless to control my breathing and desperate to tell them the truth before I lost my nerve or my consciousness—whichever came first.

Out it came, in sputtering, mournful bursts: last summer when Donovan and I had first been together, then every visit since, then everything that had happened after Liza's escape, how I had asked him to get us away, how he had agreed, how it had all gone so wrong.... At the end of my sorry tale, Kit and Daisy were shocked into silence. I hadn't looked at them at all out of sheer cowardice. I merely let the tears drip off the tip of my nose as I went on, my head bowed in shame, until I finished.

"I had no choice but to go to James." I had reached a detached steadiness in my retelling of my deplorable deeds. The emptiness of trauma stung me still but I wasn't trembling anymore. "I should have done so at the beginning of all this."

"Maybe so," mused Kit. I could tell from his muffled affirmation that he was holding his chin in his hand and his lips were mushed together in his deep contemplation.

"Do you really love Donovan?" Daisy asked in a throaty voice. I dared to look at her and saw that her eyes were shiny with tears. It occurred to me then that Daisy must feel at least a shadow of contempt, for I'd teased her about making off with Donovan weeks ago knowing full well that I had no right to toy with her dignity like that.

"I don't know," I said honestly. "I think I do." Or was it the freedom I could achieve through Donovan that I loved? I looked to Kit. "I've let you down," I realized as I saw the serious disappointment in his eyes. "You won't look at me the same ever again because of this."

"Armand," Kit sighed, sounding a lot like Graham. "You told me about Donovan the other night, when I put you to bed after Dulce's party."

"What?"

"You told me Donovan would get us out of here," Kit prompted me, "because he loves you." There was a darkness in his eyes that I could not attribute to any one thing. Perhaps my brother was appalled to think of me cavorting with another man—it was almost my worst fear, that Kit would cast judgment on me for making such a choice in a lover.

"I don't remember," I said, bridled by my insidious anxiety.

"Wait a minute," Daisy interrupted. "You and Donovan…." She purposefully left a suggestive pause follow her words, insinuating what she could not bring herself to say. "Doesn't that mean that the conditions our parents set for the Masters are forfeit?"

"It might," I replied. "If James or Donovan decided to come forward. It's not what any of us wants."

"But the Masters defaulted on their end of the agreement," Daisy argued. "Wouldn't they have to, I don't know, send us back?"

"They have no reason to safely return us home if they didn't bother to honor the conditions in the first place," Kit replied. "If our parents found out about the broken agreement and moved against them, the Masters would kill us."

The horrible idea permeated the room in silence.

"There's nothing left for us to do but let James take care of this." The air of finality behind Kit's words made me feel queasy with guilt.

"But what will he do to Donovan?" Daisy wondered meekly. I didn't want to think about that. "You did the right thing by going to him, Armie," she said after she realized neither me nor Kit would answer her question. "Our chances of getting out of here are better with James as our Master."

"I'm not so sure," Kit said. "Say James succeeds in thwarting Donovan's plan to usurp his role as the Aventine's Master—what will happen then? You asked us yourself, Armand, weeks ago when Liza jumped from the library window: what do you imagine James the Master will do when he realizes that the singular truth of his world was not only threatened, but very nearly obliterated by the actions of his own Tribute?"

I was even more an idiot to not have considered that aspect of going to James, who would lock us up and throw away the key if he managed to stop Donovan.

"It is I who have let you down, Armand, not the other way around. I should have listened to you—we all should have—from the start. There is another way to escape this place, I just never imagined that becoming a Master myself was the way to do it."

"Kit!" Daisy cried. "How could you say that?"

"Think about it!" Kit insisted in frustrated earnest. "We cannot be smuggled out, we cannot slip away in a tradesman's cart; one of us literally leaped out of an open window and still we are here, back where we started. Perhaps Donovan has discovered the only real way out for us!"

"To become part of the system?" Daisy crossed her arms. "I wouldn't consider it for a moment."

"I fail to see any other alternative," said Kit.

Suddenly, I was in the middle of a lover's spat that I'd caused.

Kit went on, "Would you rather swear into the system and gain the freedom to walk out of the front gates unhindered or stay a Tribute for the rest of your life?"

"You mean, take an oath and be a Mistress of the system that is responsible for my being here in the first place?" Daisy held her chin up. "Never. I would rather die a Tribute."

"Both of you, stop this!" I was well past the point of being embarrassed, so I shamelessly offered the old creed in the hopes of maintaining our solidarity. "We're only strong when we're together, remember?"

The words seemed to help lessen the tension between Kit and Daisy. They exchanged forgiving glances and clasped hands.

"James says we must maintain an air of normalcy in order for whatever his plan is to work," I said. "I will do my best to handle Donovan…do you think you can face him without giving up that you know his motives?" Kit and Daisy each took a moment for honest introspection. "He's a charmer," I suggested. "James says he's a master manipulator. It would be easy for you both to just follow Donovan's lead, if you should run into him between now and the end of the summit."

The old stitch pricked my chest as a necessary addendum to my confession occurred to me: If I had learned anything from this entire debacle, it was that I was of age to finally accept responsibility for my actions. Taking a lover was a prerogative of a grown man and doing so had put me past the threshold of adulthood. James would get us out of this, but it was my hubris that had entangled us all in this mess in the first place. I had to say outright to Kit and Daisy that I was prepared to accept their decision to reject me for what I'd done, no matter how much it would hurt me if they did.

"Additionally," I said thickly, "I understand if you would prefer not to see me from now on. I haven't just betrayed James—I don't care about him, not really, but if you see me now for the scoundrel I really am and don't want anything to do with me…." A sob seized me by the throat and I had to stop speaking, or I would have broken down.

Sweet Daisy crawled to my side and took my hands in hers. "I know how you feel, Armie," she said. "When I think about the part I played in what happened to Liza and where the consequences of her escape have led us, it feels like I'm being buried alive." She sniffled and pressed her lips together to keep from crying. "I understand what it feels like to want to escape this place so badly that it hurts. I don't blame you for turning to Donovan."

"I never meant for this to happen," I said. I wrenched my gaze from Daisy's, once again bowing my head to her.

"As far as I'm concerned, this is James' fault." Daisy's tone was solid as stone. "He's kept us pent up in here without windows since we were babies and has the gall to be angry when we try to tear down the walls." To an extent, she was right. James kept us in a cage and punished us for wanting to be set free.

"You are my brother." Daisy touched my chin and drew my face up so that I would look at her. "I love you. Nothing the Masters do to us can change that."

"It's true," said Kit. He seemed to pick up on Daisy's cue and reached for me, too. "Sometimes you make me so mad I could hit you, but I would never turn my back on you. We're brothers through and through, Armand."

I didn't deserve their kindness but I reveled in it all the same. I was a sorry scoundrel, but at least I was loved.

"Keeping secrets has been our undoing," said Kit. "Whispering behind each other's backs and sneaking off to affect our own designs has broken up our family. If we're going to get through this, it will have to be in unison."

"No more secrets," Daisy agreed, flashing a smile as a tear spilled past her eyelashes.

"Save for one," I said. I squirmed as I summoned the guts to make one last request, the last favor I would ever ask of them after all I'd done to put them in danger. When my brother and sister eyed me with doubting curiosity, I posed my appeal.

"Please don't tell Liza about my affair with Donovan." When I thought about Liza and how much I cherished her touch, how badly I craved to hear her voice, how ardently I loved her, I felt arrested by fear that she would forsake me and never forgive me for giving myself to a Master as I had. Punishment enough would be Kit and Daisy refusing me but if Liza ever looked at me the way I knew she would if she found out....

Just imagining it triggered a feeling that was similar to grief, like when James had told us Graham was dead. When Liza had jumped out the window and I had every reason to believe she was dead, I had barely clung to sanity. If Liza, alive, could not bear to look at me or touch me because it would make her wonder where Donovan had touched me...if she turned me away, I would certainly lose my mind.

"I promise I won't," said Daisy, who might have agreed to this only to spare Liza the pain of hearing it.

"I won't either," said Kit. "But that is the last secret we will ever keep between us."

"It's the last secret I will ever ask you to keep," I vowed. I looked between the two of them for a while; they still had their hands on me. "James will fix this," I said. "He has to."

"I believe he will," said Kit. "If nothing else, he'll get us out of it to save himself." I knew he was right, but it opened the door to dozens of other questions, mostly surrounding how our lives would ever go back to normal after the summit. The only thing I knew for certain was that my life was in James' hands now more than ever. That fact was accompanied by perilous whispers in my mind that told me, somehow, I had not yet begun to suffer for the mess I'd made.

Chapter Twenty-three

Kit

"I thought for sure he was bluffing," Armand muttered darkly as we followed Nathan along the main hall, headed to the gallery to meet our new tutor for the evening lesson James had hastily arranged for us. "Who could he have found in such a short time to take the job?"

"There are plenty of tutors around for the summit," I said. Though, looking at Armand, I had to hope James had offered our new tutor a provocative salary, otherwise it might prove impossible to retain a tutor if he was going to be saddled with a grouchy pupil like Armand.

"It feels too soon," said Daisy. She walked close to me for comfort as we couldn't clasp hands like we could have as children. "Whoever it is will never measure up to Graham's caliber."

I almost reminded Daisy that such a comment was in poor taste, given the manner of Graham's death, but I knew Daisy didn't mean to carelessly use that word. "James would have to interview candidates for a whole year if he hoped to find a tutor like Graham," I said instead.

I nearly tripped as a startling epiphany struck me in the gut—*Graham*.

"Nathan!" I blurted. Our escorting guardsman startled, along with Armand and Daisy, and turned to face me with a look of contemptuous wonder stamped on his features.

"What?" asked the disgruntled guard.

"I need to see James!"

"I'm afraid Master James' schedule is full for the day," Nathan said curtly.

"I must see him," I insisted.

"Why?" Nathan was clearly annoyed.

"What's going on?" Daisy hissed.

This was not the forum to answer Daisy, nor did I have the time to answer her. I decided to lie to Nathan and play a very risky card to get what I wanted. "Master Haitham asked me to deliver a message to James," I said. "I said I would before the end of the day—"

"It's after supper!" Nathan balked, paling.

"I know," I said. "I forgot." Nathan waved over a guardsman who was standing near the entrance to the south wing.

"You'd do well to do as Master Haitham says," Nathan warned me in a hushed voice. "And as close to precisely *when* he tells you, if you can help it."

"Kit." Armand stood over me and glared as Daisy watched me with pleading eyes. "We agreed we would not do this...." I couldn't fault him for being angry; after all, we three had just agreed not to keep any secrets.

"I'll explain everything later," I said. "I'm so sorry, I really do have to go." Nathan briefed the other guard, who took in the information with worry as Haitham's name came up. He led me away and Nathan barked at Armand and Daisy to follow him to the gallery. I trusted them to forgive me upon my return, when I would have the chance to talk them through the grim realization I'd just experienced, but for now it was too urgent a matter to waste another second not telling James what I now supposed.

Though it was precariously venturous of me to use Haitham's name as a skeleton key in the Aventine, I found it to be immensely convenient when I wanted to get somewhere fast. I'd never before stepped over the entry control protocol like this—in fact, I'd been ushered around it by the many nervous guards who were apparently more afraid of Haitham than they were James; that, or they were petrified to think of what James would do them if he faced any ugliness from Haitham because they wouldn't let me through. Either way, before I knew it, I was escorted down the familiar corridor which led to James' room. The scent of rosemary and smoked meat laced the air and I suspected that the Masters took dinner later than we usually did. Because of Armand's groundbreaking revelatory confession, not one of us maintained much of an appetite when dinnertime rolled around. Still, we ate, though it was a much more modest meal than the one I imagined was served to the Masters.

I spied Douglas as I rounded the corner on the heels of the guardsman leading the way. He was standing at ease near James' bedroom door but snapped to attention once he noticed my approach.

"Kit," he greeted me uneasily as I stopped in front of him. "It's late. You ought to be at your evening lesson. Even Liza's there—"

"He has a message to deliver to Master James," said the guard beside me. He locked knowing eyes with Douglas and tilted his chin down to convey gravitas. "From, ahem, Master Haitham."

Douglas turned on his heel and knocked softly on the door. James barked something from within and we waited a few moments as he came to open the door. There were a few loud clicks as James undid the locks before he appeared, aggravated, in the open threshold. He saw me standing between the guardsmen and narrowed his harried glare.

"What is it?" he asked, his tone icy. "You should be at your lesson." Douglas calmly explained my excuse for being there to James. As soon as "Master Haitham" crossed Douglas' lips, James went pale, took hold of my arm, and pulled me through the doorway so fast that I nearly lost my footing. James slammed the door behind me, in the faces of the guards outside, and whirled around to face me.

"He asked you to carry a message?" James asked eagerly, his expression still pallid. "When did he contact you?"

"He didn't," I answered quickly. "I just dropped his name with Nathan so that he would bring me to see you."

James sighed and leaned his head back in exasperation. "So help me," he said, "I will have white hair by morning unless I suffer a fatal heart attack tonight! Kit, you must never do that again. I've told you how unwise it is to speak his name even in his absentia—"

"I know," I placated him. I tested his temper twice in the span of a minute, for lying about Haitham and then interrupting him, but I knew he would only become testier if I didn't get to the point.

"Then tell me truthfully, Kit, what brings you to my bedroom at this hour?" demanded James, crossing his arms across his chest.

"Armand told us everything," I began. As I prepared to put my thoughts in order, I realized that I was much more tongue-tied than I thought I would be. "You told him it was dangerous to confide in Donovan—rather, you told him how unsavory Donovan's true nature is, which made me think—well, we were walking to our lesson just now and I was thinking about Graham...." I trailed off, stumbling over my words.

James' impatience only made it worse.

"Allow me to ask you a question," I posed, taking a deep breath to slow myself before I really got carried away. "Did you suspect at any point over the past few weeks that Graham might kill himself?"

James appeared to be stunned. "Why would you ask me such a thing?"

"Please," I said, "just answer the question." He averted his caustic glare for a moment and mulled over the question I'd put to him.

"No," said James. "His background was hardly dull and his history as a tutor was not devoid of the occasional outburst, but I was as shocked as the four of you were by his suicide. I'm sure Daisy told you that Graham had known tragedy in his life; he seemed to have a detached, scholarly perspective on his grief. He has since I've known him."

"But would you ever have pegged Graham as the type of man who would take his own life?" I asked. James stepped back, likely driven by his farsightedness to get a better look at me.

"This is a very disturbing line of questioning, Kit," James said. He saw I was about to urge him to answer and replied to my unspoken prompt, "I would not have guessed that Graham was capable of harming himself, no. He was a preacher of pacifist diatribe; he couldn't bring himself to kill an insect. It's why I put him in charge of you four." He watched my features meticulously for a clue as to what was going through my head.

His response confirmed what I was afraid of, that Graham was certainly not the kind of person who would surrender his life to an untimely end by his own hand—especially such a violent end.

"What the hell is this about, Kit?"

"The other night, at the party," I said. My mind was leaps and bounds ahead of my speech. Aghast, I snapped myself out of my horrified stupor and looked into James' blue eyes. "He warned me about Donovan."

"What exactly did he say?" James asked in a low voice.

"He said, 'You shouldn't leave Armand alone with Master Donovan,'" I echoed Graham's ominous tenet as a sickly feeling brewed in my stomach. The retelling had a similar effect on James. "It was the last time I saw him alive," I recalled. "He left me to go talk to you right after."

James stepped back from me as he entertained what must have been thoughts as rapid and disconcerting as mine.

"When I think about what you told Armand, about Donovan, I couldn't help but think...Graham must have known about them, right? He was the most astute man in the compound. He could have figured it out and planned to tell you?" I was rambling out loud mostly in attempt to spur James to speak. His silence was beginning to frighten me. "Armand told me about it that night; he was drunk, he said Donovan loved him. That he loved him enough to help us."

It was as though James had left his body. He stood perfectly still except for his eyes, which were flickering back and forth as though he were working out a vastly complicated strategy.

"James," I claimed his attention. "There is a lot on the line for Donovan right now, if what he told Armand is true. He stands to become the most powerful man in the system and use that power to keep the person he loves close—would you say it's possible that he staged Graham's suicide?" Even I could scarcely believe the words I had just spoken. My arms and the back of my neck broke out in chills. I was not comforted in the slightest to see a similar shudder wave through James' body.

"Graham did not speak to me that night," said James. "If he'd known, he would have found a way to tell me." I hadn't expected him to turn to denial outright. I racked my brains, summoning what details I could about that night.

"Jada stopped him!" I exclaimed when the memory dawned on me. "I remember, he excused himself to go and find you but Jada approached him and engaged him before he could reach you!"

"Jada?" James rigidly shook his head. "No. She is loyal to me, she would never act as Donovan's accomplice...." He seemed to surmise an alternative viewpoint, negating his own pronouncement.

"Liza hates her," I offered. "And she is not Armand's favorite, either. As impassioned and reckless as those two can be, I trust them enough to be wary of Jada myself." James seemed to take that into account, though he continued to stare past me as though the truth were a third person in the room with us and was gawking right at him. He weighed the allegations in his mind for a few long minutes. I could see the dread pooling in his eyes as the denial wore off.

"There is nothing Donovan would not do to succeed," James decided at last. "If he means to take my seat as Master of this place and claim Armand as his prize, there is no doubt in my mind he would remove with great care any-one who stands in his way." He swore, loudly, and startled me enough to make me flinch. I could almost feel the rage radiating off him in heated electrified currents.

I thought when James had threatened Daisy in our kitchen yesterday morning that I had never seen him so close to murderous, but as he paced be-fore me, muttering vile curses under his breath, I knew that he had just deter-mined that he would kill Donovan for this.

"Mark my words," James said to me, "Donovan will live to regret betray-ing me. He will find that I am not as easy to overthrow as he thinks."

"There are only a few days left of the summit," I said. "What will you do? What *can* you do?" James went quiet again and I voiced my assumption out loud. "You're going to kill him."

"That remains to be seen," said James, though I could tell I'd landed close to the mark. "I will have to plan very carefully. If he truly did frame Graham for his own death, that changes everything. The only thing I know for certain is what I will *not* do, which is let Donovan get away with it." In a snap, James the Master had returned to himself. "I expressly forbid you from telling Ar-mand any of this. He'll fold at the slightest pressure if he thinks Donovan is a murderer—we need him as steady as we can get him."

"We promised not to keep any more secrets," I said, frowning.

"I don't think you understand," said James, advancing on me. "Armand is not the stoic big brother you might think he is. He is fragile, selfish, and un-predictable; and despite the latest evidence to the contrary, he is not a good liar. Donovan will see right through him, press him, and Armand will tell him that I know about his plans. If Donovan was willing to kill Graham to keep his game under wraps, he will do much worse if he believes that he has nothing left to lose."

"He wouldn't hurt Armand," I said. "He loves him."

"I doubt it," James said flatly. "A primarily sexual relationship like theirs can induce the imitation of the feeling, nothing more. Love makes people stupid, and while Donovan will find that his plot to remove me from my position is the stupidest thing he'll ever do in this life, the way he has gone about it proves that he is anything but. Besides, he sure as hell doesn't love you, Daisy, or Liza. If he learns from Armand that he's been caught, he will see to it that he does as much damage as he can on his way down."

My mouth went dry. Donovan could kill Armand and anyone close to him. Liza. Daisy. Myself.

"What am I supposed to tell him about tonight?" I asked frantically. "What do I tell them about why I came to see you?"

"Say nothing. The summit is over in a few days, and I need time to think tonight about what to do. When I am able to conceive a plan, I will tell the others myself."

"Really?" Doing James' bidding was one thing, but working with him felt wrong and frankly exhilarating.

"You have my word." In an act of unprecedented comradery, James braced his hand on my shoulder. "I will take care of you boys and the girls, Kit. I promise. Remember all that I have done to keep Liza alive and believe that I would do the same for the three of you too; you must trust me and do exactly as I say."

Unexpectedly, I found myself fighting tears back. I nodded and did not speak, lest I reveal how frightened I was. James led the way back to the door and opened it, revealing Douglas and the other guard standing right where we had left them. Douglas looked straight past me to James and by the look of his pursed lips, he did not like what he saw.

"I take it you delivered Master Haitham's message, Kit?" asked Douglas, mindfully keeping his voice down.

"Oh, I received the message." James thrusted me at the guardsmen. "What was the lesson planned for my Tributes this evening?"

"If memory serves, Mistress Magdalene said something about astronomy," Douglas replied in a neutrally pleasant tone.

So Graham's favorite former student had taken his job as our tutor.

"Riveting," said James. "Take Kit with you, conclude the lesson, and bring Liza back. See to it that Nathan locks the others in the Tribute wing for the night."

"As you say," Douglas agreed. I walked with Douglas along the corridor, bound for the main hall, and the click of his boot heels resembled the ticking of a stopwatch. As I worked to stifle the panic and overall discontent so that it would not show on my face once we reached the trade floor, I let the tick-tick-tick of Douglas' boots wash over me as I resolved that for the Aventine Summit, the clock had just begun to count down. To a degree, I felt some relief when I reentered the main hall. Douglas and I moved through the sparse evening crowd easily but at a decent clip. Douglas seemed eager to carry out his orders and I was keen to see the others to give them at least an indication that I hadn't been harmed.

By the time we reached the gallery, I had successfully fixed a neutral expression and coaxed the tension out of my shoulders. Douglas led me into the wide room where we instantly shared a rush of admiring astonishment.

The overhead lights had been turned off in order to make visible the thousands of tiny lights projected onto the ceiling by a little machine in the center of the room. I looked up to see that a synthetic galaxy was over my head, swirling and twinkling in unbelievable detail. It was more beautiful than the lavishly decorated south wing had been by far—I sighed to see so many stars and even Douglas let out a little chuckle of amused wonderment.

"Could you please close the door?" Magdalene's pleasantly smooth voice floated through the darkness. "The lights from outside are dulling the projector's contrast." She was right: The glow from outside had illuminated the floor, where I could see Daisy, Armand, and Liza lying down in a circle, their heads together, as Magdalene sat nearby, no doubt to point out various constellations and planets as they loomed above.

"Apologies, Mistress," said Douglas. "Master James sent me to bring the lesson to a close." Liza was the first to sit up. She saw me standing beside the guardsman and patted Armand, spurring him to follow suit. Magdalene swept gracefully to her feet and crossed the room in elegant, sweeping strides to turn on the overhead lights, then switch off the projector.

"Kit, where were you?" Liza asked, skipping across the floor to wrap her arms around me.

"I had an errand to attend," I replied, swaying a little with Liza in my arms.

"It's nice to see you again, Kit," said Magdalene, joining us with Armand

and Daisy at her side. She wore a flowing, floor-length skirt which lent her an appropriately celestial quality. She turned her serene stare to Douglas and smiled. "Master James will be pleased to know that the lesson was over when you arrived," she said, "I was merely allowing his Tributes some time to be still and reflect while stargazing."

"It's hardly past curfew," Douglas replied, affording Magdalene a very generous smirk. "Come, Liza. Master James said—"

"Tell him I want to sleep in my room," Liza said. She'd caught Armand and Daisy eyeing me severely and was justifiably desperate to be included in whatever we would discuss once we were within the safe confines of our apartments.

Douglas gave a diplomatic cough. "I believe it's Master James' intent for you to sleep in your room," he said.

"No," Liza argued. "*My* room. In the Tribute wing."

"I don't think that would be wise," Douglas replied gravely. He was the only guard I knew of who had ever advised someone to pick her battles with James.

"It's all right," I encouraged Liza. I glimpsed a strip of white gauze peek out from under her collar and felt my palms go clammy at the thought of her in danger. "Go. We'll turn in as soon as we get back, anyway."

Liza whimpered to have to leave with Douglas. She turned with begrudging acceptance to Armand when it was time to say farewell and the two of them held each other in the usual way, in a hug that looked too tight. Her embrace with Daisy was equally bittersweet, more so when Daisy whispered a promise that we would all be together again soon.

"I'll say goodnight too," Magdalene said with a sigh. "It was a pleasure to work with you tonight. I look forward to our next appointment, pupils."

"Thank you, Mistress," the four of us said automatically, in unison. It pained me to think of how many times Graham had bade us goodnight before returning to his apartment or his home outside the compound and how I had taken for granted all those moments. I did not think to appreciate those times when Graham would arrive at the Aventine for lessons with a new book of poetry under his arm for Armand that he probably took from his own home, or new sheets of music for me that must have been tricky to procure. I had missed the lesson with Magdalene, so I couldn't be sure if the Mistress had emanated any of our late tutor's teaching habits, but the way she had concluded her lesson was telling.

Magdalene collected the celestial projector and tucked it under her arm easily, as the item was no larger than a cantaloupe, then gave us a wave as she left the gallery. Based on the looks she got from Armand and the girls, and even Douglas, I could sense that they were taken with her.

"Well?" Liza turned to Douglas. "Are we going?"

"Not until Nathan arrives to escort the others," replied Douglas, sounding bored.

Liza's violet eyes flickered to me with an unsavory knowing sheen to them before looking back at Douglas. "Is he well?" She was talking about James.

"Master James is in fine health, Liza," sighed Douglas.

"I would rather be prepared to walk into a firestorm, if that's the mood he's in," Liza said quietly, folding her arms as she pursed her lips at the guardsman.

"I didn't make him angry, if that's what you're worried about," I told her, a little cross at her sidestepping me by asking Douglas for a report on James' temperament. What difference did it make to Liza what kind of mood James was in? They weren't roommates, after all. But I'd walked right into Liza's trap by defensively offering a hint about the subject matter of my conversation with James.

"So what was the message you had to give him?" Armand asked. Douglas nervously cleared his throat.

"You would do well not to become involved in Master Haitham's affairs," said Douglas. "If you can possibly help it...."

"All right, you three," Nathan announced, showing up conveniently in the doorway of the gallery. He bore the tired look of a guardsman who had probably just sat down on his bed to take his boots off for the day when he was summoned to do one final duty, which he didn't want to do. Douglas was visibly relieved to see his peer as it meant the end of all this talk of Haitham. "Let's go."

Simply standing before Nathan was enough to annoy him, but we exacerbated his irritation further by walking slowly out of the gallery, hungry to spend as much time as we could with Liza. Armand slowed to a halt when we were about to lose sight of her in the hall. I saw Liza look back and smile sadly at him, then follow Douglas away to the Masters' rooms.

Back in our apartment, as soon as the front door slid shut, Armand and Daisy frenzied.

"Tell us what happened," Armand demanded, sounding more like James than ever.

"Haitham gave you no message," Daisy pointed out admonishingly. "You lied to Nathan just so he could take you to James—"

"We agreed there were to be no more secrets kept between us!" Armand interjected furiously.

"I know!" I fired back. "And I am sorry for this, but I can't tell you right now." I held my chin up and marched straight past Armand and Daisy, making a beeline for my bedroom.

"You're joking!" yelped Armand in incredulity.

"Kit!" Daisy exclaimed, as though I'd pinched her.

"I wouldn't keep this from you unless I had no other choice," I said, trying my best to remain collected as the two of them hounded after me.

"James threatened you," Daisy guessed. "He told you he'd do something horrible if you told us what went on."

"He did no such thing," I assured Daisy gently. I looked to Armand, who might have set me on fire with his glare, he looked so mad. "The situation is serious. I gave my word that I would give him time to come up with a countermeasure before I told you."

"The hell with your word and the hell with James!" If he were a volpine, Armand would have snarled and bit at me.

"Don't you start," I warned Armand. My hackles were up too.

"Kit," Daisy was not subtle as she slipped between Armand and me, drawing my attention from Armand's calamitous countenance to her much lovelier features. "The three of us are together in this; we need to know what is going on if this is as serious as you say it is."

I stopped just short of my bedroom door and looked between Daisy and Armand for a moment. "No," I said. "I'm sorry. James said to say nothing and I'm not going to—"

"*James said?*" Armand's raised voice was menacing enough to make Daisy flinch. "Tell us right now, Kit, or I swear—"

"You'll do what?" I challenged him. With careful ease, I pulled Daisy out from between me and my brother and I stood close to him, matching the ferocity in his dark eyes.

"This is because I kept Donovan a secret," Armand uttered. "You're deliberately keeping this to yourself—how could you give a damn about what James says you should do, after everything that's happened?"

"You're starting to sound a lot like him," I tested him. "Are you going to beat me now, because I refuse to obey your command?" I could see by the way Armand withdrew from me that I'd wounded him by drawing the comparison. "That's right," I snapped. "I can be a bully too."

"What's the matter with you?" Daisy cried.

"I'm trying to keep you alive!" I shouted. "I've said it before, I'll say it one last time—I am *sorry*, to the both of you, but I cannot and will not tell you. You are going to have to trust me enough to wait." I knew if Armand made one more comment, I would be in real danger of snapping, hauling off, and hitting him. So I escaped into my bedroom and slammed the door behind me.

I was fuming as I paced back and forth across the carpeted floor. I heard Daisy murmur something in a sorrowful voice in the hall and figured she was pulling out all the stops to calm Armand down. I heard their exchange, muffled slightly by the door.

"What could have happened?" Daisy asked softly. "It's not like him to be cruel."

"Get in there," Armand's rough voice rasped. "And get it out of him."

My bedroom door opened and Daisy whirled inside, shutting it quickly behind her. Had Armand pushed her inside? She and I stood across the room from each other and waited for the other one to speak first. I hoped she would so that I could put an end to the matter entirely, for while I disliked being anything less than affectionately pleasant to her, I was prepared to show her my teeth like I had Armand.

"Would you please explain why you were so severe with him?" Daisy asked.

"He wasn't hearing me," I replied tersely. "I meant what I said out there. I will say nothing about it until James has had a chance to consider a few things. We both agree it's what's best for us all."

"So the two of you are a 'we' now?" The darkness in Daisy's eyes put me at unease. I was too used to catching ugliness from Armand to imagine Daisy could ever be so angry; and I'd seen her mouth off to James, to his face.

"Not you too," I groaned.

"Do you have any idea how afraid I was? You disappeared to go find James! I wasn't sure you would come back!" Daisy clapped a hand to her mouth as her breath hitched on a sob.

"I'm right here," I reminded her. "I wouldn't ever leave you, not for anything."

"But how was I supposed to know?" she insisted angrily, her eyes brimming with frustrated tears. "It took everything not to fall to pieces in front of Magdalene! Not to mention Liza!"

"How many times will I have to say I'm sorry?" I wondered.

"You can save your apologies." Daisy crossed her arms to still the shakiness of her hands. "I won't accept anything you say unless it's the truth about why you lied to Nathan just to get to James."

I mirrored her stance, crossing my arms and barring myself to scrutiny. "Really?" I asked her.

"That's right." Daisy was showing me how serious she was by trying to break me with her eyes alone. I adored her, I was ashamed to have upset her, and in virtually every aspect, I could not say no to her—but I could not stand to lose her or see her come to harm. I had to obey James and keep the truth from her, if only for a night.

"I love you," I said. "Will you not accept that as the truth about why I went to James?"

"Is it the truth, Kit?"

My shoulders sagged. "Hurting me won't get me to tell you, Daisy. And it *is* the truth, the basest reason I lied to Nathan and ran to James. It's why Armand went to him too. We are trying to protect each other, so why am I being needled by you when Armie was received by you with love?"

"Because it didn't feel like my heart was breaking when I found out Armie had been lying to me." Daisy's stony resolve crumbled and she came forward, clasping the sides of my neck in her hands and resting her arms on my chest. She leaned in close enough to kiss me, close enough for me to breathe in the scent of her lilac soap and see with sharp clarity the flecks of gold in her brown eyes.

"If your partnership with James is more important than the one you have with me, say so now." Daisy was trying to undo me and I feared it was working.

"Daisy, I love you," I told her again. I thought about what James said earlier, that love makes people stupid. "Think for just a moment on how difficult it is for me to align myself with him, knowing what he is and what he has done. Do you think I would do that for anything less than life or death?"

"Life or death?" Daisy murmured urgently.

I put my arms around her and covetously held her against the front of my body. I dropped my forehead down to rest on hers and made sure to whisper very succinctly, in case Armand was listening at the door, "It is for Armand's sake that I cannot tell you. It is imperative that he does not know what I know, otherwise Donovan might hurt him."

Daisy shivered in my arms as prickling gooseflesh swept up the back of her neck. "Impossible," she whispered. "He couldn't do such a thing, Armand told us Donovan loves him…."

"Even if that's true," I replied softly, "it's a Master's love, Daze. It's selfish. He still would keep Armie here as his prize and send the rest of us away. It's all about possession for Donovan and the rest of them." Daisy tilted her face up so that she could peer into my eyes in horror.

"What has he done?"

I shook my head.

"Something awful," Daisy shared her fear with me plainly. "Kit, we can't let Armand near him if he's dangerous—"

"No," I insisted, tugging Daisy snugly toward me when she tried to step away. She braced her hands against my chest and pushed at me, driven to go to the door and get Armand, but I could not let her. "No, Daisy. It's too late to warn him. If you give him anything else to be suspicious of, he won't be able to hide it!"

"Let go of me," she demanded uneasily. For a third time in three days, I denied my love's appeal. Her struggle, however meek, excited me to cling to her even tighter and hold her in place.

"We can tell him nothing," I whispered roughly as Daisy squirmed in my arms.

"He needs to know how much danger he's in!" Daisy hissed reproachfully as she tried in vain to best my strength.

"Damn it, Daisy, I said no!" The whisper was gone from my voice now. I had lost my temper at last. "You will say nothing and that is final! Don't you understand, I'm trying to keep you alive!" Daisy froze in my grasp, my fingertips digging into her arms. "I will not explain myself any further than this: I will do whatever James asks of me, which includes keeping my mouth shut for what will probably be just a few hours so that he can figure out a way to get us out of this and I will not hear another word from you about it! So help me, you *will* do as I say!"

Her lips trembled as she tried not to cry. "Now you sound just like—"

"Just like James?" I finished Daisy's whimpered sentiment loud enough for Armand to perceive. "I'm glad to hear it; maybe now you'll take me seriously." I released her with a flourish and we glared at each other for a minute, drenched in furious and pained silence.

"I hope for your sake that this secret is worth keeping," Daisy said after a while, her heart in her throat. "Because if it turns out to be all for nothing, you will have lost me forever over this." Spurned and probably a little humiliated, Daisy turned from me and swung open the door to vanish in a whirl of long hair down the hall to her own bedroom. Armand lingered in the hall, glaring at me in the open doorway. He'd heard our struggle and clearly despised me over it.

"Seconded," he said gruffly. He stormed off too, leaving me alone in ringing silence. All we seemed to do these days was make messes and wound each other. Even though I knew that I was right to keep the terrible secret of Donovan's murderous plot to myself, I loathed the crushing guilt that smothered me like smoke. I shouldn't have handled my dear Daisy like I had, and I shouldn't have shut my brother out when he was so clearly suffering and afraid of rejection.

Dejected, I keeled over onto my bed and laid face down in a heap for a while. This apartment was missing its catalyst, Liza, and I missed her more now than I had since she'd gone to the library in the hopes of escape. As I thought of her, I reflected on everything she'd told us about our parents and the lives in Kingsfield Township we'd been stolen away from. Her mother and my father were the prominent members of the Free Factions' leadership, yet Liza was the one who exhibited signs of raw talent for it. She could coax Armand out of a spiral in just a few words—sometimes just a touch—and her mere presence was enough to keep Daisy calm and sure of herself. She never backed away from engaging our instructors in debate and she was single-minded sometimes to the point of temerity, but she was well liked and trusted.

Most of all, Liza made me feel like I was looked after without ever feeling small or incapable. I realized only in her absence just how grounded and at ease my mind had been when she lived with us.

I rolled over in bed and stared up at the circle of light over my head. Tears came to my eyes. I wished for Liza's advice on how to ask for Daisy's forgiveness, how to quell Armand's contempt for me. How to be steady and sleep tonight when I knew somewhere across the compound, James was working to conjure a solution that would keep us all alive.

I wanted to roll out of bed, go to Daisy, take to my knees, and beg her to look past the hideous side of myself I'd shown her long enough to hold me so that I could fall asleep. I loved her, it was simple. Staying alive as we navigated this minefield of a summit would mean little to me if I couldn't have Daisy when we emerged on the other side of this. She was right to question my devotion to her too. I wanted to get up right now and tell her that if she was asking me to choose between her and James, I would forsake him in a heartbeat.

I wanted to….

I had treated her deplorably. I had no right to go to her after I'd abused her like that, not unless I was prepared to tell her everything I'd promised James I wouldn't. I couldn't do it, for when I imagined alleviating the pressure on me and professing the whole ghastly, murderous revelation I'd had, I felt in my gut that it would result on standing over a pool of Armand's blood on the floor next. Or Daisy's.

James had given his word that he would protect them. I saw no other path before me than to trust in him, completely. That meant that I would have to, as I told Daisy, do precisely as James said.

Chapter Twenty-four

I hadn't listened to a single word Douglas had said. As far as I could tell, he was wondering about the projector machine Magdalene the Mistress had brought to our evening lesson, but as I followed Douglas back to the Masters' rooms, all I could think about was Kit and the apparent emergency that had spurred him to run to James.

Poor Daisy had been so pale when she and Armand arrived at the gallery. He was peaky too but knowing him, he had probably not had a good night's sleep in days. When Kit was not with them, I worried right away that some new hellish event had occurred. Worse still, Daisy and Armand couldn't tell me what had happened—not just because we were in the presence of the gracefully kind but ever looming Magdalene, but because he hadn't hinted to either of them what his outburst had been about.

I was less nervous when the four of us said farewells at the gallery door. I would get it out of James one way or another, then it would only be a matter of time before I could connect with the others and restore the transparency of our conspiratorial group dynamic. Still, I knew I would not ever be fully at ease until this grueling summit was over and neither would James.

"Well," Douglas sighed, accepting that I would not answer any of his rambling questions. "In any case, Mistress Magdalene seems like a pleasant fit for you four."

"As you say," I said. I didn't mean to deflect Douglas and his polite small talk, for he was probably the only employee in this place I liked, besides Graham or Talisa, my gymnastics instructor. I was about to offer a much kinder turn of phrase when before me stepped Haitham, appearing so unexpectedly that I bumped into him. An electric aversion to Haitham shocked me and I jumped back at once, too flustered to think to apologize for crashing into the old fiend.

"Are all James' Tributes this clumsy?" Haitham asked. He did not wait for me to reply before he took a firm hold of my arm.

"Master Haitham, I insist you let go of her," said Douglas, red-faced at the sight of the Master's grip on me.

"I need to speak with young Liza here," Haitham said, fixing his twinkling, hateful eyes on my escort.

"I respectfully decline," I spat. The old man held on to my bad arm and I winced as I tried to carefully pull myself free of his grip, which he only tightened as I persisted.

"Master Haitham, let go of her." Douglas set his hand on the hilt of the short sword he wore on his belt and my adrenaline roared into action.

"You are in no position to give me orders," Haitham pointed out. "Do you not know the laws? I reserve the right as a Master to remand any Tribute into my custody for counseling, among other much more serious reasons—"

"Such as questioning, insubordinate detention, or an immediate threat to the Tribute's safety," Douglas recited the law in smooth curtness, never once taking his hand off the hilt of his blade. I looked desperately around the now deserted main hall and realized with a dreadful jolt that I was not protected by the presence of any witnesses.

"Maybe after your brush with violence, you shouldn't be wandering the compound alone with a guardsman?" Haitham asked me, winking as his fingers curled even tighter around my arm. "Come along, girl. I wish to speak with you in private."

I dug in my heels when Haitham pulled me along behind him, even though the lack of traction from my socks made it impossible to stay where I was. Every cell in my body screamed to me that being alone with Haitham would put me in visceral danger, so much so that I considered ripping every stitch in my shoulder in order to take my arm back and get away from him. But Haitham was as strong as James, it seemed; though I was panicked, I could not get free.

"Master James has very specific orders about the treatment of his Tributes, sir," Douglas said, heading Haitham off. "I am not permitted to leave

Liza's side for any reason until I deliver her to her room in the Masters' chambers."

"I am ordering you to stand down." Haitham was inhumanly menacing.

"I am bound to obey James the Master, sir," Douglas said. "Not you."

"Stand down," Haitham growled, "or this will be your last day in service of the Masters!"

"Douglas," I said, gritting my teeth against the pain biting into my shoulder. I locked eyes with the guardsman. "Go get James. Now."

"Enough of this!" Haitham pulled me after him, toward the east wing rooms that were usually left vacant so that family members of guardsmen could visit the Aventine. I trained my focus solely to Haitham. I did not see where Douglas went but he did not pursue me. I felt like screaming but my heart was hammering too hard in my chest for me to connect the action with the impulse. Haitham let out a scornful chuckle as he dragged me along the hall behind him. "Never have I seen a guardsman act on the command of a Tribute over a Master," he seethed in disbelief.

"I beg of you, let go of me!" I sucked in a gasp of pain as Haitham swung me around a corner, tugging my arm hard to keep me close to him. With each passing beat of my heart, I felt like I was trapped in a dark studio all over again. I could do little else but follow Haitham and pray that James would intercept me.

"Not until I've gotten some answers." Haitham marched us along a narrower hall, which was tucked out of sight of the trade floor. It took him no time to find an empty office, into which he flung me before slamming the door behind him. I barely avoided losing my footing but I bumped into the modest desk situated in the center of the little room. Haitham came for me and I retreated until my back hit the wall. He seized one of my wrists and jerked my hand up so that he could study my palm under the light overhead.

"These are interesting marks," he drawled. "I know you didn't get them from raising a hand to Selenis. Where did they come from?" The cuts and scrapes on my hands which I'd sustained while scaling the rough, wooden undercarriage of the compound had healed over the past two weeks, but the marks were still plain to see.

"I was attacked." My voice was high-pitched. It was a flimsy cover and Haitham knew it.

"Do you know what happens to Tributes who raise a hand to a Mistress, Liza?" Haitham still held my wrist in his claw-like hand and he applied a precise and brutal pressure to the joint where my thumb connected to my hand. Immediately, tears sprang to my eyes and I winced in sharp pain.

"I don't—I didn't—" Flummoxed, I could not even lie badly. My eyes were locked to his long fingers grasped around my wrist and at the moment I could feel the joint creak under the strain of his grip, I worried that I would be sick.

"You're a seditious little liar, just like your mother!" Haitham relinquished my wrist and slapped me across the cheek with his flattened palm. My face burned as though it was on fire and tears flooded from my eyes involuntarily. I staggered to my right, then Haitham caught me by the arms and pinned me to the wall. "If you open your mouth to lie to me again, I'll ring your head like a bell," the old villain snarled. "Now, tell me the truth! You sent a signal to Harriet, didn't you?"

"I don't know what you're talking about!" I cried. His breath was hot against my stinging cheek as I desperately turned away from him.

"Don't you dare insult my intelligence by playing dumb," Haitham warned me. "You and your little friends were beloved by that old fool of a tutor and as soon as you caught wind of the summit, you used him to contact the Free agents!"

"I swear I didn't!" I insisted tearfully. It was the honest truth—I was flabbergasted by his violent accusations. I'd never heard of anyone named Harriet or even such a term as "Free agent" before, nor had I ever been in a position to manipulate Graham.

Evidently, Haitham did not believe me. True to his word, he hit me with great force on the side of my head and I tumbled roughly to the side, crashing into the corner of the little office. My ear rang as my eyes swiveled in their sockets, trying to even out as the room turned on its side. The thud of my heart in the ear that wasn't ringing was deafening; for several moments, I could hear nothing but my own garbled voice as I pleaded for his cessation.

"I will give you one final opportunity to tell me the truth." Haitham crouched over me as I braced myself in the corner, drawing my knees to my chest to protect myself in the little way I could.

"It's the truth!" I exclaimed through chattering teeth. My nerves were stinging in their hyperactivity, I was shaking so intensely that I felt as though my bones were humming. "I did no such thing! I don't even know who Harriet is!" I glimpsed a shimmer of nightmarish rage in his eyes just as he lashed out and took hold of my shoulder, grappling onto me right where Quinn had cut me open with his knife. Haitham squeezed me—*hard*—which elicited a low, strangled scream to rip from my lungs.

Just as I was sure I would pass out from the pain, Haitham's grasp loosened and he removed his hand from my shoulder. I choked on a sob as I tried to breathe without gasping, huddling into a tight knot of limbs.

"The only thing more pathetic than a liar is a weak one," Haitham mused. He stood up tall so that he could glower down at me, all the while looking as though the sight of me disgusted him. "I am bored to death by the would-be revolutions of young people I've seen staged over the years, but you've piqued my interest, I'll give you that," he said with a sneer. "If you intend to betray us to the Free Factions, you're going to have to do a lot better than you have been."

"I don't know what you're talking about!" I maintained urgently.

"You know exactly what I'm talking about, Liza. Rest assured, when this summit has reached its conclusion, you and I are going to spend lots of time working together on your honesty," said Haitham. He cocked his head to one side as his gaze flickered down to my throat and no doubt to the exposed white gauze just below it.

"Now, are you going to tell me the truth by your own volition?" Haitham asked. "Or do I need to persuade you?"

The office door flew open. Douglas appeared in the threshold with a firearm in hand. When he glimpsed Haitham, he raised it and aimed it steadily at the old Master, prepared to fire.

"In here, Master James!" he called. James bolted through the door and did not spare his father so much as a passing glance as he barreled toward me. I reached for him and he hoisted me swiftly to my feet.

I wanted to put my arms around him but he held me steadfast behind him.

"A gun? Isn't that a little dramatic, even for you?" Haitham asked James, as if this whole interaction was a joke to him.

"You have violated the laws of my compound," said James. "Were you not a Master, I might have you shot where you stand."

"As I told your bodyguard, I am well within my rights to question your Tribute," said Haitham. "She raised a hand to Selenis, which you know well to be cause enough to detain the girl. We were just having a conversation, weren't we, Liza?" How could he be so cool with an automatic weapon pointed at him? He truly must be a maniac.

"You have until dawn to recuse yourself from the summit and leave the Aventine," said James. "If you aren't gone by then, I will see to it that you are forcibly removed." James did not wait for a quipped rejoinder from the other Master—he shepherded me out of the room, keeping himself between me and Haitham, and set his hand on my back as soon as we reached the corridor.

"Are you hurt?" he wanted to know right away.

"He hit me," I sobbed. "He hurt my shoulder. I don't know if I ripped my stitches." James halted mid-stride to inspect the gauze covering my wound. His touch was light as feathers and he seemed relieved by his findings.

"There's no bleeding," he told me. He reached into his pocket for the container of pain-killing capsules and offered me one. I took it without question, swallowing the little pill whole. "Where did he hit you?"

I pointed to my left ear, which was still throbbing. James gingerly took my chin between his fingers and studied the side of my face, exhaling woefully to see what I knew must be a stripe of angry, red skin across my cheek where I'd been slapped.

"I should go back there and repay the damage," James uttered, his blue eyes vibrant with fury.

"Please just take me to bed," I implored. I felt like I might collapse from nerves, which James seemed to realize, so he set his hand on my back and led me down the hall as fast as he thought was appropriate for someone in my state of upset.

"James," I said, my breathing shallow. "He said—"

"Not here," James murmured. We had just entered the main hall. It was swarming with guardsmen, unlike minutes ago when it had been desolately empty of bystanders. I kept my eyes forward, knowing that if I caught anyone staring at the red mark on my face that I knew was there, I would break down. I'd never been so relieved to sweep up the steps to the Masters' rooms or to let James shuttle me to our room. My breath left me in a whooshing appreciation of my deliverance from my latest ordeal. I swayed in place, more ex-hausted now than ever. James clicked the locks into place behind us and bustled around me, checking for signs of harm that I might not have told him about. I was too impatient and in need of comfort to wait for him to finish his in-spection. I reached up and wound my arms around his neck, holding on to his strong frame for support as my weak knees wobbled together.

"What were you thinking, sending Douglas away like that?" James said with a moan, holding me tightly.

"He had to find you to stop Haitham," I whimpered. "Neither of us could have done it."

James pulled away so that he could stare into my eyes. "Is it true?" he asked. "He detained you because you raised a hand to Selenis?"

I reluctantly trusted him to keep his temper, for I could not guess whether or not he would defend his sister. I nodded and then burst into tears as I was doused in shame. "It's my own fault he took me away. I deserved everything—"

"Don't say such things." James drew me back into his arms to hush me. I buried my face in his chest as my nerves ebbed away with each quivering breath and sob. I could feel the pill I'd taken minutes ago begin to kick in and the re-lease in my muscles was like a cool hand on a hot forehead. I melted into James as my heartbeat was restored to its normal, if not more subdued, rate.

"Believe me when I say everybody who knows Selenis has wanted to knock her down a few pegs at one point or another," James said.

"She convinced Dulce to lie to us," I said thickly. "She buttered us up like pastries just because her mother said to do it." James very tactfully did not re-mind me again that which I already knew, that he never wanted us to mingle with his niece in the first place. Had we listened to him, we never would have crossed paths with Selenis.

"To bed," James said. He noticed my gradual sagging posture and guided me over to the mattress. I crawled to the middle of the bed and didn't bother pulling back the covers before curling up amid the pillows stacked at the head-board. I checked behind me and saw James standing at the edge of the bed, apparently disinclined to follow me.

"Get over here," I said. James complied without complaint, sliding across the coverlet and molding his front to my back. I took his hand and brought it to my lips, hugging his arm close. We remained quiet for a time, just breathing together and grounding ourselves in the close comfort of one another. My body gave a little shudder as the last of my adrenaline burned away and James pressed a curing kiss to the slope of my neck.

"James?" I wondered if it was strange for him to hear his own name spoken so softly.

"What is it?" he replied quietly.

"Do you really think he'll leave?" It was impossible to imagine Haitham relenting to the command of another Master, let alone his own son.

"I know that he will. One way or another, he will be gone tomorrow."

I felt the chill in his tone on the back of my neck, so to soothe James, I held his hand to my lips and softly kissed the back of it. I thought I could drift off to sleep with the assistance of the medicine I'd taken, but like the aftermath of Quinn's attack, Haitham's cruel, twisted features were waiting to glare at me on the backs of my eyelids. "There was such hate in his eyes," I recalled vacantly. "He kept demanding over and over that I tell him the truth—"

"Liza," James hushed me. "I don't want to talk about Haitham right now."

I rolled my head so that I faced him. He was lying so close that the tips of our noses touched. I kissed his lips, as they were a mere inch from my own, and was amazed down to my tired bones by how fast distress tumbled off me. James kissed me too with tender care, though I could sense sadness in him. I was determined to rouse him into better spirits, as I'd had my fill of gloom for the day. I guided James' hand over my breast and went to kiss him again, but James stilled in hesitation.

"What's the matter?"

"You've been through so much today," he said. "You're in pain. I don't think it's a good idea."

I couldn't blame him for stopping himself before he got started—a freshly battered woman who had been sobbing just moments ago was hardly desirable. But I wasn't really crying anymore, just exhausted from the wildly emotional and frightening episode that I'd just suffered. Perhaps that made it worse for him. All I knew for certain was that I wanted him to make me forget about the whole thing for as long as he could and help him to do the same.

"The pain isn't bothering me," I told him.

"You should rest," James said anyway.

"I will after." I let my intention sink in for a few moments. I then snuggled into his front and was pleased when he did not scoot away. "Come on, James."

"Liza." It was an even weaker protest than the half-asleep one he had given the night we first came together.

"Please, James." Apparently, I was a beggar—who would have known?

James heaved a sigh of forfeit and kissed me, slowly, as though he were savoring the touch of my lips on his. He sat up behind me and trailed his fingertips along my waist and down the small of my back. I reached for the band of my trousers but James stopped me.

"Let me." With just one deft motion, off slipped my trousers. James grasped my hips and turned me not onto my back, like I anticipated, but so that I was lying on my stomach. It was new of him to straddle my legs from behind instead of lying on top of me and seating himself between my thighs. James leaned over me, smoothing his hand up my back. Once more he kissed behind my neck, then the side of my throat. I reached for a pillow and clung to it in anticipation of our bodily union; and then it was upon me, and my breath left me in a great sigh.

"I was so afraid of what he would do," James whispered as we moved together. He laid his hand over the top of mine and we laced our fingers together.

"I'm all right," I assured him unevenly. It was so hard to focus now that he was inside me.

"I don't want to lose you." James rolled his hips and I whimpered with delight.

"So keep me," I urged breathlessly. James adjusted his rhythm accordingly. Having my legs together seemed to be making a new world of difference, making me moan and grunt in reflexive response to these engrossing, swelling sensations. James withdrew his hand from mine and steadied himself by holding my waist, pressing me into the bed. By the sound of him, he was gratified and having an easy time finding felicity in every thrust. On my belly, I couldn't reach him or pull him in to kiss, so I bit the pillow as tremors of a very different nature than panic overtook my body and the thick rope of pleasure knotted and tightened in my belly. I was grasping for nothing and curling my toes when that indescribable buildup released in rolling, vivid waves of sheer satisfaction.

James continued to work me relentlessly, devoted to my body in ways I couldn't count. By the time he lost himself inside me, I was ready to chase after overbearing pleasure a second time. I could not contain my very vocal response to this second coming, especially when James' arrival was so intense and possessive. James praised me with fervor and held onto me until I was still.

Only after our sex was I ready for him to curl into my back, assuming our initial positions, and hold me in his arms as we both stretched out amid the mussed sheets and pillows. Neither of us had the strength to get up and close the shades, which was just as well, because we both preferred to fall asleep under the sparkling stars reflecting in the vast, tossing sea.

"James?" I murmured as drowsiness smothered me.

"Liza?" he returned sleepily.

"Thank you." For pleasing me, for taking me back from Haitham, and for telling me the truth about so many aspects of my life—I thanked him for all of it.

"Don't thank me." James, from what I knew about his ability to fall asleep almost instantly, was not long for this wakeful, intimate moment. "Mastery is a thankless job, my love."

I smiled. I turned over in his arms just enough to reach his lips with mine. "Are you my Master now, or am I yours?" I couldn't help but recall his choice of impassioned words he'd proclaimed during his ascendancy of our union and blush. I was hardly in a state to go again but something in me swelled to think of what he said.

"You are mine," sighed James, holding me a little tighter. Whether he was answering my question or merely declaring me as *his* was unclear. I supposed that I would have to make peace with either probability. With a smile still on my face, I let sleep take me.

When I woke up, the sun's hazy glow was creeping over the sea in the distance. I felt groggy and was quite parched as I resolved to wake up, instead of rolling over to fall back to sleep. I rubbed at my eyes and yawned, turning over while arching my back to stretch my leaden muscles. James was sitting up against the headboard, staring straight ahead. He did not look over to me but reached to touch my arm when he realized I was awake.

I could guess what was on his mind. "What did Kit come to tell you yesterday?" My lover heaved a sigh and pinched the bridge of his nose, like he always did when he was thinking through something complicated.

"Essentially that the structure of this compound is more fragile than I ever imagined." James errantly brushed his thumb over my shoulder as he contemplated further. "It wouldn't take so little to topple a structure that is actually sound. I blame myself, my blindness, my disdain for any sign of the reality of my life here—"

"James." I didn't want to hear his torrent of self-loathing. "Tell me what happened."

"My time as the Master of this place is, unfortunately, likely to draw to a close very soon."

"*What?*" With wide eyes, I sat up to face him. "Why?"

"I'm not sure it matters why," James supposed. "Kit came to me yesterday to share something...I don't know. The details paint a lurid portrait of my peers—one in particular—and how they really see my role here."

"You'll find a way to fix it," I said, stunned.

"That's just it, Liza. I don't think I *can* fix this," said James. As he considered his next words, a simper flitted across his face. "What's worse is that I don't even know if I want to."

"But what did Kit come to tell you?" I asked. A shadow passed over me as I remembered Haitham's certainty in his obscure line of questioning last night. "Is it about Harriet?"

James broke his staring pose and turned his sharp blue eyes on me. "How the hell do you know about Harriet?"

"I only know her name. Haitham accused me last night of sending her a signal—he insisted that I had, and was lying to him about it."

"Did he really?" James looked ill suddenly.

"Who is she?" I pressed him.

"Harriet is Graham's daughter," James said. "She is also the reason the others are so keen on the idea of taking more Free children into the system."

"But I thought she was dead!"

"Worse." James looked as though he'd swallowed something bitter. "She defected. Graham and his family used to be the most prominent figures in the system who weren't Masters themselves. When Harriet reached induction age, we expected she would swear in and take a compound of her own in the east—one that would be virtually handed to her by Haitham—but she renounced the system, cut ties with everyone she knew, and joined the Free Factions. Graham's wife died shortly after, from the shock of it all."

Even the brief summation of the scandal and loss in Graham's life rocked me. I never knew defection was even an option for members of the system. "Haitham believes I sent her a signal…does that mean she is out there somewhere waiting to act?"

"I couldn't say, but if he was desperate enough to remand you in the middle of the trade floor for questioning, then Haitham must know something we don't and it can't be good," James deduced carefully. "It's unlike him to be careless…if Harriet is involved with what's going on out there, whatever she's doing is making Haitham very nervous. It's spooking the others too."

"I don't think he's afraid of anything." An evil man like Haitham had teased James to his face and reacted to a gun on him as though it were a child's toy.

"You are wrong about that," said James. "My father is afraid of losing his power—why else would he take part in such calculating methods to protect it?"

"That makes him selfish, but it doesn't mean he cares about the lives of all the people who are protected under the treaty you have with my parents," I replied, disarmed to hear James refer to Haitham as his father.

"Ah, but that is what Haitham would refer to as a 'common interest' with the others. They care very much about serving the system, whereas he only cares to serve himself."

"It just so happens that the system keeps him in power," I concluded. So the old man had the other Masters convinced that his fervor to reinstate the total control over the Free Factions was rooted in his desire to perpetuate a better system even though his true motive could not be farther from the truth.

"This is what he does." James' words were heavy with cynicism. He'd said it before about his father. "He weaves intricate webs of fear and deceit, knowing that the further he aligns his interests with those of the other Masters, the harder it will be for me to fight him. He thinks only of himself and I have the lives of everyone protected by this compound to consider. Luckily for me, the Masters do not make hasty decisions during summits like this as every step we take carries a great risk."

"But they're still going to go ahead with their plan to take more children?" Masters and Mistresses would clean the compound of food, drink, and space for weeks while pondering every little facet of a decision that they were largely too skittish to make, but because any alternative to the unthinkable arrangement would cost them their own time and money, they would eventually go ahead with the proposed solution! I hated politics for this exact reason.

"As I keep telling you, life on the outside is dangerously chaotic. The fear of a fracture in the system is what is pushing the Masters to act radically. All they have to do is look at Harriet Keating's brand of problem solving to see that getting their hands dirty might pay off for them."

"Harriet's brand? I thought our parents comprised the Free Faction leadership," I pointed out, speaking on behalf of Daisy and the boys.

"They do," James explained. "As they vastly outrank Harriet in experience, and Free people would never trust a girl who was born into the system, no matter how outright she might denounce her background. Kit's father took Harriet in to set an example of sorts—or so he would have everyone believe. Truthfully, Harriet was a genius in school and they'd have been foolish to turn away a woman of her ambition. She has a gift for strategy and speech, she did even as a child. I know next to nothing about her operation, but I know she has success in destroying weapons manufacturing warehouses that belong to the Masters, as well as blocking efforts to export supplies and Tributes to southern compounds. It doesn't surprise me that Haitham suspects there are spies in the system, as Harriet's sabotage usually occurs at very advantageous opportunities for the Free Factions." James had delved into thinking out loud, touching on topics that had clearly been at the forefront of his mind while he worked out his impending usurpation as I slept beside him.

My own mind was hard at work trying to fit together the puzzle pieces of all this new insight. I kept coming back to Graham and his poor wife, how they must have felt when their daughter turned her back on them. It was a twisted trade—I was stolen from my parents and Harriet abandoned hers, yet I found myself in the care of her father and she probably lived under the same roof as mine. Caustic bitterness cut into my tongue as I contemplated all the things I might have asked Graham, had I not been in the dark for my whole life about the precious role I played in the system.

"She's out there, somewhere," I mused tonelessly. "She has no idea her father killed himself."

"Oh, Liza," said James, feeling for my hand. "I'm not sure that he did."

I did not need to think twice about whether or not Haitham was capable of murdering Graham and disguising the deed to implicate Graham himself, but that did not make it any less horrifying. "That's your solution, James," I said. "You have to tell the others what he's done. If you discredit him, they might listen to you."

James peered into my eyes with wistful appreciation. "They *might*, if I have proof." He didn't and we both knew it. We sat in shared silence for a time as our separate trains of thought similarly bumped into walls of cold, refuting truth: he was stuck, I was stuck, and there was no way to get out of it. Even if there was, there was no time, as the summit would reach its end in just a few days. It was awful enough to think about what James had proposed as a compromise—to be separated from Kit, Daisy, and Armand so that I could be inducted as a Mistress and raise a new cluster of innocent children who had been abducted from their beds. At least I would have James in that scenario, but in this one? He would be removed from the Aventine and I would truly be alone...and so would he, a realization that came with an unwelcome pang of longing. I couldn't believe it. James had been right about my induction being the lesser of two evils.

My nose crinkled as my lips tugged into a frown and tears clouded my vision.

James reached to cup my face, captivating me by the soft light in his eyes. "Why are you crying?"

"Because it's too late," I said. "There's nothing we can do. And I'm afraid." Everything had changed since the night I'd followed Daisy to the library, then day by day, it had gotten worse. Soon, everyone I cared about would be gone.

"It might be too late to convince my peers to go another way," James agreed. "But there may be something we can do." He pulled me close, brushing away my tears with the sides of his thumbs, to kiss away the frown from my lips.

"Like what?" I asked, my voice ragged.

James ran his fingertips delicately through my hair and blinked slowly as he stared back at me. "I'm going to ask you something, but before you answer,

I want you to know that no matter what you want, I will do whatever it takes to keep you safe."

"All right," I said. "Ask me."

"Do you want to stay together?"

My heart decided before I did. He'd saved my life three times without question—I knew that I would never feel safe if I didn't have James with me, for whatever he was planning to do. "Yes. I want to stay together." I nodded to emphasize my enthusiasm and pressed my lips to his, feeling James smile as a calm steadiness washed over him. "But James—that means Daisy and the boys too, they wouldn't be safe with Haitham—"

"Yes, I agree," James said. He gathered me into his lap and wound his arms around me, kissing me with renewed vigor. He cradled me possessively, leaning over so that we fell onto the mattress on our sides. "It's not too late," James murmured against my lips. "I know just what to do."

"You do?" I praised him with a deep, lingering kiss.

"That's right," James said. He held me snugly to his chest, nuzzling the tender flesh under my chin and planting sweet, safe kisses there. I crooned gentle nothings to him for a while before he abruptly sat up and rolled off the bed. "Come, we don't have a moment to lose. We'll bathe and then we'll take a walk."

"A walk?" I asked, a little woozy from the whir of intimacy that I was sure had been building to something more.

"Yes," James insisted.

"Surely we have a moment or two to lose...." I twisted in bed, not ready to give up the comfort of his immediate proximity just yet.

"You're a model of chastity, Liza," James declared with a smirk, crawling back into bed with me. He placated me for a while, kissing me all over and sculpting each curve of my body that he could reach with his hands. "Up with you," James coaxed after what felt like a long while but I knew was too short. "If we go again, you'll lose your legs and we won't have time to find them...."

I groaned and laid my head back. "You can't resist shelling out orders, can you?" I asked, pouting.

"You ought to count yourself lucky that I *can* resist," James murmured. "Now come along." He kissed me one more time before sliding off the bed again, this time taking me with him.

"How many days do I have left of this?" I asked, rolling my eyes as James wrapped my arms in translucent green waterproofing tape.

"Not long, for your arms," James said expertly. He fastened the tape over the bandage on my shoulder and sealed it with a kiss. "This one, however, may need some more time." He turned on the water and stepped into the shower, pulling me by the hand in behind him. I loved the feel of his bare chest when it was slick with water. I explored his chiseled frame, mindful of the bruises that still splotched across his side. Many were still richly purple but the rims of them were now yellowing, a sign of healing. For such a savage attack, James' injuries were healing fast.

"You almost caught me," I remembered. Suddenly, the hot water raining down on me felt chilly.

"Almost?" mused James, winding his arms around me. "You seem very caught to me."

"And you seem very sure of yourself," I noticed. James was even lighter spirited than the last morning we'd spent together. "What are you thinking, James?"

"I'm thinking, I like the sound of my name when you say it."

This time, he stayed with me until I was finished rinsing the suds from my hair. Once I'd wrung my hair out, James shut off the water but did not take leave of the steamy encasement just yet. He lavished my throat with adoring, tarrying kisses as beads of water ran down our bodies. I melted in his arms and just when I was prepared to beg him to take me there, he slid open the shower door and reached for a towel.

"I resent that!" I whined, snapping my own towel before wrapping it around me.

"We have a tight schedule to keep to this morning," James said. At least he had the decency to sound sorry.

I went to the mirror to towel dry my hair and brush it out. I craned my head to the side to better work through it with my fingers before using a brush and glanced at my throat. "How is it that you don't leave a mark?" I asked, noticing that I had no flagrant dark *coso* on my neck despite all the attention James paid there. I could still see a faded pink splotch on James' neck from our first night together and couldn't help but ask.

James cleared his throat as he stepped into his trousers. "Practice, I suppose," he said.

I felt the tickle of a blush gathering in my cheeks. My naivety had embarrassed me—of course he'd had more practice than I. My boldness returned with a fury and I asked, "How much practice?"

"Not as much as you'd think," James replied easily, as though he'd anticipated the follow-up question. "Are we having that conversation?"

"I don't think so." I pulled off the green tape once I'd finished brushing my hair and winced as the adhesive pinched at the soft hair on my arms. If he quoted me a number of former paramours, I would probably cry.

"Does it bother you that I've had others?" I considered him for a moment before flashing a smile and shaking my head as I wrapped fresh gauze around my forearm.

"No," I said. "Of course not." I was tempted to point out that he was older than me by twelve years but thought better of it. I did not like to think of him with other lovers, but then I imagined James as a youth and how stifling it must have been like for him to grow up with Haitham as his father. I hoped the handsomely youthful blue-eyed adolescent I was picturing had some comfort to turn to—goodness knows, I needed him now, maybe as much as he needed me.

"I meant what I said last night, Liza." We made a curious pair, as he was now fully dressed and I was standing naked with wet hair. James carried a stack of clean garments over and set them on the sink's countertop beside me. "I don't want to lose you."

"And I meant what I said this morning," I told him. "I want to stay together." The short space between us vibrated with electricity. I saw his gaze trail down past my chin, my breasts, and then below my navel. I wondered how fast he could disrobe—and whether or not he would.

"You should dress," he muttered.

"Should I?" My heart fluttered in excited anticipation to see the haziness that clouded James' eyes.

"Definitely." He snapped himself out of his momentary mesmerized stupor. "You and I are going to have breakfast with Daisy and the boys."

He may as well have pinched me. I came to myself and reached for my fresh clothes. "Are we?"

"Oh, yes," said James. "We have a lot to discuss."

It took me no time to dress. By the time I'd yanked on my socks and swept out of the bathroom, James was at his desk paging the kitchen and shrugging into a sleek, black jacket. "Lorraine should have everything ready by the time we get there," he said.

"Do I have time to braid my hair?"

"That depends," James replied. "Do you want time to do it?"

Bashful, I smiled and shook my head. "Let's just go," I said. I pointed to my socks. "Boots?"

"I don't see why not," James said. "They're under your cot."

As soon as my boots were on, James led the way out the door and into the corridor. Douglas was waiting there, looking tired but pleased to see us.

"Good morning, sir," Douglas said to James, falling easily into stride with him. "Master Haitham is no longer in the Aventine. He was gone shortly after you left him last night."

"Good." James was not hiding any glee with his curtness—he really was glad in the coldest way that his villainous father was no longer under his roof. "There is no room for any unexpected problems surrounding his departure, Douglas...."

"He was escorted out, I assure you, sir," said Douglas. "I took the liberty of changing the guardsmen rotation shifts to ensure the perimeter remains secure."

"I'm glad to have at least one capable man in my service," said James.

"Are you well, Liza?" Douglas asked me. I told him I was no worse off and thanked him for inquiring after me. He seemed glad to hear it and even gladder when James did not dismiss him once we reached the door to the main hall.

"I'm planning on moving Liza back to the Tribute wing when the summit is over," said James in the succinct, private way he always did when there were people around. "I may be some time, discussing a few new regulations with them. I would like you to remain outside and ensure that we are not interrupted."

"As you say, sir," said Douglas. He clipped alongside me in watchful silence the rest of the way, making sure the tradespeople gave us a wide berth. I wagered that last night's fiasco had shaken Douglas, as he seemed to be focused solely on keeping me between James and himself while forcing a neutral expression.

Lorraine and her assistant were leaving our apartment just as we arrived. She afforded James a generous salutation before bustling off back to the kitchen, where breakfast preparations for the Masters were likely in full swing and very chaotic. I let myself into the apartment with James at my heels. The scent of hot sausage and baked bread warmed me as I rushed through the entryway, not stopping to remove my shoes, to the kitchen, where Armand, Kit, and Daisy were unpacking the heaps of food Lorraine had just delivered.

Armand reached me first for a greeting hug. I felt a rush of relief wash over me when he lifted me off my feet, squeezing me tightly in his arms. My cheek was against his and he felt hot, almost as though he had a fever. When he set me down and stepped back, my happiness wavered as I saw how exhaustion had dulled his features.

"Are you all right?" I asked, feeling his forehead and the side of his neck.

"I'm fine, now that you're here," he said. He'd been crying, I could tell from the scratch in his voice. Daisy came to me before I could fuss over Armand any further.

"He's just tired," she whispered to me as she held me around the waist. She released me and glanced over my shoulder. "Good morning, James."

"Hello, Daisy," said James, appearing jacketless behind us. I stared holes into Kit's turned back as he continued to mechanically unpack breakfast, item by item.

The three of them had fought, I knew it for certain. Kit was ignoring me to save face. Why else would he not acknowledge me?

"I suppose you're here to tell us what went on yesterday," said Armand, doing his best to be churlish by crossing his arms and glaring at James. My poor Armie was too tired to muster passable intimidation though and submitted as soon as James stood over him.

"Why don't we all take a seat?" suggested James. Daisy and Armand exchanged nervous glances as they silently agreed that it was very uncharacteristic of James to let Armand's attitude go by without scolding. "Kit, sit down. Leave that for a moment."

Kit obeyed, putting down the container of freshly washed and sliced fruit without a word. He turned, though he kept his eyes averted, and took a seat at the table. Daisy dropped next to him, as if her body was connected by strings to Kit's, and Armand was so determined to be difficult that he only sat when I did. James moved Daisy's ballet bag from the fifth chair where it sat in the corner and joined us at the table.

"You may help yourselves," James said, gesturing to the bread, sausage, and pastries in the center of the table. None of us touched the food—even I was too nervous to eat, though my stomach was rumbling. "Very well," said James. "I would like to be the first among us to turn over a new leaf. By doing so, as a gesture of good faith, I will be as forthcoming with you as I can be even though all four of you have deceived me in some way or another over the past few weeks."

"You want to turn over a new leaf," Daisy repeated, her tone stale.

"I do," said James. "You see, in light of everything we have found out about Donovan's ploy to usurp me as Master, I believe it is imperative that we trust each other enough to work together."

"You all knew about this?" I asked as soon as the others did not pale or balk at James' latest remark. James held up a hand to silence me—obviously they did, but he did not want to waste time rehashing the details.

"Why would we want to work together?" Armand drawled warily.

James sat back in his chair. "We share a common interest." He wielded Haitham's phrase with dark satisfaction. "After Kit came to me yesterday, I thought about how best to move forward. Extending the summit would be a folly and dealing with Donovan in the presence of my peers would make matters much worse. After much deliberation, I realized that there was a singular path ahead of us that would keep you not only alive, but together."

I wasn't even looking at Daisy and Kit to know that they sat forward in their seats, for I had done it too. My appetite had shifted to a parched thirst as I waited, my heart pounding in my chest, to hear what James had decided. I was so compelled by the spark in his eyes that I almost forgot myself and reached for his hand.

"This afternoon, I will inform the guards and the rest of the staff that Liza is being moved back to the Tribute wing in two days, when the summit concludes. I will also begin to make arrangements for Armand and Liza to meet with a Preparations Instructor, to commence their induction lessons, as the two of you are of age to do so," he said, eyeing me and Armand.

We both stared back at him in horror.

"Between now and then, the four of you will attend lessons and maintain the idea that nothing that we know of is out of the ordinary. You especially," James said to Armand, whose cheeks flushed with color. "As far as Donovan knows, I have no reason to suspect that my days as Master are limited. The summit will end after lunch, the day after tomorrow, and he will enact the schism he has planned."

I yelped, "Your plan is to do nothing?"

"You don't seriously expect us to sit through induction lessons," Armand warned gravely.

"Don't be ridiculous, of course not," said James. "Two mornings from now, while the Masters gather to close the summit, I will leave the compound and take the four of you with me."

Stunned silence rang in the kitchen. The four of us, dumbfounded, could barely react. My jaw dropped.

"But you—*what?*"

"Am I right in thinking that you didn't catch a wink of sleep last night, Kit?" James asked. "Well, neither did I. It gave me the opportunity to think, really think, about what my future as Master of this compound might entail. I realized that I don't want to be here any more than you do, and if Donovan wants a crack at my job, then he can have it."

"You're going to let him get away with everything?" Kit demanded, outraged.

"Not at all," said James, remaining calm.

"I seem to recall you vowing to make Donovan live to regret this," Kit retorted.

"I think you misunderstand me," James said to him. "I'm not going to take you to a safehouse and lie low like some kind of disgraced senator; I mean to defect, Kit. I'm going to deliver you to your parents."

I clapped my hands over my mouth. Daisy reacted similarly, reaching for Kit with her other hand. Armand shot to his feet with a wild look in his eyes.

"You're lying," Armand said.

"I assure you, I am not," James said seriously.

"You almost killed yourself trying to get Liza back after she ran away, locked us up in every way imaginable since then—and now you're going to throw it all away and escape with us?"

"I wouldn't say 'walking out' qualifies as an escape, Armand," James pointed out. "Nor am I throwing anything away. On the contrary, I intend to make use of every detail I have at my disposal to remind my peers that I will not tolerate betrayal. They can thank Donovan for that."

I couldn't believe what he was saying. "Just like that?"

James nodded. "As I said, we have a common interest. You want out of here? So do I," he said. "Now, this is our only feasible plan, but it is not foolproof. We will all need to act accordingly. If Donovan or anyone else catches on, we will fail spectacularly." He seemed fixated on singling out Armand in all this. "Do you understand, Armand? If you don't think you can keep up appearances, I can cite you for saying something inflammatory and you may remain here in the apartment. We can pretend you are being punished."

"We can keep him with us," Daisy volunteered. "We'll go to lessons together, cook, whatever we need to."

"Would that arouse Donovan's suspicion, Armand?" asked James. "I might say it's best to have you out and about, but if you suddenly make yourself unavailable—"

"I can do it." Armand perked up and interrupted James with a vigorous nod of his head. "He won't suspect anything is amiss."

I hadn't realized Armand's friendship with Donovan was strong enough to merit this kind of attention, but I supposed James wanted to make sure there was no margin for error.

"That settles it, then." James stood up from his chair and returned it to the corner of the kitchen. "On the morning of the summit's conclusion, I want the four of you to meet me in the Master library."

I blanched. "Why?"

"It will serve as the best antechamber for our purposes. There's a private entrance to the Masters' rooms down the hall from the library, one which leads to the outside. The library is out of the way, no servant will question you going there if you say you have my permission and you need materials for your lessons," said James. I looked up at him and noticed a sparkle of mischief in his eyes. "It's rather fitting, too, don't you think?"

To finally escape this place, we would have to go back to where the idea itself was born.

"If you must go all together, so be it, but it might be best to stagger your arrival so as not to turn any heads," said James. He thought of everything— we never went to that library together, maybe in pairs at the most. It would have looked odd to see all four of us march over there in two days' time.

"I think we can manage that," said Kit weakly.

"I will leave you here for the morning, Liza," said James. "Douglas is posted outside. When it comes time for your lesson, he'll escort you to the gallery and take you back to your room in the Masters' rooms after."

"As you say." I was so happy, I could have kissed him right there.

"If any of you has any objections or concerns, say them now," James said, readying to take his leave. If any of us had them, we were still too abashed to articulate them. "Well, then, I will leave you to it. Keep your heads down and your mouths shut until two mornings from now. Enjoy your breakfast."

James was gone for ten seconds when Daisy threw her arms around Kit. Kit rose to meet her and the pair kissed sweetly.

"I'm so sorry," Kit blurted hastily between fast kisses from Daisy. "I couldn't breathe a word—"

"I don't care!" Daisy enthused. She was moved to tears. "It doesn't matter anymore. We're getting out of here!"

We were getting out of here.

I looked to Armand. By his expression, he looked like he'd just been slapped. "It's true," he said, answering the unspoken disbelief he read in my eyes. "We're leaving, Liza. We're finally going to be free." The legs of his chair groaned as Armand stood, scooting his seat back. He opened his arms to me and I went to him, in shock, with a bemused smile on my face. I held on to him for minutes, breathing in the smell of his spicy citrus soap and baked bread, feeling the most at home that I had in weeks. He pressed a secretive kiss to the side of my head and held me back even tighter.

"You said it would be someday," he murmured in my ear. "Someday is just two mornings from now."

"We'll all be together," I said. I clung to Armand as my heart burst with joy. I could feel it in my bones—in just two more sunrises, our lives would change forever.

Chapter Twenty-five

Donovan the Master watched from afar as a line of servants carried the enormous easel into the Tribute wing. They reminded him of a colony of ants in their efficiency and dutiful march across the bustling trade floor, numb to the unwieldly object's immense weight on their backs. A younger woman followed the group carrying the easel with a crate in hand, filled with paintbrushes, scrolls of sketch parchment, and bottles of oil paints.

So, James was allowing Liza to move back to her apartment. Haitham would have said it was a waste of perfectly good manual labor, for in just a few hours when the keys of James' castle were handed to him, Donovan would see to it that the girl's easel would have to be carried much farther than the space between the Masters' rooms and the Tribute wing. Though Donovan did not care for the way Liza stared after Armand, he thought she might make a good Mistress soon—as long as she did not resist her preparations.

"You'll be late for dinner," said Selenis, coming out of the crowd to wait at Donovan's side and watch the servants maneuver the easel through the Tribute wing's little door. Donovan ignored his aunt and reached into the breast pocket of his jacket for his thin case of cigarettes. Selenis regarded Donovan with pursed disdain and waved the smoke away from her face. "He'll bite your head off for doing that in here," she told him, helplessly mothering her favorite sister's son.

"As if I care what James thinks about my habits," Donovan said. He'd been lingering in the main hall for hours, waiting for Armand to emerge from the apartment.

"Are you coming?" Selenis asked. Being ignored was near the top on her list of high offenses and even Donovan was not exempt from her smoldering contempt. She smoothed the sleeves of her satin blouse and waited for her nephew to respond. When he didn't, Selenis laid her hand on his arm. "After tomorrow night, when things are official, I truly hope you are a less distracted Master than you're acting like now."

Donovan replied with a pernicious glare and a long drag of his cigarette. "If you were in my position, you might be on edge too. I'm the one who has to face him tomorrow night, not you." She had some gall to nag him about being distracted, as Donovan knew full well that Selenis—despite her ice queen façade—would balk if she were on the receiving end of James' rage. She certainly would not think twice before submitting to him.

"All the more reason you should eat something and try to take your mind off it," said Selenis. She would rather have snapped back at him but she knew it was better to be a balm on the eve of such a crucial coup.

"I've no appetite," said Donovan, adjusting his focus back to the Tribute wing.

"I'd hoped you would get my daughter to eat something," Selenis said with a disappointed sigh. She followed Donovan's gaze and frowned when she realized where he was looking.

"What's the matter with her?" Donovan asked errantly about Dulce.

"*No sé*," Selenis replied. "But she won't touch her food, and she barely makes a sound."

"Well, you know how girls her age can be," said Donovan. He glanced sideways at his aunt and snorted. "Not that you ever had a jovial bone in your body when you were young," he joked, flashing his white teeth in a daring smile.

"That girl hasn't shut up since she learned how to talk," Selenis pointed out hotly. She did not approve of jokes at her expense any more than she did being ignored. Donovan had nothing to say about Dulce's malaise, he just kept peering over at the Tribute wing. Selenis crossed her arms and planted the drastically tall heel of her boot.

"All right, which one is it?" she demanded, fed up.

"Which one is what?" Donovan asked. He was getting annoyed by Selenis and her questions, which only further baited the Mistress to shut him up.

"There are three pretty idiots living in that apartment, Doni. *¿Cuál te estás follando?*" asked Selenis. Donovan finished his cigarette and stomped it under his boot with zealous resentment but otherwise did not move. Had he whipped around and accused her of cruelty, Selenis might have backed off; his lack of reaction was all too telling and made it impossible for Selenis not to bite. "It's the girl, isn't it?" Selenis asked, sizing up her nephew as he continued to ignore her. "She's tall, not usually your type, but then again she is not like the girls down south. She's exotic. I know how much men favor such a quality. And she's so young—was she a virgin when you had her?"

"I won't even dignify that with a response," Donovan growled.

"Tell me it's not the Danvers boy," said Selenis, her accent lending even more scorn to her tone. "He's prettier than most girls, I think. You might as well go for the girl after all...unless it's really Edita's son you're sniffing around after, which would probably explain why he looks at you like the sun shines out your—"

Selenis was quick to obey when Donovan snapped around and loomed over her with the look of pure, black rage in his eyes that he'd inherited from his grandfather, and told her to shut her mouth.

"What have I done to deserve such a lashing from you?" he demanded mutely, ever mindful of the busy hall he was standing in.

"I see I've touched a nerve," said Selenis. So it *was* the di Felce boy. She had to keep from showing her teeth in a sneer as she displayed her own stony reserve. "You think I care about your conquests? I don't. All I care about is what happens over the next twelve hours. I'll tell you right now, Doni, if anything happens in that time to disrupt what we have planned, there will be the devil to pay—as I will raise hell and I don't care who gets burned."

"You sound just like your father," said Donovan. It was the meanest thing he could think of to say.

"Is that meant to wound me?" Selenis hissed. "I've been hearing it all my life. It's not nearly as damaging as being constantly shoved out of the picture to make way for you and James. I am sick of the men in this family being given endless opportunities for true greatness time and time again only to find new ways of lousing it up!"

"I have no intention of lousing it up!" Donovan retorted. He was in danger of drawing a crowd. While he loved his aunt, he would not be abused in public like this by his political peer.

"You'd better not," said Selenis. She could see that she was enticing Donovan's temper and dropped her arms to show that she was backing down. "You are not as slick as you think you are, Donovan. Now, I don't give a damn whose legs you spend your down time in between, but if I can see it, then so can anyone else who bothers to pay attention to you. In case I didn't make myself clear earlier, this is my last straw with you *and* with James. If anything happens tomorrow to mess up the outcome of this summit, I will personally see to it that you are not present at the next one."

As she was one to always have the last word, Selenis left her nephew to stare daggers after her. Donovan knew he would never hear an apology from her, nor would she repeat herself. He knew that she was right to approach the next twelve hours with cautious hypervigilance, but the audacity to muse to his face about which of James' Tributes she thought he was having an affair with was over the line, even for Selenis.

Poor Dulce, thought Donovan. He could not imagine having a tyrannical, cutthroat woman like Selenis for a mother. He had just begun to wonder who might be more unbearable as a parent, Selenis or James, when someone nudged his shoulder.

"Fancy meeting you here," said Armand, wearing his usual fawn-colored shirt and pants—and as always, socks without shoes.

"I'd hoped I would see you before tomorrow," said Donovan, whose piercing teal eyes illuminated at the sight of the young man. "What brings you out and about?"

"Well," sighed Armand, "Liza is moving back tomorrow. I'm planning our meal—our first meal, as a family reunited."

Donovan could not decide whether he hated Liza's sultry stares at Armand more than the dopey, dreamy look that overcame Armand's face when Liza's name passed his lips. In fact, the Master's stomach knotted in eager anticipation at the thought of how soon he would be able to send her away.

"That sounds wonderful," said Donovan with a grin. "I'll walk with you while you shop." He kept his hands clasped in a relaxed pose behind his back as he followed Armand around the market. He loved to watch his lover sift through ingredients with rapt attention, selecting only the tomatoes that felt just right and only the herbs that smelled just so.

"I should apologize," Armand said in a low voice after a tradesman passed him back a wrapped parcel of fresh gnocchi. "The other morning, I wasn't myself." His admission came as a welcome relief, as Donovan had been petrified that his unconventional solution to Armand's plea for liberation had not gone over well.

"Was it your spat with my cousin that did it?" wondered Donovan, remembering Selenis telling him that Dulce was showing similar signs of distress.

"In part," said Armand. "So much has happened in just a few days. I haven't slept well."

"So I'm the one who should apologize," Donovan said, wearing a guilty smile. He would have kept Armand up all night and planned to try as soon as James was gone from this place.

"Perhaps." Armand blushed gorgeously. As the color in his cheeks abated, Armand collected a few other ingredients, which would cost James a fortune. "You should have dinner with us tomorrow," he entreated the Master with a sparkle in his brown eyes.

"I would be honored," said Donovan. "What about...?" He trailed off for a moment as a few tradeswomen known for their gossiping swarmed the area. "...tonight?" His whisper was heavy with alluring intent.

"I don't know," Armand replied in a similar tone. "James laid down the law yesterday. With Liza moving back, we have a brand-new set of rules to abide by—at least until tomorrow night."

"All the more reason to make our last night under his thumb count." Donovan was used to being forward with his lovers but the yearning ache Armand evoked in him was new and difficult for Donovan to reconcile. He considered himself to be a creature of habit and he had not been in a pattern of forming emotional connections to his partners when he first met Armand. There was a softness to his mouth that Donovan loved to capture, a brightness in his eyes that was uniquely spellbinding. His body too was crafted in perfection and there was a passionate, wild streak in his stock that set him apart from Donovan's previous paramours. When Donovan imagined Armand with a sword in his hand, dressed impeccably in a tailored green uniform, he swelled with desire and pride.

He was hours away from locking in a real future with this man. He was so close, he could practically taste it.

"Should I meet you in the studio?" Armand asked. Donovan was moved by the suggestion—it was the place where they had first made love.

"What a stunning idea," said Donovan. "I'll see if I can arrange for Helena to be elsewhere."

Their date was set. Armand loped off to his apartment, his groceries in tow, leaving Donovan standing with his heart full in the middle of the trade floor. The afternoon passed in torturously slow stretches, broken up by a series of little gatherings of Masters. None of them were committed to attending the final day of summit collaborations, since they were united in their decision that would be declared tomorrow. As Donovan busied himself around the market, making small talk with some of the friendlier tradespeople he'd come to know over the past month, he errantly thought that these people would all answer to him come sunset tomorrow. How poetic, too, that the sun would literally set on James' time as Master and rise on Donovan's new order. He had no reason to doubt that the people he spoke to would rejoice to trade in James for him. He would see to it that the new lifestyle for people here would be brighter and less restrictive.

And, of course, Donovan would never raise the Tribute infants he might receive like James had raised his four. Not for anything.

The time came for Donovan to meander down to the studio, now that Helena the movement instructor was gone. A devilish smirk twisted Donovan's lips when he thought of what the succulent woman might be up to this evening—he'd seen her fawning over James the night of Dulce's party and the next day, he'd caught a glimpse of something dark on James' neck. It was said of Helena that because of her dancing prowess, she was flexible enough to stretch her legs fully behind her head. *That* was something Donovan might have to see for himself someday, but for tonight, he supposed it was fitting that his uncle might enjoy a last night of excitement before he was removed from his seat.

The studio was dark when Donovan entered quietly. The office light was dim under the crack of its closed door and Donovan smiled when he reached to pull it open. There was Armand, leaning against the desk with his arms folded. His tunic was rumpled and his hair was mussed to the side, as though he'd just gotten out of bed. His eyes glittered up at Donovan in a seductive, heavy-lidded stare.

"Any trouble?" Armand murmured.

"None," replied Donovan, closing the door softly behind him. "Anything I should know?"

Armand's lips pressed firmly together in an adorable but oddly ill-fitting smirk. "No," he said. His features brightened when Donovan swept forward and bent his head in a single swoop, kissing and nuzzling Armand's neck.

"I'll have you in my bed by this time tomorrow," Donovan vowed. He slipped out of his shirt and relieved Armand of his.

"And the night after?" Armand purred, tilting his head back as Donovan dragged his teeth lightly down the front of his throat.

"All nights," rasped Donovan. Armand reached up with one hand to clasp Donovan's shoulder, his thumb resting over his lover's pulse, while with his free fingers he undid the clasp of Donovan's trousers and found the large organ there, underneath the fabric. With relish bordering on worship, Armand began to work the length of it in his hand, his lips touching Donovan's as he primed him with care. A moan sounded from low in Donovan's throat and his jaw dropped. His mouth open, Armand slowly flicked his tongue over the other man's lips and breathed a secretive, panegyric chuckle.

"Take me tonight as if it were our last time," Armand whispered, his breath hot against Donovan's ear. His urging was the hair trigger that dissolved Donovan. He seized Armand by the arms and laid him down on the desk behind them, tasting him deeply as he tore away his trousers. He climbed over Armand and brushed his lips down his chest until he reached the base of his pelvis. Without giving Armand so much as a glance, Donovan took him into his mouth. The sensations that followed were enough to make Armand put his head back with a thud and soon, he was biting the back of his hand to keep from crying out.

When Donovan could not take any more of it, he climbed on top of Armand and the two became one. The feel of Armand's nails digging into his shoulders only drove him to work him with less and less abandon, to hear those ecstatic moans and feel the chase of shivers that coated his lover's body. The finish was consuming and joyous; Donovan was not lost in Armand as he had been before, but found. It made all the grueling work he'd put in over the past few weeks utterly worth it. He saw strange sadness in Armand's eyes and kissed the younger man's temple to soothe him, rolling after to his side as the lasting tremors left him.

"What's the matter?" Donovan asked his lover.

Armand turned his head to look at him, the haze of post-coitus vanished in his eyes. "Do you love me?" His voice was impossibly small.

"Yes," Donovan replied. He sat up and pulled Armand along with him, drawing him close so that he could peer into his warm, dark eyes. "You're uncertain—why?"

"Would you kill for me?" asked Armand instead of answering the question.

Donovan's heart skipped a beat. "Why would you ask that?"

He could not know—it was not possible.

"Is it James you're afraid of? You think he'll take the news tomorrow badly, is that it?" He kissed Armand to steady his own nerves and shroud the gleam of panic in his own eyes. "I'll protect you, Armand. I won't let James hurt you," he said. He kissed the mark James had put on Armand's chin, a promising balm. "Not ever again."

Armand nodded. He caught the tear as it fell from the corner of his eye and looked away. "I'm a fool," he said. "I shouldn't have said anything."

"This is the eve of battle," Donovan sighed. He caught a loose tendril of Armand's thick hair, longest at the top of his head, with the tip of his finger and wished he could convince him not to berate himself like this. "We are lucky enough to know for sure that the battle will be a very short and bloodless one, but it doesn't mean you aren't allowed to feel nervous."

"Of course," said Armand.

"Tonight is the last we will spend in seclusion together. You'll see, Armand. Tomorrow, everything will be different."

"So it will," replied Armand. He kissed Donovan and hopped off the desk, collecting his discarded vestments from the floor of the office. "Tomorrow when the Masters declare what is to be done, I'll be with the others in the Tribute wing," he said as he pulled his shirt over his head.

"You don't want to be there?" Donovan asked with a raise of his eyebrow. "I would have thought you would want to see the look on James' face when he learns it's over."

"I'm not sure it's smart," said Armand.

Donovan bit back an oath. This was about Liza, he was positive. "I know Liza has been through hell," Donovan reasoned. "I understand you want to protect her. And Daisy, of course. But I think it may be best for Liza to see James' dismissal for herself. Believe me, he's been the hardest of all on her."

"Maybe you're right about that," Armand supposed. "I'll talk to the others about bearing witness. Kit has been so skittish, maybe it would be best for him to see it with his own eyes."

"He's sympathetic to a fault," Donovan agreed. "With or without Kit and the girls, I hope you'll come. Trust me, Armand. The unseating of James the Master is something you will surely regret not seeing for yourself."

The other Masters agreed that all who witnessed the events of tomorrow would surely tell their children the tale in avid detail, for when a legendary figure fell from power, the retelling of it in turn would become a monumental story.

"I'll be there," said Armand. He came forward to press a farewell kiss to Donovan's cheek, then lips. "Look for me."

Donovan did not want to let go of Armand, even though he knew this was the last time they would ever have to meet like this. He wanted to traipse alongside Armand, matching his slow, sweeping strides as he returned to his bedroom in the Tribute wing but he knew he would be in danger of chasing him into his room and joining him there.

There was simply too much to do tonight in order to ensure tomorrow would be a roaring success. Donovan had been a hurried slave to Armand's needs for the night and should sleep, but he knew he would never be able to hush his excited mind long enough to drift off. So he dressed, combed his fingers through his hair, and breezed out of the studio office. He remembered his aunt saying something about Dulce's discontent and considered going to call on the girl to get to the bottom of her troubles, but he was too keyed up even after having Armand to be a decent listener. He would go to his room, shower, and pace the floor until it was time for him to join the Masters in the main hall.

Jada was waiting for him outside the door of his Master suite.

"I would have thought you'd be in bed by now," Donovan greeted her quietly in a tone that was anything but warm, reaching for the key in his pocket.

"I'm on edge," said the doctor, pulling the thick, cream-colored wool sweater tighter around her waist. Donovan unlocked his apartment and held the door for Jada, who slipped inside without delay. Donovan passed her his silver case of cigarettes before removing his jacket. He could not wait to rid this apartment of the grandiose décor—how James had seen fit to furnish this spacious room with such bold, baroque pieces was beyond him. Donovan took a seat in an armchair that more resembled a throne across from Jada and watched her light her cigarette with a match she'd taken from a little box on the mantle.

"Don't tell me you're worried about James," prompted Donovan. He made a point to sound weary so that Jada might get the idea he was tired and wanted to be left alone.

"Don't tell me you aren't," replied Jada caustically.

"You of all people have the least to worry about," said Donovan. "As far as anyone around here is concerned, you're innocent in all this. I'm the bad guy, remember?"

"Have you heard from your grandfather?" Jada asked, waving away the Master's assertions with the same hand in which she held her cigarette.

"He prefers to deal with Selenis when we're reduced to solely secretive communications," said Donovan dryly. He feigned a yawn and contemplated whether or not he would make her regret referring to Haitham as his grandfather so casually.

"He sent me two more bodies for my nurses to patch up," said Jada, her tone scathing. "You should have seen the blood...."

"Would you rather he send you roses?"

"Will you quit joking at a time like this? He's on a warpath, Donovan!"

"Well, Harriet has an instigative effect on the old man," said Donovan. "She has ever since her induction fiasco. I can't say I don't feel the same about her.... She always did choose the worst moments to make her point."

"The worst moments for you, maybe," said Jada. "Harriet loves to make messes. Aren't you the least bit concerned that her latest power trip might affect how things play out tomorrow?"

"Honestly, no," replied Donovan. "And I don't know why you would be."

"If you had worked as hard as I have for a place here, you would understand." Jada tossed her depleted cigarette into the fireplace and sat on the high-backed leather sofa opposite Donovan. "One of my nurses spoke to a guard, and she got more out of him than you might like. Master Haitham went after Liza. He would have killed her if Douglas hadn't fetched Master James—"

"No," Donovan assured Jada, "he would not have."

"How are you so certain?" asked the doctor. Her sharp brown eyes were honed in on every feature of Donovan's.

"If he wanted to kill her, he would have," said Donovan. "I'm sure he thought he'd found the leak when he singled Liza out and when he realized he was wrong, he tried to frighten her into telling him what he wanted to hear."

"If he's so desperate to find Harriet, why—?"

"Jada, don't make assumptions. James' father is hardly *desperate*." Without meaning to, Donovan shivered. As a boy, when his mother had been taken by the Free Factions, Donovan had seen Haitham truly desperate. Not only would he never forget it, but he would never mistake Haitham's keenness to achieve his ends as desperation, like Jada just had, as there was a violent world of difference between the two.

"Master James had him banished from the compound," Jada said, resigned to the fact that she would never be able to argue with Donovan about Haitham's state of mind. "You know much about Master Haitham that I do not, but I know a man with a vengeance when I see one. Master Haitham might topple this whole thing simply because he does not care what he ruins, as long as Master James suffers for it."

"James is no longer fit to banish anyone from anywhere," said Donovan finally. He'd heard enough of Jada's worries.

"But is he fit to smell a rat?" Jada wondered. Her eyes sparkled with panicked suspicion. "If he caught a whiff of what we're doing, he could have gone to Harriet himself!"

"Inconceivable." Now Donovan was fed up. "If you think James would stoop so low as to turn to his childhood sweetheart to save his skin, you're even stupider than Graham Keating was for thinking he could go up against Haitham and make it out of here alive." It was a cruel thing to say, and it certainly resonated as such with Jada. "Besides," Donovan added. "James might be a ruthless bully and a fool, but he's loyal to the system. He wouldn't dream of going to Harriet."

The doctor got to her feet, glaring at Donovan as she did, and made for the door. "If I wasn't afraid of ending up just like Keating, I might have a mind to stop you myself."

Donovan helped himself to a generous crystal tumbler of whiskey after Jada saw herself out. It was the only thing to cool his temper and steady his nerves. He sat in silence for hours, staring down the dark hallway of this apartment that he hated so much, wondering where a woman like Jada Miles got the idea to harp at him like she had. What she had suggested about James was laughably inconceivable—he would never go to anyone for help, much less Harriet, if he thought for a second his place as the Aventine's Master was in jeopardy. The whole usurpation plan itself was rooted in James' vast ego. He'd never suspect anyone would make a move against him, least of all his own nephew. He was feared, it was true, but his fate had been sealed the moment his Tribute threw herself out of the library window.

"Ever the fool," murmured Donovan, thinking of Liza. She was in so many ways identical to her mother, he was almost tempted to feel sorry that he would make sure Lorena would never meet her daughter again.

In the smallest hours, as each sip of whiskey tasted smoother than the last, the darkest and bitterest thoughts writhed in his mind like thorny branches. Once he had the Aventine to himself, Donovan might ensure that none of James' Tributes ever saw their parents again. Donovan fell asleep in the warm, sinister comfort that after all these years, the Free Faction leaders who were vain enough to take on parenthood in the face of war with the Masters would finally be punished for murdering his mother.

Chapter Twenty-six

Donovan was not surprised that James had appeared for only the official beginning of the summit's closing ceremony. He hadn't expected him to show up at all and was almost relieved when James, looking grim and annoyed as always, excused himself from the final meeting with a simple "I'm sure you all understand that I have better things to do" before storming out of the congregation hall.

Only when James had gone did Donovan feel like he could breathe freely. Perhaps he was nervous about this, after all.

"I almost feel sorry for the man," sighed Alexander the Master, the copper-haired keeper of the Palatine Compound.

"He knows how this game is played," said Selenis. She eyes Donovan knowingly as he stood up too and pushed his chair in. She rolled her eyes as her nephew stifled a yawn. "*Dios mío*, go and see one of Jada's girls and get a B-12 shot. You look like hell." She glanced to Master Diego at her right and shook her head. "You'd better go too, Diego. I won't have either of you looking strung out when this goes off." With a wave of her hand, the men were dismissed. Donovan did not wait for Diego, for the old drunk's presence would sully even the most impregnably jovial situation. In the time it took for Diego to stand, Donovan was already clipping down the stairs to the Masters' chambers, seeking not one of Jada's nurses, but the strongest cup of coffee he could stomach.

"Good morning, Kit," said Donovan, his features perking up as the young Tribute approached the Master steps.

"Hello, Donovan!" Kit's greeting was enthusiastic. "For the close of a summit, this morning has been rather dull. I thought I would visit the library and track down a book for Daisy."

"Kit, if you were any more thoughtful, I'd have you sainted." Donovan clapped a hand to the boy's shoulder and grinned as Kit blushed. A chord of vigilance struck in Donovan as the Master noticed a peculiar rigidity in Kit's posture. His suspicion was confirmed when Kit wet his lips and flashed a fast smile. Donovan would have put money on it—Kit was nervous.

Could he know? About him and Armand?

"Armand made it sound as though I may not see any of you today," Donovan said, baiting his hook.

"Well, you know how Armand can be. He curls up in his room to abate his boredom, the girls and I tend to lean on the side of restlessness." The color in Kit's cheeks deepened and to disguise it, Kit reached to muss his hair and shift his weight to his other foot. His body language spelled the truth: He knew, and it took everything in Donovan not to swear up and down right there in the middle of the west wing.

"His moods can be dizzying," Donovan agreed. All he could hear was Selenis' voice in his mind, warning him not to louse up the day. He hated proving correctly any assumption that something would go wrong, especially when he would have to take responsibility for it. Very quickly, to hide the fact that he was on the verge of losing his temper, Donovan took his hand off Kit and let his arm fall with a chuckle. "I don't blame you for wanting to get a little air," he said. It was hard to erase the reproach from his tone, but if he could be kind to Liza in public, he could easily smooth things over with Kit.

"I shouldn't keep you," said Kit. "I understand you have closing duties to see to, so—"

"Do you need an escort into the Master library?" Donovan offered. He had his proof but he couldn't resist making Kit squirm to confirm it.

"James said he told the guardsmen to let me pass," Kit replied swiftly. "I wouldn't want to inconvenience you."

"You redefine fastidiousness, Kit," said Donovan, stepping back to let the Tribute make his way up the steps. "Enjoy your morning."

"Thank you," said Kit. "I hope you don't find the summit closing too exasperating." He afforded Donovan a farewell smile and went up the stairs, his ankle-high boots clomping away at a relaxed pace. As Donovan started off for coffee, he tried to keep in mind that of all James' Tributes, Kit was the most reasonable. Once he was the Aventine's Master, perhaps Donovan would be able to kindly convince Kit to—

Donovan halted mid-stride, his heart pounding and his mind whirring.

Boots.

Kit was wearing boots. James had recused himself this morning—and had given Kit permission to enter the Masters' chambers, unescorted, on the final day of the summit.

"Liar!" Donovan hissed under his breath, thinking of the sadness in his lover's voice last night. Tears sprang to Donovan's teal eyes as he realized sickeningly what last night had really meant—it was not the last night of secrecy under James' thumb, it was the last night *period.* Armand had been saying goodbye! The Master blinked rapidly, clearing his cunning stare of the disbelieving tears that had welled a moment before.

"Kit!" Donovan turned and bolted up the stairs, catching the Tribute right before the guardsmen closed the Master room door behind him. Kit did his best to hide his alarm as Donovan caught up with him. "Now that I think of it, I would be happy to walk you to the library. I really should find something for Dulce to read on the journey home, perhaps you can help me find the perfect book?"

"Of course," said Kit. He might have put the force of a dozen curses behind the allowance, but he never faltered. Donovan was impressed by his commitment to his role. The doors closed and bolted behind them, and a thin sheen of sweat broke out over Kit's lip.

"Actually, Kit," said Donovan, as thrilled as a spider who had just snared a fly in its web, "there is something I would like to show you before you head into the library." He was deviously curious to see how far this charade would go.

"I'm not sure," said Kit, edging toward fidgeting from his rapidly wavering nerves. "The library is vast. I had hoped to find the right book by midday—"

"It'll just take a moment," insisted Donovan. He felt a quiet, cold rage build in his chest. It was the same feeling that took over him when he had a blade in hand and knew he was about to win a duel. It was nearly impossible to keep his expression in check, for all he wanted was to curl his lips into a grin and watch as Kit realized that he had walked into a snare, but he could not know if James was watching. He would have to be swift and silent.

"Just this way," said Donovan. He knocked twice on the door to his left and waited, as if he expected someone to answer. After a few counts had passed, Donovan unlocked the door and pushed it all the way open, beckoning Kit to follow him. He did, and once he set foot in the room, unease churned in his belly as he recognized the space inside. The stained-glass windows, benches, and high ceilings would have been breathtaking to behold by anyone else— except Kit knew this place as a horrifying one, as it was the setting of his first meeting with Haitham the Master.

"What do you think of this room?" Donovan asked, meandering along the wooden floor and folding his hands behind his back as he peered up into the rafters.

"It's unlike any in the compound," said Kit stiffly. He let Donovan circle him slowly, watching his catlike strides with wary eyes.

"Indeed it is," said Donovan. "You see the arches there?" He pointed, calling Kit's attention to the far end of the room. "Those were modeled after the church James went to as a boy. The windows too—they tell the story of the Aventine, how the hunting grounds were taken back from the Free Factions just after the Quake. Its name was chosen because its erection heralded the assumption of absolute power. You are standing on wood that was cut down by the very first Master in the very woods this compound is built over, isn't that something?"

"Indeed," said Kit. He swallowed hard and mirrored Donovan's posture, hands clasped behind the back.

Donovan stopped in the center of the aisle, his figure framed perfectly by the arches over his head. "Won't you miss it, when you're gone from this place?" he asked.

"What do you mean?" Kit said, the color draining from his face.

"Oh, Kit." Donovan let his gaze trail down the length of the Tribute's body until it rested on his boots. "I had hoped it wouldn't come to this."

"Come to—what? Donovan, I don't know what you're talking about," said Kit. The corners of his mouth turned down as sweat gleamed on his forehead.

"You're a sweet boy, Kit," said Donovan. "But you're a terrible liar." He took two steps toward Kit, glowering down at him. For once, Kit recognized Donovan as the menacing killer he knew he was. Kit panicked and turned to run, but Donovan showed no sign of pursing him. Just as Kit whirled around, the door to the chapel closed and locked.

Standing in the way of both doors was Haitham. "Hello again, Kit," he said.

"No!" It was as though the wind had been knocked out of Kit. He froze, petrified, between the two Masters.

"Oh, yes," Haitham corrected Kit, wearing a smirk so smug it was nauseating. "I'm afraid you've crossed out of James' bounds of protection, my boy." Kit yelped as Donovan seized him from behind without warning and held him in place. Haitham crossed the room to the silver basin filled with cool water at the side of the room. Slowly, he washed his hands and dried them on a folded square of white linen.

"Let me go!" Kit implored, frantically watching Haitham push up the sleeves of his grey shirt to his elbows.

"Why?" wondered Donovan, leaning so close to Kit that his lips brushed against the boy's ear. "Are you worried the others will leave without you?" Kit struggled to free himself but Donovan's strength was so much greater, he barely bothered to grit his teeth in order to keep the Tribute in place.

"James knows where I am!" Kit hollered. He fought harder to extricate himself from Donovan's grasp as Haitham drew nearer. "He'll find me! He'll come after you if you hurt me!" It was an empty threat and Haitham and Donovan both knew it.

"Donovan is right. You really are a terrible liar." Haitham stood over Kit, beaming as he touched the back of his hand to the smooth skin of Kit's cheek. "James doesn't know where you are but I know that you know where he is. And you're going to tell me."

"I don't know anything!" Kit flinched away from Haitham's touch but Donovan would not let him get far. "I swear, I don't!"

Haitham frowned. "We're going to have to work on your honesty, Kit."

Chapter Twenty-seven

It was a miracle I managed to cross the trade floor at such a calm pace. Each time I reminded myself to keep my chin up, look passive, and slow down, my mind wandered to Kit and I felt like I could gallop into a sprint just so that I could reach him in the Master library that much sooner. It may have been for the best that I did not run, for I had donned a pair of boots before leaving the Tribute wing and I was not accustomed to walking, much less running, in these things. Tripping and falling in full view of the tradespeople would attract all the attention I was trying to avoid as I made my way to the Master library.

When I had left the Tribute wing for the last time, I had been overwhelmed with surprising grief. My ballet slippers were still hanging up in my closet, my books still marked at the place I'd left off on my desk with the intent to finish them, my hairbrush still on my bedside table…leaving it all behind seemed unbearable to me as I'd laced up my boots and glanced around my room for the final time. I'd taken up Kit's sketchbook, as a singular souvenir of the life I had lived within these walls, but Armand had vehemently disapproved.

"Are you out of your mind?" he'd hissed, snatching the book out of my arms before I could leave our apartment with it in hand.

"It's the only possession I have that I'd miss! It wouldn't be outlandish to bring a sketchbook to the library," I had tried to argue. Armand had shaken his head.

"Absolutely not. We never brought anything into the Masters' chambers, we're not starting now. This place is still crawling with Masters and prying eyes. The slightest detail could be construed in the wrong way; it's bad enough we're wearing shoes over there anyway…."

"Calm down, Armie," I'd said, carefully putting a hand to his chest. He'd been exhausted when he'd returned last night and I guessed he didn't sleep, just as I hadn't. "It'll be fine. I'll leave the book here."

Still, leaving the Tribute wing without it felt wrong. I hated to think of how much had changed over the past few weeks—I was marching to the library under secret pretenses just as I had then with only my name and the clothes on my back to take with me. I would be leaving this place once and for all, with Liza and the boys we loved, and James the Master of all people. I felt as though I were walking through a very strange dream and could not help but wonder if we were right to trust James so blindly.

Part of me warned my conscience that this was a scheme of the Masters, to make an example of us or to lure us into a trap that would spell disaster for us and for our parents. My doubts and dreading left little room for anxiety as I approached the Master steps. The main hall was still quiet, as the rest of the Masters were in conference for their closing ceremony. The guardsmen looked hungover and crabby and let me pass without too much of a fuss.

"Does sticking your nose in a book this early in the morning rank as a high priority of yours?" Nathan asked.

"Master James said I could spend the morning looking for a book of poetry," I said, pouting a little at his sneer. "I want it before lunch, when the servants will be cleaning up after the summit and in the way." I had practiced saying just that maybe a dozen times in my bathroom mirror that morning.

"Whatever," Nathan sighed, turning to swing open the door for me. My rehearsal had paid off—that, or Nathan did not care that I was lying. Once inside the Masters' chambers, I found my way along the hall. I knew I was walking too fast but I was so excited to reach the library, and Kit and the others, that I let my guard down just enough to hurry. The doorknob to the library was cool on my fingers as I twisted and pulled the door open. As though the room itself were haunted, I felt a chill and broke out in a sweat the moment I set foot past the threshold, the door closing softly behind me. I told myself, it was because I had hurried, not because I was completely terrified to be back here.

The door flung open behind me and I jumped back, my hand flying to catch the scream before it left my mouth.

"It's only me," hushed Armand, slipping fluidly inside and hastily shutting the door behind him.

I really hated this library. "You scared me!" I seethed, my heart pounding in my chest. I rounded on him. "How did you get here so fast? I only just arrived."

"I couldn't sit in that empty apartment for another second," Armand confessed. He rubbed my arm in an apologetic gesture to soothe my nerves away. "I was right on your heels. I made something up to tell Nathan and he waved me right in."

I let out a deep breath and nervously tucked my hair behind my ear. "He seemed in an unusually sour mood," I said. Armand glanced around the room over my shoulder, his gaze pausing as it fell on the infamous open window, which at present had been bolted shut.

"Where's Kit?" he asked. He had raised a good question. I turned, my heart skipping a beat as awful memories of this library flashed before my eyes. I was thankful to be wearing boots, otherwise I would feel carpet on my bare feet and likely become trapped back in time. There it was, on the other side of that pane of glass—*freedom.* Only this time when I looked out the window, I knew for certain that I was about to breathe in the cold, fresh air outside. I had to pinch myself to focus—perhaps Kit was ducked out of sight, in case an unwelcome visitor were to check inside.

"Kit!" I called in a hushed voice. "It's us! Where are you?"

The door to the library opened and Armand and I startled in perfect synchronicity. Armand cursed as Liza's wild blonde hair appeared in the doorway and James came in immediately behind her. I frowned to see Liza avoid Armand's reach for embrace but as I noticed how rigidly she was holding herself, I had to assume that she was either as petrified as I was or her shoulder was in pain today. James glared at Armand for uttering the particularly offensive swear, then glanced to me.

"Any trouble?" asked James. I shook my head, as did Armand. "Well, then," he said. "I don't see the point in wasting any—" He cut himself off with a disturbed, puzzled look on his face. He looked around the room and furrowed his dark brows. "Where's Kit?"

"He left our wing first," Armand answered for me, his tone vacant as trepidation pooled in his eyes. "He should be here...."

"Kit?" James called, commanding as ever.

"Kit!" I cried, whirling around. The pit of my stomach dropped out and my eyes immediately welled with worried tears. I led the four of us in a rapid, sweeping search of the library. James and Liza split up to check between the bookshelves furthest from the windows, Armand followed me closely to check behind the leather sofa and the other shelves. All the while, I felt a stifling bout of sobs build up in my chest.

Something was wrong, terribly wrong. Kit was not here.

I then screamed as a pair of hands lashed out and caught my wrists.

"Looking for someone?" asked Donovan, trapping me against him. His lips curled in a cruel smile as I cried out and struggled. Weeks ago when James had taken a hold of my arm, I thought I'd known strength; but as Donovan tugged me around so that my back was flush against his chest without so much as batting an eye, I knew I was in trouble. He dragged me across the carpet so that we were out in the open floor, our backs to the windows.

"Daisy!" Armand yelped, rushing around the bookshelf that separated us. His eyes locked on Donovan and he froze.

"Donovan!" James appeared behind Armand with Liza at his side. He stepped around my brother swiftly, mindfully keeping his eyes fixed on the man who held me too tightly in his grasp. "Release Daisy. Now."

"I suppose you're going to try to tell me that this is all just a misunderstanding?" asked Donovan. James took a step toward us and I yelped as I felt a sharp pinch in my side. Panic bridled me as I saw Liza's eyes bulge. She clutched at Armand in fear.

"Not at all," said James calmly, though he looked murderous. I dared to steal a downward glance and saw that Donovan had a short ceramic blade pressed to my torso, its point aimed between my right two lowest ribs.

"Let her go, Donovan." Armand was pleading as he tried to reason with my captor. The look Donovan sent him in return must have been otherworldly, because Armand stilled and seemed to not dare breathe.

"Look for me," Donovan uttered. "I'll be there. That's what you said!" He shook his head. "Such pretty promises, lover. I can't believe I fell for them." As I stared at Liza, willing myself to stand as still as possible, I felt a raging, raw heat between Armand and Donovan permeate the room. A change set into Liza's features as she watched the two of them as epiphany registered in her.

Armand had been right to ask us not to tell Liza. I could see in her eyes that her world, or what remained of it, had just come crashing down around her.

"Armie?" Liza looked to him in disbelief, then to Donovan. "*Lovers?*"

"I'm so sorry," Armand moaned, strangled by despair.

"You're apologizing to *her?*" Donovan's pitch was marred by jealous anger. "I did everything you ever wanted—*everything*—and this is how you repay me?"

"Please," implored Armand. "I didn't—"

"Shut up, Armand," said James. He turned his cold glare to his nephew. He admonished Donovan with a click of his tongue and heaved a sigh that was rank in condescension. "I think I like the look of you with a broken heart, Donovan," he said. "Maybe now you will learn your lesson? I told you over and over, you're not invulnerable to your own power plays. Had you listened to me instead of Selenis about this Tribute warfare idea of Haitham's, we wouldn't be standing here right now."

"I've just thwarted your escape and all you've got to say is 'I told you so'?" Donovan replied. "You're losing your touch, James...."

"Let Daisy go," said Armand. "This is between you and me."

"Liza." My voice came out as a mouse's. I could feel the tip of the blade poke my skin as Donovan tightened his hold on me, making each rapid breath I took sting.

"James, do something!" Liza urged.

"Be quiet." James looked to me. "It'll be all right, Daisy." My lower lip trembled as it struck me that I did not believe him.

"You don't want to hurt her, you want to hurt me." Armand stared past me straight into Donovan's eyes. "I'll come to you. Don't make Daisy pay for this." I gasped when Armand pushed past James and came to me and Donovan. James heaved a panicked wheeze to see Donovan flick the point of the blade out, slicing out as Armand advanced. His chin was nicked, directly perpendicular to the cut James had put there weeks ago. The superficial wound immediately bled down Armand's throat as he wrapped his fingers around my arm and flung me away from the Master.

Donovan wanted Armand to come to him all along; I was merely a prop. Still, I lost my footing in the struggle. James reached forward to catch me as I spilled to the carpet, Armand and Donovan grappled for a moment, and Liza let out a muffled scream between her hands to see it. James went to his side for Liza, maybe to push her behind him, when Armand hollered, "No, James! Don't move!"

Shockingly, James obeyed him.

"I could kill you," Donovan insisted, clutching at Armand's arms. "You son of a bitch, you lied to me!"

"I had to!" Armand rasped, paying no mind to his bleeding chin. I balked to see him, a lover in action, try to contain the hurricane in the library that was Donovan the Spurned Master. James was as stunned as I was to see Armand transform before our eyes. In fact, James was so astonished that he continued to hold me as we looked on, our eyes glued to the blade in Donovan's hand.

"You were going to just *leave?* How could you do this to me?" Donovan was desperate as he held a fistful of Armand's shirt.

Armand kissed the other man. James, Liza, and I had instantly become intruders on the most distraught embrace I'd ever seen. Armand jerked out of Donovan's arms but was still held an arm's length away. "I never wanted to stay here, don't you see?" His paramour still held the knife in his hand, though he seemed to be tempted to drop it in order to gain a steadier hold on Armand.

"I did everything you asked," echoed Donovan. "I was prepared to give you the world, Armand!" I heard Liza hum as she suppressed a sob and looked to her, only to see that tears were streaming down her cheeks. Indeed, Donovan was not the only one whose heart was broken in the library today.

"I doubt Armand ever asked you to murder Graham Keating," said James evenly.

I couldn't help but let out a shrill cry as though I had been kicked as soon as James' accusation fell on my ears. I had known James my whole life and knew that he only ever put charges to someone on a certainty, so it must be true. As I second guessed it, I realized how foolish I had been not to have worked it out myself. How could it not be true? Graham's suicide had been a meticulous setup on Donovan's part, a thought which made me nearly sick to my stomach. Liza too was plainly disgusted, while Armand must have done what we had not and come to the conclusion on his own. His lack of reaction was all too telling. He stared back at Donovan with a rapt, pained look on his face I had never seen before. His features contorted to make him look much older and weathered than he was, if only for a moment.

"Don't you dare say you did it for me," said Armand. He shoved Donovan away from him and retreated a few steps back until he was within James' reach. The blood from the cut on his chin dripped down his chest and stained the collar of his linen shirt. I doubted he could even feel it.

"You killed Graham?" I sobbed. "You monster!" I held the back of my hand to my mouth, my fingers shaking. This was too terrible, this would destroy Kit—

Kit. "What have you done with Kit, you bastard?" I howled. James grabbed my arm and kept me behind him.

"Don't give Donovan all the credit." The four of us turned fast when Haitham's sinister presence emerged from behind the bookshelf beside Donovan. Between his dark vestments, long hands and fingers, and knowing black eyes, he looked like a vulture. I looked to James and saw the color drain from his face, then I followed James' gaze down to his father's hands, which had been bloodied around the knuckles.

He had hurt Kit. I swayed where I stood, my knees knocking together as they threatened to buckle.

"I should have known this would trace back to you." James had never conveyed so much hate in his speech.

"You should have," Haitham agreed. "Did you think you could hide a breach of Tribute law from me? Or be able to throw me out of my own compound?"

"The Aventine is mine," James snarled.

"Not anymore." Haitham set his hand on Donovan's shoulder and grimaced down at me. "It turns out that our Kit, while he is a terrible liar, is remarkably apt at keeping secrets. It's a good thing Donovan remembered the boy saying something about a library…." His glittering eyes peered across the library to his son. "I noticed you didn't hang the volpine skin that I gave you. Does the reminder make you squeamish, James?"

"Not half as much as you do."

"Enough pleasantries." Haitham the Master flicked a pointed finger at James and Donovan took a step forward, twirling his ceramic knife around his finger. James gritted his teeth and held his arms up, staying very still. Donovan came forward and patted his sides, chest, and the sides of his legs. The rest of us did not dare to move an inch as this interaction ensued. When Donovan seemed satisfied that James was not carrying a concealed weapon, he rejoined Haitham near the window.

"You're lucky that Selenis was able to keep this quiet," Donovan told his uncle. "You're not going anywhere, but she might have had the place surrounded by my swordsmen had she not considered her admiration of you." The more he spoke, the more my stomach burned in hatred for him. He and Haitham had Kit—*my Kit*—and the last thing I wanted to do was listen to his awful, velvet-soft voice.

"You mean she didn't want to risk the others finding out," James translated flatly. "She would never be able to shake the association of your incompetence had you made this public."

"Your sister is shrewd, I'll give you that," said Haitham. He winked at Liza. "In fact, she reminds me of Lorena in many ways—"

"Don't talk about my mother!" Liza yelped.

"You murdered Graham and you've harmed my brother," Armand joined in furiously. "You will pay for this, I swear it!"

Haitham looked at us with insidious pride in his eyes, saving the more savoring glance for James. "You have sculpted them in your image, James. I feel like I'm speaking to my grandchildren."

"If I were your grandchild, I'd kill myself," I declared with amaroidal conviction.

"He may take the liberty regardless, Daisy," James said. "Was it not you, Father, who sent my guards away and paid Quinn to murder Liza?"

Haitham stared at James with a haunting, gleeful glint in his eyes. "You think I'd dirty my hands in dealing with that mad dog of a guardsman?"

"Oh, of course," sighed James. "The note that supposedly came from Daisy. You wrote it, Donovan?"

"My notebook!" The exclamation came out much stronger than I had intended it to. "You took it to study my writing!"

"Donovan's methods can be a little overly complicated for my liking," was Haitham's bored criticism.

"I thought for days about what would humiliate you enough to get unseated by the others," Donovan uttered. A taunting gleam shimmered across his eyes as he glared at his uncle. "A Master who cannot protect his own Tribute, much less from his own guard? You would have been a laughingstock."

"If you weren't a coward, you'd have done it yourself instead of trusting Quinn with the job," said James. "You may even have succeeded."

"And you might have snapped my neck instead of his!" said Donovan.

"You want to be just like your grandfather, is that it?" James fired back. "You think you can keep your hands clean while everyone takes falls for you, left and right, until there's a pile of bodies tall enough for you to sit on so that you can look down over the omnishambles you've created? Being the Master of this place is a messy job, Donovan. You'll find that not every problem can be solved by attacking it with a sword."

I could not believe what I was hearing or seeing. Liza was shaking in rage and James edged marginally closer to her, perhaps worried she would spring forward.

"It was you who killed my scouts," James further deduced. "No doubt they caught on that you ordered your swordsmen to kill Liza on sight if they found her, is that right?"

"You employ very nosy men, James," said Donovan. His demeanor was entirely absent of remorse or humility. "They are all so eager to please you, they wouldn't stop asking questions in pursuit of your infernal *due diligence*... getting your scouts out of the way was no small task, not like blaming their deaths on Harriet."

"Is that why Graham Keating had to die?" James asked. "To spare yourself the scandal of being outed as a traitor to the system?"

"On the contrary," said Haitham, infuriating us all by his impeccable impression of Graham. "Keating had to die in order to protect this system! He was feeding his traitorous wretch of a child information about the summit. Not that we could prove it, not without upsetting your ridiculous rules about how your members of staff are treated...."

"If Graham had gone to Harriet with information, he would have done it years ago and you likely would not be standing here now," said James, who clearly favored such an alternative. "The truth is, he was the most loyal man in the Masterlands and I would stake my reputation on it, no matter how sullied it is now. You were wrong about him, Father, and you damn well know it. You weren't plugging leaks in your forsaken system, you merely killed him out of spite because he called your bluff!"

The look in Haitham's eyes was purely hellish. The more I looked at him, the more inhuman he appeared and the more I felt I would be sick.

"You comforted me," Liza said to Donovan, her teeth clenched as she fought to retain control of her temper. "You watched me suffer and cry, you put your arms around me and tucked me into bed—and then you sent Quinn to kill me?"

"I'd say it wasn't personal, Liza, but we both know that would be a lie," said Donovan, his lips twisted in his trademark winsome smile.

Armand growled something unforgivably reproachful at Donovan and then said, "You just wanted her out of the way, didn't you? You wanted me all to yourself?"

Donovan unleashed his anger on Armand once more. "You think James hasn't killed for his seat of power?" he bellowed, his handsome features contorted in contempt. "Quinn wasn't the only casualty of James' term as Master here!"

I had enough of this guilt slinging back and forth. "Where is Kit?" I demanded. I did not care that my voice cracked, that I was crying, that my eyes were probably bloodshot, or that I probably looked about as threatening as a paper doll. Maybe I could be menacing for Kit—maybe that's how, weeks ago, Liza was able to conjure an aura of formidable bravery in the face of the Master who stood beside me now. Both Donovan and Haitham were standing by the windows, not blocking our way to the door at all. Though they were both murderers, Donovan was the only one with a weapon and unless his reputation as a swordsman was dead on, he could not get to all four of us at once.

If I had to make a desperate escape after all, I would. But I would not leave without Kit.

"Where is he?" I asked again, for no one had answered me.

"Don't worry, Daisy," said Haitham. "You will see him very shortly." He took a step toward us.

"Don't touch her!" Liza shouted.

Haitham the Villain let his mask slip enough to glare at Liza. "I've had enough confrontation from you foul-mouthed young people for one day. I'd like to have a word with James, alone, and if you don't want Donovan to carve up your pretty little faces, you will go with him. Take them away," he told Donovan. Armand and I both vocalized objections at once: Armand begged Donovan to please not hurt me and Liza; I sidled close to James, hoping that he would stop Donovan from taking a hold of me again.

James surprised us all by yanking Liza close and reaching deftly up underneath the side of her blouse—before I could even blink, he withdrew his hand, his fingers wrapped around a pistol. That explained why Liza had stayed so close to him and had been standing so still! He had strapped a gun to her, knowing that if anything had happened, he would be searched for a weapon and she would not be. Someday I would thank him ardently for being more brilliant and cunning than I had hoped.

"Get behind me," James said to us, aiming the gun at Donovan. We obeyed without question. "Drop the knife, Donovan."

"You would shoot your own nephew?" Donovan asked. He had gone deathly pale in the span of a heartbeat as he realized that he knew the answer to his own question.

"As surely as you have betrayed your own uncle," replied James. "If you move an inch, I swear I'll kill you."

Donovan wet his lips and nodded. He dropped the knife in his hand.

"Where is Kit?" James asked, even-keeled as ever.

"I left him with the good doctor," said Haitham. Liza hissed a venomous oath about Jada's treachery. I only cried more, worried beyond my imagination about the kinds of things Haitham had done to him. Why else would Kit need a doctor?

"Before you consider doing something you might regret, you should know that I also left your sister with specific instructions on what to do if I do not reach her within the next—" the old Master glanced at his wristwatch and sneered, "well, four minutes, to be exact."

I was going to be sick. "We'll never get to him in time," I murmured. I could feel what was about to happen next in my gut as viscerally as though

I'd swallowed a burning coal and it was slowly searing into my insides, layer by layer.

"What'll it be, James?" Haitham wondered.

"We can't leave him!" I urged tearfully. "Please, James!" I grabbed his arm and hung off him in desperation, watching him think at a mile a minute as the wind howled outside.

"Daisy, he's holding a gun," grunted Armand, heaving me off of James.

"We have to get Kit!" I insisted. "Make him call Selenis! He can tell her to send Kit up here!"

"Yes, James," Haitham mocked me. "Make me call your sister! I only hope that, in my old age, I don't get confused and have the boy slaughtered in the medical wing instead...."

I tore my gaze from the hateful old devil. "Any minute now, the others will conclude the summit and come looking for you!" I reminded James. He simply was not thinking fast enough and I was going mad under the time constraint. "If we're going to get Kit, we have to go *now*—"

We three Tributes screamed as James' gun went off. The bullet exploded from the short nozzle and struck Haitham squarely in the chest. He went flying backwards, shattered the window behind him into a thousand pieces, and disappeared from sight.

"What have you done?" roared Donovan, running to the window after his grandfather.

"Liza, the knife!" James cried. Liza stooped and swiped across the carpet, catching Donovan's forgotten ceramic blade in her hand. "Come on!" James compelled us, keeping an eye on Donovan as the other Master stared in shock out of the jagged hole Haitham's body had made in the window. We ran from the library as fast as we could. James paused just long enough to bolt the doors behind him and stuff the key back in his pocket.

"It opens inwards. It'll take him minutes to get out by himself," James said airily. He looked to Liza, whose eyes were wide with alarm. "Are you all right?"

"I'm fine," said Liza. It was a feeble affirmation—she was as all right as I was, I decided bitterly. Liza checked back with James, "You?"

James did not answer her. Instead, he studied the gash on Armand's chin. "We'll need to put pressure on that to get it to stop bleeding—"

I entreated my fellow escapists, "We need to get Kit! If we run, we can get to him before Selenis calls the guards!"

"No," said James. "We don't have the time, Daisy. We have a very narrow window to escape and...." James bowed his head. "I'm sorry, but Kit won't be coming with us."

"No!" Armand gasped. "James, please, we can't leave without him!"

"We have to!" James retorted.

Tears streamed down my cheeks and my voice reached a new level of shrill. The touch-barrier between us shattered like the library window as out of sheer desperation I clung to James, pulling at his shirt. "We can't leave without Kit, James. We can't! We just can't!"

James took me by the shoulders and fixed a grounding stare into my eyes. "With Haitham gone, he will be all right. Donovan will keep him in your apartment, and he will be safe there—without the three of you, and without me, they won't be able to risk harming him."

He had just killed his own father to make sure that Kit would be safe here on his own—and it still was not good enough. I shook my head and tried to speak against this impossible, nightmarish concept, but my sobs choked me.

"Daisy," said James. "I promise, Kit will be fine. But we have to go. If we don't, the guards will catch us and I no longer have the authority to command them. They will most certainly kill me before beating the three of you into submission and throwing you all into cells. Do you understand?"

"He's right," Armand chimed in thickly, his right hand cupping his chin to slow the blood flow from his wound. His touch was no more welcomed than James' as he reached for me, bracing his left hand on the small of my back. "We have to go, sweetheart."

"No!" I shrieked. "Armand, no! We are not leaving here without him!"

My nightmare truly enveloped me into endless torment as, over our heads, the compound-wide alarm sounded and the caution lights began to flash in measured flares. It was too late already, too late for us to get Kit.

Liza pushed both of the men aside so that she faced me head on. Her violet eyes were brimmed with tears and her mouth was quivering as she fought off her own sobs. "We will get him back, Daisy," she vowed. "I swear to you, we will get him back if it's the last thing we do. But we have to go *right now*."

James did not wait for me to agree; smart of him, because I wasn't going to anyway. But I was too beside myself to fight them off as, in turns, the three of them pulled me along the Master hall. James said we were near the exit when we rounded the far west corner but before we could get any further, James came to a sudden halt. We did the same.

There stood Dulce in the middle of the hall, wearing a simple off-white dress that fell just past her knees. I grasped at Armand, bracing myself to watch James shoot another member of his family to death, when Dulce held out her hand to reveal something shiny in the palm of her hand.

"What is this?" James asked of his niece.

"Mama's car keys," said Dulce. We drew nearer to her and I could see she'd been crying. When she looked into my eyes, her face fell in pitiful sadness. "Take them," she said to James, dabbing at the wet corners of her eyes. "They flagged your car. You'll be stopped if you take it to the gate. They'll be looking for you in the cargo vans too. You'll never make it out unless you take Mama's car."

"Dulce, you—this is—" James was speechless. We all were. "Why?"

The would-be Mistress gazed into Armand's eyes. "Because our lives are not the same," she said. "And because liberty is not a burden, it is a gift. And I want to give it to people who can do something good with it." The alarms blared overhead and we knew we had to run, but Dulce seemed to be slowing time. "I've seen Kit," she confessed. She looked to me and offered me the keys. "I will do what I can for him, Daisy. I promise. But if you have any hope to get out, you must go now."

My heart be damned, I took the keys from Dulce.

"There's a guardsman in my service," James said to Dulce rapidly. "His name is Douglas. He's dependable. If you need anything, go to him. You can trust him." Dulce nodded, blinking tears from her eyes. James leaned down and kissed her cheek. "*Me has hecho orgulloso hoy, niña.*"

"*Gracias, tío,*" said Dulce. She gracefully smoothed the front of her skirt and stepped aside. "Go now, all of you."

"Tell him I love him?" I asked of Dulce. She nodded fervently and bade me hurry after James.

Armand tarried even after I went to follow James and Liza. "I will never forget this," I heard him say. I looked back to see him kiss her before running to catch up with me. The car keys dug into my palm as I squeezed them tight, mindful not to drop them as I bolted after James, who led us through a narrow doorway and down several flights of winding, industrial steel steps. My body obeyed the commands my mind gave: run faster, push the heavy storm door open, keep my eyes open.... To leave Kit, I had to shut away the part of my instincts that was screaming and wailing at me to realize how wrong this was; that no, despite this being our only chance, I could not leave him....

James heaved open what he assured us was the last door and I knew he was telling the truth when a gust of freezing wind crashed into me. Liza and Armand had similar reactions to mine—they froze in place at the overwhelming cold, not to mention the force of the wind itself, which whipped my hair and Liza's around wildly.

"There will be coats in the car," James explained. He hovered over me expectantly and I uncrossed my arms to give him the keys. James touched a button on the handheld remote attached to the keyring and across a vast garage of large, sleek, black cars, one of them chirped and flashed its headlights. The four of us jogged over and copied James, yanking at the handles to pull the doors open and hopping nimbly up into the leather seats. My teeth were chattering as I slammed the door shut beside me. Armand sat in back with me, Liza in front with James.

"Get ready to duck down to the floor of the vehicle if I say so," said James. He pumped the car's brake and touched a button, and the engine roared to life. Heat blasted out of vents on either side of the backseat and I sighed to feel the warmth on my cheeks. When James careened forward out of the parked position, I yelped and scrambled to hold on to Armand.

"Once we're clear of the garage, it'll be safe to put your belts on," said James. "Underneath one of the seats should be something for your face, Armand." He handled the enormous car with expertise, though we were going far too fast for my liking. My stomach was already in knots over abandoning Kit, I was worried I would be sick for real.

"Hold on to me," said Armand. I saw that he was crying quietly and my heart sank as I realized he wasn't offering mere stability in the back of the rocketing vehicle, he was begging me to hold on to him because, like me, he was utterly crushed about leaving Kit behind. I rummaged underneath James' seat and found a satchel containing several cotton handkerchiefs. I grabbed one and scooted across the leather seat to Armand. I touched the cloth to his chin and he held it there, pressing on the gash, as I wrapped my arms around his middle. I kept my sobs low, knowing that I had to listen for James in case we had to duck out of sight. I watched Liza pick up the pistol from the center well where James had put it. I supposed she was going to place it safely out of sight into a small compartment in front of her passenger seat, but James stopped her.

"I might need it to get past the gate," said James. Liza put the pistol down and raked her fingers through her long hair, then buried her face in her hands.

"I'm so sorry," James said to her. "I wish it had gone differently."

"Will he really be safe?" Liza croaked.

"With Haitham gone, yes," said James. "Donovan is—" He quickly amended his line of reasoning as Liza shot him a furious glare. "He is no saint, but he is not as diabolical as Haitham. Kit just became his most valuable asset. He won't come to any further harm."

Further harm. Kit had already faced Haitham's brutal wrath. I couldn't think about how he had been hurt, but I had to trust that James was right about Kit's value now that Donovan had just become Master of the Aventine. I almost thanked James for killing his horrible father—after all, I was glad he had done it—but my tongue fumbled the words.

Our car emerged from the sheltered garage and the sight outside took my breath away. In an instant, we traveled from a concrete structure to a blindingly bright snowy forest floor. Armand's hand gripped mine as we splayed apart in the backseat to press our noses against the car window. Trees lined either side of the car, buried in thick, cotton-soft looking snow. We were driving fast enough for the landscape outside to blur together in a hazy white and wooden streaks.

"Here we go," said James. He kept a hand on the steering wheel to pick up the pistol and hold it in his lap, ready to use it again if he had to. I glanced forward, glimpsing a bright orange gate up ahead.

"Should we hide?" Liza asked. Before James could answer, the gate clicked open automatically; evidently Selenis' car was flagged to pass through this way without stopping and we all rejoiced softly as we soared past the limits of the compound, the wheels crunching down snow as we drove.

"How long will it take to drive to Kingsfield Township?" Liza asked, just as mesmerized as we were by the scene outside of her car window.

"If I could drive straight through, just over a day," said James. "Maybe less so with me at the wheel. But we will have to stop to change vehicles to make sure we can't be tracked." I saw him eye the slender mirror in the middle of the windshield, checking back to me and Armand. "There are coats in the back and maybe some blankets," he said. "Perhaps you should try to get some rest."

I blinked back at James, still holding Armand's hand in mine. "I suppose I don't know how tired I am, is that right?" I wondered. James clearly did not know what to say in response. I wasn't sure what I expected him to say, nor would I have cared if he did reply. I looked away from James and curled into Armand's chest, craving comfort above all else.

The escape I had planned was a far cry from the one I had just successfully pulled off, down to the last detail. I did not feel joy or excitement, no thrill of well-deserved freedom from the walled-in compound in which I had lived for the last nineteen years. On the contrary, even with my arms around my brother as we four drove off into the unknown wilderness surrounding the Aventine, I was fearful and despondent to an overwhelming degree. Mostly, however, I was calmed by a deep determination that took root in my heart. It was a root that grew deeper the further we drove away from the compound and I knew that I was the only person in the car to feel it.

I spent months planning to escape the Aventine and after a grueling, violent morning, I had done it. Now, as I set off with Liza and Armand to reunite with our parents, I began to ponder just how carefully I would have to plan my return to this place. If I had to, I would walk back on my own, for with or without Liza, Armand, and James, I would come back here for Kit.

After all, we could only be strong if we were together.

CPSIA information can be obtained
at www.ICGtesting.com
Printed in the USA
LVHW081052150820
663270LV00024B/2611